NEW YORK REVIEW BOOKS
CLASSICS

LETTY FOX: HER LUCK

CHRISTINA STEAD (1902–1983) was born in Sydney, Australia. She had a troubled childhood—later to be the inspiration for her novel *The Man Who Loved Children*—which was dominated by the figure of her biologist father, a man of great energy and cranky conviction who alternately encouraged and humiliated his brilliant but ungainly daughter. Determined to be a writer, Stead left Australia in 1928, pursuing a peripatetic and financially precarious career which took her to London, Paris, New York, Hollywood, and, in her last years, back to the environs of Sydney. Stead's first book, *The Salzburg Tales*, appeared in 1934. It was followed by many others, including *House of All Nations*, *For Love Alone*, *Letty Fox: Her Luck*, and *Cotters' England*.

TIM PARKS was born in Manchester, England, grew up in London, and studied at Cambridge and Harvard. In 1981 he moved to Italy, where he has lived ever since. He has written ten novels, among them *Destiny* and *Europa*; two nonfiction accounts of life in Italy; and a collection of essays, *Adultery & Other Diversions*. His many translations from the Italian include works by Alberto Moravia, Roberto Calasso, and Italo Calvino.

LETTY FOX: HER LUCK

CHRISTINA STEAD

Introduction by
TIM PARKS

NEW YORK REVIEW BOOKS

New York

THIS IS A NEW YORK REVIEW BOOK
PUBLISHED BY THE NEW YORK REVIEW OF BOOKS

This edition published in the United States of America by
The New York Review of Books, 1755 Broadway, New York, NY 10019

Library of Congress Cataloging-in-Publication Data
Stead, Christina, 1902–
  Letty fox : her luck / Christina Stead ; introduction by Tim Parks.
      p. cm.
  ISBN 0-940322-70-6
  1. Greenwich Village (New York, N.Y.)—Fiction. 2. Man-woman
relationships—Fiction. 3. City and town life—Fiction. 4. Single
women—Fiction. I. Title.
  PR9619.3.S75 L48 2001
  823'.912—dc21

                              00-012048

ISBN 0-940322-70-6

Book design by Lizzie Scott
Printed in the United States of America on acid-free paper.
10 9 8 7 6 5 4 3 2 1

April 2001
www.nybooks.com

L'expérience te manque, et malheureusement c'est
une chose qui ne s'acquiert qu'à force de sottises et
de bévues!

—*Le Paysan et la Paysanne Pervertis*
RÉTIF DE LA BRETONNE

CHIEF CHARACTERS

LETTY FOX

JACQUELINE
ANDREA *her sisters*

MATHILDE, *née Morgan, her mother*

SOLANDER, *her father*

JENNY FOX, *her grandmother*

CISSIE MORGAN, *her grandmother*

PHYLLIS, *Cissie Morgan's youngest daughter*

PHILIP, *son of Cissie Morgan*

AMABEL
DORA *wives of Philip Morgan*

PERSIA, *"Die Konkubine"*

LILY SPONTINI, *Jenny Fox's niece*

PERCIVAL HOGG, *Letty's uncle*

EDWIGE LANTAR, *Letty's cousin*

PAULINE, *friend of the family*

GIDEON BOWLES, *friend of the family*

CLAYS MANNING
AMOS
BOBBY THOMPSON
LUKE ADAMS
WICKLOW
CORNELIS DE GROOT *Letty's friends*
TOM BRATT
JEFF MOSSOP
BILL VAN WEEK
BINGHAM
SUSANNAH FORD

INTRODUCTION

"I DON'T know what imagination is," says Letty Fox, "if not an unpruned, tangled kind of memory." Though the claim comes early on in this long book, and is made what's more by one of the flightiest narrators fiction has ever produced, nevertheless the reader will immediately take it as confirmation of what he has already suspected: flagrantly unpruned and tangled beyond any unraveling, the six-hundred-plus pages of *Letty Fox: Her Luck* are the seductive and savage reworking of an apparently inexhaustible memory, its author's as much as its narrator's.

One of the most exuberant and chameleon novelists of her century, Christina Stead had much to remember by the time she came to this, her sixth novel. Born in a southern suburb of Sydney in 1902, her literary ambitions, left-wing politics, and difficult love life brought her first to London, then Paris, then New York. She had known success and failure, romance and rejection; she had worked for the Communist Party and collaborated, simultaneously, with corrupt financiers. But however complex and contradictory her career and relationships may have become, Stead's memories still tended to organize themselves around the two great stories that had shaped her life: the story of the bizarre Australian family she grew up in, and the story of the Jewish-American community she ultimately became part of. The first was a horror story with comic interludes, the second a romance with recurrent nightmares. The five novels before *Letty Fox*, all equally extravagant and daring, had kept the two stages of her life apart; they dealt with either the one story or the other. Published in 1946, after she had been resident in New York for nine years and when her literary reputation at last seemed established, *Letty Fox: Her Luck* contrives to tangle them both.

Stead's early unhappiness is easily understood. The plain, big-boned daughter of a pretty mother who died when she was two, Christina soon found herself an unwanted extra in her father's second family. "My stepmother was kind to me," she later conceded of Ada Stead, "until her first child was born." Five more children would follow. From the beginning, Stead's writing would always convey a sense of life's exhausting and oppressive excess. "Living is too much for me," says Letty Fox, who is herself more than a handful for those around her. It is as if Stead were telling us that her own explosive vitality was no more than a necessary defense against the world's threatening profusion.

Self-taught biologist and pioneering socialist, a man of immense energy and greater vanity, Stead's handsome father contrived to complicate his adolescent daughter's isolation by making Christina his confidante in what had now become the epic struggle between himself and his wife. David Stead had made this second marriage at least partly for money. The couple had moved into an extravagant mansion immediately after the wedding. But when Ada's father died, her family was found to be as deeply in debt as it had previously appeared to be swimming in wealth. Reduced to poverty, obliged to make do with ramshackle accommodation, Ada sulked. The charismatic David found her dull. Christina, on the other hand, was intelligent beyond her years. How sad, however, as he never tired of reminding her, that she was also "a fat lazy lump."

On research trips to Malaysia and Paris, David Stead, a staunch supporter of women's rights and great believer in eugenics, wrote his daughter long letters sharing his enthusiasm for the superior and slender beauty of the women of those countries. Bulky Christina yearned to travel. When she was seventeen her father fell in love with a sixteen-year-old girl, Thistle Harris, and would eventually run off with this pretty junior. Again he made the ugly duckling of his brood his confidante. Twenty years later, from the distant fortress of Manhattan, the slighted daughter took her revenge. I know of no account of father and family more generously observed or more irremediably cruel than the autobiographical novel *The Man Who Loved Children*. Published in 1940, it remains Stead's most frightening and ruthless work. At the height of her powers, she was thus able to begin *Letty Fox* with the worst of that old bitterness exorcised. She was ready to have fun.

The passage from family of origin to partner of election is the story at the core of *Letty Fox*. In that sense, albeit with a completely different milieu and a whole new gallery of characters, the novel takes over where *The Man Who Loved Children* left off. In the earlier work the heroine leaves home only in the final pages; here instead she is decidedly out of the fold and on the make. For Stead herself, as one learns from Hazel Rowley's biography,[*] this period of young adulthood was marked by the most intense yearning and frustration. It was also the period in which the contradiction that shaped her novels, or rather that extended them beyond any immediately perceptible shape, first becomes apparent.

Stead's final school exams won her a scholarship to the university, but she was ineligible for an arts degree because she hadn't studied Latin. The daughter of a biologist and man of action isn't encouraged to grapple with fossil languages. She could have chosen a science course and had her higher education financed by the State, but decided against it, apparently because she had come to associate women in science with dowdy and frustrated spinsters. The Darwinist determinism she had learned from her father had apparently convinced Stead that in the struggle for survival, which was always a struggle to win the right mate, a science degree would not be a winning card for a woman. The more biology a girl knew, it seemed, the more she appreciated that it was not biology a girl needed to know.

This disturbing lesson was reinforced, in Stead's case, by the fiercest erotic longings, desires which, if only because they couldn't be talked about in the puritan society she grew up in, she often feared would drive her mad. Would a plain girl find a lover and husband? "Hunger of the stomach can be confessed," she later wrote in a note for the novel *For Love Alone*, "but not sexual hunger." In *Letty Fox*, Christina Stead would make it her business to be alarmingly frank about that hunger. From earliest adolescence, Letty lusts. "This fox was tearing at my vitals," she tells us.

---

[*]Hazel Rowley, *Christina Stead: A Biography* (Henry Holt, 1994).

Rowley remarks that "Stead liked the hint of bawdiness" in the title's combination of the words "fox" and "luck."

Unable to study the arts and unwilling to take up science, the nineteen-year-old Stead settled on teaching, making the long journey back and forth to training college in Sydney every day. Rising at dawn, she wrote down stories of great fantasy that nevertheless show an acute awareness of what was the most urgent reality of her life: she was a highly sexed young woman after her man, a caricature almost of the traditional gal.

But she was also a socialist and a radical. Here come the complications. At Sydney Girls High School Christina had been enthusiastic when a teacher told them about the Communist revolution in Russia. Throughout the First World War she was staunchly pacifist. These controversial positions were again things she had taken from her atheist but far from clear-headed father. As he saw it, you discovered the hard facts of the biological struggle, facts that in Europe were preparing the way for a book like *Mein Kampf*, but then paradoxically, idealistically, you used that knowledge, or said you were using it, not for your own personal fight, or even for that of your race, but to further the cause of mankind in a spirit of solidarity. David Stead, for example, had established which fish off the Australian coast were fit for human consumption, where and how they could be caught. It was an important contribution. It also made him, if only briefly, an important man, the sort of man a bright young girl might run away with.

There was an irony to this, of course: the altruism of the common cause had proved an efficient way for the individual male of the species to get what he wanted, a young woman. But would the same be true for the female? Attending a politicized evening course at Sydney University, a course whose object, according to one student, was nothing less than "the reform of the Universe," Christina Stead fell determinedly in love with the left-wing lecturer Keith Duncan. Alas, she was not in a position to offer him either what her father could offer Thistle Harris or what Thistle could offer her father. Perhaps it was at this point that Stead began to appreciate the hypocrisy and contradiction in her father's position. Certainly the comedy that everywhere galvanizes *Letty Fox* is the mismatch between the idealistic rhetoric of radicalism and the biologically driven power game between men and women. Both Stead and Letty dream of the grand individual career, the generous altruistic gesture *and* traditional romantic love. Since such romance notoriously involves feminine submission, the combination proves arduous. What was required, it seemed, was an improbable stroke of luck.

Christina Stead failed to become a teacher. In the classroom she lost her voice; arriving at the school gates she panicked. Again the problem was the fear of a virginity prolonged into old age. School was a place where "a woman was not a woman." Bound over to teaching for five years to pay for her training, she had to struggle hard to escape without a heavy fine. She was lonely now. Keith Duncan and other radical friends had left for England and the wider world. They had travel scholarships. But for Stead there were no such handouts. She worked for two years as a secretary to save the money to follow Duncan. He wrote to encourage her, then to put her off. Would they ever become lovers? Every day she walked miles to save tram fares. A special and paradoxical kind of feminism was developing in Stead. She wasn't interested in rights and equality as ends in themselves, but in relation to the struggle to marry one's man.

Then, at last in England, aged twenty-five, Christina Stead did get what she would always consider her one great piece of luck in life: she met the man, that is, with whom she could combine both career and romance. It wasn't Keith Duncan. Duncan had led her on, but wouldn't commit himself. He wouldn't even take her to bed. It was Christina's new employer, ten years older than herself, who finally relieved his young secretary of her virginity. In a letter home announcing imminent marriage, Stead described him thus: "William James Blech is a German Jew of American upbringing, small, very loquacious, very astute in business and literary affairs and art, highly educated and original." Some years later, as a precautionary measure against arrest for fraudulent bankruptcy, William Blech changed his name to William Blake. It was a gesture typical of his innocent charm and considerable presumption.

Despite his new girlfriend's claims, Blech, like Stead's father, was entirely self-taught. Like her father he was a radical, indeed a Communist, though he worked for a decidedly shady banking company. Like her father he had boundless energy and optimism. And like her father, unfortunately, he was married. He had a wife and daughter. Wedding bells were far from imminent.

Once again, then, Stead was an anomalous creature on the edge of a family that didn't quite know what to do with her. The second story of her life, the second great struggle had begun. Having gratefully given herself to this man, she must now persuade him to persuade his wife to agree to a divorce. Having abandoned one family, she would force her way into another. From this point on, Stead's staunch communism, her unquestioning support for Blech unceasing political endeavors, would be a crucial part of that struggle. Indeed, like Blech, Stead would go on supporting Stalinism and Soviet Russia long after everybody else had abandoned it. It was a loyalty and a stubbornness for which she paid dearly in terms of lost recognition.

I can think of no author for whom milieu is more important than for Christina Stead, no author who works harder to create the social settings of her novels and to convey the sense that character and background are inseparable. She appreciates the irony that although the individual struggles above all for himself, and although his primary experience is that of being alone, nevertheless he does not create or even possess that self, but is very largely a product of his own milieu.

No doubt this knowledge came from being so frequently forced to change milieu herself. Having met Blech in London, so soon after arrival from Sydney, she at once agreed to his moving her nearer to his wife and daughter in Paris. She loved it. In Paris, well dressed, speaking French, with a man by her side, she decided she was not so plain after all. Place and situation changes you. Over the next few years she lived in London again, then New York, Spain, Belgium, London, and—at last a few years of stability—New York.

She made copious notes on every community she came in contact with. She changed languages, accents. She wrote books set in Australia, England, France, the US; set in the lower class, the middle class, among expatriates. Each work was testimony to her own determination to adapt and survive, to fit in; or perhaps one should rather say, to shine whatever the milieu, whatever society she chose to write about or style she chose to use. Her first novel, *Seven Poor Men of Sydney*, rediscovers and reproduces the Australia of her youth. Moving back and forth from London to Paris, her second, *The Beauties and Furies*, shows an intimate awareness of the Englishman and his relationship with France, but also a readiness to measure herself with Lawrence, Joyce, and the most innovative fiction of the century. *The House of All Nations* is entirely at home in the international banking community of northern Europe, while *The Man Who Loved Children* and *Letty Fox* are both written in a determinedly American idiom. Later in life, after a spell in Newcastle, Stead would produce a completely convincing novel of the English working classes: published in 1966, *Cotter's England* was a feat far beyond mere mimicry and suggests an extraordinary facility for penetrating an alien group psychology.

But in the decade that led up to the writing of *Letty Fox*, Stead was above all determined to fit in with Bill Blech's family, with the German mother, the expensively educated American daughter, the wife whom she must never meet, and, in short, with the whole Jewish-American community and its cosmopolitan traditions. It was here that her penetrative eye must go deepest. How else could she hope to win through, to arrive, if not at the altar, then at least at the registry office?

Letty Fox: Her Luck was the fruit of those long years of adaptation, an exuberant muddling of Stead's own girlhood memories with her meticulous observations of Blech's now adult daughter, Ruth Blech, who was a frequent visitor at the Stead/Blech ménage in New York. Ruth becomes the model, or one of the models, for Letty. She is given all the contradictions that formed the core of Stead's experience: the erotic charge, the romantic longings, the left-wing politics, the desire to be both beautiful and brilliant, to be admired and feared, to love with feminine faithfulness and submission and with masculine presumption and promiscuity. It's an explosive cocktail.

The relationships around Letty are likewise a retangling of those Stead knew best. So the heroine is given a father who, like Bill Blech, is a businessman radical, still married yet living with a mistress, who thus becomes, at least potentially, a portrait of Stead herself. Then Bill Blech, of course, was not unlike Christina's father, David Stead, another radical who left his wife for a mistress. The book is a hall of mirrors as far as possible identifications are concerned. Certainly when it was published all of Blech's extended family would see themselves in it. The only character who was unrecognizable was Letty's father's mistress: cool, level-headed, beautiful, and practical, Persia was as different from Christina as her exotic name suggests.

Wasn't this blatant mixture of fiction and reality a risk for Stead? Couldn't it perhaps lead to a breakup with Bill, to whom she still wasn't married, particularly if his daughter was to be presented as wild and promiscuous and Bill as an ineffectual father who kept wife and mistress happy by lying to them both? Reading Rowley's biography one becomes aware of an unspoken pact between Stead and Blech, the deal that made their relationship possible: she would never disagree with him politically and he would never take offense at what she wrote in a novel. It is to Blech's immense credit, after all, that he was the first to appreciate Stead's talent. Discovering his secretary's ambitions, he had asked to see a manuscript and, an able writer himself, recognized at once that it was remarkable. Her genius, perhaps, would excuse his betrayal of his family. It must be given full reign. "Dear Bill said once to me," Stead recounted, "that he would like to be to me what G. H. Lewes was to George Eliot. . . . I was not very pleased, because G. E. was not a pretty girl."

Stead would also one day remark that she only felt truly "moral" when writing, and again that she had only "felt herself" when writing. Perhaps what she meant was that in this supposedly fictional space she was free not to adhere to certain ideals, not to be coherent, to tell a clashing truth or two. "Radicalism is the opium of the middle class," announces an incensed Letty. Stead is enjoying herself. What luck to be able to say such things! And if this was the only space where she could be herself, where she could say she loved a man but found him unforgivable, or alternately that she loved a man but yearned for other men, or again that she was deeply attracted to women, but found lesbianism abhorrent, then little wonder she made the novels long and furious. They would express all the wild life no orthodoxy could embrace.

"He had some wonderful vision of the future," Letty remarks of a black man who falls in love with her, "where no hate would exist, only love between peoples and races, this was fine enough, but I live too much in the here and now; this is my great weakness." It was Stead's strength as a novelist.

The here and now of *Letty Fox* is overwhelmingly New York. Stead is determined to demonstrate that she now has full command of Bill's world. It opens thus:

> One hot night last spring, after waiting fruitlessly for a call from my then lover, with whom I had quarreled the same afternoon, and finding one of my black moods on me, I flung out of my lonely room on the ninth floor (unlucky number) in a hotel in lower Fifth Avenue and rushed into the streets of the Village, feeling bad.

Letty is always flinging out of rooms, rushing across streets. She is always full of energy and always on the edge of depression. Above all she always needs money. The long first paragraph finishes:

> Beyond such petty expenses, I needed at least two hundred and fifty dollars for a new coat. My fur coat, got from my mother, and my dinner dress, got from my grandmother, were things of the past and things with a past, mere rags and too well known to all my friends. There was no end to what I needed.

Immediately we have the picture of Stead's America, a place where love and money cannot be separated, where relationships are talked about in terms of investments and cutting losses, where people enjoy the illusion that the marriage game can be managed, and evaded, like an income tax return. It is savvy, cynical, full of corrupt life. Above all, it is brutal, since America, as Stead sees it, is that place where the struggle of everyone against everyone else is most visible and the rhetoric of concern at its absolute thinnest.

Yet it is impossible not to appreciate the gusto with which Letty enters the fray. Wondering whether she should accept a job offer in return for sex, Letty tells us: "I do not even see a scandal in this, for wide-awake women. In other times, society regarded us as cattle or handsome house slaves; the ability to sell ourselves in any way we like is a step towards freedom." Needless to say, Letty thinks of herself as a socialist. Later in the book the terms are reversed, but the principle is the same: "I had the feeling that he could have been bought," our heroine remarks of one reluctant lover, "if I had had a little more money."

Having given us, by way of introduction, a dozen sparkling pages on the twenty-three-year-old Letty's life in wartime Manhattan, Stead then goes back to reconstruct her narrator's childhood. It is here that the reader will first boggle at what Angela Carter referred to as Stead's "almost megalomaniac ambition." The "almost" was unnecessary. It is the sheer scope of the enterprise that is so extraordinary. Stead, an Australian, goes right back to the beginning of the century to reconstruct the rich New England family of Letty's maternal grandmother, the notorious Cissy Morgan, then the German-Jewish family of her paternal grandmother. Uncles, aunts, and cousins marry, divorce, and remarry. We have their foibles, ambitions, views on education, and endless improprieties. None of these are mere vignettes or anecdotes, but highly developed studies integrated in a series of interlocking stories that could well fill a book of their own. What they establish beyond all dispute is that Letty, like so many modern children, knows far too much far too young.

The satire is vast, fed constantly by the ancient struggle between the sexes and the modern American woman's delighted discovery of alimony. At great length we learn of the unhappily complex relationship between Letty's father, Solander, and her mother, Mathilde, then of his passion for the younger woman, Persia. Eagle-eyed, always excited, Letty wants to know what all this means. By the time her father leaves home, she and her younger sister, Jacky, have already learned how to present themselves as victims and make the most of being thought of as deprived. They know that compassion is a harbinger of gifts, hopefully cash.

The daughters are moved in with relatives, they are taken to England, to Paris, they write extremely long, witty, passionate letters in highly individual voices, seeking to impress their father or calm their mother. Slowly and with complete conviction, Stead shows the two sisters becoming distinct as they react first to the overall situation and then to each other's response to it, seeking individuality through complementary or competitive behavior. We see character in the making.

Meantime, stories you thought must have ended start again. An uncle you imagined married and forgotten reappears with debts and a mistress. He tries to seduce a niece. A cousin is becoming a whore, or a saint. An aunt turns up with a child, but without a husband. The book smolders, flaring up where you thought it extinguished, smoking where you had seen no fire.

But where is the whole thing going? If every form of narrative representation is essentially a convention, a pact between writer and reader as to how experience can be talked about, then it is only natural that the finest authors should be uneasy with some aspect of that convention, eager to bend it closer to the grain of their own lives. What Stead most resisted in traditional narrative was any easy formulation of shape and direction, any neatness, "the neatly groomed little boy in sailor collar," she called it, speaking disparagingly of the fiction the publishers liked most. In contrast, the exuberance and manic extension of the world that she depicts in *Letty Fox* denies any possibility of order. The work is rich and capricious, its descriptions dense, vital, and highly particularized; its only overall drift is that of Letty's growing up.

Not surprisingly, then, it is with the depiction of Letty's adolescence and young womanhood that Stead achieves her most impressive effect in this book. For perhaps three hundred pages we have been given a dazzling social satire, a tragicomic picture of a modern society where, with all traditional hierarchy broken down, the only possible relationship between people, above all between men and women, is competition and conflict; it is the mirror image at a social level of the political war that is raging in Europe as Stead writes her story. Yet up to this point, the reader feels, the whole book, bar the opening dozen pages, might well have been written in third person; for Letty is retailing stories she has heard, or overheard, stories she understands only in the most superficial fashion. The precocious girl feels superior to these aunts and uncles with their incomprehensibly muddled lives. There is a consequent narrative distance. And, as with most satires, the reader too feels a certain smug if uneasy detachment. There is something slightly grotesque about all these Morgans and Foxes with their interminable passions. Letty feels sure she will do better.

But the moment Letty too becomes subject to sexual desire, everything changes. It is as if a sane psychiatrist, chuckling over the antics of his lunatic patients, had himself suddenly gone mad. Suddenly passion, attachments, betrayals, marriage, and divorce are no laughing matter. Or they are, for there is still plenty of comedy, but the nature of the laughter has changed. It is full of pathos where before it was constantly on the edge of caricature. What had appeared to be an essentially political book is overtaken by existential concerns; the compassion Stead arouses now is not for the victims of poverty, the usual objects of public piety, but for those of desire:

> Moods of blackness and suffering passed through me, of fierce, fierce intercourse such as no flesh could bear. I got up and the fever that raged through my body was intolerable. Yes, this is the love that nymphs knew on afternoons when Pan chased them, I thought, this is the meaning of all those stories. I thought I was passionate; now, I know what growing up is. I thought, if it is going to be like this, this suffering and madness, I will kill myself now, for in the difficulty of getting married nowadays and of getting a child, that cooling cold stone of a child which stands in the hot belly and makes a woman heavy and tired, forgetting all her cruel fervors, that thing that drags her to the doors of the death-house and away from the intolerable ardors of the sun, in this slow world for women, I cannot live; I will kill myself.

Letty does not kill herself. She goes out and finds another lover. And another. Sexual conquest brings with it a gust of energy. She studies hard, works hard, she goes to meetings to discuss socialism and reform, achieving the "cheerful feeling that a lot is wrong with the universe; and it's marvelous to be able to discuss it all over a Martini." Socialist militancy thus emerges as no more than a by-product of sexual happiness. Or as a way out of distress: ("Everyone forgot . . . my troubles, and we all began to discuss . . .

the African problem."] In one of the most powerful scenes in the book, Letty seduces her father's radical and philandering friend, Luke Adams, while the older man is selfishly trying to get her to take in a Hispanic orphan boy whom he himself, in a moment of weakness, had agreed to look after. Letty remarks: "One not only felt that, in love, this dangerous man consulted his own pleasure and had no morals, but with him, all altruism vanished like smoke."

As fully drawn as any character in literature, Stead's Letty is marvelously talented, bursting with energy and youthful optimism. What is to become of such vitality, the book wonders? And so does Letty. How is it not to be spilt? In her biography, Hazel Rowley feels that this is a question Stead could not answer. The blurb to the Virago edition of 1982 shows all the feminist publisher's uneasiness with the answer that, on the contrary, the novel very frankly offers, marriage: "*Letty* is a 'powerful portrayal,'" the blurb writer says, "of a woman who might have been independent, but chose otherwise."

But could she really have been independent? What Letty most profoundly learns from her promiscuity, from her growing fear of herself and of her appetite, is that marriage is not, as her profligate family had led her to believe, merely the legally regulated collision of sex and economics. Something else is going on in the long-term union of man and woman, something to which she is inexorably drawn:

> I sometimes wondered at the infinite distance between the state of not being married . . . and the state of being married. . . . I couldn't figure it out; perhaps I was too young, anyway; but it savored to me of magic, and I felt very miserable that in this modern world something so primary, this first of all things to a woman, smacked so strongly of the tribal priest, the smoky cult, the tom-tom, the blood sacrifice, the hidden mystery. It didn't seem fair. We should have abolished all that with enlightenment.

It is in the novel's savoring, over so many pages, of Letty's growing belief, or obsession, right or wrong, that her energies must be "husbanded," that *Letty Fox* becomes more than a brilliant satire. Watching a poor working girl give birth to her illegitimate child, she muses,

> I wish I were a mother too. . . . Cornelis and all the men I had played round with seemed far away. This was the reality, and this was, truth to tell, what I, in my blind ignorant way, was fighting for, trying to make shift with one and all of them. But what chance has a smart, forward girl to be innocent or maternal? That's a dream.

How are we to take this? No doubt Letty is in earnest, but then she is perfectly capable of earnestly maintaining the opposite point of view on the next page. All the same, as the chapters accumulate and with them Letty's frustrations, we sense the growing seduction of that traditional dream, the pull of the marriage bond and maternity. Sooner or later Letty will succumb. In her case, it does not seem to be a question of choice.

The conclusion to *Letty Fox: Her Luck* is at once mockingly traditional and strikingly new. It is, I believe, one of the first novels to offer what we might call catharsis through exhaustion. Like many modern writers—Verga, Lawrence, Kafka, Faulkner, Beckett—Stead faced the problem: If our vision of the world is that it is perpetual struggle, if there is no state of harmony and propriety to which we can be returned after the disturbing events of our story (for however necessary she might have believed it was for herself or her characters, Stead never viewed marriage as such a state), then how is a novel supposed to end? Where can it leave us? Her answer, like Thomas Bernhard's after her, is to brings characters and reader to such a state of plenitude, or weariness with events, that the thing simply has to stop.

Letty moves from job to job, man to man. She is getting nowhere. A fiancé goes off to be a war journalist, then writes to say he has married somebody else. Another suitor backs out during the crucial discussion with her parents. She goes on vacation for a "trial honeymoon" with the perfect American, Wicklow; it lasts five days. Men promise to leave their wives. Out of curiosity, she seduces the elderly professor her sister is in love with. But she is getting tired of it. She throws some extraordinary tantrums. She is more and more manic, more frequently depressed. She is appalled by herself. Without a husband "a woman as strong as I am can also be strongly wickedly lazy, and forever."

But finally she, like her author, does get her one piece of luck. In the summer of 1945 she meets an old lover as tired of the game as she is herself, as tired as Europe then was with its interminable war. Everybody is quite quite worn out. Ring the wedding bells. It is not a Jane Austen ending. "Will this last?" Letty asks. And she muses: "It's a question of getting through life, which is quite a siege, with some self-respect. Before I was married I had none." At last pregnant, she concludes: "The principal thing is, I got a start in life; and it's from now on. I have a freight, I cast off, the journey has begun."

Are these closing words sardonic? Are they romantic? Or simply practical? Or has Stead somehow managed to make them all three? Rather than merely ambiguous, the novel contrives to go beyond any possible resolution. It constantly invites the act of discrimination, but only to repel it, to humiliate the critical faculty. At the end of the day Letty is both a romantic girl and a promiscuous opportunist, a happily married mother-to-be and a left-wing militant.

However we are meant to take them, Letty's final words must have echoed in their author's mind with increasing poignancy over the coming years. All too soon after the publication of the novel, Stead too would be embarking on a journey, casting off from New York's docks, but without her heroine's long-desired "freight." In the early days with Blech, Stead had twice aborted. While writing Letty she had suffered a miscarriage. Now, with the war in Europe over, the cold war had begun. America was no place for people of their political faith. She and Blech were under investigation by Hoover's FBI. They had heard that the heroine of Stead's latest novel was a young Communist.

It was hard now to find either work or publishers. Sliding into poverty, the couple moved back and forth between Belgium, Switzerland, England, and France. They were outcasts. Afflicted as ever by erotic yearnings, Stead sought to seduce Bill's friends, largely without result. She was humiliated. Critical acclaim had brought little cash. *Letty* was banned in Australia. Blech wrote some historical novels which sold well in East Germany, but it was impossible to get the money out. When, twenty-six years after they had become lovers, the couple were finally able to marry, they were living in slum conditions and Stead was advertising for hack work in the local papers. She did not mention the ceremony in letters to friends.

Stead, Rowley tells us in her biography, "had a knack of arousing hostility." Even in the days of first love when Blech did everything for her, she was uneasy with the situation. She was too used to the battle of life. She needed to make the brutal gesture, to assume the extremist position. Certainly when her husband lay dying she was not kind to him. She was dismissive of his suffering. He wasn't really sick. Afterwards she regretted it. Living exclusively on steak and alcohol, she defended his political opinions, now far beyond the pale, with renewed vigor. But she couldn't work, she considered her life over: "My life was for that, wasn't it? To live with Bill. I didn't know that was it, but it was." Needless to say all this complicated her eventual admission to the literary canon. Novels as fine as those published by any contemporary Nobel—*A Little Tea, A Little Chat, Cotters' England, Miss Herbert* —were admired but not celebrated.

It is no surprise that Stead was a very poor essayist and even poorer public speaker, unless, that is, we are to take her novels themselves as vast inconclusive essays, *Letty Fox* as the speech of someone endlessly changing her mind. The problem was that Stead could never isolate any particular message she had to get across. She wanted to seduce, but also to provoke, or rather, to seduce through provocation. The best writing, she claimed, was driven by an "intelligent ferocity" that would be able to speak all the contradictions that could not be spoken in any essay, friendship, or political movement, all the experience that risked driving a person mad if it was left unsaid, and risked driving a reader mad when it was. We must love her, in short, for telling us things we do not want to hear.

In none of Stead's novels does this formula work quite as splendidly as in *Letty Fox*, if only because Letty herself is the incarnation of this drive. Never are her men, or the reader for that matter, more enamoured of Letty than when she is unfaithful and bitchy. After her failed honeymoon with the ideal Wicklow, after her refusing even to talk to him on the return ride to New York, he nevertheless comes back to her: "I scolded Wicklow when he came to see me," she says. "He grinned, sat down on a stool, took off his hat, and remarked, 'You're more fascinating as a termagant, Letty, than as a sweet little wife.' "

As a writer, Stead is a termagant to whom one is always happy to return. I would advise a more comfortable seat than a stool. The gesture of removing the hat, do please note, is obligatory.

—TIM PARKS

LETTY FOX: HER LUCK

BOOK ONE
WITH THE OTHERS

1

ONE HOT night last spring, after waiting fruitlessly for a call from my then lover, with whom I had quarreled the same afternoon, and finding one of my black moods on me, I flung out of my lonely room on the ninth floor (unlucky number) in a hotel in lower Fifth Avenue and rushed into the streets of the Village, feeling bad. My first thought was, at any cost, to get company for the evening. In general, things were bad with me; I was in low water financially and had nothing but married men as companions. My debts were nearly six hundred dollars, not counting my taxes in arrears. I had already visited the tax inspector twice and promised to pay in installments when I had money in the bank. I had told him that I was earning my own living, with no resources, separated from my family, and that though my weekly pay was good, that is sixty-five dollars, I needed that and more to live. All this was true. I now had, by good fortune, about seventy dollars in the bank, but this was only because a certain man had given me a handsome present (the only handsome present I ever got, in fact); and this money I badly needed for clothes, for moving, and for petty cash. During the war, I had got used to taking a taxi to work. Being out always late at night, I was sluggish in the morning; and being a great worker at the office, I was behindhand for my evening dates. Beyond such petty expenses, I needed at least two hundred and fifty dollars for a new coat. My fur coat, got from my mother, and my dinner dress, got from my grandmother, were things of the past and things with a past, mere rags and too well known to all my friends. There was no end to what I needed. My twenty-fourth birthday was just gone, and I had spent two hours this same evening ruminating upon all my love affairs which had sunk ingloriously into the past, along with my shrunken and worn outfits. Most of these

5

affairs had been promising enough. Why had they failed? (Or I failed?) Partly, because my men, at least during the war years, had been flighty, spoiled officers in the armed services, in and out of town, looking for a good-timer by the night, the week, or the month; and if not these young officers, then my escorts were floaters of another sort, middle-aged, married civilians, journalists, economic advisers, representatives of foreign governments or my own bosses, office managers, chiefs, owners. But my failure was, too, because I had no apartment to which to take them. How easy for them to find it inconvenient to visit me at my hotel, or for me to visit them at theirs when they were dubious or cool. It seemed to me that night that a room of my own was what I principally lacked.

I had to leave the hotel for another reason. One of my lovers had lived there for some time, had gone away on a trip, was now coming back, and, of course, was glad of the room they had promised to keep for him in the same hotel. We had been about together a great deal, our liaison and its nature was flagrant, and I had been only too happy to make it known. Now, his farewell had been too casual and while away, he had sent another man to me, without a letter of introduction, but merely with my address on a scrap of paper and the assurance that "Letty knows the ropes." I had therefore resolved to have nothing to do with this absentee, Cornelis de Groot, unless he installed me somewhere and set up householding with me, openly. Meanwhile, I had become intimate with his friend, a very sensible, moderate man. Cornelis was too cunning and too ambitious; this is what made him dangerous for me. When with him, I behaved stupidly, incautiously, with passion, with ill temper; I was too dependent. I did whatever he wished and found him full of *sang-froid.* Both these men, Cornelis and his stand-in, were of about the same age, that is, about forty-two, too old, of course; yet with the absence of young men I could ask no questions, and in a way I learned much from these old men. I learned their weary, sentimental cunning, their husbandly manners; I found out that they were more generous than the young ones. But I was never fond of money, except to spend, and never went with a man for his money. My supreme idea was always to get married and join organized society. I had, always, a shrinking from what was beyond the pale.

I had not been out walking long that night before I made up my mind that I would do better to get myself a flat than to get company. They said the only way, at that time, to get a flat was to walk up and down the streets till you saw someone moving out. I made up my mind to spend not only this night, which was a Friday, but also the whole week end doing just this. I would stay away from work the following day (I had not had a Saturday off for months anyhow). If I did not get a flat this week end, I would take it as a sign that I was meant to accept a rather shameful (but routine) offer which had been made to me, at second hand, during the week. This offer had been sent to me, verbally, by Gallant Stack, a handsome and popular young promoter of midtown Manhattan. Two nights previously Gallant Stack had come to my mother's house, with a common friend, saying he had something important for me. It turned out that a writer who had just signed a Hollywood contract, wanted a young woman secretary: she had to be pretty, sophisticated, smart, with a knowledge of languages, and enough physical charm and social manners to make a good mistress. Gallant Stack had already mentioned my name and recommended me, and he asked my mother if she would pass on the offer as I was just the girl needed. My mother mumbled something about its being up to me, but Gallant Stack, wishing to oblige his friend, also came next day direct to me. " 'The three R's and Romance are her racket,' is what I said," said Gallant Stack to me, reporting his colloquy with the Hollywood writer. "I will think it over," said I. Shocking and unsavory as this proposition may appear when written down but not when said, it differed little from many a proposition I had received. My position with most of my employers had been just that; and let's face the facts, I liked it. It did not require any new kind of impudence for the author to send a crier round town in this way. My acquaintances in camp often sent their friends to me, and, of course, to any good-looking, smart girl they knew. It is the custom of the town. As for Gallant Stack—as he had seen some MSS., attempts of mine to get into literature, and had heard my complaints at failure, he felt he was acting the part of a friend. A writer has his time to himself, and has little to do, while I had to slave day and night to keep the favor of my bosses—and crush opposition. Stack was just a realist, a man without prejudice; and I am certain he would have taken care of me in any way if I had been in any kind of trouble. His boast was that no woman ever suffered from him; even his cast-off mistresses were helped to a new mistress-ship, a new job, or a husband by him. As for the Hollywood writer, he was not a bad man either; in this hurried world, no one has any time to seek and try out, and so one buys everything readymade. I do not even see a scandal in this, for wide-awake women. In other times, society regarded us as cattle or handsome house slaves; the ability to sell ourselves in any way we like is a step toward freedom; we are in just the same position as our Negro compatriots—and they would not go backwards toward their miserable past. One must take the good with the bad and, unmoved by the titles of things and worn-out prejudice, one must look toward the future. I feel, though, that this can't go on for a lifetime. We must bear the burdens of society on our backs just a certain way, then must set them down for someone else to pick up. This was very much my feeling at that time. I had carried the burdens of society just as far as was good for me. I was really tempted to take this chance, go to the Coast, and find a position in one of the studios.

But I was tired of work; and furthermore, I am fond of New York. It is hard to leave friends and old lovers, even when the latter have deserted. There are always the occasional dinners and the fondness that outlasts an affair that's done with. These cast-off lovers are my best friends, in a way; I have to explain myself to others, but there is nothing these men do not know. I wonder at the simplicity of people who think these affairs are bad for a woman. As for men—I don't answer for them. Men are easily debauched because they think of every woman they have had as a conquest, although it is clear that it is a mutual conquest and that each loses what each gains.

On this Friday night I was enduring that second half of living which is pure suffering. My friend of those days was Captain White, who was then situated in Washington, though his business brought him every week to New York. There was no question of marriage between us and I had agreed to leave him when his mother and fiancée came here from the Coast. The family had arrived, but I was finding it very hard to break it off; he, too. We had

scenes, reconciliations; and his doubts about his love for his fiancée, when he was with me, made me distracted. I could easily
have wiped a mere fiancée off the slate, I knew, but doubted that I
wanted him; and I had found out, today, through an anonymous
letter, that the so-called fiancée was his wife! In my upset, my
scruples vanished. I wanted to oust her; yet today I had sent him
"to the devil." I was surprised and worried when he did not telephone me within two hours of our final farewell. It was unlike
him. I knew that by now he was home with his legal woman; what
wretchedness for me! I wished I had the courage to cut a loss in my
love affairs; but a love affair is never a dead loss and this is the
catch in the business.

Going down Eleventh Street, I came abreast of an old brown-
stone house, with faint lights in an apartment without curtains
on the first floor and bright lights in the basement. An old woman,
hugging a bundle of laundry, stood at the railings, looking up and
in. I saw the first floor apartment was in disorder. An archway
separated the two large rooms which had once been drawing
rooms. The intermediate doors stood back, so that we could look
right through to trees and houses in Tenth Street. I thought,
"They're moving in, or moving out, I lose nothing by asking," and
was going up the steps when the old woman said, "It's no good
asking, I've arranged to take the place; I need it, too; I've got three
kids at home and we're living in two and a half rooms, all of us,
my husband too."

"When are you moving in?"

"As soon as I can get the men to move us."

"That'll be hard," I said softly, coming toward her; "and what
hold-up artists they are these days."

"I've got a firm," said she; "I had them for years: they moved
me fifteen times. They'll do something for me."

"For money," said I, and walked off. I went down half a block,
saw the woman had left the railings and was rounding the other
corner. I, at once, went back, had an interview with the superintendent's wife, promised her thirty dollars (the old woman had
promised her twenty dollars) to hold the place for me, agreed to
paint the place myself, exterminate vermin, and to move in in less
than a week, and so forth. It was discussed and concluded within

the hour. She took me up to see the flat, which, though cluttered up with boxes, bundles and furniture out of place, was almost my ideal; it consisted of two salons that could be thrown into one, a kitchen, bathroom, and easy access, down some iron steps, to the garden. Since they had not been allowed to raise the rent, the rent was still, officially, ninety dollars, in these days a bargain. The couple leaving the place were a nondescript middle-aged pair; the man was pleasanter than the woman, rather good-looking; they turned out to be music arrangers for radio shows. They said they had been given notice because of their pets, which they would not give up. What I had taken to be a large ornament on the white marble mantelpiece turned out to be two living Siamese cats folded round each other. A large, sickly wolfhound lay on the floor, in a back-breaking posture. A Scottie was hiding under a bookcase. The walls, I then saw, were rather smudged at about dog-height.

I slept badly that night, in my anxiety over the flat, and instead of going to work, went before eight to the real estate office. The rent of the Eleventh Street apartment was too high for me, but I gave them guarantees, references, the name of my father, Solander Fox, office manager, and his business address, Joseph Montrose & Co., a freight and chartering firm, with offices in the Produce Exchange. I likewise mentioned (though with more doubt) my maternal grandmother, Cissie Morgan, who ran two hotels, one in New Canaan, Connecticut, and one in Long Island, near Long Beach. I had luck. The apartment became mine. I was to move in within a week, whether the storage company would move me or not. There was no lease; it was on a month-to-month basis. This was almost permanency for me, whose affairs at that time were on a day-to-day basis. I went at once to survey my new premises, and had an intuition of success, good luck, all the way along.

Two doors led from the hall into the two high rooms flooded with sunlight. Between the windows looking into Eleventh Street was a mirror about eight feet tall, with a gilt frame. Above this and all round was oak paneling. At the back, other windows overlooked the garden; outside these was a terrace, which had been added. It had a glass roof. Beside this, the kitchen. The glass roof allowed light to fall into the room in any weather, so I would put my piano here. My piano, two divans (one for a bed and one for a daybed), a couple of Mother's old chairs would easily furnish this place. I turned round, a couple of rugs on the floor, a picture or so—my father had some—a few ashtrays—Woolworth's—a few wine and whisky glasses—Eighth Street—and all would be ready. I would throw a house-painting party, invite the office—show I was not depressed about Captain White's wife. Certainly, the anonymous letter came from the office. I would be launched again; everything cleared behind me. I looked in the kitchen with considerable zest. I am not a bad cook. I was, when I lived with Mother; I was not then, after having been a half-wife for several men. I was one of those marrying women who married even her casual lovers: I had a very honest instinct.

But I had not a penny. How was I to pay the rent? My position at the office was secure, I had references, but I could not put myself in the hands of personal finance companies. I had often borrowed—true, often lent—I did not always get the money back, though I am not afraid to ask for what is mine. I am generous, foolishly so when I am in the money. As for my salary, sixty-five dollars weekly, it was spent, up to the hilt, and mortgaged for months ahead, with my charge accounts and money borrowed from Mother, Father, and others. I had three charge accounts (rash Grandma's and rash Granddaughter's!) and owed money on each; one of them was outstanding, $172, for two years. Grandmother or Mother, however, would probably pay up one or other of them soon, for I would have to take one or both into my confidence; and so I could work on an account again. My argument (about the present apartment in Eleventh Street) would be that in it I would save money, for I would be able to cook for myself in the week ends; and if I made an agreement with White, or Cornelis, upon his return, say, to buy all the raw stuff for our kitchen, in return for my cooking, I would surely save the difference in the rent. I did not intend to cook for anyone but White, or Cornelis; the others must pay—no discounts. This decision was the fruit of experience. I knew that I suffered through men, and if, through some misfortune which I do not know, or perhaps (I am quite fair) do not care to remember, I have injured some too trusting man, in my Grand Tour, at least I have the argument that they made me suffer too and much more than I ever made them suffer. I have been too trusting, too generous. I shall never be a dangerous woman; I can make men love, but I cannot make them suffer. It would be much better the other way about. I have seen women able to make men suffer who could not make them love. The more they suffered the more they hung around for a showdown. In the end they did better than I, for it is strange what people will do to be able to suffer and say to themselves, in the night, "I have suffered, I have lived indeed." Well, I am just a run-of-the-mill New York girl, I cannot do this.

I divagate. At this time, I had one aim—that was to marry. I had given up going to family parties simply because cousins younger than me were married, and aunts, cousins, even my grandmother, Cissie Morgan, would look me over and quite frankly ask what was wrong with me that I had not got a man, a fine home, a good income, and children yet. Why was I still Letty Fox and not Letty What-have-you? There was no answer, for I had not even the excuse that I was ugly, ambitious, disillusioned, misunderstood, or timid; I was quite the most eligible and probably the most desirable girl in the family—well, no one ever thought to see me twenty and unattached.

Well, as to the rent: I had no chance of getting money from my father, who was quite a different breed from myself. He did not approve of my debts, although I had heard some tales about his own indebtedness at my age. Then, of course, I was not, truly speaking, insolvent, for on my twenty-fifth birthday I was to get the thousand dollars that Grandfather Morgan left for me; and, more than that, everyone has always felt that Father owed me for the shares of Standard Oil of New Jersey that were given to me when I was born and were later sold to pay for my medical and school expenses. I supposed that I would get this money when I actually got married; but on account of my vagaries in love, my family had been holding out on me; not so much giving me the forbidding frown, as secretly and tranquilly exercising their economic advantage over me; so that I felt I must marry in order to get my own property, even though I am long past my majority. My own standpoint was different. I felt that if I had the money I would attract a husband in a short time. I attracted men enough; the difficulty was that I could not keep them, and since army life had taught about eleven million eligibles what economic security is, I did not complain, because my friends, ex-officers, felt that a man needed a woman with cash, to start out in civilian life again. Young men count up; what with rents, taxes, and high prices for infants, they naturally flinch from the married state. If I could get an acceptable offer, I would not of course pay up my debts with any money received upon my engagement. These debts I considered would be rather the concern of my parents and relatives, who were supposed to look after me. No, I would put the money to some use, furnish a home and prepare to settle down as a regular wife and mother. The fact is, dribs and drabs of money must come to me from the Morgan family, as time goes on, simply because so many of the older brothers and sisters of my mother have no children. Grandmother Morgan usually paid up for me when I was really in a jam, the only drawback being that she lived too hard, was seventy-five, and still wanted to remarry.

After I had, on Saturday, given the superintendent the promised thirty dollars, an unavoidable bribe during the housing shortage, I went to my father's office in the Produce Exchange. He is a manager and perpetual understudy for an old friend, Joseph Montrose, who is in ship chartering and freights. Papa likes to see me there and to show off my good looks and cleverness. He took me out to lunch in "the Custom House" restaurant in the Exchange; and after we had chatted for a long time about the Third World War and the general fate of this lithosphere, I asked him for the thirty dollars which I had paid the superintendent. He frowned. I had a long tussle before he sighed, pulled out a piece of paper and pencil, figured upon it ostentatiously, and agreed to take me back to the office, where he would get an advance from the treasurer. I told him the address of the place and when I was to move in. I asked him if he would come and help me bring in the furniture, but he said, "I will be there, all right, but you must have the money to pay the men." I was irritated and said he had never given me a home. He stood me another drink downstairs, and it ended well, with my father merely repeating that I must not expect him to have the money for the men. I had taken a taxi downtown, and had had a cocktail before going to his office; and now I took a taxi back uptown to Eleventh Street. As this made a small hole in the thirty dollars (and this was about all I had) I telephoned to Mother asking her to meet me for a cocktail at Longchamps in Twelfth Street. She made a fuss about it, but did eventually meet me there, and sat on a stool at the bar as she really likes to do. I then asked her to lend me ten dollars for tips to the men who move the furniture. She only had six dollars with her and this left me rather short. I told her I had barely the money to pay out to servants at the hotel, and as she had disappointed me, I was obliged to ask her to pay for the drinks. However, it was all right. She told me she was visiting her youngest sister, my Aunt Phyllis, for the week end, and that Phyllis, Phyllis's husband and Cissie Morgan (her mother) were always so ashamed of her poor dress that they were always offering her small sums. I begged her to take the money this time if it were offered to her. "It humiliates me so," cried Mother. "It makes me indignant, too," I said; "but take it once." However, I dropped this fruitless struggle.

When Mother asked me the address of my new place I misquoted it, so that she would not go straight there; and though she would see it soon, I could not let her see it till I was in. My plan has always been to present people with the *fait accompli*. It is the only way to get things done. I therefore told her, as I had told Papa, that the rent was only sixty dollars monthly; I thought I would leave them in the dark, making myself out to be a good bargainer, for a few months at least, until life caught up with me. If expenses mounted too high, I would simply put it all before them and ask for aid; but, frankly, I did not expect to come down on them; I thought I would see my way clear by the fall. I would have had it out with Cornelis by then.

After all these anxious calculations I left Mother on lower Fifth Avenue to navigate her way home. She lived near the Hudson River now, in a small affair. I came back to my apartment.

I was at first almost deliriously happy. The first night, after I had put up photographs of the Morgan family, I unpacked all my old letters and books and I plunged into this stuff, this real, close-woven fabric of my youth, which was past, with pleasure. There were boxes of letters, photographs which I had kept from childhood, letters I had written to Grandma Fox, returned to me after her death, poor darling; letters which had passed between me and my sister Jacky, in our squabbles, and letters from my mother and father, who had been separated for many years. There were theater programs, menus from Paris, bills from a school I once attended in England. What a varicolored life; and yet at times I felt I had nothing to tell. There were also, of course, many packets of letters from boy friends. I had been wanting to get at these for months, just to check up; to see, for example, whether the graduated mendacity of Mr. A of five years ago, was not a perfect model of that of Mr. B with whom I was still philandering. I had come to the point when I wanted to make a clean sweep, and felt a general uneasiness about the kind of life I was leading. "A tourist," Papa called me, a tourist to men, that is. I reckoned I knew enough about life to write a real book of a girl's life. Men don't like to think that we are just as they are. But we are much as they are; and therefore I have omitted the more wretched details of that close connection, that profound, wordless struggle that must go on in the relation between the sexes. I have come to the conclusion that it must go on and that certain realities of love between men and women should not be told. I have written everyday facts which, doubtless, have happened in the life of almost every New York middle-class girl who has gone out from high school or college to make a living in the city.

2

My OFFICE friends and Captain White came on Sunday and painted the apartment. I had no time to clean up on Monday before work. My father and his girl, Persia, came on Saturday evening and helped me to arrange things. I was obliged to put Mother off until Monday evening, so that she would not meet them on Saturday, or Captain White on Sunday. Mother was very liberal about my boy friends, but seemed quite bitter about my going about with any married man, even though we were still, you might have said, still under martial order. Father came back alone on Monday night and found Mother there; and so I got all my cleaning up done, for since they would not speak to each other, except to say "Good evening," no time was lost. The next night my poor good mother came again, with my sister Andrea and Andrea's friend Anita, and so between us all I got settled in. Mother had found out the rent and said it would have been better for all of us to get a place together, but I had no consideration. She and Andrea and Anita lived in a hole over in Chelsea while Mother and Anita worked long hours at mediocre pay in war work, and Andrea did all the housework and minded the baby. All that my father could give them went to a lawyer in a certain legal affair which I will explain later—to put it briefly here, a paternity suit against the father of Anita's baby, a young war worker.

What I said in response to Mother's outcry was, "But, Mummy, you never had any consideration for us. In the first place, you did not get a divorce and so did not have regular alimony to keep us in security. Then, you were too proud to take help from Grandma Morgan, and so I never had the right clothes or atmosphere, till I earned them myself. Then, if you had settled everything as women usually do, instead of messing round in your habitual way, I believe the family would have taken you into Green Acres or Grandma's Long Beach hotel long ago, and we would all have had a wonderful home for years. Grandma would certainly have found you another husband." Mother and I had another squabble after this along the usual lines. She said I thought only of myself and I said she thought only of striking an attitude and what a gloomy, unrewarding attitude it was. "Some people, I know," said I, "say I have bounce, I am preposterous, I elbow people out of my way and am out for myself. I am, Mummy, like the King of Siam, but at least it doesn't impose on anyone; I am what I am, and I make my way in the world. But, goodness, I should have been much better off with a stepfather or with anything than with this perpetual casting back into the past. Could I bring my friends to a real home, even when I lived with you—no! Echo loudly answers no! Why? Because I was imposing on you. So I was. A youngster has to impose on its parents. I know you effaced yourself and went to the movies and all that, but was that a home? Well, you ask what kind of a home I wanted? Well, my own kind, I suppose. You're a good woman, Mummy, but we don't mix; and what is the use of pretending that we do. I know it's unfair, I don't say I'm the best daughter you could have had; but I've simply got to be on my own now. Do you know how old I am, Mother? I'm twenty-four. That's awful. I've simply got to live my own life. I know we've been over this before, but I simply boil over with it every night. Think how I live! Men make me propositions every day—this, that, and the other: none of them so far honorable enough for me to take the plunge. You don't like to hear that. I can't help it. I'm sorry. I've got to make the right start in life. Mother, I'm absolutely determined, when I find the right man, to be the perfect wife. Now you know nothing about men, Mother; and I do. I don't say I'm a genius at them. I've seen my friends marry and I wouldn't say they did badly, but how dull they look; I can't stand that lamplight conversation round the family table. There must be something better for me. So I'm browsing! You've got to let me. I've got to be selfish now in order to be a good wife and mother later on. That's why I can't live with you and the girls. Anita's got her kid and you've had three, Mother; but I have none. You've got to let me have my way."

"I'm not going to argue," sighed my mother; "you're just like your father. You can argue up and down and round the corner and still I know I'm right. However, you're far too selfish to bother about us."

I was furious with Mother. When she went I telephoned to Papa and he came over and took me to Chumley's, where I had two brandy alexanders and was at once, as usual, scolded by him, for my extravagance.

"You take too much advantage of your male escorts, that's your weakness," said my father; "men don't like it."

"Look, Papa, have I got to write to Aunt Maybell's Soul Secrets Column or something," I said, tears coming into my eyes; "I want to talk to a realist. I had another fight with Mother. Why are there good, gentle women in the world? They make wonderful mammas—and I don't pretend I'm a good daughter—but what a pain in the neck they are!"

"You owe your mother a lot," said he, of course.

"Life, love, but not the declining of happiness," said I. "I could write a book about what she doesn't know."

"Well, why don't you?"

"I would," said I gloomily, "if I didn't know so much. The trouble is that I haven't a naïve young flame, my Pegasus isn't a pony. I've read the world's best literature and the world's best critics and inspiration comes only when you're green."

"I'd like to fan your noble tail," said Papa, laughing. "Come on, lazybones, admit you're a slob and have a good time out of life. You know damn well you don't care who wins the horse race as long as you've got a dinner date."

"That's true," I said, sighing; "I'll end up yet strutting it as fattest goose round the village mudhole; I like anywhere and nowhere; it's ambition with clay feet."

My father is very sympathetic and has many of my characteristics, although not my vices; and perhaps this is his weakness. We spent a lovely evening talking over everything and Papa told me about my mother's youth (he became moist-eyed) and many other things; and as you don't know my father, Solander Fox, I have to explain that all this was told with exuberance, freshness, and astounding detail as if it had all happened yesterday, no, half an hour ago, and Solander had been a witness of it all. Not only that, my father's genius as a conversationalist is such that no one can remember later whether or not he, too, was not a witness of all the events and conversations Solander describes; the truth is, I have heard friends of my father describe events at which they never could have been present (and which, in fact, did not take place except in my father's imagination). Solander's stories are the kind which are carried all over town; months later they come back to him in a different—usually a diluted—form. Solander is prized as an evening visitor, he is a great entertainer, he has spent his life at it; he is too much of an entertainer, he has spent his talent at it. And in this respect we are very much alike. That is why we still like to go out together, in spite of the differences in our tastes and morals, and why we can chuckle robustly, argue earnestly for hours, and come home exhilarated. Of course, it is not Freudian love, for I never wanted to marry anyone like my father; I always preferred those (to be frank) more shoddy; and I had to have a man who could spend money on me freely and who can make love as an amusement.

What I heard this night about Mother was, briefly, this. Father had known Mother as a little girl, but first been conscious of her attractions as a woman when she was about fifteen and was leaving high school to go to drama school. Mother was lovely, he said, serious, absorbed in her future. She studied her roles when he was there, in a husky, ventriloquial voice which was really moving, frightening even, and which seemed to reach farther as she lowered it—a magnificent stage voice. But she had a very uneven temperament, none of that blast of energy and self-confidence necessary, and took her first few failures to heart.

I myself think she was born for the stage, and that she never got over her disappointment. She knew many roles by heart, especially out of Chekhov, Shakespeare, and Eugene O'Neill, and she often recited them to me when I was a child. At the time I thought they were her own experiences and that she had deeply suffered. What moved me most were the stereotyped words that always came so penetratingly out of her mouth. I would sit in one end of the places we inhabited—rooms in hotels, apartments and the rest—and listen to her at the other end. Her personality, full of drama, filled the apartment, and she had a disturbing quality: she unsettled you so much that you could neither meet her eyes nor return to your own reflections. It took me years to sort out in my mind which were my mother's own experiences, which were her dramatic roles, and which were roles which she had created for herself out of her own experiences. When I first read one of my mother's roles—it was Chekhov's *The Seagull,* and I read it when I was about nine years old—I was astounded and then angry. I thought my mother had stolen the words and was a liar. But I at once got to understand about the theater through this and became a voracious reader, thinking I could see through everyone in the same way; I had the impression that everyone stole some of their roles from books.

My mother was, at fifteen, a shadowy blonde, dreaming of Europe and the great stages of the world. If she thought of love at that time (said Papa) it was as Juliet or Ophelia. . . .

"She was irritated by me, who talked all the time," said Solander; "I gave her no repose for her internal contemplation of tragic and poetic parts. I fell in love with her; it seemed to me she would never come to depend upon me at all; she was so wonderfully herself." His life wrapped itself round her and his love was so wholehearted that he never doubted she knew he was coming to the Morgan house for her.

"But she probably just thought I came to spout my piece and make off," said Solander, at Chumley's.

Meanwhile, his darling, Mathilde, had fallen in love with a young actor in a Village theater; a year later with another, in summer stock, whom she met out in Long Island; and the third year, at eighteen, she met an ambitious male dancer, aged eighteen, a boy with hair of metallic blond, blue or green in stage lights. The boy was faunish, affectionate, coaxing, selfish—all that Mathilde required for a fatal passion. The street lamps under plane trees and the spring shadows in Minetta Lane, or the lights in sordid basements in the Village, forever after meant, to Mathilde, her deceived youth and useless passion for this dancer, Fred. The dancer became the intimate of one youth after another and one man after another, of young and old women, of rich and poor, but always of creatures that could help him in his career. Fred wore flowers in his hair, carried flowers in his arms, lay down in gardens in the country among flowers and looked more unreal and elegant there than most girls; with her poetic soul she saw him as he was, a flower. She could not get this out of her mind. He did not leave her —he danced away, back and away for good. Her youth was finished.

There are some people in the world who do not harden as they are the more often and the more cruelly deceived. She vacillated for years, understudied, went on the road, kept Solander in the background, and only at the age of twenty-three married her faithful lover. These were my parents, in their youth. I now took my cue and started my entrance upon the stage of life, not without the usual hesitations and regrets from my poor mother. A year after my birth, my sister Jacqueline came on the scene, and this was all our family for some years. We were quite poor, even though the Morgans lived in the grand manner. Grandmother Morgan, who was just beginning to feel her energies, and beginning to take over the business, had too much to do to trouble about us. The Morgan family was gay, preoccupied, elderly. Grandmother Fox was an old, timid, dependent lady, although then only in her early fifties.

We were as if on an island, but my mother took her maternal duties very seriously. There was a cool apartment in Sixteenth Street, which the young Foxes had taken at a high rent, to be near Stuyvesant Park. My mother, whose psyche had resembled the disturbing cavern of the empty theater before, now resembled a delicious but two-toned madonna, drawn partly from baby magazines and partly from modern painters. Her face was mealy and childlike, her eyes were gay and tender. Her heart was a newborn lamb, her curling long hair suggested cherubs, nothing in her jarred; a sepia shadow hung over her. Even when she raised her hands to her ears and cried out, the attitude and pang were perfect; now she had no doubt of herself. In this role, written for her many centuries before, she felt at ease, and she combined all the charm of an innocent young girl and of innocent motherhood.

My father poured out his love upon her, yet he was unhappy; he was an embarrassed and dubious spectator of this miracle play. When his lovely Mathilde was not worshiping her baby-in-arms, or portraying a female defending her young, or walking up and down with the child in her arms, representing to herself an unhappy and loveless woman, she was sitting in a chair behind the lowered but open blinds, looking out into the small dirty back yards, through the leaves of the Chinese plantain, and thinking distrustfully of their future. Would they have more children? Would it always be like that, looking into the balconies of a flophouse off Third Avenue? How could she make such a terrible decision as to give a child life? Now she must live for it alone. But how could she educate it? She knew nothing. How unhappy she was!

Then she was delicate and sensitive and could not accustom herself to the roughness of the housework and the nights and days without sleep. She had shut a door in herself, though, and now had forgotten forever the theater—the strange nights of acting there before the peopled cavern, all that she knew of real joy on this earth—and the blue-haired boy and all the boys before and after, not her lovers, but her friends. She had turned her back on that world of illusions, but she was fevered, empty. She must find something to do. She felt "exposed"—the child would soon see through her; the endless vigils and the battling with a rough-tempered healthy child wore her out.

She tried a few jobs, but came back to the house and her child whenever I caught a cold or fever. "I must give up everything, even reality, for the little girls," she said. "If it's a struggle for you, Sol, it is too late to think of that; we gave life and now must pay for it." At other times, she would think more cheerfully—they were a young, lucky couple; but most of the words came from others, from friends and from the foolish magazines which she read eagerly, looking for set conventional phrases which would describe her situation satisfactorily. These magazines had articles which minutely discussed her life and day, and therefore what they had to say she accepted. She began to rely upon them, while all the time, at the back of her mind, was her old experience as an ambitious, shy but gallant young girl, which had taught her very different notions. Solander humbly accepted what she had to say on my subject until it came to education, and there they began to dispute, for Mathilde stickled for the magazine and the educational cultbooks, while my father wanted us to be prodigiously well-educated, well-disciplined, and, likewise, socialists from our beginnings.

On my second birthday, my grandmother was buying and selling property on Long Island. She got home late, but turned up at my party, without presents, but with her youngest daughter, my Aunt Phyllis, a ravishing doll in her middle teens. Grandmother took Aunt Phyllis whenever she went out to meet new friends, and was rewarded by meeting at our house the two partners in the business in which my father was then engaged.

"Excellent," said Grandma to Mother, rubbing her hands over the new silk stockings her latest admirer had given her, "fine: I kill two birds with one stone; you see, this is my system: I see the family and I show off my little queen," for one never knew, she said, where she would meet the right man. New clothes for Phyllis had emptied Grandmother's purse on that day, and all I received was a bottle of sour wine, but Grandmother and Aunt Phyllis met at the house Joseph Montrose, the young merchant, who had just married, and Mr. McLaren, an elderly admirer of my father's talents, a wealthy socialist, and my Uncle Perce Hogg's friend, come to give me ten shares of Standard Oil. Said he, "A child starts off with the right idea of society if she has a little of her own; and I'm sorry you let the first two years pass without her owning something. Thus, two years have passed during which she belonged to the underdogs, and I'm sorry to observe that this has a bad effect on the character and temper in our class society."

My father remarked that he had thought of putting twenty dollars in the bank for me. Mr. McLaren said, "Do it at once, my boy; it is never too early to make a start in life, and the earliest impressions are the forming and forcing ones; let me have a child during the first seven dollars and I can guarantee its success afterwards. The lassie," said he, gazing upon my two-year-old self, "has now a small equity, and I guarantee she will be a sensible matter-of-fact young lady. Although," he continued sagely, "I will not commit myself; I'm speaking without sufficient data, no doubt."

No one hastened to add to my fortune at this moment, however, and I think Mr. McLaren felt he had committed himself rashly in this respect. He said he would counsel my father on my education, later on, to see that the effects of the ten shares of Standard Oil were felt.

When my mother wanted to send me to a privately run kindergarten, not very well known nor much respected, she found out it would cost four hundred dollars yearly, and she wanted to sell the shares to help pay for it. Mr. McLaren paid her a short visit and bore her down; he destroyed for the time being all her ideas about bringing me up lavishly. "You'll make a hothouse plant of a sturdy piece of heather or a flourishing vegetable." My mother hated him for being so plain about me. She became inconsolable at the thought of our poverty. Other mothers sent their children to expensive private schools, and made many sacrifices to do so, starving themselves and their husbands, dressing badly and having no amusement. Mother thought this the correct thing. There was no private play school to be had under four hundred dollars yearly. My father gave in and I went to "The Bairns." I had red cheeks, sparkling brown eyes, thick curly hair, heavy active limbs, and wore out my clothes, the carpets, and the furniture with my climbing and jumping. I was loud-voiced and rude, as I saw other children of my age were, and went into a screaming fit to get my way. I was uncommonly bright when it came to my own interests, and understood things relating to them, long before I could speak properly; but I spoke early too, filling the house with a rattle, a drooling and buzzing from early dawn. There was now no sign of the inherently feeble child who had made its entrance on the stage of life and received my name. Adults were obliged to bear with my roughness and selfishness and call it energy, health, animal spirits, self-expression, and so forth. I became wilder and more cruel each day as I saw them more miserable, being obliged to go through the martyrdom of me and beginning to look old, drooping and sulking, but swallowing all this that was repugnant to them. I loved shoving garbage down their withered necks, punching their fat stomachs, and treading on their toes. Mother thought I would become timid and a failure if I was scolded, I would be *repressed*!

The friends I had chosen at school, two or three healthy, loud-voiced girls and boys, had parents who thought the same. In our own minds we were already mature. The teachers and friends were almost dead, to us they smelled and looked dead. Even lovely Aunt Phyllis seemed to me at that time gross, idiotic, and elderly, and she was too busy with "love" to bother exercising any influence over me. To me, besides, she was only partly pretty; I was prettier, so were others at school. I had never, at that time, seen a pretty woman, and did not know what they meant by it—at least, I could not pick out a pretty woman as readily as I could an ugly one. But I was very fond of men, would run up to them, lead them by the hand, kiss them and ask them for things, for I soon found out that they were either charmed or obliged to appear charmed.

When I had been at this school some time, Mr. McLaren came to the house and saw me, I should say, apprehended me. He spoke severely to me, the first grown person who had ever done that. My mother took me from the room with a frown on her face; at the door she turned back and said gently that he did not understand, I was a sensitive child and might have bad dreams, caused by his repressive behavior.

"You should be careful of your attitude toward children, and not introduce foreign elements into their surroundings, you see," said Mother, "because even a moment's conflict, a casual acquaintance with an adult person, even a child, may alter a child's whole life. They are so impressionable, so ready to learn." She added that she selected her weekly floorwasher very carefully with my feelings in view and was always in the room when the window-washer was there. At this, I jubilantly burst back into the room with a loud yell, and rushing up to Mr. McLaren, squirted a mouthful of water between his plump and yawning thighs. Mr. McLaren observed that he would fan my little tail so red that the baboon in the zoo wouldn't be in it. My mother burst into tears, seeing him pick me up; but Mr. McLaren only took me in his arms, set me on his damp knee, and after saying, "One squirm out of you and you'll get the cat" (at which my mother looked very sulky indeed), began to tell me a story. It was a fascinating old-style tale about Br'er Bullfrog, told in the seductive dialect of a certain Uncle Remus. No sooner had the first dulcet sounds broken on my delighted ear, however, than Mother indignantly came over and raised me from the old gentleman's knee.

"We never tell any dialect stories here," she said, most shocked. "They only teach race prejudice; the child must not know that other people are different from us."

Mr. McLaren turned red, his gray eyes flashed; but after looking at her for a long moment, he bowed his head and said in a trembling but mild voice that it was God's own mercy I had the brains and brawn to survive such flub-dub, for any other child would be turned into a Simple Simon by such methods and why didn't they leave children now primeval jellies when they would be safe from any influence.

I burst into shrieks. My mother went out, followed by my father. When my father returned he did not argue with Mr. McLaren, to my disappointment.

They went into a discussion of systems of education, the Scottish style, old-style, and the French style, which he believed in, and the University of Hard Knocks, against the present fad for spoon-feeding and the bedevilment of parents which, it seemed, was the one I was going through. My father appeared to agree with Mr. McLaren. My mother could scarcely control herself, and put me into bed with a good many bumps, jerks, and frowns. Then she hurried out to take part, and began repeating a great deal of the stuff she and the ladies talked over when they came to visit.

"That's an undisciplined and unlettered little monkey," said Mr. McLaren. "She's been to school for nearly two years and can she so much as read or write?"

My father passed the sherry. My mother said a delicate and talented child would not receive proper attention in the public schools. They had forty, fifty, sixty, seventy in a class; it had been estimated that the teachers in a certain school had not one minute of time per day to give to each child in individual attention; and what of general health? Then, what about conservative, no reactionary ideas, brought subtly or with a shillelagh into the brains of innocent children in the public schools?

"You knock 'em out again," said McLaren calmly. "What are you here for? If you can't take care of your own children, give up the family system and go in for communal living! Can she add two and two? No."

"She has not felt the urge," said Mother; "they do not force the children; they learn the play way, they learn by co-operation; there is no urging of the individual, it leads to the competitive spirit. Education isn't a treadmill and it isn't the star system. And then we must wait for the child's need to unfold itself."

"Holy Methusalem," said old McLaren, "and has she got to wait for the urge for everything her whole life long? Then she'll know no more than her A B C when she's a hundred, for that baby will more likely be a female wrestler."

My father laughed, and McLaren told them, in their circumstances, they ought to take advantage of the free schools. But Mother spoke up for me, saying that I never would be a member of the community of dirty little foreign children, that I belonged to one sort of people and to one kind of society and their object was to push me up to better things than they had ever known, not to drag me down to the level of dirty little slum children, whose heads were as full of gangster ideas as of lice. Did McLaren even know what words those children used in the street, right outside the house? Letty had brought home two or three of them already.

Not liking to miss the fun, I raced into the room and joyously heaved a slipper over the electric light. I at once gave vent to these juicy words from my listening post. Mr. McLaren gave me an awful look which caused me to run behind my father's chair, upon which I then climbed with loud shrieks of victory. My mother was explaining to Mr. McLaren that if she now whipped me or washed my mouth out with soap (the old Scottish method apparently), I would be repressed, these words would be repressed in me for the rest of my life, and I would either take to filthy pictures years later or would become a nervous pale girl who would attract no one and never would succeed; my real personality would never emerge because they would have imposed their old-world behavior patterns upon me. "She is not over-protected," she said dolefully; "we have not the money for that, for I realize that is your objection."

Mr. McLaren listened, frowning, to this careful student-mother's recitation, and said, "It's some form of Voodoo—it's a secret society"; with my father saying, "Mac, I suppose there's a lot of Jean-Jacques in the idea, but on the financial side I agree with you"; McLaren saying, "All education should be free and every child will be spoiled till it is"; my father saying, "Middle-class radicals have a curious urge to prove they're the genteelest of all people"; and McLaren saying, "Point to one gentleman or genius!" and my father saying, "But Mathilde feels she is trying to give Letty the very best education," it all ended by my mother saying, "If you had suffered as a child, as I did, you would understand everything"; the men both looked at her and said not another word.

27

"I suppose you think that too is just compensation," said my mother, using one of the women's favorite words; "Letty shall want for nothing, she will have nothing to compensate for, and perhaps, when she grows up, her children can go to a free school. Perhaps we'll be in a different system then"; and the words dragged coldly, childishly, out of her mouth, like a distasteful formula.

Probably, however, the price of the school was too high, for immediately after I was sent to a public school, where I learned at once to read and write. I liked the school. I never tired of my tricks and of making the girls laugh and jump out of their desks, in fact, do what pleased me. But those girls were too intimidated, or too poor, I don't know what; they could never be got into the rapture of badness which overcame us so often at The Bairns. I was a great trial to my teachers, contradicting them and even quoting to them bits of doctrine about education from the talk of my mother and father. I made enemies. Many of the girls had become disciplined by this time (I was about six) and even had some ambitions. They disliked me, I upset the lessons. The ugly, ill-dressed ones admitted me, and laughed when I made a noise, though not always with good nature. For them I represented freedom, money, and privilege, and they hoped to see me punished. I let them see I didn't give a darn for the rules. These poor and ugly girls were always getting punished for lateness and dirt, and were suspected of any thefts. I suppose our mutual dislike helped them into jail, or onto a picket line.

At home I returned to my progressive school ways and in fact made such a noise around myself (my father calling me "his three-ring-circus") that I felt stouter, smarter, better every day, and felt sure I would knock the world down later on just by strutting in upon it. So many a fat and loud child feels.

In all this, I had cronies, followers, and a sidekick, in my father's words, who was my sister Jacqueline, born a year after me. Jacqueline (Jacky) wanted to be great, not famous, just great, she explained. She was a lively girl also, with yellow elf-locks, large oval eyes, and straight features, a small nose and a medium red mouth. She was thin at first, with long, thin arms, but when she grew up became like me, middle-sized and plump. She was not always as pretty as I, being graver; but she had a trait I did not have.

Her gravity threw a shadow over her face and mind, and this shadow was interesting; people even found her charming. When I was nearly seven, we had a world of our own, joky, mad, bad, self-ish, scandalous, indecent, alert. We rifled drawers, read and stole letters, faked telephone calls, spied and informed. We became pious or godless together, full of parental respect or odiously unloving together. The beginning of each of these moods was simply the words, "What will we do?" Whatever we did, we did with unflagging energy for three, four, or five days. The mood would disappear in some minute of some day and we would once more sit blankly or stand jigging vacantly round a chair and repeat, "What will we do?" Many projects were presented, reviewed, rejected, before the next project—religion, mother love, slander, theft—was decided upon. Some projects were shabby imitations of the wickedness of other young desperadoes we heard or read about in children's books.

In all this world of tumble and fun, we did not at first see that there was trouble in our family. Jacky first saw it and I scoffed. Then I saw it, and we turned the trouble into another hilarious project; we became "Clark Gable and Joan Crawford" in a hog-calling scene imitated from movie (and Reno) ideas of marital dialogue.

3

SOLANDER had seen his wife Mathilde first as a somber girl, and he had let her feel him near her for years while she was struggling to make something of herself. She became used to his loyalty, which she rewarded by a hasty lunch near his office, a walk at nightfall near her home, an arm for his arm when she needed an escort. She confided things to him and listened to his interminable explanations. She lived in the heart of things, and the rest of the world, through him, spun round her. When she was lovesick over one boy actor or another, he saw, knew, grew anxious, ran them down a little, hoped for the worst. Once he saw her in a socialist procession, wearing low-heeled shoes and a skating skirt, black on top, red underneath. She walked stoutly along, shouting when they shouted, like a brave child. Her loose hair framed her pale face, without lipstick or powder; it was the lonely face of a pretty woman who cannot understand why she suffers so much, but who knows already that she must.

Solander never looked at any other women, though he liked them and talked to them; he would think to himself that he was rather lonely at times, but "I am a one-woman man," he said to himself. He supposed he would get her at last; and when she agreed, hesitating, to marry him, after her last miserable love affair with the faun-boy, he thought naturally, "When she knows what the love of a man is, she will forget all this and love me; experiment is always unsatisfactory."

She began serious family life by keeping her baby when it started, even though they were not sure they wanted it. She thought, "This will let us see where we stand; and if it doesn't work out, one child's nothing; I'll get a divorce. Oh, to get out of the worry of the world. He loves me, he will keep me." They married. She felt a new joy and thought that now for the first time she had some reason for living. "I tried to be someone; now I see that real happiness is in being no one, in effacing yourself according to the rules of society." She had all kinds of sayings; but as no learned roles fit experiences, she wished sometimes that she had met the right man. She had no idea how much she depended on Solander, for it seemed to her she was full of ideas, when she repeated his. The art she really knew, that she was born for, by which, with unaffected, persistent work, day and night, asleep and awake, she was able to form her plastic soul to take on the shape of another's, or even force a playwright's imaginings to be reborn in the flavor of her own mind, this she neglected, as being unreal, not the real world. She threw away all she really knew and repeated political and economic phrases, correctly and credulously, but without inner understanding.

The poor apartment was now hung with children's clothes. She heard her husband air the opinions of various smart young men with whom he was infatuated (for he was an ardent lover of his friends, as well), and she wondered if he had any ability. He, meanwhile, asked himself if he were not, like many men, laughing and talking, even making love, in a mirror. Timidly each looked for another mate; such cowardly and inoffensive glances attract no one. But each said, it cannot last; and though there were tender reconciliations and moments when it was clear that they could understand each other as acquaintances, or as people living in the same city understand each other, there was nothing else between them but the children—myself a noisy, showy child, and slow-mooded, tender Jacky—and a gloomy feeling of years lost together.

Convinced that in the familiarity of the marital bed she had cheapened herself, Mathilde now tried to keep the marriage together by spending months away from her husband with the children. He slaved away in the city, attended his meetings, visited his friends, came to a house cleaned once a week, lived through the cold, the heat, and made money to keep them. Mathilde, living unhappily with the noisy, greedy, money-loving Morgans in Green Acres Inn or in Long Beach, and even up in Lydnam Lodge, the Morgan place near Clinton, New Jersey, hoped that Solander would call her back, or even take a mistress, so that she could have a complaint against him—any real misdemeanor would force a solution. All this was a vague, almost incoherent dream. She lived from day to day and listened to the advice poured upon her. Presently her relatives began to neglect her, and between themselves said, "She'll lose him." Grandmother Morgan began introducing her to well-situated businessmen. "I like Sol, but businessmen are the best providers and they need a real home, they've got to have a place their bank manager and their boss can recognize. A bank manager likes a nice home. When you're looking for credit you mustn't have ideas. People with ideas have no bank account. For every idea you have you lose a dollar. I want to see my girls comfortable. A man with ideas can't be a good provider, and an idea is a thing you can change overnight. Now, you can't lose a good credit balance overnight."

Sometimes my mother left us in the country places and with families in the city while she lived with my father alone, to patch it up. I always had a great adaptability, was a regular chameleon; I was a country girl in the country, very pert and up-to-date in the city; I did my best to be ignorant and coarse in a rural one-room school, and head of the class in town; but I was always off on some fresh tack, learning, imitating, acting something new. I hated equals. I lied about gifted, traveled, or propertied children, fought rivals as well as I could, despised those who obeyed me. As for those who seemed to ignore me, I flattered myself they did not exist. Jacky accepted all change with a reasoning gaiety. Green Acres Inn, New Canaan, and Lydnam Lodge in northern New Jersey were our occasional refuges in those early years.

4

GREEN ACRES INN was a white-painted house, New England style, with deep porches, gabled ends, and many windows opening on lawns and gardens. It was set back from the road but not too far back, for the visitors to the Inn were all of one sort—a sort that lives in the bustle made by others; that is to say, old people who would fret if they missed an automobile on the road, and who looked lugubriously and even desperately into their plates at lunch if they heard the other women calling across the soft-aired dining room, "It was a Pierce-Arrow, wasn't it?" "Yes, blue, with pale blue initials." My grandmother knew these old women well enough. At such a moment, a hostess, a young woman of thirty or so, would come into the room and ask after their health or the meals. A short grumble about the soup, and the old creatures would begin to cheer up. But they were ill-natured and spoiled, living on someone else's money for the most part, and they looked upon young women as encumbrances. They were intent upon their secret cocktail parties in bedrooms (from which they emerged with red faces for lunch), their favorite records on the Inn phonograph (Geraldine Farrar, Schumann-Heink, Caruso), their card games which started at eleven in the morning, their discussions of George Sand's love life and of the Bluebeard of the day. All their discussions ended in the condemnation of women. They were steel-ribbed ladies of fifty to eighty; to them my mother, and even their own sons and daughters, seemed inexperienced, sexless. To these avid old people, only themselves were alive and burning with sex; the rest of mankind had all to learn. There were two or three old men at the Inn. The only struggles these old women knew were for the attentions of the men, or to be invited to bedroom parties where palms were read and fortunes told. Of course, this was in

33

the days of prohibition when every man was devoted to breaking the law.

The house belonging to the Morgans in northern Jersey, was on a hillside steep, facing the setting sun and the blue ridges of Pennsylvania. Uncle Percival Hogg called it the old name of the hill, Lydnam Hill, and then changed the name to Lydnam Lodge, to the great annoyance of Aunt Angela who thought a poor man was putting on frills. It was really half a house, built by Grandfather Morgan in a moment of romance, and it looked like a grand-ducal hunting-lodge. Aunt Angela had been a Morgan girl.

Grandfather Morgan had a motto for his family: "First have a roof over your heads, the rest will follow." He bought property and houses and looked for years for a large farm, not costing much, on which he could build roofs for his family. Before his powers failed, his family was large, but by that time also he had made some money.

At length he pitched on Lydnam Hill, and bought the entire hill, a small stony knoll with steep sides, in area about two hundred acres. On it he found three farms with farmhouses, an old forge from revolutionary times, some stony cornfields, a tall wood, a small wood, some moist bottoms near a river, and The Corners, a T-shaped junction of roads at which stood some ruins covered with poison ivy and an old stone cottage. Below the stone cottage was an orchard dipping north.

Two of the farms were in good repair. On a southeastern slope he built Morgan's Folly, now called Lydnam Lodge. He poured a fortune into it. It was a museum of modern house designing. He could not get anyone to live in it. It was too far from town and it was really only one room, though that room was the size of the Metropolitan Opera House stage, so that it required a servant.

The house stood in a wood of elms, beeches, and tulip trees. A place had been cleared under them for a further extension of the Lodge, and the cleared ground was now cluttered up with vines and shrubs, a haunting and hunting place of birds, insects, snakes, and frogs. A little fountain stood beside the flight of steps down to the winding approach. By this approach were stumps of trees intended as bird roosts and bird baths, but which had become ant-skyscrapers and which contained galleries, shoots, liftwells, staircases and apartments under the bark. At the door was a slab of granite with a knocker, on which could be imitated the woodpecker or sapsucker. Down the drive had been planted about one hundred conifers, Douglas fir, white fir, and blue spruce, eastern red cedar, most of which had increased and were now about eight feet high. A runnel about three feet wide ran down the sharp hillside; there many frogs were found and there the chickens came to roost. The undergrowth was full of stumps, fungi, and small and soft plants, many of them medicinal. The farmer's hens had laid eggs all over the wood. It was not safe to venture there without tall boots and gloves, on account of the copperheads, poison ivy, and other probable dangers; but it was a lovely wood, with mushrooms, mandrakes, lilies, and full of birds.

The Lodge was a splendid building. The original house had been built on a basement and surrounded by three walls of heavy stone taken from the revolutionary forge, and above and round these stones, heavy planks and beams of cedar, and giant old riveted beams bought out of some old house, with the roof rising above the immense rafters like the upturned hull of a boat. Beneath this hull was a polished floor and a fireplace with a stone apron stretching toward the middle of the floor.

Many logs had been cut down in the wood but all had rotted and were full of ants and termites. The piles of the veranda were termite-ridden. The great fireplace on a cool day burned a pile of branches, and even sections of large logs. Old trees shadowed the place; before and during rains the old stones streamed with water and the beams sweated. The fog and moisture settled on the highly polished floor and on the waxed antiques and on the windows, whose fittings were covered with verdigris. The house linens were never quite dry, except in midsummer, and even then the high treetops and the soft woods sent down a soft, rotting damp.

Yet it was a beautiful house. Plants waved outside every set of windows except southerly, and all life was rich and prolific. Except for storms from the south, the house was folded into the hill and had no buffeting, but when storms came from the south, as they did in summer, generally in the afternoon, one could see them stalking across the near valley, up the neglected fields of tall grass, and cramping the trees. The trees were old and dangerous and should have been attended to by a forester; but after the death of old Bernard Morgan nothing was done there. My grandfather's bones later were built into one pillar of the roofed gate which was to make an entrance to the long drive edged with conifers. The rains flung themselves upon the house like a storm of light and music, sending the clouds so fast across the sky that the sun poured through; the thick crown of the wood parted and was filled with fragments of sky, and the fields all the way down the hill and the low tops at its foot and the smoky patterned fields and hills for mile upon mile tossed and shone, as the gusts poured north in a shining ocean. The house creaked and fluttered, but nothing moved, so solidly was it built. My Uncle Hogg, who lived there with my Aunt Angela, would go about crowing, "What is the matter? It fills your lungs, it clears the air." Mother visited us there, but only when she must. Both women hated it. One feared rheumatism, the other thought a tree would uproot itself clumsily trying to move in the ocean of wind, and would stumble over the house. At night too they feared. But then would come my father who, looking out when the fresh winds blew the new leaves in the sunlight, felt romantic, strong, and full of promise; and my mother silently sat on the top step of the porch, just outside the screen door, saw the great circle which had been cut in the trees for the moon to shine through, into this sculptured and furnished wood, but which was just the same—beautiful, enchanted, a treasure house; and saw perhaps the boy with the blue hair, in his coolie dancing suit, walking lightly up the hill, or wandering, with his back to her, in the smoky moonlight of the wood. My father sat by her with his arm round her waist. She sat motionless in her impatience.

Her mind was full of dreams now. For a few years before she had married, after she had begun to fail as an actress and when the blue-haired boy was leaving her, she had been walking barefoot, hideously, it seemed to her, in a bustling world, confused, hoarse-voiced, which hated her, or had no use for her. Now that she was married, even though she was unhappy, she had gone back to the dreams she had had up to her sixteenth or seventeenth year. My father did not figure in them; he was merely the one who threw the dark tent of his love around her so that she could rest away from life. She did not know this. She thought she was a naturally unhappy woman.

The world in the early twenties seemed to my father full of hope and opportunity, however. He was young. He had made connections abroad such that he hoped some day or other to realize a great dream of his, which was to go and live in Europe. At the present time, however, he agreed to do anything to please my mother and her family; and he continued with the partners, McLaren and Montrose.

Uncle Percival Hogg, who had married Angela Morgan, a very handsome but cold woman, was quite an original. They had several children, of whom one was my cousin Templeton, a handsome boy who later went into the movies. We had been visiting at Lydnam Lodge for several years, quite accustomed to the obvious disunion of the Hogg household, and were surprised and cast down when the news came to New York that Angela and Percival Hogg had separated. Aunt Angela had gone out to Long Beach, but Uncle Perce, the day Angela left him, thumbed his nose at the Morgan "palace," as he called it, and moved his things and his children into a weatherbeaten house on the other side of the Morgan hilltop. This house he called "The Wreck." He did not neglect us either. He immediately wrote to our parents to say that things must be as they had been and he wanted to see Jacky and me there, in The Wreck, every summer.

The Wreck was a weather-board house three stories high, with a dugout basement in stone; it was Hogg's storehouse, workshop, play house. Some distance away was a new garage, with living quarters to one side. This was rented to artists in the summer. The Wreck and its garage stood on the first shoulder of the hill, with an uncut field below them and an unpruned orchard lower still. They faced a wide and distant view, with roads, houses, and home woods between. A road ran down beside the house to the main road, beside which was Farmington, the farm prison. Opposite The Wreck and the garage in the lane were tall stone ruins. Trees grew from the center of the ruins. Lower down the hill was a fine stone house with some story of scandal attached to the upper apartment; I forget it now, but a nice boy named Carl lived there; and down the lane was an old family house, with dormer windows and attics, not to mention the Morgan farms, and the well-run profitable farm beyond the hill where lived the man with bull-charm, a city accountant who had come to the country to recuperate and discovered a country talent, bull-charm. The black monster lay red-eyed and suspicious in his compound, horrible to look at, approachable only by the city accountant.

Uncle Perce feared horses, cattle, and rams as much as we did, but loved meek undomesticated nature. He sometimes worked in the Natural History Museum, gave scientific lectures, or sold microscopes, according to his fortunes. His fortunes depended on official opinions, particularly those on war and reaction, for he was a reformer, a crank, an original; he called himself *The Evangelist* and *The Vox Humana.* When a piece of paper blew his way he picked it up and studied it; he said it had a message for him; he said the printed word was sacred; at the same time he sacrilegiously denounced the writings of all his rivals in botany.

He took strays into The Wreck like ourselves and an unfortunate young woman, his sister, who called herself Mrs. Dr. Goodsir. His house was managed by Mrs. Dr. Goodsir, now far advanced in a pregnancy, and his daughter Cecily Hogg, a twelve-year-old girl, a breasted, heavy-limbed child, very blonde, with a pretty mouth, but stupid and sulky. She never played with us or with her own family, that I remember, but sat looking over the orchard or the view when not working, or stood at the broken fence staring at the ivies, the things in bloom, a little dead swallow that hung from the telegraph wire, or at the boys passing. She was love-mad. We heard her talking to herself and singing, between the irregular rows of stunted corn in the Lodge cornfield, pulling out weeds, chasing small animals, and making a sort of chant of romance, sorrow, triumph. When we burst out shouting and hooraying from the far edge, where we had run behind her back, bending below the corn, her skin flushed dark red; the stain seemed to spread all over her. She said nothing, but turned and walked to the shade-knot in the center of the field. From there, too, from everywhere on the Morgan farm, you could look into a distance of miles, with blue ridges and fields. It was hard to get her to come into the house, even at night. Then, when she had jobs waiting for her, she would still be out under the stars or stormclouds, singing and talking to herself. We pretended to think she was mad, tapped our heads, and burst out laughing. We knew better than she did, however, that it all came from her longing to lie down with a man; to us all these antics were still ridiculous.

Mrs. Dr. Goodsir was quite different, this young thin woman with small hands and feet who laughed and talked to all the neighbors in spite of her situation.

Uncle Hogg was rebuilding The Wreck, using his own materials, retaining the original pattern, doing it haphazard and in his own good time. In return for this, he got the place rent-free for a year. His father-in-law liked him. Nothing suited him better. His father was a carpenter, his grandfather a stonemason. One of his rules was to lay out a job at sunrise and have it finished by sundown. He tried to induce us all to do the same: "Something attempted, something done, has earned a night's repose," he sang continuously. In addition, he endeavored to teach everyone the sciences of the field, made everyone in the house say the Latin names of living things, as *Liriodendron tulipifera* instead of tulip tree, while we were obliged to refer to the way flowers grew as inflorescences; but there was much more of this than anyone could remember. I never could take an interest in things that I had not seen as commodities in town. To be plain, I despised the country and only used it to grow in, like the plants and sheep. But Uncle Perce despised those who come to the country to melt at the sight of flowers and trees. If some visitor tried to please him by saying, "Is that a ragweed?" he would say, "I don't know the names of flowers, I only know their physiology, morphology and ecology," or something of that sort. He depressed innocent nature-lovers.

My mother and father were trying to live with each other again and had gone into a new apartment and a quiet street. We spent months with Uncle Perce at The Wreck or with Uncle Philip Morgan at Lydnam Lodge, where he was enjoying the honeymoon of his second marriage. Angela Hogg would not get a divorce: "He does not need a woman, he only needs plants." The Goodsir woman cleaned up after Cecily. Aunt Angela did not like her daughter. When she had last been out at Lydnam Lodge, Cecily, her first child, who resembled her father in all ways, came to her and said, "Mother, were you like me when you were twelve? Did you think about things?"

"What things, what things? You're gaping like a fish!"

When Cecily was a little over twelve, she approached Jacky and me one day in the early afternoon, when we were playing in the long grass, and began to question us about boys. What had we been told? How did it begin? We both saw at once, although I was then only about seven, that she had been afraid of us and respected us. By listening at doors and pretending to be innocent little girls, we had learned a lot too; but if she had learned it, it would have done her no good; she was not the kind of person to learn anything from experience.

Uncle Percival gave her his prejudices. He did not think a man could be a good statesman, for example, if that man had a mistress; he could not even be a good writer, teacher, philosopher, or trades-man if he went in for fornication. As for fornicating women, he got out of the difficulty by saying, "I speak no scandal, no, nor listen to it." Cecily also thought only the pure could love. She wouldn't listen to scandal, no one could have a good time with her. She was lonely; she wasn't human. When the boy from the stone house down the road, a tall good-looking boy, blond, with good clothes, Carl Lokart, started to wait for her at the bottom of the orchard, she believed it was love. She was invited to the stone house for bis-cuits in the afternoon too, and allowed to read Carl's books with him. Jacky and I were never invited there. Of course, we had played too many tricks down there in full view of the house. The lawn and gardens ran down to the road without a fence, and we had gone gathering flowers in the gardens without permission and given Cecily the bouquet to take to Mrs. Lokart. At another time, when two boys escaped from Farmington and the countryside was in ter-ror by night, we stole some things from the kitchen window and from the shed in order to scare the people; but we laughed so much while getting off with the loot that perhaps we were seen from the numerous windows. There is no telling now, but then we thought Cecily had told on us and we hated her. Uncle Perce, while reprov-ing us, would also give her a sermon about silly girls and calf love; and, oddly enough, when he was scolding anyone he was not such a fool as at other times, but showed a knowledge of human nature. What he said was so true that even we felt awkward, but we laughed loudly at her. Mrs. Dr. Goodsir looked sideways at her, embarrassed, and said, "She is precocious; she knows what she ought not."

Everyone came to feel she was a criminal or would end badly. The adults knew she wanted to love as they did and felt that love of the body was theirs; they watched over it. The little boys had already invited us behind the bushes, using fence language with great honesty; and like old women we knew secrets we did not tell Cecily. Somehow the boys at Farmington got mixed up in it. Straying round the roads, Mrs. Goodsir said, Cecily might meet some of those awful boys. "What do the boys do?" asked Cecily. Mrs. Goodsir was old-fashioned, modest and monitory, especially as she herself had been seduced and abandoned by Dr. Goodsir. The countryside for us was awfully darkened by our ideas of what the Farmington boys did and by local tales, as of the man who went berserk when his farm was taken away from him, and who had to be hunted by the police, the army, the American Legion, a band of armed neighbors, and, at length, an army plane. The army plane discovered him running through the long grass at night, like a bleached wolf. In town we saw the house which he had lost, and where his mind went.

There was another story of a farm far over on the other hills where everything was dead; the farm was covered with skeletons of things dead of hunger and thirst. There was a lawyer down the road who had bought up all the farms and bits of land that came into the market cheap for taxes and such. He was land-hungry, and now land-poor; he scarcely had enough to eat, but he had all this land, much of it waste. Even on Lydnam Hill there was a soft worthless bit of land that would hardly grow wood, where the cows browsed. It turned out later that an old man had drowned himself there. He just got too old, he said; and he lay down and died in the wood.

Cecily had an appetite for these stories. She loved the night. She slept out on the grass. One summer night we saw her walking naked between the garage and the house. The sky was bright with stars. This seemed awful to us, and Cecily was clothed for us in mystery and danger from that night on. But we thought her foolish too; we knew she invited the haunting, tearing hand of the road. She knew the stories of the whole countryside, especially the foul and uncanny ones; and many afternoons when she was free she spent looking across to the Farmington Institution, trying to think what life must be inside there. Mrs. Goodsir told her it was unhealthy for a young girl her age, but Uncle Perce said, "In educating the young we must make use of any show of interest," and gave her books to read about prisons and dungeons, tortures in the Middle Ages, the horrors of the Inquisition, and prison memoirs. He said it would teach her history in her own terms. She and Carl read these books down in the orchard and talked about them; at least they said they did, but up in the house, at dinnertime, everyone made sly remarks about calf love and big silly children.

Nevertheless, it was impossible not to be interested in the two lovers. Besides, with her tales and books, which we saw in her room in the attic, we had an inexhaustible spring of games. We played Torture Chamber, Torquemada, Anarchists, Butcher Shop, and Institution; and we also played Lovers, imitating Carl and Cecily, but going farther than they ever went, I suppose.

One afternoon this strange couple went to Uncle Percival and asked him to allow them to marry; Cecily was thirteen and Carl nearly fifteen. "If we are married we can live together; we can live in The Wreck or at home," said Carl. "We can still go to school," said Cecily. Hogg was embarrassed, grew red in the face with shame and gravity, and sent Carl to walk on the road while he hastened down, just as he was, in his sneakers and slacks, to see the parents. He was pleased with this important reason for visiting the stone house, for those were rich retired bourgeois who lived there, bridge players, highball drinkers, automobile fans who rushed up and down in their several cars dusting up the flowers and scaring off the birds. They sneered at Uncle Perce.

That evening, this solemn Romeo and Juliet went to the stone house parents too, and said they wished to marry—what could they do if marriage was refused to them; they were in love and could not wait all those years—five, six, until they would be too old; they could not wait. Such haste to love, even their decorum, caused a scandal. Each family blamed the other.

Jacky and I ran off to a far part of the orchard in the long grass to talk it over; we talked it over in whispers, hand in hand and almost without a joke. For several days we were in a soft pious mood. It got to be known. Everyone tried to see them and joked about them. Roars of laughter, loud quarrels came from the stone house. At other times, people going along the road talked softly, looking at our house. Most people believed that they had already mated in the grass; but the grave young couple believed in their elders and waited first to be legally wed. Shameful questions they had to answer. Nothing was decided.

5

THE WRECK was a large rectangular box with an extension on one side. A solid pitched roof covered this extension, and on the landing in the stairs a full-sized door led to the attic, under this roof. This attic had an excellent floor, but it had to be entered on hands and knees. At one time, perhaps, there had been a flimsy second story which had been knocked about by storms or struck by lightning. Uncle Perce intended to rebuild this vanished second story at some time. Meanwhile he was busy all the year rebuilding the rest of the house. Since it was all of wood and he was energetic, he could alter a door, a window, or rip out a wall or a flooring, in a day. Sometimes, when he felt sick, he worked at home developing photographs, writing a treatise; and the children, at four or five, after school, might find that there was no door where a door had been in the morning. He built a room with a lean-to roof, near the kitchen. To this he added a shed. In the shed he built benches and in a third room, no more than a closet, he built wooden beds. The shed, intended for a new privy, was cut off from the new bedroom by a right-angled passage, with two doors leading outside.

Sometimes he changed his mind about these doors and closed them up. When Mrs. Dr. Goodsir had her baby, a girl, upstairs, in the women's part of the house (he called it the Gynoecium), Templeton, then eleven or so, was given the lean-to as his bedroom. There was only an open doorway to his bedroom, and these other two doors led outside. Templeton's friends could open these doors and walk in at any time. Uncle Perce thought this an excellent idea. Later he thought not, and closed up these doorways, putting a door in Templeton's bedroom instead. Sometimes he put in and took doors out of the breakfast room. He took up the floors and put down new floors. He built partitions and pierced walls. While this was being done (this kind of job took more than one day), the women had to look after the clothes, clean the house and cook, hobbling over rubble and rafters. Stonedust, sawdust, and the fine gray dust of cement settled over everything in the house, over the curtains and the books; flecks of paint appeared in unexpected places, and even all over the bodies of the family; all their old clothes were stiffened and stained with it. Very often the table conversation was the mixing of paints, putty and cement, and types of finish, or was about the composition of paints and veneers; and was sprinkled with expressions such as plumb rule, cold chisel, stipple, second coat, mortise and tenon, three-ply, which even Mrs. Dr. Goodsir understood. At another time it would be "What makes an automobile go?" "Why does water run downhill?" Mrs. Dr. Goodsir argued and became angry; when he got to the flight of the universe through space, she wept and mentioned God.

It was interesting enough in their house, but we longed for the fun of the city. Uncle Perce believed that the movies and the theater prevented youthful minds from approaching science. It got about that Uncle Perce was godless: that was the cause of the Cecily scandal.

The rich farmer, the one with the black bull, called The Wreck "the house with disappearing doors," because of Uncle's restlessness about doors. Uncle never forgave it. The old farmer, with the old wife and the young black-haired niece, warned his niece away from The Wreck because Uncle Perce, in his opinion, was a Mormon and an anarchist. Uncle Perce attacked him venomously whenever he could.

Uncle Perce gave no presents at Christmas, because present-giving to "public or community servants encouraged begging"; in return, these "public and community servants" were disagreeable to Uncle Perce and he was never done complaining. Uncle Perce opposed indemnities for accidents, workmen's compensation, sick benefit, or anything in which the government, the community, or the employer had anything to do. "It pampered," he said. It was true, as people said, that these opinions suited Aunt Angela's wealthy family very well, but Uncle Perce's notion was that such props weakened the people. He was only in favor of self-help and compensations paid out by workers' mutual associations.

One day one of the old farmers thereabouts fell into a hole on the public road and broke his leg. He received indemnity for this and still hobbled about the farm with his old wife trying to keep a few rows of peas going and some corn. Uncle Perce took a petition round the community protesting against this pap-feeding of citizens. "If citizens were not paid for breaking their legs, they would not break their legs," said he, "and if they did break their legs, they would know better next time." All the old men came to hate Uncle Perce. The middle-aged prosperous ones did not know what to think. Some secretly agreed with him but were afraid to say so, on account of their women.

He was full of apparent irreconcilables. For instance, he thought all land should belong to the community, there should be no private landlords, and that rent, if any, should be paid "to the people"; yet he behaved with the acreage round The Wreck as he had with the hillside on which Lydnam Lodge stood, with a savage proprietorship, combining in himself squire, gamekeeper, and bulldog. Sometimes, in this spirit, he would open the place to the community. This was always for one of the children's parties, when he asked the young people of the neighborhood to come in. He did not like any boys above twelve, although females of any age were welcome.

He disliked all of Templeton's male friends. Templeton had girl friends, but being already a worldly gallant, he kept these out of his father's sight. Templeton, who from babyhood had shown the greatest pleasantest interest in all the habits and attributes of women and who until now had been a charming loving boy, began to grow thoughtful, to seclude himself, shun his father, and hold long secret conversations with boys. When a girl passed by, he could not control his passion but stared after her, his eyes darting from his head, following every motion, whipping up and down her limbs and body, his hands twisting upon themselves. Uncle Perce did all that men can do, but the poor young lover was goaded by a bite of fire. We called him "the sheikh." He did his best to overcome his energy, he worked hard and began that fierce studying which brought him to the head of his class; but we heard him turning in his bed at night, walking about and even crying.

Templeton had a friend called Jack Lack, who had a bad school reputation and who seemed to me a bully, thief, and scoundrel; but this may have been simply Uncle Perce's opinion of him. Jack Lack called Uncle Perce names and used the place, the orchard, the garage, the fence, and even the rooms of the house for his amusement and exercise. There were so many rooms that the boy could be in the place for hours without Uncle Perce's knowing it; and the house was so built that he could play hide-and-seek for a long time, when Uncle Perce chased him. The man had a peculiar hatred for the boy and, when he saw him, ran, catching up in his hand anything he could reach, on his way through the house or grounds. Dodging Uncle Perce became one of Jack Lack's games; but at times, while he was calling out after my uncle, even while my uncle was chasing him, or even when he balanced on the fence or window sill, looking far and wide over the place for my uncle, a dark grimace of pain and even rage would screw up the boy's face. Sometimes he would jump down and run away in disgust. It was as if, when he stood there, he saw that he was being forced to revolt and that he hated the misery of this squabbling life. We hated the boy and thought it surprising that smooth Templeton went with him; but perhaps Jack was another boy when out of sight of The Wreck.

Uncle Perce was like all governors; it was he who incited to the rebellion that he tried to crush. Nevertheless, he thought he was a democrat; nay, more, he believed the moot, the town meeting, the village council, to be the best form of government.

Jack Lack called The Wreck "the house with no doors." This was because he saw my uncle was proud of his workmanship on the frames, panelings, and proud of the way the doors swung and hung, without sagging and without creaking; but Jack invented it one Saturday with good cause. He had come in the morning to visit Templeton and raced through the lean-to, in one door and out the other. When he came in the evening, both these doors were gone and weather-boardings fixed over the former entrances. My uncle had not yet had time to cut the door to Templeton's bedroom which he was substituting (in fact, he was fagged out and it was not cut that day at all). Jack, in amazement, ran round hitting what was now a wall with his fists and calling, "Hey, Temp!

47

Temp!" For a moment, he supposed that Mr. Hogg had walled his son in. Jack Lack did not understand Mr. Hogg at all and was secretly afraid. The family was strange. The young woman without a husband, who insisted on being called Mrs. Dr. Goodsir, the girl Cecily wanting to get married at twelve, Hogg's doors and petitions, even Hogg's relations, Mr. and Mrs. Philip Morgan, now living in Lydnam Lodge, a young man married to an old wife—there was nothing in it that was ordinary. He pounded on the hollow weather-boarding and yelled, "Oh, Temp! Temp!" He dropped school ink into Hogg's fish bowl. He knew what Hogg told of him. He became strange, sulky, and recalcitrant, more so every day; but he could not keep away from the place or from Uncle Hogg.

But Uncle Perce feared these adventures for him, and kept writing letters to the police; the wicked youths, corrupting his child, must be put into Farmington. He named them—Jack Lack, Frank Shields, others. Templeton, at this, ran away from home, and was brought back. This was the moment when Jacky and I joined the tribe of women. Up till then we had had our own world but been free with boys, but now that the ferocity and criminality of the young boy's world bred round us, we feared the strange, leering, jeering, foul-mouthed and foul-minded brutish outlaws; and so it was to be for a few years for me. I soon again became a companion of boys and men, but Jacqueline always had a sign of this terror which enters little girls' hearts.

Once or twice Jacky and I, four or five years younger than Jack Lack, tried to get him to play our more terrifying games, such as Torquemada, but he seemed deaf, or pushed us away and rushed off with a shout. Naturally we disliked him, for we thought ourselves very attractive creatures, and some of the boys tried to get into our games, sensing secret pleasures, perhaps. We let hints drop.

One day Jack Lack, walking the rail of the new picket fence, was yelling insults at Uncle Perce, who was leaning out of a new window he was cutting upstairs. Uncle said, "Get down, you damn fool!"

"Pigg-Hogg, Hogg in his Pigsty, dirty old Hogg."

"If you break my fence, I'll kick you down the street."

"Dirty old Hogg!"

"I'll break every bone in your body, you young pirate!"

"Hogg cutting doors so the bugs can get out!"

My uncle, in a great state, bellowed, "I hope you fall and get the spikes through your belly—" We screeched.

Jack Lack continued walking the railing. My uncle thundered down the old carpetless stairs. Jack Lack had cleared the fence and was far down the road, arms and legs flying.

On another occasion, Uncle found three boys who had escaped from Farmington and for whom citizens and police were out searching. My uncle was a good woodsman and was always scouting round; when he was working about the house, he kept his eye skinned. He saw a thin smoke rise in the air one evening, smelled, calculated, and, in his soft shoes, stole down through the tousled growth of a near field to find the green hideout of the three reformatory boys. They had a large pail hanging on cross-sticks and a good fire underneath. In the pail was a stew just coming to the boil—the water was racing, a brown scum had risen, and the thin smell of the meat mixed maddeningly with the bush smell. Mr. Hogg himself was hungry; it was an hour to dinner time and he was a large-framed ravenous man who ate everything he liked and never put fat on his bones.

The man and the boys parleyed. The stew was now bubbling furiously; pieces of meat and vegetable sailed over the brown pool. Hogg could not resist looking down at it and saying thoughtfully, "Smells fine; where did you get the makings?"

The smallest, a poor, clerkly boy ventured, "We got it from the Home." The other boys looked at him and he realized his mistake.

"What do you care?" said the redhead. "Can't you go along home and let us get out of here?"

"We shot a rabbit, a bird, too," said one, suddenly; he looked sulkily at the intruder.

The setting sun shot long red rays through the bush at Hogg's left.

Hogg smiled cunningly, "Let's fall to, boys!" and he sat down with them, using a clean collecting tin for his pannikin. He showed a ferocious appetite and made the boys sit back while he lunged for the meat. When it was all gone, he kicked over what remained, saying, "Well, it was really my bird and rabbit, boys, my fire, my sticks. It's against the law to make a fire here," he said. "You'll have the woods on fire and burn all these people's homes. You only think of your bellies and thieving, that's why you're where you are."

"Is that so?" said the redhead, who had a hungry stomach-ache. There was a large-headed boy who looked fiercely at Hogg, and his eyes were bright with tears: "I did nothing, I never did anything. They just got after me."

"There's a simple answer to that," said Hogg. "Go back to the Farm and give yourselves up."

One boy snickered bitterly, one shrugged.

"Go on down to the road and get going," said Hogg, full of meat.

The boys mooched off, the one with the pail carrying it off. Hogg, to conceal his wild exultation at having eaten the stolen meat, stopped to gather a mandrake he saw. He carefully loosened the soil and brought up the strange plant, with two green leaves and a white flower and two brown roots and a white root, and which for him was *Podophyllum peltatum* (May apple), and when he approached the road going into the lower valley and came down softly, skirting an old stone fence in which he knew some copperheads lived, he saw that the three boys were talking to another boy and looking up the hill. The fourth boy was Jack Lack. For all his woodcraft, he made sounds; the boys broke and went in opposite directions, Lack mounting the hill.

"Watch out for copperheads," called out Hogg involuntarily, for at this time of a warm evening they liked to lie out on the smooth, tarred road, catching the last rays that came through the tunnel of branches. The boys looked at him and went on straight down the road. Suddenly they halted, looked down in front of them, and watched something that was moving toward the hill where Hogg stood. Hogg laughed. It was the copperhead, he knew, that was there every evening. The boys, startled, went on cautiously and hurried out of sight.

Hogg turned away from the stone heaps and made for the road, all the time looking at the ground with an expert eye. The farmers round there went about with canvas shoes, all through the fields, in spite of the danger, and he did the same, to be one of them.

He was strange and distasteful. He held them up on the roads, haranguing them about their political views and their errors. He himself, single-handed, had tried to stop them going to their mysterious rendezvous, some years before, when the fiery cross burned on the hills, and there was talk about Catholics and Jews, but out of deviltry and irresponsibility he himself at times laughed with them; a little later he would give the fascist salute for fun, explaining that this was the old Roman gesture, and would make a garden-knot in his wild, unweeded place in the shape of the swastika, saying that it was an old Greek pattern, the original of all the mazes of the world; and all this because he thought even these death-dealing frenzies of his neighbors contemptible games of the ignorant and childish, and because the world was just a vacant lot to him. The farmers, the death-riders, the reformatory boys were all the same to him. They were Other-men, Not-Hogg.

When he woke up the next morning, someone had scrawled on the picket fence, one letter to a pike, "P-e-r-c-e H-o-g-g, d-i-r-t-y d-o-g, e-t a-l-l o-u-r m-e-a-t, w-a-s-h y-o-u-r d-i-r-t-y f-e-e-t." "I know who it is," said he, and he laid for Jack Lack, but the boy kept away for a long time. Hogg forgot his enemy and went on changing and renovating The Wreck.

6

WE WENT to the local school in a bus. Jacky worked well, al-though the instruction was poor and the children were out of hand; but I joined the rowdiest and out-bumpkined them all. Wherever there was a tussle in the playground, I was in it, and would rush in and out of school, bruising head and shoulders with the toughest and strongest there. It was not to lead them, it was only to get myself known as the worst child there. Jacky did not care one way or another usually, but sometimes would go off with her nose in the air and a conceited expression. When this hap-pened, I ran to join her.

"You're a gangster, a gun moll," she would say; and I did not like this from her, beginning to be afraid that I might end up with the riffraff.

This was always my secret fear and still is; just the same, I cannot join the pokerfaces, the bronze hearts, the laurel-wreaths, the moguls and brahmins. There is something wrong with the marshal's baton they smuggled into my corporal's knapsack; it will not come out by more than a head, it is an unborn baton. Thus I seemed to lead the rough youngsters out there, but I was afraid of criticism from my uncles, my mother, and Jacky. I had no self-confidence.

Away from school, at The Wreck, we forgot this wildness and poured our brains and souls into the games I have referred to. Anything cruel and gruesome in our education served us for a framework. Torquemada was a game in which we devised tortures for everyone we detested or despised: legs sawn off without ether, hearts plucked out, flayings, singeings, scalpings, and slow roast-ing; this was nothing. The interest of this game was that it wore us out and the pleasures of a torture were soon exhausted, so that for days we would abandon the game until we thought up a new torment. Inspired by some new hate, we imagined a new torture. We had eyes put out with *sizzling* stakes, entrails thrown steaming to the dogs. We learned from Ulysses the crafty and Solomon the wise, from Puritan and Catholic, we learned cruelty, dear to young, hot hearts.

I don't know what imagination is, if not an unpruned, tangled kind of memory. I had a clear rich memory for everything I read about or heard suitable for our games, but Jacky brought in details which we had never read about and at the same time they were not always amusing, something chilling but always the kind of thing my father always called "arabesques." I have a practical mind and see little use in the imagination. I imagine only in one or two directions; that is, I can imagine what lies directly ahead of me and around me and I prepare to cope with it. I can imagine conversations in which I defeat enemies or win over friends, and apart from that, nothing; and as these things I imagine generally turn out to be venomous or empty fantasy and there is enough trouble in my world, I avoid them. But Jacky was quite happy losing herself in ideas which had no likeness to reality. She got through the world as I did, up to a certain point—neither better nor worse, and got about as easily. I would not say now that these fancies injured her chances. I compare this sort of thinking with the enormous dreams actors have. Stage characters are not real, but they have a function and they make the actors famous; therefore, in a way they're a strong reality. My mother always saw herself as some character which she nearly lived; but she lived in these characters without putting them in a book or on the stage. In one way, too, through these romances of hers, my mother adapted herself wonderfully well to her unhappiness and lived many years in suspension.

Up till last year, even, I would have ridiculed this as escape from the world; now I'm twenty-four and I can see this ingenuity is a tool for some; they can sell it, gull others by it. The greater the dream, the greater the number of dupes and gulls. Why is that? One would be foolish to overlook this strange impractical quality in mankind. If all those present constitute the fittest to survive —but really this is distressing thought. I have plenty of invention, but only when I am obliged to it. This is a very different kind of ingenuity, for very often these romancers, fantastics, are not good liars at all. They fumble it as if their fantasy were a great reality to which no lie can measure. A lie is real; it aims at success. A liar is a realist.

I can't work out the tie between this inventiveness of Jacky and her love of truth, and the connection between my contrary pair of traits, a quick wit to save myself and others in danger, and the disrepute in which the creative imagination is with me. At any rate, I easily got tired of Jacky's inventions; she went on inventing; we turned our backs on each other, would not speak for days. She saw how things ought to be, I saw how things must be. She was very late coming at an understanding of people's weaknesses, so that she could take advantage of them; but she would discuss traits and temperaments and imagine what they would do in some situation in which they had never been. I saw what use people were to me. I taught her what I could to make her more practical, but I do not think she taught me anything. I was cast, as my father says, at birth; I can become more complex, but not different.

In Torquemada we put our friends to torture; in Inquisition and Judge Jeffries we tried them and condemned them to various deaths. In Butcher Shop we hung them up by the heels, naked, and sliced joints from them as the customers came in; we reinvented Sawney Beane! We even once got the large and plump Cecily to act as a carcass for us, and this was interrupted by the advent of our angry and bashful Uncle Hogg. We had what we called a Miracle Play: we each performed miracles, being put to it, usually, to invent anything very wonderful; it was a kind of Liars' Bench. We had Bluebeard, Operations, Having a Baby, and Wedding; but as neither wanted to be the man and Templeton would only sometimes act the husband, and at last angrily refused the role, this last play was neglected and left us with a sad feeling. We loved the dressing for it, but did not like the manlessness.

At this time, we both made up our minds to love Templeton, always a handsome boy, and madly he kissed us, putting his hand out for our scarcely started nipples; but at times we threw him over for Ramon Navarro and Clark Gable. We laughed at Templeton's sex-fever; we knew it was unseasonable. We had rituals invented by us. One of them was *Oh, to be worthy*. We shared the same room on the rickety second story in The Wreck, and when we went to bed and when we got up would kneel down and pray aloud in turn, "Oh, God, make me worthy this day to get a rich man when I marry." We had whole days of holiness, when Jacky had only to look at me, when I shouted, "Make me worthy!" or I had only to look at her, when she stole the raisins; and each knew what the other was thinking, "It's not this way one gets to be worthy of a movie star." We had moments of Holiness for Templeton, foresaw the time when he would be a movie star and we would go to Hollywood and claim relationship. We would appear in all the night clubs with Templeton. At other times we ourselves would be movie stars and thus be united professionally with the glamour-boy; but he was growing dark and ripe as a mulberry, crazy, hot and slippery.

Uncle Percival had a large round garden he had spaded out of the uncut turf, with a swastika in the center; in this he put plants to instruct us. I knew skunk cabbage, golden rod, May apple, polk-weed, chicory, poison ivy, that's about all. Jacky got to know things with more poetic names like Traveler's Joy, Monkshood, Meadowsweet; but as these things did not live up to their names, I did not care about them—mostly little, dull flowers; and none compared at all with the flowers in town, orchids, gardenias, roses, hyacinths. What is the use of affecting a great interest in these country weeds? There are a few like flowering dogwood that have some looks, but how can that compare with a large, showy rose? Can those wayside asters compare with real asters, or that wretched yellow thing, Forsythia, with yellow orchids?

There are so many conventions, which I attribute to romancing. One must accept them only in order to see clearly ahead and not be confused with false rebellions. I hate all this. I don't want to be original, but I don't want to be a romantic; if I could only see clearer ahead, I'd make my way with my straight mind, for I can always look myself in the face and add one and one. The trouble is then, when I am adding one and one, that doubts and anxieties come to cloud my mind. I see the sum total but figures float in from outside and I think, "But should I count that in too?"

Jacky used to say, as we grew up, that part of my viewpoint came from my shortsightedness. I cannot see very far ahead of me.

I cannot see distant combinations of people and trees, for example. The view of couples in the distance gives you certain ideas about them. But the fact is, that when we come to things like this— love—I might as well have been born blind, for it is not couples in the distance, nor people on the next bench, that bother me; it is the man with me, and what he does to me, and if even he sits too far off, I have no interest in him. My reply to Jacky, my lifelong friend, is (now at least, it was not then) that I am more sensual than she is, and the sense of touch is stronger developed in me than in her. I must touch reality and there is no reality till I touch. In those days, in our games, I was impatient with her imagined brocades and festooned torture chambers; and if they had been present I would have seized the one for myself and, if a queen, used the other. But I am not sure that Jacky would have done either; she imagined only affairs with prisoners and ministers of state. We quarreled at our games. We were both selfish, feminine, ambitious; but I wished to be showy and Jacky had vague ambitions to be an empress, a great actress or artist, even a great mistress, some woman who ruined cabinets, turned aside the will of the people, destroyed nations.

We were both pretty enough. Some of our games turned round our looks, our lovers, our weddings, Hollywood. Those were very happy days, when we were away from our parents and living in this unshaved park of Uncle Perce. We fought and cried often. Sometimes it was about the relative wealth and value of our positions in the world, I, married to a rich man, with seven maids; she, a queen or a Dubarry. We both claimed Templeton. His grandfather was a very rich insurance man: he had a gold and asbestos mine in Canada, other properties. No one knew what he would have at his majority.

Our family, the Morgans, owned real estate, several small houses cut up into apartments, and two hotels. It now had a chicken farm that Uncle Philip was running on the top of Lydnam Hill. There was much dispute about this chicken farm in the family: they said it ruined the property. The shrill white chickens came down to the Lodge at all hours and laid their eggs in stumps and thickets. Uncle Philip had not enough help. In spite of a low-running wolf-ish dog and a family of farmers helping him, thieves came in lorries for his poultry, at night. There were not enough houses for the fowls and they lodged in the stooped old apple and pear trees.

All the property we had, between us, Jacky and I, was this, in expectations—but she and I felt rich and intended to go to Europe. Everyone went to Europe then. It was 1928. Even Mrs. Dr. Goodsir hoped that when her child was old enough she'd get a position as traveling companion, or else get a good tip from a rich bachelor and make money in the stock market and go abroad. She often talked about *gay Paree*; it consoled her for washing the dishes and scrubbing the wooden floors, and was knit into her dreams of her child. She was full of hope for the child, thought it would bring Dr. Goodsir back to her. When the child was born in The Wreck, Dr. Goodsir came, a tall, good-looking, grave man, with black hair. He and Uncle Perce quarreled, and he went away. We never saw him again. The poor mother was never able to understand why the father did not stay with her baby. In a few years she was calling herself a doctor's widow, and got jobs in that character.

After our experience with Mrs. Goodsir's childbirth, we added a new game, the one called Confinement. The teacher at the school, a woman who seemed old and worn but was probably about thirty, screamed at the youngsters and beat them on the knuckles with her stick. We would look across at each other and think of the way she would be tried and punished later on that afternoon, in our Court. We cursed her, hoped she died in agony, wished a cancer in her, or heart disease; now we wished she would have a baby and never be able to get rid of it, "scream all the time." This was a very satisfactory game: we would lie on our backs at the side of the orchard, in the long grass, smelling the blossomy air, scratch our legs against the insects, watch the blue sky and think of this interesting and even quite probable torture for the teacher. She was married; it could happen to her. We wished it on our wicked Aunt Stella; we wished it on numerous women. Serious at the thought, though, we added, "I'll have my children with anaesthetics." Jacky thought we should begin to practice then, to endure pain. I said, "Why, by the time we're that old, they will have invented something." Jacky tried to endure pain, though, for years after that. She tried to make a game out of it, but I would not enter into it. Why should we endure pain? She could not tell me. At another time, we became religious and kept beads and crosses we fabricated out of matchbook wood under our pillows. We prayed to Jesus. All this was in the hope of wearing white dresses for First Communion. I visited several Sunday Schools in turn in the hope of getting to several Sunday School picnics. But generally this required more regular attendance than I could give. We had to keep this secret from Uncle Perce, a rabid unbeliever; and our games and secret life, which we lived entirely in common at this time, became more secret; our games were wicked.

7

UNCLE PERCIVAL had four or five men friends, who were attracted by his peculiarities and talent. P. Hogg sometimes quarreled with the scientific institutions, societies, or men for whom he worked, and he then became a salesman, traveling the country and placing optical lenses, microscopes, field glasses, observatory lenses, and even arranging for observatories and planetaria. The same man who was hated by his poor neighbors, who gave the Mussolini salute for a joke, fought against the farmers in the district; the man who thought it weakened the poor to pay them unemployment insurance and hated trades unions, also fought for trades unions when the time came; the man who gave the fascist salute walked in a May Day procession. He was an ardent patriot and knew the ways to hang up the flag on July Fourth, and at the same time he opposed war and was imprisoned during World War I as a conscientious objector. He oppressed his womenfolk by making them scrub floors and fetch water from a well, and yet he was for the education, full citizenship, full emancipation of women; he thought a pregnant woman was the better for toting water and yet he agitated for Twilight Sleep and approved of the Soviet Union because they took proper care of children, and inducted them early into community life. This disagreeable man had devoted friends. One was my father, Solander, one Uncle Philip Morgan, one Dr. Goodsir himself—he had been, that is, until Mr. Hogg forced Goodsir to a wedding.

This was 1928. My Uncle Philip Morgan, who had first married at nineteen and was now twenty-four, had just married his second wife, a divorcée with a twelve-year-old son. This new wife of his was a healthy, active, tall blonde woman, a revolutionary with many lovers; she loved frankly, truly, often; her affairs were passions with her. Jacky and I wondered about this old woman who had men wild for her; and we were hiding in the long grass chewing stalks, when we heard Uncle Philip in the orchard making a confession about her to Solander and Uncle Perce:

Philip said about his old wife, "Amabel is going to have a child. I was a wastrel. I never wanted a child. But Amabel showed me the truth. I must not live for myself, but for others. It isn't a question of living for our child, but just for the rest of the world.... I was in New York on Tuesday, Sol, and walking up Fifth Avenue, where I used to walk to see those big, golden huskies our girls' finishing schools turn out, the gorgeous girls with the imperial contraltos —but the only face in my mind was Amabel's, her brilliant, ugly face full of soul and intellect. She's ugly, you might say, but beautiful. The others looked like stale blotters with nothing legible on them, not even their own names; they were like orchids that have been through too much night-clubbing and cheek-to-cheek dancing. Love affairs didn't wither Amabel: each one gave her a bloom and richer color. You know the joke about George Sand, 'My heart's a tomb!' 'A cemetery, Madame.' In Paris last year I had a studio duplex, you know, overlooking the Cimetière Montparnasse. It was that Mrs. Landler paid for it. At that time I was living with her, you know: she paid my way at Paris—she was very good to me. I wanted to study art, and she was going to pay for me. The studio was easy for us to get because some people, especially Americans, are superstitious about looking at a graveyard all day. I was not. It's a charming spot, full of trees and delicate winds, not many tall stones there, not those ugly things like cromlechs you see elsewhere; and this particular apartment was closer to the Jewish section where there were no tall stones to disfigure the landscape. It was delicious. It was a kind of eternal gentle life as you see in old pictures, like Corot's pictures.

"Naturally, at that time I did not care for Corot; he was old hat to me; and Mrs. Landler was very modern, always rue Campagne Première and so on. I loved it.

"When Amabel gets very old, perhaps she'll have that many tombs—my dear boys, I don't care if she does. A great woman's a great woman; you can't make her into a super-aerated, dehusked, vitamin-enriched, thick-waisted, white-haired mom of some subway ad. She's a great woman. What do I care if she loved before or loved again? She loves me now. Those titivated debs, with banana legs and long bobs, just go through life sighing for their empty life. You know the couplet, 'Our hearts in glad surprise to higher levels rise'? That's my life with Amabel. What do I care what people think about our ages? I must learn from life, and she is life; she will never be old, for the great are never either old or young. 'Age cannot wither her nor custom stale her infinite variety,' said Shakespeare about Cleopatra. How do I know Cleo did not look like Amabel? To hear her speak! When she speaks in a hall, to men, to women, their sex does not matter, they rise from their seats, their souls go out of their mouths and chests to her; instead of people I see there in the hall laurel wreaths and bouquets of flowers, something tossed by God to her; they are not men and women, they are the flowers of God. Yet people wound her noble heart, they gossip about her looks, her age, and her affairs! If I am born in this world only to protect her noble heart from pain, you see! I am a happy man.

"I am not madly in love at all. I know this woman and I just compare her with others. What is the use of trying to convince you? It isn't sex, you know. Sex—any couple can mate—what of it? Dogs can mate. It is something to live for. There's nothing wrong with my desires physically. But my heart thirsts so. Yet people laugh—"

"It's another frame of reference," said Solander.

"Can you imagine a woman that at her age is grandly ardent, simple and yielding?" continued Uncle Philip. "She is proud and fiery, and yet she has a sweet, modest, reluctant yielding, a shame-facedness. She says she was not always like that; her husband, that schoolteacher she was married to, made her like that. That is what she says because she's generous. She had to fight as a young girl. Such natures are not welcomed and people make game of them, or tread on them. They learn to be tough. It takes years to give them back their rich, generous simplicity. You see, she says he did that for her; and she doesn't hate him, she loves him; but he does not understand her now. He thinks she's foolish, childish. He says to her it's a sign of age because she goes with a man younger than herself. As if age counted in these things! There are tragedies, of course, between people of different generations when they love.

However, people don't care to talk about the happy affairs in such cases. They only talk about the tragedies. Because it shocks them, I don't know why."

"They don't talk much about love at all, that's the simple truth," said my father.

"I have never loved," said P. Hogg.

"And so it doesn't exist," Solander laughed.

"I don't say that; no, evidently it exists," said P. Hogg.

"I can testify that it exists," said my father.

The whole truth about my father was out by this, for Uncle Philip had put himself out to let us know: he considered it beautiful, even though he liked my mother. My father loved a young dark serious girl, with large eyes, called Persia. My grandmothers were thrown off balance by this happening—such a well-conducted man as my father! But Grandmother Morgan was too busy with her properties, her love affairs, and the dangerous beauty of her youngest daughter Phyllis, to bother about her daughter Mathilde; and Grandmother Fox was a timid lady who could scarcely admit that even childbirth existed, let alone divorce, sexual vagrancy. She never dared ask her son about his behavior. All she could do was to look at me and sigh, pull big eyes when she was with her son and sigh. How dared she ask questions about sexual matters? The mere thought, in private, made her blush.

"Don't you think about the others?" said Hogg.

"That's another thing you learn—to live for the day. When you've caught a big fish, you live for that day." Philip Morgan laughed.

"I mean, your other girl friends. Your life hasn't been a desert up to now, in spite of that story you tell them."

Philip sounded flustered, "What story?"

"Your formula: 'Life was a desert but you are my oasis.'"

Philip laughed like the winding of Roland's trumpet distant in Roncesvalles; then he murmured, "Who told you that?"

"Eleanor Blackfield."

"She was a nice girl," said Philip, in a lower voice.

"Don't you think of the trouble you made?" asked Hogg.

"They're all neurotics, they'd get into trouble anyhow."

"Perhaps they love you," said my father.

"No, I only love one woman."

"But—Eleanor Blackfield, for instance," said Solander.

"That's neurosis. They're repressed and then— But now I'm married. Do you know what Amabel said to me this morning? She's a superb woman. You know what Casanova said to his illegitimate fourteen-year-old son? His son was reticent, sulky, critical, wouldn't be free with Casanova. Casanova wasn't pleased, took him out and gave him a shaking-up. 'Look here, this is the sign of a mean spirit,' he said. 'That's a lesson to any young man. Give yourself away.' What does it matter, if there's plenty of yourself left? That's the school of life."

"Well, you do that," said my father. "You give yourself, that's all right with you."

"Of course," said Philip, "you get it in the neck, mind."

"My girl," said Solander—he went on to tell about the black-haired girl, Persia. We looked at each other, lying hidden in the grass. Grandmother Fox called her *Die Konkubine*, and Hogg had taken to the name—one of his sour jokes. He did not say it now, but lectured both of the men on normal family life.

"Society is built on the normal family, on normal community life of which the monogamous family is the basis at present. We cannot talk about the future societies of this world. Only whoremasters do that when persuading to bed." This was a stab at Uncle Philip, no doubt.

My father laughed and said quickly, "Don't tell me, Hogg, that you think we live in a monogamous, one-family society here in the U.S.A.? I don't think Morgan, I mean Lewis H. Morgan, not you, Philip, would see it the way you do. Now, why don't you look at your society, Hogg, the way you'd look at the Aruntas or the Iroquois. Now, Hogg, if you saw a bunch of Iroquois or Sioux with our organization, you'd say they were polygamous.

> " 'Now trouble brioux
> Among the Sioux
> Because each year
> A dear they chioux.'

"I don't mean wife and mistress-in-state, that's just old-fashioned French conservatism; why, I mean what they say, 'It's unlucky to be the seventh husband of a seventh wife.' Do you call that state of affairs monogamy? And to think we sent out U.S. troops to slaughter the poor old disciples of Joe Smith. It's the old story in anthropology: the conquered conquers the conqueror! Now we are all Mormons. And don't tell me you think we're going back to the one-woman convent and the emasculated man, or One Million Abelard-and-Heloises, after this carnival of jazz. 'I want to be castrated! Oh, dear, dear, I meant circumcised—that was the word! But it's too late now.' No, it's too late now to go back to being castrated."

Cheerfully, he kept it up. Both were embarrassed, Hogg, the moralist, and Philip, the many-marrier. Philip spoke very morally. My father, a decent-living, attached, affectionate man, was a pocket Rabelais.

Impossible in a family like ours, full of court scandal, to keep the various sexual knots and hitches from our sight. Uncle Philip nearly had a baby by Eleanor Blackfield, and it was only shipped out of life when he hastily married the pregnant Amabel. Eleanor was a Vassar girl who wrote poetry, came from a high-toned family, knew only girls called Butterfield, Trowbridge, van Dorp, and danced with Mary Wigman. Our Hogg and Morgan fold had not such fine white-fleeced lambs; but eligible men always are admitted among the silvertails, and Philip had become Eleanor's great love. She danced and taught dancing and helped Philip out with the rent for a long time. She was odd-looking, freakish, with transparent black voile sleeves, a long-waisted figure and long well-shaped legs, long, faunish-arched feet, long hands. Her color was putty and her straight black hair flopped over her shoulders. She had big eyes, she painted her mouth purple. She and Philip had a frenzied affair, very *fin de siècle* they thought it (in 1928). She was older than Philip by about five years. She had a devil of a temper and kept him on the jump; naturally, he needed a mother after that, and Amabel was the earth-goddess he got. But one spring, in the beginning of their affair, Philip on a river took a boat beneath a willow left afloat, incredible as it sounds, and ran away with Eleanor; and I suppose they had a loaf of bread and a flask of wine; I know they had a book of verse. How young Philip was then! He was a great fleshy romantic boy, quoted poets all day long, was always in love, and was a socialist. He was probably presentable enough too. Even when we first knew him, when he was twenty-one and married, and full-grown, he looked as if he could get women, heavy white blossomy flesh, a squarish face with blue eyes and curly brown hair loose round it, a thick strong neck, a ready smile, and a manner both consoling and appealing; and all kinds of airs he had picked up from the men he admired. He admired dozens of men, imitating them all: two he imitated were Hogg and my father.

Amabel Winslow was the subject of talk in the family, but the children did not know she was a name in society. She expected her baby in June, now dragged her heavy load in or near the Lodge. In the evenings, long before the winter snows had gone, Philip would be seen on the roads, up and down, from our high place, would be in our house with Uncle Perce, or would come up out of the distance, talking to men, women, and children. He was restless. He said he was out on his chicken and egg run; it was hard to make money. Amabel needed town and they would not turn the child into a hick; as soon as the child was born, they would turn back the farm and make off. He was constantly reading newspapers, looking for jobs, answering advertisements, and writing letters to people who might buy the farm. The mail addressed to him he arranged to receive at our house, "Care of Hogg, The Wreck" (as Hogg insisted on calling it), for he did not want to make the expectant mother anxious, but would tell her when all was ready. He received mail every day and often walked down to the post office with his answers. He now neglected the farm, after months of patient work.

"New broom sweeps clean," said Hogg; the farmer with the bull laughed fatly, said, "First he worked like a steer and now he rears at work, like a crazy horse."

The woods were full of lost hen eggs. One afternoon, in late April, looking for treasures, we came upon one nest, then another; soon we were risking our legs and even our necks in the treasure hunt. We brought back about ten dozen eggs to the Lodge; some must have been abandoned there since the last year. We then spied on the fowls and when one or other began picking her way studiously out of some glade, we marked the spot with our eyes and went for it; in this way we often found warm new eggs and stole some of these to take home. Hogg said nothing about this egg-theft, though he made an uproar about some wild birds' eggs we brought back and he was the terror of the birds'-nesting boys. He honestly thought of them as assassins. As for the hen eggs, we were poor and needed them.

This Lydnam Lodge was a folly and could never pay for itself. "Every egg cost a dollar," said Grandmother Morgan; but the Lodge was a convenient place to quarantine her children as each one reaped a wild oat; and it was a senseless delight, a pleasance which she felt she would allow them. She did not care for it herself. Grandmother Morgan, once she found she could not in any way turn the place into a boarding house, stayed away from it. She missed the clink of china and glass, the endless brushings of brooms, the glimmer of clean windows, the smells of rooms over-furnished with bedspreads, toilet covers, and women. She missed the bottles hidden in boot boxes, the crystal sets, the card games—especially perhaps the big poker game at which she herself was such a hand. She liked the complaints, the bills, the quarrels in the kitchen; she liked the cutting of lawns, the consultations with plumbers and plasterers, the quantities of goods in drawers and cupboards, the bustle of company, the thieving and picking, lashing of competitors, the brawling, the fight for life. Where can you feel it more than in a hotel or in a money game? She never objected even to what went on in the rooms, if these human frailties were kept out of sight. For that was life to her, like the secret bustle of red blood, a woman who longs and fornicates and a man who thirsts and sucks. What was there out in the country, among the chickens and plants?

Philip made trips to town almost every week, and he decided to go in for a few days around May Day. A sulky girl with a stoop came up every day from the end of the lane, to help Mrs. Morgan, Philip's wife, with the house. Mrs. Morgan did not like house-work, but was good at stews and pastries. When Philip came from town, he brought us cakes, candies, and hairbows and books. We often went to the Lodge now that we had got used to the strange woman, and had digested all the story about her. Few people visited her. She was a short-tempered woman, and if fretful or tired would stare in angry silence at unwelcome visitors, or walk up and down, spurting odd remarks, as to Mrs. Dr. Goodsir. When Dollie

Goodsir was born, we came to call Mrs. Goodsir Aunt Bette. Aunt Bette wheeled the *precious child* down to Mrs. Morgan's every afternoon that Philip was absent, for women's chat, but women's chat displeased Amabel. She had been a fighter for women's rights, but on the outside of real woman-talk, their simple preoccupation with their sex, the other sex, and their superstitions. As Aunt Bette frothed away gaily, sure that this defender of women would sympathize with her, the face of Philip's wife darkened. She would brusquely ask Aunt Bette about her work down in The Wreck, an endless job. Aunt Bette was paid a little, both by Hogg and by my father, for looking after us and the house. She never talked about the work, did it singing and dancing, as well as she could, with her tired legs, and she looked pretty and young when she took her baby for its walk. We heard her singing to the baby in the house, "O darling, O darling, O darling, O darling, O darling!" Sometimes she made up songs, "O darling, O darling, you're so sweet; my dear little baby I'll eat, eat, eat," and so she invented all the afternoon; "You've got a cruel mother, a berry cruel mother, a wicked cruel mother, a mother who hates its own little angel, its precious, a mother who is going to give it a silk dress and a satin dress and a velvet dress, all so white, all so white—tum-tum-tum—all so white—"

Her talk with Aunt Amabel was a bit more sensible, not much. "Do you think that prenatal impressions—?" "A woman I know stayed in bed eight months to have a baby—"

We loved all this. Aunt Amabel did not care whether we were there or not; but presently she would get up, stretch herself with a slow, sure muscular motion, like a lion after sleep, and begin thoughtfully to walk about.

"Has Dr. Goodsir a specialty in medicine?"

Aunt Bette never liked to answer. She felt Dr. Goodsir should not be admitted as truly living, until he came back to his child.

"Something about the glands—the ductless glands!" She had a good memory and rattled off all she could remember from his instruction in the days when they were going together.

"You have a good memory, Bette; you could have studied medicine, or bacteriology—you could have helped him in the laboratory. What can be done?"

"I—I," Aunt Bette would say laughing, with her hand over her mouth at the ridiculous idea. Then she'd straighten up, pull down her lawn and lace blouse, "I dare say I could do something if I had the chance; but now I have Baby."

"You're twenty-three."

"Dr. Goodsir would not like it, if it got about that his wife was working."

In answer to Aunt Amabel's silence, she would say timidly, "My father was too old to get big orders any more when I was growing up and I wanted to go on the stage, I wouldn't have heard of college anyhow. Besides, it ruined them putting my three brothers through college; but look at Percival—he's worth it."

"You don't complain enough," said Amabel.

"Everyone's very kind to me, very good indeed," said Bette. "I like to come into a room gay and bright, and leave a good impression. A querulous woman—what's worse!"

"Even a dog yelps when it's trod on, but not you—" Mrs. Morgan would look out the window, and the brown in her eyes glow like ruby.

"Of course, it's hard work, but I eat and I've got Baby."

Mrs. Morgan was not so happy. Philip was often away for the whole day or the whole afternoon, talking to the farmers, and would come home healthy, brown, fat and cheerful, but tired. He was known for a mile in every direction, a favorite of kitchens and barns. He knew the small flower gardens near the house, the barn and house-cats, the bulls, woodchuck colonies, tall woods full of birds, and yards sheltered by trained vines, the tool sheds and the back lots where no one ever came. A cat in the chicken farm was famous. She turned down the local toms and walked three miles to her beloved, and this, year after year. The dogs knew Philip; the boys whom others despised; the girls knew him too. He became sick of the district; scandals sprang up, but in what seemed to us a hypocritical way he was devoted to his wife. We came once upon a curious scene. Uncle Philip was sitting on the corner of the daybed which stood in the great room, his arm on the fanciful book table by its side. Mrs. Morgan was bent toward him and with her hands had tilted his face up to her: she was gently kissing every part of his face, while smiling, and he had his eyes fixed on her, quite ravished away. After a moment, one of them heard us and they turned to us, laughing, both laughing. We ran away; I, at least, felt jealous.

During this whole first week of May, Uncle Philip stayed away. In the meantime, the sulky, stooping girl from the village had come to Uncle Hogg and gone away; Aunt Bette told us there was something wrong with her and that she had said awful things about Uncle Philip—*a girl like that*. One afternoon a storm blew up, as it often does over those hills and bottoms, and Uncle Hogg sent me down to keep Mrs. Morgan company. It would grow awfully dark in these sudden storms. There was always a great noise and sometimes the wires came down. The Lodge was safe under the old wood. The rain pelted in so that it was hard to get down from the road to the Lodge, and the farmers were too busy counting their chickens and shutting doors to be able to look to the Lodge. I loved storms and liked to go and watch over Aunt Amabel. The sky was clear, high, wide, and then the dark poured over it and rains hit the house.

Inside, in the middle of the high-roofed room, it was still, but outside it seemed as if the porch would be torn away; big branches from the trees brushed the house, bushes struck the back windows, the water rushed against the house and down the hill. Uncle Philip had then been away a week and I prattled about him, while Amabel was very cheerful, and told me also about the baby coming. Night came. I was to stay there the night. About ten o'clock the telephone rang and I heard Aunt Amabel talking quietly on it. I crept in—it was Uncle Philip, in New York. She was saying:

"I am all right, my darling, but it is lonely here, there is a storm out here, the boughs are brushing against the house—" She came in, running, full of joy. "Philip is coming tonight! It's an awful trip here now so late. Poor boy!"

He came about three in the morning and she flung herself into his arms like a young girl. After this I said nothing more to Jacky about them, nor made up stories. I could not stand it. I wanted to be loved.

Uncle Philip had seemed very sweet that night, boyish, kneeling at her feet and kissing her knees and feet and hands. I tossed about thinking about it all. The next day, too, Uncle Philip was not himself and took me back to The Wreck without a word, although I babbled as usual. I became pettish and struck him.

He looked down at me, and said, "I'm a bad man, Letty dear, I'm afraid, and I'm having an attack of conscience."

"What did you do?"

"I don't think I'll ever be able to be a good man."

"Why not?"

"It's my nature."

"What have you done?"

He sighed and handed me in the gate. Then he went in to P. Hogg and seemed to have lost all shame, for he asked Hogg to please take care of the girl called Blackfield, Eleanor Blackfield. He had not stayed at his sister's (my mother's) place, as he had promised to do; he had stayed the whole week with his old sweetheart, Eleanor, in her flat in the Village; and he had been with her when he telephoned that stormy night. He was afraid she would come after him to The Wreck. "Please don't tell her I live down the road, but send her away to town," he asked Hogg. "Tell her I've gone back. You see, she thinks I live here."

Hogg flushed and he stared at Philip with fury. "Do your own dirty work. How can you bring a girl out where your wife is? I won't put my hands in the pitch. You can't touch pitch without being blacked."

But Philip persuaded him and called us in and told us to do our best for him, we were sensible little girls. "This is a lady I was going to marry. I didn't marry her and now she wants me to."

"You jilted her?" enquired Jacky, fascinated.

"He stood her up," said I.

"You've got it exactly," said Philip, taking a hand in each hand, and looking earnestly at us. "Now dear Aunt Amabel is going to be sick and have a baby and she mustn't be worried and you mustn't tell Eleanor about anything at all. Now, Eleanor is a nice girl, too, remember."

Hogg could scarcely stand the thought of it. He stood staring down at Philip. "She's coming here to see your wife?"

"She thinks my wife's gone back to Chicago!"

"You liar."

"I am a liar," said Philip. "I am a bad husband to Amabel; but I must say one thing, the girls do hunt you, you know; you must never give them a chance. Give them a chance and you'll find out."

"The girls hunt you!" said Hogg, and he told Philip about the scandals in the district: a girl three-quarters of a mile away, living with her father, was going to have a baby. He said it was Philip's.

"Now every baby in the township will be mine!" he frowned.

We stood staring ourselves out of countenance, having no idea what it could all be about. When Philip went, we spent all our time talking about Eleanor, the girl who was hunting Philip, and this was how we first saw any one of what Hogg called "his women."

Eleanor was easily persuaded that Philip had gone back to town, and she herself, seeing The Wreck, threw her purple lipstick and silver pencil back into her handbag and took the same taxi back to the station. Philip had already telegraphed from the farmer's kitchen to his sister Mathilde to fix up a story for him when Eleanor called upon her. We had behaved admirably, Jacky saying little and I pushing myself forward with a long line of interesting talk in which I skillfully wrapped up all the proper lies about Uncle Philip. I invented quite a lot; it was a tiptop performance. I was very much hurt when Uncle Percival sent me to bed without dinner, forbade me to talk to Jacky for the whole evening, and called us together before this punishment to give us a sharp talk about lies. Said he,

" 'Oh, what a tangled web we weave, When first we practice to deceive.' "

This attracted me. I skipped up to bed. Downstairs Uncle Perce and Aunt Bette indulged in that form of psychological unraveling which consists of, "She is really to blame for; he is really to blame for"; and "the parents are really to blame for—"

8

THE SCANDALS broke round them before June; the Philip Morgans fled from the Lodge to town. At first they put up with Mathilde, and when she and my father at last objected, they moved to a hotel. While the woman was in the hospital, her husband was looking for a flat, and took one in the Village among all his old friends.

My mother, who heard Philip's full confession, during his new loneliness, went to Farmington, packed our clothes, and brought us back to town. She telephoned Mrs. Hogg, who was getting a divorce, and Templeton and Cecily were brought back to town. My mother was unhappier than ever, but had a single hope—my father was to go to England, on a shipping job with Joseph Montrose for a year or so. In that time he would be separated from *Die Konkubine* and would forget her.

"But I suppose," sighed my mother, "that now it will be another one."

"There is safety in numbers," said Grandmother; "one is romance, two is adventure, and three is a shame."

The flat in Bleecker Street was an interesting nest of marital intrigue; its purpose, the recapture of my father for mother and us. Grandmother Morgan was chief of staff, although she had little time to waste on her older daughters and little enough even for Phyllis, now sixteen.

"Stella is an old maid, Mathilde has no sense, and Phyllis will get married; don't worry," said Grandmother Morgan to her cronies over the cards. She had no sympathy even for young married women; she waited for women to lose their illusions. But she was not easygoing: she wanted each woman to have a husband and children, which is nature's way. She thought even Stella would marry in time; "she'll hook some weak sister," said Grandmother.

Only three men came to the flat—Grandfather Morgan on his way to the Rice Progressive Chess Club in Fourteenth Street, Uncle Philip on his way to and from unknown places, my father. Grandfather Morgan, now too old, was a bearded, blue-eyed gentleman who spoke softly and looked like Jesus. But he walked crabwise and smiled slightly in his blue-green eyes.

"Now, I am going to Evensong," he would say softly, between red firm lips; that meant he was going to the Chess Club, we believed. He asked about my father, and nodded at the answer whatever it was, but he gave no advice; he never tried to patch up any family breaks.

While Amabel was still in the hospital, Philip brought a new friend to see us. She was Dora Dunn, a stout young woman, with red hair drawn back in a knot. Her skin was pale and freckled, her eyes green. She was smartly dressed, broad before and behind, with a soft neck in folds and small feet on high heels. She played the naïve, sweet friend, quietly admired my mother's good looks and our fine eyes, and seemed to take it for granted that she was my mother's friend.

"One of his women, I suppose," sighed Mathilde; but she liked her. Dora Dunn told her troubles and discussed her business. She engaged designers from abroad and sold costume jewelry and gewgaws in a Village shop which she owned. She had passed up from lamps, button collections, and second-hand articles with a few books on the side, to this flourishing business, invented by her, financed by friends, and patronized by girl friends who had attached themselves to wealthy men. She had a swarm of friends, of whom she remembered every particular; but she had the grace and art not to crowd our flat and my mother's sad life with these others. She always made it seem that she came to see my mother only, and to talk over family affairs. She had gathered a lot of information about the family and used it discreetly; yet her avidity was shocking. My mother, to save her solitude, had learned to rebuff people, but no one could rebuff Dora Dunn; she was overpoweringly diplomatic. She was about thirty, and for a while my mother wondered if she were not simply worming herself into the Morgan family to get orders from their clientele of hotel guests.

This gifted woman made a friend also of Grandmother Fox,

who had nothing to offer to Dora, spiritually or materially; and now my mother began to fear that Dora was after my father. Dora was unmarried; she confessed she was a virgin. She had a few thousand dollars in the bank, she said, although she needed it at hand for expenses. My mother thought my father was a weak man and that such a managing woman might get him. She watched Dora suspiciously, but it looked as if she laughed and flirted with Grandmother Fox merely to keep her hand in.

"Perhaps she really has a good heart," said my mother. Dora used to come to the flat in Bleecker Street twice a week then; each time she left she took something, a handkerchief, book, or caramel.

No doubt she was looking for a husband in her businesslike way, but she fooled Mathilde. Mathilde had met Eleanor Blackfield and others of Philip's girls who poured out their loves and hates without reticence; but Dora coolly discussed Philip's habits and looks, praised his attention to his wife, and praised his wife. It was during the summer when Amabel was nursing her baby, out in the Morgan house, Green Acres, that Philip came to Mathilde about Dora on one of those hot summer nights when people sit with their windows open but the lights out. Our windows, on the second floor, overlooked the street, still hot; noisy children played underneath. I was in bed, but not asleep.

"I want to be good," said Philip, "and I haven't been with another woman more than three or four times since I married Amabel, that's a year; you know how I feel about Amabel. But I never loved the child, Mattie, and he doesn't seem very bright to me. The trouble is, Mattie, that one of the women was Dora Dunn and I was her first man; she's in love with me, I'm afraid," and down went his voice to his boots; he sounded as if pouting.

"You can't expect sympathy from me. I have troubles of my own," said my mother.

"I don't know what to do, you see, Mattie; I've had so much trouble with girls, and you get so tangled—you don't know which way to turn. Now, this very evening, do you know there are three girls expecting me; what shall I do? Dora is one, Eleanor is another—"

"You don't count Amabel, do you?" said my mother.

"No, three girls," his voice rolled gutturally over the word, reluctant, clinging. "I had better not go to any of them, eh?"

"I don't know anything about it," and I heard my mother move her chair.

"But I promised Dora to—" his voice trailed off. After a while he murmured, "Got to get a shave."

"I haven't seen Solander this week; it's all he can do to ring me up," said my mother's thin, young voice; "I am not crying on anyone's shoulder, am I? What's the matter with me? What do I lack? If I could only see anything—but she's got no personality either: she's just a girl, like I am. I don't see it. Are there some differences to you between all these girls? Are you attracted by some characteristic—?" After a slight pause, she went on angrily, "Or is it just any kind of woman?"

"I often get women when I don't want them at all; they seem to come after me. I wouldn't say I chose them, myself."

"I suppose she chose him. I have no will power; I never accomplished anything. If I set out to get something, that's a proof I won't get it."

He sighed and got up. "I hate to stand two of them up; I don't like that. But today Dora—"

He soon went away. I heard my mother crying, but I stayed in bed. I knew I ought to feel angry that my father had abandoned me for another female, and I did my best to feel sulky; I fancied myself as an orphan; and then there was Jacky—the Two Orphans. As I saw the tragic scene of our orphaned lives, I cheered up and laughed to myself.

Mother's friends and relatives tumbled in and out of the house, tossing off advice, endeavoring to scheme with their self-centered feeble wits, shooting off their private venoms. Everyone liked my father; my mother had to put up with much mischief; those came who flatly told her she deserved it. Close friends asserted themselves and fastened themselves upon my mother like parasites. Some shared her rooms, others ate her food. She got advice on how to bring up children, how to dress, and how to keep husbands. Often when they went she would turn from the door with a piteous howl, thrusting her hands into her hair; their disturbing words ate into her mind: she nearly went mad. It was enough to have lost her husband; it was too much for her to bear these gossips and pocket Machiavellis; but Jacky and I saw it for what it was, a grotesque game, played round her, not for her, with stakes high and low, ageless, immoral, and amusing as a circus.

I was with my father, in the office he occupied with Joseph Montrose in Thirty-fourth Street, when Grandmother Morgan visited him at three in the afternoon, bringing with her Phyllis. Grandmother admired my father's business connections; Joseph Montrose knew many rich men, here and abroad; men were getting richer every day, and Grandmother wanted to place Phyllis to the best advantage. For two years Phyllis had lived with Stella and been sweet and good in the house, while she was attending high school in the city, but she had not been at home one night in those years; and now she needed a guardian, the best guardian, a husband.

Grandmother kissed and hugged me, patted Solander's hand, and regretted that Mr. Montrose was out.

"I want him to meet Phyllis, he might introduce her to someone," she said, smiling broadly and patting my father's hand again.

"Phyllis won't be hard to get off," laughed Solander.

Phyllis sat on the window seat and looked out the window, smiling to herself.

"I won't say anything about my poor Mathilde," said Grandmother. "I want you to do something for her, though; go back to her, patch it up, my dear Sol. I know she isn't cheerful, she doesn't know what to do with a man, she isn't a smart girl—but she's a good girl, pretty, and she loves you, Sol. Go back to her, dear boy; I'm very fond of you, you've always been my favorite in-law, you're almost a son to me, and I've a mother's feelings. I didn't do well by you when you were married; if you go back to her, I'll give you a *suit* of bedroom furniture—and, h'm—when you're settled down, I'll see about it—I'll see about the table silver. You never had anything out of me, I just overlooked it, dear Sol. Mind you, dear boy, I don't blame you. I know my daughter, she's the kind who is born a has-been—I wish you'd got Phyllis; Phyl is quite a different kind of girl, she knows what she's about and she has a very affectionate nature. But you preferred the quiet one. I've had serious talks with Mattie. I'm sure she'll try to improve. Living with her is not like going to the circus, I know; but she's the mother of your children—she's a mother, Sol."

My father smiled at his mother-in-law and said, "I went back to her, you know I tried, Mamma Morgan; but it didn't work out."

"Now, my dear Sol, a little practical sense," said Mamma Morgan. "I don't say get rid of this other girl, do I? But keep her in a nice place where you can visit her. I hear she's a nice girl. Mattie need never know; it's just for appearance' sake, for organization— and for the children. Letty's a bright child, Sol, the image of you, dearie, and she'll need her father, for Mattie will never be able to keep her straight. That child's full of the devil, look at the way her eyes dance: she's going to be a frisky filly, Letty is; and she needs a father's hand. I can't look after her, dearie, I've too much to do and I've got to get Phyl married. Now, Sol, you fix up a nice place for Mattie and you leave this girl behind—I hear she's a very nice girl, quite ladylike, I understand no one's ever heard her say a vulgar thing, that's what Dora Dunn tells me—and you fix this girl up and when you come back, you'll find it isn't so hard to go back to Mattie. And I promise I'll give my daughter a shaking up; I'll tell her straight: 'You've got to make a home for a man and keep it running, and be a smart dresser, or you deserve that a man should run out on you.' I'll look after you, Sol, and I'll keep Mathilde up to the mark. Why, I'm doing it for myself; I don't want a grass widow as well as an old maid. I can't look out for three more men! Not for other women at any rate." Solidly she laughed, Grandmother Morgan, kissing my father again and reiterating her promise about the *suit* of furniture, but leaving out about the silver.

As my grandmother finished her speech to my father, Joseph Montrose entered, looked sharply around, perceived Phyllis and went toward her saying, "Yes, little lady," but he turned at once toward Solander, who introduced Grandmother, now sitting there, like a great lady, beaming, holding out her hand, and flattering Montrose. Montrose acknowledged the introduction in an abstracted way, but suddenly said, "Well, Sol, this is your beautiful sister-in-law Phyllis, then? You didn't lie, Sol. Mrs. Morgan, let me tell you your daughter is a beauty."

"Oh, Phyllis is a knock-out," said Sol gaily, "but, Joe—"

Montrose had now reached Phyllis again, was shaking hands with her and eyeing her, with a fierce bright parrot laugh. Then he shook hands with her politely, turned to Mrs. Morgan and said, "Too bad I'm married! You should have told me!"

Phyllis laughed modestly, "But I am not going to get married yet, Mr. Montrose. We only came to ask you about my voice—I want to go on with my music. Mathilde was on the stage, and Mother thought—" She fell silent, charmingly, and looked at her mother.

Grandmother then unpacked the scheme she had thought up to interest Montrose. Phyllis had a sweet, clear voice of good range, and was an excellent pianist; her teacher said she could go on the concert platform with either. But could Phyllis sing *Lieder*, or Grand Opera, had she the strength of voice and body, and so forth —Mrs. Morgan was almost a home woman, lost in her affairs out at Green Acres and at the Long Island place, with another place she was thinking of setting up down south somewhere, for the winters, in Florida, perhaps. She had no time, although it was a shame to say it, for her darling youngest daughter; Sol would not mind if Mrs. Morgan confessed that Phyllis was the apple of her eye. Grandmother wiped her fine eyes and said Sol had mentioned that Mr. Montrose had friends in Paris, London, Berlin, and Vienna and could perhaps give her advice about teachers, and the cost; and more, a very important thing, where a young and lovely girl could live away from home.

"Even in New York," said Mrs. Morgan, "Phyllis must now have companionship and even a chaperone, if she is going to study."

"Certainly," said Joseph Montrose, "most important," and he took on a serious air, thumbing his chin. "A young girl," said Montrose, looking at Phyllis in a peculiar, sidelong, underhand and serious way, like a jewel thief looking at the crown jewels during a public tour and thinking, "It's a wonder the police don't look after these better." "Leave it to me," said Montrose; "young girls can't live alone—too many—h'm—we aren't all that we should be," and his lip and eye shone, he chuckled. "Yes, leave it to me, Mrs. Morgan." Grandmother then took him aside and told him that privately she did not so much care whether Phyllis sang or not; a girl's duty was to get married and if Montrose could arrange a match sooner or later, she would always be grateful to him. She had no money at hand to give away with the girl, but perhaps something could be arranged between them for one of Montrose's friends, for a nice businessman with a future, not even too rich at present; a good, solid, young man who could give her girl a nice home, fur coats, automobiles, nice furniture, she would do what she could toward helping the young man, and perhaps Montrose and his wife would accept the hospitality of the Long Island hotel, a modern one, if he felt like it, once the marriage was arranged.

Montrose appeared to accept all this with enthusiasm and already looked upon himself as a kind of papa of Phyllis. He went over, took her arm firmly, smiled at her seriously, said, "Leave it to me, I'll—do what I can—I'll—look around. And all I'll ask," and he repeated it, "will be to kiss the bride—when she marries, of course. But tell me," he said, "why such a pretty girl wants to work? Pretty girls like you don't want to go on the stage."

As soon as Grandmother had gone, taking with her plump and large-eyed Phyllis, my father took leave of Montrose and went out with me, holding me by the hand and arranging my curls on my shoulder with unusual attention. He took me to have an ice cream soda, and when we were seated at the table, said to me, "Now, Letty, I'm going to take you to see a lady; it's my girl, Persia. I don't want you to tell Mummy, because she wouldn't like it. But you're my daughter too, and I want you to get to know Persia; she's a very nice girl. I know you can hold your tongue. You understand that? It is not that it is wrong. I am quite open about it; I have no secret life. But here is where your mother and I see things differently. You are my daughter and I want you to see my new girl."

I said, "Can I have another strawberry sundae?"

"I'm in a hurry; afterwards," he said.

This put me in a bad mood and I thought at first I would tell Mother; but I had sense enough to see that nothing but unpleasantness would come to me personally if I did this, and I gradually became excited. My father babbled on and seemed very cheerful.

"Did you hear what Grandmother said?" he asked me. "She's not a bad old girl. I've always liked the old duck. I've never had anything against your Grandmother Morgan, only I think she sucked all the life out of the rest of the family. Your poor old grandfather is now a worn-out rag, and as for the rest of the family—I do not blame your mother, she is a sweet enough girl, but her

mother took all the life out of her. You heard what your grandmother said about Persia? She said, 'No one has ever said a word
against her,' that she was a perfect lady. Well, that decided me,
Letty. I thought, now I will take Letty to see her and she will see
she is no monster. For I've no doubt they've been filling your ears
with rubbish about her."

"They call her *Die Konkubine*," I said.

"Who said that?" pricking up his ears. "My mother, I suppose.
It sounds like her."

"No," I said rapidly. "No, it was someone else, I can't remember." However, he was right; it had been Grandmother Fox, who
used to be a governess in Germany, with a family at Bismarck-
Schoenhausen.

I will tell about Persia later. After the visit to the small dark flat
he lived in, with Persia, uptown, in Clarcmont Avenue (far away
from us and all our relatives), Father took me home to my mother.
They were coldly pleasant to each other, and my mother had a soft
distant manner which surprised me.

As soon as my father had gone, Mother asked me what he had
said to me and where we had gone. I said, "We went to the Central
Park Zoo." My mother hated animals and would ask no questions
about such a spot. "I had two strawberry sundaes," I told her.

"You're getting too fat," said my mother; "your father spoils
you and I have the trouble of—"

Presently Dora Dunn came in. She had taught my mother to
gossip, for she sympathized with her. Whenever she went away my
mother had a nervous crisis, and said she felt malice in the woman,
though it was hard to point out. This day my mother was cheerful
and like a girl. She said joyfully, "He is coming back to me when
he returns from England."

"How do you know?"

"Mother told me."

At once Dora drew it all from her, that Grandmother Morgan
had positively assured her that Solander, not a bad boy at all, had
promised to live with us again, as soon as his job in England was
over, "only a few months; and while he is away he is dismissing
that girl and she is going away from town to get a new job. He has
already arranged for her to leave town."

I was surprised and indignant that my father had not told me all this; and then I laughed, for it occurred to me that he was afraid I would tell the girl, Persia. All this was being schemed for her, by others of whom probably she had never heard. I began to laugh in my room; they heard me and stopped talking for a moment.

Then my mother said, "She's too quick; we were talking too loud"; but Dora Dunn came into the room, opened her fat arms to me, pushed me against her chest, and called out, "Her daddy's coming back to her; oh, goody, goody! Why, you know it is very bad for a child to feel itself rejected: it can make it quite neurotic. It can develop an inferiority complex. Now she's already a nervous enough child—"

I began to feel quite low and unhappy. Dora dropped me back among my cut-out dolls and went back to tell Mathilde about Philip and his crimes. "I must give him up; he says he's leaving her and then he goes to her. He uses one and then the other just to suit himself. I owe it to myself—"

"Philip's never had less than four or five women, to my knowledge," said my mother.

After a brief silence, Dora said briskly, "He's inhibited; he must keep proving to himself that he's attractive to women. If he had real self-confidence, he'd be satisfied with one, but such a man never knows love, because it is his own ego he's centering around and what worries him is a sense of inferiority, arising no doubt in his mother's sex history, for all we know—"

My mother got up, walked about the room, and in a cold voice told Dora Dunn that she felt ill and must lie down.

Dora Dunn continued, "And you too, darling Mattie! I've seen this Persia—"

"You have," said my mother. "How did that happen?"

"Oh, you know, I'm a friend of both parties, so it seems, but only as your friend: I thought I'd see what she is like and let you know."

"I can look after myself," said Mathilde; "and I don't care— since it's all arranged that she is to go—"

"You must shake yourself out of this torpor; it's refusal to face life," cried Dora Dunn. "A man looks for life. Now this girl isn't a coquette, and she hasn't sex-appeal, she isn't even what you'd call pretty—but she's bitchy, she's a pokerface and a razor-edge psyche, and he's probably been afraid to leave her; she has no doubts about herself, whereas you give in without a murmur. Did you even fight for him? Now, a man likes to be fought for! Did you ever see a man's open grin when he sees two women fighting about him? Why, Philip loves it. I yell and screech when I see another of his girls, just to please him. He thinks it's a compliment. Now if you were to pull a few scenes, when he's around, and—"

"I couldn't," said Mathilde, sinking into a chair again. "What's the use? I don't believe in myself. I'd have to work it up for weeks. I don't know the words. If someone would write the words for me, I could do it, but as it is—I never could invent. It costs too much nervous energy. I would be a wreck. Look at your muscles. You've got muscles like a—a coal-heaver, a weight-lifter. You haven't any nerves—I know you're right."

"Then I'll write out the words for you, or I'll get someone I know—"

"Oh, he's coming back," said my mother weakly.

"But you'll lose him again, you'll not be able to hold him, unless you make him of importance in his own eyes, you've got to give him value. Why, look how he's increased his importance by just running off with a woman—"

"Oh, I can't bear this," cried my mother. "Dora, I've got a headache now. If Mother can't arrange it, no one can. I know I can't. I'm no use at all. Wait till the little girls find out. They'll prefer her too. Everyone likes the other woman best."

When Dora went, she began to cry, out of weakness and doubt.

9

FOR YEARS my Grandfather Morgan had been talking about his lungs. Long ago, just after buying Lydnam Hill, he had even left New York for Williams, Arizona; but he had told about it in such a comical way, with his eyes twinkling, his ears twitching, and his scalp jumping under his wiglike black hair, that people had ceased to believe in it, except as a lazy man's excuse; and as proof, he had said when he came back after only ten days, from Williams, that he could not bear to see all those lungers holding up porch posts and coughing and spitting all day.

He had a few recitations about his life, which were all we knew of it. Grandmother Morgan despised him, though she was kind to him, and somewhat respectful and tender. She had been married to him when a young ignorant girl, married in a church, and for the first few years had believed that marriage with him was her only destiny. She did not wake up, as she put it, till the seventh of her children was born; that was Philip.

At one time, Grandfather had worked in the White-Brooks department store as manager. He was a tall, handsome, alert man that most women found attractive. He began to cough and use his handkerchief too much and say that the department store was full of dust. After he came back from Williams, he did not go to work again, but stayed at home, in the Green Acres Inn, to help his wife, who was then about forty and just coming out of her shell. Feeling his new lethargy, Grandmother then jumped into the saddle, began to open out the business and look for other properties, and a few years later had become the woman we all now knew. Grandfather Morgan liked to tell the story of that change, and others had a curious spittling and pleasure when listening to it, for none of them thought it decent that he now lived upon his wife. Solander, my father, saw nothing wrong in it, and was fond of the old gentleman; and Grandmother listened complacently to the old story and would help with it, though meanwhile her eyes shining so softly showed that she was thinking other things, that could not be told at all.

"A few years ago, a long time ago, Bernie thought he had lung trouble," would say Grandmother, "and he went to the White-Brooks doctor—"

And Grandfather would break in, allowing her thoughts to wander, "I was going to all their doctors, they thought I was tubercular, something like that" (nodding), "the bacillus of Koch, they called it; I went to Dr. Fawsitt—"

"Ha-ha," someone would say, "Dr. Faucet, ha-ha, now it's Dr. Faucet, Dr. Faucet and not Dr. Wasserman? And the bacillus of Koch?"

"Dr. Wasserman was it?"

Then Grandfather, insulted, would look into his plate. "All right, Philip, all right—" And Grandmother, "All right, Bernard, all right."

"Let me give you my version of the story," said Grandfather.

Grandmother said, "You don't know what you're letting yourself in for—now!"

Quietly, Bernard said, "I was going to all the doctors and I went to someone outside White-Brooks, Dr. Taylor—"

"And not Schneider? Ha-ha!"

"He's a good fella; he told me I had lung trouble, I'd be all right if I spent six months in Arizona."

"So you put two and two together," said Philip, "and thought you ought to go to Arizona!"

Grandfather composedly said, "Mother was staying for a few weeks in town for a change, at the Bedfordshire Hotel, and naturally, of course, I was at Green Acres. I was calling upon her to see how she was getting on, a few times a week; she needed rest, I just called upon her in the afternoon."

After a pause, Grandmother would say, "Just like that. He did that. He called on me. He enquired after my health. He's a fine fellow."

Undisturbed, Bernard continued, "The company doctors and this doctor Fawsitt had me running round for six months and it was then I went to Dr. Taylor, a friend of mine, very fine doctor. He said I must take the train to Arizona for six months."

"So naturally," said Grandmother, laughing heartily, "that quick head at figures got to work and you decided you should spend six months in Arizona."

"And I said to Mother," said Bernard calmly, "I had better go to Arizona."

"What do you think of that?" enquired Grandmother.

Bernard exclaimed, "In the trial, they said someone told me I should go to Arizona!"

Grandmother took a faint interest, as always at mention of the law courts and lawyers, and said, "The funny thing is he actually said to him that he must go to Arizona, and in the trial the opposing lawyer suggested that someone had told him to go to Arizona and he had taken the advice. That was a good hit in the dark they made."

Bernard, looking insulted, looked away from all of them, "All right, all right; no, no!"

"All right, go on, Bernie," said Grandmother, with spirit. "I'm just explaining to them what relation—for what's coming afterwards! You've got to explain what all this means."

"I'm explaining," said Bernard, coming back to them, "let me tell the story. I haven't told my story yet. So I went to the White-Brooks doctors and said—"

"Oh, Lord," said Philip, "you're not in Arizona yet?" And Dora Dunn screamed horsily, "He's not in Arizona yet!" and raised loud laughter. Grandmother Morgan looked at her and laughed.

Grandfather said coolly, "No, I'm not in Arizona yet. I went back to the store and told Dr. Fawsitt" (ha-ha) "that I'd seen a specialist and he said I should go to Arizona."

"Good!" said Grandmother.

"So they examined me again and said perhaps Arizona would be all right. Mother was living in the Bedfordshire Hotel; I came to her several times a week and told her every word then, at that time. After a while she went home, back to the Inn. I examined the rules of the benefit society and concluded that if Arizona was what was required to cure me, I must go to Arizona; so I said to myself, 'You take six months off and—'"

Dora Dunn yelled out, "No! Go to Arizona!"

Someone said curiously, "Did you ever go to Arizona, tell me?"

Bernard said, "Yes, I'm back." He paused as if recalling that time, and continued, "Dr. Taylor said I should go and I thought I had the right to go. So I told them I was going to spend six weeks (mark!) in Arizona."

Philip said, "Oh, my aunt; he hasn't gone yet."

Bernard said slowly, stroking his beard and looking down it, "They told me, that was all right, if I had to go to Arizona—"

Dora and one of the women began repeating, one after the other, "I just had to go to Arizona."

Bernard said, "So I got leave of absence and I took the train to Arizona."

"Are you really going to Arizona?" said Philip. "I can't believe it."

"Are you off?" said Solander, laughing madly.

"Yes, I went to Arizona all right. When I got there—"

Dora Dunn cackled, "He found he was in Arizona."

Everyone, by this, was laughing hysterically. Bernard would now look around, first at Grandmother, then at Philip.

"What are you behaving like that for? I'm disgusted with you, Philip. Look at that woman" (Dora). "You're all behaving like idiots. Mother isn't laughing. I'll only talk to Mathilde, she listens to me. You others don't listen to me; you don't listen to my story. Mathilde listens to me; she's sensible."

Solander said, "Mother Morgan isn't laughing, she doesn't like us laughing at Bernard."

Grandmother said, "I don't like to see him making a fool of himself," and for a moment her voice sounded a little like Grandfather's own, as if she imitated him, to take his side; she had some of his slippery elisions, speaking low and softer, "I don't like to see him making people laugh at him—keep on repeating—"

"Mother," said Philip, "we're not laughing at him, but with him—"

"We're not laughing at him, Mother," said Mathilde.

Solander, enjoying himself, chuckling with his Buddha expression, entreated him, "Go on, Bernard; so you got to Arizona."

"And while I was there I didn't see any doctor; and I didn't stay—"

Solander (who knew the story) said, "You made a mistake; so they wouldn't allow your claim."

"Don't rush to conclusions, Fox," said Grandfather.

Solander said, "I was just going to get to the point."

Dora called out, "He just wants us to know the point of all this."

"I'll get to the point," said Bernard. "You let me tell the story and you'll get to the point."

Coarsely, someone else cried, "So he's still in Arizona." But the word by now had lost its magic, and everyone calmed down, while he explained the rest of it, his return to New York, his taking a holiday instead at Sheepshead Bay, the fishing. Then Grandmother would take it up again, and the two of them, sending it back and forth, went through again the dismissal, the suits, the moral victory ("You call two weeks' extra pay a moral victory?" Grandmother said), first costs, appeal costs, influencing the jury by making them give a decision before lunch, and so on.

"But I made history," said Bernard at the conclusion, and this was the point, "they changed the by-laws, and they wouldn't have if we hadn't fought them through to appeal. It wasn't worth it then."

Since then Bernard had probably not gone to any doctor, and the coughing that kept him and others awake at night they put down to nervousness, faking, and advancing age; at times he collected spit in a bottle, and then threw it away again. Because he coughed so much, and read at night with a coat round his shoulders, and a little lamp, and because he walked about, and listened and peered, and made noises in the kitchen, Bernard had at last been asked to take a room in the great barn where the servants slept. He had slept there for years. He did not make friends with the servants, though some of them came back year after year (only going away for summer camp jobs), but with a gardener called Jape. If he knew Jape's surname, he didn't say it; no one knew it. Jape never got a letter. He said that many years before he and his father used to make a good living at the vegetable and flower gardens around there and had their own nursery, out of town.

Jape really did not like Green Acres Inn. He was scornful of these broken-down families, newcomers, and commercial enterprises. He did not like Mrs. Cissie Morgan.

Now, this inn, which had once been a family house, was backed by several acres of long grass and weeds. The potting sheds and the glasshouse were ruined. Birds got inside the glasshouse and battered themselves against the half-painted glass. Jape grew a few tomatoes there for his own use. Beetles and other insects grew fat and thick on the hedge flowers near the barn. It was all Jape could do to keep up the gardens near the house, and roll the lawns where the guests sat. To the glasshouse, the spiders, and the long field no one ventured. There were barn cats there that no one saw, and sometimes the little scuffling and laughter of quite a community out of the upper story of the barn. On the other side of the garden was the small partitioned shed where Jape had his sleeping quarters. It was unpainted outside, but whitewashed within, and had a brick mantelpiece, two small garage windows, an iron bedstead, and a lot of junk. No one but Mr. Morgan had had a glimpse of it, in over twenty years; and even the Morgans doubted that he had been inside. Yet sometimes Morgan disappeared altogether; perhaps he was there.

The entrance to this area was protected on one side by clotheslines with towels and aprons, and on the other by a couple of large fat black spiders with, on the back of each, a skull and crossbones. When annoyed, these spiders shook their webs madly. Jape protected them, as they protected the back yard, for he said they brought good luck and if annoyed would roll up their webs and carry them off somewhere else. But the visitors, who were mostly businessmen, teachers of English and history, and fat, spoiled wives, knew nothing about spiders and thought they were all Black Widows. At any rate, the hideous things lived in peace, with their friend Jape bobbing about in their neighborhood.

No one knew what was the state of Grandfather's health. Jape perhaps knew, but he too was an aging man, with his rheumatics, his back, his teeth, his smoker's cough. When Grandfather caught a chill, he took to his bed and coddled himself for a few days, with food sent down for him, and whatever else he asked for; and no other notice was taken of him. Rarely did Grandmother have time for him, overworked as she was, sitting up till nearly morning sometimes with her card games and then going straight on with the work of the house, and going to New York and back, all without sleep. At one time, she had been able to take one hour's sleep in twenty-four, for days together. Now she needed a little more; but caught in the floodtide of her life, running here, there, she had only a few minutes for anyone.

"My children I neglected too, and I'm a good mother," she said.

One day Jape sent one of the maids to say that a doctor must come to see Mr. Morgan. No sooner had the doctor seen him than he said to send the old man to the hospital, and no sooner did they get him to the hospital than they tried extreme measures. Grandmother had only time to see him once, with Mathilde and myself, when he died. He died suddenly, in the morning, at sunrise of a beautiful summer day, and all he said was, "I said to him—"

The whole family went to the funeral and even Aunt Amabel, though now separated from Uncle Philip, came down, in a black dress, and held Philip's arm. Grandmother had bought a blanket of roses for her husband. They recited the Lord's Prayer; a second cousin, Reverend Poote, made a beautiful speech about the old gentleman, saying things about him which sounded so true, so touching at the moment, that everyone burst out crying. I flung myself into my mother's legs, crying as loudly as I could. My father was there and went off with us.

At the funeral, standing in the background, we had also seen Jape in his best brown suit, lanky, with a black band on his arm. He looked oddly old, poor and cross, in his best clothes. It was only in his old faded blues that he seemed a nice man. Jape walked away after saying hello to several people, and took the bus home. They thought it was funny but degrading afterwards, that Jape had taken a drink or two on the way home and told everyone at length about the beautiful funeral, how fine it was, and what a fine man my grandfather was.

The truth was, though we made a great noise about it, being a very sentimental family, we had all thought Grandfather slightly in the way for years. The old women at the Inn spoke about the old man for a few days, though no one had known him, but had only seen him sneaking merrily along the old carriage drive behind the laurel bush, and many had not known who he was at all.

They were interested in Grandmother, now a widow; it was almost a fete. Within a week Grandmother had a proposal from a fashionable grocer in the town who had been her acquaintance for years. In four months, just before my father sailed for England, this propertied grocer, a stout, short, strong man, some years younger than Grandmother, had Grandmother in a flutter. He wanted to marry her at once; it was not only a good business proposition, but he loved her. Grandmother's hair was by now white as snow, but her eyes were black, sparkling, and though generally brutal or even hard, could turn tender and sweet. Grandmother at once forgot everything else in hand and asked advice from all her friends and relatives. Her children were indignant. Phyllis was not yet married, Mathilde was in trouble, Philip was getting a divorce, two or three other uncles of mine, unimportant, sedate men, were scandalized; all of them feared the influence of the new husband. For Grandmother was a gay sentimental creature who, if she threw over the Inn (which kept some of the family working and occasionally cast a spray of furs and diamonds over the family), might travel the country or the world and throw all that was hers, not into the Inn where it belonged, but to her husband.

"You have earned a rest, retire," said the willing fiancé.

"For shame, Mamma, you are old," said the children.

Grandmother was as glorious, timid, and vain as a young girl. She dashed into town almost every day to see people, buy clothes, and ask advice. At last, she felt quite distracted and announced a great family party, to celebrate her birthday, and consult all her dear friends. My father was asked to come, and while he was there they could also, she said as an afterthought, give him a send-off. Joseph Montrose, who was leaving on the same boat as my father, was asked, so that he might see Phyllis, "my little queen," said Grandmother; and many other distant relatives and friends came. Grandmother, they said, was celebrating her freedom, but she was too modest an old sinner to admit anything improper.

Two days before the party, Jape was taken to the hospital from the Inn, and without regret, for Jape's work had dwindled and now Grandmother felt he was only an expense. There were difficulties at the hospital: no one knew Jape's surname, nor where he came from. He left the hospital the day after the great party, and for a few months disappeared. His room was then opened, and in the room they found just his best suit of clothes, an old lawn mower, and an enlargement of an old photograph of my grandfather taken twenty years before and showing that he had been a remarkably handsome, gentle-looking man, with a sweet, sad smile and a face that looked spiritual. Nevertheless, there is no doubt he was far from spiritual.

10

As THE women had all advised my mother, at this great party of the family, to make peace with my father long enough to beget, and as they had given her prescriptions for having a son, and as she was so harried and hunted by them that she had no more conscience of her own, my mother sent us away the very next day to Grandmother Fox's, so that she and my father would have the last few days together.

She was anxious about the step she was now taking and thought it was for us she was doing it, and though she was almost desperate with doubt about whether it was dishonorable or not, and whether, too, this trick would bring my father back at the end of his visit, she decided to try it. She could not understand this shoddy, shameful, cruel life she was leading. It was not chosen; it was some magic by which she was trapped. She had acquired all the advertised products, love, a husband, a home, children, but she had not the advertised results—she recognized nothing in the landscape.

Her mind was torn up by advice from casual visitors and sermons that were almost rough insults. What she underwent when we were away was more like the trial for witchcraft of a helpless, gossip-ridden girl in the bad Puritan days. The relatives tried her. If she failed she was proved a worthless woman.

While this nocturnal magic was going on, and my father was receiving this love drink, Jacky and I were with my Grandmother Fox, who lived in a small apartment on the fifth floor in East Eighty-fifth Street, with her niece, Lily Spontini. Lily Spontini's maiden name was Hart, like Grandmother Fox. She was the youngest daughter of Grandmother's eldest brother, and at sixteen had come to New York to try her luck, and to live with her aunt, Jenny Fox, who was my grandmother. Grandmother Fox, who never had a daughter, remembered Lily as she was at that time:

"A beauty! I never in my life saw such a beauty! Such a skin, white as snow, red lips without paint, and such sweet eyes and such a sweet smile! Oh, I could have fainted with joy. I thought birds were singing. I said, 'Is this my niece?' And in a week, in two weeks, there was not a boy on the street but was coming round to the house, and wanted to marry her. Such shoulders, such arms, and such sweet little hands, I could have kissed every finger," and Grandmother would mumble with her withered lips, "Such a beautiful girl was never seen on the street." She scowled, thinking of the street, "It was a shame to see this girl on that street. Before a month passed a boy came to me and asked to marry her. This boy, Spontini, would not eat or sleep, until at last his parents came to me and said, 'Mrs. Fox, please let Lily marry him; he is ill and we are afraid he will die.' Lily did not want to, but she liked the parents, especially the mother, Mrs. Spontini, an Italian woman, but very nice, very goodhearted. At last, to please the mother, she agreed to marry the poor boy. She was a widow at eighteen. But she is still a great friend of Mrs. Spontini. She calls her her real mother. She goes to see her every year on her birthday, and on the boy's birthday, and Mrs. Spontini's birthday."

My grandmother, sitting in her dragging skirts and wrinkles, would sigh and again kiss her hands, looking angrily at us, "I will never see such a beauty again! Don't talk to me about that Clara Bow, Theda Bara—pooh! The men followed her in the street; Lily never looked at them. She—a girl who could have had— The boys came round in front of the house till it was like a show; but she didn't care for them. She did not want to get married; she only did it to please Mrs. Spontini, who came to her and begged her with tears in her eyes, and kissed Lily's little white hands and said, 'My darling, my dear one, marry him before he dies; there is not much left for him on this earth, and he has never had any pleasure, but he is an angel. Marry him, my dear one, and you will always be my daughter.'

"Lily married him, but she did not want to get married, and she was hardly married when he died. He only had an iron bedstead and a few books to leave her. Lily has the books somewhere in a trunk, but the bedstead she sold; she didn't want to look at it. They had no home, poor things, but lived with the parents."

Grandmother, forgetting us, would retell this tale as we rested after school, sitting on the floor, making up our stories of horrible adventure and diamond-sprinkled love. Sometimes she would come to herself, smooth our hair, kiss us, and say, "You cannot understand all that, thank God!"

At other times she talked angrily to Lily about us and about our father and mother. She did not like to have us with her, though she boasted about us to visitors. She had been living with Lily Spontini for many years and did not like to be disturbed. Lily was now twenty-eight and had plenty of boy friends, and Grandmother's mind was divided between getting her married again and keeping her to herself. Grandmother had very little money, all given to her by my father, and Lily earned a little in one of the poorest of occupations. When she first came from the country Grandmother had got her a job ironing babies' dresses in a factory. Lily had worked all the time, paying rent to Grandmother, except during the three months when she had been married to young Spontini.

For ten years Lily had been pasting labels on bottles in a workroom with about fifty girls, and had worked up by seniority to the first ten girls. She was a close friend of the wives of the workroom manager and the factory owner. Sometimes she quarreled with the girls who said she was a favorite; when, after a few slow, reasonable words, in a slightly raised voice, she would cry quietly. They were rather fond of her. She avoided all the rough ones, made friends of polite foreign girls and older women, and one or two women who read books. She talked about her relatives and "my boy friend," always looked clean and modest, had a pleased, kind smile, and never used a dirty word. Sometimes, in a chuckle, after a silence, in a modest undertone, she would tell Grandmother something bad that had been said at work. Grandmother would say, "Pooh! Disgraceful!"

Lily would apologize and gently laugh. Then, after another silence, Grandmother would laugh too, and make one of her burning, sour jokes. These silences between them, in their hour-long conversations, were like the silences between birds settling for the night.

Grandmother was a passionate party lover, mad for details of parties gone to. Lily was always visiting. Getting friends, holding them, and visiting them was her gift and her pastime. It was for this, too, that Grandmother Fox clung to her. Grandmother herself was no longer invited to family parties, although a cultivated woman and eager for company. Few understood why. Perhaps she was too thirsty for it; perhaps she gossiped. She did not invite people in return. She had always been a queer little thing, sharp, angry, and disappointed.

It was Lily who brought us to Grandmother Fox's after the great party that Grandmother Morgan gave. Mrs. Fox was not pleased to see us, we thought; but she flew and kissed us with a lot of affectionate chatter. Then she got rid of us, telling us to brush our hair while she hurried to the kitchen to speak to Lily. Only a few words were soft, and then, as usual, she spat her words out, slapping Lily into alertness, "Why did you get here so late, stupid? Well, never mind. Sit here, darling. Sit down, sit down. What's that?"

Lily's sleepwalking voice said, "I stayed the night at Mathilde's—"

"I know, I know, you stupid. How did the children get here otherwise?"

"Mathilde sent you half a roast chicken with her compliments, and said she hopes you're all right."

"Well, good, that's good. Yesterday I ate a bit of rice, and that's all. I have nothing in the house when you're out. It was raining. Yesterday Mrs. McAlan called on me. She said she was getting a good dinner ready for him. A good wife! It's easy to be a good wife, why not? For money you have honey. He goes to the stores for her. But I had celery, rice; sit down, Lily. What did you have yesterday? What did they serve, Lily?"

"We had cocktails," said Lily, as if dreaming. "I had a good supper, Auntie; don't worry. With Mrs. Morgan, you know. Soup, cutlets, cakes, fruit cup, everything."

"Ca-akes? Ca-akes?" said Grandmother, thoughtfully. "What kind of cakes? Where did she buy them?"

"I don't know. They were provided I think. From a bakery, I think."

"What sort of bakery? A good one?"

Lily's sunny laugh came through the noise of cups and spoons, "What do I know about their bakery, in the restaurant, Auntie?"

"What an idiot," cried Grandmother, "you ate them, didn't you?"

Lily clinked her spoon, and laughed, "But the cakes did not say which bakery they came from; Auntie, you're so funny. Which bakery—who knows?"

"Well," said Grandmother after a moment, "and did Mrs. Morgan like your coat?"

"It's all right," Lily said briefly; "Auntie, the whole week I had a headache, the whole week, this week."

"You don't sleep. You don't sleep. You must take your rest. You keep worrying. Now, now, darling, sit in that other chair. It's more comfortable. It's the best we have. It's that old one Mathilde gave me. She's a nice woman just the same. Look, something's spilled here. I must have it cleaned. The whole chair, yes. What's that? A hat?"

"That's from Mathilde," said Lily, "a friend of hers, Dora, gave it to her, but it doesn't suit her."

"She doesn't wear hats," said Grandmother sadly, "but she can easily get them, as many as she wants; a young woman is something different from me. What an idiot! That's nothing to laugh at. Yes, it's pretty, Lily. Very pretty. But not for me. I don't need hats. I'm not joking. I'm through, that's all, my girl. No hats, no coats, no cakes, nothing. All that rubbish. And did you see Phyllis?"

"Yes."

"When?"

"Last night, of course."

"When?"

"Last night."

"At the party?"

"Of course."

"Has she got a boy?"

"No special boy."

"Special boy—such a pretty girl as that, and no special boy yet! I don't understand it. If I had such a pretty daughter—she is nice, Mrs. Morgan, but she doesn't look after her daughters. None of them. What had Mathilde to say?"

"Nothing. Sol is staying there tonight."

"Why shouldn't he stay with his own wife? What's news in that?"

"A painter painted the living room in a different color and the bedroom, nice."

"Very nice, very nice," said Grandmother, sadly; "and the children's room, Tootsy's and Jacky's? Jacky—for a girl! I don't like these new customs. Poor children; they're so innocent. So he stays there tonight, this week?" She whispered loudly, "They made it up—h'm?"

"She hopes, she doesn't know."

"She was beautiful," said Grandmother, "that Mathilde. The whole family, beauties, even the boys. The mother used to be good-looking, but running after men—no, no, no, when her daughters are not married yet. Oh, Mattie is such a beauty, and Mrs. Morgan, never mind, never mind, she's a fine woman, though she used to dye her hair. She is very smart, a snappy dresser. And Phyllis, I never saw one like that—what a shame! But if a woman doesn't care for her daughters—but she doesn't dye it now, much better!" Grandmother sighed. "And when will he come?"

"He will come tomorrow to bring the children home."

"Tomorrow, and he's going away to England. It's my finish," said Grandmother. "All right, let him go; he can't help it; he must support his family, I understand that, but it's the end of everything. The poor innocent children. It isn't right to leave them like that. And she, that Mattie, though for an actress very ladylike. And—*Die Konkubine*—eh? Did you see her?"

"Yes, I saw her."

"All alone, poor Mattie!" sighed Grandmother; then said hastily, "How does she look? She's not pretty, is she? Who could guess? Who could guess?"

"She's not bad," said Lily.

"Who? Who? Who's not bad? What an idiot!" cried Grandmother. "She—*Die Konkubine*."

"Stupid idiot!" cried Grandmother; "did she give you something to eat? You ate at her house?"

"Yes, of course! I was invited there."

"And did you tell Mathilde? Oh, dear, dear, dear."

"Of course I didn't tell. Am I an idiot?" cried Lily.

"What did you eat? Is she a good cook, eh?"

"Yes."

"What did she give you?"

"We had a Wiener schnitzel, duck soup, salad, apple tart."

"What? What do you say? Are you crazy? Duck soup, apple tart —was it a party?"

"No, it was just dinner. I was invited to dinner."

"Was there cream with the apple tart?"

"Yes, yes."

"Was there some left over?"

"Some what?"

"Apple tart, cream—anything, you idiot," cried Grandmother, running about the kitchen in her fury.

"I don't know, Auntie."

"Don't know! Don't know bakeries, don't know cakes, don't know boy friends. Are you crazy?" piped Grandmother. "What sort of eyes? What sort of a girl? You're there, but you see nothing."

Lily laughed.

"Perhaps it was all in the icebox after and you didn't see what was left," said Grandmother suddenly, mournfully.

"Maybe!"

"And he was there, Sol?"

"Yes."

"I can't understand it," said Grandmother, softly, to herself. "It's beyond me. But she's clever. Mattie is a good woman, but too honest. You mustn't be too honest in this life. What a world! A man on the phone was asking for you! I don't know what he said— General Askas—I don't know—"

"General Askas—" Lily smothered her sweet, rich laughter; "oh, Auntie! Jimmy Brant? Who was it? Mr. Ender? Who?"

"Askas, Askas—a fine name," said Grandmother in confusion. "What is it? Russian, foreign, I don't know."

After a long silence, during which life went on mysteriously in the kitchen at the end of the passage, Grandmother said, "Were you at Rose's on Saturday?"

"Yes."

"Were you there alone?"

"No, Tony, too."

"And why not Marion?"

"Perhaps she wasn't invited."

"It's a funny thing not to invite your daughter-in-law. Perhaps they quarreled."

"I don't know, Auntie."

"That's a very funny thing."

We never had anything to do at Grandmother Fox's, in the wretched back room which was their sitting room and which looked over an asphalted courtyard. But at night we stayed up half the night, leaning over the window sills black with soot, breathing in the thick air, for drunken couples quarreled, dirty names were called out in clear voices, a place with red blinds had Chinese shrieks coming from it, and people stood in the courtyard and called up-stairs to closed windows in the tall brick wall at all hours of the night. Grandmother snored or prowled. Lily slept heavily, or got up to make herself tea. Sometimes Grandmother went into her room and the two cronies, the beautiful pony-faced girl and the wrinkled old woman with straggling hair, held councils relating to their long wedded existence.

And this night, coming suddenly out of the darkness, in the middle of the night, we heard two clear voices, "And you went and you saw she was going away?"

"Yes. Everything is being packed."

"*Die Konkubine?*"

"Yes."

"She is so clever. It's strange, I tell you."

"Yes, but he is packed too. He is going to sail."

"Yes, it is nice, it is right." After a moment, Grandmother added, "But such a clever—it is useless if a clever woman—men are taken in, and—but packed up and going already! Going where?"

Wearily, Lily said, "I don't know, Auntie."

"I smell a rat," said Grandmother thoughtfully; "now a wo-man—"

"I got such a headache, Auntie."

"Sleep, sleep, darling! It sounds right, but—h'm—you know it's all too nice."

"Why wouldn't he go back to his wife?"

"Yes, yes. And will you be laid off another week, Lily?"

"Yes."

"I say, people must work. Everyone must work. I have no money for instance—and my poor boy has to work; but it's very strange, Lily."

"Yooh! Ye-oh! Oh!"

"She got another job, Lily? She—?"

"I don't know."

"She goes and no one knows? Something wrong. No? And he goes to England? I smell a rat."

"Go to sleep, Auntie!"

"Sleep—I am too old to sleep. The old do not sleep. What do you know about it? Everyone tells me to rest—what about? You have to have something to rest about! He's like his father. A woman can do anything with him. Pooh! Don't talk to me about his father. I could have had him back, too, but I would not say the word. Pooh! Run after a man? Never!"

"I have such a headache, Auntie! Oh!"

"I'll get you an aspirin, darling. It's because you're worried about not working. I would be, too. People are supposed to work. Otherwise how can you eat? Have you a man to keep you? No!"

Grandmother got up and pattered down the hall in her bare feet, happy to have something to do in the night-time. She was heard in the bathroom, in Lily's room, and coming back to her own bedroom. In the middle of the hall, continuing a conversation she had with Lily in the last minute or two, she said, "And in Europe they're all crazy, as well! They wear fancy costumes all the time, gold braid, feathers in their hats, swords—mad people. It's like a lunatic asylum. What does he want to be there for? His father had no sense either. His father had no brains; he just got those certificates to hang on his wall to show people. Crazy, like a European! Pooh! All men—pooh! All nonsense."

Silence.

"Where did she get another job?"

Silence.

"You don't know. No, no one knows. Something fishy?"

Silence.

"I am old," said the old woman. "Running about—"

11

IN THE deep, dead afternoons of August, Mother sat with us on the side porch of Green Acres Inn trying to knit herself a green sweater. The needles and wool lay in the lap of her flowered apron. She wore slacks and a pale yellow cotton blouse. She watched the opposite house, now an inn for elegant old maids, ladies past their bearing and retired gentlemen who imitated Indian colonels, the pure Connecticut line.

The easterly porch on which we were had a private sitting room of white iron and glass for the Morgan family, or for any family which arranged for the privilege. This was the still season. Most young people were off at the beaches or even in Europe, and only a few old-timers who could not resist Mrs. Morgan, or Green Acres, or poker, were left at the Inn. Grandmother would have closed the Inn and gone away to the beaches herself, if she could have done without this crowd and her poker.

It was about four. Few people were about. Most were up in their shaded, sweaty rooms, resting. Two old ladies and a middle-aged man were playing pinochle in the long dining room, just inside the windows, near my mother. We were sitting on stools covered with *petit point*, chattering about the dump heap we had seen—all kinds of food, good things thrown away.

"Mother, why do they throw away all that bread, those chairs and things?"

Mathilde sat still and stared across the two lawns.

From within came the voice of Mrs. Polk, a neat, highly rouged old woman, with clean collars and tarnished brassy hair, "There's your answer, Cissie!"

Another old woman's voice said, "That finishes me. I'm through. It's too hot."

Mr. Manners's dull, well-bred voice said, "Isn't Mrs. Harkness playing today?"

Jacky said, "Grandmother, can I have a lemonade?"

"Go away, don't bother me," came Grandmother's rich voice, automatically.

"Your grandmother's playing cards," said Mother, bitterly, her eyes still fixed across the lawn. On a birdcage porch upstairs, two ladies had come out and were having tea under a red and white awning. Starlings hopped on the lawn.

"Big, ugly blackbirds," said Mathilde.

A car came into the drive, doors slammed, and a loud voice was heard.

"That's Looper," said Grandmother in the dining room, slapping down her cards. "She must have mail." She got up and rushed out of the dining room, calling, "Betty! Is that Betty Looper?"

There was a row of voices outside. Some new women surged into the dining room, and one with a reinforced Georgia brag, cried, "I just got one dozen pairs; they don't know what bargains they've got there. Two old maids. I saw them there yesterday and just thought! Hello there, Mr. Manners, come and see what I got and see if you don't want to buy me some more," and she thrust out her leg.

I laughed aloud and went into the dining room to see the Georgia belle, an old, fat woman, with an artificial complexion and white hair. With her were her two toadies, New York women who lived in a residential hotel and went to her room for secret drinking; she took them driving and to tea.

It was nearly five. The other women were waking out of their siestas. One came downstairs laughing and calling, "Mrs. Mason!" to the Southern belle, and two others strolling out on the veranda pretended not to notice her return, but kept their eyes stretched toward her, hoping for an invitation.

"Mr. Manners thinks I'm a wicked, wasteful woman, don't you, honey?" she said to the man. "But you know how women love to spend—though Mr. Manners is a bachelor!"

Mr. Manners smiled and cut his speed coquettishly, as he approached the women. They all looked at him. There were only two male residents at present in this half-deserted hotel and one was an old fellow in Palm Beach suits and a panama, who mumbled shamefacedly in a white mustache and otherwise spoke to none. Mr. Manners was, for them, quite a young man, not more than forty-five, tall, mule-faced, half bald, with a slow, monotonous delivery. He was a kind-hearted, stupid man, polite to the women, modest and cautious—an anxious liberal because an assimilating, atheist Jew. The women, mostly New Englanders, tough, fierce "liberals," were anti-Jew, anti-Negro, anti-Mexican, anti-Italian, but they excepted their Mr. Manners: "He is not a Jew; such gentlemen are Hebrews," said even the most ill-natured of them.

Mrs. Morgan, with her love affairs, had no more than friendly good-days for him. Mathilde, with her eyes far away, did not notice him at all; but the others, rabid, Republican, selfish, coddled this only eligible man.

Mrs. Mason, the Southern belle, made a great noise about asking Mr. Manners to sit at her table, not his own, that night. Mrs. Polk, the brittle, dismantled New Yorker, lifted her voice to say that he had never sat with her, but her voice was lost in the brass band which surrounded Mrs. Mason. Rudely she swept the women out of Mr. Manners's precincts and onto the porch, where she waved airily to my mother, "Mrs. Fox! All alone on this lovely day, honey? You want to go out for a run; you don't want to sit and brood. Your hubby will soon be back."

My mother raised her large, dark blue eyes, let them settle on Mrs. Mason, said nothing.

Mrs. Mason went to a group of wicker chairs around a table and sat down with her brass band. She shouted, "I was just saying, dearie, that you ought to go out and get yourself some of these stockings. I drove over all the way to get them. I guess it cost me more in gas than it saved, and then we went to a cunning little place for tea, out of town. We had cocktails in fact, but no one must tell Mrs. Morgan what naughty girls we were. Some time you must come with me, Mrs. Fox, honey!"

"Thanks," said Mother.

Now Mrs. Looper came stumping onto the porch. Before she was well through the dining room, she cried in her virile voice, "Mrs. Fox! Are you there?"

Mrs. Mason at once stood up and bustled off, wagging her hips through the thin voile.

Grandmother Fox, who had just come down from her room, so hastily arranged that one stocking hung down round her ankle, twinkled through the long room after Mrs. Looper, her little face quite smooth, young, and large-eyed with anticipation; "Yes, yes," she piped.

Mrs. Looper was pleased to see her.

"I have a message for you both," she said. "Come in here, Mrs. Fox," and she beckoned my mother into the dining room; "I thought I would tell you, for it concerns you more than the others—"

She looked maliciously in the direction of the front veranda from which came Grandmother Morgan's strong voice, raised to laugh down the outrageous Georgia belle, who had bounced upon her veranda.

Mother, with a languishing weariness, came to the small table, and Grandmother Fox set herself on the other side, so that each of them had her back to the veranda. The midsummer light came in over their heads and shone on their soft eyes. I have not mentioned Grandmother Fox's eyes. She had sometimes the face of a child, now smooth and white, now brown and wrinkled, changing from one to the other in a moment; but her eyes were always the same, very large and brown, sweet and tender, under curved dark brows and thick, white hair. She looked like a little girl, or a sweet and naïve old maid.

"The children," said Betty Looper, looking firmly in our direction. "The children!" But Mother took no notice of her, and let her arms rest lightly on our shoulders. Our hair blew over her thin arms.

"My daughter, Emily Blake, who married one of the Blakes of Waterfall, Illinois," said Betty Looper, "is in London and writes to me from there. She's having the time of her life, and she is a good daughter. Before she left, I said to her, Emily, write to me every single week. The boys and girls have never disobeyed me. That is how I happen to have this letter, the fifth I have had from her. Her husband has business in Paris and they're going to be there when I next hear. They're going to stay at the Meurice. Do you hear from your husband in London?"

"Yes," said Mathilde Fox.

"Ah! And what do you hear from him?"

"The usual thing, the weather, business, how are the children," said Mother wearily.

"He doesn't ask you to come over and join him?"

"He's coming back so soon."

"Coming back so soon," said Mrs. Looper emphatically; "and are you getting a divorce then?"

"A divorce?" said my mother, quivering and staring at Mrs. Looper; "of course not!"

"Well, my dear, you must either give him a divorce, or go over to him."

My mother softly, trembling, and without thought of her dignity, asked why she said that; was there something she had to tell her?

"Yes, I have something to tell you, and to you, Mrs. Fox Senior. My daughter writes to me, I will read you the exact passage:

"'I met them walking hand in hand in Piccadilly and looking ridiculously like young lovers. They seemed quite carefree and never to have heard of his wife. I spoke to them. They were friendly and asked me to their place. They are living together openly. They don't seem ashamed. Perhaps it is because they are in love, or perhaps the divorce is going through. I didn't ask.'"

My mother moaned. Mrs. Looper's brilliant, small, blue eyes were fixed on her without triumph, but in mastery. "All you can do now is to cable for information, or take the next boat. Why don't you go with your sister? I will speak to Mrs. Morgan about it at once. Unless," she turned as she was leaving the table, "you want to leave it like that? Unless you are going to Reno?"

My mother, livid, her eyes almost black, seemed speechless. Grandmother Fox said, "I knew; too clever by half. Very fishy, I said."

My mother, finding her voice, said faintly, "Mother! Let me talk to Mother, Mrs. Looper! I am not sure—at all. Mother is so headstrong, she just arranges things—" She got up; "Jacky, Letty, go out and play right away, do you hear?"

We did not move. After she had nervously commanded us to go several times, Jacky went and I was obliged to follow her. But I could see from the far edge of the lawn, where we kept in view the house with its east and front verandas, the great slow swirl of fuss and the sultry pleasure of the plump, lazy women in this drama. By now, what with Mrs. Looper's voice and my grandmother's exclamations, everyone knew.

Grandmother Fox, humiliated, sat with tight lips in a rocking chair at one end of the veranda, saying merely yes, no, and I don't know, which was very unlike her. My mother had called to her mother to come to her upstairs, but Grandmother Morgan, collecting information, had not yet gone, while the loud voices of her confidantes rang over the lawn.

Most of the women were so old now that they could not be deserted for others. Many had lost their men through the divorce courts, and some had never had any. In any case, it took only half an hour for the bubbling to die down, for cocktail hour was coming and already they were impatient with the scandal which kept them away from the room heavy with draperies, toilet soaps, and gin and whisky smells. Soon the cards would come out again, and with only a brief moment for dinner would go on till late at night, till early morning. These old women did not need much sleep.

Mrs. Looper, however, a natural governor, kept her court about her for another half hour. She left Grandmother Fox bitterly rocking in the lengthening shadows, and took those she had intimidated into the cretonne-dressed lounge. None loved her, but most would have voted for her. She was a usurper, also. This lounge belonged to the local potentate, Mrs. Morgan. A lot of people have rascally impulses.

In the conflict between these two well-matched rivals, many smaller natures had been crushed. Mrs. Looper was the daughter of an old-time farmer who made his own corn whisky. She had a gift for distilling, herself, so that she could turn potato peelings, prunes, and any debris from the kitchen and which she collected from neighbors, into liquor. She took a husband into the business and bought a seedy, downtown overnight hotel with a bar. Their son was a pharmacist, and a good bootlegger; and his daughter was studying medicine. They met good people; one son was a labor leader with a good salary, and a grandson a radical intellectual, very poor. It was a lively, gifted family.

After the death of her husband, Mrs. Looper, who had had several lovers in what she felt to be a mean-spirited hole-and-corner way, was liberated. She gradually gathered a flock of middle-aged, gambling women and ran a big card game, either in her own place or at the house of one friend or another, or in a suite of rooms in a small hotel in Chelsea. She was a gifted player, a hardy, courageous gambler and shameless double-dealer; and had even, out of the goodness of her heart, out of respect for their old rivalry, taught Mrs. Morgan a few tricks, so that she could watch out for combines in her own hotel. For, once or twice, suspicious incidents had occurred; and these hotel women were prey for the easy-lipped swindler.

Mrs. Looper's friends were women who had been free as girls or become discontented with husbands and flat life, who never read and who hated the theater. Some gambled from one year's end to the other. She had ruined some. They got money somewhere for her games. She had encouraged others to get divorced, so that their alimony would come to them regularly as their housekeeping money did not. She was not only imperturbable in face of other people's disasters, but had courage in her own. She had had a stroke and could scarcely move one arm and leg. Nevertheless, she went up and down stairs all day long, took charge of chance gatherings of people, fiercely questioned them, advised them, forbade any reference to her condition by a straight, intelligent look; and when she sat down, worked on enormous tasks of embroidery, crochet, or knitting. She made men's socks of fanciful, tartan designs, carried about with her a bedspread heavy as lead made out of innumerable squares, and was at work on a tablecloth composed of three hundred and eighty-three complicated squares of crochet cotton.

As she talked and questioned, she knitted or hooked away rapidly, working with one hand and holding the materials and needle with the stiff hand. She was scarcely still for ten minutes at a time and appeared to have excellent control of her high and hard temper. Mrs. Morgan did not like to have her at the Inn, however, for she feared she was nosing out her victims. Some of these flabby and confused women had ended up in her apartments, and some had even given up their yearly visits to Mrs. Morgan's in order to stay in town at Mrs. Looper's table, under her electric lights, to finger, with rising desperation, burning flush, and ever graying hair, Mrs. Looper's cards.

Mrs. Looper's daughters and sons were scattered far and wide over the country. She did not miss them. She merely used them as listening posts and boasted about them. She had no interest in us, nor in my mother, nor in Solander Fox.

This whole incident, which was ruin for my mother, and in which Grandmother Fox seemed to shrivel to the size of a peach-stone, was nothing more to Mrs. Looper than a pebble flung for a joke at her old enemy and colleague, Mrs. Morgan.

She already, sitting there in the lounge, discouraged questions, for her knowledge was her own, and she did not give it out too freely to the wretched suitors sitting round her. She changed the subject, spoke about the weather, politics, the rage for adopted children, pedigree, and the treatment of mothers-in-law. She was against mothers-in-law, "Meddling old carcasses, with their noses in other women's pots. Here in New England each house has a mother-in-law house to keep the old woman in—a good idea."

She always controlled and routed by her surprise opinions.

Grandmother Fox, deserted and humiliated on the veranda, sat in the wind till she could bear it no longer, and then crept through the lounge and up the stairs, not daring to use the elevator, so as not to attract notice. She was one of the unlucky ones. Two maids coming to set the tables and Mrs. Looper observed her, "Are you going to lie down, Mrs. Fox? That's right!" And an audible, "Poor little thing."

Meanwhile, Mrs. Looper was impatient to know what was going on upstairs. She rolled up her knitting, rudely left her retinue sitting there, and got into the elevator. She got out at the wrong floor, patrolled Mathilde Fox's room, and when she found the voices were too low, philosophically went to the room she had been given for the night and changed her dress. Then she manicured her nails and put rings on her hands for dinner.

Poor Grandmother Fox, who was invited to Green Acres once a year for three or four weeks in the dead season, crept out next morning to her usual post, but seemed crushed, and for once had no questions to put to the ladies staying there. However, in the afternoon about two, I heard her voice rising softly, like a breeze getting up, "Five rooms, you say? You mean, with the kitchen? Is it a modern bathroom? Oh, I can't stand—"

But Grandmother Morgan, Mother and we went into town that afternoon in the car, and Mrs. Looper kept us company along the way.

12

CISSIE MORGAN found that things were not turning out so badly, though it was a pity her child had husband-trouble. The mortgage on the Inn had been large and the interest rates high, and there were several large bills outstanding when Bernard Morgan died. She had paid some attention to his mild complainings in his decline, even when he was lodged in the old barn with the house servants; but now that she had a free hand she had undertaken retrenchments, changes, repayments and new loans, a complete reorganization of the financial structure of her business; and she was contemplating the buying of a large hotel in the Adirondacks or the building of one at Lake George, where she saw new business coming up.

She was short of money as usual, and had been glad to accept Joseph Montrose's offer for Phyllis. Montrose said that a business friend of his, interested in the Metropolitan Opera, had offered to pay the fares abroad of Phyllis and a companion; and said that he himself would have the girls at his large house in St. John's Wood for a week or two while they looked for suitable lodgings. Mrs. Morgan would pay all this back when she could. Montrose would present a bill in proper time. Mrs. Morgan told Mathilde and Phyllis that she thought Montrose was attracted to Phyllis and would pay the money himself for the sake of a few kisses.

"But see that you give nothing for it but kisses, my girl," said Grandmother Morgan to Phyllis; "I want you to look round in London and if you can't see anyone there, we'll perhaps let you go to Paris for a couple of months. You might meet a rich American businessman, or even a South American. But do nothing until you have cabled me and I have looked them up. I have connections who can do all that for me."

Grandmother cabled my father, in Mathilde's name, peremptorily asking him to send the money for boat fares for Mathilde and the two little girls who were coming to him.

"In this case the surprise attack is the only thing," she told Mathilde. "That girl, Persia, had the sense to follow him. You can have at least the same sense. He's a man with a gentle nature. You'll see the money will come."

When Grandmother had sent a second cable in her own name, saying the money was put down already and she wanted to be reimbursed, my father did, in fact, cable the money to us. It was barely enough.

Grandmother was busy meanwhile, buying an elaborate travel trousseau for Phyllis, rings, a fur coat, evening dresses, swimming suits, diamond clips, shoes and stockings, and luggage.

Mathilde had scarcely the energy to get our own clothes together, and was in tears much of the time, although all her self-elected bosom friends came in to help and to lecture her.

"How do I know he won't disgrace us when I'm there?" she asked piteously, many times. She never had much hope of anything. She refused to follow the advice that was showered on her, and to buy new clothes for us on one or the other of her mother's accounts. "What will he think of me if he sees I've put in the time on a spending spree? He'll think I'm mad, just a gold-digger."

Grandmother Morgan shook her head over this and said, "You'll never keep him if you don't have new feathers, Mattie," and even little Grandmother Fox, in these days black, withered, trembling, looked anxious and, putting her stubby claws on my mother's arm (so that Mathilde could scarcely help drawing away), she muttered, "Think of yourself a little, my dear, and my Tootsy and my Jacky. They'll have money when I die, but waiting is a long time, and they ought to have something new now."

She looked dismally at our traveling wardrobe, but bought nothing herself. To her, Grandmother Morgan was a walking Klondike, and she could not see why Cissie Morgan did not dress us as well as Phyllis. She knew nothing of finances nor of business, and saw only in the feeblest and silliest way what a fine investment Phyllis's clothes might turn out to be.

Grandmother Morgan, who had it in the back of her mind that

she might, after all, have to pay the money back to Joseph Montrose, tried to reduce expense, however, and this was where she felt that Mother was useful. She wanted Mother to act as her sister's chaperone, so that Solander, in fact, would pay back the chaperone's expenses to Joseph Montrose and Phyllis's friend Pauline need not go.

She had become very fond of this Pauline, a handsome Little Theater actress who took her on parties; she did not like to suggest it directly. Pauline had already pointed out to my mother that she was in no mood to act as Phyllis's chaperone and look after two children, especially if it turned out to be a bad sea-trip. Who would look after the children if things were black in London and Solander were really living with the woman Persia? Did Mathilde wish to live with Phyllis, receive her men friends, go out with her to restaurants, wait up for her at night? Moreover, since old Mrs. Morgan was a little tight, and, though it was a shame, had given Mathilde neither money nor clothes, would Mathilde really enjoy going about with Phyllis who was going to be a bird of paradise?

Phyllis would walk into all of these discussions aloof, preoccupied, but she asked no questions. She saw nothing strange in the arrangements that were made for her. So it had been since she was born. She believed tranquilly now, almost without vanity, that she would learn a little singing and dancing and would at once sweep fashionable Europe up into her arms. She would marry well, live abroad, do nothing but shine her life through.

She did nothing. Others bought her clothes, took her to shops, measured her, cut into cloth. Others packed her trunks, got her passports, and wrote her labels. She stood in a dream and waited for it to accomplish itself.

Mathilde, who had seemed dull to mankind during the moment of her possible reconciliation, now herself called out the activity of many different schemers; even those who were fantastics and not practical schemers began to murmur and plot.

Joseph Montrose sailed before the women. He had bought Phyllis and her companion Pauline first-class tickets for the *Samaria*. My father had sent the money for second-class tickets for the same boat. Five of us were going at the same time, though not precisely together.

Grandmother Morgan became more light-hearted as sailing date approached and thought that she, too, should visit Europe if only for a few days, before her new season opened and before she undertook this new hotel in the Adirondacks.

Grandmother Fox, who had no hope of sailing and uttered many bizarre condemnations of the Europeans, their food, dress, and other habits, nevertheless was unhappy, pattered overmuch round the house, kept Lily up half the night with her confidences. She said she was dying and would never see any of us again, and sent Lily, who was still laid off, to see us and all the others on the family circuit, to find out all she could, and to spread the news that Grandmother Fox was really very weak and might never see her boy nor her darling girls any more. The unrest spread.

Uncle Philip came to see us often, wringing his hands over his divorce from Amabel which was coming through; and saying that for a short time he had been safe, but that now the girls would be after him again; and that he only wished he had the chance to go to Europe where no one knew him. He said that he would even go on the *Samaria* steerage, to be with us, and eat the bread of humility in London, until Joseph Montrose or Solander could get him a job. He would be good. He would never meddle with girls again if only he could get a fresh start in life; or he would go away with one of the dear creatures, but only one, and start all over again where old memories, streets, dives, names, bookshops, schools, would not start up in him the endless desire, the irremediable act.

"And I would be company for you, too, Mathilde," said he, "if you felt lonesome, and while you are making your peace with Solander. For Sol's a nice boy, always was a pal of mine and you can't jolt him; you've got to let him ease her out of this, and besides, who knows, she's an awful attra— I mean, perhaps I could do something about it—take her away and see that she got another man or job or something. You know, if she had a friend, probably she would be quite willing to give him up since he's married and you're not going to divorce him—well, I mean I could be helpful in so many ways, I could even cook and look after the house. I often did it for Amabel."

Dora Dunn, making her visits two or three times a week in her well-cut linen and silk suits, would laugh, shake her fat, and say,

"I could do with a trip to Europe myself, with the whole world going. I want to see what's new, for I have plans for a shop on Madison Avenue, up in the Fifties or beyond, and for that section of town I need the latest things, with modernistic designs. These Villagers down here are satisfied with rubbish, but those people have the money and have traveled; and how can I supply them if I have no contacts?" Mrs. Morgan admiringly told her to go.

It spread and spread, a happy hunger which flattered us. I think this was the first time that I saw my sister Jacky was different from me. I knew long ago that she was more attractive though not prettier than I. When she was two and a half, I was three and a half. She pressed her nose to the fence and called, "Dickie! Dickie!"

Dickie came, fat, blond, small, blue-eyed, and smiling, and pressed his nose to the fence. Their noses looked the same. No doubt mine did too. When I called, "Dickie! Dickie!" expecting to wipe out Jacky in one word, nothing happened. Dickie's face grew serious, he gave me a grave look and went on trying to reach Jacky's nose with his nose through the fence. We still divide and conquer. I have a white-skinned, oval face, with long lashes, oval eyes, and a Japanese look; a short neck, a white pouter breast, a small waist, and a long pear-shaped back. Painters have painted my face, my waist, and the rest; but Jacky's parts, quite different, also find admirers. There is the first shock a pretty girl gets, that things in all women are alluring. I know by experience, and even I can see it. I can't help looking over every woman to see what she is peddling. I am not a fool. I know strange things attract, and when a woman is plain and unfortunate, she will get some Gala-had, but unfortunately I cannot couple in my imagination; to me every woman is plain, indeed unattractive. I am not really bad-hearted; women are my blind spot. On the other hand, I can see the good points in any young man.

Jacky is ambitious, even more than I am, but with such a wild, unaccountable ambition, you might call it a young, fiery, unreasonable ambition, the kind of emotion and urge that bring people's hearts into their throats; they feel regret for what they think they have lost.

Perhaps Jacky could have been an actress, for she has this strange power to communicate to people feelings that they have never had

and she never had either, and which makes them think they understand her. She becomes their ideal. I understand her very well.
She was not bright in school, but that was because she was distracted. She only thought of her ambition. She did not know what
her ambition was, but she longed for it like the Holy Grail. I am
sure there was a time in the world when looking for the Holy Grail
became popular, and I am sure there are always certain people who
look for the Holy Grail, although now it is not the rage. There
were always people who looked for money, I am sure, and now is
the time when everyone does, but naturally, it will pass, like all
periods of popular feeling.

There never was a time when everyone was a Romeo and Juliet;
but now girls and boys earning their own money and with five cents
to put in a juke box, warble "I love you" and press their thighs together. Yet most of them never feel love; it is just the fashion now.

Well, I cannot say that Jacky was born for her age—perhaps I
was, rather—but I know that she and I ambled along until this age,
when she was seven and I eight before any strong personal differences stood out; and then the thought of going to Europe excited
her as much as it did Aunt Phyllis. She didn't see platforms covered with flowers, but—wonderful success in some way she did
not understand, and new things: "perhaps glory," she said, "I don't
want to come back just nobody. I am now."

Jacky was more interested in Persia, my father's young woman,
than I was, and Jacky had never seen her. She made me tell what
she wore, how she looked, how old she was, whether she was sad
or gay, and she often said, "I hope I can be a man's mistress and
that he will love me madly and write me mad love letters."

I began to look round for someone to write me mad love letters.
We moved, in our private thoughts, thus from the Torquemada
stage to the stage of mad love, but while I was the one to suggest
the schemes for creeping out of the house at night, it was Jacky
who thought up the love letters. Jacky was anxious to go to England only to see Persia and the Prince of Wales, and I am sure that
she wanted my father to stay with Persia so that this romantic imbroglio could go on.

We were to sail at three in the afternoon. The morning we were
to sail, four girls came to my mother's flat in Bleecker Street, one

after the other, with valises in each hand, not to mention smaller packages—four girls, eight valises, and several packages which made a large addition to our own hand luggage which stood about waiting for taxi time.

The first girl was a friend of Philip's, Berenice, a slender, smart girl, with a straight, boyish bob. She just said she had an appointment with Phil, and would wait if we didn't mind. She scarcely seemed to know that it was our apartment. She had been waiting about half an hour and was talking casually and all good breeding with my mother, when another girl came in, a vulgar, smart, rich Greenwich Village girl, with a cigarette in a long holder, a cap and a veil, and long legs in black silk stockings. She looked surprised, and when she saw Mathilde, said, "Aren't you Mattie, Phil's sister?"

"Yes," said Mother, "do you want to see him? He must be coming, although I don't know of it, because this girl's waiting for him, too. Won't you sit down?"

My mother, irritably, went off to open and shut drawers, to sprawl on the floor and peer under tallboys. The first girl knew the second girl. We were sitting in our best clothes, with large eyes and beating hearts, waiting with the luggage for the taxi, and we heard everything.

Jacky, in whom there had sprung up this desire to be a fascinating creature, a thing of fatal charm, moved nearer to these two dashing women and drank in every word. They had not been long seated, sparring with each other in a hard, clever way, in which I have, unfortunately, long ago become expert, when a third ring at the doorbell brought in a third girl, a plain but well-fed blonde of more than middle height, in a schoolteacher's dress and straw hat, her long hair drawn into a knot on her neck. She wore a brown silk dress, carved ivory necklace, silver hammered belt, and brown flat-heeled shoes. She had blue eyes and a slender mouth which she had reddened clumsily.

She smiled confidently and asked for "Mr. Philip Morgan?"

Mathilde, now very puzzled, came out, gave the newcoming woman an armchair, and showed her where to put her bags, for she had two.

"My name is Elsie Trenton," said the woman, who seemed to be about thirty. "You are, I think, Mrs. Fox, Philip's sister, aren't you?"

Her accent was pleasant, but like school. The other girls looked at her, all the false charm fading out of their faces, so that one could look straight at them.

The first was a plain girl, with a Bourbon jaw and clever eyes, dangerous, slick, elegant, and no virgin. The second was just a Village sleeper, who yessed men, talked smut, drank and smoked too much, but felt that she was clever, sensitive and all pure rebellion, indeed (I didn't know that then, but now I know these girls so well); and the third was unlike either of them. Her simple style was something they could not classify.

My mother calmed down now, and asked the women if they would like to finish up some coffee she had left, "Only I am too nervous to perk it, one of you must make it yourself," she said.

The elegant-ugly and the schoolteacher at once came in to the kitchen to make it. They waited more than an hour and had become uneasy, when the schoolteacher said in her musical, mincing voice, "But Philip told me to meet him here and he would come with the tickets. I cannot be mistaken, for I see you are going away today, Mrs. Fox, to England."

"Yes, I am," said my mother.

"Then, that's all right," and she explained to the others, "You see, I am going with Mr. Morgan, Philip Morgan; we are not traveling together," and she flushed slightly, "but he is to bring the tickets."

Great confusion followed. For some reason, the other two girls thought also they were to get tickets from Mr. Philip Morgan to sail on the *Samaria* and all of them had their passports. But two had never sailed before and thought it could all be arranged in a minute, while the ugly one shook her straight brown bob, blew smoke from her cigarette and said, "I simply came to check up. I was abroad so often, so that I thought there was some mistake, of course; and what does it matter, I can go to Virginia or any damn place tomorrow, but I was willing to take a fling. I don't mind admitting I was a darn fool, because it was only in a bar last week he told me, but I've done it before and I'd do it again—the fugue, I mean. Why, I married my first husband when I didn't know him; we were both pickled, but he said, 'Come on, let's fly to Buenos Aires,' and we did and got married. We never slept together" (but the enterprising bride used another word) "and so we got a five-minute divorce. But what the hell, I thought it would be some fun. I think if you girls don't mind, I'll wait around anyhow until Casanova shows up."

The cigarette girl said, "This is crazy; haven't you a drink, Mrs. Fox? Can I raid your cellar or something? I don't know this neighborhood at all or I wouldn't be so fresh. This calls for something special though. Naturally, I will wait for Philip."

The schoolteacher said nothing, but with a calm face sat in the armchair. She would not meet the glances of the others, however.

Next came Grandmother Morgan with Mr. Porlock, her grocery-lover, to deposit him while she went to do some shopping for Phyllis; then several last-minute callers, and Philip himself. He came in whistling and stopped, knocked sideways by the sight of the girls. Then he said, "Hello, Letty and Jacky," and once more looked at the girls. He could hardly speak; he whispered, "What is it, girls? Berenice—"

"Well, you double-crossing so-and-so," said Berenice, with a dry laugh, "if I don't lift my left leg and go whoops upon you, son, it's because of my sex and not my feelings. Cheer up, you disintegrated old milkshake, I'm not going to drag you through breach of promise for this, but I can't answer for the suffragette sorority, and I wouldn't if I could. I have been sitting here this half hour, my boy, since I found out all about my honey, just to see how you would act in such an emergency."

She rose gracefully from her left leg, which had been curled under her, and going to Uncle Philip, kissed him on his soft, new jowl. She turned from him to the girls, gave an odd ha-ha, winked and said, "Well, go get him, sisters!"

"Well!" said the cigarette girl, sourly, "so I got a circular letter and I attended the meeting. But I'm a wrong kind of stockholder, Philip Morgan. I'm the kind that takes a train and a country bus out to Billycock, Ohio, just to put in a mean minority vote. And if no one else will have you, I will, and I'll take the trip to Europe with you or without you, but certainly with the tickets. I wouldn't marry you, on a bet, but I want to get a long way away from a place where you can abound."

Philip said, "Maisie, dear, I don't understand at all, I didn't say anything that could have led you to believe, or rather, probably as a joke, I said—"

The schoolteacherish girl took off her hat, showing her hair, lifted her eyes brightly to him, "Philip, is it true, or isn't it, that we are going to London on the *Samaria*? I gave up my job and I have got my clothes together, because it was all settled. I don't see how I could retrace my steps."

Before Philip could answer, the doorbell rang. With joy he ran to open it, and then was slow returning. When he returned a woman was with him, but this was a woman I knew, Eleanor Blackfield, who had been with her valise out to The Wreck. This time, too, she had her valise, only one, and an expensive dressing case which Jacky and I looked at first, for we had talked so much about a fitted dressing case. Phyllis had one; Mathilde and we did not.

"Well, hello, darling," said the new woman, throwing her arms without preamble around Philip's neck; "and now for the great adventure. Oh, God! Phil, it's a gorgeous day, isn't it? I said to myself coming along in the taxi, God never made a more wonderful day and it's for Philip and me, and for you, too, Mrs. Fox," she said and looked at us, but without adding our names; "I know, of course—and I do hope your trip will have a happy outcome. Are these all your friends come to see you off? Why, hello—Berenice—"

"You don't seem to appreciate a simple, but arresting fact," said Berenice. "Like many basic facts this one will throw a monkey wrench in the donkey engine. Philip, Eleanor, is in the white-slave trade. We are on the road to Buenos Aires."

Eleanor laughed. "Why not? There have been times when to me to be a white slave seemed an unattainable ideal. I wondered how people did it."

Berenice took out her tortoise-shell cigarette case with its gold monogram, the whole thing a studied public insult—offered this studied public insult to all present, and said, "Oh, sure. Very neat. But are you paying for your ticket yourself? Can Philip pay for us all? For he has offered, apparently, I judge recklessly from appearances, to take us all to England on the *Samaria*! And I think a brawl is due. I for one—"

During the brawl that followed, my mother ran to the phone

which was in the entry. The entry, fortunately, could be reached by a door into the kitchen which was whitewashed and usually kept bolted. She telephoned the first person that came into her head. That was Balan Froggart, an old friend, an actor who had risen to fame, who had sent her a bouquet this same morning. He said he would come at once, taking a taxi because he had a benefit performance in the evening and had to sleep a little.

When she came back to the room Philip had disappeared, for with a dramatic talent suitable for this kind of situation only he had, after stamping about, holding his hands to his ears, kissing all the girls in turn, offering to help them with their valises to the taxis, turning his pockets inside out (to show that he had no money and no tickets), and pulling out his handkerchief to wipe his sweating forehead, this attractive young fellow had suddenly rushed to the door, pulled it open, said, "Fight it out amongst yourselves," pulled the door to, and disappeared. The girls had too much sense to follow him and were seating themselves to have a good cry when Mother came in. She opened a package of chocolates, most acceptable always, and saw them disappear under her eyes.

Scarcely fifteen minutes later, while she was herself helping them to an understanding of her brother Philip, the prepotent, irresistible, beetle-browed figure of Balan Froggart appeared. He got them around him, like a crowd of autograph-hounds, kissed my mother, offered them drinks in his apartment and free theater tickets, told them to be good girls, told them that if they had been good girls, they would never have got into this jam, sang the "Jamb on Jerry's Rocks," told them he was himself an eligible, if unreliable bachelor, and rushed them out of the apartment into a taxi which he declared was waiting, and left a last message for his friend, Solander, which was, "Tell Sol, Philip had the right idea; only ladies should live under a king. Come on, girls."

13

My FATHER was at the boat, and for one night took us to the Strand Palace Hotel, a resort of Americans in London, where you could then get bed and breakfast for nine-and-sixpence a night, baths free and breakfast up till eleven in the morning. Breakfast consisted of about eight courses; those taking it were able to economize by doing without lunch. There were three or four hotels run on this attractive system by the same concern.

My father had engaged, for the week only, board and lodging at a respectable red brick pension near Hampstead Heath. The air, he said, would be good for my mother and for us. Mother cried at being left there like a widow or divorcée, and asked how she would ever explain it, saying they would think she was a mistress or a deserted wife. Father said that he had already explained to the woman that he worked permanently in London, lived in chambers, and that Mathilde Fox, his wife, had shortly to return to the U.S.A. for the opening of school. "And that is true, Mattie, isn't it?" he asked; "I cannot afford this living in separate quarters and do not want the children educated here."

At first he would not tell my mother where he was living, but then gave an address and asked her not to call upon him there. There was no telephone and never anyone there in the daytime.

"She is there," said my mother.

My father at first denied this, but afterwards agreed that Persia was there.

"Why do you do nothing but lie to me?" cried my poor mother. "It is all built on sand; I have no one to turn to."

"I lied to you to save you pain."

"I have no one in the world to turn to," said my mother, pacing up and down. "You brought this girl over here, but not me. You don't give me a chance."

"She is looking about for another job. She's very ambitious and is studying to go to France or Belgium to work. Montrose offered her a job here with me."

"Montrose! He said nothing about it to me; he told me—everyone is against me! As soon as her husband leaves her, everyone insults a woman and lies to her; they seem to think she's a two-year-old child. Really, they don't care—she is dead to them. What a position to be in! Dead to society! How can a dead woman like me bring up your children? Soon you'll want to give them to that woman. She's a concubine, but she's alive. People are interested in her. She has power. That's what they're interested in. I understand everything, but too late! But I never had any luck!"

My mother, crying, sat in a corner of the room on a straight chair, placed there beside a tall green and yellow pottery vase, painted and fluted like a waterlily. It was about three feet high and held a stick and an umbrella. Everything in the room was, to us, beautiful and strange: the Nottingham lace curtains, starched stiffly so that they almost stood up by themselves; the lace doilies on chair-heads and armrests; the two hassocks, one lemon-colored velvet, one red plush with a basket of flowers; the marble clock with gold pillars holding up a dome upon which a Cupid stood on tiptoe. China ladies and gentlemen in flowered clothes stood beside it. There was a tall mirror reaching to the ceiling, and the mantelpiece, broad as a reredos and very much like one, had carvings, shelves, niches, openwork; and in a glass corner cabinet was a collection of fine, tiny things in china.

While this conversation was going on, Jacky and I were spread flat as weeds in an aquarium, against the glass of this cabinet. There was an old woman on a chair, a night stool, a guitar, none more than an inch long, and a collection of china dogs, all the size of fingernails; much more beside this. Our father came toward us, his pale face lighted up by his large, gentle eyes, and said, "It was on account of those little dogs and that child in the swing that I took this room, I tell you; I knew you kids would be nuts about them."

We laughed loudly and tried to open the cabinet. My mother cried and said, "And you won't stay here even tonight, Sol?"

"I cannot; there is no room here," he said in despair; "perhaps we will make some other arrangements before you go back, but you must go back soon, Mattie. I cannot keep you all over here. You know what I am getting. Montrose paid for my fare, but he took it off my salary and I ended up the first week twelve pounds in the hole. And now your trip—such a wild thing to do —why didn't you write to me? You take your mother's advice, Phyllis's advice, Pauline's advice, but they don't pay your fare, I notice."

"I spent nothing," said my mother, weeping; "as you see, the children have nothing new. I am ashamed to take them down to dinner."

My father laughed, "I think they can compete with the English and so can you."

"They all think Americans are so rich and we look like beggars."

"Rich Americans don't stay here."

"I do think Mrs. Montrose could have asked us out for just one night or two," said my mother desolately; "she asked Phyllis and Pauline, but not me. It is ill-mannered. And as for Montrose, he came to see me several times and brought candy for the girls, and now I find that he was only interested in Phyllis. Probably that's the whole story!"

My father laughed, "Oh, Joe's not a bad fellow, but he expects some return for anything he puts out. That's the usual thing, you know. Your own mother, Mattie, is not far from that class herself."

"I'm the Cinderella," said my mother.

"No, you're married to a pauper not a prince," said my father, tenderly. "Maybe Mother Morgan could do better next time."

"It's no laughing matter."

"Do your hair and fix your collar, Mattie. Go down to dinner and I'll come and see you for dinner tomorrow night. I'll arrange to have my dinners here."

"Oh, what will they think, then, Sol? I had better say you're my brother."

"What a poor thing," said my father, coming to my mother and kissing her; "what a coward, and what a silly, timid woman."

"I have no home, nowhere to turn," said my mother, putting her head on his chest. "Sol, what will I do? You're all I had. You understood me and now you have left me. Life is so uncomfortable now."

"I'll come back tomorrow for dinner," said my father, suddenly.

He kissed Mother and then us, and smiling his great smile and making several codfish, salmon and toad faces for us at our request (for he was very good at frogs and fish), he left quickly, leaving with us an impression of black and white, a plump comforting waist, small coins in dark pockets, and love. If Sol did not love Mathilde, he loved us. I felt a faint disdain for my mother, no doubt. She often said we did, when she complained.

We stayed in this place for two weeks, and by that time Joseph Montrose had made the following proposition to my father: that Pauline, Mathilde, Phyllis, and the two little girls should take a large flat he had found. There was some furniture in the flat and he would provide more. Pauline and Phyllis were to have four of the six rooms, and we were to have two. When my mother returned to the U.S.A. Montrose would take over the whole flat and pay for it all, unless my father had any other suggestion. As my father would have very little rent to pay under this arrangement, my mother would do the housework and cooking, but as she would have company, and be able to receive visits from my father without having anything to explain, everyone agreed to the idea.

Mrs. Montrose felt it very respectable that the sisters should live together, and Mr. Montrose explained to her that he hoped to reconcile the separated husband and wife. He explained this to my mother, too. My mother was reconciled to Joseph Montrose, although she scolded him for having deceived her, "Why didn't you tell me, Joe, that woman was living with him in London?"

"Wasn't sure myself—didn't enquire—give you my word, Mattie, never knew for certain," and he smiled, pressed her knee.

"But you gave her a job, and all the while you were pretending to be my friend."

"Look, little girlie, she came to London; she's used to my business, and I like to do a good turn. I'm giving her a good salary so that she can learn languages and get to the Continent as she wishes. I'm really helping you."

"Why can't you tell him to leave her?"

"Well, you know my respect for you, but—"

We saw a great deal of Joseph Montrose. Mrs. Montrose came once only, seemed pleased with the flat, and went away giving vague invitations to dinner. She did not care for Jacky or myself, that was plain. But Pauline and Phyllis were invited to dinner at their house the very next week, and came home, gracelessly roaring with laughter over the house, the way dinner was served, and the manners and conversation of beauteous Mrs. Montrose. She was beautiful, but dead. Her dinner was dead, all drowned in water. She had a butler and two sons, all dead, with *etched* British accents.

The following week Joseph Montrose visited Phyllis and Pauline, but not us, to my mother's surprise and mortification. After this, Pauline and Phyllis went out a good deal with Montrose, and at times Pauline would come to my mother and say, "Joe is coming this afternoon to see Phyl; I think we'd better give Phyl a chance to talk to him alone, don't you? She is so good with men."

This went on for some time. We would shut our door. Pauline would go out. Montrose would come and hold long conversations with her, and also short silences, for Montrose was a hurried man. He was a bull-necked but fair-skinned and clear-eyed man at this time, about thirty-eight, broad, stubby, muscular, with a jutting chin; the nose a solid promontory over a slender, pretty, but manly mouth; a sweet flitting smile; the face of a hasty, egotistic sensualist.

It was not long before Aunt Phyllis began to think of marrying him; and then, when Pauline was in, we would be called in for a conference with them. Sometimes we all sat there on the chairs and divan, Pauline, Mathilde, and two little girls, and we listened breathlessly to the love dialogue of the previous day as told by Phyllis. He said Ada, his wife, had never made him happy, but kept a sour, dull home, had never loved him, and had nothing to say; she was always asleep. He was looking for a wife and would make Ada divorce him; he was madly in love with Phyllis.

"He talks about nothing but love. He's very passionate."

"Does he really know anything about it?" asked my mother. "He's always so quick—"

"He said he never loved before; this is the first time. He says I have hooked him. He says I am the oasis in a Sahara."

On other days Montrose seemed far away; Phyllis doubted his truth. What should we all do? Montrose was paying for Phyllis's education, but he was mean, Phyllis thought. He wrote to Grandmother Morgan asking to be repaid, every month regularly. Phyllis had already slept with him many times; she saw no way out of it. He was not her first lover. She did not love him, but she liked him. It was entirely a question of whether he was to be trusted, and whether he would divorce his wife. If he did so, he would be able to give Phyllis all that she wanted. Mrs. Montrose herself had diamonds, furs, silks that she never used, plate that she never used, a big house in which she never entertained.

"I'd be very different; he'd enjoy life with me."

"Perhaps he's afraid of the expense, after all," said Mathilde; "he's a wise child, and you say yourself—"

Pauline had one piece of backward wisdom, "Phyllis should not have slept with him so soon."

Pauline never was able to follow this advice herself. Pauline said further, "He took me in a taxi this very week to buy the bracelet for Phyl, and I'll be honest with you, he made me a proposal in the taxi."

"What sort of a proposal?" asked Phyllis, merely with curiosity.

"What sort do you think? Not to get married!" Pauline laughed. "I said I was your friend."

None of us believed this, of course, but I could see Mother and Phyllis had no feeling against Pauline. They sat thinking Montrose over as a marriage proposition.

"He has this weakness," said my mother; "he is a Don Juan. You'd never have a moment's peace."

"What would I care, really?" said Phyllis. "All I want is to get married, then I'll manage very well. I expect him to leave me free, too, after all. He's already quite old for me; I'd have a good time."

"I don't think you ought to go to her for dinner," my mother said heavily.

"Wouldn't it look funny if we refused? She quite likes me and she loves Pauline. Pauline has ingratiated herself." Phyllis laughed, "Besides, don't you realize I don't really want her husband? I'm just looking for someone eligible. I'd be very pleased to get someone else."

Pauline approved of this; my mother, herself, did not see how she could turn down Mrs. Montrose's rare invitations. Mrs. Montrose pitied her for her misfortunes, and had many hard words to say about my father leading a wicked, wanton, adulterous life. But my mother's cold sorrow did not please her. Mrs. Montrose preferred the two lively women, Phyllis and Pauline. Mrs. Montrose loved to turn her old dresses, boasted to Joseph of her thrift. Pauline saw it infuriated him, and she helped Mrs. Montrose to re-make several old gowns, in order to help on Phyllis's chances.

Grandmother Morgan had sent over a few checks to reimburse Montrose, but now felt she must come over herself to see how her investment was going. Mother, following Pauline's advice, had lied, saying she and Solander were living together and asking for money for household furnishings; the money had not come, but Grandmother Morgan cabled suddenly that she was coming to London on her way to Paris before the opening of the new season, and this was followed by a short, lively, and ill-spelled letter, in which Grandmother advised Phyllis to keep Montrose at arm's length and told my mother that Grandmother would try to mend her marriage for her. She also wanted to get away from Mr. Porlock, who was pressing her to name the wedding day; she added a postscript:

I'm tired of Eddie (Porlock). He isn't a real sport. I couldn't settle down with him. He doesn't see I need life. He talks about Darby and Joan which means old people living old. Not for me. Also, what is always the case, there's another man, that opened my eyes to Eddie. The boys are against this new man, Sid, and I want to see what you think, Pauline, with your experience. Love to Mattie and Sol. Cissie Morgan.

My mother at once telephoned my father, and told him that to save her face he must at least live with her for a few weeks; Grandmother was coming over, and expected to see the family re-united. Eventually my father promised to see what he could do. Another cable arrived, giving my grandmother's sailing date, and Mother, feverishly, in tears, begged my father to have a home for herself and us, if even for the few days her mother would be in London.

Cissie Morgan had one lover after another, begging her to marry him; Phyllis looked after herself, and what would *she* look like—worse than even Stella, the old maid. And, said my mother, if my father wished to avoid endless family discussions, even if he did not want to live with her, the best thing would be for him to pretend to live with his real wife for a few days. And then she said, sobbing, he could go back to the woman who suited him so well.

My father agreed to take some rooms in a central London hotel for a few days. Since he was not rich, and had to send money to his mother, pay for our rent and expenses and keep a home for *Die Konkubine* going, he could not afford more than two rooms in the hotel; one was for us, and one for Mother and himself. Nevertheless, he did not join her when it came to the point; they parted each night after long discussions which lasted till three or four in the morning.

My mother was never able to lie, and when Grandmother arrived in a new outfit, with new furs, and when Grandmother had completely thrashed out the Phyllis-Montrose situation, with Pauline and Phyllis, my mother began to cry (in our new hotel rooms, and while my father was away at business) and told the whole story, that she had lied and that even this was a façade, a sham for Grandmother.

"Does he sleep with you?" asked my grandmother at once. My mother was weeping.

"Of course he sleeps with her," said I, who was reading a book in the corner; "they have only one bed, and he doesn't sleep with us, and he stays here until two in the morning."

Grandmother smiled and patted my head. She gave me a ten-shilling note and told me to go down to the sweets counter in the hotel and buy myself anything I liked, a box of chocolates, a big doll. As soon as she thought I had gone, or even before I had closed the door, she said squarely to my mother, "Well, Mathilde, he's yours; he'll never go back to her if you have sense."

"Oh, heavens," said Mother, "it's so dreadful."

Grandmother said firmly, "Women are supposed to have children anyhow. What are you doing in life? She hasn't had the sense to have a baby yet. Until she does he'll never marry her. He's too poor to keep more than one family. Wear him down. And the other thing."

"He'll say I've trapped him."

"You are supposed to. Why do you think laws were made? Otherwise all our fine feathered friends would be running out on us all the time. Your father, you know, Mattie, had some cutie or other the whole time as far as I know. I simply took no notice. Men invented the tourist business. We can't take notice of that. The only trouble with modern women is they take it to heart. Forget it. You marry a man. You expect him to keep on bringing you candy and flowers. Forget it. You can't get men to wear their home address on their—collar. Never mind, though dogs they are! Don't be a fool! You've got to get yourself another baby. Wear him out. If you don't take this chance, I can't do anything more for you. I can't worry about you at my time of life. I've got Phyllis to get off; I'd like to marry that old maid of mine. What am I doing with an old maid?" She laughed, and moved her chair. "You must be anemic, Mathilde, and Stella's too tough, too bossy." After a moment, she added, "But Stella had bites, don't fear, she had her chances, but she's difficult to please. Now Sol himself—"

My mother said, "Oh, don't rake that up. I didn't take Sol from Stella. That's her imagination."

"Suppose you did? I wouldn't blame him. You're better looking and you used to dress lovely. Not now. You ought to brighten yourself up a bit. Get yourself a new hat—I'll pay for it—"

"Oh, Mother, surely you don't—a hat! What's the use!"

"I know what I'm talking about. You get yourself a new costume and a new hat and put on a bit of powder, and don't forget—the other thing—"

"Oh, I don't see what all this is. I want a man to love me. I love him."

"You talk like a high-school girl. That's all over, for the time being. Wait till you're an old woman like me." She laughed knowingly, "Right now, Mattie, you've got to think about your future and getting some security for the little girls. You don't want them to be insecure? It's your duty. I have no sympathy with this about love between decent, married people, with children to bring up. I want to see you with a good rent-payer, a good provider, a man to keep you in nice clothes and send the children to nice schools, and give them nice clothes too, so they can meet the right boys. It's selfish to keep crying about love, love. Look at Sol. He talks about love, love. Do you care about that? You see? You don't care about his love, love."

She laughed solidly, "I'm the one who can afford it, love, love. I can pay for it. I've got the time and money. I wouldn't be so crazy —knock my head against a stone wall before I had money in the bank?" She laughed aloud, "Go on, wake up, you crazy fool, you're just a kid. When you're forty or forty-five, it'll be time to think about necking and—" her voice softened—"love—and men—and all that. But you've got to get Sol back right now and that's the whole problem. Leave the rest to God. He'll take care of a decent woman, who takes care of her family life."

"Then I'm to have no life of my own!"

"You must sacrifice yourself for Tootsy and Jacky," said Grandmother heroically. "I swear to you, Mattie, I never had anything serious to do with a man till all you children were grown up. I had a sense of duty."

I heard my mother crying, and ran off downstairs. As there was a doll there which cost twelve-and-sixpence, I gave the woman seven-and-sixpence for it, telling her Grandmother would pay for the rest. When she gave me the change, I bought some bull's-eyes, licorice, and a pair of Irish crocheted gloves, just my size. When I ran upstairs and showed these to my grandmother, impudently laughing and cuddling her solid thighs, she stared a moment. Then her clear, brown eyes smiled. She turned to my mother who was looking forlornly at me, and said, "Mathilde, just look at this kid! Come on, kiss Grandma, you little monkey. What'll you be now? An embezzler, a counterfeiter? Signing my name to checks? You'd better not, you little devil. I'll warm your little tail for you. Don't you do so any more, do you hear? Mathilde, I wish your kid was in your place for a week or two. She'd get her daddy back, wouldn't you, Letty?"

"He will come back," I said.

"How do you know?" Grandmother asked.

"He's sick of Persia," I said, noticing how keenly this hurt my mother, and laughing somewhat. "She nearly had a baby and she was sick, but he didn't want the baby, so he'll leave her now."

"Little imp of mischief," said my mother, breathing hard, staring at me. "How do you know this? Who is Persia?"

"Someone told me," I said.

"Who, who told you?"

"I heard Lily telling Grandma Fox in New York."

"By the way," said Grandmother Morgan thoughtfully, turning to my mother, "have you heard from Mrs. Fox?"

"No; why should I tell her how I'm living and the situation I'm in. She never liked me."

"In cases like this, women always stand together," said Grandmother seriously; "sit down and write a letter to her, Mattie, asking after her health and say Sol is so anxious to see her. Besides, you should. She's your mother-in-law. I don't believe in family quarrels. Families should stand together. You see, also," she said, twinkling, "you could find out something, maybe! Write! Wire! You're anemic, I think. No sense of business at all. You were right to try to be an actress."

"I was a failure," said my mother.

"Oh—" cried Grandmother, blowing out her cheeks and taking a few strides up the carpet, "fiddlesticks! Everyone's a failure till he succeeds. If you die before you're married, you're an old maid too. Ha-ha! Fiddlesticks! Write to her; send her my love. Say I'm anxious to have her at my new hotel in the White Mountains the very minute it's opened. I have a special room for her, little white curtains, a tree right outside the window, ground floor; she doesn't have to climb. Everything nice. Running hot, cold. She can have a bathroom to herself if she wants it, tell her. I don't have to make good if I don't open the hotel, do I? What do I care? I'm doing it for you. Tell her there's going to be a swell crowd there, all furs, diamonds, roast chickens, apartments with bathrooms. Ha-ha! Tell her anything. I'll make good if you get that boy back, Mattie; I'll give you a *suit* of furniture. Now, catch the mail. Wait, I'll go down to Montrose's office and ask him to send a cable for me. I'll tell him, never mind. I'll manage it—give me her address. I'll cable, cable. She'll be tickled pink. You write. Now, mind! I've got to run. Good-bye! Write! Write! Give her my love. I always think of her. How's her arthritis?"

Grandmother rushed out, a flurry of skirts, furs, and a breeze of heavy, expensive perfume, a strong satin prow, and a strong satin stern.

Since Grandmother started her own love affairs so late, it's unlikely that she found out the value of her peculiarities. By that time her figure though tightly bound was besieged and taken by middle-aged flesh, strong, irreducible.

There is a lot of superstition about what is beautiful in a woman; only a grown woman, with considerable experience of men, knows what is really attractive. I saw a model in an art class, a white girl, with the figure considered ideal in our America, and in fact, in this year, she had been chosen the most beautiful model. She had a silly, pink face with her nose in the air and a wax smile. Quite naked, she was safe from rape or desire, while a fat coarse dragon in her tight satin made the men stir and laugh. I have noticed this, too, looking at myself, standing without stockings, in a short slip, with my hair down, before going to bed in a strange place where I have not brought my nightdress. Perhaps some men enjoy my maturity in prospect, while I am still young enough for them. They think of all kinds of things, most unpleasant and dishonest; that is what they call knowing women. I used to be very unhappy.

Who said, "Love is prostitution of self?"—Baudelaire. He went to whores and so he thought thus. For these men, too, whores are the most romance they'll get out of life, and if they meet a girl who is not wanton, they wantonize her in their minds. Yes, but I cannot think it of them when I love them. But there are dull moments when I ask myself what I am to love such wantons. Is this what he meant?

But the time when I learned all this was when I was eighteen and nineteen. Now I am not a woman to be generally handled by this type of man. At this time I was speaking of, though, when I first noticed Grandmother's figure and observed that I was a little like her, my idea of love was not fleshly. I merely thought I would be a little queen and pulverize them, ruin them, make them cut their throats, tread on their bleeding hearts, kick them, laugh (as Jacky and I often laughed out hard, mirthful cackles), and fall swooning in the arms of some matinee idol.

None of my daydreams was secret. In one of them which I told very often, regiments of men stood before me, dreaming of my favors. I went down the line, selecting one, throwing out another. All kinds of reasons occurred to me. I loaded them with blistering insults. They fell on their faces and howled, or fell backwards and mangled themselves in some juicy way.

The questions of love and marriage, which appeared to be the only questions in the feminine society we lived in, now began to form the conversation my sister and I had. There was room for speculation. Our female friends did not know the answers to most of their own questions and this entertained them, too, enormously. They had always plenty to talk about. For example, they never knew what attracted a man to a given girl. They could discuss this for days. The reasons they gave were very instructive for us. Jacky would sit, very attentive, with her eyes wide open, trying to picture the girls they spoke about; thus,

"It's because she was fresh; had no one before—because she knows how to handle men—knows the tricks of the trade—has that baby stare—is so naïve, he feels ashamed—is a blonde; has those great, dark eyes; knows so much; knows nothing—started to have a baby—did not saddle him with a baby—"

Impossible to become corrupt in this school for girls, for no one had the recipe for anything. Even Grandmother's recipe for getting Solander back had not yet worked, and Grandmother didn't seem to care much.

My father and mother went away with us for a week end to Folkestone. They roomed together, but this didn't cure their separation. When I reached London, my parents went to their different addresses. On the way down Mother had expressed a delicate reluctance to sleep with my father when he had come straight from the arms of "that woman"; and then she had cried bitterly nearly all the way to Folkestone, that it was so degrading, and it was this, perhaps, that changed their week end. My father then told my mother that he was not actually living with Persia any more, while Mathilde was in London, and out of respect for her feelings they had both thought it better to live separately. And Persia had gone on a trip to Antwerp for Montrose. She would work there for Montrose.

"And will continue to do so while I am here?" said my mother, astonished.

"Yes," said Solander.

My mother made no reply, and cried no more. Even toward the end of the day she began to laugh and pull our ears playfully.

My father told a joke and she laughed; at Folkestone they went straight up to their room.

My mother was quite pleasant on the way back, though she clouded over as London approached. Outside, she hailed a taxi and said to my father, "Let's go straight home, I want to change the girls' dresses. Then I'll put them to bed and we can go to the movies."

"I am not coming with you," said Sol. "This was a little vacation for us."

Mother, almost without taking thought, groaned, "Oh," and flung herself on my father. People looked, we both went red, and Jacky began to cry. My father comforted Mathilde and then said, "That's enough, my dear, now get into the taxi."

My mother bawled out, in a strange, affecting contralto, "Oh, don't leave me; don't leave me!"

After a few more words, Solander tried to put her into the taxi, telling us to jump in, and we anxiously scurried in, but my mother, brave in her desolation, cried out to the taxi driver, "Oh, don't go yet, my husband's leaving me. He's sending me off while he goes to another woman. My husband's left me. What shall I do? Oh, don't go away till I make him come home with me."

And she turned to the people passing out of the station, saying, with her eyes full of tears, "Help me! Help me! My husband's leaving me."

The men hurried past with eyes full of shame and curiosity; the women went even faster, blowing, waddling, with wooden faces. No one came to help my mother. She looked wonderfully handsome, with her face all black and white, smudged with tears, and her brown, curly hair loose on her shoulders, so I could see looking out of the taxi door, but I was deeply ashamed and said, "Mother, Mother, everyone's looking!"

"I'll come to the hotel with you, but this must be the end," said my father. Mother at once bowed her thin shoulders and stooped in among us, while my father gravely gave the address to the driver. Night was falling. My father sat with a convulsed face, staring ahead; tears were in his eyes.

"Your happiness is built on my ruin," said Mother in a low voice.

"Do you think I am happy?"

"And you are ruining your children for that woman. What future have they?"

"I don't know what I'm doing," said my father.

"She is only one; we are four. What is love now? We're too old for love," and my mother began crying again.

When we reached the hotel, my father said quickly, "I'll pay the driver and take Letty for a walk. I want to get her her comics. Jacky, go up with your mother, I'll be back later."

Then he began walking quickly away, while I ran and panted to keep up with him. He said to me, "Letty, I can't explain things to you because you can't understand the lives of adults. I'm just going to have to do what seems the right thing and trust that you'll understand years later—if they don't poison you against me. That's the wrong word. I don't mean poison. I mean your mother is very unhappy and she sees only her troubles!"

He then said he was going home to his chambers to telephone, was taking me with him because he had little time, and that, therefore, I would see Persia.

"I lied to your mother to keep her happy, and I have lied to Persia to keep her happy. I'm in a mess of lies and I'm an honest man."

"Why, Papa?"

"And you must lie, too, in order to keep your mother happy. You must not tell her what you see here in my home. Tell her nothing. Tell no one anything. You can do that. But I am taking you with me because I can't lie to you little girls, really. That's all."

"Don't you want to live with us, Papa? Don't you love us any more?"

"Stop that," he said angrily, "those aren't your words."

I hung my head with shame and irritation. How clever he was! When we came to the chambers, in mid-London, we climbed three or four flights of stairs and reached a top floor. Under the attics was a furnished apartment with two or three rooms. It was hard to say whether two or three, for the bedroom was an ingle.

Persia, with her glossy hair loose, in a blue dress, kissed my father heartily and chattered away without any suspicion of scolding. I was surprised. As usual she took no more notice of me than if I had been an adult. She did not say, "Darling little Letty," or

"What lovely eyes," or any of the things to which I was used. I sat and stared at her jealously. There was nothing special about her and she had not even good manners. She jerked about. Her voice went brittle or thin at odd moments. She grimaced and jumped in excitement. She seemed a schoolgirl. She used no endearments with my father, but it was, "Sol, Solly, Sol," all the time. My father laughed, jumped about also, showed things to me, told jokes, and said it was a pity I could not stay for dinner. I looked very black.

When my father went in the bathroom and shut the door, I told Persia that all four of us had spent the week end at Folkestone and that my mother and father had slept in the same room.

"Did they?" she said, and looked at me steadily. I continued, "We had a lovely time, we went to everything, and we met people we knew in America and soon we're all going back, Papa said."

Persia said nothing, but looked at me.

"Mummy and Papa—"

I was glad that Solander arrived at this moment, for I had run out of ideas, and I now wanted to see the fireworks. Persia went on talking as if nothing had happened. I was puzzled by this. For a moment I had a queer feeling that I had dreamed it all, that I hadn't opened my mouth. Presently, we went and, "Good-bye" said Persia, coldly. Probably, she never mentioned my revelations. It seemed strange to me that the first blow I had struck for Mother disappeared in this magical way. I could not tell anyone about it either. My father left me at the door of the hotel.

When I came upstairs, my mother merely looked gloomy, and said, "He must think I'm a child."

I sat in full view trying to convey to Jacky by signs that I had again seen *Die Konkubine*. I wriggled and became mirthful, for Jacky had never seen the fabulous creature. At last Jacky came over from her book and I whispered, "I saw *Die Konkubine*."

"Oh, you're a liar!"

"I'll tell Mother what you said."

We were both sent to bed. We rushed off. I described exhaustively my short visit, but left out the piece of mischief I had done. This great deed I kept to myself. Jacky must have lain awake a long time with her eyes shining. She murmured, "I wish I could see her."

"You'll never see her," I said. "You can't tell lies and you would tell everyone and so you will never know anything."

"I would never tell," said Jacky sadly; "she must be glamorous."

"She's just nothing. She's stupid. She doesn't know anything. Nuts to her," I said jealously.

"I hope when I grow up I can entrap men. What must it feel like? I think I could feel like that! If with one glance from my enchanting black eyes—"

"You've got blue eyes. I've got black eyes."

"My witching blue eyes. I, Letty! I wish I was Cleopatra. And walk along sinuously, with cloth of gold, covered with flashing gems, and I would come up to King Solomon—"

"You're mad! That's the Queen of Sheba."

"What was her name?"

Although I was the infant wonder of our family, I did not yet know *Balkis*, so I ripped out, *Phylloxera*, which my father had been talking about, "Phylloxera was her name."

"No," shouted Jacky, "Cleopatra—in a barge—yes—with cloth of gold trailing in the water and gems. She was in a barge, I remember. Solomon had a temple."

We had stood for hours in the Art Museum at home studying the painted queens. After a moment, Jacky said dreamily, "But you know what I like best? The burial of Alaric! They turned the river and now it flows over him. The river Busento. I don't know where it is," said Jacky sadly, "is it a real river?"

"Yes," said the infant wonder.

Through the high window, that high window that looked out over half London, I could see late evening coming, and in the light, Jacky's smiling face turned toward me. The dark made her eyes seem very large. She looked at me burning with passion, "It is a real river!"

She loved me, because I made some of her dreams come true, I suppose. And that was the hold my father had over us both. He knew. And isn't that why we adore men; in four words, We think they know!

14

JACKY AND I, with me for guide, would go downtown to the office in which my father worked with Joseph Montrose and watch the workings of this simple, large, empty machine. My father seemed happy, young, and even foolish. He dictated rambling letters to Persia in order to show off to us. He wrote to everyone I had ever heard of in America. He wrote long letters weekly to his mother. She must have been surprised at all the mail she was getting. She, too, began to write her stiff, disconnected notes. Now, having been egged on by all, she began also to beg a little, to hint that everyone went abroad, but not she; that though the Europeans are mad, of course, with their gilded coaches and feathered hats, like Cinderella and cockatoos, still an old woman might get a good laugh out of it all; though what an old woman wanted it for, she could not tell, an old woman was perhaps an old fool; she was not such an old fool as to want to go to London to see the King! A cat may look at a king. Yet, it seemed strange that poor people went over to Paris nowadays, stenographers, shoeblacks, really everyone, girls in Woolworth's. They became rich on their shares and started talking about the Rue de la Paix, and had their anecdotes, quarrels, bargains, lovers. All but herself; and Lily, of course. But Lily was an idiot. It was no pleasure to be in Lily's company all the time, no joke at all. Lily, of course, was a good girl, but what was a niece to a son? To her sweetest little honeys, Toots and Jacky? Well, she would probably die without seeing any of them again, and she had been so ill recently, with the heat, dust, the choking all the night—though that poor Lily had done her best, one had to say that for her—that she feared she would never see her darlings, her blessings, again. All this came, of course, not in the letter, but was doled out. September came, ended; my father was remorsefully writing fervent letters to his mother, begging her to take the next boat, "You write *yes*, and I'll cable you the money."

This was madness, if we were going back to New York; but at present my mother had made no move and everyone advised her to stay. She did not welcome old Mrs. Fox's coming.

"She lives only for herself," said Mathilde, "a woman with a son does not care for other women."

But Lily Spontini knew a boy who had gone to London, and encouraged her old aunt too.

We had moved away from the hotel and were back in lodgings. My mother was now very much alone. Grandmother Morgan, after going to Paris and getting some new ideas for menus and clothes, had returned to New York to look into her affairs. Pauline and Phyllis had little time for her. Phyllis was dissatisfied with Joseph Montrose, believed no longer that he would marry her, and was now going out with a blond American gentleman called Dave, who had run up a large expensive apartment house near Hyde Park, which was now full of modern couples, well-kept mistresses, and girls on the make, brave enough or businesslike enough to speculate on a high rent. The huge building was called, on brass plates, Chippendale Mansions, but popularly the first word was affectionately shortened. This was not Dave's only venture. Dave now came to visit Pauline and Phyllis at times arranged by them. He didn't seem to mind this at all. He listened to Phyllis play and sing, and said the girls should go to Paris or Berlin. He suggested an act for them. He knew something about that business. Strangely enough, when Mathilde heard about this, she was pleased. She was sick of the shabby Montrose entanglement. Joseph Montrose, also, seemed pleased about the new idea. Dave, who had never met Montrose, agreed to put up some money, so that the girls could live cheaply for a few months in Paris, to study singing and dramatics and learn enough French for an act. Phyllis was to get money from Grandmother Morgan to study at a well-known Paris school of music run for Americans in the Place des Vosges, a delightful old square, where everyone would be very happy.

My mother became unusually animated. She said to Solander that there was no point in her staying here. He neglected her, she wasn't comfortable, and she was humiliated. Pauline said the children would do better to go to a French school, pick up a foreign language, and go back to America next year. Then poor Mathilde would have doubts and say, How would the children adjust themselves to American life, after they had lived abroad? Perhaps their parents' selfishness would ruin them. The next morning she would get up quite cheerful and argue that in Paris she would look after her sister. For Pauline seemed a little flighty. In fact, Mathilde was sure Pauline had slept with Joseph Montrose on the occasions when she pretended to go and consult with him about Phyllis's career and Mathilde's troubles. Mathilde knew Montrose—"He held my knee and showed me his wallet," she said, with a faint sparkling smile and provocative flush, to her husband one day. Solander looked gloomy. "What is one to do? Ignore it or split with him forever?" Mother was softly flattered, "Oh, never tell him I mentioned it." After a silence, she continued.

"Let's meet in Paris in the spring," said Mathilde, in a rare, lyric moment. "Perhaps, Sol, you'll have got over this obsession by then and we'll see how to start over again; and if not, my mother's coming back in the spring to Paris, and she can take me back, and we'll shake hands on it."

"I agree," said my father thankfully, and seemed quite to love her.

At this moment, he got a cable to say that not only was Grandmother Fox coming over in answer to his repeated pleadings, but that it had become possible for Lily Spontini also to come because of a small amount of money received from a relative dead in Canada: "Only enough to come over and go back, but she can find something to do in England, I suppose. She isn't very smart, but she can do jobs that other people would be too proud to do. That kind of girl can always find something."

Grandmother Fox named the boat and asked for the money. My father looked harassed. I don't think he had thought Grandmother Fox would come. His letters to her had been romantic outpourings.

Grandmother Fox and Lily Spontini were on the sea, only two days out from England, when the October stock market crash came. Millions of toy balloons burst with a loud noise and a number of people who had taken a trip overseas found themselves stranded. The anecdotes began very soon after, about those who were saved by a miracle, a day, two months, before. Grandmother Morgan was again ruined; Phyllis's protectors had no chance of being repaid and Pauline and Phyllis at once set about getting an engagement in a private club or night club somewhere on the Continent or elsewhere. Grandmother Fox and Lily Spontini had no stocks or bonds but had a real daily earner, Solander Fox, to depend on, and so were neither richer nor poorer. We were in the same situation. Everyone else, who did not commit suicide and had no wage-earner, began to live on debts. The Americans left London and Paris, and the U.S.A. came in for the first knock-out blow in living memory, one which soured it forever. But some managed to live in the old carefree way and we were among the survivors. My mother put us to a cheap Catholic school in Paris recommended by Pauline. By Christmas we had rosaries with crucifixes under our pillows and started praying at night, not because we were taught to, but as a new play; and Jacky had another romantic variation. She wanted to be a Greek Orthodox. We were now sopping up Dostoevsky, and Aunt Pauline took us one day to a wedding of some White Russian friends, and we saw the onion-shaped towers of the Russian Cathedral. "It's the Queen of Sheba idea in Church work," I thought. We then played "Christ is Risen!" "Letty, verily He is Risen!" This accompanied by kissings and preceded by a procession; "Christ is Risen!" (Kiss, kiss.) "He is indeed, Mother." This was a play that could go on for hours. Everyone played it, adults too. It was absorbing. We double-kissed everyone.

Mother was glad to be in Paris. In France, even at that time, the position of the married woman was still such a sure thing that "Madame this and that" had a condescending voice and was superior to "Mademoiselle this and that."

Mother had become languid, temperamental, and had put on weight. Pauline kissed her repeatedly and told us not to bother her.

We were scarcely installed in Paris in a hotel near the War Ministry, a quiet and respectable quarter, when we received a letter from Uncle Philip saying that things were very bad in the U.S.A.; that he had been again pursued for debt and back alimony; that Grandmother Morgan had given up the idea of her White

Mountains hotel; that there was a back-to-the-land movement and Perce Hogg had taken advantage of it by establishing a community, called Parity, N.Y., where men could go who were hunted by their ex-wives, the whole idea having been suggested by the farm-prison he had seen at Farmington (and that Philip would just as soon be in jail for good); and last, that Dora Dunn, that most reasonable of women, had suffered from the panic. The man who had been supplying her with money had thrown himself out of a window upon finding that his secretary had stolen his money to play in Wall Street. Dora had closed her shop for a few months till the world got on its feet again. She had first gone to Parity, N.Y., to organize things for Uncle Hogg but found it hard going. Uncle Perce had no job, didn't care, was living on vegetables, letting various poor relatives clean the house for him free (as, Mrs. Dr. Goodsir), advocated free love without practicing any kind of love, and thundered about the suppression of the businessman and the merchant. Dora could not take it. She thought she had better come abroad and see how things were, since no one else was coming abroad now and everything would be cheap. The American buyers had all fled home; she would be the first one for the new goods. At the end of his letter, Philip said that he was running away with this splendid girl, who was not a Greenwich Villager, like so many of his friends, but had a mind of her own, made a fine living, was a sensible radical, did not believe in tying a man down, would live just as he, Philip, chose, and had her own plans for the future. "You can't get bored with a woman like that." This fugue to France was a sort of trial marriage, which they both thought suitable. Nothing might come of it. Happiness might. She admired Philip, thought he had an excellent business head, though she did not understand his poetry (Thank God, said Philip). She admired his genius and she had a general sensitivity which enabled her to understand him, in fact, quite well. Besides that, she was not the woman to lean on him; and even if he left her, would not crumble, but would keep on being the same woman. "The wonderful thing about Dora is that I cannot influence her; at last I have found a woman who is herself! I don't compare her with anyone who has passed out of my life. I have a loyalty to anyone I ever loved, but here is a woman who hasn't even a *velléité* for the past attitudes of women. She engages life in a fraternal combat."

This was Philip's ordinary style. He added a postscriptum to say that Dora's friends, some liberal and farsighted Jewish people, had given Dora the money for the trip, but that Mother had given him his fare and he would have to pay her back. As far as he could see, he would marry Dora. It looked like a reasonably good future and he was tired of being a Greenwich Village esthetic bum. "And it's good for any man's soul to get away from the U.S.A. now! First, they were on top of the heap and now that the crash of material goods has come, the dreadful vacuum in their souls—their hearts! They had nothing but the Elk-accepted, and Love as Permissible in the Oranges." My uncle further asked Mother to find a lodging for himself and his new love, "Say it is for Mr. and Mrs. Morgan."

However, my mother would not agree to this. She found two small lodgings, one for her brother and one for Dora Dunn.

Scarcely were these found when we had a telegram from Le Havre saying that they had arrived and were on their way to Paris. We went to meet them and saw a fatter Philip and Dora Dunn oddly changed; paler, plumper, and foolishly a girl. Her attachment to Philip was too public; it made us uneasy and aroused our jealousy. It was not the attachment of the young wife, or of a clever girl like Aunt Phyllis, but of the neglected woman. But she was not neglected! It was like an unpleasant discovery about someone we knew. Yet it was all a mistake, a passing phase. Uncle Philip seemed bored with her. He was anxious to get to the Left Bank. He rattled off a dozen names of painters and poets, all of which I had learned before the night was over, for I had his fatal facility for proper names. He had adopted the idea that he ought to be a painter and would go to painting school here, perhaps later to the Beaux Arts. As a painter he would not only become a connoisseur and be able to help Dora in her business (they kept this up), but he might be able to imitate, at low cost, models from Europe, learn modern design. He felt sure he had talent. "Esthetic perception is a general gift, provided you have all five senses." Dora seemed to agree with this, but she was a lumpish thing.

Mother said, "She can't keep him, she's gone soft, and she's lost all she had. It's quite right what they say about women, all their talent comes from the fear of being an old maid." She sighed, and said, "I wish I'd even had the talent I deserved on that score. I'm

143

just a failure all the way round. Personally, I don't believe in female talent. I think we ought to be trained how to hold our men. When you come down to brass tacks, that's the secret sigh of every woman, and it's the only way she can be happy."

Aunt Phyllis and Pauline had no time for this philosophy. Aunt Pauline said, "Believe me, you have to be a Machiavelli to keep a man once you've got him; that's no time for getting gooey"; but, as in this case, any philosophy they had was tactical, and arose in moments of defeat, or in those pleasant relaxed hours when active people summarize their experience, but only to fill in time, because they use physical not mental philosophy. Of course, if we had to act on our findings (for I'm one of them), life would be dull. But no, our motto is that of Napoleon, "Go into it and then see; *On s'engage et puis on voit.*"

I don't know how Pauline had got the three months' rent which was payable in advance, but she had taken an apartment in a side street in La Muette near the Avenue Mozart, a *garçonnière*, composed of two rooms with kitchen and bathroom, well-lighted, gay, with two entrance doors. Both sides of the flat looked into alleys. The rent was rather high, since *garçonnières* (flats for bachelors) are sought after, in Paris, by broad-minded mothers and aunts, for their sons and nephews not yet in a situation to attract solid fathers to marriage. One could often see a plump aunt and plump mother in their best afternoon clothes and Rue Royale hats, with sly maternal smiles, invading these little furnished flats on an inside court. Pauline and Phyllis had good taste; and, since their furnishing was not yet complete, they engaged Dora Dunn to help them with bargains in modern interior decoration. I do not know at all where they got the money for this decoration. We had none. Dora had none. Pauline had none. Phyllis only got a small allowance from her mother, and a little from Montrose and Dave. Naturally, there are all kinds of guarantees one can give for furniture got in advance of payment. Furniture companies even propose these plans as a social act and a kind of saving in retrospect; so I say nothing more.

Phyllis knew she must learn her business, for she was too young and innocent. She knew she could be trapped; and under Pauline's tuition she worked quite hard to learn to manage men without her-

LETTY FOX: HER LUCK

self being got. She did her best to become a flirt, a coquette, a heart-breaker, a woman on the make. It is hard to do this; one has to be cool and brittle. I know now, from experience, how hard. Many men make money and spend it all on their passions. Some are able to keep it and have dime and nickel passions, a kind of safeguard. Some women are able to have greater and more frequent passions, it is not all dollars and cents, and this capacity is their capital when they make love their career; Pauline could love, Phyllis not.

My mother sent back a letter to Grandmother Morgan about Phyllis's progress, and although Grandmother had plenty of troubles at home, she hadn't lost her head so far as to forget her marriageable daughter. She evidently was not pleased with Phyllis's affairs. Phyllis was too young. Grandmother approved of Pauline's management:

Phyl needs a stage manager. If she were in Hollywood she'd have an agent, and she'd have to go out and meet men, wouldn't she? We are strangers in Paris and Phyllis can't get any notices in the paper. Maybe Paris is no good for Phyllis. Ask Pauline yourself. I am asking her too, when I send her the check she asks for, whether she doesn't know any journalists. Why can't Dave do what Pauline suggests and get Phyllis on for a turn in a musical? You must invite him to tea, Mathilde. It is all a question of business risk, after all, and then he likes her. My God! You got to market peaches in the season. Why the Society people don't put their girls up for more than two-three seasons, and then they put their pictures in the paper with Chesterfield and Pond's. Even Miss America has to be put over with personal appearances, Hollywood contracts, and a slap-up Atlantic City advertising-men's pow-wow. Then what do they get? Well, some get a man the same as you and me. It isn't easy to get a girl to meet the right man. You got my word, I won't forget anyone who does a little teamwork. She's all that's left to me, Mattie. I love my little Queen. My God, Mattie, you want your sister to let her chance slip by? A woman's only got one.

My mother wrote to Solander and asked him to approach his partner Montrose about clothes and a stage career for Phyllis, just so that she could meet the right men, and so that her beauty could be seen by as many as possible. Solander wrote back, "Montrose isn't exactly against the idea; he says, 'The secret of success in sex is exposure.' "

My father promised a letter from Montrose. The letter came with a small amount of money. Montrose said he, himself, would be over in a few days, also, and would help with his acquaintances in Paris; "I like Phyllis's idea of earning her own living. This is a fine thing for a young girl. Later, she knows how to take care of her husband's savings, and of course, I know she doesn't intend to go in for a music-hall career." He wrote to my mother, "Just the same I think we ought to all put our heads together and write to Mamma, and think about little Phyllis getting married. She must at least be married a first time very soon; she is too susceptible and doesn't know how to make the best of her opportunities."

Meanwhile her friend Dave had come to Paris in response to letters from Pauline, and was taking her around, introducing her to cabaret managers. Phyllis made many conquests, but few were willing to give her a try-out. They thought of it as a joke, and she got no engagement, except for a single night. One cabaret owner, an Armenian, forty-five, had fallen in love with Phyllis and would marry her. He had wanted her as a mistress and would have had her, but for Pauline's management (said Dave) and now was ready to do anything, go the limit for Phyllis. At any rate, Pauline and Phyllis could eat and drink every night in the cabaret, without paying, and were always to be seen at the bar. We were all very glad at this news, even my mother, who forgot her troubles and thought that some woman, her own sister, in fact, could make a success of life. She wrote a cheerful letter to my father and asked him to come to Paris to advise her, Phyllis and Pauline. My father was hard pressed for money. Montrose, naturally, expected him to pay for his traveling expenses. He had, as well, to pay for a home for Grandmother Fox and for Lily Spontini, who had not yet found a job. Lily had at once dug up a young man who would marry her if Solander Fox would advance him three hundred pounds for a toy business in Bevis Marks. He also needed a little money to clear a misunderstanding with the police in Paris. There were the expenses for Mother and ourselves. Joseph Montrose had asked him to reimburse certain extra sums that he had been obliged to pay out for Pauline and Phyllis during the establishment of their home in the *garçonnière*, and which Grandmother Morgan had so far refused to pay on account of the situation in the U.S.A. More than that, Uncle Philip had written him a private letter asking for money. He had gone to Brittany and was stranded there with his girl, Dora. Moreover, Dora was pregnant and had to come to Paris to see a midwife. Solander wrote:

Philip asked me not to mention this to you as he is afraid you will scold him, and I am only mentioning it so that you will realize it is almost physically impossible for me to visit you, much as I should like to do so, my dear Mathilde. You know, also, that I must live, and I live quite poorly. I am thinking what I can do to cut down my expenses, which have mounted incredibly, and in ways no one could have foreseen. It almost seems as if everyone who had nothing to do in the U.S.A. has come here and put himself on my payroll. And what do I get out of it? Very little! I haven't been to the movies in ever so long. I assure you I am wearing an old hat that someone in the office gave me. Don't think I am complaining. I just want you to know since you are still getting a large part of my salary, and we still have the children to look after (that is, I am your husband), that I am hard pressed, and I don't want you to write me a letter of blame.

My mother reread this letter many times, and let others read it. She was happy because he spoke of their relation, husband and wife, and because Solander had so much money to pay out. She foresaw that he would soon be so harassed that he would have to pack off most of his dependents and partial dependents to the U.S.A. and would have to return to us in order to make both ends meet. She wrote him a serious, short, friendly, and tender letter which she also read to Pauline (now become her confidante), in which she asked him not to worry, told him what economies we made. We were very badly dressed and quite a disgrace at school, and she herself was ashamed to sit in a café because no one believed she was an American, but a Frenchwoman, with her restricted wardrobe, and also she was the victim of improper advances; she begged him to send his mother and Lily Spontini back home. What were they doing in London? They could not enjoy Europe! She also asked him to send a check to Philip and Dora Dunn so that they could return to Paris. As soon as they did, she would ask Pauline to look after Dora Dunn and she would speak to Philip. But she felt my father himself ought to come to Paris to straighten out all this; that the money so spent would be a saving in the end. She asked my father if his trip abroad had really been worth while, for here he was saddled with these parasites, of which she admitted she herself was one; but what could a married woman do under this system? Perhaps under socialism she would not be such a burden, a ne'er-do-well, a failure and a parasite. Perhaps the best thing was for them all to return, together, or severally, to the U.S.A. However bad things were there now, she had heard that you could get an apartment for nothing, and that the landlord would paint and redecorate, even without rent, because he feared to have no tenants at all; and he was willing to wait for the rent till things should pick up.

Looked at in one way this is a bargain for us; we need little; and perhaps now you have suffered so much you have got over your obsession. At any rate, I insist upon your coming to Paris. There is much to talk over. And if you think of me at all, and I suppose you must, you owe it to me, Sol. I am so uncomfortable here. I have no one to turn to and am in the midst of all this uncertainty. I am most uncomfortable in the quarters in which I am now living. I never was any good at managing the children, who need a man, especially now, and especially Letty who is beginning to know things and realizes that her own father has abandoned her. She will probably always have a sense of inferiority about men, not only because I am such a failure and can't teach her anything, but because her Grandmother is so showy, and so Letty would tend to retreat. Also, of course, because she will say to herself that she has been abandoned by her own father. You know how the father-image is the first man-image in a girl's life. I don't know what effect this will have on the children.

In a P.S. my mother said that I was sick and needed special care; that French dentists were notoriously bad, and she had heard from her mother, Grandmother Morgan, that a dentist in New York related to the family, would treat my teeth; that is to say, put on braces and look after me in a visit once a month at only one hundred dollars a month.

Since the child is in a sense an abandoned child, I feel we ought to do all we can to improve her health and physical appearance, as well as to educate her properly so that she will not have too much feeling of inferiority. I realize I have lost out. But I am a mother, and must think of my children's health and I think you should too. You cannot be so obsessed with your personal happiness that you have not a moment for your children.

This was the essence of the letter that my poor mother wrote with much pen-nibbling, and many tears and much feminine advice, to my father. It happened that my mother was at a disadvantage all this time. She was acting almost alone, for she had only the advice of Phyllis, who did not care, and Pauline, who was always in a hurry. Meanwhile, these two girls and my Uncle Philip were writing to my father, sponging on him, usually with no mention at all of my mother or us. Yet what was their relation to him except through us?

About this time my father had an opportunity to come to Paris to work with a correspondent of J. Montrose in the international shipping business for a certain time; and he came in order to save the trips backward and forward, and to see us more. For my mother, being ill at ease, had put us both to board in a pension with an aging French woman named Gouraud, a peasant, who was very saving and very exacting. From her we learned French, manners, and in her house we became slim and neat. This was a good thing at a time when I was growing into a bouncing, successful girl, with a figure like a barrel. Pauline used to pay me a visit twice

a week and became a great friend of Mme. Gouraud. She learned at
once all the French recipes. Pauline had been brought up in a convent in Canada. She was an excellent housewife, not only according to French ideas, but because she was naturally so. Mme.
Gouraud, when Pauline was in the house, brought to her our
stockings, pinafores, and dresses. Pauline mended them, embroidered them, made new cuts in old dresses so that Jacky and I were
now quite in the fashion, although poor in clothes. This was a
thing my poor mother was unable to do and Mother often left
Pauline as her deputy in all these things. If we were sick, Mother
came, naturally, but, feeling herself to be such a failure, she thought
she was doing us a greater service by putting us in more competent
hands. Pauline spoke excellent French and soon had a Paris accent.
She improved the accent we learned from Mme. Gouraud. She insisted upon taking us out with Phyllis and my mother, and taught
us all how to order things, how to eat them, and how to drink dinner wines; how to speak to waiters, to chauffeurs and attendants
in theaters, and girls in shops. She gave us rules for acquaintance
and friendship. She had no knowledge at all of literature or art, but
knew a good deal about what was current and fashionable, and had
picked up dozens of friends already in the *lively arts*, journalism,
stage, dancing, radio, cinema, publicity, agencies, and the like. She
saw our different natures at once, and characterized us:

"Letty will be a success and is, in fact, unable to endure defeat.
Jacky is a romantic and will live for a great passion even when she
hasn't one. Neither of these girls is suitable for American life, for
Letty's good looks are not dollar-beauty, and Jacky's ideas are not
dollar-talent. You would both become, down there, just ordinary
neurotics, but, of course, that's a bit of an ideal over there, isn't it?
The neurotic is fashionable."

The bills she ran up for our sober, decorous clothes, were sent
to my father, as were the debts Pauline encouraged my mother to
incur, for house linens, house silver, and the like. As my father had
often said: "If I had had a real home with you, Mathilde, I would
not have left you and the girls—" Pauline reasoned that my mother
would be doing best for herself and us if she spent a good deal of
money. My father had deposited twenty thousand francs out of his
salary, to provide funds in emergencies, and to make my mother

feel more secure in Paris. Pauline's view was that he intended her to spend this for the establishment of a home. She also borrowed some for the wants of Phyllis and herself. Only my mother held back, out of timidity, "I'd look so stupid waiting there with a house full of furniture and two children and a French servant, and no man. What would the servant and the concierge think of me?"

"My God!" said Pauline, holding her hands in a French manner. "My God! Is that what they teach you women in America?"

"Listen, Pauline," said my mother, "you've been in America. Don't do that. I wish I were back home and had no responsibility. That's the unfairness of it; all this responsibility with no one to help me, and everyone suspects at once what is wrong, the French are so quick."

She wrote some of this to my father, even about the silver and linen she was going to buy; for my mother was one of the feeble, and Pauline was gradually getting her way. My father at once wrote back to say that he was indeed moving to Paris, that he was bringing his mother to live with us, he thought, and perhaps something could be arranged, and he begged my mother to make a home for us all. He said that he could not bear the expense any more; even his personal happiness was as nothing compared with this awful burden. He added that he had sent the money to Uncle Philip and that he wanted my mother to find them a cheap lodging, and to look for a midwife who would get an abortion for the woman. "At least do this for me, Mathilde, if you have any interest in me."

My mother became distracted, "My Heavens! He makes conditions for returning to me. I must look after Philip's women, and have that old woman here giving advice."

And she was very forthright about Philip's behavior. He must have doubts of his sexual powers, she said, if he had to prove his charms so often to himself. He must fear he was impotent if he had to get up the bellies of so many women. However, with much grumbling, she went out and found a place for the couple, but this time, together; for, she said, she certainly would not look after the woman in her false confinement, and Solander would no doubt expect this of her; "I hate that copperheaded frow, she elbowed her way into my confidence."

Certainly, Dora Dunn, when she reappeared, seemed to have lost all her looks and assurance. Pale, pimply, fat and anxious, she sat on café terraces with my mother and Pauline; her blue eyes and red eyelashes were wet all the time. She said she was going to England to have her trouble or her baby. She had not made up her mind, and she did not want Philip to be forced to marry her, although he had promised to do so. She refused to go to medical friends of Pauline and left for London before my father arrived. Philip hoped every day to hear of the miscarriage and, meantime, held hands with American girls he met in the cafés. A good many of these were stranded, or had lived beyond their allowances, and expected him to help them pay their rent. One lived in the hotel in which Mother lived in the Rue St. Benoît, a reddish blonde, handsome, thin, well-dressed girl of about twenty-five who looked very prudish, the kind who is driven mad by this very look and is very raw in her ways of getting men.

Philip was, of course, taken in by all women, and as well by this kind. He paid her month's rent out of the money Father sent him for Dora Dunn. Mother was angry, but at length promised not to tell my father, if Philip would reform. Philip, meanwhile, was carrying on a fervent love affair by letter with Dora Dunn, whom he imagined as being in agony, spiritual and physical, through loss of her child. She wrote to him saying that she would spend a few months in England with the uncle who had brought her up, Mr. McRae, and who, she thought, was going to name her as sole heir of his business and lands in the Midlands. "The old gentleman looks older than I remember him, acts as if he already had a stroke, and I think I had better stay with the man who was more than a father to me."

Her writing was open, ornamented, loose, her spelling bad. Her manner was confidential to all.

My father now paid a flying visit to Paris and stayed with my mother at the Hotel St. Benoît. Pauline, who kept Mme. Gouraud up-to-date in this affair, told her that, according to Pauline's instructions, my mother "made every effort to show she could love him and even went too far, to such a degree that on the Monday morning Solander got up out of bed and said, Mathilde, you care nothing for me, only yourself. I must go back to London, I have business to do"; and my mother, clinging to his neck and begging him not to leave her, did not succeed in making him stay. Pauline did not speak of her own failure which I heard from my mother. Pauline had said, "Don't let him see you looking such a frump, and the regulation woman with a grudge. Get a new hat and suit and silk stockings, and cross your knees high. Smoke a cigarette, order cocktails and let him see you're a very attractive woman."

My mother weakly let herself be persuaded and went off to a coiffeur called Rodolphe, who had his own ideas about how to dress the hair of American women. He regarded them as flotsam among his customers, never expected to see them again, in fact, despised them as no ladies; and Mother came back looking very ordinary indeed. He had turned her into a Middle Western wife summering in Paris. Yet my mother was, as Solander said, "of all countries and ages and could as well have been a Japanese beauty or a Spaniard."

My mother then went to an address in the Rue St. Honoré recommended by a businesslike American friend, one of the sort who fancies herself a buyer and likes to get commissions. She bought a blue suit of striped woolens, which made her slender and tall figure look fat and broad. It was not a regular French house at all, but one run only for Americans and English people. My mother did not know this, and her commission friends did not, either. At any rate, the whole thing, the coiffeur, the stockings, the shoes, the gloves, and the striped suit cost a lot of money, looked expensive, and made my mother out to be quite a different woman. We were young then; we were surprised and impressed; but we felt strange with this thickset young woman. No doubt my father felt the same. Furthermore, since he footed the bill, he made a criticism. "Why do you come to see your husband in this feather and fancy blouse? Do you think I can be brought back, Mathilde, by an expensive hat and a blouse with a frill?"

My mother was embarrassed.

"I'm not a lover," said my father, "to be brought back by a new hat. That's an idea women have, but it isn't the kind of idea you usually have; and I think you have been listening to the usual female advice, or reading some magazines: How to Retain Your Husband's Affection!"

My mother tried to unpin her hat, but my father stopped her.

"Don't do that now! I don't care whether your hat's on or off. I know you, Mattie. I know what you look like without anything on; what does your hat matter to me? And I know what you were like as a girl in that little skirt in that socialist procession. Do you think I care about all that? I suppose Pauline and Phyllis got to work on you—" He laughed gently. "Look, Mattie, what's your idea of our future? If you expect to live with me again, you must have thought out something. I wish you'd guide me. I am very unhappy. I don't like to spoil your life, and I know you have the girls to bring up."

My mother at once began to cry, "How can I have a plan for the future? Pauline wanted me to get furniture and we even went to Christofle and bought some silver as I told you, but why should I interrupt the girls' schooling till I was sure? You don't seem sure. You didn't break your relation with that woman. You let your mother live in London while you're living with a mistress. I don't see why I should make plans when I have nothing to look forward to. This will happen again and again. Mother said to take you back and let you have women on the side. My pride doesn't allow me to do that. I want love, or nothing. I don't want all this compromise and sly glances. I don't want my old school friends to laugh at me. Why must I be the only one to suffer? Oh, God! Nothing ever went right with me. I have no luck. I wish I were hard and self-sufficient like Letty. She'll always get what she wants. She feels quite secure though she has no father, no family life, nothing; no money, no decent schooling. She's forced to move about from one country to another, for I'm not able to look after them, feeling the way I do, and living here without a husband or a home, but Letty doesn't mind at all. She's made to survive, that girl. As for Jacky, Jacky's a dreamer. Nothing means anything to her. I don't know what that child thinks about. I envy her. She finds compensation for everything. Both your daughters are like you; they can find compensation in life, but I'm not so lucky. I know I've been beaten. And why? It's just bad luck. Everyone says, 'What a pretty woman,' and I can't get a single man after me—"

"Well, thank you," said my father, smiling dourly. "I just asked you if you wanted me back."

"Oh, what's that? That's a sense of duty. You're just too much of a coward not to say it," said my mother, weeping and touching her large eyes with her handkerchief. "You'd really rather live with that woman and have no responsibilities at all. You pretend to be a socialist, but it is only to escape your responsibilities. Once you have had children, life is all over for you. It is time for you to think of them. But you want to be a child forever; you are looking for a mother. I cannot be your mother. That is why you left me—"

This conversation went on for a long time, but in the end my father returned to England, and Mathilde was glad she had not taken the apartment with all the rooms and all the silver.

Dora Dunn was somewhere in England, writing letters which made no mention of the child. Philip spoke of going back to the U.S.A. alone, but he was unhappy. The winter had come, very severe in the U.S.A. and everyone was downhearted. People were hungry, futureless, there were suicides and miseries. France and England really looked better.

My father came to Paris from time to time, and we often did not see him. In the spring he was going to Antwerp to work for a correspondent of Montrose. Montrose came to Paris to see Phyllis and Pauline, and Mathilde thought that Montrose had even made advances to her, late one evening, but I am not sure that my mother knew what were advances and what gallantries. When my father complained of the expenses, my mother said she would send the children over to London to him; we could live with our grandmother. But, instead, my father sent my Grandmother Fox to Paris. The cold weather and uncertain heating of London had given her pains in arms and legs. She came to Paris and stayed with us in the pension of Mme. Gouraud.

She was much changed, older, complaining, almost demented. She stayed in her room much of the day, resting, fumbling with clothes, sleeping. At all times of the day and night we heard papers crackling; there were little packets in newspaper and string everywhere. Whenever anyone came, Grandmother would run up to them with an open, childish smile, ask after their health, and then beg for stamps to write to her son who was far away and neglected her. Her niece also, she said, Lily Spontini, who had returned to the U.S.A., did not write to her; God knew what she was doing. She was a lazy, stupid girl and—Grandmother would apparently forget what she was saying. My mother was frightened by her and would not come to see her except when she was urged to do so by a letter from Solander. Grandmother Fox continually asked after her and had many anxious conversations with Mme. Gouraud. "Who ever heard of a mother not living with her children?"

Mme. Gouraud consoled her impatiently, agreeing with all sides. When my mother came, the courageous old peasant reproached my mother gently for not making a home for us, "What must your husband think? He pays out the money and he sees no home."

And when my father visited us, she reproached him, too, but in another way, "Poor Mme. Fox is quite distracted, just a young girl, and needs guidance, and your mother would be happier with you both than here. She deteriorates. It is all moral suffering, not physical."

But Mme. Gouraud was anxious to keep us with her, while the household was being reestablished. Meanwhile, Mme. Gouraud hinted, he would do well to glance at the Pauline-Phyllis ménage. "Mme. Pauline is charming, but too continental for this young American girl. My opinion is that she should go home and marry very soon."

At other times she proposed husbands for Phyllis: an architect, just come into prominence, who had seen Phyllis at Mme. Gouraud's house; a young lieutenant ("but it isn't practical, just a love affair"); others, amorous but unsuitable. "She is handsome enough to marry a very rich man, but she must content herself with one of another generation, rather mature so to speak. This is only natural. If she had a home to which to invite them, as, for example, if you and your wife were living here together (I am making no suggestions, it is a thought which occurred to me), she ought to find a husband very soon. Furthermore, I recommend it. She is receiving too much undesirable attention, will have her head turned, and who knows—young girls are very foolish—rich men expect to marry virgins."

My father told Mathilde to write to Grandmother Morgan and let her know that Phyllis was in danger. A certain man hanging around Phyllis, both Montrose and my mother thought to be a white-slaver. She attracted the attention of a very peculiar old woman in a cabaret. Phyllis herself said wildly, that she could not hold out much longer, she had to get a man, so she'd get married if they'd find her a rich man. She didn't mind an old man if he liked company and would take her about.

My mother had many friends who visited her and met her in cafés and these offered her different advice about my father; in general, they plotted feebly to reunite the couple.

"Persia's really stupid not to have a baby by him," said many of them, "but, after all, my dear, that's your chance," and each word was a stab to my mother.

Things were all very simple to these philosophers. They ate with my mother; my mother bought them drinks in the café; her pocket money dwindled, vanished. Mathilde lent money to Phyllis and Pauline, always in trouble. Pauline occasionally got jobs in cabarets which paid poorly in order to use Phyllis as bait there. Pauline was twenty-five, tired and corrupt; Phyllis still shone with her lovely youth, an apparently voluptuous virginity and unsatisfied longing for men. She had learned a lot from Pauline. They had parties at their flat near the Avenue Mozart, lasting sometimes three days, and most of the guests were men; sometimes Pauline packed Phyllis off to Mathilde while she had her own parties.

It was the corrupt Pauline who prevented Phyllis from becoming the prey of these men, some of them being very Parisian, elegant and delightful. "I must watch your sister, Mathilde," she said; "American women—look, I don't want to insult you, but it's the truth—set up to be sex-careerists, but the plain truth is they fall the first time they get drunk or their senses are tickled; the sugary appetites of children. I don't let Phyllis get too drunk, and I watch her like a hawk. I've saved her virtue several times already. I'm a different type; I'm passionate. Her only danger will be when I fall for someone suddenly. I might disappear. Things come along which are irresistible. I think, Oh! God, this might be it, the grand passion. Then I throw up everything—and then your sister would be in danger, for pretty young girls in the U.S.A. are brought up without the faintest ideology—simply this: Get a home, get a husband who is liable for alimony. That's no way to start a marriage. Here they are more professional. But, my dear, the fact is that if I disappeared one day you must at once take Phyllis under your wing. She's as safe as a barnyard chick with vultures."

Pauline wrote to my father in the same strain when asking him for money, and talked sentimentally of my mother's virtues and of us. "Poor children, they are quite out of hand and Mme. Gouraud, good soul, is a bit grotesque."

Then she would write about Grandmother. Once Aunt Phyllis wrote my father a headstrong letter accusing him of living only for pleasure and neglecting his children's futures. Things happened to be tight that week in the *garçonnière*. Phyllis said Solander must send more money for his wife and neglected children.

Lily wrote a gentle, sad letter saying that Solander had never given her pocket money while in London, otherwise she would have stayed. She reminded him, allusively, of the nice young fellow with the toy business who had failed her since Solander had only got him a credit of one hundred pounds, not enough. Now he wanted Solander to guarantee him as an immigrant to the U.S.A.

Everyone wrote to Solander. He had many sympathizers; and as, at the same time, they managed to convey as an afterthought, or in a postscript, that they understood his troubles, that my mother was rather prosy, and that they themselves were ashamed to ask him for the small check which was nevertheless the only thing they would have to live on for the next week, my father spent all of his money and went into debt. This was good for him, said the adherents to my mother's cause when she heard of it. It would re-unite him to my mother, and all they did was calculated to bring us all together.

In the spring my father moved to Antwerp. Grandmother Fox had developed the persistent dry cough of the aged. Solander offered to send her to Switzerland to be treated, and she accepted, while saying she was too ill to take the journey alone. He himself accompanied her to Zurich for examination, left her there, and returned to Antwerp where he was living in the old town, in a single room at the Metropole Hotel with *Die Konkubine*, who also worked in the office with him.

My mother also began thinking of medicine. She went at once to stay with some American friends in the south of France, near Grasse; and these friends, named Pample, now wrote to my father saying my mother was seriously ill, probably tubercular, and needed care. They thought that it was not pulmonary tuberculosis, but something worse, some bone decay; and in the letter was a note from my mother, saying she must have money to pay board to her friends, and for X-ray photographs.

Uncle Philip, who lingered on in Paris trying to pick up an acquaintance with artists, and to pick up some artists, also wrote to say that Mathilde was very ill and that he must make the journey south to see her. He added that Dora Dunn had inherited a little money from her Uncle McRae, who had just died; that a son had been born to them; that Dora Dunn was coming back to Paris leaving the child with a nurse, and they were to be married. Philip could not return to the U.S.A. because his first wife wished to jail him for arrears of alimony. What could he do? His mother was not at present in a position to support him at home, or to pay his back alimony. He felt it would be cheapest for all concerned if he went and stayed with the Pamples at Grasse. My father paid for the return ticket for Philip to Grasse, writing, "I cannot go, Phil; please let me know your own opinion. Mathilde is unhappy, but I do not like to be blackjacked."

Dora Dunn arrived in Paris during Philip's absence, came to see us, took us out, pleased us, and quarreled with Pauline, who felt that her rights were being invaded. After several quarrels, Pauline and the wife-to-be made peace and had serious talks about reuniting our father and mother. "As for the young woman, Persia, we'll find someone for her; she isn't fussy. Evidently she believes in free love," Pauline said; and went on, "I could do something for her, but you see I have just arranged for a concert tour for Phyllis and myself—Vichy, Aix, Marseilles, Alexandria, Constantinople. If this works out we will be starred in cabarets in Dresden, Munich and Berlin! It's a great opportunity. Phyllis is not a wonderful singer, but really magnificent physically. I have a small voice but am an accomplished cabaret singer, and we can get by on that. I am glad to go, also. I am on the point of losing my head about a French vaudevillist here; that's not in my schedule at all, my dear, and I know myself; I'm a perfect fool. My God! And Phyllis, that raving beauty, will never know love. She won't even know whether her sables are genuine or not, but she'll get them genuine, I don't doubt." She added, "What luck you have, you American women! Men who pay for everything and don't ask for accounts.

Yes, it's Protestantism. The men believe they've done their wives insult and injury by sleeping with them. They must pay forever! They must pay their mothers because their mothers suffered to have them. And as for the women, my child," she said to Dora, "they want to get married, naturally. But they behave as if they are disabled for life as soon as they're married. They go in for man-sweating. Every man, legally related to them, must pay through the nose. The law allows it. Oh, Golconda of women! And then one's not obliged to stay with one man. Not at all! A woman can try one man after another and each one's obliged to pay her for the privilege of sleeping with her, but only, of course, after he has stopped sleeping with her: it is, sleep with, or go to jail for alimony. It's incredible," she declared excitedly. "Never in my wildest dreams would I have imagined a country where men went into such sacred frenzies of self-abnegation. All the same, they don't know love in the U.S.A. No, they are all miserable—the men, the women. They marry without dowries, so they think they marry for love. But afterwards—I'm not a philosopher, I can't explain all that. But I know I am happy. Comparatively, I am a bad woman. So some people say, but I have passions; men love me. It's the reason for living, don't you think?"

"Yes, yes," said Dora Dunn, "but Americans love! Philip loves me madly, and to think I might never have met him! It was quite by accident. When I first saw him I thought, I wondered, Who is that hulking boy, sitting there drinking too much, he looks like a Greenwich Village bum from the Middle West. I went and sat by him, and he started to talk to me. I was surprised at how agreeable he was to me, smiling at me, charming, you know. We were together from then on. It was—you know. I still get cold sweats at night when I think I might never have gone to that party. I only went to please my friends and backers, the Gropers. He was a friend of theirs, and at first I didn't think he'd suit me at all. I didn't like his record. And then he seemed weak. But he says he needed me."

"That's obvious," said Pauline, pleasantly, "and tell me about your darling son, Bernard."

"I called him Bernard, after Philip's father of course; but he looks like Philip—"

"I can't conceive why Philip wasn't here to meet you. Of course, he had to go to Mathilde, who is sick."

"I wrote to him that I hope we'll get Solander and Mathilde together again now: we must protect the marriage. I arrived earlier than I expected, though. I made arrangements with the nurse in England—"

"And are you satisfied? One has to be careful with these nurses. You know, these baby farmers—unscrupulous, murderous, avaricious—"

"Oh, this one was recommended to me by my uncle, Mr. McRae. It was a friend of his. My uncle will bring me news of dear Bernard. He adores him."

Pauline said curiously, "They are very level-headed, the English and Scots. For example, he didn't mind your going there without a husband and having a baby? But—good gracious, isn't he dead?"

Dora said, "Not yet. Someone telephoned me—it was a practical joke. They said, 'Is that the McRae Heiress?' I was so relieved to find out dear Uncle McRae was alive. We were always like father and daughter."

"The world's mad nowadays, anyhow! No one can ever be surprised at what happens," sighed Pauline; "but I am very, very happy for you. And since the parents of these children, Letty and Jacky, are such infants, and I am obliged to leave in a few days for my concert tour with Phyllis, I am delighted that some relative of theirs is here. Frankly, no one knows if the old lady will return and she is quite senile; and as for Mme. Gouraud—a peasant, my dear, and an old maid. And you are so intelligent and a mother. That makes all the difference."

Dora looked at us uneasily. She was plumper, but had much of the girl-about-town in her, still: "If no one comes, I'll ship them to their father."

And looking anxiously at us, that evening (she stayed in the pension with us) she sat down to write a letter to my father, asking what should be done for us.

It will be seen that we did not lack for friends and intimates, and that everyone was concerned for us. We never at any time felt lonely or neglected, but, of course, we soon learned that we were to be pitied, and I, especially, would complain about the absence of my parents. I understood everything, I thought. My father was self-ish, my mother lazy. Mme. Gouraud once or twice called us in her brisk voice, *Mes Orphelines*. We felt cheerfully that all women lived in a pension of tears in a whirligig of infinite possibilities as to husbands.

15

THIS WAS 1930. I was nine years of age, my sister Jacky, eight. Solander went to Zurich to bring back Grandmother, and I heard it said that during this time Persia, his mistress, was lying in bed in the Antwerp hotel, and had miscarried, with intent, of another child. My father did not go to her, but came straight to us with Grandmother; and leaving Grandmother with us, set about looking for a flat for all of us. Mathilde was on her way home from Grasse with her brother. Pauline and Phyllis had already left Paris, and were playing in a small hall at Vichy. We had a brief cryptic note from Pauline: "Phyllis has so many admirers and is keeping her head."

Solander waited till Mathilde arrived in Paris, showed her the flat, which she disliked, installed us all in it, taking us away from Mme. Gouraud, and then left for Antwerp. My mother cried at this, but Solander said that Persia was leaving for Switzerland, where she would get a job in the League of Nations, and that we would hear no more of her. Nevertheless, he had to return to Antwerp where he was now situated in business, and would only visit us in the week ends. Mathilde would not live in a town so dismal, old-fashioned, and strange. She had managed to pick up some French, but could not make another attempt at outlandish speech. Mathilde refused also to live with Grandmother Fox; "How will we ever make a go of it with two small children, a mother-in-law? You've been very thoughtless of my comfort, Solander," she said; "it is easy to send money to transport people back and forth, but the fact is you are just following your whims. It is easier to send money than to think, and it is I who have the burdens of looking after the house, arranging meals, and trying to fit in a cranky old woman and two restive, spoiled girls. I cannot look after all these people and the best thing you can do is to hire a maid for me, or else to send for your mother's niece, Lily Spontini. She could live with us, and look after the children—"

My father would not agree to this; and his mother, who was happy at the idea of living with her daughter-in-law and with us, would not hear of it. Two weeks of this life was enough. Grandmother, who seemed much younger, nevertheless had bad habits. She murmured to herself, walked about at night, and was always timidly appearing, with her eyes larger and more inquisitive in her pale little face, asking questions that angered my mother. When my father visited us for his week ends, the old woman went to her room and sat there, so as not to be in the way, and we would see her white head, small and low, like that of an aged child, looking timidly around her door. She was afraid and muttered doubtfully, "He is nervous. She, the poor woman, is nervous! No wonder. Who would blame her? It isn't right. They don't lead a regular life. It's not right to be living in a strange city. Children should be brought up at home. Poor woman, no wonder she's nervous."

She always said this when my mother scolded her, and would run with her head down, her eyes darting to one side, to the kitchen or bathroom. Sometimes she lost her temper, and shut her door with a bang. My mother complained that at night the old woman walked about on tiptoe in her nightgown, listening—to what? We did not know. My father found board and lodging for his mother in a place run for Americans in the Boulevard Raspail, and he would take us out with her once a week during his visits from Antwerp. When my mother asked him if *she* had gone to Geneva, my father answered that she had. We were unhappy! We had wild moments when Jacky and I, who by now both spoke French easily, ran away from home for a couple of hours to see some monument, or some actor, or telephoned numbers we found in the telephone book and announced that a husband or wife had left town for good; or telephoned famous stores, where we bought things on our mother's account, and the rest of it. At other times we quarreled. Our games fell to pieces. Jacky criticized my mother's taste in apartment decoration. I slapped Jacky for this treason. I stole letters from my mother's drawers, and Jacky called me a spy and sneak. Then we would come together again to imagine ourselves nuns in a convent, and get up at night to pray. We began two diaries which we never worked on afterwards. We invented a play from school (we were now in a French primary school) called *The Happy Crusader*. A happy crusader, returning full of honors and riches after ten years, is met by a smiling wife and eight children.

"I see you have been faithful to me," says the Crusader.

"Yes, these are our eight beautiful boys," says the wife.

This play, produced before Dora Dunn, Uncle Philip, Grandmother, and our parents, had such an instantaneous, unwarranted, and suspicious success that we could not be induced to give it in public again. We heard Uncle Philip and my father retelling it for months afterwards. My mother found it silly. But upon our next visit to Mme. Gouraud, who had become a close friend of the family, we boasted of it, recited it, and received a blow, "What childishness! Don't you know that a wife can have only one baby when her husband is away so long? Only one, and even then—"

I said, "Mother is having another baby and Papa was away a long time." All heads turned at this kind of talk.

Within a month after the return from Grasse, Dora Dunn and Uncle Philip were married in the Mairie of the Eighth Arrondissement, the Pamples, American painters, coming up for the ceremony; and after a few weeks of whispered conversations, we heard that we had a young cousin named Bernard at nurse in England, the son of Philip and Dora. This, with the episode of *The Happy Crusader*, and some gossip we had heard about *Die Konkubine* (that is, by listening in corridors) and the advice long ago given to our mother and her new pregnancy, had given us a strange idea of marriage and cradle days, and we produced some odd, dramatic sequences which we found in the end began to bore our friends. Our French friends, especially, were not at all amused and began to give my mother advice, "Letty, especially, is quite a precocious little girl—"

I thought this referred to my school talents. I was book-smart, as Grandmother said proudly. Jacky did poorly in school. But she had taken to hanging round the color and brush merchants. She, for the first time, began to know things that I did not: *charcoal, aquarelle, sanguine*. We learned dancing now; she danced better than I. I was heavier then, and had a fair promise of broad, powerful loins.

I called myself Spanish; evidently I was not, as a thickset little girl, a graceful dancer. I became turbulent, jealous, and cruel. They thought I hated her. No one could understand the change that had come over me: "Growing up," they said.

For the first time I saw that I might not be forever the best, and that people could go their own road without paying attention to me. I found this cruelly hard to bear. It had never seemed to me that Father, Mother, or others could have reason to look at any other than me. I had always thought of them as my father, my mother, my grandmothers, and my sister, and never thought that I was only their daughter, her sister. Once, at about this time, I saw Jacky run across the street. I could not see why, being even then shortsighted. I crossed over too, and saw that she had run into a dark and deep shop full of canvases, frames, and brushes. The name on the shop was Bastien. She was speaking freely, breathlessly, using her hands, to the shopkeeper and his wife:

"Yes, Miss Jacqueline!"

She turned round and saw me standing in the long ray of light that thrust into the shop, dusty, heavy, and yellow as a beam of new-sawn wood.

"That is my sister, Letty," said she.

How inferior I felt! I retaliated in the evening by saying she visited strangers and annoyed people in all the shops: she spoke to men on the streets. Enquiry was made and this passed over, but we received a solemn talk about not talking to men on the street and not visiting strange people. Our eager, mystified conversations about this wiped out the hurt.

Dora Dunn and Uncle Philip were now Mr. and Mrs. Morgan, but this had not conferred upon them money for the rent. They had moved away from Paris after the wedding, for a honeymoon to Corsica, with some money that my father advanced to Philip (upon a verbal assurance that Grandmother Morgan would repay him). My mother begged my father to do this for Philip. She believed that Dora was solid and would make him work. The best thing was to give him this last fling, and then send him back to work. She pointed out that Pauline, about whom some strange stories had circulated, had proved a good influence for Phyllis, who was now earning money for herself instead of taking it from men, and that things were on the upcurve. Although we had to pay for Grandmother Fox in the "American Courts" on the Boulevard Raspail, we had saved the money that would have been spent on Lily Spontini's trip and on her toyshop fiancé, who was still writing hopeful letters.

"A little more such saving," said Solander, "and we'll be in the poorhouse."

"And we are saving the money we spent on board, lodging, and tuition at Mme. Gouraud's."

"Tell me how rich I am," said my father, laughing.

"And," continued my mother, "you must be saving money in Antwerp."

"How do you mean?"

"The girl! Has she gone to Geneva?"

"We lived in one room. I live in one room," said my father gloomily, "there is no change. It is the same room. There's little difference in rent."

This was an unfortunate remark, for my father became serious for the rest of the evening, although, as usual, he came in to wish us good night, and tell us one of his long, extempore tales, baroque, worldly, extravagant—improvised Mark Twainery.

They drove us to go to see Grandmother Fox. She had a small room, with a pale blue wallpaper and almost entirely occupied by a country wardrobe, a bed, a chair, a washstand, and her worn-out valises. On her window sill stood two pot plants in colored paper.

"Who brought those? Aren't they lovely!"

"A lady," she muttered, "a lady, a nice friend. She likes to visit me. A very kind lady, an American lady."

"Aunt Dora?"

"Aunt Dora," said Grandmother, with respect, "no, poor woman, never mind, she did quite right, say nothing about her. She's a good woman, she's a mother, never mind—"

"Mme. Gouraud?"

"Mme. Gouraud! She wouldn't spend that much, not that much," said Grandmother spitefully, her face twisted with greed, very bright and pink, "she came here with her dinner in a bag; an old lettuce; she goes shopping for bargains. Give me the oldest and cheapest, I'll make soup, she says, and carries it all the way home. Trust the French for such pennysaving—pooh!"

"What lady brought the plants, Grandma?"

"I don't know her name. She didn't tell me, and I didn't ask. I didn't think it polite. If they don't tell me, I don't ask."

A week or two later I had a moral inspiration. I would visit Grandmother without being forced to, poor lonely old woman! She ought to live with her own, some said, and she herself quoted long conversations with legendary persons she knew, as follows, "The Spanish woman, a nice woman, said to me, 'Oh, Mrs. Fox, I can't understand such a nice woman as you, so thoughtful, living all alone, and your son and daughter-in-law and two grandchildren living so near to you—' "

She reported this sentiment as echoed by most of her legendary figures, in words appropriate to their characters.

On this Saturday afternoon, just after Solander had arrived in the house, we set out and were about to go into the American Courts when I saw someone I knew in front of me, and held Jacky tightly by the arm.

The person, a young woman, walked into the American Courts with a package in pink paper, in her hand. She wore a pink coat and skirt, had a straw hat, and carried an umbrella.

"See that girl—woman! Look quick, you dope!"

Jacky stared.

"It's *Die Konkubine*!"

How Jacky stared! Then her face came around to me, transfixed. It was like the annunciation.

"Oh, I wish I could look at her. Where's she going?"

"To see Grandma," I shrugged.

"How do you know? Perhaps she lives there."

After a minute, Jacky stared at me again.

"Grandma doesn't know her!"

"Of course she does. Everyone knows her."

"Then let us go in," said Jacky, pulling away and starting to run toward the door. "Quick, before she goes."

But I had more savoir-faire than my sister. I was intrigued.

"Can we wait here till she comes out, Letty?"

"No, come along."

Persia knew me. Persia was not in Geneva. Grandmother knew she was not in Geneva, yet Grandmother continued to hold conversations with my mother, of this sort, "Have you heard anything about—the other one?"

"Why should I have? I don't ask questions about her. It doesn't interest me."

"Did she get a job there—wherever it was?"

"I tell you, I don't know, Mother."

"It surprises me that she got a job so quickly, and in French. She must be smart."

"She's smart enough. I wouldn't worry myself about a girl like that."

I now realized that Grandmother Fox, who had seemed to me a simple, silly woman, just an old woman, was an evasive diplomat. But why didn't she tell Mother what she knew? How interesting intrigue was! I didn't tell Mother what I knew, for I was too busy fitting things together. I got Jacky away from the American Courts by saying we would both go to the canvas and paint shop. It was quite safe for us to go together. I said, "You must never tell Mother or Papa that you saw Persia."

"Oh, no," said my sister, clasping her hands together, and shining at me. "Oh, thank you for showing her to me."

She skipped along the street, dropping my hand, her long, loose, fair curls dancing on her shoulders. She was singing softly to herself. She sang, "I saw *Die Konkubine*, the pretty *Konkubine*, the darling *Konkubine* . . ."

We did not know what this word meant. It had a foreign, interesting sound to us. The following day we all went to see Grandmother. Jacky did not make a false step. My father seemed quite as usual. A box of chocolates with a pink paper underneath it was on the table. Grandmother offered it to us and to Mother. Mother ate a lot of them. At this I laughed, and my father laughed back without knowing why. After we had got outside, I pretended I had forgotten to kiss Grandmother and ran back.

"Always some new trick," said Mathilde, who had been disagreeable all the week end.

"Grandma," I said, running in and bussing Grandmother fiercely on both cheeks, "Grandma," I cried, climbing up on her and tussling with her in a way that frightened her, "Granny, Granny, I saw her yesterday—she came here—"

"Get down and behave yourself," said Grandmother with surprising command.

"And she brought you those chocolates."

Grandmother looked at me for some time vaguely; she didn't seem to know I was there. Then she muttered, "Yes, a nice American woman. I don't know her name, she doesn't tell, can I ask? Perhaps there's some secret behind it all. I don't ask people's secrets; it isn't right, I think. Perhaps some tragedy; one never knows. There are lots of tragedies in lives. It is not right to ask—"

I stepped forward, looking excitedly at her—I was already the same height as this small, old woman, "Grandma, Persia, she came here, I saw her—"

Grandmother Fox seemed deaf, "What? What do you say? She talks, but I don't understand a word! Getting old, that's what it is. I hear nothing. Perhaps people come, and I don't know their names. They don't tell me or else I don't hear. I like chocolate. I said yesterday, Miss Elsie, when you go out would you mind stepping into the candy shop, *la confiserie*, and getting me some chocolates? A nice woman, a schoolteacher who is studying here. A respectable woman, but not like the other one, she is a very good woman—"

I watched Grandmother for a few minutes with sparkling eyes, but she turned her back and busied herself with some of her little parcels. She forgot me.

"I hear nothing; I don't know names either," said Grandmother.

"Good-bye, Grandma," I said, remembering them waiting for me.

"Yes, yes, good-bye, good-bye," said Grandmother, without turning, "always good-bye."

16

FATHER AND Mother quarreled each week end, made up, and went to a café and a movie. My father said, "You said you would try to adjust yourself; you said you didn't want a child."

"It wasn't a trick, but I have too much to worry me, nowhere to turn."

"How long are we going to live in such uncertainty? It's terribly serious."

"I suppose you think you have made a sacrifice? I don't think so."

My father would say nothing to this. Mathilde would suddenly cry, "Oh, give me a little more time. I can't make up my mind. It'll be too late soon."

"Perhaps that would be better."

At other times she said that he owed her compensation because he had taken her out of the labor market as a young girl, and that now she was not only old and unacceptable, but knew nothing. She gave him a letter she had received from her sister Phyllis, marked *Alexandria, Egypt*, with a postscript for Solander, "How can you be so heartless, Sol, as to leave poor Tootsy and Jacky without a home, or even bread to eat? What is to be their future?"

Solander said, "What on earth are they doing in Alexandria? Do you know what that town is like? I am going to get Montrose to send them a cable at once," and he sent off two cables, one to Egypt and one to Grandmother Morgan.

There was a lot of mail. My mother would read a page or two of these letters, all from women friends, and then throw them in the drawer of her dressing table. She had lost interest in life. She visited no one, sat for hours taking the sun on café terraces, and rarely visited Grandmother, who had retreated into a great silence of anxiety. Grandmother, for some reason, feared this new child.

To get the information they all withheld, I now read everything I could lay my hands on, and all my mother's mail. Dora Dunn, now Aunt Dora, had written from Corsica:

My dear sister Mathilde,

... You must keep him up to the mark, and tell him so. My advice is, never to release him and make him pay you all he can. He won't like her so well when he has to pay through the nose for her, and as you know, it is mere carnal feeling and money with men, not as with us, where we have a social duty and our children. You see, my dear, she has been getting everything, his company, his money, and you sit here abandoned and lost, without any security. How do you know he will not desert you and go off to the ends of the earth with that woman, and leave you and the darling children starving? Do not let him think you will let him go without a struggle. Men have more pride when they see we value them. My dear, we must be practical, we women. Do you think Philip would have married me if I had not been firm? Now I have my family to think of and nothing would induce me to let him go. It would not be fair to him. Now, Mattie, don't be an idealist. Tell him you're pregnant. Sol is a great sentimentalist and has some sense of duty, and also of what is practical. He is not going to keep you and three children and that woman. If I were you I would say nothing about the woman. Let him have her! Men always do this. Make him live with you and let her be the one to suffer. Nothing is too good for you. You are a wife and a mother. You have given life. Nothing is too good for us, once we are doing our duty to the state. We are not girls! We are society! Men are nothing compared with us, when we are mothers. We must protect our young. Your husband is obliged to keep you, and if he will not, go to a lawyer, and the lawyer will see to it that he pays, and if he will not, don't be soft, Mathilde, clap him into jail! We have our children to think of. I have had my eyes opened. I found letters in Philip's pockets. I recommend you to go through Sol's pockets too, so that you can keep track of everything. We are always deceived. We must stop at nothing. We women must stand together. Would you believe it that while I was away having my baby in England, Philip was writing love letters to a wh—— of his in New York. He invited her over here to meet him—Eleanor Blackfield. I find he is still corresponding with this ——— and using such expressions! He intended to use her for his own satisfaction and then me and perhaps others. How do you know Sol isn't like that? Do not trust *anyone, any man*! They are all beneath contempt. There are no words for what they do. All we can do is to protect ourselves. So never divorce him, dear, you are doing him *no favor* and do not let him out of your sight. As soon as he is out of sight, be sure he goes to her! I would get a detective if I were you. You are entitled to do anything to protect your home. Marriage is sacred. It is a bond. A decent man does not go back on his bond. You are holding him to his word, that is all. Do not be a fool, Mathilde. . . .

I read this letter to Jacky in one of the long, quiet evenings when Mathilde and Solander had gone to the movies. She listened to it in utter silence. At the end, she asked, trembling, "But if Papa stays with us, he need not go to jail?"

For a few days however, we shook the dust from the chandeliers with our shrieks of laughter. *Make him pay or clap him in jail!* we shouted apropos of everything. *Off with his head and clap him in jail!*

"What's the matter with you giggling idiots?"

The frenzied pair skipped out of this room into that, with "Clap him in jail!"

Our cautionary tales ended with this punishment. I now systematically searched my mother's drawers for these conspiratorial letters, and read them with my sister. We lived in an agreeable fever of excitement. The adult world was more interesting than we had ever supposed, and as to marriage and babies, these things began to make sense to us at last. When my father next came, it was I who searched his pockets as Dora had suggested, and to my intense surprise found the following letter from that active young woman:

My Dearest Solander,

Please, dear, can you send me our month's money, 500 francs. I am supposed to get some from England from Mr. McRae, and Philip from New York, but dear Mother Morgan is coming over here so there will be an interval, and we have not received the last promised, as yet, so please, dear, send it to me as soon as you can. I really wish you could let me have 750 francs or 800 and then I could get us out of here, and we could get off to New York, for home is the best place. We can both work. I wrote to Joseph Montrose, whom I met in London and found very friendly, to write to you about this, and they are supposed to write to you from Green Acres, to help me out, in case we are in difficulties, but I do not know if they have. Anyway, send me the month's money AT ONCE, dear Sol. If you are not in Paris, then send from Antwerp as soon as possible, and send to me, as I am more reliable in money matters than Phil, who is wasteful. Hope you are well, also Persia, and please answer me soon, Sol, as I need the money. With lots of love and greetings and not forgetting Persia, and dear Mother Fox. Affectionately,

Your sister-in-law, Dora.

P.S. Dear Mother Morgan is coming over here to take Phyllis back which is a good thing. She is running wild. Also she has a good husband for her, she says. Ten thousand a year.

I do not know whether my father sent this money. Presently the honeymooners returned from Corsica, very poor, and put up at our flat. Philip was a good cook. Dora said that soon she would have another dear little baby. Solander, quite distracted and tender, said his roof could cover one more, he supposed.

Grandmother Morgan arrived like a thunderbolt in Paris. Cables flashed between Paris and Alexandria. Money was sent to the enterprising cabaret team (which was admittedly penniless and living off men by this), and Pauline and Phyllis were soon back in Paris. Pauline looked a little rakish, but brighter than ever, while Phyllis, tranquil, radiant, was no longer a music student. She had the self-possession of a woman. She sat calmly in our dining room, saying little about her surprising adventures, except, "We met nice men everywhere. In Marseilles a rich man was very nice to me, but he was too old. I like the East very much, but it was not clean enough; every morning Pauline gave me a prairie oyster"; and she declared to her mother and sister, in our presence, "I must marry. I'm not a real singer, and I don't want to work hard. I can't hold out, Mamma. I'll go crazy."

Grandmother had just the right man for her, a young, good-looking man, with business ability: "I guarantee him," said Grandmother. She took her peachflower home on the next boat, and only a few weeks had passed when we received photographs of a lawn wedding, and Grandmother's ecstatic letter: "Phyllis, all in white satin, with her sweet innocent face, looked like a madonna at the altar. We all cried for joy—"

Phyllis, at the altar, had her head swathed in a turban of lace which would have ruined any but a beauty of the first order. But we pored over the face. "How pretty is Aunt Phyllis?"

Mother sounded tired, "Mr. Montrose says she is one of the prettiest women in the world, and I suppose he knows."

"Oh! Oh!"

We spent days in dreams of her and our beauty. The inconsistencies, plots around us, were forgotten. If Clark Gable had seen Aunt Phyllis would he have married her? We pored over cosmetic advertisements. Finding myself too small, I sent for a brochure, "How to Have a Lovely Figure in 16 Days."

17

THEN DOWN came the house that Jack built. There was a series of extraordinary events. We lived in mystery and doubt. We did not know from one day to the next whether we were to stay in the flat or leave it. Mathilde could not make up her mind, or did not know. For a week my father had been in Paris to settle affairs with my mother. Each night my mother said he could go, and then said he could not. He looked very ill. She cried; they stayed up all night; he hurried off to work. We went to school and came home, or went to Grandmother's when we were told. One night my father flung out of the house, and did not return.

"Is he in the river?" cried my mother. "I am a horrible woman, selfish; what will happen to us all? I made a terrible mistake."

We cried. At daylight she put on her hat and went somewhere. She came back very somber. In the evening Solander came home and there was dull but agitated talking. "It is too late," Mother repeated, "but I didn't mean it this way, Sol." In agitated words she somehow explained her impression that life was a sordid intrigue into which she had been forced.

Looking out of the window of the salon, I saw a miracle. "Jacky, Jacky!" I called softly. There was Persia in the street. It was incredible. She walked into the house. Someone came to the door and rang. We put our heads into the broad passage and saw my mother opening the door, my father some paces behind her, and the girl there.

"Good evening!"

"Good evening! Come in," said my mother. "I expected you."

We were shut into the salon.

"Perhaps we are all going to live together," said Jacky.

"It is against the law," I explained to her.

I bit my nails, not understanding why Mother had not dressed up to meet her rival. Persia had on a pretty, blue-gray coat with a fur collar, wore white violets and new shoes. Her eyes seemed very clear and large. She was calm and radiant. My mother wore an old pinafore and blouse with canvas sandals, and her face had that washed-out look that you see in young actresses on the street in the daytime. The fatal three sat talking, and one heard nothing but a murmur. Soon Persia went. The door was unlocked, and we set the table for dinner. At dinner my mother suddenly said, "Your father is leaving us in a week; he does not love us."

"That is not true. I love you all." My father sighed.

"But you're a slave of this woman."

"A slave? Perhaps I am."

"I ought to drown myself and the children," my mother cried, wringing her hands. "Or if you did, it would solve everything."

After this, there was much noisy trouble in the night; my mother wanted to go to the river, "because she was like a girl who had got into trouble."

"God damn it," said my father; "you'd rather I took a street-girl, so you could be safe."

"So I would," wailed my mother. At the end of the week, my father walked out of the house at four in the afternoon, taking nothing with him, so that we were in doubt about his intention. He did not return. In the morning, he came back with a taxi, for his bag, and then went off after kissing us, with tears in his eyes, and taking my mother by the hand. His face was set, however; and he said, "There has to be an end to this."

"You're in her power," said my mother. "I'll kill her; we'll have a home."

But Mathilde and we went to Mme. Gouraud's. My father, whose work in Antwerp was then over, returned to London, taking with him Grandmother Fox and, doubtless, Persia.

Grandmother Morgan, who had taken a great taste for Paris, once more returned, and took back with her her daughter Mathilde and Jacky.

We were thus separated; Pauline put me on the train and I came to London by myself. It was understood that I was to live with Grandmother Fox. There, however, I found my father living in a regular householding with Persia and Grandmother, who looked a little strange, but much younger. It was a fine apartment on the top floor of an American-style apartment house, with a long corridor like a gangway and as many windows as a yacht cabin. There were three bedrooms, the ceilings sloped; the flat looked out all over London. The kitchen was furnished with every conceivable thing, and Grandmother Fox, though whispering and wandering as usual, had this one happiness. She sat in the large, splendidly furnished kitchen all day, or visited the bath arrangements which were extensive and in separate quarters. Merely to tour this part of the house delighted her. We were all out most of the day and she had this undreamed-of place to herself.

I had a surprise in the shape of a letter from Jacky. She told me that although she missed me, she felt it was a good thing. "Do not write me in detail about all that is important, experiences with the other sex—your emotional life; I can understand you, for I also know about this now; and as you know my letters are supposed to be handed round to everyone. I feel well. I am pretty. (But they say I am not very well, it is my chest.) A boy sent me a *love letter*. Mother is going to write to Papa about sending me to Santa Fe. Of course, you know about the baby, our sister, Andrea. I cannot understand Papa. Now Andrea has no father. I no longer admire you know whom (D. of K.). I am getting to understand things. It is settled for me to be on my own; they speak to me as if I were grown up." Grandmother Morgan might bring her to Paris in the summer. In the meantime, she was to go to a private school in New York, where children learned art and had special instruction; and later she might go on to the Music and Art.

I wrote Jacky a nasty reply, in which I boasted of my London school, of how good I was in French (better than the English children), and that I, too, was going to a special school, down in the country, run by a Lord and philosopher. This was not true. I had just heard it mentioned. I told her about a play that I had written; I was in the school quarterly with a poem.

Solander went to work in the City, and seemed happy, if quiet. He took me out a good deal and had a good effect upon me. I was a spoiled child, and no one had taught me manners but Pauline. In Paris I had become an elegant child, and now knew how to behave, but in London I had to drop some of these manners, which were there artificial in a girl of ten or so. I was supposed to be simple, frank, and not too clever. I easily picked up these ways. In Paris, on the one hand, they had sternly repressed any fantasy, exaggeration, or show in my composition. I was supposed to describe what I saw like a scientist, an anatomist; whereas, here in England, all that they required was "an original note"; that meant something you perceived that no one else had perceived. I easily changed my ways in this, too. Once more I had the pleasure of being a novelty, a prize pupil.

My mother wrote to Solander frequently from the United States now—she had not done so before. She seemed confident that he was coming home to her soon, and I believe his letters told her so. *Die Konkubine* behaved in her usual casual style and even brought an admirer to the house, a young Welshman, of blue-black coloring, something like herself. Grandmother Fox encouraged the budding infidelity; but I heard my father and Persia laughing about Grandmother Fox's schemings. Grandmother Fox was outraged and complained to everyone about her son and his paramour. "What do they do?" people enquired. "They laugh," she said; "they laugh," she wailed; "all day, all night, jokes, fun. Is that what life is for?" "They laugh at what?" "God in His Heaven knows what they can find to laugh at all day and night."

Mother told my father that the separation was doing my sister a lot of good. There was no one to compete with and she was encouraged to bring out her individual talents. The price of the private school, about six hundred dollars yearly, was nothing when you realized how well Jacky was getting on. The simple fact that she did not have to compete with me was enough; she now had no sense of inferiority. On the other hand, my mother said, English education was so far behind American, that she thought my father ought to give me some special tuition, too, to make up for what I lost in home influence. "If the child feels she is getting special treatment, that some fuss is being made over her, she will not feel so humiliated at living with an old woman, and being apparently abandoned by father and mother."

My father replied that the taxes in the City of New York paid for tuition for children in the public schools. He received some indignant letters from various members of the family, and even

Grandmother spoke to him anxiously, knotting her old fingers round a letter she had just received from America about "the poor children, who need love." I had a sense of injustice and behaved badly, doing just what pleased me; but I sided with no one, being equally insulted by all.

Presently, Mathilde said that she was coming over with Grandmother Morgan in the spring to London to see me, show me my little sister, and probably to take me home, and she felt I was being neglected. "An old woman can do nothing for her, and Letty was always spoiled and headstrong."

Grandmother became very excited. She had a letter from Mathilde. She said the household must be broken up, for she and I must not be found living with Solander and Persia. My father put off the separation from day to day. Grandmother slept badly, pleaded with him, and wept to herself. "What will I say?" she kept asking. "I'm too old for this. It is madness to speak of happiness. Happiness comes too late; there is no happiness. Oh, what will we all do?"

Though I was in good health and well treated, I was once more becoming a wild, thoughtless little girl.

Meanwhile, Grandmother prepared the way as best she could, at home. Grandmother, lively and talkative in streets and parks, soon picked up friends. We began to hear accounts of her conversations with them, and the incidents of their lives which always fascinated and surprised her.

"Miss Slattery, you know my friend, the old maid, whose brother is a policeman on Ludgate Hill, a policeman, pooh! I don't care about that—" "What do you think? Today, my friend Edie, you know Edie, she works in Swan and Edgar's. Swan and Edgar's, what a name! I always say to her, Swan and Goose. She laughs."

Grandmother invented excuses for giving them tea in the kitchen, but her secret reason was that she felt the rest of the house belonged to the grand people, that was to Father, Persia, and me. But, poor thing, when Persia's young male friend visited them, she showed him into the best room, and was so youthful, pink, happy, imagining she was saving the family, and that we would all soon be reunited, that she forgot who Persia was (perhaps she sympathized with her—who knows this?), called her "My dear," and told him how clever Persia was about the house. She told everyone that her young companion, Persia, had a nice young man paying attention to her. Naturally, this fascinated our visitors; they asked her about "her friends." Persia grinned. Grandmother at once became inextricably tangled in a web of conflicting romances. She was so proud of the Morgans that she loved to brag about their social life, money, properties, and grand connections, like the Hoggs. People asked me about my mother. My answers did not match hers, no doubt, and I, too, was a prudent liar. I had too much to think of to brood over the little indecisions of my parents. I was glad to be free of Jacky for a while and I was so busy trying to argue my father into sending me to the exclusive experimental school, run by a famous Lord and philosopher, that I let things run their own way.

Grandmother's homespun plot came to light at length. One day I heard some strange conversation in the kitchen, and after that I observed Grandmother and her friends closely. In the first place, Grandmother was proud of her friends, but never let them meet each other. Then, though she talked of their affairs continually, she laughed at them. If they stayed away, she worried, and thought of them with greed, but once they returned to her, she satirized them. If they invited her out, she was flattered, pressed her dress and mended her gloves, but she fretted, saying, "What does she want with me; what do I want with her?" She was witty, cultivated; she saw their faults. Yet Grandmother felt humiliated if she lost any of her friends, however poor or ugly. She prepared for hours for every visit, arranging her room, running up and down to the kitchen a hundred times, muttering to herself. She was always ready too early, and sat on a chair waiting, with her hands in her lap, like a little girl in a picture, waiting for a party.

There was an end room, built like a tower, looking over two sides of London. This was the largest of all, and my room. I stayed there quietly reading my comics and girls' annuals.

One day Miss Slattery came. She was a healthy, unmarried woman of about forty-five. She lived with her brother and his wife and told tales about them which irritated Grandmother, who only cared to know how many children people had, how many rooms, and how much money: wishing to know their social status, not caring about their sorrows, their cat-and-dog life. This time,

Grandmother entertained in her bedroom. Tea time came, and Miss Slattery said loudly: "I'll ask the girl to make tea for us."

She went to the door of the room where Persia was lying reading on the divan covered with an Indian weave, and made her request; but Persia said, "I don't take tea, thank you." Confused, poor Miss Slattery repeated her request, which met with the same reply. The big, ungainly woman scurried to my grandmother and told what had happened, but Grandmother, whose ears were sharp, knew already. She muttered, "Later, later! I'll make tea. Poor thing, she's tired."

They conversed in undertones. Miss Slattery said twice, "She's lying down. She's lying down on the divan in there!"

Grandmother reassured her. Then I heard, "She is tired. She is tired. She works. Very hard."

"What at?"

Grandmother's pride rose. "She's learning library work; it's very hard. You have no idea."

"Really! In the evenings?"

"In the evenings—in the daytime."

"Really? You give her time off? You're kind to her!"

"Why not? Why not? A nice young girl—"

"Very kind!"

"She is very clever, very clever—"

On the way to the kitchen to get the tea, Miss Slattery paused in the open doorway (the door had been taken off long ago), and looked effusively at Persia sprawling on the divan, "I hear you're very clever at library work, evening study. I admire that! Trying to improve oneself is always the best thing."

"Yes," said Persia.

"Do they pay well for library work?"

"Not so very well, but it gets you a permanent position. The work takes three years or more."

"Oh, then you must be very clever to do that when you're working as well."

Persia looked at her strangely. The old woman rattled on impertinently. She lowered her voice, "You don't want to do some extra cleaning, do you?" she enquired, like a conspirator.

Persia put her legs on the floor, "What do you mean?"

"I know someone—my sister-in-law—needs someone, just for a few hours a week, and I see you have extra time. They're easy-going." She nodded toward the kitchen.

Persia grinned. "I don't intend to make extra money doing house-cleaning," she said, and suddenly put her hands across her belly and hooted with laughter. She fell back on the divan, swiveling her eyes up at Miss Slattery. Miss Slattery seemed offended, "I just thought I'd put a little extra money in your way, and naturally—"

Grandmother stood in the kitchen door, her ear cocked, and with a grave, crestfallen air. I burst out laughing, "Miss Slattery wants Persia to go and clean her sister's house!"

Miss Slattery turned an unfriendly face to me and then went with dignity toward the kitchen. She said to my grandmother, "I said, if she had time to spare. I see she has time on her hands. I was not trying to take her away from you."

Grandmother scolded, "She has no time for such things! She is doing library work, I told you."

I did not grasp it, but it was funny. The women conversed in murmurs. Miss Slattery seemed angry. Persia sat on the divan with a nasty smile which reached to her ears.

When Miss Slattery had gone, in a bad temper, Grandmother came to the door of the dining room and began a very agreeable conversation with Persia, first praising Miss Slattery, and then laughing at the squabble in her brother's household. I said, "Miss Slattery thinks Persia wants to go out cleaning."

A silence followed this. Grandmother, with a humiliated expression, ran into her room. She came back presently with a petticoat, to Persia, "Oh, my dear, you are so clever, such clever fingers. I do not know how to take up this hem—it hangs, whatever shall I do?"

"Sew it up!"

"But, my dear, I am old, crippled by rheumatism—"

In the end Persia unwillingly agreed to do it for her. Miss Slattery did not return for some weeks and Grandmother worried endlessly, at last writing her a letter. But she had been away to Folkestone. She must have talked things over with her family, for this time she treated Persia with more respect, and though my grandmother tried not to leave her alone, she managed to get a moment to speak to Persia, "You have a maid in to do the work, don't you?"

"Once a week," said Persia.

"Yes," Miss Slattery nodded; "you must have thought me stupid the other time. I didn't realize you were the housekeeper. I think you're very nice to her, the old lady—" she nodded again, with a smile, "a bit difficult?"

Persia did not answer; and Miss Slattery, after hovering distractedly, went back to her friend. This time Persia walked up and down the corridor while the ladies were having their tea in the kitchen. I laughed to myself, to think what would happen when my father came home. Nothing happened. Persia said nothing. I would not have been so patient, or would not have been able to bide my time, whichever it was.

In the summer my mother came back to England with our newborn baby sister, and visited us, as she had said. Solander was out, but the three of us were at home. My mother came unannounced and alone. When Persia opened the door, my mother stood there looking very beautiful in a new dress and hat. She said, "I suppose you think I'm an intruder?"

"You're always welcome," said Persia, and showed her in.

Grandmother, with a pale face, came running, quite out of breath. I threw myself into my mother's arms. We all three went and sat in the kitchen, Grandmother's reception room, and Persia went off as usual, to her books. There were long conversations that evening, in which Persia took no part. She behaved as if nothing had happened. I was taken away that night to stay with my mother, and saw my little sister Andrea. I thought the baby was delicious. I thought my father would be sure to love her. I held her in my arms for hours; oh, a little baby in my family! I chuckled with happiness.

But it turned out that Dora Morgan had come to London with Mathilde and proposed to go back to the United States at the end of the summer with my mother, if she went alone. Dora Morgan was again with child; Philip Morgan was again unfaithful. The intrigues began again, but this time I listened to their plots with a certain reserve. I was anxious to keep Andrea with me in London, if possible; Dora Morgan helped me at first by getting up a household with Mathilde and the baby Andrea.

Dora Morgan had persuaded Joseph Montrose to give her money for the trip, on the promise that she would bring Phyllis with her. Phyllis was dissatisfied with her young husband, a poor money-maker. But Phyllis, since tempted by a new prospect in the matrimonial market, had not sailed. To my indignation, my father provided the money for us, and went off to Scotland with Persia. Yes, he was selfish. Mother and I took the baby to see Grandmother frequently. The cat was out of the bag; but Mother ignored the cat. She pretended to us that Persia did not exist. Grandmother was not left alone, for Edie, the girl who worked at "Swan and Goose," went to sleep in the apartment at night and was promised a fine present when the wandering couple returned.

Joseph Montrose, Pauline, all the old crowd visited my mother and me, and one day Montrose brought with him a young nephew of his who had just started to practice medicine. He declared that Mathilde needed medical care, and at once. With the help of everyone, my mother sat down to write a fatal letter to my father. He had said he would return at the end of a week, but this was a lie, he too was feeble. Everyone was feeble. My mother sent four close-written pages. The words were more Dora's than hers, and she, on Dora's advice, addressed it to Persia. It said, "You cannot kill me as you tried to kill my child," and so on. We thought it very dramatic and expected this letter to do the trick.

Persia and Solander did not return for two months. Later I found out from this Edie what had happened. With Grandmother running anxiously up and down the corridor (she, of course, knew all about the letter), Persia read the letter, gave it to my father, who read it, handed it back, and looked to the young girl, waiting for his future to be pronounced, so to speak. Persia took the letter without a word and enclosed it in her hairpin drawer. After a long silence, my father said, "You must answer her."

"Why?" asked Persia. "I don't answer letters."

Later in the day my grandmother heard her ridiculing Mathilde in an airy way. "She says, one who gives life is sacred—well, well, so every hen and sow is sacred." She laughed. My father agreed,

"Of course, it's a ridiculous way of talking. You, too, could have had a child by this, but you stood by me."

Apparently Persia said not a word about his having betrayed her with Mathilde, during Mathilde's stay in Paris. She only laughed, "Children, ha-ha. We can all have one once a month. How can they be sacred? Plums aren't sacred to the plumtree."

We all waited for some time; no one had doubted the outcome. This was Mother's last card. It was all quite hopeless. She had lost. My mother, desperate, sent a message to Persia that she would shoot her. Persia sent back, "Tell her I will shoot her too!"

"Did you tell her you would go back to the United States with her?" asked Persia.

"Yes," said my father dispiritedly.

"Well," said the girl, "I know; your mother told me." She laughed. "Never mind; it's all over."

It was all over. My mother returned with Dora Morgan to the U.S.A. and took up her place in the ranks of unhappy, futureless, abandoned women. Her role was one more written out for her, slicked over, acceptable. Once this agony was over, she became quieter. She never tried to do anything again, except demand support, which also was an honest employment for women.

Meanwhile, Dora Morgan went to Mexico to have her new baby, because her uncle, Mr. McRae, had gone there for a visit. Everyone now knew he wasn't dead after all; but no one had seen him, or her son. McRae was an oil finder, and made a lot of money prospecting in California and Texas, very often in old and abandoned fields. He was now an old man. He had lots of nieces who expected money from him. Graduates of Sandhurst and Dartmouth were hanky-pankying with these nieces, waiting for the old man to die to see if the girls would be rich, and Mr. McRae felt a responsibility toward the girls, who were all sickly in love. Dora explained all this, and said that if she did not show herself, and her lovely child-to-be, and tell her sad story to McRae, her own dear children would be deprived of her expectations. She was a tigress mother, Dora explained. She had become one of Mrs. Morgan's favorites. She had visited Philip's first wife, begging her to go to work and turn back the alimony, not to jail Philip, as she threatened to do. She had been kicked down the stairs by the former wife's lover. All manner of cruel things had happened. Now she went to Mexico, had her baby, which she named Cissie after Grandmother Morgan, and came away, leaving the baby there to nurse. She explained that since fate and society were so hard toward mothers and their young, she must be deprived of her offspring until she could make sufficient for them all to live on; Mr. McRae had found a wet nurse for little Cissie Morgan.

She persuaded Grandmother Morgan to give her money for her business, which she started up again in Lexington Avenue, with the further help of her friends (the Gropers); and with money begged from Montrose (to whom she had promised Phyllis the very next spring at the latest), she kept the home going. Philip was said to be in misery. He had told her, when he married her to give the child a name, that each would live his own life; there would be no prison-marriage with them, modern people. To this Dora had agreed. But now she said this was nonsense. Then she had not known what marriage was, nor what motherhood was. Society was based on work, decorous living, respectable principles. Philip only worked occasionally. When a girl winked at him, he went to her. Dora found shocking, foolish, boyish letters in his pockets.

"Eleanor, my lust for you is as great as my love! I am no different from the old days, and at the mere thought of you I can't eat or sleep, and my . . ."

Here he spoke of the sexual prodigies he would perform if he lived with her. He proposed to run off with her, "I have made a great mistake."

Dora had heard by now, of the four girls with the eight valises; of all the girls who had preceded her in temporary wifehood; she was righteously bitter. But after the first moments when she disliked Philip and thought of divorce, she hardened with her victory over these other women; and with her motherhood; she decided to go her own way. She'd chain him to the kitchen table before she let him go to his fancy women.

"What he wants from them, I can give him, and he must give me, and the children that come of it he must work for. The law allows me and the law forces him—he married me."

My mother loathed her, and yet thought of her with wonder; "a terrible woman," said she.

Grandmother Morgan said, "Poor woman; Philip is not all that he should be, and she knows how to manage him, which is more than I can say for the others. She's a good business woman."

I went for about three months to an expensive private school in Devonshire, the one I had pestered my father about. We had scientists, writers, philosophers of standing to teach us, and there was no odor of the schoolroom in it. We lived in "life," in the laboratory, in the theater, and in the private life of adults. There was not only a sense of free love, but much ethics of a free, liberal, idealist sort in the school. The owner of the school carried on the ideals of Shelley and Wollstonecraft when it came to love and married life, and the teachers were young, gifted, austere, and fond of youth. There were few pupils; they were of both sexes, and as I was now reaching puberty, I knew a different world. We talked about love and the marriages, free love and legally recognized, of our teachers. We fell in love with each other, and lay on the beds or lawns in pairs, miming a full adult life yet far away from us.

In accordance with the English tradition, we were supposed to experiment in all things, write, dramatize; in all ways, create. As I was experienced at this, I did very well, but no better than many of the others. They were mostly children of divorce, or of separation, or of free-love unions; there were some by-blows of celebrated persons. The school teemed with talent, with a devil-may-care insolence and gaiety, intelligence, and youthful, timely maturity which was different from anything else in my life; from either the wildness of middle-class American private schools, with the senseless union of "co-operation" and "lack of inhibition"; or the routine pressure of French schools.

In one year I had almost forgotten my sisters and only thought of Mathilde in connection with the man question. This made her interesting. I no longer believed in Aunt Dora's principles. Sometimes I thought I would never see Jacky again, and sometimes I hoped I would not, for Jacky had changed very much. She had become a new personality. I feared her. I had lost my one subject. In my school all were carefree, haughty, spoiled, self-indulgent, ambitious, and yet uncertain of their future. Yet we were happy. We didn't feel our age, or any problems. The children lived in an intelligent, open community, with a touch of luxury, a Utopia which severed us from the community. We were aristocrats. In the small town near by, people drove trades or belonged to the *working-classes*. We were above everyone in the world, including our parents. We were the creators, also the critics, we learned that creators, critics alone may be.

I wrote a play which was performed. This was ignorantly Rabelaisian and was, in a nutshell, the vision of the medieval church held by Protestant youth; its name *Muns and Nuncs*. This, a pageant in verse, my first, began with the Muns groaning in their solitude, followed by the joyful announcement of the *Primus* and *Secundus* that the Abbess was approaching with her *Nuncs*, for a long visit. Followed a cheerful scene of the Muns furbishing up the old place, the entry of the Nuncs, and some indecorous scenes of feasting. It ended with the gay clerics pairing off, rounding the great hall and mounting the staircase; finally, the farewell to the Nuncs, with some of their offspring. The Muns kept the boys, the Nuncs went home with the girls.

This was not ill-intentioned. It was supposed to be libelous, outrageous, shocking, but not insulting. We all believed that this was how things were, more or less, conducted in, say, Chaucerian times, and that this was how, at least in part, the ecclesiastical houses were recruited, with bastards, rips, superfluous heirs, and unmarried women; and that men like Erasmus sprang from such loins. A Rabelaisian time, my masters! But such was the adult world to us—every day of the week.

18

SOLANDER expected much from me. He already happily arranged, in his head, a marriage between me and a young duke at the school, who was only one year older than myself. I fell in love with this duke; we made young, ribald love; and for a year or two after leaving, I wanted to go back, as I really dreamed of marrying him, for he was the boy of highest rank at the school. Every girl there had this dream.

At length, with all the extra expenses, and the high fees charged by doctors and dentists to children at such a school, Solander had to withdraw me. My mother, hearing of this, asked for me to be sent back to the States.

I traveled by myself, under the special care of the Captain, the Purser, and a stewardess on a liner, and reaching New York in summer at the age of thirteen, felt myself a woman of experience.

Jacky was at the wharf to meet me. I hardly recognized her. I was far developed, with promises of good looks, and a turbulent, gay, ambitious face, bad manners, no doubt, restive, overbearing. With my mother was a pretty girl, with long hair, well-shaped eyes and mouth, a vain, nervous face, clouded with shifting notions, whims; a face delicate, but uneasy with temperament. It was, I saw with shock, my sister Jacky. It was not the same person. I had no confidence in her. No doubt the disappointment and jealousy of this moment affected me profoundly, and formed one of the reasons for my becoming so bold, arrogant, and coarse in the following years. I saw that the world of things I had learned abroad would not do; I dropped it from my shoulders and set to work to learn whatever would make me a success here. I knew I was sharper than Jacky; experience did not hurt me and it stunned her; it would not alter my looks, while she would droop. I did not fear

Jacky's competition in popularity, but it seemed to me another person had been substituted for the girl I knew. She looked sly and I saw a sort of plausible charm, partly acquired from the local slick fable of women. She swung her curls, was a pretty, feminine dresser, coquettish, snobbish, looked sideways at all the young men and laughed. When I boasted that the young Duke had kissed me, and lain by my side on a cot, she stared at me with well-bred astonishment. "I would never do that!"

It was humiliating. I answered this with bounce and invention. I said he had proposed to me. She accused me of vulgarity and lying. I said she was a parrot, a pet, an actress, and in French, "What a comedy!"

She had not forgotten her French. We quarreled; I called her prig and man-mad. But I set to work to shine in school, for I had always had the best reputation for scholarship in the family—the only reputation. Most of my cousins were soft, satisfied materialists. They already went to dances, had beaux, were leaving school and having a good time. The family, inspired by Grandmother Morgan, spoiled them and smiled fondly at their misdemeanors. There wasn't a serious face in the family. But as I also had reasonable good looks, I hoped to do as well as they—indeed something better than that.

Solander, who had *left* me, as my mother and aunts said, had always talked to me as man to man; his rapid, ribald hurricane of humor, his merry exaggeration and explosion of honest anger, his kindness of heart, always took me by storm.

An obscure but general ambition had been implanted in me by him, or was there to begin with. There was nothing to hold me back. Grandmother Morgan did not know one grandchild from another. My mother, though still young and sweet, was pale and uninteresting, and whenever any subject was mentioned which referred in the least to love, marriage, divorce, children, and the like, she had a sick, beaten, or dull and bitter look, and seemed to turn her back, not only on those who had injured her, but on the world. It was true that no one but my father had ever been very kind to her; and this had gone too.

Grandmother Fox, to whom I wrote sometimes (I must admit, generally before my birthday, and in time for Christmas), adored me more than Jacky because I resembled my father in the face. My father's nature, recklessly generous and unprejudiced, was made to spoil me. While trying to give me serious instruction and to make me honest, in a broad strain, reminding one of folklore, he invented so much, and so often revealed to me the seamy side of things, though always in a cheerful way, that I was more likely to become a satirist, or comedy playwright, or buffoon, or scandal-columnist than anything else in the world. I think at this age, before their daughters become serious-minded frumps of sixteen, or giggling flirts, with their stout bosoms and childish romances, all fathers expand genially and try to do their best for their daughters. Afterwards, at about fifteen and onwards, the relation is better forgotten.

I never was a puritan, and the wild, high spirits I had, which were only touched off by company, and the opportunity of showing off, made me the life of any party if I had no proper competition. But a fiber of Mathilde was in me, too. If any girl were present, bolder and richer than I, quicker with men, I became dull; I drooped. I was often defeated because I would not fight. If I did fight, it was out in the open, fiercely, with brawling and shouts; never in a sly manner, or with slow conspiracy, or with silence. These are methods I despise. They are cold-blooded. Yet, of course, with some, as Persia, they work. I am simply too impatient. There are all kinds of methods.

That summer, I was simply a tomboy, hurling myself about the town, when in town with Mother; and about the garden at Green Acres or at Long Island, to the annoyance of the guests. They did not care for me. Jacky sat on a stool or the bench and read books. The ladies did not like this either, but said she would ruin her eyes. She would simply get up, seriously, and walk with her book to another place.

A male schoolteacher, about thirty, from a preparatory school, took an interest in her when he saw her reading epic poetry, and they went for walks and talks round the garden.

When my cousin, Edwige Lantar, came to the place for three weeks, all this changed. I left off amusing and instructing the old ladies with my chatter; Jacky gave up her books and her thirty-year-old schoolteacher. Edwige was going on for twelve, but seemed

to be fifteen, though small, and with a bird voice. She was a reddish blonde, with a spotless, fair, firm skin, and of a pronounced,
delicate plumpness, with unusual proportions, small waist, wrists,
hands and feet. Though I was jealous of her, the whole family
talked of Edwige. I had never seen her. She walked on high heels,
with her small pointed nose turned away from us, although she
had seen us; she had a slender neck. When she had finished her
walk, she came toward us and looked at us with a little smile. I
spoke to her in my usual bubbling style, showing no concern nor
respect, but I felt uneasy. Her eyes stared at and into me; they
shone exceptionally, like polished glass, and were of an impene-
trable light blue. She laughed continuously, like a mechanism;
pouted her small, red mouth and smiled affectedly, while vapors
passed over her face, but not expressions. There were no expressions in her voice, either; she tinkled up and down. She behaved
like a doll and watched us all the time. She looked at us sweetly,
lifting her face in childish appeal, and at the same moment, her
voice would take on a metallic ring; and, as she watched us, trying
to make out what we thought, her eyes showed something beneath. They flicked back for a moment, showing behind a burning
heart, almost mad with selfishness, dangerously alert.

I don't mean we saw this all at once. Jacky merely disliked her,
but something in me was astonished and afraid. After she went to
the house, I stood looking at her back going away, and gulped. She
was not really very bright, but shrewd and more immoral, as it
turned out, than any other person I ever met. She understood she
was immoral, and she said, one must be. The world was like that,
it was the only way to get on. Everyone was, she said. She instanced
everyone we knew, grandmothers, nearest relatives, friends, she
showed them to be relentlessly but mindlessly wicked monsters
living a predatory life of self, and turning a pious, smiling face to us.
This did not shock her. It was so, she said. She said she intended to
do what she pleased in life. In the meantime, she played the part of
a charming, pretty little girl to all the older women, and became
their favorite. They were no more able to discern a wretch and
criminal than children are; yet children and good women are supposed to sense everything. Dogs, too; and of course dogs like only
their food-givers. From same conditions spring same results.

Edwige had this unnatural soul, and had learned all the tricks of her sex in her profession; she had one. She was a model for young girls' clothes. She played the innocent under the apple bough for magazines, and held straw hats, by ribbons, in advertisements. She had photographs of herself, which she carried about with her, all these ones of charm and flutter, and some secret ones which she showed only to us; in these she was naked. With burning cheeks we stared at them.

"You must have them to get on with men," she said, "and all women's careers are from men. Only pretty women have any careers and although I am not a woman yet, I soon will be, and my figure is good enough already, as you see. You're too fat, Letty, but you will whittle it down, I suppose; you ought to diet, though, or no boy will look at you. No one wants a piggish lump of suet—"

She never spared our feelings, but spoke direct, out of cruelty. "And you, Jacky," she said, "are almost plain. That way you screw up your face to look sweet, and all that bunk, will never get you anywhere with men; perhaps with some high-school boy who'll want you to go out in his car, or buy a soda—you have no glamour, you don't look like anything. You could be all right. You're the grave wide-eyed type, but not photogenic.

"You must get some photographs," she continued to me. "You must take dancing lessons; but not dancing for a career, that makes everybody ridiculous, they get to have wooden faces and muscular legs."

"What will you do with those photographs?" I asked, trembling.

"I give them to people I know, to show in Hollywood. Someone or other will be attracted and try to do something for me. I am not quite formed yet," she said, looking critically at her picture, "and I won't be perfect till I'm about seventeen, because this is the age you put on weight, but I will do. The thing to watch is your hips; if they are right, everything is right. You must have a very small waist now-a-days, just like a boy of ten's; then you must be their type—it changes every year. You soon feel yourself on the dump heap."

She told us what she had picked up in the studios in which she worked, though undoubtedly not all. She treated us as children. My foreign learning, my hoydenish romping and loud, gay talking, my qualities of leadership, made no impression on her. One day when she saw Jacky reading, she picked up the book inquisitively, as if she had never seen one before, and asked what it was; was it a best-seller? Then she asked if Jacky was going to imitate it, "change the names, bitch up the situations a little, if it is a best-seller, then send your version to the slick mags," she said. She could not understand that there was any pleasure in creation. In her intense, limited, keen idea, everyone was always working consciously for their own ends, all of them either marriage, or moneymaking. "I'm going to be a success," she declared several times. "I'll get everything I want."

Beside the frog pond, watching us but not listening to us, letting expressions scurry over her face which were not for us, but to be used on others later on, perhaps tonight, perhaps in ten years, Edwige calmly told us abominable things about adult life. Jacky and I had just entered it, and Edwige, not yet; but she knew what crimes and terrors it had, just as marine biologists can know about deep-sea things with tentacles which they have never encountered. She explained everything to us. One afternoon I happened to think of *The Happy Crusader*, Muns and Nuncs, and the Torture Chamber plays of our childhood. I felt ashamed. Edwige, two years younger than I, would have stared to hear about them. They seemed to have no meaning. I thought, how could I have been so stupid, stupid without meaning, so inexcusably childish? It seemed to me as if my childhood had been one long parade of vanity. Then I remembered how unhappy I had been at times, suffering from the insults and well-meant stupid advice of adults, the shock I had had when I had seen Jacky on the wharf, the pleasure at the idea of marrying the young duke, surprise at Persia's strange ways, and all the rest of it, how I had won debates at school, and received prizes in school concerts, how popular I had been on shipboard coming over, sitting at the Captain's table and reciting French and English —I had a record too. Of course, I was older. I had lived, also. But when I thought again of my sharp, heartless, brassy rival, Edwige, who was two years younger, and of whom my grandmother was quite fond, I again felt stunned with defeat. Everyone was charmed with Edwige; with our elders she behaved like a saucy sweet baby; we did not know how to give her away.

People who are very corrupt always fall lower and lower; they have no backbone, for they are afraid of making fools of themselves, or being taken in by some fine-sounding words. "Yes, I know all about that," they think. Then they always engage in the vilest schemes, supposing them to be the most amusing.

It's necessary to be moral and have principles, even in a really evil setting. It is the only thing to pull one through. When temptation comes, one can't resist it; but one needs moral stiffening in the inevitable disappointments. Who can face his own truth? At the first glimpse of this truth one must fly to the Ten Commandments, or the Thirty-nine Articles, or whatever is your pet Voodoo. Most people are so weak, however, or so deformed by training that they can never take a chance. I take my bearings and then steer for land, but I don't read the Bible in a storm. Bibles are for the camp fire. I adopted some cynicisms myself, but always for one reason, because I hoped to please someone, especially a man. It is not part of my nature. When the usual misery comes in a love affair, that I call the heart's-death, I am able to resume my life just because I believe both in the "inevitability of accident" and the "recurrence of the normal." Life goes on!

When I went back to school in New York in September, I was ready for adventure, social, political, amorous, any kind. Members of the Morgan family were always coming to town, and when Mother would not go to the theater, I would; so that I saw a show almost every week, sometimes more than once a week. I was fourteen. My memory seemed to have no limits. I knew quotations about almost everything ever mentioned in conversation, so that I was a prodigy to myself and to my teachers. I planned a career for myself as a professor, or a writer, or headline journalist. I was no schoolma'am. I was getting to know life and thought myself very advanced, put on airs, hinting that I knew things I did not.

I wrote to Grandmother Fox, who loved me feverishly, and who wrote to Mother very querulously, about home-coming. My French words were no affectation. I was not yet quite at home in American:

Dear Grannie,
I am writing to you on my new typewriter. Mother bought it for me.

We are now living in a furnished *appartement* and will stay here until the end of June. It seems that it is very hard to get an *appartement* now, so Mother is waiting till the summer. I go to a very nice school. It's tremendous. There are more than seven thousand girls. I take a lot of crazy subjects, but only a few decent ones, such as English, French, and a few others.

Write to me about London. What is it like now? I don't feel so homesick for Europe, any more. But I do hope you come here.

I am making a whole lot of new friends. I have some boy friends, too. And, I'm taking ballroom dancing lessons. I got mad the other day, because someone would have taken me to a dance, if I had known how. So now, I'm learning.

I'm quite active over here. We are having a nation-wide student antiwar strike, and I'm helping with it. I went to a meeting, "Against War and Fascism" at Madison Sq. Garden, and I had a good time, because it was very interesting. My address now is Riverside Drive. Later on I will give you my summer address. I myself do not know it yet. Mother wants me to go to camp, but I don't like the idea much. Wouldn't I look cute, in a middy blouse, playing football? You remember my figure? But they have a different idea here of what young girls should look like. They should look like bread sauce. They like them to look what Papa would call "galumphish." Of course, Jacky could not look galumphish, but I could. Jacky, too, is not anxious to go to camp. She hates the idea of living ten to a room; it is something like that. Then, she has a weak chest. Seven thousand in school, and ten, fifteen, twenty in a bunkroom. This is a mass-life, but I am accommodating myself to it. It is fun, too.

I've changed a lot since I left England. I'm a lady (or think I am), now. I wear lipstick, high heels. I even have a pair of blue shoes, especially for a new spring gray suit. Tell Papa I'm a Communist, but a Bad Communist. I use a lipstick made by a Russian nobleman, Prince Matchabelli. (It sounds Italian though.) That's where his hard-earned money goes. Alas, as they say in Shakespeare, it must go elsewhere, too, and it is a shame, but how am I to live? Also, Jacky must go to a dry place for her cough. I think it would be nice to see you here.

There is a very good play in New York, called *Waiting for Lefty*. Perhaps you've heard of it. It's about a taxi strike. With it is another play about Nazi Germany, and it is very good.

You'll forgive me, I hope, for not making this letter longer, but I also want to write to Pauline who is again in Paris, and to Mme. Gouraud.

With lots of love,
LETTY.

P.S. Grandma Morgan is going over to Paris some day soon. Phyllis is getting a divorce in Reno. I suppose you know Mr. Montrose is in town. Love to Mrs. Montrose.

Mother waited bleakly for letters from my father to "tell her his plans" and scarcely ever wrote except for money for her three girls. I got as used to her wretched story as a nurse in a drunk ward, I suppose, gets used to the awful stories of drug and drink addicts. That doesn't mean they don't suffer. It just means you have to live, too, in your own way, and harden yourself. Mathilde always asked why she was ever born and why no luck had ever come her way. I felt, in my rather strident way, that my life was my luck. I could make the best of it.

At school I shifted from group to group—there seemed to be hundreds, and as many social strata as shelves of hell in the Inferno. I had no guide, but I was too young to want one. I don't know what the young want; I only know what I wanted. I wanted, in a way, to be truthful, to find the truth about myself. It's hard indeed for youth to be truthful; revelations never seem moral. Adults lie in order to be moral.

I was looking for the group where I could shine, no doubt. My life was not entirely voluntary and instinctive. I really sought, and found at last, the group in which I not only shone then, but could shine now (although it is no longer shining). I was able to write very well, but could not stand the moonstruck, literary girls who were afraid of boys and did not know how to dance. I never wrote mashnotes, nor poetry. I could not do artistic dancing. I drew, but not well (Jacky drew well). I could not sing at all, played the piano dashingly, but badly. I was taking dancing and piano lessons, but so was every girl I knew. And as for that, we all fell in love with our music teachers, who were young men favored by Greenwich Village groups; we were drawn to their classes by groups of excitable young women who were promoting them, and we flocked to their Town Hall concerts.

I was approaching the Village. I did not intend to waste my life on aimless, accidental love affairs as Uncle Philip had done. I despised his adolescent lovemaking and his poetry. He knew nothing, although pleasant, kind, and too charming altogether; so charming that he could not resist trying his wiles on everyone, even me. We always kissed each other passionately, and my feeling was never that of a niece.

At school I found the political circle to my liking. I must confess, it came very natural to me. I was bold, with a crisp and carrying speaking voice; on my feet, my ideas flowed fast and free. The mere act of opening my mouth caused me to think. Happy gift! There was only one political group, the radicals. The others, perhaps, dimly believed some vague routine they had got from their relatives; these were not ideas, but a shameful inertia, a dull hope of comfort. Action, thought, youth, where there is generosity too (important qualification), mean only one thing—radicalism. A Tory youth is a youth speculating on his future, that is all. He is not much better than Edwige; in fact, he has less observation and daring. As to women, they are, of course, timid. They are afraid they are not good-looking enough to get a husband, or will be horribly bored by a job; so they stick to churches, ritual living, and Mamma. But a glorious and noble thing it is to be a radical when you are young. And why not? You do not have to worry about the rent! Out of doors then and try to do something for humanity. It is all very well for the rich to say humanity is rotten, and for natural frauds and criminals, like Edwige; and it's all very well for certain queer persons of whom Jacky is one, persons of obscure unpopular talents, to dream their lives away, masochists who like to swim upstream, but *active people* in youth should be *ashamed* if they do not try to change the world, but cling to their aunts' skirts and their grandmothers' coffins.

To keep some semblance of life into middle age like my father, into old age like Grandmother Morgan, that's rare! The great queens and Venuses of history (the plural I know is Veneres, but one can't say that) are a hundred times better than the mousy girls who die at the altar and become wives and mothers, model of the year, slated for the boneyard. Dreadful thought! It is like being a sardine in a school of sardines. You can't tell one from another. What imprint do you leave in the ocean wave? The children of such corny cowards are probably worth nothing at all, just fit to make clerks, buy aspirin, and whine at the taxes.

As for mass-action, I am all for it; but I do not intend to be canned in cottonseed oil. I do not intend to be eaten, if I can help it. Then, if I feel this about myself, why shouldn't I feel it of others? Why shouldn't I try to stop others from being canned and eaten? For that is all they are good for if they listen to the words of wisdom of the conformists. Well, this is a stump speech. I rattle on. The mere thought of making a speech, and my thoughts do flow—I do make one—this is an example.

Although dissatisfied, ambitious, unruly, a great trouble, and at the same time, no doubt, a blessing to my teachers (for I did good work and got it in on time and also went in for all kinds of extracurricular activities), I felt I was not getting on well enough at school. I wanted to do everything at once. I thought the school system did not suit me and went to my teachers, to suggest changes. I said, "There should be a sliding system of classes, one ought to pass up or down weekly." I felt myself cramped, and I resented the presence of girls who read the New York gossip columns, listened to the radio, mostly under-bred, silly and poor girls from the Bronx and Brooklyn to whom the gossip columnists, the radio plays, and Hollywood scandal represented the high point of metropolitan life. They paid no attention to the lessons, did not care about getting marks, and when they did not fill in their times with the above, told dirty stories (but washroom smut it was), and talked about boys. I certainly did not wish to be celibate. I wanted to have a love affair, and had a good idea of how it ought to be conducted, but the boys they went out with, soda-shop heroes and drug-store jerks, depressed me. They were deflowered behind a movie house and lay together under the boardwalk at Coney Island. Can women really pass their lives with such men, I thought? To have to marry some such weed and moron, and pass your life with him from then on because you're poor, worn out, and have kids—this is an underworld. Everything that hurried me away from that cruel prospect was good to me; my financial luck convinced me that I was very superior to these five-and-ten humans, getting their Shakespeare out of a juke box and lucky to get legally married to a taxi driver.

I didn't spend any time on these girls. Frankly, they did not exist for me. I scarcely saw them. They were badly dressed, and without taste. I was badly dressed too, that is, for the group I was in, the daughters of the middle classes, the "medium price class" as my irreverent papa said; but was not without taste, and there was always the thought that things might get brighter, that Grandma might suddenly give me twenty dollars, or Papa might decide to make Mother cut the rent and so have more to spend on us. Whenever I went to Green Acres or Long Island, I felt depressed, for there they felt it a great shame that Papa did not give us the proper things; I don't have to describe them, the things that are advertised for college girls in all the smooth-paper magazines. These visits were not good for my morale. In between I was happy and intoxicated with my social success.

My mother persecuted Jacky and me to keep up our correspondence with our father, and most of these letters were written with a money motive. This was natural, as the Morgans persisted in their single notion, that if Mother loaded Papa with debts, he would be forced to return to this country. When I was some months over fourteen, I wrote to Solander, from camp,

Dear Papa,

I am having a grand time here. Saturday night we had an annual sing. Instead of the poetry song competition, this was more of a pageant representing the evolution of man; in 6 Freezes which, in turn, came to life and showed the spirit of the time and its contribution to our modern era. Directed by one of Martha Graham's group members, Beth, one of the counselors, it attained depths unseen by most of the audience, but nevertheless present. Naturally, she's a comrade.

The first Freeze was the primitive one. Not the prehistoric

brute, or the Negroid jungle inhabitant, but man at the beginning of the famous Darwinian link. Dressed in scanty, ruddy,
earthy browns and reds the Freeze began. Previously an
announcer had read a prologue and 2 stanzas relating to the
age. (This was done before each tableau.) Then, an invisible
chorus recited in chant (not original, but plagiarized from
Van Doren's anthology). Then the tableau came to being and
preceded to expand its surplus energy, to show its freedom
and straightforwardness, its lack of inhibitions. At the conclusion, the lights went out for the second Freeze. The Archaic
Freeze was remarkable, because it really conveyed the spirit
of Egypt, Greece, and Rome. It had the 2-dimensional flat-
ness, the bas-relief effect, of the Egyptians. The robes of blue
and green showed the artificial getting away from nature and
the civilization and debauched culture already arisen.
During an interval of the dance, the invisible but not celes-
tial chorus sang a Pythian Ode to Ra, the Sun God. (Sounds
as if I were at a tea, saying, Oh, yes, Albert Jones, the painter,
you know.) Then the 3rd Freeze, the medieval representing
the omnipotent power of the church. It began with what
looked like a painting by Leonardo or Raphael, with the
inevitable Infant Jesus. Then the monks expressed their
dance motif as the suffering martyrdom, sacrifice of the
period. A stained glass window as a background. A Bach
church song by the camp prima donna. The music for the
chancel, Borodin's "In a Convent." (I thought of Hugo Wolf's
songs, but it would have been impossible to get them.) Finally, so enmeshed in its cleverness and devotion, the church
falls to a doom which has not yet been repealed.

4th Freeze. The Court. This was more pantomine than
dancing. Though the costumes were reminiscent of an English or German court, by the heavy brocades and brilliant
hues, the period was the Spanish Inquisition, this last recognizable by the ominous braun garb of the monk of the affair.
A typical intrigue, arrogance, despotic rule, absolutism, natural causes of a revolution all trodden under the garb of court
intrigue. (Remember my play of the name?)

5th Freeze. Romantic. Not the mushy, popular conception

of the epoch, but the splendid, materialistic, awakened romanticism of Shelley and Hugo, the Napeolonic Age and the War of 1812. The dance, naturally, had to symbolize curving, flowing flare, high-waisted flimsiness and ephemeral and evanescent charm. Yet, something less esthetic and airy floated through the dance and gave it a true consciousness.

6th Freeze. Modern, clad in RED evening gowns, the modern divided itself into 2 parts. 1. Lazy—the rich, sensual. 2. The social view, the awakening of youth, its sudden realization of power, its foretelling of the future. At the end, the inhabitants of each age, simply clad men and their mates of the awakening age, corrupt and brilliant citizens of Rome, somberly clad and somberly thinking priests of the time of Charlemagne and, eventually, the Borgias, decorative and ornate courtiers of Ferdinand and Isabella of Castile, flighty and sensible romanticists, and the contradiction of inhibitions, releases, retrospections and futurisms of modern youths, all of these gathered in a homogeneous group which sang the new camp songs, songs to Mrs. B. (you don't know her—she really is a lovely person and a true mother, besides being a shrewd business woman and one of the most well-educated persons I've met). Song to our head-counselor, Betty; song to all the counselors, and song to Rosie, junior dancing counselor, who's been with the camp for years. (There's a secret, she's a C.P. member.)

The sing took everything we had out of us, but before that I'd been having an exciting time. First, we play tennis, volley ball, basketball, and go canoeing a few times a week. Swimming twice a day; I can almost do the crawl and am beginning diving. If I keep it up, next summer I'll be able to take my junior life saving. Then we have dramatics. The big play is going to be *Lysistrata*, the Aristophanist anti-war play. Dancing, music, hikes every Wed. and arts and crafts, where I am secretly making Mother a leather engraved book cover. It's costing $2 but she'll like it. Then camp is liberal. Here's an example of the schedule: Monday night—club night: dancing, dramatics, pioneering, everything. Tuesday—boating. Wed.—dress up and games. Thursday—bunk night. (Each bunk in turn entertains.) Friday—concert. Saturday—the play of the week. Sunday night—camp fire and a reading of the Weekly Newspaper, to which I've contributed at least 2 articles every week. If I come back, I'll be editor next time. If I weren't so young, Mrs. B. would make me a counselor in training. My age would annoy the seniors, however. But—(this is confidential) Mrs. B. thinks I am more mature than the 17- and 18-year-olds.

Your letter brought up two points to be cleared up. 1. If you don't come back to the U.S. soon, what of Grandma? And why can't you come, anyway? 2. Your letter was dated Aix-les-Bains, July 20. Your envelope, in your handwriting, was postmarked London JULY 20. You seemed insistent to let me believe you're in Switzerland, when you're in London. Why? What are you trying to hide?

I've just finished Turgeniev's *Father and Sons*. I loved it, but it put me in a singularly dejected and dippressed mood. Added to that, Cecily's death! Did anyone tell you? We were at camp and it was hard to write and hard to believe. She could not marry that boy. They wanted them to finish college and they both tried to commit suicide. She hung herself from a beam in "The Wreck." He must have helped her, for he was there, lying on the floor and had shot himself, but not enough. He is getting better, but she is dead. He will be charged with murder. I can't face it. No one can. They all say she was mad and selfish and so on and they must have done something wrong (that means, made love), or they wouldn't have felt so guilty and had to commit suicide. I can't see why making love would make you commit suicide, and this to me is a lot of *jibberish*. I don't think they really know why, or they don't want to admit. Lots of children my age want to get married. At camp we are all in love. We see their parents married, and we don't understand why not. Aunt Amabel's little girl (you remember Amabel—that was in Uncle Philip's past) is terribly spoiled, like all the children of real radicals, they are the worst spoiled of all. They let her do and say anything, and they tell everyone. She's quite a brat, but nice, soft, blonde hair and all that. She told her mother (aged 7—the girl I mean, her name's Joanna) some boys wanted to (unmentionable word) let's say initiate her, behind the bushes. She asked her parents, well, if I can't now, *when*? They said, wait. She said, I suppose that's another of the things that only you grown-ups can have? Everyone thinks it's so *cute*. I'd spank! But anyhow, adults really don't know what's going on in submerged youth these days. We protect you from the awful truth.

I'm just talking like this, but I feel terrible about Cecily, and so does everyone, and Uncle Percival Hogg has no explanation; he has a lot, but his chin is hung on his boots, and he tries to blame it on everyone, but not on himself. Aunt Angela says it's his terrible example. Example of what? Everyone talks baloney.

Please come back to the U.S. It's terrible here, because apart from the community life, and the sings and the newspapers, all that, there are these other things. We seem to live more than our parents. Or, I don't know, maybe that's how parents live.

I'm writing baloney. I just discovered Shelley's *Prometheus*. Is that a masterpiece of Marxist theory and dialectics?? and Poetry! If you do come back try and smuggle some books and new art in on your ticket—yours! From England, I mean.

I appreciated your analysis of the European scene for me, though I admit things look extremely bad for, not only the Spanish and French Popular Fronts, but also the pacifists. However, I do not think there is any danger of war for at least six months. If only the fascists could be crushed, what has been accomplished by the leftist gov. is or would be an advance toward a more radical cabinet. I was one of the few Y.C.L.'ers selected for duty on the honor guard at the C.P. Convention. We got in free, dressed all in white, and paraded around. Madison Sq. Garden was packed. The enthusiasm after the nomination of Browder and Ford was something to make you feel inspired and grand. After each nominating speech there was $\frac{1}{2}$ hour parade ovation and we ran way up even to the uppermost balcony, and paraded around. The sight of 25,000 faces clapping as you clench your fist and themselves singing the Int'l is something hard to be missed.

At Camp besides Margot, my friend, who was in France, only not when I was, we have 3 Y.C.L'ers, 2 C.P. members and a few sympathizers, among whom is Dr. B. (He is a retired professor; his functions around the camp are pretty much the same as Grandfather Morgan's at Green Acres before he was taken ill, and the same is true of the husband of the Ranking Counselor, who is a retired musician. They sit around and grin knowingly when their wives do their acts.)

I suppose you heard of the death of "Argentina"? I wept for an hour at the news, and felt blue for a long time. Margot too.

Please write more often. Mother is well. She has not rented the apt. and is waiting for DEFINITE news from you to select another one for the Fall. Will we be allowed $25, 45, 75, 100, or 125 a month for rent? I am not trying to be funny. Please give me a sane address and a clear explanation of what you're up to. I don't mind living hand-to-mouth, but there are *four* of us and *Jacky must go away*.

I'll write again just before I leave camp and after when I find out if I've passed my exams. I'm studying American History and English by myself. Please send me the Cambridge entrance requirements, courses and lists in general of all needed for admission, living and study. That is, if you still wish me to go there. If you do, we'll have to count in my living separate from Mother, and you'll have to calculate what she and Jacky and Andrea will cost you here. That is if you still count on us living like this. I might like Radcliffe, but it has not B.Sc. Regents. If your monetary status is low, I suppose I shall pig it in Brooklyn College. Do you remember the $5,000 of Grandmother Fox? Why don't you give it to her to spend, so she can live where and how she likes and furnish a little place for herself comfortably? She speaks of wanting to live apart from you, with that English girl she knows, who works in Swan and Edgar's. This is my own bright idea— honest, cross my heart—not "inspired," as you sometimes think. This girl Edie that I saw, that I know of, comes from nice people, radicals; they are even related to some good family, I don't know which, and Grandma is ashamed not to have a good place to offer her, although she is poor. But the girl is 28, wants to get away from home. That I understand. I'm not for the united family. (Good thing, is so? Ha?)

Lots of love,

LETTY-MARMALADE

Always in a Jam.

P.S. Is the article on Spain in the *Sunday Times Review of the Week* by the same Blank of Harvard you inspired in London? Have you anything to do with it? Your doctrines, I recognize! You're a great deseminator, aren't you?

P.P.S. How is Mr. Montrose and everyone we know? Dora Dunn (Morgan) is talking of getting a divorce. She now despises and neglects Philip UTTERLY. But she says the thought of the children makes her stop. Then, going to Reno is expensive and New York State is a scandal it seems, and to marry you must get a court order, and it's all an imbroglio. But, of course, that would be Philip who would have to get the Court Order, because, believe it or not, Tall, Dark and Handsome is in love again, and goes to work to prove it. Oh, why do I know so much? (Because what you know here, makes what you know in those corrupt England and France a laugh!) Well, because I am your dotter, Pop; and you know so much. But, it didn't do you any harm. (Or did it? Answer me that one day.) And again (it's time),

Your dotter, LETTY FOX.

P.S. Mother says it is "Frieze" not Freeze; well some of them act frozen.

The $5,000 mentioned was of great interest to us, as Grandmother had promised it to Jacky and me on her death.

19

M<small>Y</small> S<small>ISTER</small> went out West with Grandmother Morgan not long after this. They visited Aunt Phyllis who was about to kiss the column in Reno, and after trying Albuquerque went up to Santa Fe. All this traveling about was not necessary, but Grandmother was curious about the entertainment given to visitors in the hotels there. She found some friends for Jacky to stay with in Santa Fe, left her there, and made her way to the Coast; the jaunty old belle not only hungered for new scenes, but thought she might drum up business, even establish a hotel, and might meet some presentable rich men of her own type. "I am sick of local men," said Grandmother.

Santa Fe is, among other things, an art colony and a little palace of American culture; under its astronomical skies are sierras and sun-bitten plains, on which old nations spilled blood and died. My sister was intoxicated with happiness there; her particular genius visited her there. She did not write to me very often; she said the fine mountain air which was curing her was hard to breathe, but she was healing. Everywhere she was taken for older than she was. She had entered her teens. She now drew away from "street-kisses, those slight touches in the dark—to me now this is banal; I know it is not love; though I don't despise it—I don't despise *anything*." About Christmas 1934 she wrote to me:

Dear Letty,

I waited for you to write to me about the marriage of the Princess, to send my answer on that, but I can wait a long time it seems. I am getting slowly cured at Santa Fe; I cannot come to New York now. I'm under doctor's orders which are, still, that I must take a complete rest. A single visit wears me out, as well as the least change in my routine. Of course, it is partly the altitude, which is enormous. I have been feeling funny since last September and didn't manage to get fat and still had fever, thus I could not come home for vacations or birthdays and such. Poor me! Write to me quickly about everything that is happening in your part of the world—and even, is it always the same part? A stupid thing—some people die here. I read about burials with such interest! Do I think I am going to be buried? Probably; but it is with pleasure I read about them—and then I should like to be somebody, to be buried with ceremony. Hélène Boucher was the fastest woman in the world and beat the altitude and endurance records. The requiem mass took place in Napoleon's chapel which you and I have seen! You know what an immense honor that is! She is the first woman buried in the Invalides! All the aviators were there, Détroyat, the handsome, the others. The Invalides was full of *white flowers* for this woman, she was cited on the order of the day. I feel marvelously happy. She earned this and they recognized her; she is a heroine. A film star is nothing to compare with that! If I am not famous, too, why live, why die? How splendid life is when you have such possibilities. I see to the *full* all the possibilities of living. Today is a wonderful day—a dry winter's day—I long for the spring; you do not know Santa Fe, you look from the Cerro Gordo (Plump Hill!), it looks like Jerusalem, it lies in a bluish haze in which swim trees and white walls and mud cabins in a flesh-colored crease of hills, which suggests birth—somehow—and between a few streaks of cloud and these dark glittering clear trees, the sky is so blue; bloody light (the Blood of Christ) spreads down the mountain, in the fall. One wants to run about on the hills in a thin fluttering dress—but I can't run a step. I don't think anyone can. You are not supposed to gallop the horses. There is a lovely Mexican girl here with an Aztec face; she rides astride and looks fiercely ahead or aside as if she could see through the rocks. She never looks at me. Perhaps she is jealous; I am certainly good-looking too. I go out to see her ride by. But each step one takes is an extra burden on the shoulders, heart, and lungs; one feels like a pack mule and then how disgustingly I am writing, heart, lungs—I am ashamed to think of such things. What I said above, about the death of this woman, has made me think. Thinking about someone dead, one says, Why is he dead? You will say (materialist), "Because he doesn't breathe, because his heart has stopped." But why doesn't he breathe, why did his heart stop? It went before. Perhaps, you'll say, it was worn out, along with the other organs, the veins, the lungs, the brain. But—what now? I know the mechanism of the body is perfected; and since it stopped, it must have at one time *been set in motion*! There is no perpetual motion in our physics! It couldn't have been an accident that made the first men breathe, that is, that all this immense stupefying mechanism started to move by chance. And then the whole thing—for example, not only how many roofs I see when I look at my little Jerusalem, but how many other eyes these two little pieces of me can see and with them communicate! I am staggered. I think it's marvelous and I can't stop myself thinking that God must exist; don't send me jokes about this Idiot imagined by the Ironic thinkers; that he might well exist and lead a vegetable life of his own, without any more influence on us than a tree in Thibet. I know how they think, the Ironic thinkers, like Voltaire; their preoccupation (with God) perhaps shows they are sure about him—probably they're only trying to cure us of our weak, babyish ideas about God; trying to make us think the way they think. I cannot believe such Great men do not believe; and for contempt of that Idiot God which they despise, I have it too; but the God of my eyes, I believe in. About Voltaire—if you haven't read anything, read *Candide*—read it, marvelous! I read everything in the bookshelf in the dining room. I don't think I told you that I met a prince here, Prince Wolkovski, and my first impression of him was that he is *irresistible*! He is staying with his family in a rented mud-palace at the end of Acequia Madre. Imagine a room covered with sabers and fencing-irons, etc., of all countries and times, old ones of the fifteenth century, above all, the saber of a Tsar, a samurai sword, a

Chinese double-edged beheading sword, daggers, a woman's stiletto to hide in the bosom; I was enthralled. How I long to possess a pair of foils; I begged him to tell me where I could learn fencing. He laughed aloud at my astonishment and was charming to me; he gave me two records, *La Tosca*, "the stars are shining," a Russian song, "All Russia is under snow," and a Russian foxtrot. He went to a university in the U.S.A. and told me all his impressions. He is a friend of several American and French writers, but only chic, correct, and rich ones. His description of radicals made me burst out laughing, for he does not know I *know* one: they are people who don't wash, don't pay their bills, and are impossible as friends because they quarrel. We talked about Russia and I asked him if the Tsar wasn't a coward. He smiled, saying I was awfully violent and that the profession of a Tsar is to be behind the lines and that it is for the generals, who are his aides and lieutenants, to be in front. A chief must save his life. This was a new idea for me; I do not know what to think. He lent me some books. His looks are very Russian as well as his accent. I drank some vodka with pepper in it and he was amused because I insisted on the pepper—according to him, "my throat is very Russian and I might even be a Russian young girl from my looks." This pleased me enormously, it is only in this way that we get confidence in our charm— so I had a wonderful afternoon with a fascinating man and afterwards they told me I could brag about it (as I am now doing) because he is rarely so pleasant. His father was a high general in the Tsarina's army and it seems this is a very great honor; his mother, whose photograph I saw, was a marvelous beauty and he has personal photographs from the Tsar and the Tsarina. I drank wine with him yesterday marked 1908! In spite of all this, I am not becoming a White Russian. But I am delighted to know him. This is really the kind of friend I want to have, at least until I know the world better; then perhaps my taste will be *faultless*, but it is not now. Enough gabbling for today; au revoir. Write to me. I want you to. I am at Santa Fe until further notice.

Your Jacky.

P.S. And when I came out of the house, the Aztec princess was passing by on her big bay mare, her face as inscrutable as ever and white kid Wellingtons on, and her legs brown underneath. I have never been so happy as here.

P.P.S. I was going to tell you all kinds of things about the Princess, and about Carol of Rumania; I am in touch with people here who are close friends of both, of course, they are all related, by marriage. Well, about the Princess—all they say is *absolutely true*. And, in addition, before the marriage her relatives never paid their bills, but lived on afternoon teas and dinners and only bought evening clothes and afternoon suits and stayed in bed till midday; and they didn't pay for any of them; they had no jewels at all, not a single automobile and they did not give one wedding present at any time! And this is the second time; but the first time the Princess married a Prince who was overthrown within six months and had no chance to send any money to the family and they feared they would *never* get her sister off. Also the famous Prince of ——— whom I always loved so madly, or so I thought, was very friendly, in fact, intimate with the Princess who is now married to his own cousin, in fact two depraved society types together—so depravity inbreeds, does not spread; good! I am sharp because I admire him so much and so I blame him. I am not making any more collections of photographs, with two exceptions, Katharine Hepburn and Joan Crawford. Andrea will be happy—tell her to take all my dozens of Boyers, Garats, Gables, Coopers, etc. A surprise for her. At one of my friends' here, there is a Peter Paul Rubens guaranteed *authentic*! It is a long low mud-mansion behind trees; you enter by a bridge over the ditch. You are invited to dinner and afterwards the hostess, who is very imposing, and in a white lace gown, draws back a black veil—there it is! I looked closely; I do not think it is a Rubens. I did not dare mention my suspicions to others, but I have heard whispers since— Then, there is a formidable, frowning building on the hill, it is terrifying, like that of a bloodthirsty Mexican king or chief; but a painter lives there. Oh, how delicious, noble it is to be wealthy, I get a wild exultation, some are vulgar, but there is no need to be. I look out at the slopes, the roads, the fall of the mountains, the view, and the treasures my hosts own—"the loot of centuries" you say—oh, to possess —the joy—the mad fervor—and yet I collect nothing but photographs and autographs. I am not an egotist. But, to possess beauty! I shall never have the money unless I marry a prince or an aristocrat or a wealthy artist for I could not be content with what is vulgar. I look at myself now in the looking glass and say, "I am beautiful, but am I beautiful enough for that?" I am also learning drawing from a gifted superb marvelous woman, full of raging pride, scornful, rough—you can see she has dreamed of fame and of conquering everyone. They say she was a great beauty. She is only here for the winter. I look at her and think, "I won't admire you, Mrs. Headlong, my darling, I won't hero-worship you, I won't kiss your long feet, for you are a Tartar, a demon, and I do not intend to bend the neck to anyone, not even my husband the Prince." So I don't admire her. The woman I am drawing is naked, young, but not a girl and she is twisted with grief, horrible and yet lovely because she is a young voluptuous woman. They say I should practice more on the living model, before I can manage such things. Young people want to do tragic brutal active things, but they say, there is beauty in repose. I am impatient with repose. I am buying reproductions in color and am studying not only the modeling but the basic designs and am shocked to see the simplicity and almost vulgar force and plain meaning. I dare not point certain things out to people. I am dizzy. What is art? *Jacky*.

Another Day. I had not the strength to go to the post office to get stamps and no one had any. Besides, you did not write.

King Carol is in all sorts of involvements; cannot travel, cannot move from one country to another and it seems his wife controls him *absolutely* and is really very brilliant, a woman of state, like the Pompadour. Only to think of it! I regret I could not go to Rumania. I know so many people now who know Carol. I am promised an introduction if I travel there. I met a Rumanian priest who lives in an orthodox monastery at Jackson, near Detroit, and he is a remarkable, dazzling, strange and—dangerous—man; dangerous to women. I can tell now. But I cannot tell you all the people I meet; and I only speak about the interesting ones, for I am *turning my back* upon everyone who has not done something brilliant, extravagant, courageous, adventurous—for what is the use of living otherwise? Only I, so far, have done nothing. I go to meet them, and lose myself with them, I am charming, very bright, but when I come home the illusion is broken to pieces—there I am, just a pretty young girl, very pretty—but what of it? You do not feel this necessity, Letty, because of your exuberance. I have not exuberance but fever; is it just a physical fever? I am invited to the monastery. The cure here is absolute. I will certainly soon be well. Poor Papa. About Mme. Lupescu, I hear wonderful tales about her courage and *brio*. I admire her. I shall try to get a signed picture of her. This is all my life—I am very happy. I am obliged to consider only the best, finest, most brilliant men when I think of men fit to be my husband, for it must be someone to increase my happiness, not to make me miserable; and I am not looking for a husband to liberate me, or give me a home, as many miserable girls are—I am free already and my life is glorious (yes, except when I say it is *wretched*), and I would not shut myself up except with a superb man, a man beyond men—a prince, recognizable by anyone in the street, as a prince—or even a savant—but he must be handsome and have money too. I cannot live in a side street; I cannot be discontented, as a woman, for I must have a spotless, absolutely chaste married life and everything must be delightful. I try to reason out (but vainly) the steps by which a girl like you came to your view of the world—sameness, a geometrical pattern, women in overalls at machines and men talking about dams and cross-country trains; no traveling, no objets-d'art, no beauty, no folly, no great passions! It is incomprehensible. I am obliged to say to myself, it is a mere fad. But I am always your Jacky.

20

GRANDMOTHER Fox had been away from the U.S.A. for some years and feared to die abroad. She wanted to come home, buy a lot, a headstone, consult with us about the lettering, and die among us. She would be happy if she could think her female relatives, aunts, cousins, nieces, and her daughter-in-law with grandchildren, of sex female, could come to visit her when she was underground. She loved Lily Spontini like a daughter, and Mathilde because she had been betrayed by a man; she loved me because I resembled Solander and was her first grandchild, and Jacky because she was a sweet, feminine girl, and Andrea, my six-year-old sister, because she was, maritally speaking at least, posthumous; and then, because we were all female.

I think she even liked Persia too, for I heard her say to her once, "When you have little girls of your own, my dear, you will understand; that I know."

Then she had strange notions, come in her old age, that they would take away her citizenship because her passport was old and her mother had been a German, and everyone now hated the Germans and, "There will be war, there will be war," she said, as she had said since 1919.

My father, in return for her kindness to the family, had got an immigration number and arranged financial backing for Edie, "the girl in Swan and Edgar's"; and in the spring of 1935, Grandmother sailed with this girl to New York.

The girl was an experienced trimmer and finisher of women's dresses. Though Mother was displeased with Grandmother for living with Solander and Persia, we all three, and with Dora Morgan, who was then in New York, turned up at the wharf to welcome the pair. I turn aside here to say that Uncle Philip at this moment had attempted to leave Dora, but the agile-tongued shrew had so rounded up the family, that Philip had this week returned to her, who had all the appearance of being his fateful woman.

Grandmother was pale, having lain in her berth the whole way; but Edie, a tall, brown-haired woman of twenty-eight, souring and tanning somewhat with a work-woman's spinsterhood, looked conceited as ever; she did not so much as glance at the skyline. "I saw it in the movies," she said disdainfully, "long ago, years ago." Edie was lively, with quick speech, smiles and glances and sudden turns of humor; spiteful, wise, cynical, all in a sentence. She seemed very fond of Grandmother, who leaned on her arm, and with a liquid glance upwards of her lovely brown eyes, called Edie "nearly my daughter." Mother took a dislike to Edie, complained of her wretched Cockney accent, which mingled rapid, vaudeville notes with a strange dragging middle-class affectation.

Dora, again pregnant, extremely active, loved to run about everywhere, showing her belly to people, talking about her three other children, the boy in England, the girl in Mexico, and a boy, Tony, Dora's youngest, in Green Acres (the only one anyone had actually seen), and complaining genteelly about her husband, Philip: "I am tired of his crocodile tears."

Philip was threatened with jail by his first wife for back alimony and seemed not to care. "I believe he would go to jail to escape me; it would relieve him of his responsibilities," said Dora, in quite a warm tone, with pink cheeks, a jolly manner, and a dress that reminded you of Mary, Queen of Scots. She put her hand just below her waist and smiled tenderly. Though everyone in the family but Grandmother Morgan had become wary of her, because she never left any house without taking a gift with her (a cough drop, a tube of toothpaste, "merely as a token of you, dear"), it was hard to condemn her. What was she? A wife and mother; and Philip, a philanderer. She had been just lately to see Amabel, who was trying to get Philip back, with the idea of sympathizing with her over Philip's bad ways. She was very indignant, for this powerful woman, with the aid of her two brothers, threw her down the stairs. We never knew whether this had really happened. We said, by this, Dora was a mythomaniac, the latest polite word for liar.

At this time the U.S.A. was being overwhelmed by a new polite language, a sophomore neo-Latin, which my father called *acadamese*, and which concealed everything unpleasant in terms pseudo-scientific, generally pseudo-psychological. This was partly the effect of translations from persons writing in German, e.g., Freud and Marx, whose works were translated by verbal-parallelists (not translators) into an astounding polysyllabic jargon.

In the so-called *sociological* sphere, English words were built up in the German fashion to conceal things. For example, this was the time when the poor and hungry began to be called *the underprivileged* and the rich, the *overprotected*. Radical views on the part of the poor were called *maladjustment*; the use of the imagination was *escapism*.

Thus Dora, a liar and fraud, everyone called, rather tenderly, a mythomaniac. It was partly anger. Philip, no doubt, had an ulterior motive in marrying her. He had always been seriously interested in women apparently able to keep him and themselves. He had always had bad luck. Now Dora had given up all thought of business, thrown away her talent, and devoted her unusual energies to tormenting Philip.

Dora at once tried to insinuate herself into Grandmother Fox's sympathies by patting her waist, as I say, speaking of her dear children far away, and of Philip's wickedness, "But you always told us, dear Mother Fox, that men are like that and I did not listen to you. Oh, I know better now, dear Mother." They sat at tea in the back room in the St. George Hotel that Grandmother would occupy for one night with Edie. Edie, at a loss, casting round, blabbed to us about everything; she looked to us, without trusting us, for some support. I do not think she ever trusted any American. Dora told how Philip would shortly go to jail for alimony and leave them destitute, so that she would be thrown entirely upon the charity of Grandmother Morgan and her relatives by marriage. Mr. McRae, her uncle, had gone on a world tour, a thing she regretted, since he was surely using up the money which she so much hoped (and what was wrong in such a hope, in a mother?) would come to her own dear little ones. This made Grandmother Fox thoughtful. She said, "To put him in jail is not nice; a father should work for his children. Idiot! Does she think he can earn money in jail?"

Dora beamed, "How kind you are, Mother Fox! You understand

me so well. Philip has not used me properly, but, after all, he is my husband, and I will allow him to work for me and dear Bernard and Cissie and Tony, so far away from me, and the new one I carry; I am not vengeful. I will take him back. I know what he has done to me, dear Mother Fox, using me and then using other women, just as it suits him, and often I thought to myself, Better he should be in jail, he'd be away from them and he'd have a chance to think over what he's done with his life! But, after all, I must think of my little ones too, I am a mother, now; I must not consult my own feelings of revenge. A girl can do that; a mother not. No woman can understand how things really are, till she is a mother."

"Yes, yes," said Grandmother Fox, in a worried voice, "no doubt, no doubt." She suddenly became irritated, "For God's sake, how could she? Eh? How could she understand? You expect my little Letty or Jacky to understand things like that? Thank God they don't. Youth is for enjoyment."

Dora laughed lightly, "How right you are, Mother Fox! How true!"

There was a silence. Dora continued, nonchalantly, "But he likes living in England, doesn't he? Oh, I don't think Solander would ever come back here. I do not think he would ever live here again. And then he has all his friends there, all his friends—"

Grandmother was silent for a little while; then she murmured politely, "Do you like it very sweet?"

"Not too sweet."

"Oh, dear! Perhaps it is too sweet. Taste it, my dear."

"No, it's all right."

"Are you sure it's not too sweet? I can put in more tea."

Impatiently Dora said, "No, no, I like it this way."

"Well," said Grandmother, "much ado about nothing, as Shakespeare would say."

Clink, clink, went the spoons. Dora said thoughtfully, "Poor Mrs. Bowles! You know Gideon Bowles's mother? They are expecting her to die."

"Who is Gideon Bowles? Who knows all these things?"

"Gideon Bowles is that dear old friend of Mathilde's from when she was in the theater."

"The theater—I don't know—" said Grandmother crossly.

"Poor Mrs. Bowles is dying now—"

"Is her son with her?"

"No, he is in California."

"What is the matter with her?"

"She got a stroke."

"If she is healthy, she will linger," Grandmother said fretfully. Dora said, "Philip went to see her. The daughter is very good to the mother. Gideon Bowles visited Mathilde, but they say he is very good also to his mother. But they say the daughter is better."

"Really good? Is she? I cannot tell you this, my dear. I never saw any of them."

"Gideon was very good to Mathilde and she is so lonely." Grandmother, after a silence, said, "Too sweet is no good for me." Dora said, "Thirty-five! Think of it, a man that age who hasn't a girl friend; do you think that is natural?"

There was a long silence; then Grandmother said thoughtfully, "You see, Dora, I don't like this material. It fades. Very, very natural—a daughter, a mother—oh, a stroke you say! Well, she may linger for years. And the daughter—nice, nice—and the son, he loves his mother, he cannot marry. You see, my dear, I knew a case, five sons, they loved their mother, they did not marry."

Dora said, "Ah, I heard all about it; and if you ask me, that daughter is not so well either. He is fond of his sister, they say. Good, very good. I do not think she has been well for years, that girl. She had two kinds of operations and got hurt internally. They say she had one she lost—she wanted to lose, of course—and I think she was operated on once mysteriously—she does not look well, she looks nervous, that girl. Too much devotion to the mother is not good either. They cannot marry. Yes, twice a week Gideon Bowles was calling upon dear Mattie; a woman is glad of some company."

In the silence, they drank. Dora reflected and in a maudlin voice began, "Since Letty came back to America, she is not the same child at all. I think Mathilde wishes she would be more attentive to her mummy. Then living in the Green Acres hotel— she learns bad manners; and is quite spoiled. And Jacky is getting too much attention. But then she is an invalid. Poor, poor child."

Grandmother remained silent. Dora pursued, "And Jacky reads

so much. She hurts her eyes so much. And not a good scholar, either. Reads, reads, reads. All the time. I told her not to. She needed care. A brisk talking-to. Mathilde—you know, Mathilde—Mathilde wished Letty and Jacky were nicer to their mummy. And Andrea—dancing, pulling up her skirts—"

Grandmother seemed to be dreaming; she murmured, "No, because if they go to a nice school, they will meet the right children; but so, in hotels—yes, they are very naughty—"

Dora said, "That little Letty loves to go to the movies too, every day, and to the theater—I never saw a child so spoiled—"

Grandmother became entangled, out of loyalty to her grandchildren, "It is—because, you see—if she reads too much, it is because—you see—yes; yes, they are clever, but naughty! Hotel life is no good. Andrea—oh, mm, mm, really a little beauty—well, what do you—well, let them be."

"That Madame Gouraud," said Dora soulfully, "there was a good manager! How she kept those girls in order; and even Mathilde—even a good influence for Mathilde."

"She is a very practical woman and a good manager," said Grandmother, suddenly wide awake.

"And what do you hear Solander is doing? Mathilde heard he might come here."

Grandmother sighed, "He may be long away—it is no joke—all alone—"

Dora said, "You can be worse than all alone; Philip is not a good husband, and he is there in the house with me."

Grandmother gabbled suddenly, "You never know a person if you do not live together. There are plenty of people very nice and very clever because, you know, a too clever man may make a very bad husband. Yes, yes, I know whereof I speak. You should never pick a man who is too clever. I know. Because those men are spoiled by women. Yes, my dear, entirely spoiled."

"Philip had so many women."

"I could not tell; I could not. No, my dear. A sealed chapter, as they say. Some change; some never change. They change, yes; but when? When they can do wrong no longer. Don't tell me—once, yes—"

"Yes, they are converted when they are old men."

"You know even the famous, wealthy author, Tolstoy. He was a military man, a Russian officer. He had women."

Suavely Dora now egged Grandmother on, "Ah, you mean to say a woman-chaser then?"

"Woman-chaser! Woman-chaser!" scolded Grandmother. "He could not remember them all. He had plenty of legitimate. As for the others! Then he wrote against children when he was old. A nice crook. A famous man, indeed! Too clever by half! So do not trust men, my dear," said Grandmother in the gentlest voice, "they are all the same. When I was young. Oh, dear! He was very independent and clever! And what he said! But you could not put your trust in it. Sometimes they are clever too, the innocent children; but if they are boys, you cannot trust them. First, what is it? Only a boy, only a child. Ah! what nonsense. It wastes your time. Yes, none so blind as who will not see. I see. I have a lot of experience, my dear. A fine talker, a fine man. Tolstoy, indeed! Shakespeare, too! Thoughts are cheap. Words are cheap. All women, or most, are fit for marriage, but no men, very few. A sad, sad waste, yes, indeed; I know."

Dora's voice became rascally, "Yes, after all, you should not try to control one individual, should you? If they do not want you, you should go on and live your own life."

Grandmother responded to this with a cautious silence. Dora continued in the same voice, "Now Philip's mother, you know, she liked to have a good time. She is not dyeing her hair now; it is all pure white. But once, I hear— and why was that? Well, we know."

"Oh," said Grandmother, dubiously, "I don't like that, do you?"

"You know there are many women at Green Acres who dye, and you know they like a good time."

Grandmother hurried on, "I don't dye; if I don't please people, I can't help it."

"This is not a good influence," said Dora.

"If you see an elderly woman with blonde or brown or black hair, you can bet your life it is artificial. Bad taste. They must take me as I am," said Grandmother.

"And others who do not like a good time," pursued Dora, in a firmer voice, "are sometimes, under everything, very selfish. They have a selfish life. Or they are weak. They waste themselves on their own troubles. Everyone has troubles."

Knowing that this referred to Mathilde, Grandmother remained silent. After a moment, Dora sighed, "Poor Mathilde, she does not feel fit for looking after a house and those spoiled children; not their fault, but a fact is a fact."

Grandmother murmured vaguely, "Will you eat this? No? Then I'll put it away. It keeps better."

"If she puts him in jail again," said Dora composedly, "what will I do? Where will I be? For him it will, no doubt, be an improvement. I have no home for my little ones. I am the sort that never cracks. My business training, you see, keeps me at it. I sit straight; I don't lounge. I'm in the best of health, and not even morning sickness, just a little fatigue."

"Morning sickness," muttered Grandmother, with distaste, "well, everyone has it."

"So why not let me stay with her, if he is not coming back?" Grandmother, who understood the whole plan in this moment, murmured, "See this nice little box? I'll keep it for wheatenas."

"Yes, very nice. I will have a roof over my head, no extra rent, and when baby comes, it will have a home. And I can do everything for Mathilde. She has let things slip. The same rent covers us both. And think of the advantage—she will have no trouble at all. I will look after her, after those three girls now. They need it."

"I don't know," murmured Grandmother; "she does not like company."

"So I wrote to Solander, you see," said Dora, with composure; "and I am waiting to hear what his reaction will be. And believe me, if he agrees—for it will save him money too, you know—"

"How save him money?"

"Well, you know Mathilde cannot see my little ones starve, and she helps us out, and so she is obliged to get extra from Sol. This is only because Philip is a bad father and does not work. You see, I would never beg. I can work. I know my way about."

Grandmother had become a trembling, old leaf standing on end in the dark room. She pottered to the window, and waved at a little boy across the court. He was peering from the dark bedroom opposite. She smiled and then frowned, "Sweet; yes, but when he grows up—another one—" She had mastered herself and came back to Dora, "You see, my dear, I know nothing about all this. I am all alone. No one bothers about me. They tell me nothing. I cannot advise you."

Tactfully, she got the conversation away from Mathilde and Solander. But as soon as the corpulent, red-headed woman had gone, Grandmother began to shake all over; for she had been hoping all along that Mathilde would ask her to live with her, and that she could send Edie, the English girl, to a hostel. She muttered as she arranged her pillows for a sleepless night, "I am dying, on my last legs and she, a stranger, Mrs. Nobody-knows, from Nowhere, she is to stay there." She continued, "I'll leave my money to Jacky and Letty, and what will happen to it? She will grab it. Mathilde is asleep on her feet. Sol is away—a fine rogue he is to me—I'm all alone—Lily Spontini—an idiot—she hopes too, she hopes, she's hanging on for it—pooh! I'm too old for such disgusting people. I see everything. None so blind as him who will not see. I see."

After a quarter of an hour, she hurriedly pulled on her outer things, took the bus, and arrived after dinner at Mathilde's. There she had a serious talk with Mathilde. She found her daughter-in-law in a weak state of mind; "I can't look after them," she said fretfully, "why shouldn't Dora? I hate her; but she's strong and capable. And I owe her something, because Philip's my brother."

"All she wants is my money. What am I talking about? What money have I? Just nonsense—I'm getting old. But suppose Solander comes back! He will say, You don't want me! He does not care for this woman. She's a thief!" suddenly cried Grandmother, twisting her hands in a frenzy. "She told me, Sol can give his money to me and you can give your money to me, I'll manage it for the whole family."

Mathilde stared at her superciliously. Meanwhile, the poor old woman, in her decline, went on imagining fresh terrors and giving them utterance.

The doorbell rang, and I admitted Aunt Dora, who gave a flash of triumph at the two uneasy women sitting in the lamplight. She cried, "Dear Mother Fox! You should be tucked in by this. The world traveler! What a brave little woman! But you wanted to see Mattie about something!"

"About what? I have no business; I am too old," exclaimed Grandmother. It was easy to see that Grandmother Fox was bent upon protecting our five thousand dollars. But Dora Morgan was not upset. She said, "Where are you going to live, dear Mother? A woman of your age cannot live in a hotel. You're so used to your own home and your own things."

"I don't know," said my grandmother, most worried, and looking askance at Mattie. "What does Edie know? She doesn't know anything about this city. I can't go anywhere. She's used to a fine home."

"I will find you a place," said Dora; "naturally, I shouldn't be running about too much, but I carry well, very well. I never have morning sickness; I'm made to have a dozen children, Mother Fox. I love them, I love children. And a woman's made to bear children. I feel nothing, not a qualm. And the last one, darling Tony—only one hour labor pains! Just born for it, eh? So it won't upset me at all to look for a place for you. Now why don't you stay with dear Mathilde for tonight, and I'll ring Edie, and by tomorrow we might have found you a place; and if not tomorrow, then the next day. And I promise you, dear Mother, I won't overstrain myself, at all."

Aunt Dora then handed Grandmother over to my mother, who was put out of countenance, for she could not say no, and bustled away to work on, or with, Edie.

The next day she had really found an apartment suitable for my grandmother's resources (she had a little money from Solander and Edie was willing to pay something weekly). It was up in the new district of George Washington Bridge, in Audubon Avenue.

My grandmother, who hated slums and suburban areas, and would have preferred above everything a flat in Times Square, was not at first displeased. Everyone said this area leading to Jersey would develop and become very modern. Nevertheless, the place she had was a miserable affair, on the ground floor (of which she was very much afraid), unfurnished, and looking upon the street, without an areaway intervening, and upon a court in the back, so that it was easily accessible to burglars.

Grandmother became quite crazed with fear, and muttered continually. She could see that her neighbors were poor and lived from Saturday to Saturday. They were blowsy women, about twenty-eight to thirty, already quite settled in housewifery, poverty, and the mixed ribald-moral views on life with which such unhappy creatures comfort themselves. Mothers, wives, decent women—yes; but Grandmother Jenny Fox was unhappy with them. They were often of Italian, German, or Jewish origin, and they did not even understand her culture; and what is more, she only now realized that to them, to all women, she had suddenly become old, a rag of flesh, carrion, on the dump heap.

Her reminiscences of childbirth made them laugh. So long ago, and only one! Or was it two? The stories did not match up. And where was he, the one? Far away, she said. She had a rich daughter-in-law, she said; and the daughter-in-law had a mother so rich, you couldn't count it, she said; and when the grandmother died, which God forbid, the daughter-in-law so rich and beautiful (with such a pretty face) would come into something, *she said*. But who lived with her now? A foreigner who couldn't speak American at all; a German probably, the way she talked. This Edie. Edie itself was certainly a German name.

My grandmother was very unhappy. She had no furniture, but two iron cots and two old armchairs which Grandmother Morgan had got out of her basement, and an assortment of old kitchen things which various friends had contributed. Grandmother wept about her poverty. This was not calculated to impress the Italian, Jewish, and American wives alongside. It did not go at all with her stories of traveling in Europe. She had been a governess at Bismarck-Schoenhausen? Ha-ha. The old lady was a bluff; crazy, said one, meshuggah, said the other. "But, I'm telling you, absolutely crazy. Old women get like that, and it looks like she has no boy at all. No one comes to visit her. Where is this rich dotter-in-law? It's all a fake, they get that way. A bluff, that's all. Well, maybe she has a boy, who knows, but he never shows up. Something wrong, you think? Who knows, maybe only a loafer, a no good. Either a gangster, eh? In jail? No, no, she is a nice woman. So a nice woman can't have a gangster, eh? Ha-ha-ha-ha!"

Poor Grandmother sat at the window above the asphalt, in the hot evenings, fanning her pasty little face, listening, with no lights on. She heard everything, she forgot what she could, and invented stories for the next day. I will tell them—I will tell them—and, at night, she turned on her pillow—why does he leave his old mother alone like this? For a black-haired girl with no children, a nobody, not even money, nothing! Why? What use to have children? A son they say; better, a daughter. A daughter stays with her mother—they understand each other. A son goes off with a black-haired girl who flops her curls at him; she knows nothing, and he's a smart man—or was. A college graduate! But what does it all matter when a girl with long black hair, like a high-school girl—what does she know? She doesn't care because she doesn't know. Young, too young. They don't care for us, and who cares for us? I'm old, I'm old.

A stranger, Edie, nice, but English, cares for me. Mathilde doesn't care for me. Why should she? Look at the trouble my own son caused her! And the children, dear little children—it's no use asking anything from them. They have their life to lead. We lived ours. Let them be. They shouldn't have our tears mingled with their little troubles. Poor little things. No father. Grandmother often wept.

In the next room lived Edie, more and more discontented. Her wiry, brunette type did not appeal to New York men. She did not know the right answers. She had a whining, pert way. She looked about for work, but couldn't join the union till she had a job, nor get a job till she joined the union, so she said. Though she was a legally admitted immigrant, she now wanted to return. She had seen New York at its worst, with its dust, heat, abrupt, rude, overworked men, and painted, rude, overworked women; its sex laxity and roughness. In certain society circles, girls were supposed to kiss men and think nothing of it; it was all a part of their training. Here, girls were supposed to sleep with men and think nothing of it; more than that, provide the bed, sandwiches, and beer; and never expect even a telephone call of thanks.

"Look, baby, this is just between you and me; we won't make anything of it?" and "Say, we're a new country, we haven't got all those fancy manners they have over there; we're new, we haven't got the time."

Dreadful land. She wanted to return to her "nice, comfortable home." In the hot evenings, after she had wandered all over town, wearing out her feet in her cheap, high heels and feeling the misery of the girl who isn't the local type, she would return to the whining old woman who had tried to rest during the heat, and who had lived on porridge or a little chicken soup, or a bit of a chop, "What can I eat? What can I do? I'm old!"

She paid her rent out as agreed, and saw her money dwindling. She began to be angry with the old woman. She found out the truth about the old woman's son: Solander and Persia were not married. Her respect for the old woman dropped. She met Lily Spontini, complained, and found a friend. Lily knew her old aunt. She had been jealous of Edie, her supplanter. Now she said, in her slow voice, soft and obstructed, like someone in a nightmare, "I'd like to come and live with you, too. You know I've always lived with Aunty. We got on all right. I know how to manage her." She laughed gently, "She's difficult, but we get on all right. I'll get another cot. Where I live, I'm all alone. A furnished room. I don't like it. Now my cousin Bert, he's so silly, I don't know what's the matter with him, something wrong, maybe; he tried to get in my room the other night; he said he's got no place to sleep. He said the cops are after him. He's crazy, I think. When I went to work in the morning, there he was on the landing asleep. The next night he tried to climb up over a roof next door, a garage. He called to me. I looked out and there he was in the moonlight. And he don't seem to know he does wrong. He said, 'Help me in, Lily.' Of course, I wouldn't. I'm his first cousin. So I don't want to live alone. You see it's inconvenient, and men follow you. You know," she said, "the man on the bus last night, coming up, asked me my address. 'Is this where you get off, girlie, what's your street?' he said, and he said he signed off at 128th Street and to come to the barn, or he'd come to meet me. Now he could easily find out where I live."

With a vacant smile, Lily looked at Edie, asking for help. Edie was delighted, "All right, you want to share the rent? I can't stand the old witch any more, pore old thing. She mutters like an old three-times-three-make-up-nine."

"It's worry," said Lily, kindly.

"Yes, I know she means well," said Edie, "but you know she always lied to me; she said her son was married and I don't know what."

"Yes," said Lily dreamily, "yes, she says things, poor Aunty."

Grandmother Jenny revived to find her dear Lily with her again.

Lily brought a few things from her room; and bought a bridge table with four chairs she saw advertised in the daily papers, modern style, nickel tubes and leatherette. Lily dug out curtains from Grandmother's boxes that were known to her and that Grandmother had carried round with her from apartment to apartment for forty years or more. Some of them came from the Bismarck-Schoenhausen time, when, a young woman with old European notions, she had begun to collect a trousseau; and these particular curtains, which had never been used, fine thick muslin with tatted edges, Lily now hung. She put up two pictures a boy friend had given her, one showing Pierrot, white on black, and one with a Columbine asleep under a tree.

On the Saturday morning, when Edie was helping her zealously, the first time she had ever helped in the house, Lily confessed timidly, "This boy friend, he's English, too; he wants that I should marry him. He would get his citizenship if he is married to an American, and he wants my cousin Solander to give him a little money to start with, only a loan and he could go into a toy business, a leather business maybe; I told him handbags, but he calls it saddlery, that's what they call it in England." Timidly, she laughed. "So, I thought if I moved in with my aunt I would save the money. And, you see," she said, "my aunt and I have lived together so long, it is a pleasure for me anyhow."

After tacking up the two pictures which they both loudly admired, Lily added, with an even more broken and breathless accent, "And Mathilde, she is a nice woman. I haven't nothing against her, you know, and the children are nice children, but they have their own troubles, and they don't want no bother with my old aunt. It's natural. I was lonely there in the furnished room; and then the men follow you. They want to know, 'Where do you live? Do you live alone? Haven't you got any family? Can I come and pay you a visit?' I want to get married and have a nice place. I was married, but I lived with my husband's parents. They were real nice to me. But he was dying, and he died in the bed with me; and there was no other bed—I didn't have no real home."

She laughed, a sweet, troubled laugh. Edie looked at her narrowly. Edie was herself a poor girl needing money to get married and she was not convinced that Lily was really naïve. They both knew, as hundreds of people knew, in the Hart-Morgan circle, that Grandmother Fox had five thousand dollars. Lily said somnolently, almost whispering, "Did you see Persia? Before you left London?"

"Yes, of course, I saw a lot of her, and especially him." Her bad temper betrayed her. "He didn't tell me they weren't married."

"Well," said Lily, easily, "they will be soon, I guess. Maybe she'll have a baby."

"Before getting married?" Edie was severe.

Lily laughed, "Well, why not? I wouldn't blame her."

Edie said, "Why, the old woman would never leave her money to an illegitimate baby." She gasped slightly, in excitement.

Lily plucked at her dress. She answered in a dreamy voice, "My aunt hasn't any money. She hasn't anything to leave, illegitimate, not illegitimate. You think they wouldn't come to see her, if she had some money to leave?" She laughed frankly, at Edie, "They aren't slow, the Morgans. They're some lively crowd. Where money is concerned. Friendly, too. Good sports. They are all right. I got nothing against them."

She laughed with pleasure.

21

THE GIRLS quarreled and would not clean the flat. They were both disappointed that each had to pay the full rent, agreed upon separately, with Mrs. Jenny Fox. They lived in the same room, and that room was, after all, the living room, into which the hall door opened directly. They had no privacy and it was ten dollars weekly.

Grandmother Jenny, tormented and half-crazed by the worry about money and the presence of two noisy young women in the place, with their cooking, complaints, and washing, harassed them and muttered at them.

When Lily was laid off for an indefinite time, and the two girls had nothing to do all day, Grandmother entered that region of personal misery and isolation which seems like madness to others. She hardly recognized anyone; she shouted to herself in the kitchen. She thought of the way she had lived in London, of Grandmother Morgan's hotel and of our place. We were now living in a place on Riverside Drive with five rooms.

Grandmother Morgan's youngest sister, a childless, married woman in her early forties, who lived in East Orange, had taken Jacky for an indefinite stay. I lived with Mother and my little sister. To Grandmother, it seemed that there was room for her with us, and that she could have been a nurse for Andrea. She did not know how old she was. Her neighbors did not believe her stories about Riverside Drive. She tried to forestall Edie's gossip and Lily's naïvetés by saying, In London, she had lived like a queen, with a housekeeper and a maid, with her son. But now she had no news from her son, perhaps he was dead. He was wandering in Europe. What was he doing? Something he could not tell her?

Perhaps others had news. She had none. God knew what people did these days in Europe. He would return no more to the U.S., and had abandoned her. She began to complain about her two young women. Lily was lazy; Edie would not pay the rent and told lies about her. Edie wanted to go back to England.

Lily Spontini visited everyone. She went from one person to another at all hours of the day. She had hundreds of acquaintances. Sometimes she induced Mathilde to entertain Grandmother Fox, even though my mother now hated the old woman who asked so many pressing questions about Solander, and who begged endlessly to live with us.

Grandmother dreamed of Mathilde's meager invitations for the whole week before. Looking very worn, she would arrive at last at our place on a Saturday and receive my fierce caresses, which were cruel, not kind. The lamentations she made over the fatherless Andrea were so heart-rending and adroit that Mother pretended as much as possible that Andrea was sleeping; or else she sent her to a neighbor. Grandmother, clothed, in her right mind, would sit, chat, and soon begin to beam with hope.

"Well, my dear," said Grandmother, "if you only would pay me a little visit! But why should you? Such a hole! Not for you. Not nice neighbors.

"But, Madame, at last here I am with the Herrschaften! Do you know what that is, Mathilde? It means elegant company, in German. Well, if you know it, you know it, Mattie. Is it a crime to tell you? And have you been enjoying yourself? You must enjoy yourself; what use is it to cry? I did not say you cried! *Misunderstood, we gather false impressions.* That is a poem, my dear. You know I would not— Have you seen Phyllis's new boy? She's marrying again I hear. Well, what kind of a wild animal is he? What sort of a puppy, Mattie? What? What do you say? I don't hear you! I'm getting deaf as a post! ... What about next week? I *am* paying attention. (Like a post.) What? She says something, she even hollers at me—I don't hear anything. What is he, Mathilde, a businessman? What kind of business—there are all kinds? *For the third time—* very well, but I didn't hear what you said the first time. So he's coming here next week? Next we-ek? Um? ... I can't help it, my dear; you don't understand . . . and Lily tells me you were at your mother's and then you went with her to visit someone, Dr. Burning. Burning as a flame, ha? And did you like his lady, his wife? What? No family? No sweetheart either? A bachelor, eh? Does he live with his mother? And why not? . . . Ah! I see, his mother lives in the Bronx? In an apartment, I suppose. What sort of an apartment, Mathilde? . . . I know you didn't see it, my dear, but you must have heard. How funny you are, dear! . . . Has she three rooms, four rooms, four rooms and a kitchen—that's what I mean? I mean, how much rent, now? . . . Well, because he's a medical man, he can't talk about apartments, you mean? That's rubbish. Probably, three rooms and a kitchen, don't you think? Enough room for him—but who knows what he does? . . . Listen, my darling, it's very unpleasant the way I live—you know that— you have seen—a shame for you to see it, a pigsty! Well, the other day, Lily came in, little Lily, my Lily, you know I call her my Lily." She laughed, "My Lily, Mrs. Spontini. She said, she'll clean up the place a bit because she was free now, laid off for three weeks nearly—my tea too, she forgot the tea, for she didn't get her strike pay, but she will bring me new tea, never fear. Then she wanted to visit her mother-in-law, so I had a bed empty—oh, such a fine mother-in-law no one ever had, what do you think? Probably the mother-in-law is better than the daughter-in-law in this case. Well, not all are so good. But sometimes the daughter-in-law loves the mother-in-law, a nice, quiet woman, better than her own mamma. There was a case in my own house when I was young. Oh, dear, dear! I think of it now. It was a young man. He came to hear me play the piano every day. He loved Beethoven. He had a real musical sense. Where is he now? When young, they're all nice. Probably I wouldn't like him now. But then he said, 'I love you better than my own mother, Mrs. Fox.' She was no good. A fly woman. No wonder, eh? . . . What did Lily tell me now? Pooh, all her tales—I can't—a head like a sieve, I've got. Yes, now I know. She said her mother-in-law has three rooms and a kitchen all for herself. Too much. *It-is-too-much*, said Lily. How stupid! She drags her words out of her mouth. For thirty-eight dollars monthly. A palace, she says, really, a palace. And Kirkland Avenue. Where is that, Mattie? That's Coney Island? Not a nice quarter? But in summer, just think, you get the air; the houses are all empty she says, to let; you can get bargains, and think of the air. Well, it's fine for children. But for old people like me—what do they want with sea air? Naturally, if I could—that's really a bargain, thirty-eight dollars and a palace and the sea air. I love the boardwalk! And think of how the children could play there and on the sand? Well, for summer only, naturally. Also I hear the chicken is good, there. The Jews like it so much, you get plenty and cheap; cheap and good. They have nice taste in some things, you know. Chicken is excellent for children. Meat is too much for their stomachs, especially in summer. . . . Once in London, she—what am I saying? A lady friend of mine, a nice Irish woman, brought me a little half of chicken. You need it, she said to me; you're old and can only take little, light things. In some things, you see, the English are nice, refined; they are thoughtful. But, of course, she is only a stranger. What does she really know? Well, Lily brought me this piece of chicken, a breast it was, with the compliments of Mrs. Spontini, her mother-in-law. Very thoughtful! But it wasn't much, not good, not good quality. I know how to buy better. I could buy a whole chicken for a whole family and you would see something—naturally, for a little piece, you don't get the best quality. Why should they? And then . . . Yes, yes, yes, talk about things like that. She talked for an hour about Mrs. Spontini and the breast of chicken. It was nice of course, but not what she made out. Yes, yes, she loves her mother-in-law. That's a very odd thing, but some do. I said, Why don't you take your mother-in-law a breast of chicken? It is not her place to give you breast of chicken? Well, she said, she is rich. Stupid! Thirty-eight dollars is certainly not a high rent. . . . Yes, yes, and now Lily must be careful with her money. The boss signed with the C.I.O. See, he bought a machine worth a thousand dollars, and he saves so much, his cost is one-tenth of what it was. And then Dinkle, Lily's friend, the manager, said Lily must be laid off for a while. . . . I, do you hear, I say a worker, do you hear, a worker works; a worker must work or have money. I have no money; what next? . . . I told her. She said she was in the Bronx and saw a job in the paper. Then she went to the address in the Bronx and she met a boy from the factory. He told her that she must go back, the strike is finished, and when she puts in an appearance, she'll get strike pay. But she got there too late. She was terribly disappointed. She ran, but it's too far. And you know, with something tied on her, a picket they call it, she goes up and down, up and down; and then she gets tired of it. I tell her a worker must work. . . . Now she will go back to work. In the meantime she went to see her mother-in-law, she had the chance, and she was able to bring me back a breast of chicken. Well, sometimes strangers, you see, are closer to you than your own. Why is that? They see you, they like you and— What am I talking about?"

She paused. After a long moment she looked at my mother, who had stretched herself out on the sofa, with her eyes closed. In a gentle voice she enquired, "Yes, but now I remember, Mathilde; never, never did you care for it, did you?"

My mother said at last, "For what?"

"For chicken; yes," said Grandmother Fox, fumbling with her fingers, her face downcast, "now I remember everything. I'm getting old. I forget things."

My mother made no reply.

"You see," said Grandmother Fox, "that English girl is young, that Edie, from Swan and Goose; she can eat anything. What has she in the icebox? A cold sardine. Ugh! Not in my condition. And Lily—that idiot—I don't know where she eats. Well, I'm better off at my age eating oatmeal, that's the truth. What do I want with chicken? A breast is very nice, tasty; and if you have a wing, you can make soup, too, which is very good." Grandmother became excited, "If you know how to, and I do. But where in the world is one to get a breast of chicken? They want those things for themselves. People don't give away gold nuggets, either. No, no. It's a good thing I can't eat such things any more. That piece Lily brought me now, that her mother-in-law—"

My mother sprang up, and said, "Mother, I'll kill myself if I hear another word about chicken. I'll get you one. God save us! You'll drive me mad. Why don't you come out in the clear and ask for it."

"I ask?" said Grandmother, gently. "And why should I ask

when I can't eat such a thing, at least, generally? You see, my dear, I am old now—"

But the talk dragged on and on. Grandmother went away grievously disappointed, and looking as if she were eating her heart out. Mother was remorseful too, afterwards, and sent me to the house the next day with a fine broiler which had come that morning from Grandmother Morgan's. Grandmother Morgan sent chickens, cream, eggs, and other things every week, to her numerous sons and daughters, and even to those divorced from her sons and daughters.

Grandmother Fox was fussed, pleased.

"Oh, dear," cried she, "and you came all the way in such dusty weather to bring a chicken to your grandmother? I know who loves her grandmother! Ha-ha! Perhaps better than her daddy; perhaps better than her mummy; perhaps better than Grandmother Morgan, eh? Ha-ha! Never mind, don't answer it. I know what I know. We mustn't be inquisitive with young hearts. No, no. It isn't right. I ask no questions ever. That is my rule. And now, darling, my own precious, did you hear from Papa? I—nothing! Not a letter. God knows what he is doing. Is he well or sick? Is he alive or dead? I don't know. Here I am all alone and he doesn't ask about me. Do you write to him, my darling?"

We went out to the kitchen and when Grandmother had hacked a leg off the chicken (she was not strong enough to cut it and had at last to get my help), she became herself again, years younger; and said, "Here it is, much ado about nothing, as Shakespeare said! Well, and what does he say? Soviet Russia's in a bad way, isn't she? What does Papa say? They will make war on Soviet Russia, you will see. I know—I've been over there. They're no good. Tyrants. They don't like socialism at all. They're afraid. The people might find out something. And Hitler! Ugh! What a monster! Look," she continued thoughtfully, "see what I do, you have this, carrots and this, a meatball, and a bit of tomato soup—will you eat, my darling? . . . What time do you get up? I get up at seven. They—young and sleep so late. Pooh! Look at my self-baster. Ah! that is something they have special in America. But in France I got this chopper. It's the best in the world. Well, each place has good and bad. But Hitler—there's something altogether bad—well, well—you are my angel. But you must work, Tootsy."

Grandmother, plump and young, in the possession of her chicken, was no longer the dusty hag of Audubon Avenue, but had become the self-respecting old lady of our London apartment.

22

ONCE OR twice out of kindness I went and stayed with Grandmother, when Lily Spontini was absent. Lily often spent nights with her girl friends.

I shared the sitting room with Edie and slept on Lily's iron cot. It wore out my patience to stay in the dirty, wretched place, into which vermin crept and which was covered with street dust. It was hot in the heat, cold in the cold. Shouts and cries entered it on both sides. The bathroom and kitchen were not more than compartments in a dark passageway. These compartments, into which hardly any light came, were full of women's old dingy clothing, half wet or rough dry. The drains were clogged. Boys and men living in the house knew the trick of the broken door lock and could push it open. At night the girls pushed the bolt which hardly held in the eaten wood. Yet these apartments were considered of quite good rank, and there were even women who thought Grandmother well off having an apartment to herself which she could rent out.

It was intolerable to me. It was weeks since Edie had spoken a word to my grandmother, and after one night of it, I felt that way myself. Only a weakling would put up with it, I thought, despising Edie. I scolded Grandmother and told her to move out at once and send the news to my father. She must live decently.

Grandmother was broken with disappointment, and with the idea that "there were no more stops on the line; she was almost at her terminus." I asked the English girl why she treated Grandmother so badly, and then she told me strange tales about the old lady, which I was unable to believe.

"She's a liar, a hypocrite, a cadger, and sly as a fox," said Edie. "She gets letters from her son every week and saves his money by sweating us. And that Lily is loose—gone to the bad."

This unlikely description of my dear little grandmother, and Cousin Lily, who were both merely poor strugglers, worried me. I thought, Am I mad, is she mad, or is Grandmother mad? Then the poor girl went on to tell me of her own troubles. She began to speak glowingly of the home she had left. She told about the home Grandmother had promised her in America. I think poor Jenny Fox had been dreaming of living with Grandmother Morgan.

"And I, who lived in luxury at home, was not satisfied," said Edie; "well, for instance, she told me that for a dollar here, only four shillings, you could be dressed like a princess, and at the same time wages were so high that every girl could save money and get a husband. Working girls went on world tours or to the Bahamas or to Paris. And, of course, I've seen them myself."

I said, "How could you believe such things? You must know if wages are high, prices are high. I thought your sisters were so-cialists. One of your sisters is even a communist. I know. I've seen her selling the *Daily Worker* in Baker Street, London."

She said, "I never troubled my head with such rubbish and I didn't think they should have. Attracting attention; making us look queer."

"I'm a communist," I said.

"You," she answered sharply, "what difference does it make to you? You've got two rich grandmothers and a wagonload of other relations. It's real selfish of my sisters to bring that trouble to the house. The police came once." She continued, "If you saw what we had at home. Axminsters, Chippendale furniture, and Wedg-wood. We've an Adams door, and it's on one of those quiet, lovely squares—"

She went on with her dreamy description, breaking into it with her sharp notes, which made it very real.

"How long have you been living there?" I asked, in surprise.

"For years and years. My youngest sister was born there. I went away and lived with my married sister, but I came back to it. They were too selfish."

"Yes," I said, smirking.

"You see, married people get very small-minded. The least thing they flare up. To pieces, they go to pieces like an old chair; the dust flies. Any little thing that goes wrong and they want to throw you out and it's all over. A fine friendship—finished. She's the same, your grandmother. It's the petty life. Just to go out and pick in other people's plates. That's not much of an aim in life, is it? That was theirs. And never took me. Out of the money I gave them for the rent, I got nothing, a bare roof over my head. Nothing like I had at home. They must have thought I was cracked. The village goose; born to be plucked. I always remember your father telling me, in London, you can fool the people the one time, but you can't fool them all of the time. Have you heard him say that? It is true. It is true. It is true. Isn't it?"

"That's not quite it, but—yes."

"I've often thought—"

"But the sentiment is more or less right. It's this way—"

"True, right you are," said Edie, "not a truer word. Like I said to my brother-in-law, I am not as green as I am cabbage looking. I thought my society would suit them. What a nice compact you have. Is that real? Things are expensive here. . . . And there's no hot water here most of the time. I can't stand it, I tell you!"

"I'm darned if I would."

"You don't have to. Anyhow, I'm fed up with this gold coast. I'm going home. I've got things better at home. And no strange men coming in. I don't think it's right, if your grandmother does. A young man sleeping in the kitchen, with two young women here."

"What?"

"She says it's her nephew, Bert Hart. And a policeman on the opposite side of the street, all day, two days now, watching for him, because he did something. A nice young man, sweet she says; because he brought the old fool a cream cake."

"Say," I said, "don't talk about Grandma that way. She's old, but not a fool. What's this about a cop?"

It turned out that Bert, Lily Spontini's cousin, had climbed in at their front window in this apartment, nearly killed Grandmother with fright, and had slept on the floor of Grandmother's room until morning. They had come knocking at the door saying that a man had been seen climbing in at the window. Grandmother said no, and looked such a frightened thing in her crumpled white flannel nightgown and her little white pigtails, that they just gave an appreciative grin at the two girls in bed, and went out again.

But both the girls were wide awake with fear. They believed that Grandmother was harboring a criminal intentionally. He hid in the flat and slept in the kitchen. He was a pretty boy, seventeen, dark-eyed, cowardly. He said he had taken some pictures from someone's apartment. "They asked me to have them valued and now they say I stole; perhaps I misunderstood them."

He told Grandmother she had plenty of room and that he would move in till he found a job. He had a pretty girl, with a ten-thousand-dollar dowry, on a string, just round the corner and would bring her to see Grandmother any day now. He left the apartment by the back window at nightfall to go and visit his girl, and came back after the movies were out.

Grandmother sullenly hated Bert's elder brother, aged thirty-five, who was "a loafer and was pulling twenty dollars out of the air, on relief, just like that and would not have his young brother with him." This man had had the misfortune to visit poor Grandmother, without a cream cake.

This was not all. A foreign woman, old, but younger than Grandmother, was persecuting her every day, trying to get space in the flat. This woman was a White Russian. She had been a revolutionary, she told Grandmother (when she discovered that Grandmother was an old-time socialist), and had run away from home as a girl and gone to Moscow to learn what to do. Later on, a worker in a district council, she had met her husband, who had become a general under Denikin—

"Don't tell me another Russian General," I cried.

But Edie, in perfect good faith, went through to the end.

They had one son, aged ten, who sat all day on the toilet seat and read. No one could get in; but the boy was "brilliant and it was the only place he had to himself!" They were being dispossessed this week; the sidewalk was their next address. My grandmother must, must share her home with them. The woman elbowed her fiercely, "What right have you to a roof when others have none—think—an old man, a young child! Throw these boarders out. They have money! Make your son get you a larger place. You say he had a palace in London!"

Mrs. (General) Rode was a woman of great force, a terrible pest; she would not go. Everything she wanted was not only her right, but part of a Bill of Rights for Mankind. The husband, a bent, mean creature, came for her sometimes. She spent the day in the flat, browbeating Grandmother, and eating her poor victuals. When she went, Grandmother had not the strength to eat anything, but sat with dark circles under her eyes, a face of stone; and she became troubled in her mind.

The accusations that Mrs. Rode invented against Solander took body before her. Thus she sometimes thought Solander was a libertine and wastrel who laughed at her and spent her hard-earned money. This was nothing to what Mrs. Rode said, for Mrs. Rode could begin at nine in the morning (when she came with her husband for her morning tea), in the tone of a prosecuting attorney, and timed herself so well that her peroration would wind up exactly at six, when she was obliged to go and cook lentils for her husband. They went to bed without tea at night and without bread or light, simply because Grandmother refused to have them there. Jenny Fox was even glad of her nephew's presence in the flat. Mrs. Rode had been a little easier to get away. But she told Mrs. Fox that her nephew was a scoundrel, and would be in the jug in two weeks. She laughed to scorn the story about the ten-thousand-dollar dowry.

"He wants your money! Old women are afraid of burglars, and it is always their nephews who kill them."

Grandmother lived in horror. But Mrs. Rode was not a vampire. All she had in mind was to get a little bit of Grandmother's floor space for herself.

Grandmother was flattered because the woman next door often knocked on the wall to know if she could come in and talk to her. She was a lovely, young wife, Grandmother thought, with two beautiful children; "a pleasure to look at them." But what did she really want? She wanted to keep the children's clothes in one of the two unpainted wooden closets the girls had put in; "I have so many children and there is no closet space in these miserable apartments."

I listened to this, lying on my back, with my eyes on the ceiling. I could not let Edie see my feelings. I was puzzled, too. I knew now Edie was a liar. She must have forgotten that I had once been with Grandmother to the place she lived in, in London. It was in a black street, one block long, off Wardour Street. On one side was a brick wall, enclosing a yard. On the other were narrow tenement houses in very bad condition. It was one of those slums, rich in returns to ducal owners. In the basement of one of these, completely below ground-level, was a two-room flat running back and front. In the front room, Edie's respectable and honorable family had attempted to arrange a friendly sitting room. It was clean; a fire was generally necessary in the grate on account of the damp and cold; and two little china vases stood on the mantelpiece. The sisters grouped themselves round the mantelpiece and people looked at the vases. On a bookstand were the usual English classics: Bunyan, Shakespeare, the Bible, one volume from the *International Scientific Series* (this was *Hummingbirds*), something on the Russo-Japanese War of 1904, a novel about the Indian Mutiny, some Dickens, and some socialist classics. On the mantelpiece were communist pamphlets and standard works. A red cloth covered the table. Apart from tables and chairs this was all they owned.

The father was dying of tuberculosis, and one of the daughters had it. The mother was dead. The girls filled the room with life and one was quite plump, but Edie had sat mournfully to one side, dark, slender, and dissatisfied with everything; ashamed, as I now knew. As for me, I despised them all. I never could stand anything poor, wretched and ugly. If I am a socialist, it is just because of that.

I came home to tell my mother about all these would-be boarders. We both wrote very indignant letters to my father. Why should Grandma live in this misery? Where was her money? He must come back and get her a better apartment.

23

HERE IS the last letter I received from Jacky before she rejoined us. She had now left the aunt and come home to Green Acres to live with Grandma Morgan. Grandma was holding another pow-wow there, because she had received a marriage proposal, by air mail, from an aged physician in California. My belief is that Grandma never intended to marry, at her age, but used these romances as a means of keeping her by now middle-aged and married family round her in her declining years. Jacky's letter ran:

GREEN ACRES INN, NEW CANAAN
OCT. 20, 1936

Dear Letty,

Here I am! Merry Hallowe'en! I am sending you a parcel (an Indian doll) and wish you the best, as, to become the secretary of an American Stalin. If I haven't written to you, here's the reason. Aunt Phyllis and her latest husband, Bob, were here at our place, Green Acres, for the week end. When your letter came, everyone wanted to read it. "Letty is so cute." If you recall the text—it wasn't showable! Pretending to hand it to Aunt Phyllis, I dropped it in the frog pond by accident—only, by the same accident, the letter became quite smeary and I forgot where you would be for Hallowe'en, and Mother only just got here. Here is the reason for my silence. Mother's visit is dull and of course they discuss family affairs. They ask, "How are we to live?" Grandma paid up at Santa Fe! We only have the money Papa sends us and he is not a moneymaker. Mother has money from Grandfather's estate, but cannot get it from Grandma Morgan's brothers, as they want it for the business. We have so many expenses and poor Mother, as you know, spends up to the hilt. And yet we do not live like princes and do not throw it around and Mother just dresses in that black and white and is absolutely white-haired. I myself don't see why she doesn't dye it, as they all say, but she thinks it would look as if she wished to marry again, which, of course, would be shocking. They say she had a dreadful life; Grandma and Grandpa were so busy making money they had not a moment and Grandma *lived* twenty-three hours a day, only not for the children. Mother says when she wanted money for a new dress, at eight years old, she used to go to the pinochle room and pull Grandma's dress: Grandma always just answered, "I meld," or something. We are supposed to be going to *Mexico* with Dora and Uncle Philip next year in spring. It is very high (Mexico City). Philip chose this because we will all be rich with the exchanges. Mamma says it is because the girls are so pretty. Philip says he wants to help Papa; he is fond of Papa and says Papa is a very good, kind man. He told me privately he *knows Die Konkubine*! He has known her since the beginning, but Mamma does not know this! Philip says she (D.K.) is nice! But I know now he sees everything from the standpoint of his own moral weakness. Consider this!

From the political point of view! I am nearly fourteen, am very proud, have got fat, have great hopes not well defined, how could you expect me to be a communist? Isn't that for the depressed? I don't understand political views except on the part of the wretched, of snobs, or of people like you, with a vague hope of success. Think it over a bit; you think it's wonderful of you to fuss about the unfortunate, you want to give them a sovietical happiness. Put yourself in their place instead! Would you like to lead a life regulated from one end to the other, work from this hour to that on this day or that without any choice on your part? Would you be happy? Wouldn't you go mad thinking that the entire world had a life built on your design, hour for hour, day for day? To be forced to stay where you were, never to travel, to be tied to one job, one set of meals, one type of entertainment (oh, I saw some agitprop—I won't say a word of what I think), to belong to a political club, to be bored to death with political duties and the impertinence of one hundred thousand citizen critics and commissars coming to tell you how to draw and write: and all your equals! I invent *nothing*. I met a boy whose father and mother were there. They have nothing to fear, they are rich liberals and can pay for everything; they had the best of everything; just the same, the food was terrible, and the bedbugs (I have to write this awful word), in the hotels: and—much worse, I cannot write it. They took away their photographs for *inspection*! But this is not the main thing, I admit. I deny the beauty in a soviet government. Literature—art—where are they? Aren't they life? Otherwise we are ants and bees. Read—you'll realize—the poetry and prose are nothing. Of course, I put this old trickster Gorki on one side, he's a dilettante, who does not believe, who goes from place to place and is fêted everywhere, has no rent to pay. When they asked Baudelaire the source of his genius, he replied—leisure, liberty—where could you find piquancy, originality in your infernal Russian paradise? Genius is not an automaton which produces, salivates, and digests at regulated hours when you press a button. How could you describe the world if it's unknown to you (because *the world* doesn't punch the clock)? What reasonings could a writer or artist have in Russia? False, based entirely on his imagination! Our world, he doesn't know. Their world is inhuman. And why write? All writing would be identical! What is writing? It is to see the "cases" around you and make a book about them explaining the causes of suffering and love; it is not to support political doctrines. I simply state that I don't care for the exasperating "benefits" of communism. I prefer to suffer and beg.

You foresaw this, and you said to me—Fascism would be equally intolerable to me. I am an American, in other words, quite incapable of putting up with any such systems. That's true. Now, I admire Stalin as much as Mussolini, Gorki as John Dos Passos, Leonardo da Vinci as Delacroix. I am not prejudiced. A friend of these people we know—who went to

Russia—have a house in 55th Street and have Delacroix, Gauguin, Picasso, Matisse, Van Gogh, Cézanne originals, also some El Grecos of dubious authenticity, but one certain Rembrandt—you see they have no *ax* to grind, they have everything—they have a friend in Paris who was a high official in the Veterans' *Croix de Feu*, and who knew a communist who had much protection in high official circles (can you imagine it?) and he spent 150,000 francs yearly on 15 casual mistresses, one queen of the harem and one legal wife, the whole regiment lived very well—and that, Letty, is a communist! Very nice. I don't doubt it appealed to him. But that is Mormonism! I don't think you'd care to be even the legal wife in such a *garrison* of women. You must look *reality* in the face. And this golden calf, which you would have adored, once elected, you can imagine, how he will fill his pockets! Well, he'll have to!

You say you know the theory and I don't know a word of it. Well, that's true, but fortunately, I know the *practice*! If the U.S.A. or England become soviet, my child, the best I can wish an enthusiast like you, is that you will be one of the ones on top. At least better for my sister Letty, just the same, to oppress, than to suffer things like that! I am getting an autograph of *James Joyce*, and will give it to you for New Year's. He is nearly blind and walks very slowly with a stick, but pretends he can see. Oh, the God of eyes, he is not a kind God. I must confess I don't like what I said to you about this last year; I do not believe any more in the God of eyes. How childish I was. Look at the paper I am using! I got it from the Green Acres desk just now; I love the gold initial, but alas, it is not mine. I read Gorki, Gide, Merejkowski, Dostoevsky, Napoleon, Goethe, Dos Passos, Dreiser—so much. I am half mad with the excitement and joy of living. You see, I could not bear for them to take it away from me and put me in a factory. I read from morning to night—I get quite breathless and pale, but don't stop. "Look out for your eyes! My eyes are wonderful!" I read Delacroix's journal. Now I am *sure* I am an artist. I got all the books I saw mentioned in the Columbia University yearbook for the first year (I mean I am getting them one by one) and I am reading them all. Oh, the thirst for knowing things! I love it, I adore my life. When I go there, I'll say, "Put me in Second Year!" Of course, they won't. Imagine I am to go to Hunter and I will know so much more. I am swallowing the classics alive; Victor Hugo, *Les Misérables*, bad art, no art, socialist art, I should say; what a sickly creature she is, and of course she marries well—pooh! Yes, and I myself a year ago was talking about princes— according to myself then, he (V.H.) is right, young girls are sickly and I was one. Then Jack London (I like animals), *Life of Talleyrand*; Spinoza, I am trying to understand and think I can, but it is the beauty of man and Spinoza's style more than his ideas, though I am now become an atheist and *understand* this. Then I am collecting gramophone records, Tetrazzini, Caruso, Geraldine Farrar, Nellie Melba, Emma Calvé; and I have ninety-eight autographs. I write to them, as soon as I read a review or critique (good or bad, for some famous people have started out with *bad* reviews), but it is only if the critique, good or bad, gives me that glorious burning feeling of the soul that tells me, I am in the presence of genius. Oh, genius! It is my life. I am living only for it. One day I will meet a genius, or more than one, male and female. I have seen all the plays in New York this month and every new movie. (Here followed a list, with annotations upon the love relations and marriages of all the actors and actresses, as well as glowing commendations of all the roles she had seen them in.) Martha Graham, etc., etc. I am saving every penny I can to get the autographs of some of the *illustrious dead*, like Napoleon (that's impossible, unless I charm some of the possessors of unique collections, like Prince Wol-kowski—but he did not give me a fencing foil, after all), Duse, Oscar Wilde, Duncan—you see how ambitious I am! Life is really maddeningly *delicious*! All this makes me mad with enthusiasm for things as they are now. I do not find life dreary, you see, and long for some other system—and I can't believe that you do. No need for any revolution. I read Paul and Virginia; how delicious it is, how true, this beautiful, pure, dazzling, innocent love like brother and sister—I could feel that; that is how we wish to feel. Look how Shelley suffered! Yet I suppose there is a great temptation to really physically love and the probing of a love to its depths, however bitter, must be *unlike any other human experience*. But I will be quite satisfied with a noble friendship, with some great and glorious, or noble and splendid man; I would be quite satisfied to find a man, or rather a young man, who could feel this with me, utter equality, and at the same time, rapturous love on his part, unconscious, exalted gallantry! I love, that is the secret: he loves, that must be the secret. So you see I have no time for conventions, processions, placards, meetings, reports to the secretary-general and all the dreary paper-shifting which you *ignore*, for you are just inflamed by your own speeches. You simply wish to feel the excitement of crowds as I wish to feel this grand, splendid, etc., etc., love; and will you ever feel like me? I do not know.

I will visit New York from top to bottom next week, and all by myself; they have agreed I can now go about alone! I am going to all the museums and all the art shops and visit all the shops, to know what is going on and get to know everything, but do not think I am supine; I have resolved *not to follow anyone*; I must not even admire the old masters, nor take the classics for granted. I am myself an artist, I must accept nothing. I must get to the bottom of everything. What is the basis of criticism? I have so much to talk to you about—about life, what will happen to us in a few years. We are women! That is important in our lives. I have thought about it, things one cannot write. People read your letters to me and I must warn you certain things have come out without any fault of mine. You are so dizzy, you write about "romantic contacts, emotional experience, and a casual kiss which I can't forget"—as if it were necessary to write this. Aren't we much alike on this side? I'll ask you about your work, life, friends, theater, cinemas, books, grandmas, and others but not all others, unless we are alone—and even about politics, if you must and if you don't try to convert me; above all, we will talk of the sexual life but not in public. We'll have a long serious conversation about it—it's necessary, for we are beyond where grandmas and mammas can help us—and of course, it's profoundly fascinating. Don't bring up politics at our first meeting! I only saw you once in these recent months and you brought it up. It was so strange. I had a feeling we didn't get along. Terrible. Perhaps politics will separate us for life! If I saw any chance of that, I would *pretend to be on your side*; and what advantage would that be to you? I mean, I am thinking of your *political honor*. We are all well: we'll soon be together again. I am looking forward to it—and afraid. Oh, I hope our separate experiences have not separated us already. I get on well everywhere; why not with you?

Your Jacky.

BOOK TWO
ON MY OWN

24

OUR FIRST few hours, at our home on Riverside Drive, flew past, and we seemed to be happy and united as before, with many new and intoxicating aspects of life coming up between us, as Jacky said. But unfortunately that very evening we had to leave for Green Acres Inn for the New Year's party, and I did not have a word with my sister till the following day, on the train back home. I had grieved her and she herself was pale and lumpish with late hours and the unpleasant experiences at the Inn—for the party, which was nothing out of the ordinary, had seemed a debauchery to her.

I was nearly sixteen. I knew I had never looked so pretty as I had at the traditional New Year's party at Green Acres.

Grandmother Fox had been alone with Lily over the holidays, in the Audubon Street flat, for Edie had gone back to England and had written us a letter to say how happy she was.

I felt like a new girl. Is this, I thought, real girlhood? Well, though fifteen years is a long time to wait for it, it's worth waiting for. My confidences to Jacky of the day before seemed childish.

Mother had stayed out at Green Acres and Jacky and I had come back to be together for a day before going back to school. Jacky was very pretty by now, but not my type; and she had a curious line which was strictly not beau-catching.

"Time," said Jacky, "is all we are taught; get through exams; hurry up and get through; get a job, succeed; youngsters in kindergarten are catching up with you! Be in style, be *à la page*, go to dances at the right age, get a beau and get married, neither too soon nor too late—don't you think so?"

This was in the train, coming home. I yawned, "What if it is so? So what? There are times for things."

"Yes, but they've cut us up until it's nothing but *rites de passage*! Play school, pre-school, school, high school, and the rest; soda-shop gang, teen-agers, subdebs, debs, brides, young mothers, is that a human life? And that not for a class, but they try to put it over on the whole one hundred and twenty-five million— It's fantastic," said my sister. "We've got no time. It's an express train. Everything's just speed, just getting there. That's the only thing. They never say, 'Throw everything away; join a lost cause!' "

"So what?" said I, beginning to whistle through my teeth.

An old lady looked at me angrily. This pleased me. It was only recently that old women had stopped patronizing me and begun to hate me. I bounced like a tennis ball. If she knew what I knew— she probably did, and she hated me for having it now when she was as good as dead. "You're a gilt-edged pain in the neck," I said to Jacky; "you've got the goofiest line I ever heard; why don't you stop that sophomoronic philosophistry? Your head's in the clouds with the cuckoos."

My sister said something. I sang to myself. I felt I had seen everything. I was sure, myself, of the only thing worth being sure of—I was a hit with the boys. I had for the first time been able to tackle them en masse, and the results were, shall we say, satisfactory. I couldn't bear the company of my little sister. She kept talking like a Hunter College girl (which she was to be). She was stuffy, straitlaced; and not a whiff of sex-appeal about her, although later she would be all right, I thought. She wore her hair like some pictured woman she had seen, bright gold hair in a long even braid round her head. At the other end, short socks. It looked odd. No one but a future Hunter College girl would have thought it up, I told her; a combination of high-mindedness and girlishness which would tell anybody the kind of girl she was, a sonnet-writer, an artist.

She said I thought too much about boys. I told her I was taking physics, modern history, geometry, and English and at present knew a lot about electromagnetism, but I didn't wear a sixteenth-century hairdo and bobby socks. She became scarlet; her eyes flashed. She told me I had been drunk the whole week end. This was true, of course. I gloried in it; yet, it seemed a bit sordid to me.

I left Jacky to poke about at home, very angry with me, and

said I, at least, was going to visit dear Grandmother Jenny, who was all alone and always gave us five dollars for New Year's. Jacky did not want to pay visits to anyone; she said she had a headache. When I passed the street window, she was already sitting in the window-seat with a book. It was snowing, clear, bright, three in the afternoon. How glad Grandma would be to see me, I thought. I bought her some flowers and a small box of chocolates and then regretted this, for I had spent all my pocket money during the holidays, and Papa kept me short. I burst in upon the old lady, who flushed with joy.

"Oh, the lovely snow," she cried; "Merry Christmas and a Happy New Year, my darling, and look, wait, wait, I have something for you!"

I danced with impatience. It was some old trinket. I threw it on the bed without opening it, so that she had to pull at the clumsy wrapping herself; "Look in it, my darling."

She insisted upon enquiring after everyone; wistfully, for she had wanted an invitation to Green Acres. Because we had been there, she seemed to think it had been a children's party, or one of those boy and girl affairs you see in children's books—white dresses and sashes, and Eton jackets. I decided to let her see life, out of deviltry, not really out of badheartedness. She'll be happier if she knows what it's really like, I thought; she certainly won't be sorry she wasn't there. I laughed; I danced. "You should have seen me dancing, Grandma!"

"Oh, I wish I could have been there, Tootsy."

"I had eleven boy friends; they all danced with me."

Her face brightened, then fell.

I cried, "Oh, Grandma, I have to admit I had a good time. I shouldn't, I suppose, but it really was, Grandma. I don't mind admitting I got good and drunk, but that's what New Year's is for, after all, isn't it? Green Acres was simply stacked. They were sleeping four in a room and they even turned the servants out of their beds, and put guests in the barn and in that old place belonging to Jape and even in the garage. Everyone was crazy to get into the place. Grandmother always gives them such a swell time. They had Tommy Goodman's band and three other bands going all the time. Oh, I had a swell time—"

Laughing, I was watching Grandmother's face. It was the oddest mixture of shock and envy; she began to look crushed. I went on malevolently, "At first, I was all right, then I had four long drinks one after the other. That didn't seem to do me any harm. I sat down to dinner. We all sat round the long table, and half-way through dinner I just got up and went across the floor and kissed a boy I saw sitting there. I don't know why. I just kissed him and came back to my seat. I didn't even know him. And when I got up—oh, gee, I suddenly realized, well, I wasn't—quite sober; I wobbled. But I got back to my seat all right.... Then we danced. Errol was there. He went down with me. You know him—I told you—he begged to go down with me. And it was a good job I went down with him. No sooner did I get there than I saw Bobby Tompkins; he walked in and pretended not to see me. Well, such is life. Can you beat that? I told you all about Bobby Tompkins, the boy who was out with me when I met the cop in Washington Square, who wrote a poem and said he must have been thinking of me all the while, and Bobby—oh, I told you anyhow. But try to see it! Pretending not to see me. Presently, he began walking out again. All right, smarty, I thought; now, I won't see you. So I averted my face, and I pretended not to see *him*. Well, so life goes on.... He went out and he didn't know if I'd seen him or not. I wonder what he'd think of if he'd known I did it on purpose. Well, came the dawn.... I was doing the Big Apple. Errol was my partner nearly all the evening, although I danced with a couple of other boys I'd just met, and there were a couple of old guys about forty or fifty tried to make me, and I danced with a couple just to kid them, but I wasn't really having any; no gray hairs in my beer, I said to myself, and I said it to them, too; not quite that, but pretty much that. They got it anyway; but everyone was so stewed that they'd just go and try another girl. And back comes Bobby; and out goes I! I just walked right past him, staggered would be a more appropriate word, I suppose. Errol was holding me up, I must admit. I just said, 'What's new, Bobby?' He was too shikker, poor kid, to know what was what. I guess he'd been practically passing out all along and hadn't noticed me at all. It's just possible.... Well, we went out and we walked up and down; we had to walk, the elevator was going all the time, or maybe someone was necking in it. I guess that was it; and we looked in every corner—well, frankly, for a place to neck—and we couldn't find one place. Everywhere we went there were a couple of kids necking, and even more than necking. Gee, much more. And kids wasn't always the appropriate word. Finally, we had to sit in a corner of a sort of storeroom right behind the kitchen, where there were already three other couples. Overcrowding—Malthus, all that."

"Where was your mother?" asked Grandmother in a gray kind of voice.

"Oh, Mother—she had a couple of long drinks, she can't take it the way I can, and she passed out—out of sight," I emended, seeing my grandmother's face. "I don't know where she was, sleeping, I guess. She was dancing a bit with Mr. Bozo, something or other, but she got dizzy and went off the floor. Grandmother was in full sight, however. She didn't let up all night. So I felt no qualms about staying—and I guess I wouldn't have, anyhow. Well, after a bit of necking, we wanted another drink to jazz things up a bit, and we went back on the floor. I don't know what time it was. I would have been tired of Errol by that, although he's a swell kid, but frankly, I hardly knew who I was with. I just had to have someone to hang on to; and my recollections are, there were more than Errol. What did it matter? We were too drunk to even talk. No one could have made an improper advance, believe me, Grandma. We went back on the floor after the drink; the swing band was hopping away. I felt sorry for the poor guys. They were a swell band, but they just had to keep going. Mr. Masters, that's the manager, you know, paid them three times the usual rate to get them that night; and they knew what to expect. When we got on the floor, we found we couldn't dance, so we just trucked and shagged."

"What's that?" enquired Grandmother, in alarm.

"Really, Grandmother! You're not serious? You're not joking, are you? Why, all the kids, even round here—look out in that court-yard any time— Look! That's trucking; now I'll show you shagging; that's shagging."

"So you were trucking and shagging . . ."

"Yes. Then I got sick of Errol and I said, 'I say, I'm sick of you, Errol, let's get a couple of other guys.' He said, 'Okay,' and we went to look for a partner for Errol first, because I can always get anyone, partly because I'm Tommy Goodman's employer's grand-child, I suppose, or maybe—I don't know—not worth the inquest. Well—Jacky had disappeared hours before, I don't know where. Anyway, there was Edwige, nearly passed out, and I dumped Errol down beside her and left him mushing her. He didn't know she was only thirteen; no one would. I went off to look for someone. There was a kid there, was hanging round me all the evening. Dizzy they called him. Dizzy said, 'Let's go some place, kid.' I said, 'Okay, but remember, I'm not the age of consent.' He said, 'No fooling?' I said, 'I wouldn't fool you, I'm only sixteen.' I didn't dare tell him not even that; quite, that is. 'Well, there's something I want awful bad,' he said. 'Me too,' I told him. What's the good of beating round the bush, Grandmother? You may as well know what life is these days. We've got to be realists. Otherwise, you and I'll get into those mushy, old-fashioned conversations where you still pretend I'm a little girl. It saves all the baloney, too, between the girls and boys; and if a boy tells you what he wants, he certainly isn't deceiving you or seducing you, or anything. It's all darn clean and honest."

Grandmother looked as if she had been a French woman just hearing of the Battle of Waterloo. I laughed and kissed her on the cheek. Her cheek was dry, cool, ruggedly soft like an old peccary glove. Her eyes were dull.

"I'll put you out of your misery, Grandmother," I said tenderly; "I am still as Mother delivered me to the world, though how I can't say. I guess that age of consent or something—I don't know. Or, I ought to tell the truth I suppose. We had some liquor; we went and sat in a car and we both passed out. I didn't catch a cold —not even that. A hangover! Oh, boy. Well, there you are, I did a plain, unvarnished tale deliver! And you've got to stand for it, Grandma, for I'm grown up now and there's no turning back. No standing with reluctant feet, you know. So let's you and I get along all right, eh?"

Grandmother kissed me softly, and with a very lovely expression, called me her turtle dove; but she was worried, I could see. I believe that she wrote to my father that day. This led to an interchange of letters. My mother spoke a good deal about the wildness of children in the States, and the immorality of local family life, and family ill-health. This was not the first time this had occurred; but now my father had finished his job in England and was ready to come home. Some members of the family had wild hopes that he would leave Persia behind. He did not.

Mathilde was again visited by more serious members of the family circle, and advised to come to an understanding with my father, a separation or a divorce; the latter would be more profitable. This was treated in a more sedate manner than before because Philip Morgan had just been jailed by Amabel for back alimony; and the serious side of married life had appeared again to these spinning heads.

It was reported that in the cell, Philip met Percival Hogg, who had been jailed by Aunt Angela.

"I shall never pay that woman," declared Hogg; "even if that makes this a life sentence. It's against my principles."

"Well, well," said Philip humbly, "I feel I'm being punished. I haven't been too nice to the girls; I suppose at times—"

"Rubbish! Trash! Twaddle!" said Percival Hogg. "Pay a woman who doesn't sleep with you? What are we coming to?"

25

MY FATHER returned with *Die Konkubine*; and to save rent, Grandmother and Lily went to stay with them, in the face of the whole family. Lily visited and did not mind; Grandmother was ashamed. Now, the old woman made secret visits to Mathilde and us, bringing us her last poor treasures, one by one. She fancied all the Harts, her relatives, were waiting for her death, to rifle her trunks; and even the woman and Solander only waited to throw her carcass out of the house: "They caught a bird with a broken leg in the courtyard and fed it, but it died; the next day they threw it out in the garbage can: that is their idea of things!"

She brought her French meat chopper, her American self-baster, even her little boxes with old handkerchiefs saved for twenty years past. Already Mrs. (General) Rode had followed her to her new roost and taken away a brass spoon; the others, not so bold, merely waited.

Mother tried hard to be patient with the rapidly failing woman and to please her with food she liked well. But now, nothing had any taste.

"Borden's," said Grandmother Fox, "not everything is good either, even with advertising; the French also, some say good food, the best—some, is yet the smuttiest—dirtiest—all over the world, my dear, is the same, for nothing is nothing. You must not look for bargains. Tell me, Mattie, what is the Ukraine? Now, my brother Theo Hart was there; also in Kazan—the name of a place. Oh, he liked it very much, but the food—he travels and then he comes back home and marries—don't speak of it. That Vera! In taxis with men—all the time. Theo said I was to go with Lily, my Lily, little Lily, Mrs. Spontini, to his place. Why should I go to Vera's place? But this I must say, she acts very nice. An educated woman, no doubt— Who can understand? She says he is no good—

to her— Is that a reason for being a tramp? My God! In taxis—a regular Mary Sugar Bum. My dear, what is the use? A lovely boy and marries—h'm— And Solander was a lovely child. Oh, what a lovely boy, a genius—yes, pooh, I say. A genius runs off with— They are nice apples you have, my dear, but in October we must ask—apples are such good fruit. A woman told me—on the avenue —she has four rooms and a kitchen, told me on the promenade, you know on Morningside, she had intestinal troubles, because the doctor said take—she is cured—take only scraped apples. Yes, just so. It isn't dried out. Well, tomorrow will be warmer, but cloudy, says the newspaper. Is the *Post* a good newspaper? Yes? Ye—? Yes? Yes, who knows? All the lies. The shops are full of spring chickens. Perhaps at Thanksgiving Mrs. Morgan will send you a couple of spring chickens, eh? But what is the use? My appetite, I have none. You do not understand, my dear. Old is old. Young people do not understand. It is God's blessing upon earth we do not understand everything. A wonderful big pineapple your mother sent. This I must say, that your mother, Cissie Morgan, is not stingy. She has a good heart. Yes, my brothers, you do not know them, Uncle Theo and Uncle William, like stones they are. They were in France three years—not a word! Like stone; what is the word for potatoes, they asked me! *Pommes de terre*! What sort of a word! In Rome do as Rome does, I said. Rome! Rome! All the priests are swindlers of course. That is not the question. The Spanish cannot speak foreign languages. But they are good neighbors. I had one once; yes, you see, all the volunteers go in Spain and they all speak together. Yes, people can learn if they're not stupid. Ah-ah! But let me tell you, that's not the only thing. She, Persia, can speak French, and now she is learning Spanish! I said to Sol, 'What does she do at night, always out?' He said, 'She's at a class.' I'm old, but not stupid, I said, 'A class, always learning, always a pupil? I know what I know.' 'Mamma, this is propaganda,' he said, and he laughed. Laugh! Laugh! I know. She's clever, all right, but she's too clever. Chekhov wrote in a very simple language; everyone could understand it. That is to say, every Russian. Foreigners, naturally not. Now, Russian, she does not understand. She could not. No foreigner could. So smart as that—no. The wind in my room is terrible. 'Do you like your room, Mamma?' he asks.

Do I like it? Do they ask me when they move? Pooh, fooey—but a nice neighborhood. Not a nice view. But in the neighborhood, on the promenade, very nice people, a very fine gentleman, that's quite another story."

My mother said coldly, "Will you have some coffee?"

"If it is fresh."

"I don't reheat it."

"Reheat it: well, that to me is poison. I can't take it. That's another kind of thing, altogether."

"Mother, I asked you would you have some coffee!" (A pause.)

"Is it fresh? Who knows? What is she talking about?" (A pause.) "Not if it is reheated. I'm very sorry, I thank you, but I can't."

"I told you it was fresh."

"Well, if it's fresh. . . . Reheated, you say? No. All right, if it's fresh, but you say—" (A pause.)

"Here's your coffee."

"So late in the afternoon? I don't know, my dear. I don't sleep." (No response.) "Tea is better. Is it fresh, anyhow?" (Mournfully, low.) "They don't tell me. I don't know. I know nothing!"

"Drink your coffee," said Mathilde, "it's getting cold."

"Cold, hot? What does it matter? I'm dying, my dear!"

"Mother, please don't keep saying that. Every time you come—"

"My dear Mathilde, if you knew—" Grandmother let out a great cry, with a fresh voice, a wail; "I can't keep going any more; it's all over, my dear."

When she had had her coffee, she calmed down, grew bright in the face, and unwrapped the china teapot she had carefully brought from home. It was an old painted teapot, cherry blossoms on white, that I had seen ever since babyhood. "It is for you, Mathilde. I want to give all my dear ones something, for the time is coming on me, and I don't want her to get it, nor any of them. Theodore's wife keeps writing to me—and Lily asks me, 'What will you do with your money? What will you do with your fur coat?' No, no. It is for my friends."

As she sat there, evening came on, and the coffee had a bad effect on her. Her fancies began to torment her. "I cannot tell you. You would never believe what they do to me. It is torture. They keep everyone away. Theodore came and she stood all the time in the corridor—the woman—with a broomstick, ready to hit me, listening to what I say. I speak in German; she does not understand, but she watches the least thing; she will hit me."

"Mother, what are you saying? I don't believe it."

"You don't believe it? You do not know—who knows? She hit me with her fist here on the shoulder, and knocked me down in the corridor! I lay on my back. I called. She stood there and she looked at me; she laughed. In the evening he came home, Sol, came home. She told him and they laughed at me!"

"It's impossible, Mother! This is a lie."

"Oh, my God! This is what I suffer and it is all a lie because you cannot understand. No one can understand such a woman—"

"But," said Mother, "Lily is there, she lives with you!"

"Ah, when Lily is there," said my grandmother, who seemed delirious, "naturally she is too smart to do anything. Too smart is no good, my dear. Lily sees nothing. Lily looks in my drawers. She counts what I have. She puts rotten fruit in my room. People come to the door to see me. *She* drives them away—she will not allow anyone to come to see me. And the house, the house, wind, dirt—I cannot explain it, my dear, to you, I am starving; they buy nothing. I starve; I am thirsty. I cannot sleep. And at night they make noises to keep me awake. The icebox is always empty. They do not drink coffee or tea, they drink beer, wine. The coffee she gives me is old stuff, poison, they are throwing away. Oh, my dear, I cannot tell you; I am dying. She pushed me on the floor and now every day she stands there with a broomstick. She says, 'If you tell anyone how I treat you, I will hit you with a broom.' She threw the china on the floor and smashed it; and all I said was, 'Can I have a little bit of sugar, my dear?' I say, my dear, for I am afraid."

My mother, terrified, said, "But Solander is there?"

"He is there? He does what she likes. She winds him round her finger. He kicked me the other day. I asked him, 'Where is my money?' He said, 'It is all gone. Never mind. Don't ask. I kept you, didn't I? Don't ask,' he said. I began to cry. He kicked me. I fell on the floor. Then they went into the room and laughed. Oh, dear, dear, dear; and I'm dying!"

"Mother," said Mathilde, "don't you think you ought to see a doctor?"

"No, no, no; what would he tell me? That I am old? I know it! Every man's hand is against me. Why? You do not know. Because I am old. No use. Let us die!"

In the end Mother got rid of the weeping old woman. When she was once settled in the bus and had kissed us and received the cake we had for her, she seemed herself again. She smiled, smoothed her skirt, and looked young, her cheeks flushed, and her eyes sweet, innocent and bright.

"She has forgotten what she said," said my mother, taking my arm, "and you must forget. I don't wish that woman any good luck, but I guess she's paying for her tricks."

A week later my Grandmother Fox was dead. It was only then that Mathilde had the sense to see what had been the matter; that death had been at his tricks. I was afraid, "Do you get mad before you die?"

"Some do."

I shivered. At that time, now, when I think of the dreadful day, I love my grandmother more, through horror, than through affection. It was not fair, and this was not she. And I thought, When I am old will I remember this? I am her blood; I will watch for every sign. For the worst thing about it is, that sometimes without any such excuse (for she was trying to keep off death), I am pretty much of a liar and fraud; oh, what have I said at times in cheat and deceit? And then I thought about my New Year's story! Did she think that about me? Letty is lost, a loose girl probably, she thought (with her old-fashioned morals), a wanton, a drunkard, and she loved me with this selfsame horror. But I love her all the more, because of my fear? I hope not.

I hope Grandmother was not so complicated as I am. But I suppose all human beings are pretty much the same, except Elks and D.A.R.'s and that sort.

She must have loved me, for she left me the proper amount, twenty-five hundred dollars, and the same to Jacky; but it was all verbal. At the end, she had begun to think bad things about me, too, said my father; and during the last month she had told strange stories about me; he would not say what. In her last three days she was lucid, kind, loving to everyone, even to Persia; the fever seemed to have dropped. The only thing was that she cried all the time, in a clear, intelligent wail, like a person who has just lost a child. And the last day, she said, "Persia, my dear, call Sollie. Sollie, you can get the doctor if you wish. And ask for Big Lily and tell Little Lily to come home from work, and whatever I may have said, remember I do not want a headstone, but an urn."

That evening she died in a hospital. My mother and I were there and no one else. In the afternoon, the nurse told me, Solander and Persia had been there, and Persia, who was taking her a glass of water, had slipped and fallen on the polished oilcloth and wet her skirts. "What bad luck," cried Persia. "Oh, what terribly bad luck." Grandmother died at sunset, exactly as the last rays were shining level in the window. Two other women were in the room, a blonde and a brunette, both middle-aged. They were excited by the event; it was a gossip item for them.

Grandmother said, "Is that you, Letty?"

I said, "Yes; Mother is here, too."

Grandmother said, "Yes, but what is the use?"

"Grandmother—"

"No use—" and Grandmother expired. I burst out crying.

There were eight automobiles. My mother and I rode with my father in the first car, and Persia, with Gideon Bowles, that old friend of the family, rode in the last one.

At the funeral, we all stood together; Jacky, myself, Mother and Father in the front; Persia with Gideon Bowles stood with strangers in the last row. My father, my mother, Jacky, and I did not acknowledge Persia, nor her escort, Gideon Bowles, although we all stood together on the steps as we waited for our cabs. Yet Persia, Gideon, and Papa went off together, while we were left alone, after Papa had handed Mamma into the taxi with a polite good-bye. Mathilde sat in the taxi in a bitter silence; Persia had wished her good day when they first met, and Gideon Bowles had once been her, Mathilde's, close friend. How treacherous the world is! He had consented to second the outcast Persia on this sad day.

As we went home, someone, I forget who, asked about Grandmother's inheritance. Someone else said, "A good thing that Vera Hart did not come; I should have ignored her." A third said, "I suppose they'll get a smaller apartment now; surely they won't keep Lily Spontini on—" Someone said, "Shh!"

Lily, who had lived with my father and Persia during this time, as a companion for Grandmother, came to visit us on the second day following. Persia had told Lily that Grandmother wished the money to come to Jacky and me, but there was nothing written down; and Lily was to get nothing. Lily smiled timidly when she said this. However, Persia had offered her the fur coat and what furniture she liked, out of the old woman's room, because she now had a prospect of marriage. Lily's man friend was a drug-store clerk, slightly lame; she had met him when she went in to get some headache powders.

In the meantime, Lily was to stay with the couple in the same apartment; "I am invited," said she, hesitating, with her timid smile. She was meek and kind, saying nothing about her disappointed expectations. She had already spoken to Persia, and in a week would move into Grandmother's old room, to be near the front door, "so I can answer the bell"; and would be separated from the couple by some rooms, having now, in fact, almost complete privacy. Her former room was now her sitting room. She became rosy, and softly smiled at the prospect.

She cried for a time; but she said, "What times I passed with her when they were away, I can tell no one! Many days I came in from work and found her asleep with her head on the back of the chair. I thought she was dead. What would I do? Poor Aunty," said Lily, "she was kind, she was nice to me; she called me her daughter"; and then Lily laughed. "And the way she scolded me, believe me, she thought I could not look after myself. But, Mattie, the way she was crying every night, 'I am dying, I am dying, I'll never see the sun rise'; and the way she used to say when they were away, 'I'm too sick, Lily; I hope the sun doesn't rise any more for me; I can't get through the nights'; that was bad. I felt so sorry, I used to cry."

Lily told us how it was during the first days after the funeral. On the night of that day there came Big Lily, one of poor Grandmother's oldest friends; this was a niece almost her own age, the daughter of Grandmother's oldest brother.

"Strange it is," said this woman, "that your mother died so long after her twin sister, Solander!"

"My mother had only an elder sister," said Solander.

"No," said Big Lily, "but you have forgotten; she had a twin, a very pretty woman, who did well. She married a man who owned a chain grocery in Detroit. She was always hurt; for they did not think of her, when they were doing so well!"

Solander said, "She had an old friend, Mrs. Bettelmans, in Detroit!"

"That was your aunt!" Big Lily laughed. "So you really don't know!" She continued, "But I suppose she was humiliated by it: they neglected her, and then when your father, Sol, was divorced, she felt ashamed of herself, having lost her man, though he (I make no criticism now, God knows) was the guilty party. She never would admit to being a divorced woman and it was a long time before she told Mrs. Bettelmans; then she said she was a widow."

"Yes, but my father is long dead," said Sol.

"What?" cried Big Lily. "Your father was always large as life and twice as natural! Didn't he ever write to you? He lives in Montreal, and he has two children; grown up, now, of course, and married. One is a fine woman, pretty, Eleanor; she was here and came to see your mother. Your mother gave her my address, for she said you did not wish to see her; you could not forgive them. But I think poor Jenny Fox did not know how to explain about Mathilde."

"My heavens," said Solander, with tears in his eyes, "don't tell me that my poor little mother concealed all this from me? Poor, poor little thing! What she carried in that little head—what troubles, what disgraces—life is hard!"

"She never told much," said Lily Spontini.

"I have a sort of family then—she was ashamed of all that," said Solander, glumly.

"Naturally," said Big Lily, "she was a timid little thing," and she wiped her eyes. "I loved Jenny. If your little brother had lived, I suppose she would have felt better; your little brother—your big brother. Two years older than you he would have been now. I'll never forget the year of that accident when you were scarcely seven months old, and your poor mother—he ran out into the street—"

"Lily," said Solander, "what do you mean about my brother? Did I have a brother? This is very important to me. I thought I was an only child."

"Of course, you had a brother, Gilbert," said Big Lily, looking at Solander suspiciously; "you knew that, at least; why, your mother had three pictures of him. I've seen them."

"Gilbert!" cried Solander Fox. "She has a picture—she had a picture—but that is my cousin Gilbert who died—"

Big Lily murmured, "No, Sol, that was your brother. Jenny was quite broken up. She blamed herself for leaving the door open. But you were only seven months old, and she pulled herself together for your sake."

"Oh, poor Mamma," said Solander, putting his head in his hands, "I never knew!"

"At that time," said Big Lily, "your poor mother, Jenny—Jenny, dear, poor Jenny—such a little thing—" she wiped her eyes. She sniffed and said, "Poor Jenny had a beau, but she was afraid of men, and she led him quite a dance, without knowing it, I suppose; she could not make up her mind. She distrusted men after the way—well, let bygones be bygones—your father was nice enough to his other wife. They just didn't agree; that's a bad thing. Now I think a woman should choose her own man. You know that when your Grandfather Hart, a man with a black beard, a terrifying sort of man for a small young woman like your mother, arranged the marriage with your father to suit himself, because he liked Fox, your mother was afraid of the whole thing, and ran away. But they brought her back."

"Look," said Sol Fox, "well, it's all right, Big Lily, just go on; I see I don't know anything about myself. I understood my mother met my father while she was teaching languages."

"Yes; your father was then a herbalist, and your Grandfather Hart was a pharmacist, and wanted to go into partnership with this young man to make up some tonic for men's hair; it gradually dyed it, without hurting it, and made it grow, too. Naturally, if you can get the smallest results in a hair tonic, you can make a fortune. This young Fox really had something, and he had been selling it for about three years from a little basement workshop he had fixed up on the West Side somewhere. Oh, I remember it all. It was whitewashed, damp, all brick with an earth floor; some coconut matting spread on it, two benches, and some canvas chairs, and a little motor going, 'Um-pla-um-pla!' and some colored stuff swirling in a big basin. That was all your father had then before he got the support of Mr. Hart."

Solander Fox got up and started pacing the room, but he remembered himself, smiled at Big Lily and sat down.

"Well, go on, Lily," he said, "tell me all; you see I thought I was somebody else."

They all fell silent, thinking that his mother was just dead.

After a while, Solander said, "Perce, what do you make of that? We knew nothing about the poor thing. All these stories, to hide all her shames, you see?"

"We do not see what is under our eyes."

After a long talk, Big Lily said, "I should like to have some little thing. Something to remember Jenny by." Thus began the tumbling of Grandmother's possessions. Lily, feeling she should not intrude, stayed in the living room. There were medicines, years old, for heart, rheumatism, liver, headache, eyestrain, with a pair of old spectacles with silver rims, a gray hair knotted in them; a lavender sachet, cheap scent given to her by her granddaughters, photographs of relatives, a little box "for wheatenas."

Everything had been washed and folded. The bundles of paper with which Grandmother Fox had occupied herself feverishly for years were neatly arranged.

At three of the next afternoon, the doorbell rang and Theodore's wife, the dreaded, gay Vera blew in. She must have weighed a hundred and ninety pounds. She was dressed in lavender voile and a big straw hat, with purple gloves and she carried a cakebox in her hand.

"Persia!" she cried, enthusiastically, ignoring Little Lily, for the moment, "poor Grandmother! Poor Jenny Fox! I could not get to the funeral yesterday. You know I have to work, the afternoon is my time on; and poor Theodore! He felt he had to go to the funeral. Why not? Blood is thicker than water. I said, 'Go, Theo!' Look, I brought you a cake! I thought you'd probably need something, and have nothing in the house! All this upset! Yes, yes, and this is Little Lily's room? I've never been to see you—I often thought of it—"

Persia apologized.

"It's all right," said Vera, putting her at ease, and with an intelligent smile, "Sol likes to be with you at home in the evenings, it's natural, and I myself, what time have I—?"

The intelligent woman managed to get a smile from Persia too; for few of the family would admit in conversation even after all these years that Solander really liked to be with Persia; Lily Spontini was the only one who dared to affirm it publicly and laugh at it.

"And now let's eat the cake," said the woman in purple, "I'm hungry. I had lunch, and look at my waist—but this cake won't make an extra bulge, and if it does, you won't be able to pick it out from the others. What did Jenny leave? I'd like something for a memento. Let's have some cake and then I'll just look through, don't you see—I know her prejudices; she was a dear old thing, old-fashioned, and I know what she'd like me to have. Have you given away anything yet?"

"No," said Persia, "I'll get a plate for the cake."

Little Lily sat down cheerfully with Vera, one of her old friends, and they clattered away, Vera keeping her ears open but not able to distinguish what Persia was doing. She was taking out the fur coat and hiding it in her own linen closet, for she intended it for Little Lily. Then she came back, with a serene look, and saw that Little Lily and Vera had finished the cake between them, and were looking very gay. Wiping her hands elegantly upon the napkin, Vera got up briskly and asked to be allowed to go to the old woman's room. She went first, with Lily after her. Persia stayed behind. She heard Vera's astonishment:

"Why, she had nothing! Fooey—those bloomers! Old woman, eh? This is yours, Lily? Well, there isn't much to take. What did she do with it? Gave it away to Mathilde? To whom? Worthless trash! If I'd known that's all she had, I wouldn't have come. But I had to pay a visit. What old women keep—what's in here? Ha-ha! Look here. Old bits of elastic—no use—there's nothing I can take. But I must take something. This sewing box is no good; it's unglued. This table runner—it's not worth anything, but I can't go away emptyhanded."

They went through the closet, and through her old paper valises, "Where are all her clothes? She had some clothes? Her fur coat?"

Lily sighed, "I don't know; what did she have? She didn't have so much."

"But I've seen dresses—"

"You couldn't wear them!" They laughed.

"Probably she felt her end coming—I've seen a lot of these old dames," said Vera genially; "they often know. They start to give away things and that's the sign, because they're all old misers."

She gave a ringing laugh, which stopped short, "I'm forgetting where I am. You're getting the room, eh? Lucky. No rent."

Presently she came out with a wretched cotton table runner in her hand, "This'll do; it's only for the remembrance," and in two minutes she was off.

That same evening Mrs. Rode, the White Russian, was there, stony and bitter, saying that Mrs. Fox had liked her, but turned against her in her senility; she must have something to remember her by, in fact, she demanded it. She was cold, her child was cold, they were dying of poverty and an old, dead woman had no use any more for anything. Lily and Persia let her in to rummage. She came out, disappointed, with some underwear.

"What did she do with it all?" she asked bluntly. "I knew she was going and looked through long ago! Not enough left now for the moths to eat."

The next morning, Dora came to pay her respects to the bereaved. She took two blankets from the dead woman's bed for Tony to take to camp.

The woman next door came in, shamefaced, and said that she had often run in to bring Mrs. Fox a little cake of her own baking and now she would like a remembrance. The little coffee pot, which made just one cup—she had often admired it; or those two pretty flowered cups and saucers, which were Grandmother Jenny's own.

During the week some two or three other disgruntled friends or relatives appeared and turned over the pauper's belongings of the dead woman; toward the end of the week two had to go away with empty hands. There were no more pickings; what was left was not fit for charity.

When this was all over, Lily became the heiress of the fur coat, and took it to the furrier's to be remodeled. Lily confided shyly, at the end of this account, "You see, I have a real boy, he's quite interested in me. He thought I might get some money from Aunty Jenny when she died; but he is not mean, not that sort, and when I told him they gave me the fur coat he was quite pleased; he says, 'It will do'; and then Big Lily likes me too and he likes Big Lily too."

Mathilde asked, "Didn't Mother leave anything?"

"There isn't any will," said Lily, "but I am told—I was told—by someone, that Jacky and Letty are supposed to get twenty-five hundred dollars each when they marry. It is nothing on paper—just a promise—"

"A promise," said my mother, dispiritedly, "and the old woman told me in her last days that those two had spent it all already—but, of course, who can believe such tales? I don't know where I stand! And what about Andrea?"

"Andrea—" Lily's mouth fell; "I don't know," she said stupidly.

"She must have thought of Andrea."

"I don't know," said Lily in fright. She soon left.

26

THE IDEA of this money gnawed away at me. I needed clothes, money for parties and presents, though my theater tickets and movies and cocktails were all paid for by others. I wanted corsages and taxi-rides and more than could be provided for by the boys I went with.

I saw what happened to the girls who looked poor, talked poor, and went poor—they went poor, semi-colon; and they got no invitations, period. They didn't live; they dragged along like an amoeba, rather, like a slow-worm. (I don't know if that's really slow.) The amoeba, that was I. I surrounded everything and then looked at it; if it didn't suit me, I exuded it, negligently. I was doing well at school, too. I couldn't see where girls got the idea that not to wear lipstick and not to go to dances made you brighter.

I was in a special class for themes; I was leading member of the school paper, and slaved in the publications office from morn till night; became, after two issues, an expert at dummying, writing headlines, rewriting, getting pally with the printers and writing fill-in poetry when I needed two extra lines; I learned, without tears, how to prostitute my talent, putting in little things to please the faculty adviser and editor. I turned poet, toured the radical sheets with my output, having imitated, without effort, T. S. Eliot, Ogden Nash, and perhaps Abe Lincoln in some of his worse moments. As for the rest, like every other literary-minded brat in the U.S. of the day, with Jacky as my detested and derided competitor, I was at work on the great American novel of the youth of 1936, which seemed to us then decidedly fifty years ahead of anyone born fifty years before.

We knew how to be not only iconoclastic, but smooth and level-headed about it; we had a sense of humor and could wind up an exhortation with a punch line. That is, I could. Jacky never was humorous. She lacked this quality. She intended to move into history with all sails set. She took things seriously, and I was always telling her that we'd both wind up on the barricades, only she would get shot, and I'd get the editor of the *Daily Worker*, whoever he might happen to be. Jacky told me I was shallow and an ape; I said she was like the tarpools, profound, black mud. She was a bit pale at this time, with sunken eyes; and she did not like the boys I brought round.

I swallowed every new book; she pretentiously made notes on the classics. I read *Personal History* by Vincent Sheean, which bored me intensely; *Mary, Queen of Scots*, by Stefan Zweig; much ado about nothing, as Grandmother would have said, for it apparently didn't occur to that pale-loined son of the upper-upper that she might not be the white-faced angel which he made her out to be; but this, of course, was peach melba to the mammas in the book clubs; then another book, overwhelming in its superciliousness, *Eyeless in Gaza*. I had been to a British school, and I had never seen a man so anxious to show that he had been to a British public school, that he knew a thing or two about philosophy and literature and that he was one of the Huxleys, of the inside-inside. And then, *Good-bye, Mr. Chips*, sweet, and the depressing *Ethan Frome*.

All this from my diary of that year; for, from time to time, I did keep a diary, with every intention (of course) of publishing it. It seemed to me it was a pretty easy way to write a novel about yourself. Just jot down a few notes, and later on, get it typed and give it a title. But now it is only a paragraph to me, for I had a queer sort of luck in life, which didn't depend at all, as I thought at that time, on the Sunday columns of the *New York Times* book section.

Things moved fast. I saw all the movies, including *The General Died at Dawn*, which we all touted; for Clifford Odets was the man who was going to take the revolution to Hollywood.

In many things we saw *soupçons* of class-consciousness. I yearned to write for the *New Masses* as a literary or film editor— I tried to improve them by correspondence; "You had better step down a step," I wrote to them, "in the ladder of understandability and unassumed sincerity." I thought I would be there in a year or two as a junior editor.

New York was lively. There were Roosevelt and Landon to be listened to, special Y.C.L. training schools. I went to one; and upon coming back, enthusiastically explained to *everybody* what the communist stand was on Roosevelt, grabbing what threads I could of the floating cobwebs of political explanation.

But while a stalwart in public, I was dissatisfied when by myself. I even felt the things at school were only half-explained. A thirst for the real explanation of things took hold of me. I hardly had time to worry about this. I read *The Last Puritan*, saw Gielgud's *Hamlet* twice, in the hope that the "let" would be in the second performance (the first was the opening), *White Horse Inn*, and the W.P.A. Negro theater rendering of *Noah*.

I wrote abroad to Mme. Gouraud (not a good choice) for copies of the *Humanité* to show to communist friends. I got fat, then lost sixteen pounds, spent all my monthly allowance in the first week of the month, and at length determined to ask my father for some of the famous twenty-five hundred dollars.

Everyone in the Morgan crowd became interested in this attempt; they egged me on and asked for news. Everyone doubted that the money for Jacky and me existed. I began the campaign astutely, in my usual manner, by sending Solander a poem written for the occasion.

Dear Sol-Papa,

You complain with all my literary efforts I never wrote one to the author of my being, the co-author, that is. I am touched, co-author, by this complaint and here is one for you:

> *U.O.I.*
> *One's one, then two and later, there are three;*
> *Then two subtracted, leaves a count of one,*
> *The adding was result of chemistry;*
> *And the subtraction profit is to none.*
> *I was not born of mathematic strain*
> *And had to be laboriously long taught,*
> *To solve quadratics, which makes worse the strain*
> *Of multiplying debts when I have naught.*

Christina Stead

> *If it's not clear, I'll draw a diagram:*
> *To wit, to buzzard, wanton, wolf and lewd*
> *Misogynist, misanthropist, I am*
> *Feloniously indebted; to be crude*
> *I could pay all in kind—this would be rash;*
> *They'd call it their per cent, and still want cash.*
> —Letty Vulpes.

Yours for purity, insecurity. This, I made, quite new, for you. I am even so devoted as to attach the original from which the above was on the typewriter wroted.... Please, Papa! Your Letty-Marmalade hollers: let me have about one hundred dollars—(to begin with).

L. M.

Every magazine in the country was on my side. They all showed a slick, amusing Powers model gouging money out of smooth Papas for clothes, automobiles, hairdos, and society colleges.

Grandmother Morgan thought me not only *cute*, but became quite anxious about the money. Jacky was even *activated* so far as to write a note to her father, in which she enshrined the gem, "The conception of pocket money has grown for young girls."

I was behind this letter. These five thousand dollars were an interest in life, something to live for. I must admit that at times I made it appear (to my friends) that the entire sum was for me, on my graduation, marriage, or whatever I had in mind.

Solander simply wrote back, "Letty, you are too flighty to handle big sums of money." This was the first time I felt toward my father, not as a child, but as an adult. I was furious. I took a taxi over to his house and finding him in, with Persia, I began to abuse him for withholding my money from me and let him see how badly I was living. Girls with real homes did much better than I; I not only had no real home to ask my friends to, so that my chances of marriage were reduced, but he was actually sitting on my property. When was I ever to get it? He put me off with cold and severe words and promises—when I showed some self-control and had chosen a profession.

As to Jacky, he said he took no notice of her note. It was I who had prompted her to write it. I could not resist a grin at this. My sense of humor lost the battle. We ended by laughing together. However, I decided to use him as we used Congressmen and Senators. I began to send him postcards daily. I'm of an indolent nature; this didn't last long; also, Solander took no notice of me. I sent him a study of the Whodunit I had prepared for school, called "Who Killed Everybody? Or, the Mystery of the Mystery; No One Cries for the Corpse." There were three pages of speculation, ending with the plot of a detective novel I said I was writing under a pseudonym and a paragraph I intended to include, giving away my real name. The speculative work was entitled, "Economic Bases of the Whodunit," and the pseudonym was Abernathy Evans as the last paragraph told:

All butlers end rather nastily, especially truly high-class Yankees, entirely vapid and natural simpletons, in stories, largely existing to titillate youths, vicious, untrained, lacking perspective, eternal sophomores, who have overlooked nearly every essential, dumb so-and-so's demanding orthodox unpleasantness, gilded hangmen.

(Sigd.) Letty Vulpes.

My father telephoned me, "Well, come over, you bloody fool, and let me know what you want money for"; and he laughed.

I suppressed the joy and expectation which now kept rising in me, for Papa and I always got on well, and the interchange of our ideas, always much the same, was like the babbling of the Schubert trout stream when we were in good mood. All this because of the bursting of the money-sacks. I defended Solander three or four times in one week. I could see his point of view, entirely. Yes, he has the money, I thought. He's a true, good man. My gracious, if a man had to rule his life by these women ankylosed in matrimony, where would he be?

Grandmother Morgan, Phyllis, has a right to kick over the traces, but not Solander? What does my mother do with her life, I asked myself. Better to be Lysistrata, Diane de Poitiers, Catherine III, than Phaedra, Mariana in the Moated Grange, Ophelia. My spirit rushed toward my father, and I understood him utterly. How we had misunderstood him all these years, in our petty way! A man fights the world, makes money for his family, and they sit at home, mope, and criticize. They think up plans for plunder, and all around, life welters. But they are not life, as the poets say; they are corpses. Yes, all except, of course, young girls who have found out the secret of living, which is, that you must live for the day, have no regrets, and take as much of life as you can get; also, not to accept old saws, old wives' tales.

I telephoned my father the same evening, and went to the house to dinner. I got there on time, for I knew it was one of their complaints against me, my "C.P. time." We had cocktails; it had the air of a celebration. I became excited.

"Don't drop dead," I told Solander. "I know I'm very nearly pretty, but really, I've often been told so; and I've already been painted by a Hungarian painter. Oh, boy! has he etchings! But real ones. By Rodin; he says it's Rodin. I told him, they're very *moche*. That hurt his feelings. He said to me, 'I can't pay for Félicien Rops, you know. I have to live on my work.' I said to him, 'Why don't you make etchings yourself?' He said, 'I have no model'; and then he asked me to pose for him, on account of my interesting figure. I assure you, Papa, you scold me for not dieting, but I have a good figure. Well, I went to the place, he put his wife and sister out of the studio and I undressed—completely—and he made some drawings, not etchings. He says I'm unique, and in a way, beautiful. That is how I know. Don't be shocked."

"Well, go on, fair skunk," said my father, laughing, "how does this entitle you to one hundred dollars?" He became serious. "Try to keep fixed in your mind how your poor old grandmother made that one hundred dollars and all that goes with it. Not by getting undressed for Hungarian worthies."

I burst out laughing, and then became serious, for I saw he expected it of me. I said, "Oh, Papa, sooner or later I must tell you the truth; it may as well be sooner. I have met the man, I am in love, and it's for good."

"Not the Hungarian, I hope!"

"Oh, no, Papa! This is innocent, the real thing."

But Persia was there, and I was really in love, so I waited till she had gone into the kitchen. To tell the truth, on this first occasion,

I felt properly a young girl and embarrassed. I said, "Papa, I've met some people you'd really approve of, this time, not my childhood friends, Selma, Linda, Celeste, who are in jams most of the time, but some people I met at the special Y.C.L. school and a friend of theirs is an Englishman—no less—a descendant of George III. I mean, spiritually; he thinks we're terribly inefficient over here. He has surprisingly fresh ideas about us. What's his name? I don't know, really. He's always in a crowd. It's Clays, but I don't know whether that's his first or his last name. He's a lanky one, older than any of us, twenty-four or twenty-five, madly fascinating, handsome; and I am almost the only one who can understand everything he says, but he is a rapturous *raconteur*, Papa; he can talk by the hour and besides, he's a wonderful kind of socialist, an Aclandite, that's after Sir Richard Acland. They believe in giving away their estates and nationalizing everything and dividing up the land and putting in a new Domesday Book. Doesn't it sound, Papa, like the eve of the French Revolution? What a slap in the nose for us if the British went socialist before the Great Democracy, eh? He says it can. I have never been so thrilled, and it isn't a crush this time; it isn't like the Duke and the English school. This man could be a duke and he's almost blue-blooded, at least some relative of his is a relative of the Silver Stick in Waiting. I am mad with enthusiasm. Alas!—there's always an alas with a man— he has a girl friend here, and furthermore, he's been married and is getting a divorce. The girl who introduced me, Hilda, she seems to be living with him and expects to marry him. I regret to say, she's not bad, but she wears flannel underwear or something. She and Clays Blank-Blank conduct themselves like husband and wife. It makes me feel so terrible—I mean, I really am in love with him, and I *know*—I don't blame you for not really believing me, but you know how it is. Well, I don't say Blank-Blank out of respect for his wife, or because I am afraid of the Gestapo; I just don't know his name. He told me, but I didn't get it, there were so many people there, buzzing round him; he was the lion of the party and Hilda told me she enjoyed it; her people up in White Plains think it so rude to be a radical, and here is this Clays Name-Name just the rage of New York, and if she goes with him, she meets people her parents couldn't possibly meet. He has spots on his tie, soup spots, not polka dots, and a greasy overcoat. It's because he's a younger son, or something, and anyhow, that's very British, isn't it? I don't mind. Well, frankly, Papa, it's for him I need the money—I mean, to dress up for him, because this is IT. Hilda lends him money because he doesn't get enough and anyhow what does a radical get? And, worse is to come—I wrote him a poem! You see? Don't think I'm getting soft in the brain, but it's serious. When you compare Clays with the silly boys, only eighteen or nineteen, who don't know anything, but talk about the riddle of the universe and turn their heads away in the coffee pots, so that the girls have to bleat to their wilted collars, and who say, 'Yers, yers, I suppose so,' and can't take a cocktail without getting rough, and sit for half an hour in a booth, and then say, 'How about it, kid!'—well, I mean I'm just giving you a vague idea—I don't mean this actual thing really happened to me—but it could—well, Papa, it isn't in the same world. They are puppies. He is a man. You know English education is so different. It expects them to be men; it doesn't tolerate puppyishness. Here is what I wrote for the Great Unknown!"

Ravishing my handbag, tossing out lighter, cigarettes, compact, letters, and all the rest of it, I produced:

TO THE GREAT UNKNOWN

> *I heard the guy's wonderful chronica*
> *And in passion wore out my veronica*
> *(That's a sweatrag to you)*
> *For I'm all in a stew*
> *(And what in the heck is his monicker)?*
> *He's seen villages Bessarabi'an*
> *And he's yachted along the Aegean;*
> *He stopped in Epirus*
> *Without ere a virus—*
> *Is he Bert, Cyrus, Shamus or Ian?*
> *Is he Spoffski or Wilson or Ehrlich?*
> *Is it Jones, Brown, Smith, Robinson? Rarelich*
> *I have seen a poor woman*
> *In straits so inhuman—*
> *Is it Murdoch? MacRoy? It's gefährlich!*

"I gave him a copy. Papa, I could spend a lifetime with him. He walked me home yesterday evening. Of course, Hilda tagged along. We talked about the Whodunit, about Clifford Odets, *Studs Lonigan*, the great American novel, everything. He has a new opinion on everything and so keen. He told me how I should dress. It's a funny thing, but owing to my training, I guess, and I'm not flattering myself, at least I think, I got on much better with him than any of the others, and certainly understand him better than Hilda. But Hilda worries me. I hate to admit it, but she's really pretty. Your offer of a Christmas gift, Papa, is greatly appreciated, but I do hope it will be a substantial one, for if it is just a box of hankies with a card, I shall make more sarcastic allusions to the deity above than all the preachers of Christmas Eve and all the society types, 'Oh, God—My God,' and the java-joints 'Jeezes Christ,' and the prolet-writers, 'F'Chrissakes—' Because, seriously, Papa, I need some of dat doe, and I'm askin' you, Lord, not ta let me down. I've got a wardrobe that needs replenishing from the Louis-Kans up, and, this time, no joking, I met a man. I'm serious. I met the right man, Papa, I want you to see him, too. What does it matter if I'm only sixteen and a half; that used not to be so funny. There's no regulation age for meeting the right man. This is it! I need some dresses. I'm coming to see you, to see you, and then again for my money. I really need it, Papa. I'll tell you all about my secret life and Pharisees in the spring. I admit I'm discontented. A time comes when you hate school and you feel they're just not trying to teach you about life, but filling in time till you get your graduation. Now, you asked Mamma to find out about my friends, Linda, Celeste. I could not tell Mamma the whole truth and nothing but the truth, for Mamma would think it terrible, but you will understand. You'll be surprised to hear that I'm friendly with both of them, though I think Linda is wrong, domineering, and at times strangely stupid. She reminds me a bit of Jacky—and I don't think Jacky is getting on so well; I never did believe in one-sex colleges, but you know that. Anyhow you are right in one way, Linda is just the same and she goes to two-sex institutions. I like her, and I see her occasionally—but that's enough. She wrote a lousy poem for this term's magazine—boy, is it lousy, but I published it, I had the yes-no. Selma is nicer than she ever was, but she is getting in with a crowd of youthful neurotics, who've all turned Lesbians for the fun of it, and several of them have been foiled in attempts to commit suicide. Though Selma's pretty strong, I don't like that influence round her. She's beginning to pose too, and says she could be abnormal sexually if she wanted to, too, and I'm worried for her, because she is a swell kid and I guess the one with the most talent here. None of the girls will ever be as dear to me as Celeste —by the way, her brother Bobby, the one the girls used to hang around, that used to hang around me, was doing party work out in Michigan and then in Alabama, and while distributing leaflets was arrested, beaten up, and sentenced to a year on the chain gang. He was released after local mass protest and is still doing work in Kansas City.

"Well, if you must know, I just received my report card for midterms; my English exam mark is ninety-six, highest in the school, Papa, and my daily mark, ninety-five, history, geometry, physics in the nineties not so hot, but the things I learned in backward old Europe helped me up the ladder. I'm editor of my unit paper and Friday we're putting out an issue on Spain; swell—the opinion of my section Organizer. Well, I mean I am writing and I am normal sexually and meeting the right people. Well, now you know why I want to sting you for expenses, but you can count it out of Grandma's money."

Solander said, "Yes, it's as clear as mud."

Persia shouted, stolidly, "Dinner's ready."

I can never stand frustration. I looked at my two enemies, my eyes shining petulance. I thought, I'd like to sink them both in the sea—but how? I'm a helpless minor. And if I weren't a helpless minor what could I do if the money didn't exist? I didn't even know where it was. I said angrily, "Where is it, in a safe-deposit, or a bank, or just where?"

But I was ashamed and even afraid. I ate my dinner gloomily, while my father teased me about my expenditures and my love affairs; and I at last flung at him, "I'm taking riding lessons, if you must know. Clays's family has an estate, and he's never even heard of a girl who can't ride. I've got to have a habit. Clays wants to go riding with me. Well, I might as well be frank. He's invited me to some relatives of his, who live at Chappaqua and I wanted to go for the week end. It's quite all right, I assure you, they're not the kind of people to put up with any monkey business. But I've simply got to have the trimmings. And I want to learn golf."

Persia and my father burst out into good-natured laughter. This was all a lie, this story, which I had made up during dinner, outraged at my failure to get what was mine; but the exaggerated absurdity of it, I suppose, touched them, for after some conversation in the kitchen, while they were fixing up the dishes (I never helped with such things; I hated all domesticity), my father came in and said very seriously, "I'll give you one hundred dollars and I don't give a damn what you do with it, but let this be the last. I don't know what you want it for; I just know you're a crazy nut, utterly spoiled, but I'll give it to you anyhow. But remember it comes out of your grandmother's money."

"One hundred dollars," I said. "Why, the program I just outlined to you would cost much more than that. My teeth have to be fixed and I've nearly contracted for some reducing lessons and lessons in deportment; it's a course. I went and saw the man and he said he would undertake to make me over completely, manner, voice, figure, style of dress, for four hundred and fifty dollars. Add that to what you want to give me, and I'd barely have enough."

Solander gave me a shrewd look and said tartly, "Think yourself lucky at your age to get one hundred dollars."

He looked green about the gills and would not give it to me then, but fixed a date the same week when he would meet me in the Café Lafayette and give me the money.

I went away in a sober mood, thinking how much more than that I needed, but I was calmed, and able to think of my father with good sense. Of course, if he gave a spendthrift like me one thousand dollars, I'd certainly throw it all in the gutter, or give it to Clays, just to buy him away from Hilda. Hilda had not much money. She was supposed to be studying at N.Y.U. but had decided to become an artist, and she spent the money on art classes and just wasted it. It occurred to me, as I walked down the street, that I would soon need the money for college, anyhow, and that it might suit me to go away to the country, say Ithaca or Wisconsin, so that they would have to give me a proper allowance.

Then I thought, What about Clays? The best thing is to tell

them, If you want to keep me in the city, give me an allowance; it will be much less than it will have to be at any women's college, and I can dress worse in New York than in any other place. In this town the girls wear ordinary street clothing; at those other places, the bird-brained flibbertigibbets wear anything that's advertised in the slick magazines. I didn't like the company, either. I wanted to be metropolitan, that was the crux of the matter. But, for example, Barnard horrified me, although I could make the grade there or elsewhere. As soon as I got home, I sat down and thought over my career.

What would I do at college? I could do anything. The high-priced careers attracted me, since I could insist upon handling the money myself, and the prestige was so great; but the women became so dreary. On the other hand, I was besieged by the temptations of Vanity Fair—throw college away, and go in for the arts, or for journalism. Clays was a man who, even if I married him, would not worry too much about keeping me; I'd have to keep myself. I had not one preoccupation, but three: an allowance, my career, and getting married early. I intended to put behind me, as soon as possible, the danger of being on the shelf; that would be one step forward. An allowance would be number two; a career was then called for, but what about the family? I wanted a family, too. I didn't want to be done out of anything. Any such loss makes you feel such a fool, and I couldn't endure the idea of simple and awkward girls doing better than I in the ordinary things of life. "Love should be taken like a drink of water." Everyone who has even kissed a boy knows that is an absurdity. But there's a place in Zurich where wine pours out of a faucet in the automat; mountain wine, local wine. In a sense, all the good things should be on tap like that. That's how life appeared to me—the big rock candy mountain, if you only knew how to approach it.

My brain was active; it was all on account of Clays; it seemed evident to me I had a future. What should I do? I only asked for some occupation in which to expend all my powers. I felt as if my baton were growing out of my corporal's knapsack, just like a tree.

A few nights later I began to fill in the papers for several colleges, and my pen would keep falling from my hands as I suddenly saw life before me. How dull the last year of school had been! I had spent a good year of my life among children, all wasting their time. I put a record on my phonograph and started a letter to Solander.

Papa, what is your profession, professionally speaking? Shipper, broker, wanderer, writer, economist, journalist, plumber, or agitator? Refreshing choice. Kindly underline that which desired and also that which actually had. And don't underline *plumber* in blithesome mood, because, if you want to know, I might want to go in for medicine and they've got professional background considerations now. If your grandpappy and pappy were doctors, then you have, mebbe, a right angle on the profession. This sounds sinister, and it is—hush—to keep out the J-e-w-s and the *poor*, they say. I vouch for nothing. But I was not told this by a J-e-w, *Je débine les potins*. Hush! With my teacher, I'm playing a Beethoven minuet, a Brahms waltz, a Bach prelude, and soon begin the *Moonlight Sonata*. I am getting value for the money, so are you. Stop that snickering, Papa; I chose this parlor trick my own self and if you don't like it, it means it doesn't like you. But, smartypants, I also know the whole of FLAT FOOT FLOOGEY and am certain that you don't even know what the hell I'm batting about, to use your expression. I'm eclectic, buddy. Pardon the flippant tone. I'm worrying about *The Man*, my dress needs (which I hope you will look after); I just finished reading Milton's *Lycidas*, and Barbusse's *Stalin*, you'll agree a bit different; and I feel nutty. School tomorrow, and I haven't slept for three days, not since you promised me that money, which won't half cover what I need. I'm not just a wastrel. I mean that literally, I haven't slept. Why? On account I met Mr. Right. I'm going to bring this perfect specimen of manhood along, even before I find out his name. I haven't seen him for three days. I'm serious, Papa. What I want for Christmas, I found out long ago. The most gorgeous book of Diego Rivera murals, some dollars needed—and I can't take this all out of the centum of bucks you have kindly said you'd give me. (And which are greatly appreciated.) My soul opposes this mercenary call—but, oh, Papa, if you were young like me! (Oh, the fine touch! You'll admit I don't crawl on my belly for that $150 bucks I need— yes, that's the sum I really need in earnest. The market has gone up. I am serious about the horseback riding. And the rest—girls' stuff.)

> Lots and lots of love,
> LETTY-MARMALADE,
> always in a jam.

My father put off our appointment, but sent me one hundred dollars, and scolded me for trying to raise the figure. The next day I lent Clays twenty dollars for he badly needed it, and I found out his name—perhaps my name, as it would eventually figure on my tombstone! It was Clays Manning.

I am always truly grateful; I am a goodhearted girl. I wrote a song of gladness to my papa on a piece of pink toilet paper which I got out of Aunt Phyllis's bathroom.

> *Des sentiments en rose—*
> *Cent fois merci*
> *mon cher ami*
> *plus cher qu'amis,*
> *mon cher papa*
> *(tarantara!)*
> *pour ton chèque-ci*
> *et dans la vie*
> *des soins gentils*
> *à l'infini!*
> *Fin en demi-deuil (comme les ris-de-veau)—*
> *je te caresse*
> *avec tendresse*
> *tu peux me croi(re) (faut ici accent de la barrière)*
> *si quelquefois*
> *mes manigances*
> *et viles tendances*

t'attristent, te blessent
sois un brave mec
et cette fille laisse
tomb-
> *er-*
>> *a-*
>>> *vec-*
un grand bruit sec! Plan! Plon!

P.S. His name is just like him—it's Clays Manning! Isn't that terribly English and romantic. He is the only man in the world looks good in floor-sweepers, that's tails to you, and he looks as if he ought to be at least Sir Clays Manning, Bart. I am certain he will end up as an ambassador, although he is only a socializer of the land at present. I want you to meet him. You would get on like the Babes in the Wood. He told us all that juiciest latest about Mrs. S. and the King. When you said only a small minority has mass sympathy for the Spanish people, take for instance, Friday eve., Earl Browder in his weekly broadcast spoke on Spain and announced a meeting at Madison Sq. Garden with three Spanish envoys as main speakers? It was jammed, and $15,000 was collected —in one evening. But you're right, most people don't know the difference between a loyalist and a rebel.

That defeatist attitude among U.S. communists, which you condemned, and on which Clays agrees with you, is fast disappearing—the knowledge of the great task ahead of us, after election—the building of a farmer-labor party has stirred the radicals to enthusiasm. I suppose there are a few blasés, but that's a remains of the twenties and is an accepted evil. My marks are not exceptional. I must tell you I have been missing school a bit to see Hilda—well, that means Clays and another friend of theirs, Amos, interested in the farmer-labor—I am sorry, Papa. Won't do so no more. Still my average is 85. I am concentrating at present on a report for English which is to be a monumental thing. We are supposed to hand in reports on the life and works of 5 modern poets (in itself quite a proposition!) but I am taking the whole imagist school, this is at the suggestion of—again, Clays. You must think I am goofy, and it includes: 1. Origin (symbolists of France, am using Mallarmé, Apollinaire). 2. Development and so on to 5. Interpreters, Ezra Pound, Richard Aldington, D. H. Lawrence. No more. Papa, when can I bring up this gentleman? It's serious, serious! For me. This farmer-labor man is called Amos. It's incredible, isn't it? I'll tell you what Hilda says about him, he's a beanstalk and he's a Casanova, but she calls him "Scrofulous Amos."

Ta fillette
LETTY-MARMALADE.

Clays Manning was getting a divorce from his first wife, an American girl named Jean, who wrote crime stories. Clays was a journalist, at present working in New York but hoping for Washington. Hilda dogged his footsteps, and always stood at his elbow like a shadow. She was a conceited little thing, who could sometimes look very pretty, and that worried me. She had been educated near Paris and spoke French as well as I did, and she had run away from this elegant French school when she was fifteen. She was older than I, but only twenty, while he was twenty-four. I was more spirited than Hilda, and not so babyish and clinging; but she had him, and I couldn't bear it. The way she put her arm through his was simply an advertisement, *He's mine.* And I knew she expected to marry him, when he was divorced. The situation was that he was divorced already, but it hadn't taken, or wouldn't go in England and New York State, and a lot of other things. I hoped they never could get married. Hilda had got some job writing captions for comic strips, and made half a living. She got a little money from home, too. Still, in order to find out about them, and in order to get friendly with Clays, I went to see her.

Hilda wore Alice-blue dresses, and used to wind a lace scarf round her thin neck. She didn't seem to care at all about dress, but she had style. She was the opposite type from me. She gave me quite a setback. It seemed that there was the daughter of a Lord in London, who had the right to call herself "The Honourable," whether married or not, and who was mad to marry Clays as soon as his divorce was clear.

"And even before, she'd probably take the chance," said Hilda.

Of course, she knew by this, she had sniffed it out, that I wanted Clays too, and she knew I would be interested in The Honourable Fyshe in London. Then—worse—they had lived together. This was frightful. When I heard that, I simply went home and cried in a heartbroken way. What could I do against those callous, brittle, elegant brutes, who are quite immoral and will do anything for their own way? I knew all about them. This Honourable Fyshe was only twenty-three and very lovely, said Hilda. That was the reputation she had. She was quite a famous beauty, and she got herself up to look very girlish, though you could see her skin fading from debaucheries, and she had gray in her hair already. But she was the kind, unfortunately, who looks very elegant with gray hair, young; and, at the same time, the premature gray had made her cynical, bored, and wretched, all in a swanky way, so that she had the most devastating air you could imagine, of the corrupt, penniless aristocrat. Of course, she rode to hounds.

She had a higher social rank than had Clays, even with his relative who was Silver Stick in Waiting or Elementary Black Rode (I do *not* remember). Just how it was, Hilda explained to me, but I no longer remember. You could work it all out by looking up Burke's Peerage, she said.

It seems that not only was this Honourable Fyshe able to keep Clays on a string, but there was a really horrible creature that he had lived with at one time, Caroline by name. He didn't want to marry her, but she thought she'd give fate a shove by calling herself Mrs. Clays. I can hardly bear to think of it even now. She prided herself on knowing carpets, furniture, and all that, because she pretended they had very good rugs and stuff in their family mansion; so she made Clays go round with her to all the shops and galleries. She's the kind that's convinced it can pick up bargains, pitting herself against all the Armenians and Persians who've been in it for generations. It all went with her sense of importance and she thought the Duchess of Dumbcastel's niece (which she is, unfortunately) had a natural instinct for everything, and of course, "The earth is the Lord's, and the fullness thereof, the Lady's."

This Caroline used Clays in this way. She picked out a couple of rugs at a gallery near Victoria after having shown Clays as her husband; and had them sent to her flat as "Mrs. Clays," but couldn't pay for them. She pretended she had a right to use them two months to see if they would wear, and said quarter-day was coming and by then she'd know if she had been cheated. Then, because she's the niece of this Duchess, she put on airs, and thought she had a right not to pay; that's the Curzon Street atmosphere. She just said, "Let him take the niece of the Duchess of Dumbcastel to court!" She thought he would be afraid.

The Armenian kept sending her bills, first to her parents' home, because she lived there and used her ex-husband's name there. In her flat in town, where she lived with Clays, she used "Mrs. Manning." Presently the man found out about that and sent bills to Clays. Well, the man tried to scare her (as if the English aristocracy were ever afraid of bill collectors); she scolded him over the phone and called it a "try-on" and was insulted; but at the end the Armenian said he'd take back the carpets. Caroline refused to let him have them. He left them there a bit longer, to try to collect. It was a sale after all, and she is a connection of the Duchess of Dumbcastel.

Well, that's how this Caroline lived, and how she furnished a place to attract Clays. "Of course, it is awful," said Hilda, "but what worries me more, is The Honourable Fyshe. She is so beastly corrupt, and doesn't give a damn for anyone, and Clays is mad about titles."

"How can you say that?" I cried indignantly. "Such a man as that. Look how he wants to give up everything; abolish the king, abolish the nobility, and divide up the land."

"Poor innocent," said Hilda, "if you think that has anything to do with a man's preferences. Do you know how our chances are in getting men? Rank comes first, then money, then fame, then right at the bottom, looks. Of course, I'm talking only about eligible girls, about girls like us. The U.S.A. is jammed with lovelies—where do they get? There are so many in Hollywood, they can only get jobs in coffee pots; and so many here in New York that they're elbowing each other out of the model agencies; and you get used up there in two years because of the competition. Beauty is simply nothing. But if you're famous on the stage, or have a title or money, you can get on in Hollywood, or get married."

I had to admit this was only common sense. "And so this Honourable Fyshe is going to marry Clays, you think?" I asked Hilda.

Hilda looked gloomy. "The only consolation is," she said, "that The Honourable Fyshe can't bear to leave London, except for short forays to Como or Nice or Florida, or the Channel Isles, wherever she has a reputation for beauty."

"Is she so pretty?"

"A reputation for beauty is a different story; beauties often don't have it. You are all right, Letty, but have no reputation for beauty; no one is attracted to you by common talk. The Honourable Fyshe is quite plain, but so taking, when she moves, it's like a wind, or water; your heart turns to water, so he says. And then, think of her money!"

All this talk made me feel miserable. I was a nobody. I was at home. I did not even have a basement flat to which to invite Clays. He never had a home. Girls with flats seemed to attract him. He simply couldn't afford to be always putting up hotel rent. Then he liked company. He could not live alone, and a warmhearted man cannot bring himself to make love in a hotel for transients. He prefers women with flats. Furthermore, Hilda said, "The most attractive thing in a girl is accessibility."

This remark struck me with great force. I was not really accessible. If I had been—I believed, at any rate, that I would know what to do. In the meantime, as we were often a foursome, I was obliged to spend some hours almost every day with Amos.

Hilda could hardly bear to look at Amos. He admired Clays and aped him; he even tried to ape a British accent, and when Hilda was away visiting her parents, Clays would go out with Amos, and even stayed in his room, for the company. When Hilda returned, she removed Amos's things from her flat with a *pair of tongs*.

All this made me simply desperate. I went to my father's apartment one evening, after dinner, threw myself into a chair and told him I had to have some more of my grandmother's money. He must give it to me.

"Don't you ever intend to give it to me?" I asked. "This is just an excuse, saying you'll give it when I'm married. I don't know that Grandmother said this. If Grandmother were alive and saw that I needed it now—now, not when I'm married, she'd say to give it to me. I haven't even an evening wrap! Do you expect me to get an escort just in my school dress? You've no idea what the girls spend on dress nowadays. They have a decent home, their parents live in a regular way, and they have all they want. If their parents want to divorce, they don't; they think of what a young girl needs. Their parents give parties for them, and think of them a little. But if you can't do that, just give me the money. I've got to have it. Men won't visit me if they see Mother and my sisters waiting for an official engagement. They feel like steers huddled up in a compound and waiting for the brand."

My father, very coldly, told me that I had never shown any ability to take care of money; that I threw it about like water and was like my mother, grandmother, and all the Morgans in that. I then told my father that I owed $362 already, and I had to have money to take care of that. One of the accounts was outstanding a year.

"I don't care about your debts. I didn't authorize them," said he, without even asking who had, for I suppose he knew that, as usual, it was Grandmother Morgan, who had ruined her entire family by allowing them to run accounts in her name at the big midtown stores. It was really $262 that I owed. I hoped to get the extra one hundred dollars for myself. I needed this badly. I flashed out at my father, "I am obliged to get into debt because you give me nothing like the proper pocket money. I have no dress allowance; Jacky has nothing. Grandmother said nothing about your keeping it till my majority. If you want my idea, you haven't got it at all. You've spent it all. That's just what Grandma said—you'd lost all her money."

I began to cry that I was broke, had spent everything on parties, taxis, and the like (but it was so little!), and that I loved this man and would do anything to attract him. Couldn't Father understand that, and couldn't Persia understand it? I went into the bedroom to powder my face, and heard Persia say, "Oh, heavens, I'd give it to her, and have done with it!"

I came back with a cheerful expression. He said, "Letty, I'll give you a little allowance. I suppose you'll only learn how to manage money by having some!"

I looked at my father with emotion.

"Papa, I'm a beast and a brute, but you've no idea—I can't always depend on men to pay my bills; I do the best I can—I do as well as anyone."

"Gold-digger!" said Solander.

"But if you don't give me any pocket money, I have to gold-dig," I said.

They laughed indulgently. I was softened. I immediately thought of all I had secretly gone in for—piano lessons from the young pianist now fashionable in the Village, subscription concerts, for which I had borrowed money; and then I thought, not of paying these debts, but of what I must take on.

My father set a date, two days later, when he would give me my first money. We met in a little French restaurant on Lexington Avenue. At the table he handed over the bills with a secret flourish, and at the same time I saw his face and his big eyes, rather drawn. He looked seedy. His shoes were dusty, the trouser cuffs were frayed. His hair was turning gray. I felt a twinge of pain, and dropped my eyes. But the first thing I did was to buy two heavy gold-washed bracelets, in quite poor taste, which I had seen in a little shop near Thirty-fourth Street and for which I paid too much.

27

YOUNG, HEALTHY, and handsome—there is nothing of which a ten-dollar bill cannot cure you, thought I to myself, the next day, as I saw the blue eyes of Mr. Clays Manning fix themselves on me in twinkling speculation.

"My grandmother left me twenty-five hundred dollars," said I. (I did not mention the money she had left to Jacky.) "She was afraid to see the Angel of Death standing at the bottom of her bed, and kept a night light on. She slept in the daytime. Then, you know, her room was full of old fruits and vegetables and other things that people brought her, even coffee and soup—why? Because she said she was starved and thirsty at home; and what was that? That was Death starving her, don't you see? And you know at the end she said people were waiting to beat her with broomsticks. And what was that really? That was the scythe-handle of Death waiting to mow her down. She said my father stole her money —but it was Death who was waiting to steal it from her. I see it all now: at that time we thought she told lies. But it was all the truth. Her inward eye saw everything. Death came, and took first away her sense, then her outward eye, then her hearing, and left only an old vegetable in place of all that. When she died, everything had gone; worn out like an old clock you can't repair. It was the one-hoss shay. It was because she saved. I, on the contrary, will throw away."

Hilda laughed and Clays said, "And did you get the money—but no, I suppose you've got to wait for the crock of gold!"

"Oh, no," I said airily. "You know this isn't Europe where girls are in leading strings; no; I have it now. I can get it when I want it."

With this, I opened my purse, and showed a fistful of bills.

"My God! It's enough to make a man a gold-digger," said Clays thoughtfully. "The fact is, my darling, your old man needs twenty dollars. Lend it to me, do."

"Oh, yes," I cried joyfully, for Hilda did not have even twenty dollars on her.

"And now, Letty," said Clays, "buy us all some drinks. Come on, I want to see you throw it away. Can you do it? I don't want you to be a tightwad."

I did not pay any of my debts; I contracted others, for I saw the possibility of paying them all at some time or other. In all, I lent about eighty dollars to Clays, and was very happy to do so. He became attracted to me. He thought my stories smart and quaint; we agreed on politics, almost, and I was fascinated by his patter. He was a born *raconteur*.

As soon as I could, I dragged him along to the prize exhibit in my family, that was Solander, after all, and to my regret, the two almost fell into each other's arms; I tried to break in with my political truisms but might just as well never have been born.

Well, time passed. My marks were not good by Christmas. I was madly in love with Clays, and, incredible as it all seemed, he was in love with me. He rarely mentioned it, for he always had too much to say, and I always had too much to say—about literature, the world, the weather, his stories, but we were in love, and I had a feeling when I was with him that I never had had before.

I scarcely saw my sister Jacky or Mother, and Clays was rather surprised to learn that I had two sisters. I kept Jacky out of sight. She was still at Hunter College, high-minded, full of poetry, her studies, and her teachers, behaving in a silly way about the one or two men teachers they had visiting, and brothers of her friends. She was at the awkward age in everything. But even I had to admit that she was attractive. She had a queer face, but a dazzling skin, large eyes, a longish full turbulent mouth, full even at the corners, and her loins from behind made a sculptural rounded hexagon, of the greatest voluptuousness, which we all admired. She could have had a "reputation for beauty," but she was robust and her expression was rather sulky. She did not know how to please a man, but sat opposite to him, drilling him with her serious eyes and crisply shooting her ambitions at him. They laughed at first and called her "girly" or "baby," or something; they got nervous at last, but invited her out for a ride; she was only at first duped by their sudden affection or abrupt insulted silences.

I did not trust her with Clays, for Clays was an eclectic; and many Europeans expect young girls to be serious. They do not expect them to be the enslavers of Mamma and the ruin of Papa, which is pretty much our ideal. I was a realist and did my best to live up to the local ideal while retaining what common sense I could. I loved Papa; I often regretted my weakness toward him; I rarely upbraided him for not making things easier for me. The truth is, I am weak. I love people and I am not sure enough of my own virtue to criticize others; this is the best fruit of vice! The moral person should never govern a family or a state; but I trust in the future, the belief in abnegations will have passed away and we will have no more of these dry-skinned governors.

I was a social type; Jacky was prim. We quarreled a good deal at this time. She did not understand me. She rejected all political ideas and social movements, and went in for metaphysics. I did not understand her, either. I thought she was confused and slow; but I admitted she had quality. Something might come of it. She was not really a rival of mine, but one can never be sure with a pretty girl. You never know when she's going to see sexual truth; when she sees this, she knows as much as you, practically, overnight. Why do I say, pretty girl? The ugly girls, too. I'm not sure they don't know more than we do, they often get more men. It sharpens their wits, they have to know more and it becomes a kind of Aunt Sally contest with them—how many did you score?

I kept Clays from home, where he would meet Mother (who told uncouth anecdotes about my youth) and Jacky (who had $2,500).

It happened that about this time, Christmas, Hilda had to go home to Saratoga, N.Y., for she was out of a job, and her parents were old-fashioned and rather well-off, wanted to have her with them. She left, with many tears, and after some heart-rending scenes with Clays. He liked her well enough. As far as I know—I could not face it at the time—they spent a second honeymoon, a very tragic one, at her flat. I should have liked to have taken over her flat, but could not persuade either Father or Mother to let me live on my own. They thought I wanted to be "accessible" and my father cautioned me against my own tendencies, "You know I don't want you to suffer, but I don't want to see you a wanton."

This sobered me a little, but they did not know how I was suffering, and I could not tell them. I had already been through as much as Mother, it seemed to me, during the days of Hilda's farewell to Clays.

Now Clays and I were left alone. Clays was at first depressed by Hilda's departure and her natural sorrow and affection. She said she loved him and he seemed to believe it. He didn't know it was just the escapade of a wild young girl. Naturally, no man can admit that to himself. But he had an elastic nature, and next time he was on a visit here from Washington (his new job was there), he came to me, simply telephoning and expecting me to go at once to meet him, just as if it had all been arranged between us. It was so unaffected that I hadn't a twinge. He was using Amos's flat. We saw a lot of each other. I behaved with natural joy and may even have been a bit weak and feverish at first, because I had had *grippe* over the holidays. Also I felt that now I faced a decisive year and could not play round with my studies any longer. I wanted to go away to college and at the same time wanted to get married. The holidays had been quieter than I had expected. Clays was away. Amos had made a few passes at me, but I was having none of him then. (Although, later—but that'll be bad enough when I get to it.) I saw three plays in the holidays: *Idiot's Delight*; *Reflected Glory*, a little doodad whose chief merit seemed to be that Tallulah Bankhead was in it. And last, through no fault of my own (Amos took me), *Promise*, a new play adapted from that worthy masterpiece (by the masterpiece-maker) M. Henry Bernstein's *L'Espoir*. Oh, what a lousy play; but in it Sir Cedric Hardwicke, Frank Lawton, Jean Forbes-Robertson. The acting was all right, but it was New Year's Eve, and you couldn't hear because of the tooting of the horns outside. An enjoyable three hours! And Amos trying to hold my hand and snuggling up against me. I went out with Selma, Linda, and Celeste, who were together in the audience, just to get away from the cuddlesome Amos. I began to think about him what Hilda used to say. He not only imitated Clays, but nature had made him a kind of loathsome copy of Clays. He was like a transparency of

Clays, through which you could look at another man. We all went to Childs, then to my house, and we had a good time there, because (I don't quite mean it this way) Mother did not get in till 6:30; but I was through with going out with other men. The two boys who joined Linda and Selma were only nineteen and no use to me after Clays. Of course, we all kissed and necked and said things we didn't mean, but I knew it for what it was. Then, Clays returned. I saw no more of Amos, though he must have been somewhere in the offing all the time. I met Clays that night by accident, but how fatefully, at the Madison Square meeting for Spain. Ralph Bates was there, and said he was going back to fight soon. When he sat down, they applauded, especially the trades unionists, and some Y.P.S.'s behind me snickered, "Oh, that's the C.P. line."

I got into a heated argument, so that I missed the next speaker. People were shishing. I should have known that our American comrades of the Socialist Party had not learned the lesson of their European friends; and could not even understand the idea of a people's front. They were just in it for the hell of it, or to meet the boys, or to feel soft and warm, wrapped up in old, acceptable ideas, such that even the F.B.I. novice wouldn't give them a second thought.

The main speaker of the evening was the ambassador to the U.S., Señor de los Rios, formerly Minister of Education to the new government. Alas, there was a song about him, a bit anti–popular front, "de los Rios, socialist with the white gloves." He spoke for a solid hour in Spanish.

Afterwards, I saw dear Clays, head and shoulders above (most of) the crowd. We went away somewhere together to have some coffee, and he not only talked madly in his usual style, calling everything, in his delicious way, "preposterous"—"preposterous little man," which meant everything from a very small man in a loud check suit, to a social-democrat puffed up with his services to the working class—but told me the news from Washington. He sang his songs, "Socialist in White Gloves" and "Four Generals," all in Spanish, though I can't guarantee the accent, and asked me to lend him some money. I was delighted to do so, but had so little in my purse that I blushed for myself and my family.

For Christmas I had got twenty-five dollars from Grandma

Morgan and Mother and Aunt Dora between them, and still had this in my purse when I went out with Clays. I daresay he thought I was made of money and he didn't think it strange for, by now, he knew how everyone threw their money round in the U.S.A. and how everything was for the children and youth.

I was, meantime, torn about the idea of college, Antioch, Cornell—N.Y.U.—and what profession: medicine, sciences, literature, languages? If languages, I had to take up Greek, Latin, German, Spanish. All I knew was French. I started Greek and Latin with Clays helping me, but this did not get very far, for he was always here and then there. We had very little time together. He could not tell me when he was coming, and I am afraid that this term I did very badly in school.

This allowed me to discuss my future with Clays, however. He wanted me to go in for foreign languages, so that I could get a job abroad in the embassies or foreign economic services, or as a journalist. Then he said, "And if you're smart, you can help me, don't you see!"

One thing led to another. He said his divorce was nearly cleared up. His poor wife, the crime-story writer, had gone through another divorce, just to free them both, and she was not asking for any alimony. There really are some decent women in the world. Their romance was all a mistake, but dramatic enough. She was one of two sisters from a New Orleans family, and supposed to be very pretty. I didn't think her so pretty, actually. She was upstage and conceited, but she was tall, well-formed, and had an air that would impose on some men.

She had met Clays by accident in Washington. They took a plane trip to the Coast together, and stopped off somewhere to get married. A few months later she was sorry, and he was sorry, too. They fought like wildcats. This always made me anxious, for I had seen flashes of temper in Clays. He was Lord High-and-mighty at times, and would begin to speak in a totally incomprehensible English society manner. I was afraid of him, then. Out at the Coast, she had got herself a job writing crime stories. She was good-looking enough, even in that town, to interest the cops, so that they gave her first chance when some murder or horror story broke. Clays and she had bought a fast car, and she now purred and whizzed through Los Angeles and out into the San Bernardino with her husband-to-be at the wheel to protect her. Naturally, Los Angeles (and, in fact, all Southern California) is a Yukon for crime-story writers. Nevertheless, the competition is keen, because there are plenty of disgruntled film writers there. It's a hard life, and this girl went in for it. But she was making out pretty well, and had decided she preferred this to Clays. Of course, she was twenty-two, and, I suppose, life had lost its gilt-edge to her.

I asked Clays about The Honourable Fyshe and about Caroline. At this, he grinned, "Do you want to marry a virgin, Letty?"

And this was how he asked me to marry him. I rushed home to Mother.

"Mother, my life story only has two lines in it: She met an Englishman named Clays Manning, who asked her to marry him."

"And then she dropped dead from joy," said my mother, grimly, "God forbid! So you think your life is over now, you poor child. At sixteen."

"I'll be seventeen next February. Clays will get a court order and we'll be married in Connecticut. Or he won't, and we'll be married in Jersey. Or with a court order, he can even be married here, but only after a year—I think it is. But you don't know about all that. We ought to go to a lawyer."

"At your age!" said my mother, grimly. "Who was his other wife?"

For as Mother was very sharp about divorces, I had never mentioned Manning's previous marriage. I told her the story and that I was quite innocent, but my tongue slipped, and it came out about Caroline, for she was the co-respondent.

"What are you letting yourself in for?" asked Mathilde; and was set against Clays from that time forward. At any rate, I had set a date for bringing him to the house and Mother could not refuse to meet him, nor would she battle him; but she set it all down on my father's account and said that it was because of his life that I was already set on the same path. And then she spoke gloomily about what she would do, if my father was so mad as to let me marry. What would she do for an apartment? She could not bear to live in a small place with the other girls; yet she would lose the money given for my keep. She did not suppose Clays would want to live with her, an old woman (she was forty); but perhaps I could remain with her and Jacky while Clays was away. By this she had cheered up somewhat, for she realized that I would have to go through college, even if I were married; that Clays would be most of the time in Washington and even in London. He was obliged to return to his source at times, both to see his chiefs and to see his family—and, I don't doubt, to see more secret connections. For almost every Englishman is a working patriot, though his politics are not those of the Government in power. I didn't then ask myself what would happen to me if I were such a patriot as Clays. What a situation! Under Two Flags!

My mother thought deeply about the Mannings' divorce. It fascinated her. This was a piping hot subject at that moment in the Morgan family. Not only were Philip and Percival Hogg still in jail for alimony (Hogg was *still* in jail, and Philip was *again* in jail, there was a difference), but Aunt Phyllis was bedeviled in a sad way. She had remarried a man named Bosper, who had been divorced. Aunt Phyllis had now a baby boy and was being sued by Bosper's former wife. The suit was a complicated one. Bosper was sued for bigamy, Aunt Phyllis for false pretenses (calling herself Mrs. Bosper), and an attempt was being made to call Aunt Phyllis's child a bastard. Bosper was resident in New York State; his first wife had obtained a Reno divorce, alleging that she was a Nevada resident. The first wife had already remarried, and had a child of this remarriage. The second marriage was a runaway marriage. The second Mrs. Bosper had been a married woman. After divorcing her husband, a New York women's magazine editor, she had run away to Florida (during her vacation) with Bosper and being offered the alternative by her first husband, divorce, or be divorced, had divorced her husband, a resident in New York State, and she resident in Nevada, and had remarried in New Jersey. Six weeks after the marriage she had left her second husband, charging intolerable cruelty, and had gone to Reno for a second divorce, there receiving a liberal allowance in alimony. She asserted she was a real Nevada resident, anxious to establish herself there as a magazine correspondent, and report the doings of the fashionable divorce colony.

However, Mr. Bosper began to make big money after this (in

the fur business), for the war in Europe was not only making the shipment of furs difficult, but also raising the (unavowed) prices. This money he put into a home, diamond rings, and furniture for Phyllis and her baby, paid for in one-dollar bills, which he carried in a valise.

The first husband of the second Mrs. Bosper (Mr. X) had now remarried in Connecticut, but this marriage was at present illegal in New York State, for he had been the guilty party.

The second Mrs. Bosper, now twice a divorcée, once Mrs. X and then Mrs. Bosper, saw an excellent business in dresses and coats opening up; everyone now thought war was coming. She needed money to start the business. The remarriage had brought her in a good yield, but she needed more. She asked Mr. Bosper for additional alimony. This was refused. She sued for it, but at this moment the judges seemed hardhearted and she was turned down. The second Mrs. Bosper (once Mrs. X) now sued Mr. Bosper, alleging bigamy. She said Mr. Bosper had married the first Mrs. Bosper (Anne) and, somehow illegally, had obtained a divorce in Reno; he had not really been a resident of Nevada, but a New York resident, and the divorce, of which his wife was not notified, was obtained under false pretenses, and was not acceptable in New York State. He had then married her, Mrs. X, who was legally divorced and they were legally married.

He had obtained an illegal divorce from her, and was in arrears of alimony, for which she now sued in New York. But she further claimed that he was not divorced at all, and had married, illegally, Phyllis Morgan, who, therefore, used her (Mrs. Bosper's) name and obtained money and credit under it, and filched away the real Mrs. Bosper's friends by misrepresentation, while, of course, their child (Phyllis's and Mr. Bosper's) was a bastard, and could not normally inherit Mr. Bosper's money.

Mrs. Bosper II (formerly Mrs. X) hoped to collect a small sum from Mrs. Bosper I, from Mr. X, and from Mr. Bosper II. She was suddenly warned, however, that if she won her suit for back alimony (which she was about to do), she would be unable to obtain a decision in her other suit alleging misrepresentations in divorce proceedings, thus losing her basis for blackmail. She illegally agreed to drop her charges, however, upon payment of a round sum of ten thousand dollars, although she had previously alleged a felony. This was arranged.

Mathilde was bitter in lament over the wickedness of the world, but the rest of the women were openly discussing the profit of the alimony game, which now took on complications that they, in their simple, old world ways, had never suspected. They had simply divorced men and lived modestly on men's labors during their respectable lifetimes; but here were brilliant female gamesters unmarrying and remarrying, seizing parts and profits. The women were as shocked as huggermugger sidewalk traders are at the bold feats of speculators and profiteers on the exchanges.

Mrs. Looper said it was better than poker. Mrs. Morgan said she hoped the women didn't get too clever, because Green Acres, most of the year, was kept running on the weekly board of middle-aged women who were put out of the way by their husbands on neat little alimonies; it was one of America's own particular Asia Minors, a relative of London's Lancaster Gate and South Kensington, and the refuge of similar superstitions, race-superiorities, palmistry, and flagwagging. If all these became conspirators and monsters (well, if pigs could fly) of fraud, said Grandmother (though she was not opposed to self-protection as such), the men would become irritated, arise in their might, and cut down the juicy little game. Then, "We girls should remember our place," said Grandmother Morgan solemnly to her two married daughters and several of her friends. "The men marry us, keep us and our children; give us allowances, buy life insurance, and leave us their money and even hand us alimony! But all for one reason, and one reason alone. To buy us off! They don't want us running the world; they are willing to pay a lot, so they can run it themselves. It's insurance, as I see it. Now, if we start plundering the men, if we burden the trade with more than it can bear, it stands to reason that Congress or the Supreme Court, or whoever does these things, don't you see, will start to go over the situation and we will get either no alimony at all, or else no divorce (which would be awful, girls, after all), or else a uniform law; and there are no pickings when there is a uniform law. You see what we women have now, in the U.S.A., is an arbitrage business; we make pickings, even a fat living out of the differences between state laws, an excellent business, considering there are forty-eight states and not only a difference in the laws, but a confusion in the minds of judges, lawyers and divorcées."

"In my opinion," said Mathilde, gloomily, "there should be no divorce. What good does it do anyone? You marry a man anyhow."

"You have no divorce," jeered my grandmother cheerfully, "and look where it's landed you. That is no solution. We girls can only go on getting freer. But not by gangsterism, don't you see? I know there are a few pioneers who will get away with it, like this bird, Mrs. X, but you'll see, there'll be a moral wave and we'll be swept up.

"And," said Grandmother, pulling out another stop, with her great *sang-froid* and good faith in the world, "there's my poor, darling Phyllis, my little beauty; she should never have had a cloud in her blue sky, a woman men should kiss the feet of, a natty dresser, smart, a good wife and mother, and she gets herself into all this trouble; and how she has cried, my darling. We must also, don't you see, stand together, for our daughters. We must not let these harpies and speculators—these women out for what they can get—" My grandmother coughed.

"Where did you get those openwork stockings, Ada? They certainly slim the leg. Do you think if I went there I could get some? You see, I have no hair on my legs, and I wear the sheerest of sheer, but I could do with a pair of openwork, too, for Muron says my legs are one of the most beautiful things about me."

Grandmother simpered. Muron, a broker, was her latest beau and wished to marry her. Grandmother broke off all thought of alimony to plunge into a rose-and-honey account of her romance.

"I would go right off with him tomorrow to City Hall but the boys are so harsh to me, and Stella says it's ridiculous at my age. I want you to come out to Green Acres. I'll throw a big party. We'll have a big get-together; and," she continued gleefully, "Muron's a real good-time-Charlie; that is when I'm there. But other times he likes to sit home—maybe too much. I don't understand what is the matter with the men; they all show their age. But Muron is real nice, good-looking," said Grandmother; "and perhaps this time I'll throw my cap over the windmills. A woman can't live alone forever. It isn't natural."

Thus ended Grandmother's instructions on alimony. Grandmother was delighted with my own prospects, and lectured Mathilde. I must get married; I was a lively young girl, and girls knew everything these days. I better get married before it was too late, she told my depressed mother.

"If only her father took some interest in her," cried Mathilde; "and where will they live? Letty can't live all alone in an apartment."

But she was unheard, for the ladies were all over me, wanting to hear about the rich Englishman.

Grandmother left. She had a date with Muron. The ladies seeped away in her wake and I was left alone with Mother, who indulged as usual, in Poësque visions of my future and hers, not to mention Jacky's, my father's, and so forth.

On me she bent a profound, cold eye, for when Mathilde had tried out the line, "She is too young to know the realities of adult life," Grandmother had hawked, laughed, sneezed, and said, "She's getting too restive. You'd better let her have her head. I know, I remember—"

Grandmother said no more and became grave. It was now no longer admitted that Phyllis, the matron and wronged woman, had once gadded about Europe; and if anyone mentioned Vichy or Cairo, Phyllis preferred to be as ignorant as any woman in the cornbelt, as we conceive it. Mathilde, too, had reached that stage and age when a lazy woman finds it more seemly to forget she ever had a desire or want. Still the thought was there, and not only was I before her eyes, but my cryptic sister Jacky, who was not taking sex in her stride. Mother was even morbid about Jacky, who was doing well enough in the usual subjects for the punch-drunk, history and English, but knew nothing of the modern world or of her contemporaries; who never went to the theater unless the family took us; despised politics; who repeated all the gossip about the male teachers. She criticized them, and satirized them. I tried to make Mother take her away from Hunter, which seemed to me unhealthy, because all girls together, but Mother said it was I who was unnatural and unhealthy.

My final argument to Mother was (about Clays) that she knew I was too young to have the experience of college. This, simply because a professor she had admired at college had said youths ought to go out in the world and get a job and know something about mankind, before they started learning the higher arts and sciences.

I said to her, Why couldn't I take a few months off, try married life, wander about a bit with Clays, and return to college in the autumn, a young, married woman. My mother made an outcry at this, saying I had no idea of how a married woman was shut out of the lives of young girls, despised and treated as a pariah. Indeed, all married women were pariahs from life itself, said my mother, unless they consented to behave like Grandmother Morgan, members of a joyous, ribald camarilla, hardly women, more like men. Where was a place for a married woman in the world today, groaned my mother, wringing her hands. She wanted me to have my playtime. And what about children? Did I realize that they might come—too soon? Why not, was my argument. It would be fun to have them, and get them over; then, by, say, twenty-four, I would be a settled woman and have a career. My mother said, little did I know what I was letting myself in for. Why, this carefree, but far from heart-free man I was marrying did not even stoop to make the promises her children's father (that meant Solander) had made to her; in fact, he practically proclaimed himself a rogue with women.

Perhaps, my mother enquired with a sad sneer, I intended to be like my maternal grandfather, my paternal grandfather, my maternal grandmother (for Mother could not blink the fact that Grandma Morgan was not entirely chaste), my Uncle Philip, and various other relatives, not to mention my own father. Yes, it was a nice pattern they had in marital relations today, and perhaps it suited a girl like me; although, thank goodness, Jacky showed more of her mother in her, and Andrea was an innocent child.

Mother felt she had not acted well toward me in letting me run wild all over the world in free-love schools, and in not insisting upon my going to Hunter, too, where I might have thought of studies for a few years at least, and seen that all the girls in the world, of my age, were not engrossed with dances and sex.

At this, I spoke up and remarked that I did about twice as well as Jacky in studies; that I also had a social life, and was all that a young girl should be, pretty, agreeable, safe with men, and not wasting my time over the poetry of a strange vegetable like Peter Varick, the professor with whom all the girls at Jacky's college were involved. Involved by hate or love, what difference did it make? What sort of a man is a man who gives lessons to young ladies, said I, mimicking young ladies. Peter wore pants, but he was a vegetable, a yam or clam, or something; quite close to the vegetable kingdom, at any rate.

My mother stretched out her hand! A fog came over her fine, blue eyes with their clear blue-whites. She cried, "What can I do if the father is so negligent?"

I would cut up as a wanton, end up living with the man, she knew—with my father's encouragement, I would certainly do that.

"And apparently your father approves of this semi-vagabond?"

I jumped up, and threw my arms round her neck; "Oh, Mother, thank you ever so much. I'll never forget it," for this was Mathilde's peculiar way of saying yes.

"I think I have some rights," said my mother, at once, "and that is that your marriage must be secret, or nearly so. If you knew what you're letting yourself in for. Going to college next fall, a married woman. They'll laugh at you; you'll be out of everything. There isn't a mother alive will let you talk to her daughters."

I stared at her.

"I know, I know—too much," said Mother in the exact words of poor Grandmother Fox.

"All right. We'll only tell a few friends."

My mother said sarcastically: "You forget he's not divorced yet."

This was so. My father and Clays, very much the same in ideas, of course, thought it quite simple that I should marry, and I was mad with enthusiasm at having this side of my life so neatly settled.

I threw myself into my work with such energy that I bewildered teachers and secretaries of societies. I sprang to the top in everything, realizing that I could not keep Clays unless I showed a great ardor in politico-social life (I say this now, but at that time I did not know there were any other kinds), and determined to make a splash, if possible, later on, on the Continent, or in England; nothing was too much for me.

There were many nights when I slept only three hours—homework, meetings, chewing the rag after meetings, accidental conversations on street corners, restaurants, bars, and Greenwich Village cellars where young people lived; giving out leaflets and rushing to bookshops to get new publications; work on the school magazine, selling the *Daily Worker*, or leaflets, organizing rallies. I had time for it all, and school, too. That was the effect of love and expectation upon me. I suppose it would be upon everyone. Fulfillment is the secret of energy, not self-sacrifice; at least for my type.

Clays and I had seen, as in a vision, Clays an attaché, or secretary to some embassy abroad. I started out, not to fit myself for this so much, as to already take part in it.

I turned out to be the most brilliant girl in the class in economics according to the teacher, but did not get the very highest marks, alas, on account of these outside activities—but I did not regret that then, and I do not now. I then felt for the first time (with Clays, and my marks not so bad) that I had something to do, what some people would call a destiny. That was not my view then, and if it is now, it is because I have become more sentimental, because older. At twenty-four I have noticed people start to become sentimental; they forget all they have learned and congeal, not into any essence of themselves, but into some requisite atom of the social group.

Last year I was at a reunion with some alumnae of the high school, and after, we went to a bar, all in red plush, to have a talk. Some of the girls were married, two already divorced, and all sorry.

"Are you beat?" they asked me.

"Not yet."

"You will be soon," they said. "We've given in. You've got to live the way people do. You can't hold out."

I did hold out; I will hold out. But why shouldn't those who are weak hold out, too? That's the question. This world is made of ex-chimpanzees, not ex-champs, after all! What is the plural of Joe Louis? There isn't any. That just shows.

I wrote about this to my darling Clays, then in Washington. As well as my other works, I had time to write him every two days, at least. My letters were full of my active life and indignation—for the most part, indignation. Why? I was a hotpot, forever bubbling, said Clays. But this fever and ferment was my life at its best. Fever to others, life to me. Never did I wish to be past this fitful fever. I lived for the day, for the hour, only to enjoy it better. For thinking back (like my mother) or ahead (like the philosophers) makes you languid and lazy.

Of course, perhaps, I was just a pocket edition of Grandmother Morgan, with some higher education! This was how she lived. In her later years she picked men younger and younger; in their mirror she saw that she had more years to go. How clear it is!

I wrote to Clays (whom, for fun, I called Sir Clays, he was the parfit knight),

My darling *Sir* Clays,

...We had a debate in economics on the legality and ethics of the sit-down strike, and I was on the affirmative; that is to say, they are both legal and ethical. As you predicted some time ago, oh, seer (by courtesy of Marx), the wave of strikes is hitting the United States, and the workers all over are becoming more and more labor-conscious, and realizing that they have rights too, and are setting out to get them. Labor is marching on and growing very fast, despite the opposition of the typical bourgeois "mistaken liberals" who claim that sit-downs will lead to Fascism, because the middle-class will be *aroused* by this "destruction of property rights" (ha, ha, ha!). This feeling is echoed by my dear Republican history teachers, who point out with sadistic pleasure the rise of a group of all of 50 vigilantes, as if every new thing in history, as if every new force of progress and democracy (yes, in our supposedly free land) had not always been attacked by the forces of reaction. Our teacher said that the vigilantes are a national institution. This must embrace a very small scope of the nation and even if it were true, who encouraged the vigilantes, dear lady! who started them? My Eco-teacher is Trotsky-ite, not mistaken, but a real one! It's too much to always give them the break and call them Trotsky-mistakenites. She infilters the duckiest notions into the class; as the class is special, and supposedly for the bright girls, they have taken care to include very few members of the real working class in it (we have plenty here), so that the snug, comfortable brats are all too willing to receive the bad idea. The working-class girls may not have had all that leisure to read Marx (they generally have to wash the floors in between times), but oh, boy, they know what is so and what isn't, when it comes to the wage scale, ticklish proposition, for example. I have the biggest arguments, and go up afterwards and discuss Marx (I know nothing of him, as you state, but she knows still less), and so life goes on. . . .

My darling Clays, I am not sighing and pining for you. This is an unusual love letter. I would, though, if I had the time, so don't take offense. I can't see you pining for me, either, but I hope you do. You have more experience than me in pining—I know your record—so I hope you pine somewhat from mere habit. What a shame that I can't tell everyone! But what fun, too. I love to look at all those simpering brats and think—oh, baloney, what do you know about that thing they pronounce in the movies LERV? I'm getting sticky, my boy, and I move on.

I am taking Art-ah-Art. We have been studying, in one week, what should take at least a year. We are now supposed to be able to identify romanesque, byzantine, babylonian, greek, gothic, renaissance, neo-classical, and such forms of architecture—the truth, we cannot. Also, now we are going to Painting. I like this better. I have to make special reports on Leonardo da Vinci and Jan van Eyck—that's all. I know you'll laugh at me, but "it's the custom of the town." I am taking J. van E. because I saw the *Adoration of the Lamb* myself, with mine own eyes, and she doesn't usually have reports on him. She reminds me of a person who builds a house without foundations; because he is the true founder of the Dutch school. Of course, I'm dying to take El Greco, but she said I had enough.

I am going crazy. The Y.C.L. is being reorganized (again) —I approve of the idea that communists should be human beings; that in their relations with others they should be tolerant and broadminded; that they should do as the world does because they can thus convince more people of the efficacy of another world (not the preacher's, the Marxist's)—

but I am sick and tired of the idea that people join the League, not to be told anything about communist theory, or to be trained in any way for the struggle later on, or to make them better Party members when they grow up. Oh, no! You must not scare them by doing anything but having meaningless discussions. You must forget that you were a communist and make the League a "mass organization" with NO PURPOSE (essential)! with little or no chance for Marxist education, and with the already established leaders remaining the already established leaders; the Leadership—God Bless 'em, over the water! Still 'n all, I am trying to educate myself—I should love, love to go to France, Spain, England—with you—learn something—how little a girl knows. When we see men conforming, how worse than bad! For we are supposed to regard men as the tigers, the outlaws, the "beloved bandits"; but, actually, are they? Very few mavericks, in my experience. But the theory still goes, among these (soon-to-be) horned heads, that the maverick, the leader is what women admire and choose, in order to carry forward the best of the species, or something of that sort; actually most of my classmates, female, have their eye out for the willingest, not the best. It's a tattle-tale gray world, my masters. Well, there'll be no sense in sexual theories until women start telling their minds; and, of course, until they have some; that'll be when they abolish the ads, for all the kids I know get their ideas from the ads; but even at that, what they choose men for ain't at all what the boys think. But don't start asking me why I choose you. You know why! I couldn't resist you. That's terrible. I don't want to think about it.

I am coaxing Mother into giving me, for my birthday, the collected works of a gentleman of the Bourgeoisie known to fame as Lenin. Then, maybe I can start catching up on you. (This IS a hint.)

You will probably think I am just a loony kid gone intellectual, but I just felt like writing to you. You are the only one to whom I can tell my whole life. What a pleasure that is, what a relief! Don't let me down. I am giving myself away.

Every book on etiquette, not to mention on *How to Attract Men*, tells you to do the opposite. Meanwhile, I am listening to the dances from Prince Igor; my taste is crazy, but it and you make me feel freer and less nervous than I have in months and months—and years. I think I grew up fast. Jacky is still at the idolized-professor-of-English stage. His name is Peter "Varnish"! Poor kid! She thinks men are gods.

> Yours
> LETTY-SCHLAGOBERS
> (easy to whip into shape).

Clays wrote back, among other things:

I'll throw you out if you say *all over* which is German, instead of *everywhere* . . . and a friend of mine (in the Foreign Office, so many of them are; it's the old school tie operating) explained the Nazis to me this way: "It's you communists that brought it on, it's the reaction." Don't ask me, dear Letty, why I go to see him. Gilbert (that's him) always knows when war is going to be declared; and it always arrives on time. I don't even need Marxism when I know Gilbert. I don't make any inferences.

> Lovingly, Clays.

P.S. Why *Sir* Clays? Do you think that a handkerchief and a tourney were love? That was adventure! This, that *we* have, is LOVE.

We spoke of our marriage, but we waited for the double divorce, which Jean, his wife, the crime writer, had not managed to get. This was not malice. We had asked ourselves if we ought to wait so long. While we were asking this, a letter came from the wife, saying that she expected us all to be free very soon, as her parents were paying for a Mexican divorce and she was even then in Mexico City. I could hardly believe it. It was like hearing that Europe was free. Do these things really happen? Underneath the excitement and joy, I had felt down in the mouth—marriage was really too hazardous these days, I sometimes thought, and I thought of poor Mother. I now wrote to Clays:

I have had a new, different kind of feeling in the last few days, which I hope will be permanent. At last, I have lifted myself out of the tenseness, general apathy, and self-consciousness, the occasional rising into periods of hysterical work, and the general feeling of *malaise,* which I've had for months now, and is what I most have, that resembles the kind of young girls they write about. I feel like a different person. The only thing is that too many people around jar on my nerves, which is new; and that I like to be alone. However, don't think that's too bad, I feel a strange kind of peace; though I'm still so young, a feeling that I'm not as immature as I was, in order to convince myself that I can really accomplish something, I am making plans for a book. Don't laugh! I know it'll never get anywhere as a work of art, but if I can complete it, I'll feel that perhaps I have potentialities as an author. I mapped out a plan a few days ago, and I've just been working on preliminary notes, haven't got down to work on the actual thing and won't for some time. What is the right way to begin? It's a story of a group I know very well; a group of girls in high school with some fancy flourishes of my own. The most I've done is writing a page-long character sketch of each girl and her family, ten in all, and in working out a fantastic theory about the riddle of the universe which one of the boys is supposed to hold. I have a kind of knowledge that young men of twenty or so indulge in theories about riddles of the universe; tacked on is a conversation where he says he can't believe in God; and he goes about telling every girl the awful news. This one's name is Bobby —but there is more than one. I know it sounds crazy, but if I can get it done by the end of the summer—that is if we're not married—I'll feel happy.

There is a strange tenseness in the air in America, it seems to me! Families parade along the streets on Sunday in their new suits; discussions go on as usual, but, maybe it's just because I live in a big city, but everyone seems to have a feeling, conscious or otherwise, that something big is going to happen, something startling—I don't know what. A lot of the pseudo-intellectuals, the dilettantes, have been

wandering about lately in a high fervor of seething excitement, because of the profusion of lectures by Thomas Mann,
Harold J. Laski, etc. There is a general meeting of each other
at meetings, at the New School, at dinners, at Mecca Temple,
and a cheerful feeling that a lot is wrong with the universe;
and it's marvelous to be able to discuss it all over a Martini;
just as the intellectuals of fifty years ago discussed it in the
Closerie des Lilas, or something, over Pernods. Life at school,
as a consequence (consequent by comparison), is becoming
more babyish and disgusting, as life outside of it is getting
richer and more full-blooded. One gets a sense of waste, of
foolish indulgence, of "why am I here," every morning when
contemplating the mature faces of eighteen-year-old cherubs
who wouldn't know a serious discussion, except on boys, if
they were listening to one! And a feeling of the broadness
and wealth of material in life all around, except for the class
one is attending.

And is *this* growing-up? Each change, I say that to myself.
But it's usually some awful symptom—but if *This is It*, then
it isn't so bad. If this letter, into which I have put my real
thoughts, seems weak and adolescent to you still, well, tell
me and I'll weep suitably; but if it isn't, show it to others
and say, my girl,

LETTY FOX FECIT.

P.S. Author's swelled-head already!

MAY 8, 1937

Dearest Clays (not sir),

You can't imagine how thrilled I was to get your letter.
Though I think I am getting less sentimental and childish
every day, yet I have such a longing to go back to Europe,
though it is so changed now, that it is incredible. I have been
living for the past two months, as if in a daze, all sorts of
things happening to me, a very *mouvementé* period, and yet
I don't quite feel as if I were all here and (don't snicker) as if I
were going to get married. All I know is that I am dying to go
back where you came from. This is not the influence of books,

nor, strictly, of you. All the books, for instance, about Europe that I have read lately, except for Erich Maria Remarque's *Three Comrades*, have, on the contrary, made me want to stay in America. And yet, I want to go. However, there is an obstacle and that is Mother. Not that she is opposed to the idea of my going so much, as that she wants to know many things more. First and foremost, she wants letters to her from you, not to me, telling about it, and with more details. She is hurt, really, at the idea of your having written so much to me, when she does not know your exact status (this is so ironbound but it is natural), and she would have to be consulted anyway. She wants more details and she wants to know who is to supervise me and be responsible for me, not a person always actually with me. But you travel around so much, and now you want to fight for Spain which is so splendid, but which is so much anxiety for me and her. And she wonders if I would not be better off with her. I don't think so; I'd rather be there, even in Spain, and you know I mean that. Oh, what an end to my life if even I died in Spain! This is not all romance to me, as you cruelly put it one evening when we were walking down Eighth Street. I am a young girl, but every young person lives so much in these years of change. School doesn't match up to life, and if your eyes are open you see it. And then, parents separate, and you aren't nursed in those old illusions; and far from being a dreamer, it's impossible for one to "come a cropper," as you always put it, for one knows everything. I don't mind dying, if I die gloriously, I mean this. "One crowded hour of glorious life is worth an age without a name." And more than that, I shall have been your wife—at seventeen; and I shall have been a student at the Sorbonne (I adore this suggestion); or a worker with you at Madrid. I can hardly write, the pen is falling out of my hands as I think of it. Oh, really to do something! I have done all I could, but it has been committees, conventions, articles—I sound like, *blood, fire and the sword*, a fire-eater. Don't pull your cold, superior Oxford airs on me, Clays; I am just a fiery, gallant person, given a chance, and, I suppose, the Hectors and Achilles-es, were like me, only more so. You won't "be settled and in charge of me," Mother says. It sounds as if I'm feeble-minded; and to her I'm a child. Also, what is to become of her? She would like to go to Europe and take Jacky to give her a chance, but Andrea? My father will have to give me the $2,500 if I marry you (when, I mean), and Mother will persuade him, if she can, to give Jacky hers; or part of it, to get an European education; as for Andrea, she was posthumous maritally and financially speaking. It's a shame to deprive her of it; but we need it too. Jacky wants a different career from me. She wants to go to art schools and wind up at the Beaux-Arts. She's only just fifteen, not old enough to go with you and me, and she is rather young in some ways, younger than I was; and I know now, I was fairly young for fifteen at fifteen, though I didn't think so then. If you would write to Mother quickly! She has got up all sorts of fantasies since last night when I got your letter; that (for example), when once I am over there, Jacky will want to go; and Father and Persia will want to go; and she will be left all alone with only a baby and a poker-playing and alimony-racketeering bunch to fall back on. She's dreadfully afraid of them, and has tried all her life to be a fine, cultivated woman. So, it is, of course, rather hard on her. At the same time, I don't intend to stay here and let you go to Spain; and I wouldn't think of trying to persuade you against Spain. It is a wonderful opportunity for both of us. Then, stupid things. I can't go right away. My orthodontist (brace-doctor to you, you vulgarian, and we have specialized even braces in the U.S.A. I'm just doing your sneering for you, at the glorious old stars and stripes, *not* stars and bars as you say, probably only to annoy, I started out to say, my orthodontist) has not yet completed his work. I can't go with you with hoops on my kisser, and I have oodles of work to be done. But I would follow you in September. Oh, heck, you hear the voice of maternal authority. I am under-age, and all the foregoing, or most, is what Mamma says. What are we to do? Perhaps a *pension*; but when you could get away—and you say you could sometimes, at least to get to the French border. I'd have to travel. If I went to college there, I'd either have to be in a kind of Latin quarter which Mother is dreadfully against, or in *externat surveillé*—why, that's simply impossible. And do you realize they have passports and *cartes d'identité* and they'd all know I was a married woman? I could pass as a young girl, so they'd expect me for decorum's sake to live with a respectable old dragon. What am I to do? Do you really think I should like Montpellier? I do object to having my freedom curtailed. Why, this is one of Mother's objections to marriage at my age for me—I'd have no girlhood. And it is true! Isn't that your real objection to my studying in Paris. But, of all evils, we must choose the least. And then, perhaps I could persuade Mother to let Jacky stay with me—though since the now hush-hush episode of Aunt Phyllis, I doubt if the Morgans will like this. And I must know more. First (you know, you have been there), what are the subjects one studies in *Philosophie*? Second, must one go to the Sorbonne afterwards, to study and get one's *licenciat*? You know I'd like to go to a co-ed school, or I'd feel so shut away from the world. This world nowadays is really a bisexual world, *both* sexes are fighting, both political, both social. I'm going to become a hell of a prissy, blue-stockingish prude if I live segregated. And why? It was all very well to segregate the girls before. Now, they have all kinds of people to segregate; so I don't want to live in an internment camp when I'm not (yet) any of the proscribed races, religions, politicals, and so on. You know I couldn't be sex-avid now, but I still feel a kind of restraint when I'm out with men, although no one would believe it of me. And I blame this on the American system of "dates," etc., etc., where everything is prescribed, hairdo, conversation, baby-talk from the girls, yessing the men; and second of all (as they say locally), I don't get along with girls, so very well. I don't gossip. Perhaps I'm a cat, as you say! But I don't gossip and can't bear giggling over boys, and, What did he mean when he halted at the door? And this is girl stuff. The prospect of being very respectable, in a ladies' college with girls growing moldy and getting that iron-gray complexion that means hope is dying, while they concentrate on

317

Greek roots, fills me with horror. So I'd like maybe, my son,
to live in Paris, where there is some maturity and people can
let loose via the intellect and the arts. I don't mind *La Vie de
Bohème*, but not local sex; for the only way they let loose
here is in sex alone, and that's what they live for; sex in
every form, in stories, thought, action, innuendoes; and
every darn word in the American language has come to
cause a hyena laugh because of its double meaning (that is,
they don't care for the real meaning). This is a tirade and I'm
being humorless. I know. But think, just the same, what it
must be to be a relatively young person with everything
ahead, in some place where there's a hope in society (not just
in types of automobiles) for a better kind of life all round, intellectual as well; and where people think it's all right to be
brainy; and that the brainy aren't loony and that the brainy
aren't bad sports; and that sex isn't some variety or other of
"feelthy pictures." I am tired of a place where instead of getting out the old family album, they now get out the old
Oedipus complex that made them what they are today! It's
the same, but not in such good taste! Wow! I am not in my
best parlor fit. There is something wrong, when I begin to
yell, *What is Truth* and *Up the Labor Republic*, as I am now
doing. So, you see, you must write to Mother and Father, and
everyone else you can think of, in your most sporty style—
for, let me tell you a secret, you bowl them over when you
get going on all fourteen cylinders—and help me out of
it. . . . I will leave out all my usual gossip about May Day,
Madison Square Garden, and other society notes. I presume
by this you know what happens on May Day. . . . I took your
advice about my girl friends. My best friend at present is
Isabel Cartwright; she does awfully in school, but writes real
poems. She seems dull and yet you can go out with her every
day and talk and talk—and I am very much tempted to tell
her all. She is ugly, long horsy face—and she suffers! But she
is an adult at seventeen, just like I am; and I don't have
to behave like a Mexican jumping bean or talk itsy-bitsy, to
prove I'm not a pain in the neck, which is a relief.

Your Letty.

I blushed for this letter when sent off and fancied Clays would give me up; but he came at once to New York, getting special leave, and visited my mother and father—two separate visits of course, for these warring powers could not meet, except by special arrangement.

Now came the letters and papers from Clay's ex-wife. What joy! But she warned him his marriage would not be legal in New York or in England. She had no money to come to New York State to get a proper divorce. The present trip had been paid for by her family, who were very angry with Clays. They had always had great hopes for their beautiful daughter, expected her to make a career in the movies, or with some rich man.

Clays's residence was both Washington and New York, mine New York; but I was under-age.

"Be careful of bigamy," wrote his ex-wife.

"A figamy for bigamy," said Clays.

I cried. My mother and father were very anxious indeed. Aunt Dora who came in, of course, having a great nose for smut and trouble, said, "I suspect her motives," meaning those of the ex-wife.

"No, no," said Clays; "she's a fine woman."

"Go and live with her then," I sobbed.

"Must I live with every wonderful woman?" asked Clays.

At this moment, Clays received a message that he must be ready to leave for Spain at any moment. Since he had decided to go there he had got himself a job as special correspondent, and "they expected things to break at any moment."

Clays now plunged, and asked, Would my mother and I come to France, and wait for him; or would we risk the separation? I did not like this idea, though Mother did. He would have to be on the spot (Madrid or any designated place) for ever so long, and there was, after all, only a faint likelihood of trips to France or England. Once there, our movements would be uncertain; for all his friends in embassies, foreign offices, and points to windward and leeward of the world, couldn't assure us, or him, papers when they were wanted. And all because he was an avowed radical!

My mother was in the dumps. She was in no mood to go and sit in cannon mouths, or under the red flag or under the skull and crossbones (for that's what it all seemed to her). She was sick of ill-starred im-matrimonies. A stormy time! I said, "What is all the trouble about? We'll live together and I'll go over unmarried and go to the Sorbonne while waiting for him."

This was the first time I felt an overwhelming desire for him. I had thought of marriage and knew what it was, naturally, but at the thought of losing him I felt something different, a jealous fire. Then, he had made his promise to me before so many people, and before my family; he could not let me down. This publicity has a wonderful effect, in itself causes passion. This is age-old, just an auxiliary to true passion—but how powerful! I never thought of his defrauding me, though others did, and said so. I felt that sureness that Persia must have felt all the time. Marriage bonds and guarantees mean little when you feel that. No sooner did I feel this, than I forgot all the innumerable not-impossible she's and he's that might cross our paths, and fell into the Great Illusion; which was that Clays alone would suit me and I must have him at any cost. I stormed, turned into a shrew. "I must and will go with Clays to *Ultima Thule*," I said.

Jacky thought this was splendid, and began to take my side. (She now regarded me as a party girl.) Clays said, "In little more than a year you'll be eighteen, and legally a woman then. What I'm saying is queer, but not underhand, because it's for your mother to hear. We can't pretend we're in the nineteenth century. If I live with you, I'll marry you. We'll be bound. But I won't promise to marry you, if you don't live with me; not because I have other intentions now, but because I know the world, men, women, and myself. If you live with some other man, you'll marry him; and I'll be in Madrid, but out of your life; and the same with me. This is the truth about passion, though you don't know it, Letty, and, probably, Mrs. Fox doesn't like to admit it. I wouldn't say such things normally, but our whole lives are being decided here and now, and we'd better be clean about it."

"This is impossible," said my mother; "I'm not a prude, but I don't care for such speaking in front of my daughter."

"There are old standbys," said Clays, not unkindly, but in his superior way, "which don't help us at all."

"Whatever I say, no one will listen; everyone will do just what suits them," said Mathilde.

"Very well, then; it's left to you and me," said Clays to me. "We will go out to talk this over. I am sorry to cause you any anxiety," he continued to my mother; "but as you are unable to come to any decision, we must do it ourselves. We will see Letty's father."

"I am left to myself in a moment like this," said Mathilde.

My sister Jacky came forward, a flush flooding her pale, serious, but fleshy face; her eyes flashed. She took Clays's hand, not mine, though she looked at me friendly, and she said, in German (from Heine's poem *Der Asra*),

> "And the slave said: I am called
> Mohamet; I am from Yemen
> And my family are those of Asra
> Who love, and die of love."

He held her plump, white, and rather pretty hand too long, patting it. Then he came away, saying, as he jammed on his journalist's hat, "She's going to be sweet, too, Letty. One of the bemused. Of course she'll be unhappy, I should think. Depends on the lucky chap!"

"Why? There's a chance she'll go to Paris and study art. That's all she wants, and the Great Lover!"

"Not much! Not much at all! Is she strong? Not any trouble?"

"She fancies she has. But that's only dreaming. She's always reading old stories where women always had tuberculosis."

"Yes, but that long neck—and her complexion—white and quite lovely; transparent, waxy, clear as possible—"

"You must now forget other women, your Steepleship!"

"I can't forget them. But I won't betray them, or you. I'll get you some Parma violets—I adore them, don't you?"

"No; but they will do."

"How saucy!"

"I'm not going to be meek with my husband."

"Your husband—now, that's just what we've got to talk about!"

We went to a Stewart's Cafeteria near Fourteenth Street. This was a stolen trip and Clays had to be back in Washington. Could I go with him? He could put me up, perhaps; he didn't know. I had never spent a night away from home at the famous "girl friend's," and knew that my father would not forgive this, either. He gave me every liberty, but would despise this kind of trickery.

"Well," said Clays, "then I must come to you, but can you arrange a night away somewhere; for don't you see, once we are —man and wife, to be frank—they'll allow you to go with me, to France, anywhere; and it isn't exactly rape."

"It's screwy," I said, hesitating, wanting, after all, a wedding with parents in their frills, and champagne cocktails at that Longchamps near City Hall.

"I've got to run," said he. "Look, Hebe, I'll send you a telegram and you fix up that girl friend, for you know I'll have to be in and out like this, and if we can get married, I'll fix up the boat ride; and if not, you must come after me, but we won't be separated. Fate weel naut zeparate zem. Gracious," he said, in that lovely way he must have got from a charming, foolish mother, "I must fly." And he flew.

Ten days later came the telegram. I got it just before school, cut classes, and rushed off to buy myself a wedding dress. I used one of Grandmother's accounts, for I had nothing left of the $150 (I had lent a lot to Clays and Father had refused to give me any more); I bought an ocher chiffon, with some colored satin ribbons wound round the waist, and rushed home to bathe.

I spent an hour brushing my hair and looking anxiously at the short white wool coat I had to wear with the dress. I never was one for doing things in advance, and had not one thing ready. I told Mother simply that Clays was coming, and perhaps would marry me that afternoon.

Clays jumped off one of the first cars at the station and came striding toward me with that forked, humped, and undulating gait of the very tall. I was dumb with my feelings; no doubt even my color went. I stood quite still. He flooded me; the dam broke; I trembled all over.

"A cab!" said he.

We got in, and I still had not said a word. He looked at the string of beads.

"Nice," said he; "the old boy was decent—let me off. I told him I had hooked a beauteous New York society girl. You look lovely in that faeces color. I'm so excited. Isn't this all preposterous? As soon as we get a ha'penny between us, promise me you'll always have a faeces-colored dress. But I forgot, we're going to live on the hop, rather, aren't we? Not even time for a toothbrush between plane and machine-gun shots—have to learn to do like the blacks you know; they have wonderful teeth; rub them on a bit of fiber when they do anything; they chew up caterpillars, I think. Worth it, to have their teeth—I mean the Aruntas. And we'll have to learn to manage like birds you know, wipe our beaks on fences."

I said nothing.

"What's wrong? You're supposed to repent at leisure, after you're married. Good God! You're not starting to repent now? You've got the entire future of the world to repent in. Your child and grand-child and great-great—they can all hear the story of how you ran off, to your cost, with that preposterous Clays Manning; but now, now is too soon, my darling."

I laughed now, "I'm coming out of it. Too much excitement. Are we going to get married? This is my wedding dress, Clays."

"Oh, charming," he said, flurried. "Well, we're going to run off, my dear, if you want it; but we must tell Pappy and Mammy, odd as it all sounds. My divorce has not come through yet, and we haven't time, and I've got to go—you'll have to trust a Briton—"

"You know, now we have the united front—"

"Yes!"

"Politically, I mean."

"Even with George III? With The Man with the Umbrella?" Saying this, he stopped the taxi at an address in Bleecker Street, before an old tenement, newly brick-faced and made up into high-priced flats for artists. I had been here once or twice to visit friends in college.

"Let's go in here," he said.

He had a key, and we got into a flat on the ground floor, with one very large living room, and a series of three closets in a dark passageway, run up out of thin partition board. Curtains were hung here and there; everything was old, and covered with scaling paint. There was a name on the door, one I knew and respected, a writer who was now in Spain.

"He sublet this to Joe," said Clays, mentioning another well-known character, "and Joe is in the country at present, staying at

Jake's. Jake and his wife are in Hollywood and cannot sublet on account of bad times, so they gave him the place free just to keep it up, and I can have this place for week ends free, until Joe finds a sublease, or himself returns."

"This is new," said I.

"Yes; I told him my predicament; ours. And now all we have to do is go and lay down terms of surrender to the previous generation."

"Or present them with a *fait accompli*," said I.

"We'll visit Mamma," said he; "no representation without rights. I'll brush up first."

After brushing up, he bought me wine gloves and red roses, and some carnations for Mamma. We telephoned her from the bar where we had drinks and spoke to Pauline, who was with her, giving sage advice about me. Clays bought a bouquet for Pauline. He kept me firmly in one hand, and all these flowers in the other arm as we reached the house. I was quite small to "His Steepleship!" I found myself within the old doorway with a tumult of feelings. A discreet old gentleman who lived in the house, and was always going out to affairs or concerts, passed us and smiled. I heard my father's voice. He had come from work, too.

Clays was very gay with all, and quite chattily discussed his matrimonial tangles. It was "preposterous." He might not be out of them for a year—longer. He would be away; "I lead a risky life. You may think of her as the airman's bride. You give her in me a love which she may never have again; and you may have the pleasure of seeing her a beautiful widow of seventeen or eighteen. Perhaps I shall hop this mortal twig in short order. I may say I consider it quite proper."

They argued it up and down. It was naturally hard for even the most liberal of the four (Dora Morgan was there still) to agree to free love. Finally, Clays took me out to walk and to eat.

"End of the second chukker," said Clays, "and no score yet."

"Oh, Clays, why did you start all this? It's just a mess."

"Then what's your idea?"

"Let's run away, now. Not go back."

"My own decision, Hebe. But I want you to be sure. I had visions of you making up your vacillations too late and following me, on the spur of the moment, all round Spain; while I, obedient to the whims of Mars, chasing the canards of Rumpus, left you far behind. I saw you sleeping alone under the Spanish stars, and I, not alone, but in caravans, trains, coaches, motorbuses, inns, water cellars, barns, ditches, ruts and caves, attics, and hiding underbeds, kissing the wormeaten boards and flagstones in lieu of Letty; and tempted by those black eyes and those high pouting busts—"

"Clays!"

"You must be inured to the truth."

"What makes you think I'd do all that for you?"

"My ex-wife would have done it. She was that sort. She's quite a grand girl; but of course, you're better, so you would have."

This cast a gloom over me. I didn't think I would have, but on the instant became persuaded. I murmured, "What you are is such an olio of romance and rococo sentiment, pathos and vaudeville, that really I must believe in my knowledge of human nature to take you at your word, Clays. Don't kid me, I'm going to cry again any minute"; and I declared I was ready to throw myself into the land of fire for him. Let him just get the passport. He became hotter and hotter, interspersing his declarations with regrets for wasted time, gladness that I was born no later (for then I would have been much too young for him), and making allusions, so raw, to the night coming, that I felt something like sharp knives in me. He kept referring to my virginity, and to how little I knew (for all my supposed, but innocent wildness) of life and love; and how exalted and at the same time sordid and bad love could be, till I felt more than drunk.

"I'm tired, worn out, Clays. I must go home."

"All right. Here's a cab. Home, James!"

In the taxi he squeezed my hand and said, "How you love me! It's wonderful! You've really got me!"

This made me angry. He seemed stupid and animal. But I felt so sick that I was determined to bring things to a finish, so that I should know where I stood, both with him and with other men, always afterwards; "so that they cannot tease me," I thought to myself. I had nothing to wear to bed; but so suddenly to bare myself to a stranger did not upset me, for I was in a coarse, glum mood, and hardly counted him. His eyes were glued to me, and I saw myself as he must see me, a stumpy, young female, whose legs came out like columns from my white shirt. We got into bed, and I threw myself into his arms quickly. It was just as if I had done it every night of my life.

What a surprise! We rolled there, smoking and uneasy for some time, when Clays, with shocking calm, told me that his excessive love had made him impotent and that we would have to get up and sit talking for awhile. I was abashed. I sat with downcast eyes, blushing. Suddenly it occurred to me that I must telephone my parents. He looked after me anxiously. I told my parents I had gone out dancing. At once, he brought me back to bed and, taking my hand, showed me where to put it; and then he declared that he had been up five nights in succession, with only three hours' sleep a night, and had been beating up the town to get his papers for Spain, and anxious about his divorce and me; and that all this had an effect even on a young, strong man in love; I must forgive him. Many were the apologies he made, but in a manly tone; and laying his head on my breast, he went to sleep. We got up at seven in the morning, hungry, disquieted, and worn out.

Clays was supposed to return that day to Washington, but said he would risk another night. His friends in the office would stall for time and let him know immediately if he was wanted.

From the café where we breakfasted, I rang Mother again, and found that Pauline had stayed the whole night with her. It was Pauline who came on the phone and told me I had better come home at once with "the man" and see them.

When we got there, it was ten-thirty in the morning. Mother was asleep, having been put to bed by Pauline; Jacky was home from school, but Andrea, my little sister, had been packed off to Grandmother Morgan's with Dora Morgan, till the scandal should have been mopped up.

Pauline was delighted to see us; "So you spent the night with him, naughty girl! You thought you would pull a fast one, wicked child! Well, darling, I am really your friend, and you must rely on me. But Mother, naturally, is horribly upset. You cannot understand that, you are only a naughty child. But he is the one to blame," and so on.

Pauline's remains of a French accent made all this sound quaint and cheering.

At the noise, my mother rose and lumbered out of her room, in her amazing way, bringing a thundery atmosphere with her. As she stood in the doorway and surveyed the scene, I felt once more her grand stage power. As soon as she was with us, her bad temper poured into all of us. We stood dumb before her.

"Well," faltered Pauline, "go on, Mathilde; you said you would be nice to them. Besides, frankly, it makes little difference what you are to them. It is all over."

"Come here," said Mathilde to me, taking no notice of the other two; "you can't expect me to be very pleased to see you! I suppose you knew I should be very worried all night? And I suppose you know you should have asked my permission to do so crazy a stunt, before going off? Instead, you notified me this morning that it is a *fait accompli*; and, of course, I can do nothing about it. And then, you're here without giving me any of the information that I, as a mother, or even as a guardian—for the name of mother doesn't seem to have any more influence with you than the name of wife with your father—"

My mother lost her way for a moment and stared at me with her lustrous, morbid eyes. Then she recollected her role, which must have been rehearsed in her mind in the long hours of the night; or long before, perhaps.

She continued with so much talent that it merely had seemed a dramatic pause, "It has not been an easy or pleasant time for me, all this folly of yours, Letty; and I have had no comfort from you at any time, for you are quite selfish! And, knowing what you do about my troubles, it does seem to me that you should have made some kind of an effort, even if it cost you a little discomfort, to keep me as free from outside worry as I can be. By that, I don't mean that you should have done this thing secretly, but you should have taken me into your full confidence before doing anything so unexpected, unusual, and—irreparable. You have subjected yourself, you will subject yourself, I know quite well—to all kinds of inconvenicnces and perhaps dangers, which you cannot possibly foresee; and which he, no doubt, did not trouble to point out to you, though he has been a married man, and knows all about it. I do not like you to marry a man of this experience and way of life. He cannot give you any kind of comfort; he cannot even marry you!"

My mother turned her eyes to Clays, for I was standing my ground, though consulting my boot tops more than my mother, with my eyes. I felt myself a very little, guilty girl. My mother's echoing voice continued harshly, "You have given up school for the week; that, I presume, is unimportant from your point of view?"

"I am going back to school. Clays said I must study and graduate."

"Oh! Clays will allow you to continue school. That's very pleasant to know."

"*Ah, mon Dieu!*" I cried passionately, in French, so that Pauline would be all for my side: "*Elle me dit ceci; c'est tout ce qu'elle a à dire; et toute la nuit l'autre murmurait, Je t'aime à la folie, je bois ton corps, j'aurai tout de toi, je t'avalerai jusqu'au sang; des mots fous, voltigeants; de la passion, toute la nuit.* He loves me and she does not love me, that is all. What else am I to think?"

"Yes, you are both suffering now," said Pauline, rapidly, in French.

"It's a fine day in my life, and she brings rain, cold, dust," I cried. But Clays and Pauline intervened and brought us together, somewhat. Also, even I knew that Mother was weak and helpless; that this dramatic scene which she had gradually evolved had nothing behind it. All her strength went into these strange characterizations or impersonations. She had nothing left for life. She could not stand up to anyone; and, as she gloomily said at the end of the discussion, "What does it matter what I say? I wonder you came back here. You always get away with everything, Letty!"

Clays and I now found it proper to vanish. It was not till I got outside the house that I suddenly heard Grandmother Fox's voice ghostly whispering in my ears, "Much ado about nothing, as Shakespeare the great dramatist said."

I mentioned this to Clays, to tease. I felt injured; but really, his failure was a thing I would not have told for the world.

"You are lucky," said Clays; "you can still turn me down if you like."

"My goodness! That's not the kind of thing you can explain to your mother. I am sunk, just as I am."

I went back to the Bleecker Street flat to read, listen to the radio, until Clays should come back with our dinner. I could not bear to touch the flat: the bed lay in disorder.

Clays came in with what was required for the occasion: cold fowl, wine, fruit and flowers.

"I am no poet," he said, "but I thought up something for you and I present you with the sole poetry of my life:

"I, the thirst, thou the wine!"

"Is that all?" I burst out, laughing.

"Well, I could enlarge on it; I could say:

"I, the thirst and the cup;
You, the wine and the riot."

"It would be better if I said that to you; the cup, that's Letty."

"Well, at times like this, we think for each other."

Well, I thought, this is really my wedding. But it was not so. We were just in bed, and he had just begun to fulfill some of his promises to me when the telephone gave one of those long, signal rings and he was obliged to answer it, being not only a journalist, an electric spark jumping when the line was vitalized, but also A.W.O.L.

"My darling," he said tearfully, signaling to me from the telephone.

I heard his abrupt tone change. He became interested, he agreed. He laughed, "It's damn inconvenient; but I'll be there, if it will really be only half an hour." Then a laugh; "I was not sleeping alone. You hit it. See what I do for you."

With this, he turned from the phone and began a fraudulent lament, "My darling little Letty, I know it's simply preposterous, but will it be all right if I leave you here for half an hour? Well, it will take an hour, all told, and I'll race back, but I've got a chance to see this particular chap—it's Blank, of all people. He's leaving town for Paris, and he'll hardly see anyone. It's been arranged for me by a frightfully good pal. They found out I was away and he managed this, to screen me; and it is a scoop anyhow. Not only this chap, but the paper would be frightfully miffed if I let them down."

I lay still, choking with rage.

"That's right," said he, kissing me, "now take a little snooze, while Papa nips out. I'll be back before you know it. There's my darling darling— Gracious, I must fly!"

He nipped out, after dressing rapidly, with a good many winks, nods, and blown kisses, all of which I received with eyes of rage and scorn. I lay still in bed, thinking everything over. Was a young girl ever treated like this, I said. Spasms of fear and pain tortured me. Was he fooling me? Was he a pervert of some sort? Was I really ugly? Perhaps I did not attract anyone! What should I do? Dress and go home, tell the humiliating story, and be received back as an unfortunate? Cut my throat? Run away? Pretend I had quarreled with Clays? But—"my reputation"! I said to myself. If I had been a stray of the streets, he would have treated me differently. The business would be over long ago. Does he doubt my virtue? Is he afraid? What is it?

This lasted a long time apparently, for when I got up it was near morning and Clays had not yet come back. He would never come back, I now fancied. Perhaps he was a lunatic. I suppose I was not the only woman who wondered this on her wedding day, or just before it. Who knows? He is a stranger!

But Clays returned, apparently as fresh as a daisy, about seven in the morning. He had dropped in at a Turkish bath for a couple of hours, for a pick-me-up. "So far I've cheated you of your rights," he said, nonchalantly. "I thought of you all the time. Blank was quite talkative; gave me three hours, not one; and even made jokes and laughed at mine. I'd never heard that he was amusing. He takes himself very seriously. He doesn't know the world—at least the newspapermen—look upon him as a mountebank and a crook. Isn't it the truth? All great men! Even embezzlers and cutthroats."

He lay down while talking to me, stretched his arms out, then round his head. His face was merry, drawn, dark, his eyes bright. He yawned, shut his eyes and was suddenly asleep. I threw myself into a chair, but in a few minutes went out into the long room. "Was ever woman in this manner wooed? Was ever woman in this manner won?" I asked myself, as I stumped up and down. No, I am sure not. This outrage was for me alone. Yes, I must be uncommonly unattractive, repulsive even. I smelled of dull girlhood, simply. But to attract him, must I get first another man? And to get the other man, another man before him; and so on, *ad infinitum*?

With a thousand different starts and pieces of luck such as I had assuredly had in my life, I had got myself into a thousand jams and traps quite unique. Yes, there are women who look for trouble—that's called, *taking a chance*; and there are the children of the poor; and there is the suicide squad to which my mother belonged, hell-bent for misery; but I was a happy-go-lucky, confident, credulous, and even magnificent girl in my own way. I could not work the whole thing out. What was wrong? Fate threw everything at me—I had a better time than Mother, Jacky, or Andrea. The separation of my parents had turned out to be a Christmas tree for me, so that I had twice the chances most girls of my sort have; and now? Why, I even hooked a man like Clays Manning—and now look! Asleep on my non-nuptial couch, dead to the world, and—don't mention the rest!

Well, I thought, perhaps it's all a warning. I am still quite young and can learn. It was pitiable.

Another telephone call summoned him from his sleep back to Washington; this might have been foreseen. He had only just time to dress, catch the train, and hug me crushingly, kissing me all over the neck and face, telling me I must never breathe a word of our accident (he called it) to anyone; he would grab a holiday in a few days, and we would go away somewhere. He promised it to me if it was the last thing he did on this earth. He promised also to cable his father in England to try to get some money, so that he could, perhaps, expedite divorce matters.

"For we are going to be married soon, and it's forever and ever," said he; "you're a wonderful girl, the best in the world."

With a lot more of this, which I wanted to hear, and which gratified me somewhat, he jumped into the train. He had given me some money, which I took, of course, and I took a taxi home. But in the taxi I burst into tears. I was sobbing when I got out, when I came into the hall, and could not stop for an hour.

I just threw myself on my old bed and lay face downwards crying. My mother came softly behind me, and said: "What is it? What can I do? Letty, I'm your mother. Tell me everything, poor child. You're my daughter. You can trust me. I'll help you."

But I could only tell her that Clays was coming to take me on a honeymoon, and she could not see anything to cry at in that. At last I could see by her remarks that she supposed the experience with Clays had unnerved me, and I left it at that.

28

I WAS LOW and Mother utterly depressed, on account of my past with Clays. She chewed it over at the table; her friends came to view me. I went after school, therefore, when I had no dates or meetings, to my father's. He had, by now, gathered round him a large crowd of new friends. He was a gay, ribald, talented man, who was not very sure of himself; exactly like myself. If a mean wit sneered at him, he was cast down; if some flimflam praised him, out of boredom or vanity, Solander was delighted. He embraced people; he laughed with his wide mouth, showing all his funny cream teeth, and tears of joy flowed out of his eyes; exactly like myself. Some people thought he was a genius. I was not averse to this opinion, for if those were the signs of genius, I had them too. I could not be a cynic. I preferred to believe in people. A good many of the people round my father came to get ideas from him, or to have a free entertainment; for, say what you will about radio and the movies, the theater and vaudeville, with their movement, color, and real life, and their full-length living portraits, are sky-high above them for pleasure and inspiration. There were few real wits or original *raconteurs* round my father, not because there are so few, New York being the chief bazaar in the U.S.A. for such talents, but because each one (like Solander) needs his own audience and his own addicts; and those addicts crowd out other entertainers.

I heard from Clays every few days. He was making preparations for going away and expected to spend a couple of days in New York, but could no longer think of the country honeymoon. He seemed wild about me. He told me the place he had picked out for us, if we had a week end, was a charming place in a woodland, near a lake. In the lake was an island, and on the island two cabins which could be rented by guests, at a slightly higher rate. There was boating, golf, riding; for it was mostly used by busy young couples on real or week-end honeymoons. "To hasten on *The Night*," said my lover, "I send you a poem, my first, and it is simply called —*To Eve*, which means both Evening and Woman, but woman means you." The beginning of *To Eve* went—

> *Copper goblet Hebe bear*
> *Thrice-filled, to the thirsty stars;*
> *Mesopotamian scimitars*
> *Sulky seraphs flash in air.*
> *Simoons drink the fishless lakes*
> *The grass devoured in sand remains,*
> *Old cities die in shifting plains*
> *The sun to him the ocean takes.*
> *Clubfoot stems and hairy leaves*
> *Flowers, seeds, gemmae, thalli, plants,*
> *Leopards, lambs, all celebrants*
> *Of innocent love, ye now by Eve's*
> *First curiousness must bear and die*
> *As she; the kingly cockatrice*
> *His hissing mail hath unwound twice*
> *And startles the phalanstery.*
> *Ruby tree like blood doth shine*
> *In* jus-primae-noctis *murk;*
> *In all the shriveled bowers lurk*
> *Carnivorous eyes that wait to dine.*
> *And sexless sentinels shake the night*
> *With sapphire bayonets fixed in guns*
> *Their bores like our star-shooting lenses,*
> *Hand mortars large as God's best suns*
> *All throwing diamonds in cadenzas.*
> *(But he has taken the best gift, Adam,*
> *Walking softly with his madam.)*
> *Fast shut now, the delicious gate—*
> *With trembling hair, our mother white*
> *Leads breath-filled Adam by the hand*
> *On sticks, shards, stones, till weary quite*
> *He falls, all spent, upon the sand*

> *But thinks not Eve to reprimand.*
> *The angry God one thing knew not*
> *This thing thought not to take away;*
> *He knew not youth and age as they,*
> *He could not really curse the spot.*
> *Self-willed world-owner, all things lent*
> *To all-obedient idiocy;*
> *But gives for stealing from his tree,*
> *The hangman, cops, war, death and rent.*
> *He tries to interest take, in pain;*
> *The loans retaken, he's bereft;*
> *He fears the one who did the theft,*
> *He re-creates them, Abel, Cain.*

And the very day I received this, Clays left, with only twelve hours to spare, for Spain; he gave me a seal ring but I was not his bride. Mother was quite impatient with this or anything that was not a-b-c. Nevertheless, with pride, I showed my ring and my poem, not only at school, but ran with them to my father's ribald company, filled, usually, not with aesthetes but with those drifters of the big city, publishers, readers, and other idle wits who fortunately have time for drinking, eating, witting and whoring. They are not a moral lot to throw a young girl with, nor are they really vicious, but are a sounding-board of the city, as is Wall Street. As I was meeting publishers, or publishers' salesmen and publishers' readers, my thoughts turned more and more toward literature. I thought that I should get used to good society, Clays and I might cut a good figure here or in England or in France—or even in any country, say Italy or Turkey, in which we might live—if Clays really turned out to be an attaché. I thought a great deal about the expediency of our friendship for the Soviet Union; for the fact is that, with all his education, his birth in a foreign embassy, and his traveling, Magdalen College, and the rest of it, Clays would have to pant for his attaché-ship a bit if he remained a friend of Russia; the British Empire was still operating at the old stand. But Clays was young and so was I; we had not the sordid preoccupations of the adults. We did not want things to remain *in statu quo* for our lifetime, like the septuagenarian senators and congressmen and the heads of the Elks; because, actually, things had been changing since we were born, and we were enthusiastically used to it. Although our parents (my mother, I should say) worried about my *sense of security* (a cant phrase of the time), none of us had ever had that; and it was rather the struggle that made us strong. Some reporter (Clays told me) asked Karl Marx to define life in one word—well, a dopey question if ever there was one; but trust a reporter, said Clays, to think up the most vapid stunts in the world, anything for a byline—and K. M. said, "Struggle." And what else indeed relates me, *Letty-Marmalade-always-in-a-jam*, to the plant in my window box (not put there by me, but by my Italian superintendent) if not this Darwinian word?

To proceed. I was always in such good form at my father's, and always so soggy at my mother's, that I preferred one to the other. Having told Father this, I heard him say, "And why not? Doesn't everyone prefer Life to Death?" This was his view of his own life, and he had reduced it to very simple terms. Mathilde was *death*; Persia was *life*. This was uncommon simplicity in the big city.

At Solander's and Persia's I met, among others, a young advertising man by the name of Gallant Stack, a radical from Kentucky, who made part of his fame by ridiculing *southernisms*. He was a bold, political radical certainly, and *exposed* himself very consistently; but a lot of people disliked him without cause. He was handsome, powerful, blond, gay, and reckless. He gave the impression of being a slob without being unclean; perhaps it was the loose-neckcloth idea of elegance in him. He was both a country boy and a gentleman, and successfully cultivated the pose of a Southland Squire. He had other idiosyncrasies: he told wonderful stories, some original, and boasted about the size and power of his male parts, with much joviality and good nature. He would relate how he told stories in small-town living rooms, while wives shifted and fanned themselves and glued their eyes on his extremities, the while, in fact, he felt the disseminator showing all its unusual dimensions, for this was the effect of wine, ladies, and fun upon him. When someone (a woman) would laugh with him, he would say instantly, rising and coming to stand over her, with boorish good-nature, "When do you want me to come and see you?" If the husband or brother were there, he thought it very gallant to say,

Christina Stead

"When will your husband (or brother, or friend) be away? Any evening you are lonely, let me know, and I will not disappoint you."

This bouncing rustic gallant was so direct that at first I was obtuse, for I could not believe he was saying what he said; it was the drift of his stories that enlightened me further. I had always considered myself an indiscreet person (although an excellent and consistent liar), for, on occasion, if annoyed by a person, I might blurt out his characteristics to himself; but I certainly had never blurted out my own characteristics, failings, and misfortunes to others, as did Gallant Stack.

It was my father's forty-second birthday on this occasion I describe, and there was quite a gathering, chiefly of men. There was Gideon Bowles, the old family friend, a tall, strong man of forty-odd now, with thick black hair, clear hazel eyes, and red lips. He had been thin and a black-and-white dresser. Now a few visits to the Californian coast and to Mexico had shirted him in pink, red, or blue; and his suits had noticeable checks or stripes. He was an architect. He had built a Camelot castle on one corner of a crossroads in Beverly Hills, and a Riviera dream in ice-cream pink on the other. He designed fountains, gates, paths for these houses with the liberality of a dope fiend. For years he had been a modest, crushed, thoughtful man with darned socks; this was during his mother's lifetime. She had recently died and now he was bumptious, tipsy, and coarse; and his affairs, which had been kept hidden, now came out in all their misery. He was such a grand, tall, simple fellow in appearance, and spoke so of his mother, that the girls believed in him. Now one of his girls was with him, a tall sawney called Alice, who had been his mistress for a long time. She had a terrific lust for life and slept with anybody almost— priests, organizers, salesmen, stewards on boats—but was succulently jolly on her best days. She should have known better, but now she hankered after this Gideon. I was a wise child and knew my mother was sorrowful too, because she had thought he was her best friend. Sex is a mystery to me still.

There was also a rowdy goose-fleshed blonde who had had three husbands, who never smiled, and shouted commands at people; and Luke Adams, a pinched, nut-brown man with a monkey face and thick black hair. This man Adams was taller than he appeared to be. He stooped and shuffled, and he appeared to be careless of his body, in mind devious, silent, resentful; but he at times also seemed sharp, humane, passionate. When one came nearer, one saw that his clothes were clean; they were simply poor and did not fit. He believed in bargains and would shop for days for a cheap shirt on the East Side, or in some godforsaken hole in Jersey or in Brooklyn, rather than get the same thing round the corner. He had this gift: when he stood near a person and wished, at that moment, to express good feeling, a gust of heat was felt. If it was a woman, she was simply scorched by him, for women he was an open hearth; his eye lengthened, melted. He was a well-known trade-union organizer, a cartoonist and pamphleteer. At present, I looked at him from the outside, with curiosity, respect, and timidity. I had certainly not yet got over my timidity with men, and the experience with Clays held me back.

My father, who should have been secret, in a short time began to laugh, gesticulate. He lost control of himself in his earthy good humor, and told them all about Clays. "Letty's bound to marry into the English aristocracy! When she went to school, only eleven years old, she used to bed down with a duke, but that was in the daytime, and I saw her as the future Duchess of Greenshire, the Duke liked her very well—"

"He liked nearly all the girls very well," said I, with unusual modesty.

"The Duke was fourteen then," said my father, "and I thought if I kept Letty around there a few more years, I would be father-in-law to a duke. But now, I'm going to be father-in-law—and in point of fact, illegally am father-in-law—to the relative of a knight-baronet, and knowing the incest committed by the English upper classes, note I mean social and financial incest, Miss Paula Fitz-Broke marrying the Birthday-Honored Sir Oodles Lucre and the sister of Sir Oodles marrying Mr. Maudlin Degree, who is first cousin of the Duchess of Handmedown, whose son will marry Miss Angela FitzBroke—since this is the system, in England, I expect in a very short time, after the Spanish Civil War and all that, or even before, to be related to almost everyone in Burke's Peerage and the Cabinet. I don't know whether you know that there is a rule in England that at least fourteen members of any

Cabinet, if you trace them out, are really first cousins or first cousins of first cousins. It's impossible to avoid it; and if they're not first cousins, they sit side by side, in the administration of industries, and eventually become brothers-in-law. Thus, when Clays Manning does his duty by my daughter and makes her an honest woman—I regret to say it is now necessary—"

"Papa!" I cried.

"Well, my dear," he said, "if you stayed all that time with Clays and you are still a virgin, I should be very much surprised," and he laughed.

"Jesus, Solander," said the slow, thoughtful voice of Luke Adams, "you ought to give her a break!" And he turned on me his secret smile.

"Is it true, kid; is it true?" cried Gideon, in his whisky baritone. "Are you married, or thereabouts? Let's celebrate this. This calls for a drink. Let's all drink to Letty—what's his name? Manning. And will you be Lady Manning?"

"He is not a baronet," I said. "He's just a tramp; a red. Of course, the family forgives him, because in England they allow Oxford boys to champ their wild oats a bit and be reds for a couple of years. They think they'll coax them round. Clays—" But with this name on my lips, in this company which had just heard all these details of my private life, I could say no more, and blushed deeply.

Luke Adams smiled and came impulsively to my side, putting his arm round my shoulders. "Jesus, Letty," said he, "congratulations; what's he like? I'm glad. What are you going to do while he's in Spain? Gee, I'm sorry—it's a pity."

Meanwhile, Gideon had routed out glasses and got a bottle from Persia and was pouring out drinks all round, rummaging ice from the icebox, and splashing water into the glasses. He poured his own drink last, made it strong, and this he raised for a second, "Well, good luck, Letty!" And he downed the drink.

They had been talking mostly about politics, collective security, whether France or the U.S.A. would intervene in Spain in any way, the hopes for Russia's intervention, food for the people, new books; but now they became gay and got on to stories and conundrums.

Gallant Stack said, "Do you see any resemblance between a

LETTY FOX: HER LUCK

constipated owl and a soldier? Well, there isn't a real resemblance; the soldier shoots and shoots and sometimes hits. I knew a woman, this is true," he continued smartly, "she kept a call house; later she got married, and came in to see me, when I was in her town again, all fluttery, and showed me her ring. I said, 'Well, Mamie, I suppose you're keeping your business on.' She flushed angrily and said, 'He ain't no pimp; I'm retiring. He'll run it.'"

Gideon Bowles laughed loudly and slapped his knee at everything, making rude noises in his hands and mouth, and washing it down with liquor all the time. He now horned in with one of his horse stories going about town.

"A man down in the streets of Louisville, or Frankfort, Kentucky, near the big Derby track, that is—this man is going along the street on Derby Day, or else during the morning sprints—have it your own way, and the man hears, 'And to think I used to be at even money right there!' He looks round, but the street is empty except for a milkcart with an old horse in it. He takes another step and hears, 'To think I used to start from scratch and get to the post first every time!' And with it, a heartbroken sigh. The man starts, looks round, and the horse says, 'Yes, it's me. To think I used to be a coming wonder as a two-year-old!' The man, aghast, stands by, and when the milkman comes out of the house, he says, 'Say, your horse can talk!' The milkman says, 'Oh, him! You can't believe a thing he says. Has he been at you with his lies?'"

He continued, "Say, do you know this one? A man with a dog goes into a stable to saddle a horse for riding. The horse says, 'Oh, let me alone; I'm too tired to take you out this morning.' The man says, 'Can you talk?' The dog says, 'Yeah, he really don't talk bad for a horse; it's kinda wonderful, ain't it?'"

A woman from Washington, a polite miss in her forties, stared at the crowd now laughing at this incomprehensible local joke. They went on with their horse stories.

Gideon slapped his knee and shouted, "Two zanies meet each other and one cups his hands and says, 'Guess what I have in here.'

"Zany No. 2: 'Brooklyn Bridge.'

"Zany No. 1 looks at his fists, and then, 'No! Ha-ha!'

"No. 2: 'Woolworth Building?'

"No. 1: 'No. Guess again!'

"No. 2: 'National City Bank?'

"No. 1: 'Na!'

"No. 2 goes crazy, but finally says: 'Six race horses?'

"Zany No. 1 looks carefully in his fists, and then says, defiantly: 'What color, though?' "

They shouted with laughter. The Washington secretary looked very much surprised and a cloud of anxiety shifted over her face.

"An Irishman goes into St. Patrick's," shouted Gideon, "and he says, 'Give me a whisky-and-soda!'

"Priest: 'Shh! This is a church!'

"Irishman: '*Give me a whisky-and-soda, I say!*'

"Priest: 'Shh, shh! This is a holy place.'

"Irishman: 'I don't care what place; I take a drink anywhere, that's me.'

"The nuns pass two by two.

"Priest: 'Look, man, see where you are, see where you are! Shame on you!'

"Irishman: 'I don't care about your floor show; give me a whisky-and-soda!'

"Priest: 'I'm ashamed of you. Aren't you a son of the Church?'

"Irishman (ashamed): 'All right, I don't want you to think bad of me; set 'em up for the girlies too.' "

The Washington miss, who wore a pretty old-fashioned straw hat wobbling on her head and a dark thin veil over her ears, so that she looked rather like an old Italian painting, now said, with timid eagerness, "That's very good. Do you like limericks? We go in more for limericks in Washington."

"Go on, Miss Oaker," said Persia.

Miss Oaker straightened herself and recited,

> "*There was a young girl called Bathsheba,*
> *Who passionately loved an amoeba;*
> *The affectionate creature*
> *Had little to teach her*
> *As it tenderly muttered, 'Ich Liebe.'* "

Gallant Stack laughed romantically into Miss Oaker's eyes and said, "That's a honey, but do you know this one?

> "There's something gone wrong with Papa;
> He shows tastes both odd and bizarre;
> He brings home bears and camels
> And other large mammals
> And leaves them alone with Mamma."

Miss Oaker laughed tremulously and leaning forward toward the handsome grass-gallant, she cried, throatily, "Oh, I know some really good limericks.

> "There was an old sinner named Skinner
> Who took a young girl out to dinner..."

She continued her Washington limericks for some time, her cheeks becoming pinker and her eyes prettier all the time. She had a trusting girlish manner as she leaned into the pool of floor out of which grew the company's legs.

"You don't mind if I go to the bathroom for a breath of fresh air?" asked Solander hilariously.

Luke Adams and I sat there mute. The three-husband woman hurled loathsome obscenities into the company from time to time, but without laughing; and the corn-haired girl told a joke or two which had the appearance of having been peeled out of one of Gideon Bowles's pockets, full of tobacco crumbs and old papers.

"But I, just the same," said Gallant Stack, after looking at Luke Adams, whom he enormously respected, "am a romantic. At home, when I was a grown man, I used to go out for walks at sunrise with a little girl aged seven who simply loved the sunrise. She'd wake up an hour before dawn just to see it coming into her room and she was always down there waiting for me. The fields there are wet and green; and only cows and hedges about, mostly. And I used to go for moonlight walks at the University of Virginia with a very old lady who was the mother-in-law of one of the profs. She was infinitely charming. 'Under this tree, as a young girl of sixteen,' she would say, 'I had a romance; and on this little bridge, after I had played the harp, I stood pretending innocence, while I waited for a very flushed young man to find me and tell me he loved me. I was quite cool and unruffled. I thought myself a queen then. I used to think

341

of the opera, you know, and the love stories of queens, and think, That is I!' There never was a sweeter woman than this old woman; she was one of the most beautiful women in the world. Do you realize, the most beautiful woman in the world becomes very aged?"

Meantime, Gallant Stack, by standing up, boxing the compass, courteously ogling the girl, and by changing his position with one excuse and another several times, had placed himself next to the woman from Washington, Miss Oaker. He took her hand, and said to her, "Did you hear in Washington about the forgetful bee who forgot where he laid his honey?"

When the company had stopped its roaring, he continued, "But I am more interested in romance; I am really a romantic. A knight went to the Crusades (that's an old legend), and came home after many years, weary and broken. As he neared his liege lord's castle, he saw a little bird on the path with a broken wing, in the way of his horse's hooves. He got down, picked up the bird, and put it in the tree. It turned into a lovely fairy, who said, 'Noble knight, well hast thou lived up to thy knightly vows, to succor all tender and weak things, and, though thyself tired and famished, scarce able to mount thy steed, yet rememberest thou thy promises made before the altar of thy liege lord's chapel and in the Holy Land, etc. And I will grant thee one wish; think well, for it can be only one.' Said the knight, 'I have no need to think about it. I am old and tired but have a great lust for life. I want to be in one respect (which he mentioned) like my horse.' 'Granted,' said the fairy; and the knight perceived that it was so.

"He arrived at the castle. They were overjoyed to see him. He advanced to kiss the king's hand and was allowed to kiss his cheek, while the cooks went out to kill all the shoats and bull-calves available. Thereafter, for three days, there was much merrymaking. The knight observed that during his long absence many pretty maidens had come to the castle, or perhaps they had just grown up; and he went round chucking them under the chin as was correct in these old-fashioned days. They responded nicely, and in due time, it was noticeable that they were very much attached to him, so as to neglect the other knights in the castle. Even the queen was much interested, if not, as rumor had it, positively infatuated. Enquiries were made, but no answer was forthcoming that seemed satisfactory. In the end the king came to the queen and said, 'My dee-ah, do you know what makes the Chevalier so interesting to women? No weaving has been done in the women's rooms for a brace of weeks.' 'Yes,' she said. 'What is it, my dee-ah?' 'Well, of course, I know only by report,' she said, 'but I hear that he could not be better hung, my dee-ah.' 'But this is quite a new thing,' said the king. 'Yes, only since his return from the Holy Land.' The king then proceeded to the knight's chamber, where he found him sleeping vociferously; and after assuring himself that the thing might well be as reported, he shook him and spake thus, 'Sir Knight!' 'Darling,' muttered the knight. 'Awake, Sir Knight, it is your king,' said the king. The knight threw himself from the bed to his bended knee, a commonplace feat in those days, and which the knight had practiced regularly since he had come home, though not strictly with the king in mind. 'Cavalier,' said the king, 'tell me whence come your marvelous powers.' The knight related to the king all that you know.

"This amazed the king; and he thought, And this place is not more than a few hours' ride from my own castle, and not in the Holy Land. Though, 'slife, I should be willing to start even for Jerusalem. Well, just after midnight, he steals from the castle, saddles his horse in the dark, gets things on somehow, and sets forth, in higgledy-piggledy array, true, but still he's riding. He travels four hours, the sun gets up, he travels all day, gets tired, turns back, is exhausted with looking, and when nearly home, there on the ground he sees a little bird. He throws himself from the horse, puts the bird in the tree, and the fairy appears with, 'Noble and gracious king, thy most kingly action, etc.,' and he can hardly wait till she gets to the end of it. As soon as she gives him a wish, he says, 'I want to be like my horse.' The fairy looks surprised and says, 'Are you certain?' Yes. 'Granted,' she says; and the king rides home. The knight and the king then lived happily ever after, and the ladies went back to spinning and carding."

Miss Oaker looked much puzzled at this medieval romance, until Mr. Stack whispered in her ear, when she blushed and burst out into the immoderate laughter of reticent women.

"Did you hear," shouted Gideon Bowles, "of the woman so thin that when she swallowed an olive three men left town?"

Then followed some olive stories (the things around which legends and stories collect are unexpected); and then Gallant Stack, who was rather drunk but in a Tom Jones fashion, said, "And I am always fond of fairy tales. Do you know the one," he asked Miss Oaker, "of the young princess playing with the golden ball by the fountain?"

"I'm not sure—"

"She dropped it in, wept; it was returned by the frog, who said she could have it if she promised to take him home and put him in her little bed. She said yes; but forgot. But at midnight he came, flip-flop, and reminding her of her promise, and of noblesse oblige, he obliged her to take him in. On the stroke of twelve, precisely, he changed into a handsome prince. You'd be surprised at the difficulty she had, in the morning, in convincing the queen, her mother, about the frog and the ball."

This went on for hours; they told the original *Shaggy Dog*, the original *Little Audrey*, the dog, horse, pigeon, and zany cycles, as far as they knew them; and hundreds of others, and not all of this order, zany or indecent, but long local romances sung out of his own experience by the green-acres troubadour, and some surprising incidents related by two young sculptors, young giants, who ran a studio together in Maine and owned a station wagon which they drove about. They could not get themselves or their works into anything smaller. One of these sculptors told true horse, dog, and pigeon stories which had happened to him, like, "A taxi driver could not find the address and drove me round for hours, till in despair he put me out in a blind alley and there at the end was a dead horse, all blown up, with a red flag stuck in it."

The other one told true adventures, long and fascinating, excruciatingly convincing, except that each account ended by his saying nonchalantly, "Well, that isn't true, you know, I haven't really a brother at all," and so forth.

The party was a great success. Persia still retained some youthful looks and had a fondness for men.

Gallant Stack, who was married, was preparing the conquest of Miss Oaker; it was not difficult. He bragged with pretty boyish frankness about his success with ladies and its simple cause. The medieval legend was just a curtain-raiser to more naked stories of his own prowess. He was obliged in his business as wine salesman and publicity agent to roam the country. He did good business visiting college towns where the professors liked to think of themselves as sherry-tasters; and while he got the men drunk with samples, he raised a flush on the ladies' faces and a luster in their eyes by his stories. His accounts of their behavior were quite improper. The women present at Persia's party themselves rustled and tried to keep their eyes from starting.

Sometimes, he would break off and tell about the beauty of his wife, a strange little wanton with beautiful breasts, which she talked about as much as he talked about his particular beauties; and at other times he would give the impression, by his accounts, that their home life, in the humble flat that they occupied near Gramercy Park, was a good-natured saturnalia. He went on and on, trying to get himself pictured by the women as Don Juan, and when one of them remarked, "My husband is going away to Chicago this week end—" he stood up, turned to her with bright eyes and said, "Then I'll come and visit you," and laughed, turning his fair plump face to the company coolly and continuing, "And I will make good, and so I would tell your husband if he were here! If he objected, of course I would not come, except by the fire escape."

He departed with Miss Oaker on these words, leaving the other woman staring after him, flattered, startled, and on her face the beautiful mantle of the loved one.

I went away with Gideon Bowles and his sawney girl. Gideon Bowles, from his post far above me in the night air, belittled Gallant Stack, telling sneaky tales about him. Gideon left the sawney at her place, promising to come back in half an hour and spend the night with her, after he dropped me at my mother's.

"I want to see Mathilde," he said, slapping his lips together greedily. "She and I have been very good friends and I haven't seen her for months." But at the door he stopped, held my shoulders hard, kissed me on the lips, and then laughing boldly he strode away, saying, "Give my love to Mathilde, dear," and the whole thing was an imitation of Gallant Stack.

Mortified by the persistent looks during the evening and the casual touches and kisses of these dull devils, I went to bed in great misery, and resolved never to go to my father's again. My father was a good-natured man who never restrained his company. I said to myself, "I am the same myself, I don't know the limit either. I hope it's really a sign of good nature and not of weakness; at least in me. In a woman it might just get to be weakness, and I don't want to get into loose ways." I thought of Persia sitting there, surrounded by men, taking it all in, saying nothing indecent and amusing herself so slyly. "I prefer," I thought then, "to be a generous fool." No doubt, the fairy heard me, for it was granted.

29

I WILL try to tell the wretched episode with Amos, a friend of Clays, as it was then to me, and not as I see it now. I thought myself in love with this man. What is worse is that I always think myself in love. I have had relations with men I did not much care for, but only for one night or two. These men, afterwards, meant nothing to me; they were total strangers, or less; I thought very meanly of them. I cannot tell if I have ever been in love. It seems to me, at times, I never have been; perhaps only once. I am not counting as this once my affair with Clays, because that was the fruit of girlish ideas about marriage, which were given to me by the family and society. I don't know if I loved Clays. I loved one man, I believe. We'll get to him later.

Amos, whose second name I leave out, for the sake of his various brides, was then about thirty, a weedy, insinuating blond who wrote very badly but was quite a rabble-rouser when he spoke, and easy with women; at once, full of soulful regrets, common sense, and simple lewdness. I don't know whether he was born this way, or learned it. His own story was that he had suffered a lot with women as an adolescent, and had been kept in the background by his mother, a woman who went after men. But he was nothing repressed when I met him, although he still had about him this shadowy sorrowfulness, and apparent reticence, while telling all, which is so dangerous for women. Women have lots of secrets, because there are all kinds of women; but they are, after all, foolish, because they must become mothers, and any man who finds this out and uses it is a dangerous man. This is what I mean about Amos. Of course I did not know it at first. Another point is, I suppose, that no man is dangerous till you take an interest in him.

He was a professor, as they call these ignorant men with fresh-water degrees, in a small college outside New York. In this same college there were also brilliant and original men, who were either too idiosyncratic to conform or who were struggling for a footing. The one most smiled-upon in the academic world of his small town was Amos, a rawboned hick (I hate to write it) from Illinois, who flattered himself about Lincoln and his own hard struggle. He had a couple of degrees, and the favor of the faculty. He found a faint radicalism judicious and supported the Labor Party for the time being.

During the summer of this year (after I was seventeen), I easily persuaded my mother and father to let me go away to summer school, not only to help me out in the coming year at college, but because I felt so lonely without Clays. Clays had written me one letter from a town, or village, in northern Spain, in fact on the French frontier, and then had got to Madrid—and then nothing but his reports which I read, under a *nom-de-guerre*, in the news-papers. I read the papers frantically, feared that all the time the telephone and press building would be blown to atoms, and fretted myself so much that my marks came out very badly. I was unable to keep the whole story to myself, and let my many friends know that I had a fiancé, in Spain. I was quite grown up now, much more mature than the boys around me, but I knew their world from top to bottom, I had all the local talk down pat, and (perhaps my contretemps with Clays helping) had developed the proper manner with the boys, a sidling, caressing, flattering attitude, with upturned face, baby voice and charming pettishness (carefully practiced by us all), and a friendly smile for all lewd gestures which was so successful an act that I had many boy friends.

"For," I said to myself, said I, "these young divorcées are enough to make you sick: they lose their husbands through knowing no other men, and I will never be like that. I will know men to keep my husband when I get him."

It was the old Eve, I suppose. I had to live. I was nearly eigh-teen. My father was no longer obliged to support me at eighteen; I could be in the university at eighteen. Why be a baby in anything? But I had the Old Scratch in me and felt obligated to try to get every boy who came under my notice; friends of girl friends, boys with poses, boys with peroxide bleaches, boys who pretended to be aesthetes, and even ambivalent boys who had a yearning interest in girls and reminded me of lapdogs. The most dangerous boys for me were the political-faction chiefs, for I could often beat them on their own ground, and when they would go away in a huff, I would feel desperately that I had lost them and would run after them. At the very next meeting, I would roll my eyes, go peek-a-boo and amen all they had to say. Besides, to me, they had the most prestige.

A good many of the girls, by now, had secretly had their photographs taken naked, to show to their male friends. This had shocked me long ago with Edwige: I did not think the world could keep going another day if such corruption were known. But now I, of course, had these photographs in my possession too; and several boys, the ones who dabbled in art, had painted my picture or used me as a model for charcoal or pencil sketches, sometimes nude. I had a fine head, powerful and sensual, with oval eyes, thick hair, and the kind of skin that gives back the light, but it was my figure that they hankered after. I nearly was seduced by one or other, when I became his model, allowing him to sketch me as I lay or stood, languidly, heavily, a naked virgin (no one knew this) on some hot afternoon, or in some overheated flat, or even in some cold flat, that the poor aspirant had tried to make richly depraved with a couple of cushions and pictures. The pictures (etchings, oils, drypoints) were often of other nudes, and sometimes the work of the talentless artist himself. They belonged to cheap art classes for the pleasure of seeing the naked model, but the models were real models and had their points. I was jealous of them, but when I observed that none of them was as I was in my particular beauty, after all, I took it more philosophically and began to tease the boys themselves, with their lank pale faces, so longing and so stupid. For they had really run through every experience, they thought— and once you think that, of course, you know nothing and you are done. Now, there's a feeling I never have had.

One, Ken, said, "I'm a hedonist, you know, Letty"; and I, knowing quite well all the girls who had preceded me, and having even seen his bad sketches of them, making them ugly, too thin, or too fat, or droopy, or sprawling, in his portfolios, sighed and felt pain.

"I don't expect you to marry me," I said, laughing with difficulty, "for standing, sitting, or lying. This is Art for Art's sake."

"No, no, that—" he waved his lank hand and turned his teased blond face from me, "at our age—we can only enjoy. Have you any other object than full experience? Later on, the libido is confined. Let joy be unconfined." He continued languidly, giving a few inexpert dabs at his line-drawing of my breasts. "My last subject had a curious shelf-form here, she was a Negro of course. She was quite perfect for her type."

"You are so detached, you dog, that I really don't feel naked at all; that's no compliment to you!" I laughed with some hardihood, for I had just made up my mind to leave him. He was shilly-shallying, but he put the shilly-shally on my conscience.

"Women are always naked before men," he said in an exhausted tone; "their thoughts meet through their clothes, you know; it is really no surprise when a woman undresses before you."

"Good, but Renoir didn't think so."

"He was an old man," he said contemptuously; "you see, he had no chance to see women but professionally. Frankly, look at one of his paintings with an unprejudiced eye and you'll find them all the same. One feels he became enamored, through the eye, of one model—that's so common with old men. It is much better to prostitute the eye as a youth, you see, for that forms the artistic sense, breaks up the lines; you know the theory that art is based really on the feminine form."

"Ah," said I, obscurely stung, "and woman's art—"

"Feminine art," he sighed, "is there any?" He added a last disfiguring stroke to the academy for which I had so obligingly sat to him, without a rag on. "Women's art is limited by their timidity. And then they scurry too much, too much interested in the drapery—in a different society of course, where they would have contact with the flesh—more frequently—"

I sat down, pulling my little pink shirt over my head disconsolately, and after a while (the dark was coming) I said timidly, "Ken, what is to be with us?"

He yawned, got up, put away his pencil, and looked critically at some sketches of me he had made the day before. "I don't seem to get you at all, you've a difficult figure, it's really out of drawing."

"Ken, I asked you—"

"You must decide, you know."

"You are not exactly the great lover, are you?"

"Love is just excess baggage for moderns," he said, most carefully attentive to his chin, which he observed in a mirror. "Of course we agree on that. I know you're a girl with experience. Naturally, with an ordinary virgin—"

"You know, Ken, I must confess something; I am a virgin—"

He smiled, "Oh, I know about everything—I'm broadminded." But he smiled at himself in the mirror, not at me.

"Ken, I am really a virgin. Don't be so broadminded."

He turned stiffly. "That's the craziest story I've ever heard."

"Well," I said, stubbing my bare toes on his dirty old imitation Persian rug, "it just happens that it's true."

He sat down in an old chair that he had painted white, and stuck a bit of red silk on, and looked at me profoundly, through the gathering dark.

"So that's that," I said, dismally.

"I guess so," he said quietly; oh, the practiced little calm and cold, in the dark. He was used to farewells. I was crying quietly, and brushed my hand over my eyes. He must have heard my sniffs, but he did not move. I finished dressing.

"Well, so long, Ken," I said, standing in front of him and hoping for some kind move.

"Well, thanks for everything," he said, getting to his feet and going to the door with me. He bent and kissed me with cold lips.

I had to see him at N.Y.U., where I took evening courses, in the cafeteria, in the bookshops; I saw him that week and the next going round with other girls, who had that silly vain expression that I suppose I had had. I sat at tables in the cafeteria with crowds of girls, among whom were five or six, whose so-far-virgin bodies he had drawn; that was his simple technique. He sat at a table apart, with some other girl, looking at us vaguely, or above our heads—always dim, remote, and somehow unreal. Perhaps he did not look at us and scarcely thought of us, all pretty girls (for he was an artist) that with his dull contempt he had made to feel like a dusty crowd of hens. I wanted to leave the university and get a job somewhere where no one would know my shame, to make it

351

simple. For, as usual, I had told everyone the whole story and everyone supposed that he was (at least) my second great experience.

Thus, when summer came and I had the chance of going to this summer adult camp where classes in politics, economics, and literature were being organized, I was very glad to go. Some of the serious girls from college were going, including Isabel Cartwright, the ugly girl who was still my best friend, and I even agreed to let Papa take the money for it out of my grandmother's money, although I did not think it fair—for Clays and I would need it all. I resolved to make him give it to me back later on. Perhaps he would do better, or Mother would get a divorce and another husband, so that she wouldn't be such a burden on him. I knew that Grandmother Morgan was always hunting for a husband for Mother; not very energetically perhaps, for she always told people her daughter Mathilde was "pretty but slow." "She likes to be a back number," she would cry cheerfully. "She takes a pleasure in being a pill." I had little hope of Mother's remarrying. The only hope was that Persia and Solander between them would make a financial go of it.

It was called Camp Lookout, in the Ramapos. The arrival day was tremendous fun. I forgot all my troubles and found myself with a totally different crowd, most older than myself but not better informed, men and girls who had been to this camp for years. Most of them were radicals and New Yorkers, interested in all that interested me. I had quite a good outfit of clothes. I found myself one of the prettiest girls there and in demand at once.

I could have had a bunkhouse with three others, two girls of my age and a woman, but I had not been there more than two hours when I met Amos, Clays's friend who had been a worker for the Farm Labor Party. He was one of the lecturers at the camp, and quite a figure. It seemed he had been there for years and everyone knew him. He created a simmer of excitement, not only because he was well known, but because he was supposed to be a heartbreaker and had appeared this summer without his third wife, a woman of twenty-two, who had actually been in my high school when I was there. He was separated from her already, it was rumored at once, because of his wandering eye (to be polite), and was only waiting for his divorce to marry another girl, still younger. This devourer of young women was himself only thirty, as I said, and not good-looking, but with canny sweet ways that made you feel sultry at once.

Seeing I was going to be quite a success at this camp, I suppose, or because I was, for him, an exotic type, or because I already had a reputation as a sex-type (I can't say which), Amos came up to me, and after we had danced together a whole evening, he asked me why I shouldn't spend the summer with him. He and I would live outside the camp in town (he had the right to do that and so had I if I wished), in some cabins or boarding houses affiliated with the camp, or which sold chickens, eggs, and such things to the camp. I agreed at once. I knew him; he suddenly resembled Clays strongly. I liked him; and I was flattered that, with all his experience, he picked me out of the whole camp. I knew he had met his wives at camp. I must admit, to my shame, that for the time being I forgot Clays and thought, "Perhaps that was just a flash in the pan and this is the real thing; for there is no romance about this man, he is willing to live with me at once, this looks like sincerity and the lightning flash."

To tell the truth, I can hardly remember the arguments I thought up in one night to persuade myself to live with the man. He knew his way about and the very next day had fixed it all up, so that we moved that day into a kind of cottage, which he had occupied in previous summers on the outskirts of the township. Here, we were not conspicuous, and needed not have callers; and here we were accepted as a respectable part of the camp. He would present me, he said, as his future wife to the local people. It was well known by this time that he was getting a divorce from his other wife. He told the neighbors it was on account of religion, since there had been a dispute about religion before he married the other girl.

I said to him, timidly, "What about the girl who is waiting to marry you?"

"Don't put your trust in rumors, Letty! Who told you that rumor? And look, let's not look ahead, eh? We'll see what we shall see. Aren't you game, baby?"

"I'm game."

He smiled at me and we went to town to get our supplies. This, all before we had so much as been alone together, except, so to speak, on the dance floor, on the boat landing, and in the garage. Of course that night we were alone together and I became to all intents and purposes really his wife. I got an unwarranted sense of permanence and a feeling of union from this circumstance, and went about fooling myself into a great passion.

I did not write home for a long time, about two weeks, and then, after some anxious letters from my mother, I wrote to my father, just to get it off my chest.

O Progenitor (No. one), or, Dear Solander!

The delay in my writing to you was not due to my natural laziness, habitual Foxian sloth, customary Morganian languor, occasional slowness, etc. No, no, I just couldn't remember your new address, and it seemed too difficult to write to you without one; and then the title of the farm which you grace with your dual presence? Kronstadt? It cannot be. You call me a lousy pseudo-intellectual red, and look at you; called after a movie! *You* say that I should quit riding perpetually after the hounds of culture (it is really *to* hounds, you know) and you leash them up and make them pull your carriage. I can think of a lot more high-class jokes but this is all phony. I have given up culture for hard work; believe me and don't come anywhere near this alleged holiday camp.

Here I am an ardent red, being whipped into a lather every day because I don't work enough, me, can you believe it! The devotion to the party and good old K.M. out here is just wearing me out—everyone lives it, breathes it, does it, agitates it—the Russian specter, the Bolshie menace, you know what I mean—only we reds know what it is. For the others, it's just parlor tricks, magic lantern. I have been put into harness and am forced to the sad position of being forced to read—carefully, for I have classes—*Value Price and Profit*, *Wage-Labor and Capital*, the *Dialectics of Nature*, and reports of congresses. I have just read a book by a naïve socialist, the first ever, Upton Sinclair, *World's End*; he does think pretty straight, but not well.

I am stalling for time; I think my style shows it. Of course you (and I guess someone else, who is a quick figurer, as I have noticed—shadow-boxing again) must have figured out for yourself that there is something beyond the charm of the scenery holding me here. I won't claym (interesting typographical error, Freudian slip, the kind that always shows—I meant to lay claim) to being celibate—I'm not. In fact, . . . dots . . . well, I'm living with a man. Isn't it awful? Or don't you think so? I remember all your speeches, and I'm still doing it, and knowing what I'm doing at that; well, of course I know. But this is, Papa, and dear Solander and Progenitor, no light little inamorato—I don't seem to know this word—of two kids in their teens. This bozo is over thirty, has been married twice, and is a professor at a small college in a neighboring state, in the city of Khardump, in the province of Leftova, you know. And—this is the rub, this is where he hails from, this city of K. in the province of L., and where he likes to be. We are spending a very pleasant summer, but I will be back in the fall.

I don't intend to start settling down seriously now, and I don't want you to worry about too much permanence. You must think it queer, about Clays, but this is the truth about that affair—Clays and I did not ever actually get together, it's too crazy, the whole story, you never would believe it. I felt like a dog with his tail between his legs, what kind of expressions am I using, my style is pure Freud, and you simply don't know what I went through. I do want to marry Clays, but things went altogether haywire. I guess it happens to other girls too, because everything seems to happen; but somehow it doesn't seem possible.

About the man; I suppose we will both have pangs at the end of the summer, but I am coming to realize more and more that, unfortunately, the life for me is either an activating big-city life or an organized rural life (and I think the latter's just romance, I couldn't stand it), like the Pamples, way back in the South of France there. Mayhap, you know, if I could get to Clays somehow and we could travel, but forever —well, that would be different from anything else. But I can't think of Clays now; he has gone right out of my head; I'm most ashamed of it, and yet not unwilling. I'm happy in a way. Only one thing grates, and that is I'm no small-town gal, and although I'm peaceful and content now, I could *not* live my whole life with someone who has nothing of the cosmopolite in him—anyway his third wife won't divorce him, or is making so much trouble it gives you a headache. And where have you heard that before?

I hope this hasn't shocked you too much, maybe not at all because you thought it was all over and done with; I'm suffering from rather belated thrills, I admit. As for me, I'm glad it occurred here and now, at a time when my whole introduction to life with males and real (as distinguished from nominal and relative) relations with them can occur without any necessity for concealment, or one-hour rendezvous or indecisive tête-à-têtes—"Well, you must make up your own mind, Letty." Oh, the Lochinvars!

I'm going to feel restrained at home, in the fall. But with all this, I have a certain longing to be home. It has proven to me how nice it is—and the oddest thing of all is I miss *you*. I'll be there in September, but not before, because I'll delay the return. Mamma and I will take up our petty way, and fight about what Jacky's glooms mean and whether Andrea is precocious. Oh, gosh! Aren't we all precocious? But Mamma has a wonderful faculty for forgetting each one as she grows up; and that's how eventually you get to be a grandma I suppose. (Mamma doesn't, mustn't know.)

Well, answer me soon. Much love,

LETTY-MARMALADE.

P.S. I had two letters which threw me, both, in different ways. Clays at last wrote to me from Madrid! What excitement. And I couldn't show it to anyone! I am sending it to you because you like Clays; and he is the only man I ever met who is worthy not so much of me as of my destiny, if I ever do anything that isn't absolute trash. The other letter is from poor Jacky, who just proves she is my sister—to sum up in one word, Jacky-Jam. More anon. She isn't like me, thank goodness. She couldn't take it, I know. She believes in love, but like Paolo and Francesca.

L.F.

P.P.S. The only thing that would make me marry Amos would be to find out what it's all about, I mean marriage and all that wife stuff, so that I could make up my mind about everything. I'm awfully young and could make even a big mistake and repent it. The worst is—I *know* he isn't as good as Clays. But where is Clays?

This was a long time ago and it seems queer to me that July nights, the thick rustling black of wayside windbreaks with the stars above, and young people singing folk songs in lighted lodges, the tunes of "Lady Isabel and the Elf Knight," and "East Texas Red," and "Long John," the lovely youngsters in their floppy outfits, and all of it, the sounds of my real honeymoon, should be connected with this Amos. Yet if he'd been free, I would have married him.

30

Jacky was bound to fall in love with a professor. She was a girl who wanted to achieve something. She was mad to go to Europe and thought she would be a great painter. She hated to walk alone along the streets, because she was by this (when she was nearly seventeen) a very pretty girl, and the boys whistled after her. She thought she was far above them and never answered them. She thought of marrying someone noble, a genius; and it wasn't marriage so much as the genius, the kindred spirit.

She wrote to me in the summer vacation. She wrote to me from the camp at which she was counselor. She imagined I was bound, spiritually and physically, to Clays, and that I was going to be a figure in the world, with his help. She wanted my advice. She wrote in French (for we had kept up this habit since France):

> I'm going to tell you my love-troubles because I think now you won't laugh at me. I am most unhappy. I volunteered to be Counselor; I needn't have done so. It was an effort to get out in the world. You reproach me with being a nose-in-the-air, with "not hating myself." But I am cruelly unhappy. They are dull, insane, with their way of living; they only think of sex and there is a lot of it, underhand. It isn't that I don't understand it; but I don't like that kind. They seem to think they have a right to tear up everything because they are young; they pretend a ferocious happiness, a madness; and pretend to hate and despise everyone, old and young, except just their own little gang. I am pretty as you know, and have a *genre* of my own; and I am approached every day. They expect me to sleep with them, quite simply, without any love, or even decency, just to prove I'm one of the gang. It's like an

underworld. It's unimaginably tough. But these are supposed to be nice people, young middle-class girls and boys. What a terrible outlook! Getting married to someone with money, getting some girl to *lay* and all that kind of thing; jokes one doesn't hear anywhere else. If anyone says one word about the mind or love or such things, it's a horse-laugh; they think you're mad.

They're beginning to think there's something the matter with me; and the crudest of them just put it down to virginity. I'm crazy because I want to study, because I want to be a great woman. I despise them and hate them and I am surprised at my weakmindedness in coming away like this to "know life." What a stupid idea....

More than that, of course, I am suffering from love. I am madly in love with that professor you always call Peter "Varnish." A boy I met somewhere writes to me, says he longs for me, and all the time I long for Peter "Varnish." If the letter were from him! If I could see him even; if I knew what he's doing this moment; if he thought about me; if he could love me! But I remember his attitude to me. Now that I know, when I have my wits about me, that he does not reciprocate, my pride (and I have a great deal) produces a kind of tearing inside me. I hate myself because I don't sleep, because I think about him; for reading nervously all day; for nursing my mad ambitions; for not wanting to see anyone, and for hating everyone. And I hate the world in general, or rather I have thoughts of this color; not always hate, but not pleasant, because I know I am not ugly and not stupid; beyond all that, I am capable of loving with all my strength; and I have the pride to say that I have the right to think that someone, some day or other, will see it.

And must I wait till he sees? This makes me feel like death. I will tell you something I did this year, long ago, in spring. I went out with a man a lot older than I am, someone we both know, fascinating, a ladykiller. L.A. are his initials. It was night. We stopped under a lamp, near the El in Seventeenth Street. He passed his arm across his body and drew me to him and our arms formed a love-knot, a pretzel. It was rapid but timed, a practiced, practiced gesture. He kissed me. I can't describe to you what it was like. Perhaps all love-kisses are like that, but I have an idea he is unusual. I did not love him, but at that moment fell passionately in love and went on walking with him.

One night when Mother was ill I left Mother, everything, and ran out in the streets with him. Mother never said anything about it. She just thought it was the spring and that I was a crazy young girl. She forgave me!

That night I said to him, "My heart is full of love for you, L."

He said, "I don't know what's in my heart, Jacky."

I said, "Last night, I wrote a poem to you," and he just said, with his troubled troubling laugh, "Do you know, with all the women I've known and loved, Jacky, I've never written a love poem and I've never written a word of love, nor a love letter."

I said to him, "But I don't care; I've got to tell you what I feel," and I told him, "*Thou art chief among ten thousand.*"

After a moment, he laughed again, as if even more troubled (but he was not, I saw his face), and he said, "Now don't you think you're exaggerating, Jacky?"

You see, I treasure this conversation. I knew it was wrong. I know you shouldn't tell a man, and must use a kind of calculation; I was too proud not to give everything, and I will not calculate in love. But now I am wiser, I cannot lose "Varnish" with such tactics; and then, unfortunately, I have not even kissed him.

I am only talking about myself. But I do it because now I feel that my state of mind must in part be yours; I feel better if I think we are both love-stupefied at the same time—it's a good thing, isn't it? I understand very well your irresolution and troubles about Clays. It is because we wait too long. It's very painful to have to accumulate these tender sentiments for a long time (and have to pretend to be darling little girls and cute teen-agers), hold them inside you, for what does it end in? You then begin to feel this love for Mr. B. or Mr. C. It's bad, from any point of view.

I am happy to think of the good-natured way you receive my exaggerated confidences—I only say that in apology, for me they are not exaggeration, they are the truth. The truth! Believe me, I love you, Letty, and all you do; you're a friend of mine, better than any other. During the years just past we had to disagree; our natures are different. I want you to be happy, and I understand that you have suffered very much and that upsets me.

I have an idiot here, who takes charge of me, is infatuated with me: she is called McGogue (it doesn't seem possible) and she has an absolutely flat chest. I look carefully even in her swimsuit—nothing, not a shred. The poor creature is all gray, dried up and Anglo-Saxon; what they mean by that word, you know; and I boast of my Welsh blood. Can you lose your figure once you've had it, just by staying an old maid? There's another one here, with a nice figure, pretty, not bad at all—but after all, women, women! Three days ago I became a slave, the slave of Tolstoy, *War and Peace*. There is, in a nutshell (wrong word), exactly the life I want to lead —I can't put it down; and this is the tenth time I have read it. Oh, what splendid, passionate, brilliant life, mad with follies, wickedness, etc.; but, at least, life. It's the passionate sincerity of the book which intoxicates me—one feels the author never writes anything he hasn't felt. That is my idea of art, too; and then what a conclusion does one draw! One must experience everything? Can a woman stand so much? This is a man with a soul as deep as the sea, and then look how strong he was, rich, owning property, loving women, and think of the age he lived to. But he tyrannized over everyone. He took other people's lives too. Do you think that is necessary, to be really great? You must read it, Letty. You must understand Natasha, who is the most feminine woman in the world. You must hear young people as they talk in Tolstoy's book; you'll stop at every phrase with tears in your eyes—"it is true, profound, it is our life." He is dead, he knew us; they are living, they see us every day and they don't know us. And then, written with a powerful rhythm of thought! And all accompanied with a beat in the language that is absolutely magic. I see it all unrolling itself before my eyes—well, I'm boring you.

In spite of the work I have to do for school, I am devouring everything, and it seems to me now that I have never worked with my head at all—can I think? I am reading the biographies of men like Keats and his letters to get to know, *How did he feel, who was he?* (And also, Am I like that?) and I am reading the books of the first great saints of the church, to know the same thing, *What did they mean, what kind of men were they, how did they lift themselves up in those ages of confusion?* What is anything? Don't you feel you haven't learned anything? And afterwards—I think I see a light, and then I go to sleep with my ideas more mixed up than ever. . . . It's extraordinary that Mother is so unhappy. She ought to leave town and travel a bit. We could get along all right and there are, God knows, a thousand relatives to take care of us; and you're to be trusted, practically a married woman; and as for me, I'm Miss Puss-in-the-Clouds. Give Mother all my love if she comes to see you; she won't come this far to see me. If you don't care for this kind of confession, I know you, you'll be kind enough to tell me so and we'll shake hands over it, exactly as many years ago. Imagine, an idea came back to me from those days—or was it Tolstoy? Or, more frankly, it was an idea I've had for some time. What if I should write a book? I tried. Fortunately, I had the sense to see it was all wet, but I kept some passages which were better than the others, and I'm keeping them to show you, my *only confidante*. When I reread them, I am surprised; they seem very good. But can they be? Impossible.

It's late. Excuse the heart-throbs. Write me a letter and I'll be very pleased. It's frightful here. Have a good time.

JACKY F.

Tear up this scrawl! I am *not* writing for posterity right at this minute.

31

I HAD too much to do to write to Jacky; none of my affairs could be written to anyone. I arrived in town at the end of August, knowing what the first feelings of motherhood were. There was no doubt about it. My friend Amos took it very calmly; and on my asking for it, gave me money to come to town and make certain arrangements; but he said he was too poor, that he was obliged to pay for his wife's divorce and a previous alimony and that I must return the money. He knew, of course, that I had my grandmother's money. (I told everyone!) My poor mother would certainly have lectured me bitterly about my wasted life and many follies, and her weak and tender nature would have suffered intensely from this misadventure. There was the fact, too, that I deceived her about Clays and then about Amos. I therefore came to Solander, who put me with a friend of his, and in every respect was cordial, cheerful.

I found letters from Madrid awaiting me, and at the very same time I had in my body the child of another man, the only man I had really loved, to speak the truth, up till then; I did not want to lose the child, but I did not want to marry its father. I was not afraid of my future. My parents were kind, and I had money of my own. I had determined to have done with school, and if I had been very strong about it, I could have had this baby. I am too slothful by nature and never can buck public opinion; or rather, never can do anything eccentric. It was odd to feel myself not really *myself*, for I had at once changed completely in nature and felt superb, wonderful. When anyone spoke to me, I swung like a big bronze gong, it seemed to me, and rang triumphantly as if the person had struck my rim and an immense joyful sound like a shout of laughter came inside; and it wasn't that I, only, heard it.

I met my old pal, Bobby Thompson, in Topps', Fourteenth Street, while I was trying to make up my mind about my and the baby's future; and he said, "Well, Letty, you've changed completely, you're just kibitzing me, you're razzing me, I've never seen you like this, I'd like to see you like this all the time, you're absolutely tops this way." He went on to say it must be my summer; and I fancied, then, he must have heard something. However, I knew it was not the summer, but Amos's child. It was the triumph of life. I didn't merely live; I rang and rang; and I had almost no feeling for the man who was the cause of it. Naturally, no one wanted me to have this child. At bottom, I knew it would be a folly; and I had plenty on my score.

The day I was operated upon, I received a letter from Amos, as follows:

Dear Kid,

Your Ma-ma! Ma-ma! has me worried! She sent this enclosed letter which I opened, and I sent her a telegram taking your name in vane. I hope she will let it rest there. In any case, you had better ship a letter out here for me to send to her from camp. I will not be able to hold the fort endifinitely. Life here is as usual, except for your sad absence, for which they try to console me but cannot. Sleeping (alone) (!) disagrees with me. I was ill yesterday. Tell me about what has happened to you. Have you had enough of this dump? There is nothing to write about from here. Charley and Bob say send you their love. (Platonic, of course.)

Afftely, Amos.

A day later. Nels Belles, I forgot to mail this. Just got your letter. Will write later.

A little later, I was in a different mood; and so weak as to cry when I saw little children on the streets. It was too bad; and I even regretted "my child." I was anxious about Amos, of whom I thought persistently. I thought of him as lonely, sick; and fancied he was worried about me. After a week or two he wrote me another letter.

Dear Kid,

I'm glad everything's O.K. by you. Here, not so good. I am very lonely and have been ill again. I was in bed three days with temp. 104 and missed your cooling hand. I thought you were coming back here. What happened? Same old routine here; and I don't like being Kissless Amos; am not used to it. This is not a threat but the flesh is weak. About you I have fleshly pangs of *course*; and spiritual ones. I don't like to get people into trouble; it ways on me. I have some very bad moments which I know you know about me. I wish we could get together now—tonight (!). My experience with women has not been happy and you understood me very well for the kid you are. You sent me a sweet letter—considering— considering what (!)? Better not say, eh? You will always be a dear comrade to me, even if you decide not to come back. Make up your own mind. Don't feel badly. You had me, that is something. If I have enriched your life, let me know and I will not feel so bad; I think this was some sort of a real expearience for you. I am still not well and these things way on me. I have not a cent; and it has been only half a summer, you know why. You went away. I don't want to mention such a thing, but I am badly in need of d-o-u-g-h, and if you did not use all that, please send me the remainder, and when you can of course—but I'll try to make out till you can get all. Did you let your Papa and Ma-ma! into the secret in a young girl's life? Now it's all over, can tell? Tell Papa you had to borrow that money from someone. I seem to harp on it, you know it isn't so. Write to me. I don't sleep well, thinking about things.

Your comrade, Amos.

This letter upset me. I thought it reflected a genuine distress of spirit—which perhaps it did, in Amos's own way. I wrote a sympathetic answer saying I would get the money as soon as I could; but I thought it a bit injudicious to ask Papa for it right away as he would naturally think Amos ought to be concerned. I said, "Why don't you come back to New York early so we can talk things over?"

Amos at once wrote an even longer and more pathetic letter about his troubles and his poverty; and as I have, of course, alas, a remarkably kind and undignified soul, which knows few such notions as "pride, dignity, woman's rights, resentment, righteous indignation," I squashed whatever faint hints of such feelings I might have felt and was all for flying back, with whatever money I could scrape up, to console the inconsolable one. What prompted me, above all, to do this was the odd behavior of some boys and girls who were starting at the university that year with me, and whom I had already met in the streets. A lot of them had not been away at all. Their attitude to me had changed. The girls glittered toward me and had that sorority air; the boys were inexpressibly amiable and made improper advances. It did not occur to me that the grapevine telegraph might have been at work, or that Amos had betrayed me in a casual way; I had yet to learn that men always broadcast their conquests, and I walked in the oldest feminine illusion in the world, that men love, as naïve women do, those whom they have met in the flesh.

My most persistent admirer now was Bobby Thompson, who had reached his full height, about five feet ten, and was dark, pale, arrogant, nursing a small mustache, and was well-dressed, with fine, pathetic, yet ironic eyes. We talked about the value of college to people of our experience; should I keep on at college? Should he? But his father and uncles were doctors and he would be helped by them. Later on, when the young physician has so much difficulty, in the matter of setting up an office and in the getting of modern instruments, and pleasant, well-trained, pretty young nurses, his family could help him. Yes, college was dull but it was the way out: Bobby and I had known each other since play-school days; we had known each other's riot, since Grandmother Morgan's famous New Year's party. We lived in the same circle, talked the same music, art, books—we ran in the same pack; within a few weeks, he had come with me to my father's and my mother's houses, and it was the old boy-meets-girl, as far as most of my friends and relatives were concerned. However, at college, where he was quite the cafeteria-king, the girls only laughed unpleasantly when we went by, talking eagerly, and all these sidelong sneers and snide sotto voces which came my way so needled me that I made a serious attempt to make Bobby mine. He was pleased at first, for he thought I would fall to him easily, after the summer-school episode. I had suffered great pain when getting rid of my baby and intended not to risk that again; so I was more careful than I ever had been; and Bobby, putting it down, naturally, to coquetry or to the failure of his charm, made more vigorous attempts to get me to bed than he had supposed was necessary. Even when he left me alone for a few days, I did not get into a fever as I might have done, because I had other things to worry me. Amos was now back at college, but was short of cash. His previous wives and the present one were manhandling him for their allowances, lawyers were writing him letters, and the poor fellow was greatly in need of the money I owed him. I did write saying that he must wait some time for the full amount, and my natural weakness betrayed me to this extent, that I said in one letter: "You see I cannot tell anyone it is you I owe this money, Amos, since there are so many old-fashioned people who would think it so shabby—" but I am glad to think that this was all I said to Amos about the money. Amos wrote back quite a desperate, a whining letter, in which he said he had a chance to spend the week end in New York and that if I did not get the money, he must ask my mother if it could not be paid back. He wrote:

> I am so despirited and despirate that I cannot see my way clear to letting you have that money, Letty; I know we were good friends, but your people have the money and it keeps me awake at night thinking they have it and I need it. You know, I can put it to them this way, which will protect both of us, I can say, I do not know what that money was for; I lent it to you because we were such good friends, but now I am simply despirate and must have it back. I have three women on my neck. I am sorry I ever got myself into this mess; women talk about love and they do not mean it, they only wish to harress you. I will lose my position if they start to come to the Chairman of my Department which is what one of them threttens to do. You were always so understanding, so sweet for a kid and it was because you were such a kid I felt a kind of responsibility and I lent you the dough;

but if you could see me now, the way I am, you would try to get that money. I am coming to New York the week end after this, can you have it by then. What about that dough your grandmother left you? If I had not known about that I would have known I could not get that dough back. I am in an awful jam. I will telephone you, at your mother's place. Think of a good place to meet. Or will I pick you up at Columbia?

As ever, Amos.

I suppose there was no reason now why poor Mother could not have known about my misadventure, but it was an accepted thing that she did not; and one lives so often and so curiously by accepted things. Again, I had sympathy for Amos, although I knew by now that he had not a strong character; and even the way he spelled "despirited" was so like him, brought him so much to mind, that I had not the heart to expose his weakness to my parents. But I was very pushed to think where I could get two hundred dollars. There was another reason with these—actually, by the kind offices of Solander's friend, the whole wretched affair had only cost me one hundred dollars and I had used the other one hundred dollars partly to pay off a long outstanding bill at a city department store and partly for a fine suit of black marocain, which had set me back forty-five dollars. Whenever I had to explain such miraculous appearances in my wardrobe, it was easy to say I had the suit from Grandmother Morgan or Aunt Phyllis, both generous spendthrifts who would not give me away, in any case. My heart troubled me and I wished I could sell the suit. I telephoned Aunt Phyllis, but she, naturally, had several closets bulging with things she was waiting to discard and only wanted the very latest in clothes; she would not be seen wearing a suit that cost only forty-five dollars. She haunted a circle which knew accurately the price and origin of every suit and dress in town. I had a typewriter, and offered to do some typing for some of the boys; but they showed by their behavior, if not in words, that they expected me to be paid enough by their kisses, or more. When at last Amos came to town, and we met in the Sixth Avenue cafeteria, where we thought we would be safe from my family, and I sat down next to him at the table, with that strange feeling of middle-age and custom and tranquillity which came from our having started a child together, I felt my heart beat hard; for I supposed what I felt were wifely feelings and I was really afraid of what he would say when he found I had only amassed ten dollars for him. These I silently pushed over to him, across the round table. He took them up, stared and looked quite wrung; he said, "What am I to do? I came to New York for the two hundred dollars: I have wasted my fare."

"I have no money," I said, bursting into tears.

"We'll have to take it up with Ma-ma," he said gloomily; "she gets plenty of allowance from your father for you four; I know what divorced women get, and it goes up when the girls are going to college; she can spare it, probably, out of the next two months' allowance."

"I suppose you think she'll use every ounce of energy getting the cash for your ex-wives," said I, wiping my eyes.

"Is it my fault?" he asked gloomily. "Besides, I'll put it this way to Mamma: I knew about the baby but couldn't be sure it was mine; only, out of gallantry, I lent you the dough anyhow; I'll say that. Besides—who really knows? Eh?"

"You're so cheesy," I said, my heart sinking into my boots, not on account of the forthcoming interview, but because men seemed to me, at that moment, a cruel illusion. I had not only been loyal, but had confessed my girlish follies to him in loving nights with him.

"I don't mean you were unfaithful. I mean, it's the best way out, to say we've been living in free love—then no one can get mad with no one. See? Isn't that the best way, honey," he asked me. "What can we do otherwise?" We talked it over for a long time. I went to his hotel room with him, for I could not at that moment resist him, and I fell once more, which made it quite impossible for me to argue against him. He, at last, went away with my ten dollars, saying that I must do the best I could. Some anger stirred me and I wrote him a letter that very night, saying that I could not understand his claim, for I had resolved to drag the whole thing out into the glare of family publicity, in order to get, out of pity, those dollars that he demanded; but he only wrote back coldly, saying that I was well known as a "party" girl and that he had no means of knowing the child was his. Nevertheless, in all this, I did not dare go to Solander, to expose what kind of man I had fallen in love with; and this shameful correspondence went on for months. At length, he did not answer one of my letters, and there for some time the matter rested. I was so sweet and yet chaste with Bobby Thompson all this time, that he became rather fond of me; we were always together. I, unfortunately, finding him so kind, fell in love with him; I needed a comforter of my own age so badly. To him, I would not have to explain my way of life, nor the way my studies were falling behind, nor my debts, nor anything.

We all had them—the loves, the debts, the agonies: it was so wonderful to just walk with him in the dark, or sit with him in a drug store, or sit in the park, under the trees, and talk pompously or fliply and yet know we had the same troubles weighing us down. Dear Bobby! I longed to be married and in a safe harbor as some of my girl friends were. I felt, it is not far off, this year I will get married, too. Approaching marriage, as I thought, I felt as if I were approaching a splendid great white woman, blushing with youth, I felt quite warm with pleasure. Oh, to be married and understand what life was about; how magical, I thought.

Bobby persuaded me that it would be better for me not to go on in college but to look about for a job. He said I'd get nothing more out of college. He really understood me, and he had no illusions about the academic game. What should I do though? I had to have some project before I dumped this idea in Solander's lap. Should I start off in writing? I returned to my idea of the Whodunit; and inspired by another book (*Verdict of Twelve* by Raymond Postgate), I decided to write one called *The Twelve Uncaught*. Looking back on my secret life, I became troubled, wondered what kind of secrets everyone conceals. Everyone of the *Twelve*, I thought, in every jury, perhaps has an actual crime, or more than one, on Heaven's true account. Has everyone? Has a good, laughing man like my father? It seems impossible. And poor Mathilde? She cannot have committed a crime! But didn't she steal Solander from her sister Stella? That is what Stella says; and perhaps it is true. These were terrible thoughts and I began to feel I was penetrating life's *heart of darkness*. I did not see it like Edwige Lantar, my wicked young cousin, as Satan's invisible world made visible. No, this life was flesh of my flesh, I knew; I was wicked just as other people were wicked, not more nor less. But what depths and flaws, even what a chaos in me, I now seemed to see! Life was a heavily smoked glass through which to look at the sun. But I never had any dreams of sainthood; I just felt, it was hard to be a model of virtue, in the lovely world of the flesh and the devil, which was, to me, the only true aspect of the world. I know my sister had a different view. But I could not accept it; and even now, when I am nearly twenty-five, the age of inevitable maturity, I cannot accept any view of the world but my own. The others seem disagreeably primitive to me, tentacular, feeble, like something Mesozoic, or H. G. Wellsian—he was much affected by the ancient emanations of the mud banks of the Thames!

This book, *Verdict of Twelve*, I regard as a clue in getting through my labyrinth, for it was given to Jacky by her Prince at Santa Fe, and in it she had drawn a profile of one of her distinguished friends, a remarkable woman no doubt, a poet and painter, who had an adobe palace at Santa Fe and in New York had a studio on Sixth Avenue, where she gave art classes which Jacky attended at night and on Saturdays. Jacky at this time was working as hard as I had ever worked, but only at painting and at literature. She had not my effervescence, but went in stern pursuit of her hobby. She had become more caustic and spoiled in her ways than ever I was. Were we both spoiled brats, or is everyone like that? I suppose parents like it. I'd let my youngsters knock things to pieces if I thought it showed the tumult of invention.

To be honest with myself (a momentary and, with me, morbid pastime), I was jealous of Jacky's progress in the arts. I proposed to leave school and take up commercial art and commercial writing, in order to plunge into life and to beat Jacky to it. She had a cheap sketchbook already full of park and subway sketches, in a manner that had begun to be her own. Some day soon, I thought, she'll sell one of them and there's something lucky about her, she'll at once begin to make good. She won't be satisfied to be a filler-in for a recognized comic-strip artist.

My parents, Mathilde and Solander, were bitterly opposed to my leaving college. Both agreed that if I did so, I had no hope of getting my grandmother's money, until I married for good and all. I was a wastrel, a tramp, bum, ne'er-do-well, in their opinion; I received quite a trouncing on this occasion. I went back to college, sulkily, saw how I was received by the demi-virgins and the pimpled youths, and went straight back to Solander to tell him I could not stomach that society any more.

"Say what you will, Papa," said I, "you may call me a loafer, I am, but I am not a giggling, hard-boiled virgin; and I have lived with a man, I am a woman. I have got to get out of this cookie shop they call a university. It never would suit me. I've met the products of this renowned bakery, and they are not as smart as I am right now; you know yourself what the general opinion is of the prof and the teacher? Donkeys, things with long ears. And what's the end-all of their teaching, to make me like themselves? Have I got to spend four years at the university trying to educate my teachers? I've done enough of that at high school. I promise that if I'm left high and dry by life, and nothing else happens along that is better, I'll go back to school at a later age; but to a decent school, mind you, not to what is called a university, jammed with adolescents, most of whom don't even know how the sexual act is performed. For that, with work and child-getting, and mental creation, is, Papa, the chief adult activity; and believe me, they don't know what any of those four are, not even this simple and delightful one."

"Well, what will you do, you bum?" asked my father, laughing.

"I'll write," said I. "I'll get things in the *New Yorker*, then I'll write a book, and then they'll take me in Hollywood. I'm young, I'm good-looking, and I'm smart. I can learn any technique. I'll forge ahead there. You'll soon see me at one thousand dollars a week."

"Don't take my breath away with your idealism," said Solander, laughing heartily.

"Papa!"

"All right, you no-good. You can try it. But if you make this an excuse to be a girl about town, I'll be after you and throw you right back to the universities. Also, remember, you have to make your living; that's the purpose of all this, I understand."

"Oh, Papa! I already know two men on the *New Yorker*! One wants to marry me but I don't like him, poor fellow; it's his friend I like; and he, naturally, is married, and doesn't want to leave his wife."

Persia laughed, saying, "I thought there was something too abstract in this proposition, but now it has come down to recognizable Lettish terms."

I grinned sourly. Perhaps there was something true in what she said; but it was Amos and my foolish weakness for him, and my pangs of motherhood, as well as the man on the *New Yorker*. However, it had been the *New Yorker* fellow who had given me the ideas about Hollywood.

As soon as I was free of college, I asked my father for the money he would have had to spend on me, in the first quarter, to get myself established. He gave me a little of it. I then started going to Jacky's art class. I felt I could easily beat her. Here I met her teacher, the celebrated Lucy Headlong.

32

Lucy headlong was then a woman of about forty, lanky, handsome, with visible jointings, like an old Dutch doll, with graying bronze hair and the skin of a sundried windfall. She was dashing, with a strident voice and expensive arty clothes. She was said to have been a raving beauty as a girl; and even now, her small face, formed on a delicate regular skull (which was beginning to be visible), and her large sea-blue eyes, wonderfully shaped and set, gave her days of beauty. When I first saw her, I mentioned my father and his lively circle. She appeared to take no notice of my conversation, but carried on in the outrageously rude, almost insane manner of an acknowledged chieftain. Yet she directed her wild airs at Jacky and me. It soon became evident that she preferred us to all the others in her class. She had puzzling ways, however, that could cut you to the heart. She was capricious; and just as you fancied yourself her friend, she would swerve blithely, even blatantly, to another member of the class, male or female. I could not place her and had great distaste for her. My gentle Jacky had almost fallen in love with her. "A woman of genius!" Jacky cried joyfully. As for me, I could not help thinking of certain airs adopted in England by girls bred to the upper classes—the high-pitched brutality of voice, the elegant sweetness always at call, the selfish caprice. "She loves no one on earth," I said to myself, "but her husband and crazy family."

Adrian Headlong was a columnist, well known for his pure style and his empty head. He was of good social origin, harked back to some hero of our history, like old Chisholm, or the original Chicago porkpacker; and though broken by years, was still quite a figure of a man, sculptured head, long back and legs, broad shoulders, and the proud swinging arms of a gorilla. He had fierce blue eyes, and when he entered a room and stared genially, one felt a presence; "I am Sir Oracle, and when I speak, let no dog bark." Yes, alas, there was too much of that about Adrian Headlong. Mrs. Lucy adored her husband in a highspirited way.

I soon saw that Mrs. Headlong liked to show us off to the rest of the pupils; she caused us to chatter about England, France, and our foreign schools. We were, for her, young women of her class. As she had at first been attracted to Jacky, but was irritated by Jacky's natural coldness, I set myself to win her; and soon, with my fire, yielding charm, and verve, was able to do so. We both received an invitation to spend a long week end at Arnhem, her country place in Westchester; but as Jacky had a chance to go to the Museum of Modern Art on the Saturday with the man she still adored, Peter Varnish, she refused and I, with enthusiasm, set out from Grand Central to visit my teacher alone.

Arnhem is near Croton, and over the Fall Line marked by the Hudson. Without imagination you can see the ice age there. My father had seen me off, and at the station adjacent to Arnhem on the New York Central line I was met by Lucy Headlong, with her car.

At first you mount a long way from the river steeply up to a plateau which holds woods, clustered hillocks, a lake and a road from which slope away bare wild fields downhill on one side, with winding paths leading to hidden dwellings; and on the other are upward slopes with houses, cabins or palaces visible, sheltering behind the crest of the rise. These were declivities like parts of Normandy that I had seen as a child; and orchards which keep falling through apple-loam to unseen valleys.

We were now far away from the river. Miles away, it appeared, at intervals, pushed off beyond hill bottoms and over paddocks. Now we were below the crest, in the woods on a mamelon. Now we dropped over this and came into a low country that must have once been marshy. We had come down from the high grounds on switchback roads and the houses on each side had changed in value. First, there were shacks and cottages in a town, then villas; then the houses of artists, stone farmhouses with attached studios and wooden cabins, just as surely home and studio combined. Beyond this, country houses and then the massing of trees as we proceeded toward the low grounds; behind these trees hints of great houses; and visible, in slashes, ancient natural ponds.

On an undulating road at a dangerous turn, a driveway opened and a little wooden arrow, rustic style, said—A. S. HEADLONG. A few hundred yards back we had passed one of the large ponds, nicely banked and surrounded by fine trees.

Lucy Headlong was a fast, nervous driver. She took the dangerous curve and the turn-in neatly, however, and coasted into a private park, beyond a lawn set with birches, a turfed hill, and a Japanese garden with a rivulet and bridge, to a great house, the flagged driveway running two ways in a heart shape, toward the door. A third road ran off into the trees, to stables.

She brought the car to a stop before a side door, in a wing offshot from the great Norman house. All around were planted thickets. The house stood on a mound which fell away steeply to lawns, tennis courts, and the pond.

"This is your place?"

"This is Arnhem," she said very offhand. Then she laughed, "I built it!"

It was impossible to praise it. It was magnificent. We went in through the door and saw, through an arch, a great Norman hall. At the other end, windows and doors, all in glass, in steel frames, blazed out across mound and lake. White walls, beams of great size, an open roof, a fireplace, a staircase and a gallery, and long tapestries of a very dull yellow. It seemed to me that this heroes' hall bore some living quarters on its upper deck, like cabins. The rest of my life flew past me as if I were in an express train; it went glittering past and dwindled in the distance. Joy and love sprang up in me, ambition. I had known how to deserve and win Arnhem! Now, at this moment, my real life was beginning.

Mrs. Headlong had already gone out to some domestic quarters behind a small door on another level. At that end of the gallery was a coffee room, perhaps, looking toward the birch lawn. I did not want to seem to be staring. I pulled off my gloves and went to the glass doors. When Mrs. Headlong returned, I said serenely, "Oh, how lovely your lake is in this light!"

Mrs. Headlong seemed pleased with me. She took my hand, "We'll go swimming there tomorrow, if you like, or we can row; but it's badly overgrown with weeds just at present, and the boys ask a dollar an hour to weed."

We entered a corridor in which were several guest rooms of different sizes, with bathrooms. At the end of this, three doors; one, leading outside, one, to a linen closet, and the middle one opening upon a winding staircase. Mrs. Headlong smiled and took me by the arm, "This will be your room, I think. Do you like it? You can have any one. We will be all alone, for Adrian is in Boston. I had two prepared, one for you, and one for Jacky; so choose. You will be all alone in this wing, but that staircase you just discovered," and she smiled, "leads into a dressing room, off my room."

At this I could not restrain myself, and went off into mirthful, but respectfully enthusiastic admiration.

"Shall I show you the way? If you are restless, you have only to unbolt the door and come upstairs. The switch is here; and you can have Adrian's room, which is off mine."

I said, flinging myself in an armchair, "I love a big place; I was always happy at Green Acres."

"What is Green Acres?"

I saw everything in a flash. Jacky must have met Mrs. Headlong through Solander, who probably knew Adrian Headlong. I answered negligently, "It's a place my grandmother has in Connecticut."

"Has she other places, too?"

"Oh, yes. One in Long Island—a small place in Florida."

Mrs. Headlong seemed pleased. She gave me a frank smile for the first time and said, "Now, little Letty, do you want to change? We are all alone. I am tired and have invited no one for the week end; though, if you are lonely, we can visit anywhere you like. I have friends, just across the way, everywhere. We can wear slacks and sweaters. I've got things that would fit you, if you want other things. I've got seersuckers and even a land-girl costume that would fit you."

"I don't think it would," I said, indicating my figure.

She did not like to be contradicted; I saw that. I looked at her with sweet appeal. She smiled slightly and said, "They are old, you needn't bother about them. They belong to a friend of mine. My friends leave their old things here, so they can pop out for the week end, if I'm having a quiet time."

She then showed me my bathroom, next door to the bedroom: a room in green tiles, with green silk curtains, a design of water lilies. On the wall above the bath, as a splash board, was a fresco painted by herself. It was, like all her works of that kind, frank, bold, hasty, trite—girls, swans, lotuses.

"It's so nice," I said, naïvely.

This seemed to please her well, and I felt my timing was excellent that afternoon. I was like a cat on hot bricks, however; my skin prickled as in extreme heat, for I had never heard that Lucy Headlong had such a place. Why did she teach in the great tumbledown studio on Sixth Avenue? Evidently, not for the money. Her advertisement was modest, and her prices very low. Ninety-three cents took in one lesson, with model, paper, and charcoal provided. Mrs. Headlong excused herself to order dinner and speak to "Washington" she said. Washington was the gardener.

"We'll pick our dinner tomorrow, ourselves; but now we must have what is in the kitchen."

I sighed. I hate to pick my dinner, but rich people fancy it's either curiously rustic—or economical. I did not risk a remark, but smiled. She left.

No one appeared for a very long time. I climbed the outside stairs to the gallery, found a summer library, a niche for table games, and then the apartment of the Headlongs; bedrooms, showers, dressing rooms, and a long sitting room, glassed in on all sides, overlooking a wood on the next rise, the tennis courts, and the boat house. This was a solitary room. One could live there and forget the world. I came downstairs by the spiral staircase.

In the dressing room I found, as indicated, the clothes Lucy Headlong wanted to lend me. I tried them on. They did, in fact, fit me, and were clean and new pressed.

Lucy Headlong seemed to me to be taking a long time. I wandered out in the Norman hall, dressed in some other woman's outfit, a homemade dress imitating the Spanish, in yellow, white, black, red, a small design with a yellow ground. I stood in the wide, white arch and saw Lucy Headlong waiting at the fireplace on a school bench.

"Hello, there you are," she said, cheerily waving her hand; "I've made drinks. Do you like Manhattans? If not, tell me what you like, and you shall have it."

I preferred Scotch and soda, but did not say so. She had the Manhattans mixed in a large glass jug with ice floating in them. I detest this cocktail this way, but I was cheered to see about a quart of it.

"Do you expect someone?"

"No, this is for us. Didn't you tell me you were a stout drinker?"

"Oh, yes."

She glanced at me as she busied herself with the glasses, "Yes, yes, it's just what I thought, child. And tomorrow we'll try the velvet slacks."

I burst out laughing, "Papa says I look terrible in slacks."

"Papa says? Well, perhaps you do." She laughed. "We'll see. But if he says so, no doubt you do. You're very fond of Solander, aren't you?"

"Oh, yes."

She set her teeth together in an odd smile, quite savage. The night began to close in. I heard no sound from anywhere. I had not seen Washington, the gardener, nor any of the servants. We finished the drinks. We talked away, and Mrs. Headlong was friendly and courteous; but now a fit of embarrassment had seized me. I had been examining myself during the past hour or so, and I could not help asking, "What does she see in me? To tell the truth—I hate to do so—I'm quite an empty bladder, just a balloon full of air and dried peas, I rattle; but she's a well-bred woman and a millionaire, it seems, not to mention having a reputation in her own right. This must all be a gross mistake. Was it Jacky she wanted? Jacky has quality; I am what I am, but no soulmate." I sweated for half an hour.

I already foresaw the end, a dismal Monday morning, parting apologies and courtesies, the cold handclasps and the dislike on both sides. I jangled. There was a humming along my nerves. I said quite nervously, almost losing control: "Can we go out and look at the lake; look at the metallic luster?" and I continued to speak anxiously, "How primitive it looks; it's been this way for ages I suppose, since the Ice Age; it looks like the Ice Age," and I shivered. I went on feverishly, while she agreed with me and smiled kindly at me, "How chill it becomes! It's Indian summer. How awfully, awfully still!"

She smiled, "We are alone. Don't you like it?"

"It isn't that. I'm not sensitive. I don't infold at nightfall," and laughing, I raised my eyes to hers and saw a strange, deep, beautiful look on her face. Her eyes were searching me. How good, sensitive she was. How much the *grande dame*! Yet, simple, industrious; trying to avoid the sloth of easy money.

I hurried on, "There's an abnormal stillness in all this country, I've noticed. It is deathly. You feel the dead are round, and I don't mean the recent dead, but, say, the Indian dead. People who died in the winter, in their tents; died of wintry hunger here. I suppose a lot died here, after all," I said, looking around me anxiously.

The grass was, by now, almost black; the lustrous lake had turned from chemical greens and reds to olive, and now was slowly growing black.

"There are dead here," I said.

"Minds die near here; there's an asylum for the criminal insane near here."

"I'd go mad stuck away from love, wouldn't you?" I said.

A faint star showed. The sky was pale, tender. She smiled and said with consideration, "We'll go in if you feel uneasy. You know the penitentiary is not far away; is that it? Would that make you afraid at night?"

"Oh, no!"

"Well, we will go in anyhow. Tomorrow morning, you will see it all in sunlight."

We had dinner, a Spanish stew, on the oak table in the coffee room, to save steps for Josephine, said Mrs. Headlong. I saw Josephine now, a middle-aged, dark-haired, sober Irish woman, in the traditional cap and apron. With the stew we had a light Spanish wine, which Mrs. Headlong got out of a cupboard herself, taking some keys from her room; we had black coffee, but no sweets.

We went back to the Norman hall. Mrs. Headlong, before our early bedtime, said, "Perhaps you will be nervous in such a big house, all alone, the first night, so I think I will show you over it. You will know where everything is, and will not be afraid."

I said, with a blush, "I have already explored those parts near me."

"Yes, I know. I heard you walking about."

We went upstairs, and, by the gallery, entered a suite of rooms used by Mrs. Headlong's half-grown children, all away at schools, their nurse and governess; linen closets, toy cupboards. From these rooms an easy staircase went down to the playroom, from which three doors led, one to the kitchens, one to the coffee room, and one to an outdoor dining room. There was a wooden gallery outside the great kitchen, from which stairs led down to the garages and the men's quarters. Still another exit from the kitchen led to a foyer in which was a powder room, and this again led to the entry in which I had first found myself. Yet, because all these were grouped round the great hall and were divided into wings, everything was clear.

"I shall not be afraid now," I said.

Mrs. Headlong took me to my room, showed me where the books were, and, in her elegant boarding-school style, bade me good night. I drew the heavy curtains over the windows, both sides, and sat down. I heard faint movement upstairs. Not long afterwards, Mrs. Headlong came down the inside stairs, in her tailored negligee, and said we must leave the door open to the stairs so that I could use it, and that I must come at any time of the night. I said I really wasn't such a coward as all that.

I read for a long time and then put out the light. The windows in steel frames could not be entered from outside, and there was nothing but starlight, very faint over the woods. Laurels and hollies grew near the house. It seemed very stuffy, but I was afraid to pull back the curtains from the windows. I lay in bed under all that stone in the thick silence and laughed at the lavish hospitality, the great house. Yet I was oppressed. The spirit itself stifled. Not far away was an insane asylum. What did the servants do at night? Did they creep down all those staircases? I felt they hated Lucy Headlong. But why? She was kind—indeed. I had never heard such stillness, and asked myself if it had something to do with the Fall Line. Here, the land was truly under the influence of the last ice. I knew that on the other side of the Line, the bush bloomed soft, round and green, and rustled and sang all night. Here, the northern silence murdered all sound. All the things round the house I had seen had been smothered, and would come back in the morning, vampires, to deceive with a fair show.

I started as just outside my window two voices began, a man's baritone and a woman's light, hurried speech. The woman said something nervously, and the man assented. The conversation went on. I got up and looked out. Anything better than the thumping heart, the thickness of the room's night. It was rather clear now, a moon was visible. The sounds were made by frogs. My glance traveled over a boulder, a rock garden, a roof, the dip of the hill, and swam in the innocent mute lake lying down there, and becoming lighter with the moon. It is simply, I said to myself, the absence of noise. I'm one of those town lunatics, like they have on the Grand Concourse, who can only sleep with four radios blaring out "Three Itty Fitties," at two in the morning. I drew the curtain to welcome the wood light into the room. The walls took on faint flesh and I settled myself to sleep. I could not sleep. I became lighter in spirits. At intervals throughout the night I switched on my light to read. I read natural history, the latest best-seller, anagrams, anything that they had in the room; but could not keep my attention fixed and would soon turn off the light again. Mrs. Headlong was not sleeping, for when I rose I noticed, after a while, light from above falling through curtains. A nervous night.

For a long time the frogs went on talking, "It's eerie here! It's eerie here!" and the bullfrog, after a meditative silence, "I know! I know!" Then the nervous frog again, "It's eerie here—it's eerie." The bullfrog seemed to consider it, when he answered consolingly, "I know—I know!"

Later in the night, when I had ceased putting on my light (for I saw that when I put on mine, Mrs. Headlong put on hers, no doubt to comfort me), later, I leaned against the bed head and listened to soft sounds in the moon-washed grass; animals, scurrying feet, ghosts of animals, animals the Indians had known? But harmless, gentle, slipping by. The night passed. I got up early and it seemed to me I had not slept.

"Did you sleep?" asked Mrs. Headlong, when I came out in my borrowed land-girl suit, feeling quite fresh.

"But did you?" I asked, "I saw your light," and I went on to declare that there were gentle ghosts about, rustling like spring leaves. This pleased her very much.

The day passed uneventfully, but as easily as the night had. We took a long ride through that dull, wooded country with its sunken roads and lakes. We visited an elegant farmhouse or two where we had drinks. Mrs. Headlong pounced about, full of glee, making a grand, aristocratic clatter. It seemed to me that these people were all stuffy and snobs, for they were quite cool to me. I could not help my uneasy feeling that this week end was a kind of mistake, and that, no doubt, all these people thought I was a poor girl sponging on a rich woman.

The evening was dull, but agreeable, for this same boisterous and bold woman, who handed out insults when it pleased her, in a royal way, had also a cordial art, and could behave, even to me, a girl of no particular charms, moneyless, as a sweet and humble friend.

"If you do not sleep tonight," said Lucy Headlong when she took me into my room and unobtrusively arranged things for me, "come and tell me; you will get an aspirin."

"Oh, I wouldn't disturb you for the world."

"I rarely sleep," she said, with a nervous but earnest air.

This night was like the one before. The frogs conversed; the moon rose, a little brighter, the airy hours scuttled past. Animals swarmed up and down the slopes of the mound, but delicate-footed, so that, quite entertained and friendly, I looked out of both windows endeavoring to see what kind of animals they were; but I saw nothing. I lay awake, but not uneasy, and rose frequently to look out the windows at the woods, hopping strangely, very lightly, full of girlish bliss, from one place to the other.

The room this night was bathed in dry, pale light, for I had left the curtains wide. I knew, now, no one was about. I would throw myself on the sheets for a while and would take pleasure in trying to seize the unseizable fancies in my head, and again get up, even trying to read by moonlight. At many hours in the night,

I saw the poor woman's light on, falling through the slit of the curtains.

It was the third day that was strange. To fill in time, Lucy Headlong said she would paint my portrait. I had not slept, and yet felt lively and delightfully childish. I behaved in a confiding and childish way.

We went out into the home woods where, some hundred yards away, in a clearing, breasting another mound, we found a building with stables in the lower part, and a loft; and above that, a studio. A large sheet of canvas was spread on the hill between staves to throw the light into the room. Above, the roof was partly glassed. There was an alpine balcony and sliding doors on one side. She kept most of her supplies and canvases in closets in the walls and on a high gallery, reached by a narrow, carved stair. A door led to a wall closet. A small window looked out over the undulating country. On the balcony was a bed covered with a native rug.

When I came down, she brought out some of her canvases for me, including several self-portraits. One showed an exceptionally fresh and enigmatic girl, in a Velasquez court costume.

"This is you—what beauty!"

"I was not bad-looking once."

"This is simply a beauty! Much better looking than I am," I said.

She smiled slightly, "You are all right, Letty, and you are young —whatever you may be later on, now you are perfect. I am not good-looking any more."

"You are very handsome."

She made a face, pulling her jaws slightly apart, with a beastly rictus, so that she looked both insane and dead. A fierce light shone in her eyes and her skin showed all its yellow; one could see the hundreds of fine wrinkles in her delicate, but aging skin and flesh. Gross persons have great wrinkles; these beauties who are taking on the clothing of contempt they will wear in old age, have these fine webbed crow's-feet, an infinity of small wounds. Now she pulled her face another way, with her fingers, she thrust her face close at me; I had a moment of terror, staring at this face with eagles' eyes. Then she drew off, and turned her back. Without seeing any more, I felt that she was frenzied by her age. A painter knows better than another how she looks. It took her some time to calm herself; then she turned back with her usual, lady-like smile.

"Sit you here, my little Letty," and she arranged me so that the light from the canvas on the hill fell on me. As soon as she had taken up her post at the easel, she was occupied by her craft, but I was conscious of her unsought, tender, thoughtful friendship, and a soft air of gratitude and affection, I am sure, was moving from me to her, much of this morning.

"Speak, speak," she said to me, explaining that I must speak about anything, so that my face would be naturally animated and my gestures natural.

"Don't lose the pose, though."

It surprised me to find how easy it was to monologue by the hour. It was delicious. If I stopped, after a moment or two, she would say, "Go on, Letty; tell me something; I need the anima-tion," and when I had started up again, her gaze traveled back and forth in the same busy way.

What was my conversation about? At first, it strayed. Then per-haps, because she abstractedly said, "Who was he?" I began to talk about the men I knew. My father—she said, "You're very fond of your father, aren't you?"—my handsome cousin, Templeton Hogg, now an aspiring Little Theatre actor, hoping for Hollywood—in a quarter of an hour I had arrived at Clays Manning.

"Go on, go on," said Mrs. Headlong. "And he is in Spain still?"

There was something soothing in the morning and our occupa-tion and I was light-headed through not having slept, although by no means sleepy. I began to confess. Soon Mrs. Headlong knew all of the Manning affair, and became vividly interested in Manning. Her face lighted up, she cast sympathetic smiles at me, and said, "Well, such things can happen to anyone—anyone," and her teas-ing eyes danced.

"Well, go on," said she, "and now you are waiting for Clays?"

My late misfortunes kept me silent for a time. She noticed this, put down her brushes, surveyed her work and me and then, putting out her hand, "Come, little Letty! We'll go and have drinks and lunch!"

She again made a quantity of cocktails, which she brought

outside to the stone terrace, on the lake side; and we sat in summer chairs under the tall walnuts.

"What a contrast," thought I, "with Grandmother Morgan's rowdy-dowdy out at Green Acres."

Here, not a thought, not a word, not an action that I did not want myself; silence, and great wealth, beauty, peace, and singular admiration. Mrs. Headlong watched me, "You like it here? And yet you don't sleep! Shall we go and visit this afternoon, so that you can sleep, or shall we just stay here and relax?"

"Let's take a ride and visit!"

"Anything; anything you like," she said at once, cheerfully, "and if you miss your little Jacky, I'll telephone or send a telegram for her." She leaned forward, "Shall I send for Jacky, dear? You're lonely."

I laughed outright.

"I miss Jacky? I miss anyone? I do not miss even Clays. I'm ashamed to say it. Of course, I'm restless, lonely, in a way, all the time. I need men, and then when I have them, they're unsatisfactory. I don't know what I want, of course. But I've lost the taste for men my own age. And when I look at older men, I have my doubts—what is it, exactly? It's difficult to make a start in life."

She became more serious than I was. She began to tell me about her affairs. Her life was famous, romantic, adventurous. She had been everything a woman should be—an artist, a radical, had lovers, husbands, children, money, philanthropy, doctrines, follies; a woman who did not despise any kind of life.

I went on, with "Luke Adams—"

"Luke Adams!"

"Oh, yes, you knew Luke Adams!"

"What could a girl like you have to do with him?"

But although everyone admired this gallant and rather strange artist, man of many adventures and loves, brave, poor man, she blackened with spite.

"Little gutter rat from the slums! Mad with vanity! Only thinks of the size of his fan mail. Yes, I know a good deal about Luke Adams!"

But it was clear that none of what she knew she had known in love. She said viciously, spitting the words out one by one,

"He's a little upstart; he's made a name for himself by coddling the prejudices of the half-hewn and the lame-brains. Is it an honor to be born in the working class? I mean, not in socialism, just now. He pretends it is. Richard III had the decency to regret that he was a misshapen brat—he hated his mirror—but not that ugly monkey-faced wizened brat, that Bowery lambstew tosspot."

I said, amused, "Oh, I rather like Luke Adams, he's a friend of my father."

"Solander and Persia Fox should have more sense."

Persia Fox! Never had I heard her called that till now. I looked with surprise at this woman, without prejudice, and thought, There's a great side to her nature. She's been through stormy loves and half-ruined lives. She's milled finer, perhaps, than I. A second later I asked myself if it wasn't just her money working on me, for I'm not in the habit of thinking others better than I. It's a weakling idea. No, even a millionaire of the persuasion feminine is not better than I, I thought. I smiled babyishly, in my malice, "They say he has many women loving him."

"No doubt he tells it himself."

It was mere kittenishness. I passed on. I noticed she criticized many men—I suppose a talented woman does, not obliged to flatter their image. Or is it money? I remembered the truth about her —she was paying an allowance to a previous husband. Naturally, she had not a particularly dependent view of men. Though her present husband suited her well, a successful town intellectual of good tone and welcome everywhere, people still laughed at him if she so much as bought him a bottle of wine.

"Lucky for him to be kept so well," they said, "talking on his wife's money; I could do that." The men were jealous of Adrian Headlong.

She went on with her affairs, eagerly, baring her life to me, "My first husband was a Hungarian, a fatal man. I can't look at him now without qualms and he's been married twice since. I got tired of him, and I determined not to be under his thumb. Palyi was irresistible," she said delightfully, "it cost me a lot to divorce him. I went to Mexico City to do it. He came down there and wheedled round. When I went back to New York I went to see him, against my better judgment. His room was in a hotel near Central Park.

He was living on my money then. Why not? I gave it to him. I didn't like Palyi to live miserably. A delightful creature like him. Soft, insincere, but charming as a girl. On his wall were etchings, all indecent naturally, and to the point—you know, the only thing that interested his direct mind. Direct action was his way. I said to him, 'Palyi, that's mere tiddlywinks. Casanova had a patent armchair that tilted back and had arm-grips.'

"He at once pulled a long face, and his irresistibly melancholy brown eyes slid about, 'Lucy, I can't afford the exotic.' "

She laughed, "Palyi, Palyi," she murmured. "Terrible for me, bad for my peace of mind, and my morals. I danced after him for a year or two, think of it. I remarried him. Think of it! He wasn't so pleased. He became morbid. He sat in his room and was depressed. He cried. Naturally, I wouldn't let him have his etchings on the wall. He sat at the window and waited for me when I went out. He dropped flowers on my head when I came in. That was the town house—you know it—Fifty-fifth—he sat on the second floor and dropped petals on my head. When I got upstairs, he'd throw himself on the couch and look at me, 'Oh, I've been waiting all day for you.' How cunning he was!"

"Was that cunning?"

"Of course," Lucy Headlong cried irritably, getting up and taking strides. "He knew I couldn't stand that kind of mamamouchi. He just wanted me to get rid of him again and to get back his allowance."

"Where's Palyi now? I don't know his other name!"

A shadow crossed her face for the first time; "He's married again, of course," she said, without a smile.

After a moment, she came back and poured me a drink, "If it's too watery, tell me. But the one you remind me of, Letty—well, not exactly, you're strictly feminine, you know—not exactly, just something about the foreheads—you have a fine forehead, and then —no, it must be the forehead; everything about you is distinctly not male. The hair? Perhaps that too!"

She sat down, and told a fine-drawn story of her second marriage, and the man I reminded her of—her phrases transparent, broad, natural and clean, new cambric. I understood as the story went on that it was not a marriage by law, yet, it was in fact, of her

senses and inclinations. Then came Adrian; and now, "I'm a pris-
oner of his kindness."

Her small face had become tragic, the eyes sunken. She ran her
hands through her hair. I remembered having seen my mother do it,
but here, I thought, Oh, here is the queen; my mother is just an actress; Lucy Headlong is the firebird. Down she comes and drinks
up men's souls and bodies like milk and nothing puts out the fire.
But I looked at her composedly and mentioned the birds settling
in the trees. I was slowly learning not to give myself away in any
company except that of a man, and as for that, foolish as it was, it
was my business. The lean, wary game in sex was not mine, and I
despised it. I smiled artificially at my hostess and she went on in a
low tone, to tell me who it was, the one who had maddened her
with love, two years ago. It was a famous man, one of the best
known in the world.

"I stared at his ears which were long, open, and animal, and filled
with hair. Eventually, I cured myself in this way. For the sake of
both men, I could not make a scandal."

I became sober, thinking of the treasury of knowledge that was
there, that I needed so badly in my own affairs. Why not make use
of it? She was in every sense my friend. She had bridged the gap of
our ages and made herself mine. I said, with some hesitation, "You
have a lot of experience in love, so to speak; I'm not really asking
for myself, but just from want of general knowledge—what would
you say is the axiom of the love affair? One doesn't know that kind
of thing."

It seemed a stupid, blundering question. She looked at me doubtfully, but was searching for something. In a moment, she said, "All
I know is, that when you want to get one person, it's another person who falls in love with you."

Certain incidents in my own life made me nod my head,
"There's nothing you can do about it."

She smiled, "But it seems to me, from what you say, you
must know."

"I don't know—"

A silence fell between us, full of this penetrating and courteous
question, " 'And now, you, my guest, tell your share.' "

She pushed across another drink. I twiddled the glass in my fingers and lifting my eyes which I felt soft and full, I said with the utmost naïveté, "Mrs. Headlong, I have had, really, no experiences, but those I have told you."

She started, "It's impossible! Not the way you talk! You seem so very much the modern, sophisticated—" she halted.

I took up, "The overdone young woman, the girl about town? I do; but that's play-acting. My mother was an actress once, don't forget. But I never had the velleity of the stage, and I just bring it plain and subtle into private life. I acted little girl, I acted young girl, and now I act knowing girl."

Mrs. Headlong withdrew into herself. After a moment I began once more about the fish in the lake and the corn in the garden behind the yews. But I did it with sophisticated weariness and even rudeness, as if to dismiss too intimate a subject of conversation, raised by herself. She took this humbly, and now spoke of lunch, "Josie is off. I must do it myself. Let's go into the kitchen, or would you rather stay here?"

I went in with her. The kitchen was the length of two or three ordinary kitchens, winding a little, as if, in fact, several rooms had been thrown together; a buttery bar; a serving foyer. Two doors led out of the serving foyer, one to the nursery dining room, one to a powder room. The disposition of this powder room was such that Lucy Headlong could make any kind of exit from her guests, from breakfast room, kitchen, nursery, outdoor dining room, or general foyer, not to mention a few others, and find herself in a private make-up room. Wonderful for a fading beauty!

Beyond this serving foyer, lined with handsome dressers and cupboards containing heavy serving ware, stretched two kitchens joined into one. The first had the dinner ware and the preserves and the ordinary wine that the servants perhaps could get at, and the second was the cooking and washing-up kitchen, where stood the usual things. From this the staircase led down to the paved yard, a kind of castle-yard, and the garages were below. I hung about, feeling this domesticity unworthy of us. I'm not the kind of woman that can mess in another woman's kitchen, or in any kitchen. I'd always lived in hotels or apartments with Mother or some woman to wait upon me, and there's nothing bores me more than the false intimacy of the kitchen. Nevertheless, there I was obliged to be, hoisting myself against some cupboard or other, fiddling with egg-timers and oven-holders. Everything had been left ready by some servant. We had cold fowl, salad, Barsac, cheese, and coffee. Afterwards, Lucy Headlong washed the dishes herself, and I made no move to help, for this is a debasing relationship, this hanging together with gummy gaiety over the greasy plates and steaming bowl; a woman looks like a waiter with a towel on her arm.

I wandered out onto the lawns, and looked for the tabby cat, supposed to have her hide-out in the gardener's toolshed. I saw Washington wandering sulkily in the distance. He took no notice of me.

Mrs. Headlong soon joined me, in no way put out by my behavior. I saw that I had been right. Rather noticeably, I examined my small, white, plump hands and manicured nails. She was in a pleasant mood, and I thought to myself, There is only one method in this life, and that is to overrule; altruism is a confession of ugliness. I could see that Lucy Headlong had all her life done just this, and that her present mildness toward me was perhaps a result of her advancing age. How old was she? At least forty-three.

"Would you like to go to a cocktail party? While you were consulting the daisies on the lawn the phone rang, and we were invited to the Dichters'."

"Who's that?"

"Don't you really know the Dichters?"

"No; you forget, Mrs. Headlong, I don't know anyone. My background's an ordinary one. Anything I have I owe to myself alone. You know what that means—the self-made woman."

She smiled, "What wonderful arrogance, and how I love that in a woman," she said, stepping sprightly in the direction of the garage. "Come, let's drive about, and then we'll drop in when we please, when it suits us, to the cocktail party. Tell me, do you need anything, lipstick, a scarf? Go into my own little powder room which is just outside the kitchen at the bottom of the broad staircase."

"I know where it is," I said, with mild and shining insolence. "I looked; I looked everywhere in your beautiful house."

"Yes, you have taken it to yourself, bless you, little Letty," she said, "I know."

I had now got over this feeling of surprise and wonder which made me nervous when I first came. We drove through the beautiful afternoon, through high and low roads and visited many beauty spots.

About five, I think, we came to the cocktail party; a crowd of nondescripts squashed together, knees and glasses touching on dirt-stained divans and chairs, in a couple of little rooms, with cigarette ashes on the carpet. Perhaps my manner showed what I thought of them. I was treated coolly and did not get into talk for at least half an hour. I sat holding my glass.

The Dichters, poor German exiles, with a fantastic shoddy happiness of their own, in their poverty and fame unknown here, scandalized me with their Bohemian life. Everything was harem-scarum, sketchy; the carpet was worn and had been thin to begin with, the books were dog-eared, the shelves of plain white pine thrown together, and the house was a mere shack, with a lean-to kitchen.

After a while, I felt it necessary to say something, and the middle-aged woman beside me began to converse with me, asking polite questions about Lucy Headlong and myself, how long had I been staying, did I know her well, did I like the house, and whether I was staying alone, or there was a house-party, and how long I was staying. The woman seemed timid and sweet, but in retrospect, I resented her questions. I must admit at the time I was only engaged in playing reticence and hinting at the casual intimacy of my hostess and myself. I mentioned someone, some people we all knew, and I soon became the center of a small circle. But I was bored. The men had a strange and poor look, with the sunken eyes and the strawlike hair of the starved intellectual; a distressing feeling. Their conversation all seemed to me to say only one thing: How hungry I really am, and all my sacrifice has brought me only one thing, I am hungry and therefore distorted. I could not stomach their opinions; I smelled the unclean attic upon them, the exile driven out in horror, fear and dirt; the creature without clothes to his back, or a roof over his head. Besides, there were two or three hungry curs prowling round us and these were lifted onto the laps of the women's dark, long-wearing dresses. Round me, some people discussed with ludicrous surprise and ignorance some animal they had seen. It was just an opossum. They had never seen one. I had seen plenty on Uncle Hogg's farm. At length I laughed, and told them what they had seen.

I went up to Lucy Headlong, and asked her if we could not go soon. Evening had come. I longed for our tranquil cocktail under the trees, above the lake. She looked toward me with her society woman's air and said, in a brief whisper, "Soon, just a moment while I take leave," and shortly I was out of that hole, and we were speeding away. A few people came to wave us good-bye, but most sat there, hardly answering us; everything about the place was dismal and dubious.

"Who are they, and do you really like them?" I asked my friend after we had gone some distance, and had lighted our cigarettes. The air of the hilltops had blown away all this sadness from below. She looked at me in surprise, "You didn't like it? If I'd known, I would never have taken you there. They are old friends of mine," she continued apologetically.

"They don't seem very friendly."

She waited for a long time, pointing out views between trees and down glades; then she said curiously, "They offended you?"

"I don't mean that. No, they were nice, but they're awfully slow, don't you think? I got a funny impression, that was all. It was dull, odd—"

I don't know, to this moment, why I said a thing so out of character; it was the result of days of unquestioning comradeship. She said quickly, but not sharply, "Then you shan't go there again, if they don't amuse you."

"Oh, I'll admit, if you don't mind, that it was—boring—I don't like Bohemians. I'm very prejudiced."

She was again silent, running the machine fast and slick through the upland. She said in a hesitating way, then, "Did they say anything you didn't like?"

"Oh, no, just so dull—"

Nothing persuaded me to this rudeness, but the consideration with which Mrs. Headlong treated me. There were instants when I felt she was companionable, but I never felt myself her equal for longer than this.

We came home. A local couple came after dinner, the young

man being a rising dramatist, one of those socialists who are extreme puritans, who detest all satire and have nothing of the Molière in them. I had an amusing time nagging and upsetting him, with my easygoing and cynical views of human nature, and saw Mrs. Headlong smiling all the time, with her small head on one side.

Afterwards, Mrs. Headlong and I were in excellent mood, laughing at the naïveté of these soft, pliant men, who are born and trained to compatibility and success.

My hostess said I must sleep in a room upstairs, near hers, not her husband's, but a studio, opening out of her own room, and reached by a small staircase, so that it looked out from the roof. Here, said she, I would neither see nor hear the soft animals of the night, probably not even the bullfrog. This suited me. I had been frightened without knowing it, in the well of stone and silence. When I put out the light and looked upwards, I saw, floating like a sail on the ocean on a dim night, the bellied canvas which protected the room from the direct light of the glassed studio roof. It floated and floated, more and less visible, according to my thoughts. It was sometimes like white woman's hair floating; sometimes, like a cloud. On this side of the hill, too, something slid past, a larger-bodied animal this time, but it was far below me, except on one side, where the slope approached the window. There were four windows, two groups and two single ones. The curtains were wide open all night. What haunted me was my imagination; it was not fevered with projects, anguish, regret, disgust at myself as usual, but calm and rocking as a rowboat on a shallow bay into which the tide is flowing. It went on moving all night, but always in the same place and no form of fantasy came to me, and no misery nor idea. I began once more to enjoy that gentle endless insomnia in which the other nights had been passed. But now I was the victim of some physical irritation, and the desire for love, without the dream of any masculine body, began to fill me. It started like a pinpoint and spread; it ran through my veins. I thought about my discomfort, but did not dare put on my light, for fear of waking my hostess; the doors between our rooms were open to get the breeze. Between us was the staircase and a round place opening into a bathroom, but the light from either room would fall upon the staircase. I lay on a wide studio bed, invisible from anywhere, but I could see the light on the staircase when she switched it on. She, too, was restless. The strange spirit of the place kept us awake. For there was unquestionably a haunting here, or it might have been another kind of life that was here, the life of a local wind, or a sweet miasma from the ancient ground, or the thickness coming from the trees, or it might have been something ineffably inhuman; but a kind of life.

It was not terror, and never once did I think of Washington, the gardener, or the too easy access to the servants' quarters, or the lunatic asylum, not far away. Nothing moved in the woods, but the scuttling animals round the house. All night, in the corpse-pale moonlight they moved, thought, hung about the foundations, and then footed it undangerously away. I did not sleep. When I got up in the morning, I found my skin luminous, my eyes languidly bright, and my hair finer than it had ever been; of itself it fell into delicious tendrils. At breakfast I made a joke of my extraordinary life here, and said, "But perhaps it is possible to live forever here without sleeping. There is a fluid at night which comes into you and lifts you out of yourself."

She gave me a kind and rather twisted look. The grimaces which had troubled me on the previous day were tumbling now about her face and body, so that she moved out of ordinary perspective. I said, "Do you know, Lucy, I should like to go home. I feel there is something here which does not suit me, although I look well enough. May I go home?"

"You may do anything in the world that you like," she said, "but would you like me to send for Jacky instead?"

I hesitated then, "No, I must go to work, I suppose. This is heaven, but I am not yet dead, unfortunately, and I must work."

She laughed. "Well, this morning we will work on the portrait. I will see you this week in town, and when you like, you will come out again and let me finish it. I have a feeling about it. It is going to turn out all right. You know, that's something you're never sure of, till at a certain moment, the conviction comes—and if it comes, then it is so."

This morning was passed in the outdoor studio. I packed and she drove me to the station. She bought me my ticket and some magazines to read on the train, though it was a short ride. All this still made me quite uneasy. I said to her, out of my embarrassment, "Lucy, I don't know if there's something wrong with me, for I know there are plenty of girls who take everything thoughtlessly, but I am not used to such generosity. I suppose it is because of the wreck of my family life, and the fact that I've always had to knock about, in a sense."

She kissed me, said, "You'll come out and I'll spoil you again," and sent me down to the train.

33

IT WAS hot in town. My whimsicality dropped on the way in. I found my sister Jacky at the station to meet me and take me home. I was out of sorts, sharp with her. She innocently plied me with questions about my fabulous week end. I said curtly, "Mrs. Headlong hopes you can go next week end; but I shall not. Let her start a picture of you!"

Jacky was breathless with her questions. When I got home, I threw down my bag and lay upon my bed. When Mother came home and questioned me, I got up and answered her curtly, glaring at her, walking up and down, and holding my waist with one hand.

"The heat's unbearable," I cried, and went into my room; but did not lie down again.

I first walked up and down and stood against the whitewashed wall trying to cool my face and body against the plaster. I threw myself upon the bed. I had visitations, dreams. I saw myself walking in a cool park and embracing the cool, slippery stem of a large tree; I saw myself swimming under a river and holding on fiercely to a jutting rock, covered with mosses. I held in my arms the mossy stele of a forgotten terminus in a Roman field; some goatish head looked down paternally upon me. Moods of blackness and suffering passed through me, of fierce, fierce intercourse such as no flesh could bear. I got up, and the fever that raged through my body was intolerable. Yes, this is the love that nymphs knew on afternoons when Pan chased them, I thought, this is the meaning of all those stories. I thought I was passionate; now, I know what growing up is. I thought, if it is going to be like this, this suffering and madness, I will kill myself now, for in the difficulty of getting married nowadays, and of getting a child, that cooling cold stone of a child, which stands in the hot belly and makes a woman heavy and tired, forgetting all her cruel fervors, that thing that drags her to the doors of the death house and away from the intolerable ardors of the sun, in this slow world, for women, I cannot live; I will kill myself. I believed that what I was suffering was then the first attack of adult passion, but I could not think of anyone else, not of my father, of Mathilde, nor Grandmother, nor Persia, not of anyone but myself, and my tortured body. I went back to the plastered wall and kept knocking my head against it; block, block, block, went my blockhead.

"What are you doing?" my mother called out.

"Oh, what I am suffering—" I cried, pulling my clothes straight and, with a knitted cap in my hand, rushing toward the door, "Don't ask me any questions. Living is too much for me."

"Living—?" said my mother, with extreme disdain.

"Living without love."

I banged the door after me. The streets at first seemed cooler than the house, but this passion, new to me, this fox was tearing at my vitals. I felt as if any moment I would throw myself down in the dust and let the stones tear out my flesh; let pedestrians tread over me, for my passion could only be cooled if my flesh were in a thousand pieces.

I dragged myself along, with an appearance of haste, and did not dare look at anyone, for if the passer-by were a woman, I hated her so much, for her being nothing of a man, that I would have liked to rip her cheeks with my nails; and if it were a man, I wanted to throw myself upon his welcoming breast.

Here were trees, unlike the trees of my visitation, but things I longed to embrace, and children in their baskets I longed to tear out of their swaddling clothes and run off with, holding them fiercely to me, pressing them like grapes into my hot chest; and here were horses with great, broad chests that I could hold to mine and here the grass of a front lawn, a church—only to throw myself on it and feel the coolness of the earth!

Thus I walked for hours, madly, with my cheeks flaming and my hair flying. My heart thumped; I was dead tired, but my cruel passion was not exhausted. I, at last, came home. It seemed to me that once there, I could take off all my clothes, bathe my skin, and even lacerate it, tear it so that the boiling blood would rush out.

Nothing could satisfy me, of that then I was quite sure, and I wondered what I would do when I was married to some man in a solitary home and these dreadful loves, the love of those who die of love, overcame me.

I reached home in the same state, behaved furiously to my sisters and mother, spent a long time in a cold bath, and came out raging. This went on for three days. But by this time I had so outraged everyone in the house that I could only go to my father's place for company. He never took things hard, and that cool individual, Persia, always laughed at me. On the way up in a bus, the air from parks and the river blew upon me; I felt that I was getting better. I asked myself, "What was this visitation?"

But I did not know. I wanted for the first time to catch Persia alone and ask, was love so, in adult life; well, not ask it, but guess.

Persia was glad to see me. I could answer the telephone while she was out marketing; and scarcely had she gone when Luke Adams, the cartoonist, rang at the doorbell and walked in, shaking himself like a shaggy dog and embracing me casually and genially, as all women. He was a shabby, dark, thin-faced man whose personal beauty poured out of him intermittently. He made men and women love him and behaved with the nonchalance of the coquette. He made moves to catch his prey; but once caught, he left them to themselves, knowing they would be tamed. He had a pack on his back which he was taking to the devil; once he caught your soul, he was done with you, though he had a certain possessive feeling—would not let others steal you—my merchandise, he thought. "They," he thought, "will cry at my funeral." He had, nevertheless, a manly heart; brave, free, beyond a certain point no one could possess him, though everyone seemed to be allowed to love him to this point. He possessed himself. Dangerous possession. He had the art thus of pleasing women without troubling himself at all, and perhaps thus came the strange legend he had about his women: "I do nothing really; women attack me."

He troubled men and women. He was the possessed. He had that possession they all longed for. He had liquid, squinting, wise smiles and the unreassuring predatory absences of the cat. Hardly anyone in the country called him Mr. Adams, but Luke.

He kissed me as a matter of course, and in kissing him, I put my arm round the small of his back. He drew away and looked at me with a yellow gleam, but seeing how it was, an accident, he smiled and went into the dining room where he took off his pinched and stained hat and threw it on the floor. He tumbled his books, satchel, and newspapers on a chair.

"Well, little Letty, how's school?"

"I've left school. I'm looking for a job."

"Oh? That's smart! Something intellectual, eh? Or a typist, eh? You've changed since I saw you! Seen a bit of life?"

He smiled and spread his newspaper, his eyes chasing down the columns.

"Not intellectual! Advertising copy, perhaps. My grandmother knows people in Lord and Taylor, Bonwit's—that sort of thing!"

He lifted one eye, laughed, "Good! You ought to see what kind of a fist you can make of it—hullo!" and he returned to his reading. He looked up to say apologetically, "They're—uh—expecting —where's Persia?"

"Mr. Adams! Why do you ignore me! I'm not a child. I'm a woman. I was a Y.C.L.'er—I wrote plays—I'm a human being too."

He looked at me over the top of the paper, smiling quizzically, "I noticed you'd changed; you've been knocking up against life a bit, is that it?"

I frowned. He grinned and went back to his paper. Presently, after considering me, he folded his paper, took a pint bottle of whisky out of his satchel, and put it on the table.

"Don't get mad, little Letty; I brought this along. Thought Perse might have a nip. She likes it. Do you know where the glasses are? Are you allowed to drink, though?"

"I'm a two-bottle man," I cried, running for the kitchen.

"Two bottles of orange juice, pickled sunshine, eh?" he chuckled, and from the end of the passage I saw him casting his eyes sidelong at the newspaper. We had a couple of ponies each and Luke began to sit toward me, with his hair tousled and his eye merrily fixed upon me, "You're a pretty girl, Letty. How's that Clays? I read some of his stuff. Good stuff!"

"Clays is all right. But he's a long way away. I'd like to go over and join him."

"Be a *vivandière*, eh? Be soldier's mate? That's all right."

"Be a gun-moll. But I'm fighting here too, for Spain."

"Ye-es," he said, pouring some more whisky. "Where's Solander?"

"At work."

"Well, he'll be home soon, I suppose."

I looked him over. He was unshaved and one tooth was missing in front; he looked rascally and downtrodden, but he didn't seem to know it. He beamed upon me.

"Have you had lunch, Luke?"

"No-o. But I had late breakfast."

"There's some cold chicken fricassee out there; do you want some?"

He said Persia would feed him when she came. She always did.

"I'll heat it."

"No, no, I—"

"Yes, do, Luke."

He gave in, was ill at ease, and after a minute took up his paper and began to read it. Everyone knew how badly he ate and how sick he was with his chest. I heated the food in a rough sort of way, and set the table. I said, "I see there's some black bean soup, too. Would you like that first?"

He said genially, looking at his paper, making a concession, "All right."

I had already heated it, set it in a plate, and now put it before him. I felt the service, which I had never done, suited me badly, but I did it, because he looked so poor. He was genially awkward, but sat and ate, waving his hand, however, and saying, "If Perse comes and—she'll wonder—she wants it for dinner, maybe—?"

Although irritated by waiting upon him, I went and got the chicken and sat down to look at him eating. He put away his paper, "Letty, you're a good cook!"

"A good canned cook."

He put down his spoon, and felt in several of his pockets. At last he brought out a couple of packets.

"Look, some phlox seeds. Why don't you put them in your window boxes down at home. Girls like flowers."

"Thanks, Luke, but I don't want 'em. I hate watering things and no one else would. Give them to Perse."

When I brought in the chicken and the coffee, he looked at it, with hesitation, "We oughtn't to rob Perse this way."

"You mean, she wouldn't feed you?"

"Oh, that's true, she always has something to eat. Sign of a good woman, Letty."

He laughed reminiscently through his chicken. I told him I didn't care if I cleaned out the larder, for they wouldn't care. They didn't live that way. When he had finished his mouthful, he felt through his pockets again and brought out other little packets from several; "Do you do any cooking yourself, at home?"

"No. I hate the kitchen!"

"Well—" he said. "Well—anyhow," pushing the packet at me, "anyhow give the packet to your mother. Saffron's good, rice dishes, paella, fish, Spanish dishes. Mm!" and he went on eating.

"Oh, look, my hand is bright yellow!"

Luke looked for a few seconds and the meaty palm I showed him stuck out boldly. He mumbled, "See you don't waste it."

I laughed to provoke him. Luke said, "He's a Spaniard. He lives behind the shop. The man who gave it to me. His brother mends watches. He plays the guitar. He's saving up to see Mexico, *mi tierra*, he calls it."

"Yes?"

Luke said, "They came in through Miami and tried to get a job, but they chased him away; they don't like them down there, or any other South Americans. They think they're a kind of—uh —Negro."

"Yes."

"He says he doesn't like the women down there"; Luke shook his head. "Poor girls," very intimately, he went on; "no free women there at all, slaves in marriage, slaves outside marriage."

"I know, it's the same here."

Luke took no notice of me. He went on eating his chicken and looking at his plate intimately. He murmured, "And then the outcast—women; the pariahs; you know—" he did not say the word, "and even some of the wives—stupid, slovenly, go about in dressing gowns with their hair in wisps—fah! slovenly. And the gutters—smell, you know."

I said I was never there in the South, but I had heard. Luke continued quietly, "But a good climate, it's very healthy; the children ought to be healthy. The Negroes love children; the Spaniards too; all native peoples."

Luke Adams had a wife with wispy hair and with one stringy child and I was embarrassed, but not he; he was not referring to his family. He murmured instead that this Spaniard with the guitar had adopted a ten-year-old boy that he had found hanging round the Union Hall, a Spanish boy whose parents had died in a bus accident. He slept sometimes at one place, sometimes at another, sometimes in the Union Hall. Now, he slept with the Spaniard, Antonio, and his brother; and they had no place but a curtained-off place in their shop, where they were not supposed to sleep, but which they used for their living.

"So," said Luke Adams, "I took him, of course. But now Elsie doesn't want him. I don't blame her. He's noisy—of course; can't settle down. I thought—Perse and Solander might take him. Or perhaps they know a place in the country, he needs the country. Thin, nervous—"

He chewed at the last chicken bone, and his tooth-lack showed as his long, dark lips curled in a confident smile.

"Thought they might be glad—there's a bed here." He had become quite cheerful.

"I don't know," I said, much displeased. So the saffron and the phlox were for that.

"Perhaps your mother would have room—no boys—perhaps she likes boys," he ventured, with much simplicity.

"My mother—doesn't care for strangers."

"No, no," he grumbled. Then he became angry.

"I took him to Cassell's, and they said they had no room. When I went to stay at Mark Handel's he took me all round the damn town looking for someone to put me up. I could have slept with little Mark—his son, that is. I said I'd take the boy."

"Where was Elsie, your wife?"

"She was—" he waved his hand, and after thinking, said deeply, seductively, "In the country, we have a little place, good for children. Children need air. And I thought Leon—that's the boy—but naturally, she had enough on her hands."

"Where are you staying, then?"

"I was at the Union Square Hotel," he said resentfully, "and they gave me a little room, like a box without a window. Jesus!" He looked at me.

"Then Leon—the boy—I left him with Ethel Brown, a woman I know in Brooklyn. I met her at the meeting—a meeting I was at— she has a heart as big as a whale," and he repeated, staring reproachfully at me, "big as a whale!"

"Luke!"

He looked up quickly, with a smile, "Yes?"

"Luke!" But I shook my head.

He smiled eagerly.

"What is it, Letty?"

"We're guests, girls of my age, we have no homes. If this or that were my home, you could have ten of your adopted children there," and low, I added, "and not even adopted."

"Letty!" he cried, "come here. I would kiss you, but if I did—" and he did so. I broke away. "So you'll take him here or down there for a few days? It's only till we get a decent place for the poor kid."

He had begun to walk and had reached the wall. I came to him against the cream wall and held my face up to him; he laid his long, dark lips against mine, and this was the first time that ever I was really kissed. A spark flew between us and I became a woman of fire. I felt the shape of my limbs from within; they were dark, round, pouring downwards with the blood. I trembled. I thought at the same time, Can I learn from him to kiss like that? But this is it, I thought; oh, the rest—poor men—

"A little girl," he said, with a wondering voice, "just a little girl."

He stood against the wall, himself trembling. I kissed him beside the mouth. He said, gutturally soft, "You're wonderful, Letty, you're a wonderful girl."

It came so mechanically from him that I thought, This is the thing he says, and I simply echoed him, "You're wonderful to me, Luke."

"Letty, Letty," and in a deeper voice, "Letty!"

"To me you are so wonderful, Luke; I've always thought about you."

"You're sweet, Letty, you're sweet."

"You're a great man, you're different from all other men, every-one knows—everyone feels it—you are a man. What we mean by a man."

He broke away with a sob.

"Don't go," I muttered.

"I must go."

"Don't go."

We embraced again, nearer the door. He had, strangely, col-lected his hat, his books, but not his satchel. Luke looked down at me, and put his hand on the roots of my hair on the forehead. He cried fervently, "I could give you everything—everything in my life. I want to tell you so much. If only I could talk to you. I want to love you, Letty, I want to—" he muttered and muttered, words deep and obscene.

"Why don't you, Luke?" I said, quite drunk with him. We were at the door. He had jammed on his hat and slightly opened the door. He looked round at me with wild, black eyes, his hair fly-ing. He looked as if he had just come out of a street fight. He smiled and bent toward me, "The boy—is it all right? Can you really take him? Persuade them. I can't face them—now. I'll be back, after dinner."

"I'll ask them, but for how long?"

Luke said carelessly, "Oh, a few days—till I get the ticket back —to where I got him from, southwest, a—place—here he'd be all right. Good company. Good food. A clean place to sleep. You've no idea what a difference that makes. Nice boy."

"I understood he was a regular little hobo—"

"Just had no opportunity, he'll be all right. Just tell Solander. Well, I'll tell him—but you," he leaned forward mysteriously, "you break the ground."

He sauntered over and rang the elevator bell. I went out. He tangled with me again, his eyes maddened, "I want to love you, Letty, I want to love you."

"Will you come and see me at my own place?"

"Where's that?"

The elevator had come to the floor, and he scribbled the address in a small breastpocket notebook.

"I'll get round there sometime," he said, smiling.

As the lift was going down, Persia and Solander came up the stairs. They had seen Luke Adams in the lift, and they found me as I was then standing, leaning against the wall, inside the door which was on the latch.

"What's the matter with you?" said Solander. "You look mussed up; you look tousled."

"No; Luke was here, and he's coming back after dinner."

Persia let out a cry, "I thought he was coming for dinner," and in an ill temper, went into the kitchen. When we entered the dining room, the bottle of whisky was standing on the table, with the plates, glasses, and the rest of it, and Solander said irritably, "What? He ate, and you had drinks?"

"Can't I hide anything from you, Papa? Oh, that Sherlock."

"Well, you look queer, and here are the remains—now you clean the place up. It looks like an illicit love affair," he said, looking me in the eyes.

I laughed, but I was frightened when I saw my appearance in the mirror.

Luke would be very angry with me when he heard the result of the night's negotiations. They refused to take the orphan boy, Leon, into their home. Solander said, "This is just the anteroom to my keeping him forever. Everyone knows our Luke. Nothing doing."

I went home early, in a fit of passion, like nothing I had felt before; I was madly in love with Luke Adams. A hopeless affair it was, for he was forty, newly married after a wanton life, and with a young child; he had settled down at last. But I now knew I had never even known what love was before; and I say now, a Lovelace he is, no doubt, but this is the only man I ever met that I really loved fatally.

I did not escape a homily. My father went out with me, and I was glad of that. I was not now used to walking about the streets at night without a man by my side. But my father took me to a cafeteria, brought two coffees to our table, and told me he thought I was getting into loose ways and I must look to myself. As to Luke Adams, he was a married man and a well-known libertine. What could he offer me? I looked at my father with exasperation. This kind of man, the loyal one, does not understand that a woman does not need to be offered something—for my poor father supposed I wanted a home, an income. And as to the married state in which Luke found himself, I scarcely thought Solander had the right to comment upon that. I kept silent; but my father continued, I must find a job and settle down to work. He would give me no more money to waste.

"What can Luke offer you?" he asked irritably. "I see you're going to turn into a bum, unless I spank you."

I laughed blackly. What could he offer me? Marijuana; but you can't explain that to Solander.

Papa refused to go home with me, and I bussed drearily all the way home. I tossed about at night, thinking over my sins—but after a short time there came back this flame, the love between Luke and me.

Jacky had said foolish things to him and been turned down by him, on account of her youth, perhaps. Many other women had had him and lost him. I hoped I would enjoy him. For the first time I was really in love. As to his wife—she had the leavings of many women and who could believe that Casanova would be faithful? Who worried about her?

All through the night I was kept awake by the fire in my veins and the kisses I had given Luke. Morning could not come too soon. I made up my mind to look for a job the next day, for in idleness I could not live. The life I enjoyed at that time was too fierce. Besides, it was clear I needed a place to myself. I was nearly eighteen, and was more than mature; I even began to feel weary of the wandering life; oddly enough, a young woman in her parents' home feels a wayfarer, a stray, even while she is glad of the services given to her.

Luke Adams telephoned me the next morning at my mother's house, to ask if my mother would be willing to take in the orphan Leon. I said she would not, but I would do my best to place him that very day. We had thousands of relatives and friends. He was very cheerful, and his self-deprecating, sweet baritone made everything between us seem a sign of intimacy. He said he must see me soon, and always with the doubt in his voice, as if, on a moral issue, I might lose him. He might experience qualms. As for me, I felt none.

His wife had come from the Jersey flats, an easygoing consummately arrogant small-town daughter, a greasy-chopped slob, with unwashed hair and a continual smile. I had held her child on my knees when he was a fat good-natured baby. Now, starved and filthy, neglected and put upon, he was a wretched, peaked lad, a gutter urchin. He slept in filthy shirts, and his mother dressed in rags, but always with the same calm air; she believed herself to be a queen among women. I had no feelings of shame toward her, nor had any of his women, I suppose, but not till now had real rage filled me about Elsie Adams.

Before, we had laughed at her and deplored her housekeeping; only now did this bitterness gnaw at me. He was mine. That was his fatal charm, he gave himself at once to a woman; he was always hers.

The next day he telephoned me again about Leon, and now, in his troubled voice, said he'd like to see me, when would I be alone in the house; and I thought he wanted to avoid Jacky, for he was certainly the "L.A." of her summer letter. I gave him a time; but just before the hour, my mother whisked me away. The next day I made an appointment (he telephoned again) and this time it was my father who took me out for cocktails.

I had been paying visits all over town, and through Dora Morgan had heard of a woman, Susannah Ford, married to a second husband, with a boy, eight, who had a house in Jane Street, and an extra bed. She was a "real radical" as they said, and would certainly take in an adoptee of Luke Adams, for the glory of it, and because she was always a friend of men. She had some money and threw it about, to husbands, radicals; and wasted it in parties. I went to see Susannah Ford, let her know of our family's connection with Luke Adams. She agreed to take the boy. I almost ran out of her house in Jane Street to telephone to my dear one. I could hear him throw his hat on the floor and tramp on it, in his glee, "Three cheers for you," and then the strolling, teasing tone, "Mrs. Fix-it, eh?"

"I can always fix it, Luke."

"Oh, yes, you are a fixer," and with his interest picking up, he asked for the address and circumstances of the woman in Jane Street. He would take the boy there that night. I said, "Susannah's got an eight-year-old boy, and he's a louse. 'Little School Barn'; he's got a gilt-edged certificate he got last June that he can make zebras in striped wax; he's a piece of cheese."

Luke trilled his trullmaker into the phone,

"Don't be acid, Letty; you're a real cat; I never knew."

I had so much to disturb me that I could not sleep. My father's scoldings upset me. He was unnaturally good to me, not, I am sure, because he had been like me, but just because he had not been like me. He did not want to distort a nature so different from his own. When he reprimanded me I thought about it far into the night and knew I needed a guide, and that I should follow his advice. I am not immoral. I suffer too much from what I do, and from the smears of others, to be that. I am not hard, crass. I am soft-hearted, foolish, willful, even, in a way, too moral; I suffer very much from the imagined consequences of my acts. Very often nothing at all happens; all my sweats and tears have been for nothing. Then, indeed, I feel like a fool. No one knows what I go through.

On this occasion, I had my black hours, not of course, for that long-jowled wife of Luke's, but for my lost youth—for Luke was forty and I knew we could not make a go of it. He was far too old; I felt disgraced at times to be so much in love with a man of that age, and yet, it was love. I thought, will I ever feel that burning, aphrodisiac kiss again? I'll marry, but it'll be a queer thing to marry a man and live with him when he can't kiss like that. That, too, will be a compromise; and this is where my struggles came in—why should one compromise? If you've compromised you can't give an absolutely clear look at people, that look that is a knock-out blow.

On another count, I had trouble. Jacky had come to life and caused me much trouble by wanting to argue with me about doctrines. I had always had a lot to say, but did not care for arguments in my own home. Jacky approached the social question through art. Was art better or worse before, during, after the French Revolution, the Russian Revolution, and so on? She did not read pamphlets and books like me, at express speed, tossing them off, and able to repeat their arguments word for word. She devoured them fiercely, but halted at every second word—"I don't agree with this." It bored me. I was supposed to chew the fat with her through the long winter nights in the isba; that was her idea. It went against the grain. I refused. She now wanted to confide in me.

I had received an invitation from Lucy Headlong for the week end right at hand, for the finishing of my picture. I wrote to her that I could not; I was drawing up suggestions for selling town outfits to out-of-towners, to be sent out in attractive leaflet form to wealthy women in Peoria, Washington, St. Louis, Dallas, and such places, and, to pursue my higher ideals, was planning a novel upon a rebel hero—John Brown, Robespierre, Lincoln (too much written about, but *autodidact*, the most interesting for a woman), Saint-Just, Byron, Dimitrov—yes, The Hero. The objection, that a woman should not write about a male hero (for she loves him too much), seemed of no account, now that I had loved several men; and I must admit that at this moment my experiences appeared to me in a new light, as the most valuable experiences of all. It was by them alone that I had begun to appraise men.

There was my grandfather—but he was so much the old, effete man—Percival Hogg, Uncle Philip (whom I had never understood till now), and my father. For the rest, the world had been filled with storming, mouth-opening males of whose acts I had understood nothing. Now, it was becoming clear to me. There are puzzles you get, as a child, out of stockings. You rub water on a piece of paper and pictures appear. My picture of the universe was now appearing to me like that. Now were appearing the Luke-Philip parts, the Amos parts. I had never yet met another man like my father and perhaps it was lucky I had him for a father, for he wasn't the kind of man I met in daily life, nor was ever likely to meet. I saw quite well the path I was setting out upon, "the path of libertinage," said my father; and this was one of the rare moments when I caught hold of my own tail and saw what I looked like to others. But for persons of my sort, it isn't a thing one can do. We proceed from great folly to giant error and hope for a great stroke of luck. Also, we sometimes get it. We are not the kind to toe the line and keep our distances. One day, it's a famine; the next, a feast. We see little difference, we suffer in the one, and enjoy the other in a great boisterousness. I prefer it! Do me something, as they say.

Jacky turned my hair gray with her nagging at one word and another in some simple pamphlet. She had no notion of joviality. She peered at concepts.

I was working on a leaflet with my new boss, Mrs. Patrice, one of the heads at the Tweed and Silk Shop, Madison Avenue, and sketching out a novel on Robespierre. I asked Mrs. Headlong could not my sister Jacky take up her option now, for she looked fagged after the summer spent as counselor at a camp. I had alternatives, too; one job offered in a foreign-language bureau, but I could not see myself as a clerk or translator, and one, promised to me in Hollywood as a junior writer, if I got something published in the *New Yorker*. Mrs. Patrice was one of Grandmother Morgan's clients at Green Acres, and at her more elegant hotel in Long Island; but really I had got the introduction through the Second Mrs. Bosper, Aunt Phyllis's hated rival. The Second Mrs. Bosper was a young, handsome, shining, and amusing girl; and as I happened, when I met her, to make some derogatory remarks about Aunt Phyllis ("she was now settled down into middle-aged lard like any mamma on the cake-flour ads"), the Second Mrs. Bosper took to me, and offered to get me a place in business. It was she who took me to Mrs. Patrice. My several rough drafts for an advertising campaign pleased this dashing lady well enough. My titles I thought fetching:

Consult your home engineer; he built the streamlined model
   —he'll like the streamlined You.
P.S. We are dressing—
I'd rather be lovely than President—
Personalizing you—
Make every entrance a personal appearance, but don't make
   your dress the life of the party—
No wish fulfillments in dress—
Dress—the melting pot of the arts—
The shape of things to come—
Don't oversell your best points, but consult them—
Don't flatter yourself, and others will flatter you—
Dress, the first of the lively arts—
Build your dress on the bare essentials—

With this went snappy, modern paragraphs into which I poured all my practical imagination, experience of France and French women and knowledge of women. Indeed, it suddenly occurred to me, I had met thousands of women in my life and I was the kind that criticized every one of them, hence most fitted to be their marriage broker; for that's what dress selling is, in the heart of every woman, marriage broking.

I was astonished at first at my facility in this line; but then I realized I was a well-set-up and a well-oiled machine suited to any of the lively arts of the day. Hadn't I tried the epic poem at school, the detective novel, when the radical journals started to consider them a people's art (or the opium of the people—they didn't make up their minds), a French satiric and indecorous play (*Les Loups-Phoques*), imitations of Verlaine, Baudelaire, and Laforgue, when it suited me; and could I not turn my pen to anything, editorials, pageants, and arguments full of slogans as a plum pudding of raisins! Yes, I was much fitted to live in my own age; a great gift. I felt, as I sketched out a scheme for the Robespierre novel, or considered my conquests in love (I had won Luke Adams and Clays Manning), strewed my sketches from Headlong's school, good, vivid things in charcoal, on the carpet, or wrote a one-acter against Intolerance—as I did this, it came to me that I was born to make money and would probably end with my name on a door in the plushy sections of M.G.M. I'm a realist. Yet, I was not so blind and deaf to the finer things of life. I had serious struggles with myself and consider that any failures I endured came from this struggle with myself, for at the same time I felt energy and talent superior to the paying of super-taxes. But whatever I took up, I must shine at it, that was the principal thing—always to be the best!

I had much to worry me. I was nearly eighteen and my life was confused. It was October. The struggle round Madrid kept me anxious and I was in the thick of the fight for intervention on the loyalist side in Spain. Stories were coming through on the life of the Madrileños—Clays was in the heart of it. I had his articles and letters. I felt a heroine, once removed, yet humbly too, knew my part was feeble. I still loved him bravely, best, as a woman should her husband. At the same time, I had now loved Amos and been through troubles with him, but—why this doubt? With doubts one never gets anywhere at all. Go into it and then see! And then came this lightning flash with Luke. One not only felt that, in love, this dangerous man consulted his own pleasure and had no morals, but with him, all altruism vanished like smoke. He was the moonlight wraith, the demon-lover, the eternal Adam, the faun with his oaten pipe.

When I did not hear from him over the telephone, I bit myself and ran round in circles like a wounded centipede, and every bite was poison. I could not, in fact, endure my home, where those three females, my mother, Jacky, and Andrea, lived in the age-old female way, apparently contented with their sex's condition. I understood only too well my Uncle Philip, who must run out in the streets, with tears in his eyes, hoping for the dear lip, knee, eye, hand, and floating hair. Luke had a curious quality. Everyone knew of his affairs stretching back, as far as I was concerned, into the mists of pre-history. This, with his inordinate genius for passion, made him impersonal, or disembodied, yet the miraculously united lip, eye, knee, palm, which the thirsting lover seeks. Luke was a Stromboli; with him alternately came silence, then the spurt of fire in the legendary air. As to Amos—a poor, wretched thing, a stand-in; he only got women because there are too many hungry lovers.

I had enough trouble at this time, with my incontinence and my shame for it, my father's exhortations, my mother's lamentations, fear for dear Clays, my passion for Luke, and letters from Mrs. Headlong; and Amos. Amos now began to dun me again for the money he had lent me; he needed it, and I had met at a party at Susannah Ford's house in Jane Street, a young girl, who said that her mother was marrying Amos in the fall. I suspected that Amos needed the money from me to make some show in the new apartment. This woman was rich and could set Amos up in his own place with plenty of furniture, silver, and linen; she had been a chaste divorcée for many years and had fallen madly in love with him; but, I suppose, Amos had a few debts, or needed a wedding suit. Although I felt enraged that Amos should still apply to me under the circumstances, I did my best for him, going to my father again and asking for the money, but telling him for whom I needed it. My father flew into a passion and threatened to write to Amos. I said, "Don't do that; I prefer to cut a loss, Papa."

My letters from Clays filled me with girlish love and at the same time I became fretful when I found he was not above telling me that he was now in correspondence with The Honourable Fyshe and Caroline, "Mrs. Clays"! The men are so weak on these scores—one can never trust them. Last of all, I had a syrupy letter from Lucy Headlong, which I flung aside, when half-read.

O my Letty,

I'm all agog to read your love letter to Robespierre—for what else is it? Won't you, young girl, tell the truth and say you admire great men? But no, I make no interpretations for you—what you will do will be right; you will know how to be austerely revolutionary. Besides, we can overcome the inclinations of the flesh when we want to; and if not, why should we, women—by what law indeed—?

Oh, do go to California, child, if you can—Yankee lust for life—the frontier still—the Barbary Coast and Eldorado—hot blood, high adventure—(etc. etc.) And, oh, what hope in Spain —the bloodfed—pridefed fires of Spain—if you should go there—rub shoulders with the real type of woman to which you belong—(etc. etc.).

And your home, the charming drooping dove, Mathilde— and if another place, where? Will you furnish it?

Dear pretty Jacqueline, we have brusqued each other, and now are as it was in the beginning, and she, too, must come next time and you will feel more at ease, for you love your sisters dearly—(blah-blah). One of these days when you're tippling alone at the *Lafayette*, telephone me in my town house, where I am often, to be with Adrian—(blah-blah).

Do you remember your Goya dream, little Letty, the bald-headed men and the lovely Spanish girl with skirts gathered round her hips—yourself, of course, but, why—(etc. etc.) and through the *brouhaha* (as you said) you heard—(etc. etc.).

Good luck to Clays. He's a good man and good men are hard to find, as you remarked. Yes, good luck to him.

LUCY.

In annoyance I threw it on the carpet and then picked it up with a pair of tongs and put it back in the bottom drawer of my desk, which I dragged up with my toe on the handle. What possessed the old woman to write in that strain? "Almost like a love letter," I muttered. "I wish men would write love letters."

34

SUSANNAH FORD was—she is—a square-shouldered, finishing-school, natural blonde, with sharp features and several fur coats. She wears hair jewels, diamond bracelets, and puts her money in ventures she thinks radical. Every day at that time she was taken up by her radical activities, her eight-year-old son, Blaise, her lawyer, her hairdresser, shopping, and her psychoanalyst. Her psychoanalyst had the newer part of her day; she went every morning at ten. Her son, Blaise, went to a psychoanalyst for children twice a week. He had been a sensitive child, it was said, nurtured in progressive schools; he needed now an expensive witch doctor, by which I mean his psychoanalyst, to initiate him, as early as possible, into the sexual troubles and social discontents of the tribe. Blaise was an unbearable infant. He had been given to understand that the whole of society revolved round his *reactions*. When I came to know Blaise better, I saw he was a lazy, good-natured boy without much drive, greedy rather than sensual. He had no sexual troubles at all; he was just a wastrel. It had all begun with his mother's pretending that he was deprived of something or other because his father had "left him." This was current jargon in the Village. Since so many women were divorced, there was an entire new philosophy to fit the case of these pensioned young women, too idle to seek new husbands.

I found myself a furnished room at Susannah's. My mother was glad enough to disgorge me. She felt I was a bad influence with my sisters. I now had a steady job with the Tweed and Silk Shop. I moved some time in November, in wintry weather, to the Fords' house in Jane Street. By good luck, they had the first floor front free.

It was a small house with a large front room and a small back room on every floor, a corridor running between them outside. I now occupied the first floor front, which had a fireplace at the back, an archway in the center, and a bay window with lozenge panes. I put my new small typewriter on a solid table right at the front window, and the very first afternoon sat down between the heavy curtains to work at my novel of Robespierre. I had a notebook at my side in which I jotted down, from time to time, the gag lines and ideas that occurred to me for my feature-writing work. I wrote, so:

"All styles arise out of some economic upheaval; e.g., short skirts after war because there is little cloth."

"*For the well-dressed woman!* This is a Byzantine civilization, the patterns of speech, dress, books, the same, no one desires an irritating originality. Anything inspired is in bad taste, inept."

"How to put this in gags, hits?" I had confidence in my agility. I imagined myself riding two saddles at once—advertising and scholarship. I found it equally easy to write the propaganda and the Robespierre. I wrote:

N.B. to myself:

"Find a new gag, e.g., Orchids to you. Time marches on; this type."

"Why American women are not so well dressed as French women with the same income?"

"Aphrodite was, in a sheet, a perfectly dressed woman, but she wouldn't become Miss America today. We prefer dress models to sculptors' models; do not start figuring from the Venus de Milo up."

"Don't get uplift from a rash buy, if you want to be smart. You don't buy a steak because you need a psychological uplift."

This is the dreary stuff I wrote in my first days in Jane Street, already seeing a golden future for myself, as an advertising writer, or a buyer. I wrote:

"Buying and wearing clothes is a business, a life business; a regular business. Your friends are your competitors; don't let your competitors buy for you!"

This was my last sartorial aphorism. I looked at this remark of my own and began to sweat. I was on the slide. I read in my notebook:

"A little frock—it's feminine to wear high heels—Sunday

best—the latest—a woman with a touch of white—do men like shape in women, or dollar-bearing clothes?"

How low had I sunk already? To ease my conscience I began instead a story for the *New Yorker*, where I knew a blond young man in neat suits, who seemed very fond of me. He was the kind that I would not marry and did not even sleep with; and he promised to do much for me. So, wishing to see my name in print in the paper, and hoping I'd get thereby a pass to Hollywood, I set to work to write one of those New York jargon bits: LIFE IS A TERRIBLE STORY or, *Vas vaist doo, vas vaist doo*?

"Across the courts, Mrs. S. comes in her flowered and quilted dressing gown at eight-fifteen A.M. and says—

" 'Nu, barin, barinya, vaist doo what that is, Henry? In Rossian, is Barin Lord, Master; Barinya, that is die Madame . . . Nu, hite-a day, the sun shines. Nu, what is it? Ich bin a so vernickt from mine krankhite. Kaput! Kaput! Abattis! Yes, *abattis*, the French say. Hör, Henry! you must to die Madame explainen; sie most ihr Mamma zu clean die zimmer hite-a helpen, warum ist mine Back all in pieces. Ach! So weak—vot is die use? A living corpse, wirklich, a living corpse. Ich war so kaput die ander Tag dass I could not mine name spellen. . . . Nu, so vot is it? Old is old. Listen, Henry, though a zo feel fun! I was thinking. Oy, was a Deep in Detroit, Michigan, Mr. Lacher, went to the Polygram, aber doo vaist shone, vair dey play polo, polo, vaice ik? Zu de Polygram ist er gegone and a boy hat him geschlah! Er hat it earned all right. A zoll thief! Vass for frechheit? "You will get fifty cents, a dollar perhaps, maybe," to me he says. What could I do? He begs, he prays, "You will do me a big favor," says he; what is half a dollar? I vass in de street mit Henry in de baby carriage. Ich hab de boy nit gezane. Also, seine Madame auch—ha! a solche daughter und die mutter war a zair stolze Fee. An animal. Really! Nu, ich can nit it helpen. So I go in de court. I sit, I wait. Dann asks de Jodge, "Oh! Mrs. Schmidt," says he, very polite, "and iss it true?" What can I say? Der Lacher, hat zelt zine tale. And he looks. Yes, to me he said, "Do me a groser gefall, please." Bitte! Bitte, Madame! Indeed! I am villing! But vass vaice ik? I say to de Jodge, "De boy is a very roff boy, dass vaice ik, aber ik var nit zu de Polygram." What for shall I lie, Madame? Der Lacher, hat zair goot gevoost dass ik can nit mit a baby carriage zu de Polygram gane. De Jodge, auch. Und den, ik kom home kvick. She was a nice woman, a Mrs.—dass ik vaice nit, ist terrible—life is a terrible story, Madame— Ik hob all's fairgessen, a head like a cat, she war a goot friend of mine—yes, Mrs. Johnson, a Svede, but she war a zoll kind—she comes to me— "Oh! Mrs. Schmidt," says she, "if you have to go to de court, I will look after your dear little boy." She looked him after, but er hat nit mir die half-dollar gegeben. A solche steal-thief! Ach! Ik vaste mine werter. Ik vaice, ik vaice! Yoonge, yoonge, a zoll dombbell life—ik vaice—ja, Henry—warum lachst du, mein kind! Ja, without fun, life is a terrible story.' "

Across the court from the Fords' were a German mother, Mrs. Schmidt, Henry, her son, and the daughter-in-law, a Yankee girl, who provided each day and three times a day such material. Henry came home for lunch. The daughter-in-law, a chipped blonde, whose surface was worn off, although only about twenty-six, was doing some comic-strip continuities. She was a retired pillow-girl, by which I mean one of those female youngsters like me who choke the big city, hanging out their shingles in ones, twos, or threes, in rooms with kitchenette and bath, in the fashionable districts, and who make up their furniture-lack by colored cushions, pillows, and lamps.

I could work twelve hours a day. Free, now, at night, I worked hard. I typed manuscripts for publishers, did easy literary jobs, and wrote my letters. I read books sometimes for nights on end and was able to make up for it, in a week end. I sometimes, exhausted, bloodless, would fall into bed, singing with joy for my ability to work myself to a standstill. I regretted nothing. Most evenings, however, I went up to the sitting room of the Fords', where my new friend, Susannah, her departing husband, Brock, and her probable lover, Aleck, sat and disputed about things political and artistic. It seemed to me that both Brock and Aleck preferred me to Susannah. Brock was a tall, languid brunet, with fine eyes, and a caressing manner toward all women. Sue said he disappointed her at night, but I am putting mildly what she told in detail. Aleck was a tall, mild, blue-eyed boy; on his head a close-fitting cap of crimped blond hair. He worked in a chic dress shop, and wished to be an artist and have an exhibition in Fifty-seventh Street. He took taxis to and from his work, and knew no places in New York but Madison and Fifth, Fifty-seventh, Fifty-eighth, and certain addresses in Park Avenue.

I was much taken by Aleck, while it was Brock who would come down to my apartment, if Susannah was out, and tell me his marital troubles.

Susannah had been going to a psychoanalyst for months to avoid a break-up, yet she preferred Aleck to Brock. All of them solemnly discussed this subject at night as they discussed Browder, Herriot, or Chamberlain. The little boy Blaise also listened to their marital discussions. At this time there was a widespread notion that middle-class life could only be an endless series of painful experiments, and that children should be prepared early. Many parents, like the wicked Susannah Ford, with this excuse, took advantage of their children's innocence and unconscious purity, to parade all their sexual vices before them. Susannah hung pictures from *Esquire* in her son's bedroom and handed him back, with an indulgent, dulcet laugh, a packet of "art photos" she found under his pillow. "He mustn't be repressed, especially now," she said. I complained that the little scoundrel made passes at me in the passageway. "That shows the result of our training," she said complacently, "he is no introvert."

I could write a book entirely about Susannah Ford, who was the ornament of her time, in the sense that an ornament is something hung upon the essential and receives a good deal of undeserved notice. She was handsome, had some influence in expensive schools, made the family move when the boy moved from one school (which did not understand his psyche) to another, so that the poor child would not have to travel, for traveling gave a child a sense of impermanence; I mean, in this sense she was a devoted mother. I said to her, "How is it the damn schools can't understand him when I understand him only too well?" She read the books headlined in the leading newspapers and also in the *Daily Worker*, subscribed to the rebellious weeklies, had all the medical and pseudo-scientific fads, was easily persuaded to place half her estate in an enterprise owned by a radical party, in such a way that she could never ask for accountings, because this poking and prying was unworthy of a radical; and at the same time, was sharp with her husbands about alimony; in every way thus, she tried to be a required woman, to conform to all the current notions in society. She cherished notions of service to society and thought she was a left socialist and an aesthete. She had fetishes on the mantelpiece and Gauguin, Soyer, and Burliuk on the walls. At the same time, she was a wicked woman. *To free his libido* and her own, she talked to her son about the Oedipus complex, that is, about incest; and in this strange way, tried to attach the boy to herself. She brought this child and Luke's orphan child, Leon, into conversations about the sexes, trying to surprise their miserable secrets, so that she could make them part of table conversation. Meanwhile, she lived daily with her two mates, Brock and Aleck, and one or the other slept on a studio couch in the living room.

Often, I called upon her in the afternoon, when I came home from consulting with Mrs. Patrice and her artists and printers; and knocking at the door of the second-floor flat, found poor Aleck much discomposed, while Susannah was nowhere to be seen, though at home. Aleck found his situation humiliating, and began to tell me his troubles, when he found that Brock did the same. It was at this time that Susannah took that dislike to me which she continues to this day.

It was winter and almost Christmas. The wind howled down those black streets so near the wharves. We (Susannah and I) had planned with Aleck and Brock and the children, Leon and Blaise, a fine Christmas party. I had been invited to my father's, where Persia had a tree, and to Grandmother Morgan's, to the hotel, and to Arnhem, in Westchester. I knew I would have plenty to eat and drink at the Morgans', but hated those drunken parties which had seemed so sophisticated to me a few years ago. I only cared for the party in my own house, here, in Jane Street. I felt sure, now, that whatever man Susannah let fall, Brock or Aleck, I would get. In fact, they both loved me. I was, indeed, wretched in my love affairs at this time, and was looking for consolation. I had quarreled, one October night, with Luke Adams, who wasted my time. I never forgot anything to do with this man. He caused me so much pain; and every wild joy I had from him I paid for a thousand times with shame, the shame of being abandoned and the misery, the misery of the confident young beauty who feels she is just a telephone number in a little book.

It was a Saturday afternoon in October, just after I had moved to Jane Street, when Luke turned up there. He was newly shaved, cleanly dressed, and smelling sweet. After about an hour, during which he kept repeating, "I can't stay long, I've got to go," and kept by him his coat, satchel, and umbrella, I got him to accept a drink and gradually took from him his coat, hat, and other things. When I brought the drink I smiled almost tearfully and with that tearing woman-voice which comes unasked out of my throat, said,

"Why are you so mean to me, Luke? You don't telephone me. You come here suddenly after a long interval. It seems to me there are unwritten engagements. The unwritten ones are the best."

He said, "I'm not mean to you, Letty; it's just that I'm afraid of you. You're a dangerous girl, you're a lovable girl, pretty too. I could fall in love with you. I don't want to; gee, I've only just settled down after a life of wandering and where would I be? Jesus, I can't start wanting you. That's terrible; I've been through that too often." He shifted uneasily. "Haven't you got some wine, Letty. I thought you always had some," he laughed good-naturedly. "Do you know what I want to do, stretch out for about half an hour on your divan. Do you mind? I haven't had any sleep in nights. That hall's filled with smoke, they all smoke pipes, filthy pipes, Jesus," he laughed; "where's that fruit you had last time I came, eh? What happened to you, Letty? I thought you were so hospitable?" He laughed and stretched himself out; then stretched out his muscular brown hand, "Thanks, Letty." I put a cover over him. "Thanks, Letty"; his voice was at once sleepy, between a smile and a yawn. "Thanks, dear." He turned his back to me. I thought a moment, and went out, quietly shutting the door. In a quarter of an hour I was back with wine, fruit, and chocolate cookies which he liked. I put these in two bowls which I stood on a little table near him and I resolved to lie down myself, for I had slept little the night before, having been disturbed by Aleck's tender advances. But at the sounds I made, he turned round, saw the wine, sat up, stretched out his hand, and pulled me to him, "You went and got those for me? Sweet—Letty!" and he pulled me onto his knee, kissed me, and fell sideways with me on the bed. "Gee," he kept murmuring, "gee if it weren't that you were so young, you're too young for me, and your daddy, what would he think, I could—" I hung to his lip and gave myself up to this delicious pretense of wrestling; he kept murmuring, "Solander is such a fine guy, we mustn't worry your papa, must we," and I kept saying, "Oh, Papa is so wonderful," while we entwined like two stout vines that are still growing and have nowhere to hang but to each other and are feeling persistently for the strongest hold. But suddenly while we were so profoundly entwining, he said in my ear in his smiling voice, "Let's get up, Letty, I mustn't, I mustn't—" and he rose, carrying me with him, so that we sat on the edge of the couch. He stretched out his hand, took the jug of wine and said, "We'll drink wine instead; I must remember you're a young girl." Thus, I knew I was to be disappointed by him again, and I wondered how he could bear to cheat, but said no more. We sat at the table now and drank a quantity of wine.

He went away, with his slippery backward smiles and grimaces of his dark face, saying, "You're a dangerous little girl." "Come back and see me soon," I cried. "Ah, Letty," said he, and went through the door into the street. I saw him passing the window with hunched shoulders under his overcoat; he spat into the gutter. He looked old and chilly. My appetite was sharpened for him; I telephoned him two or three times before he came again, and then he came unexpectedly. How soft, genial, hesitant his voice on the phone at his office: it amused me to hear his chary, wary tones when I spoke, "Is that Luke?" "Ye-es, ye-es, who is it?" One night at eight he telephoned, "Are you alone, Letty?"

"Yes, I am."

"Well—perhaps I shouldn't come."

"Why not?"

"We-ell," a soft laugh, "you're all alone, Letty; that's dangerous."

"Well, come if you like."

"I suppose I shouldn't."

"Make up your mind, Luke."

"No, I shouldn't," a soft, dolorous laugh.

"Luke!" I cried, "why don't you come? I'm all alone."

"Well, maybe, I will."

I arranged things to look as if I were working on my Robespierre novel (not waiting for him); and put out some brandy which fortunately I still had. Sitting, typing expertly at the window, I perceived Luke Adams, mooching along the sidewalk opposite, taking stock of me. When he came in, he said paternally, "You weren't waiting for me, you were working; you're the kind of girl I like, Letty."

"Oh, yes; since you couldn't make up your mind."

"My mind. He-he!" He threw himself in the corner armchair and beamed at me. I picked up his coat and hat; I noticed his clean shirt and new shave. "Have you some coffee, Letty? It's getting frosty," he rubbed his lean hands together. I made coffee, brought it to him, pulled down the blinds, and drew a straight chair close to him. When he had drunk the cup, he said gently, "Come here, little Letty. A real woman! I bet you're a good cook. You'll be a good wife. You won't spend money on clothes, or movies, you'll just stay at home and mind the children"—he chuckled—"and sew a fine seam. Or perhaps write short stories, eh, for the slicks? Eh? Isn't that your ambition?"

"Luke," said I, "why are you putting me off?"

He laughed, "Sit here, on my knee." I sat down, a stout young creature, and felt uneasy enough, for the chair sloped deeply backwards and I was being slid onto his chest. I kissed him on the face and on the throat. "I love thee," I said in French.

"Je t'aime. I know what that means," he said.

When I got off his knees, he rose, chuckled, "I must go; it's late."

"Did you come to see me to talk over the world situation?"

His eyes cleared, he pulled off his hat again and laughed indulgently, "You see, Letty, I'm a married man."

"Let me love you—let the fault be mine."

A wild light came into his face, he threw his hat on the floor and put his arms round me. He said rapturously words which I cannot put down. He muttered, "I'd get on the bed with you, but I know what would happen."

"Only what we want to happen."

He held me, his face turned up toward the ceiling and the words of rapture tossing out of his writhing dark lips; he became less incoherent, "I could spend the night with you."

"Why don't you?"

"But you see, I am married; I want to be honest. And then I don't want to go through all that, Letty—if I could have you for a night or two nights, then I could forget you—" I listened, with surprise and irritation.

"I want to go away with you," he said, ardently, "for a whole week end." I almost danced with despite, but kept smiling and murmuring at him, "Darling, I am almost French, I know so much but I am afraid of you—" At each sentence of mine he yielded a few feet, softened a little.

"Why afraid?"

"You are only an American, Luke; probably you don't know anything about love; I'd be afraid with you, to—"

"What do you mean?" he said, no longer smiling.

"You probably know nothing about all the ways of making love."

"Letty—at my age—" he said, coolly extending himself and looking fixedly, cynically before him.

I knew his caution and even his egotism was part of his age, his forty years. I never had had to do with an old man before; I felt myself repulsed by his curious coldness; and yet with all his gestures and strange looks, he encouraged me to further play. I could see that he wanted to give himself to me, but that he wished me to coax him, as if against his will. The reason for this was plain. Presently, with a shadowy, almost regretful smile, he suddenly slid his clothes from his smooth limbs, but this was not done, when he sprang to his feet, standing straight, his eyes starting, muttering, "Listen, someone at your doorbell: someone is coming here—"

"No one is coming here; I won't answer, Luke, Luke—"

"Listen, shh!" he said, putting his hand in anguish on my head.

"Come to the end of the room," I whispered, "throw yourself on my bed."

"No, no, not there, because there, we—"

"Yes," I whispered, "there it is out of the lamp light and lamp shadow: there's no silhouette."

With a wild air he went there, and at first, as his springing to his feet had brought my lips against his naked thighs, he dragged me after him, for I was embracing him, and there I was on my knees dragged at his feet for a step or two, like a woman worshiping her pagan god. I kissed his bare knees; then I laughed, seeing the disorder he was in, how wild, almost unconscious, so that there was no longer any barrier between us. I let him go and followed after him; he lay panting, murmuring words beneath his breath, and I began to kiss him all over, saying softly, full of joy at my triumph, "I always thought of kissing you like this; I dreamed of it; living alone would not be so hard, if only I did not dream."

He murmured words which precipitated me upon my knees in adoration, for I had resolved this night to conquer him rather than to think of my own pleasure; I did my best to fill him with love and joy and had the satisfaction of hearing him say my name many times, at the very moment when I thought he had fainted, so that I knew that he had been obsessed with me, too. It was me he had thought of, not others. His voice filled me with passion; I experienced a new and unexpected pleasure at this unselfish love of mine and I had a cunning hope too that I now really owned him. When he left, I smiled languidly and threw myself back in a chair at the window to watch him pass. His coat squatted on his back in the early gray morning: the streets were filled with a miserable mist; I saw him spit seedily in the gutter; he was unhappy because I had no coffee made and he was hungry. For some time I had no word from him and was disappointed; and yet I hoped every day to hear from him, I felt he loved me; and I seemed to see him, making plans for a week end, even an hour together. Wintry weather came; in spite of the icy rain and snow, he would go off to his shack in the country to be alone, and I expected to be invited there. True, he shared his shack with another man. I dreamed of us lying embraced in the icy upstairs room, of even climbing through the manhole into the freezing attic, but anything to be alone, for we were so hot for each other that even this would be a pleasure. I thought of the whole company walking at night, and our touching hands in the dark and how he would halt behind some shed or tree in the freezing dark, so that he could embrace me. This did not come about.

About Christmas, he came back to the house and invited me to be present (though not to go with him) to a New Year's Ball given by some union; and I said I would be there. I was in low water and could not dress as I wished for this ball, but when I saw myself in the large mirror which stands in the foyer of the hall, I saw I looked very handsome; I wore a long red dress with a white fur borrowed from Aunt Phyllis. I was like a great flower in this dingy place; and among these working girls. As an escort I had taken along Bobby Thompson, to whom I had breathed no word about Luke; but somehow or other he had a suspicion and was in no very pleasant mood. Another boy I knew came up to me and began laughing, saying, "You look as if you're on the make."

"Oh, I am," I said.

This made Bobby more attentive to me. We walked around the upper gallery; dancing was already in progress downstairs on the big smooth square floor; they were doing the Big Apple, the Conga, and the Rhumba, which was just coming in as the rage. I thought we ought to go down and dance, since when Luke came he would see me in the arms of a handsome young man, and this might stir his sluggish senses. What worried me about Luke was that he was not jealous; for every man I had known, even when he was not much attracted to me, would show jealousy when I was with another man and would struggle to get me to himself; but not Luke. I was not sure that my appearance there with another man would not simply give him an excuse to neglect me for another six months. In imagination, I heard him saying, with his sweet, sultry smile, "I could see you were not lonely." But, of course, I went and danced with Bobby, and had almost forgotten the man of my heart, when I looked across the hall at some groups of older men who were talking together and I thought, "What a handsome man; is he South American?" before I recognized in him Luke Adams. I looked at him for some time silently, rather surprised to find that he was so handsome; but he was conscious of me. He had a secret which I had surprised. One side of his face, being much handsomer than the other (the other was drawn and showed his hungry years), he did his best to keep this glittering, dark, full cheek, with its patine of sexual beauty, toward the woman he wanted to attract; and I now saw that, apparently all unconscious of me, he moved gracefully, as he talked, the few inches that were necessary to keep his beauty in my view. I said nothing of this to Bobby Thompson, but I could not conceal my wild exultation at this discovery, and Bobby naturally supposed that he was having this effect upon me.

"How beautiful you are tonight; I hate to pay compliments, but—" I saw that he was falling in love with me but would not admit it; and full of glee, I did my best to conquer him too. Thus, he followed me upstairs, after the dance, in a dream; and I felt sure that Luke Adams would soon follow. This he did, always pretending to be unconscious of me. But now he had in tow his ugly, clumsy, plump wife who was very ill dressed in a dirty housedress. When I saw her, I flashed round, turning my back to them all, and indeed I felt quite sick at heart at the sight of her; for Adams had plenty of the hypocrite in him and always pretended a joviality and decorum in public toward this woman, which seemed to me in the worst taste. Everyone knew that she was his disaster: other women called her "the scourge of God"; and said she had been sent to him, to punish him for his ravaging of so many fine women. It was as if a plate of oatmeal had been stuck in the middle of a banqueting table, otherwise covered with wines, fruits, sweetmeats, and splendid dishes. I sat down in a booth with Bobby, and as he did not think to get me a drink from the crowded buffet, I waved to the other boy, who had said I was on the make, and he at once brought me what I wanted. Bobby understood the rebuke, and he became sulky; but I, thinking only of Luke, did not care what he felt; and this supreme indifference gave me an added charm in Bobby's eyes. He was, alas, a typical New York college boy, the only son much spoiled of two doting parents who did not care for each other and had stayed together for Bobby's sake. Of course they had to make much of Bobby to pay for their sacrifice; he fancied himself a young prince and was usually a most disagreeable and difficult, though much sought after, escort, because so handsome and usually in funds. I had my fill of this kind of man, but I knew how to handle him fairly well; and I was not so absolutely dependent upon him as the usual sighing college girl. These boys make a regular traffic of their sex, taking up girls and throwing them away at will, twisting them and making martyrs of them, just because they have and withhold what the girls are sighing for. Naturally, this did not work with me; and I knew Bobby for what he really was, a sulky, weak, and lazy boy, that some stronger woman could manage, once she had, by some sleight-of-hand, got him to marry her; he was, of course, quite frankly looking for a girl with money, for he did not care to work too hard and yet he wanted a professional career.

As I sat there, in the booth with my two admirers, I saw Mrs. Adams coming up to me, and this made me feel almost faint. I greeted her with unusual modesty. She sat down and said, "Letty, Luke is over there."

"Is he here?"

"Yes." She smiled as if she knew that I knew; then she said, "Don't you want to see him?"

"Yes—of course, but you see—" and I grinned at the boys.

"I'll bring him over," she said, and lifting her heavy body off the seat, went away. Presently the couple came back, Luke laughing chastely and good-humoredly with his wife. He stuck out his hand, "Oh, hello, there, Letty; I did not know you were here." His wife left us together and the other two boys hauled off and began to talk over some things that interested them. Of course, I taxed him with avoiding me and having no affection for me, and he only smiled, said caressing words, and said he had been busy, but some day, some day—I saw all my fantasies about going out with him to his shack had been mere daydreams; and this upset me, for I do not like to waste my time in such things. Had he really forgotten that he had invited me to this ball? But half an hour later, when the entertainment began, I saw another part of his game. The lights were turned low and people crowded into the boxes upstairs, to overlook the hall and see the stage. People pressed about me like the ghosts in Richard III's tent; they rustled, it was warm and delicious, and I saw, with my heart in my throat, Luke standing on a chair just beside me and leaning over me. There, beside me (I had not observed them all moving in), was his wife, and in front of her, against the wall of the box, a sad-looking woman with fair hair who was the woman Luke had lived with for years before his marriage; and behind this trio was a dark, vicious, neurotic girl who was one of Luke's light-o'-loves; while I sat at his feet, almost and beside me were my two men. Tableau. Mrs. Adams was speaking to the fair-haired woman with a sisterly superiority and yet a stiffness which showed that she knew who she was, she knew who I was, and so I suppose she knew who they all were, the five or six women of Luke's that he had got round him there. He stood over them on the chair, husky with a cold, crooning the songs in his broken voice and an unpleasant gaiety in his voice; and I thought, "He's a famous Love-lace, we break our necks to get him; but is this the truth, this aged croak and this lewd shameless behavior, getting us together, the creatures who—" I did not now care about the wife, but I was upset by the fair-haired castoff. I knew she had worked for him for years, when he was ill. Would he be grateful to me and remember me, simply because I had kissed him once or twice? I did not want him; I had no wish to live with such an old man, used up by so many affairs; and the hollowness of my life appeared to me as I sat, sang, and laughed in the yellow and ruby lights that came from the stage. It was the lovely old opera picture, pretty women, sharp-faced and handsome men in a box in the half-dark; and I could taste a kind of filthy dust in my mouth. Yet when the lights came on, his wife and he insisted upon our sitting together at a small table, while he got drinks for us; and I wondered if she had pleasure from looking at all these women she was humbling; I had to admire, unwillingly, her nerve. As we stood in the foyer to go out, I in my coat again, he came up beside me and we made a fine picture, I saw us in the mirror. I looked beautiful then, excited by the evening, and I saw hungry regret pass over his face. He moved nearer to me and I felt his scorching fire dart out and lick me; but he made no move, not with hand or foot. He muttered, "You're pretty, Letty, I'd like to go along with you," just as his wife came up.

Some caution in me made me not so much doubt his words as try to think of them addressed to another woman. I "tried them over on my piano." If he had been younger, I would have swallowed everything. And all the time, as I walked along with Bobby, and felt Luke's charm, I was thinking, do I have to listen always to these old serenades? I felt throughout my adventures that I was only looking for the right man; if I had found him, I should have been very glad to renounce all these affairs. I had to admit it—the dangerous Luke was the most negligible of affairs.

I thought with gloom of the time, when I was about fifteen, when I had thought I could manage men. Now, the barrier between men and women had come up, the question of marriage. No man I knew wanted to marry, and for me it had become desperate; not, of course, to enjoy men, which makes it the only resort of timid girls, but to give myself a start in life. As it was, I was living spiritually and mentally, from pillar to post (pillow to post!) and from hand to mouth.

In these dark days Susannah Ford, for all her faults, was a good influence upon me. She believed that public discussion made all things moral and easy to bear. She not only teased out every strand of my affairs (for I told her all), but dragged me back into what was a sort of social and intellectual life. She forced me, with good-natured fanaticism, to think of every popular substitute for snake-oil and soul-balm. Led to believe that Freudianism would keep her chaste, she wallowed chin deep in psychoanalysis; and also took mudpacks for her complexion. She was so engrossed also with her troubles between husbands and lover, and with trying to regulate the love affairs of her friends (usually this meant to steal their men, though almost a naïve, blind theft), and she believed so rapturously in any man she chanced upon, if he were crooked enough and persuasive enough to cheat her and get her money from her, that in her house, at least at first, I plated my sensitive soul in the rich, thick, wholesome folly of thoughtless, bodily living. Here was a woman who lived as I did and was none the worse for it. New come from life in a female house, with a defeated and lazy woman, and two young sisters, I began to see I had my own place in the world. I had grown up.

Susannah made me free of the house. I had expected, on taking up my residence in this house in Jane Street, that Luke would seize on the excuse of Leon, the orphan boy, to come and see me regularly, twice a week or more. But Adams was delighted to rid himself of his responsibility and stayed far away from Leon. Susannah's eyes had lighted up when she first had seen Luke. Everyone in the room could see that she marked him for her prey! Luke, too. He had smiled, shifted his legs, cast his dark eyes down, and afterwards he had said to me, "Susannah's a nice girl, she's got a heart as big as a whale—but, you know, she wastes her time— I've known girls like that—"

At first Susannah, then, watched and waited for him; perhaps that too kept him away. My need for a diversion was keen. Luke was the *homme fatal*. He only understood lechery. I understood him for a heartless coquette, yes, cold, for all his flame. The whereby of his daily food and roof and his pleasure, were all his concern.

The struggle to suppress my feelings, difficult, since I have a nature, open, frank, and bold, and my unreciprocated love, produced whirlwinds in my blood. Once or twice he dropped in on me when he "happened to be passing." One evening, I turned on Luke and scolded him for his ways. He opened his eyes, laughed and drawled out, I was a witch, a danger to men, a termagant queen, a lovely shrew; "You'll get on all right, Letty." As I saw that this excitement pleased him, I boiled and bubbled—but at what cost to myself! In the end, I realized that no matter what happened, he was the winner; my sufferings and outcries were merely pleasurable drama for him. I tried to tear Luke Adams out—he was much deeper rooted than I thought. It was like tearing my veins out one by one.

I gave him a short history of my love adventures, so that he would be easy on that point; but he deduced from this account that I could look after myself and hence worried about me less than another.

Some nights I came home late from work, to Jane Street, and looked from the street, over the little railed areaway, into the broad double windows of my flat. Often I hoped to see Luke there. He was never there. Once, I saw his back, in an old man's crouch, as he turned the corner of the street. I ran after him, at length shouted, "Luke! Luke!"

That was the kind of thing I would do, ruining my game after weeks of continence. Luke was, in all, a tease, a hound of love; he worried and gnawed the heart to death. Luke would leave me half seduced, which was one of his cruelest, most telling trullmaker's tricks. He would take himself off, murmuring something about his wife, my young girlhood, his respect for my father's friendship, the presence of Leon in the house, and several other modesties and moralities; and at the door would turn with pain and yearning in his eyes and, holding me to him, whisper that he loved me. He had the boldness to say that he loved me, he needed me, and was in a fever fit thinking of long nights with me. I was at my wits' end. I knew that while Luke found consolation for black hours and heart-stings in his wife's arms, I found none anywhere. I decided to break with Luke at any cost. All the cost would be borne by me.

This was my own fault. I bragged about my conquest. One of my acquaintances, a union organizer, David Bench, a gawky fellow of the Lincoln type, reproached me with it. It was strange to hear this tall man's shamed whisper above me, "You let everyone know—you don't try to conceal it. And if you even go out with that man, people suspect you."

David himself seemed to love me, but he was ashamed of me. I thought he was jealous, and that he had an interest in me himself. Sometimes, when I look back at my relations with David Bench, it seems to me I behaved with him as my slippery friends with me. "I loved her, she loved another, and he in turn neglected her for another." Heine says something like that. This is love.

I seized the occasion of a union dance to break with Luke. He had half asked me, which was his way. We went out into Jane Street; we walked along one street and another holding hands, making for Washington Square and then Union Square, and all the time Luke murmured and talked about sex. That was his pressing way, not love, but the end of it. He began by saying, "I have been thinking about you all the week."

"What were you thinking?"

"I was thinking of you"—his voice dropped and dropped—"all the week."

I fancy he prepared his speeches and only used what was long tried and tested.

"I'd like to go away with you for a week, Luke, to your shack."

In the dark I saw his flattered smile. Then he said, "I've loved so often and I'll love again; life is never done with us; you love better the more you love."

I said, "Yes, but I'm a woman; it's different."

I was haunted by the thought of Jacky taking perhaps this same walk with Luke and hearing these things. He said, "But, Letty, don't you love this boy of yours—Clays—eh? Or is it Bobby Thompson?"

"I love them and love you too—I don't know how it can be; but it is."

"Yes, I suppose it can be. Ye-es—"

"You are not the same, you're kind of impersonal—you're Adam."

"Adam? Adams—oh, I see."

"No, Adam, the first man. You make me Eve."

He laughed, "Adam!"

"Hello, Adam."

He laughed, wonderingly, "Adam!"

The hat sign opposite said Adam Hats. He laughed: "Adam Hats, says the sign, Adam Hats."

He bent down and kissed me. After a while he said, "Now I am very sleepy."

"Oh," I cried, offended.

"I am sleepy."

I cried, "Oh," again, but in a different tone and pressed myself to him.

"We ought to continue this discussion somewhere else—in bed," he said.

"What discussion? I think we agree."

But the rigmarole flowed out of him, "Men and women—" he said softly.

"There's my place."

He said: "There are hotels too—everywhere; no one would know—that night your father came in—not nice, Letty. You must think about your father."

The signs said, Rooms, $1; Smoor, $1.

"I couldn't."

"Of course," he said, in a low, considerate tone, "I couldn't take a girl like you there."

"But I've got a place."

"Well, you see, Letty dear, I'm known about there; my friends live in that house on the top floor and I wouldn't want my wife—and going out with you is just a holiday—you know, for me you're a dangerous girl—" gutturally he rolled the endearing word *girl*, "a dangerous pretty girl."

"Oh, damn, I'll forget you, that's what I'll do," I cried out.

He looked surprised.

I said, "It's the old tease; you don't care for anyone outside the thrill. I'm just marijuana to you. See what you said, 'A holiday.' This is blind man's buff and no clinch. I'm looking for a man, and I tried you out because I'm wild about you. I'll tell you now," I said madly, losing all discretion, "but if you don't say the word, I don't care, I'll take anyone, even David Bench—I won't stay chastely waiting for you, like a good little girl. I suffer too much. Let's go in here," I said, pointing to a café in a side street, by now quite famous, a smoky little den, with paintings by local artists on the walls; "I've got to settle this."

He willingly went in, put me before him, opened the door, treated me with deference and with what I would have sworn (if I hadn't known him) was love in every intonation. I said: "You can't give me the runaround."

He said, appearing to be much troubled, "You see, little Letty, I'm a married man, dear, and you're such a sweet youngster, and the sort of girl who always gets me, and if Elsie weren't a mother—"

And again the fascinating guttural. He shook his head sadly. "But these things are real, Letty, motherhood, family life— We don't think so. I believed in free love at your age. Practiced it too. You don't want to be bound down either. Not at your age. And then, think of Clays!"

I swallowed my cocktail in a gulp, and raising my voice, bawled him out.

"Faker," I said. "Social fraud! 'It will be better for us in another world.' I won't stand for that song. Motherhood."

And under this head I reproached him with the stories about him that everyone knew, the women seduced, the homes broken; and even with her children which I had held on my lap and longed for. I said, "Love's free, but children aren't free; men get all there is to free love and women are robbed of their children."

And for the moment, hot and lusty-tongued as I was, it seemed to me I wanted and desired nothing so much as a hearth and home. He raised his eyes presently, saying: "Why, Letty, you're quite a strongminded girl, aren't you?"

The woman who was at the cash desk near me frowned at me. She hated me from the first, and she said: "Ssh!" I turned upon her and said, "Is this a free place or isn't it? I've heard enough family brawls here to know. I pay for my drinks. You shut up. This place is for public entertainment or it isn't; and I'm entertaining the public."

A man beside me, quite drunk, with two floozies, laughed, "Some temper."

The waiter said, "Take it easy!"

Luke shuffled his feet, but he finished his drink.

"Take it easy, Letty! Let's get out of here."

I said to the woman who was still staring at me, "If you don't like the way I behave, I'll get some friends of mine in the N.M.U. to come in and louse up your place for you."

"Heh, Letty," said Luke, laughing frankly; "you devil, come on, let's go home."

I tried to read his eyes, my desperate love rushing back into me, but no sooner were we out in the damp river air than he, buttoning my coat at the throat and kissing me on the lips, said, "Letty, don't you think you're getting a bit wild? Maybe you ought to go back and live with Mathilde, eh? You're too young. Life's hard. I don't think you can take it, Letty."

"I can," I cried, dashing my hand to my eyes so that I wouldn't cry, but I did cry. He piloted me toward my home. He came in with me, and I clung to him, "Oh, stay, dear Luke, oh, don't tease me so much," but he kept murmuring, "But it was only a holiday from morality, Letty, last time; we couldn't overstep the bounds, we'd both get into trouble. I've got to go, dear."

I threw myself on the studio couch, face downwards, and sobbed loudly into the coverlet. I heard all sound cease in the little Ford apartment upstairs and with renewed energy gave out heart-rending sobs. Luke stood by, helpless, saying, "What do you want me to do, Letty, what can I do? I can't help it, dear; it's the way things are."

When I had cried myself out, I sat up, with my pink, fluffy face, and looked at him. But he picked up a brush, brushed my hair which was loose on my shoulders, took a little packet out of his pocket and said, clearing his throat, "Here's a bracelet, Letty, that I won in a lottery up at the Union; it's for the sick benefit society, I won it—here, it would look just right on you—like all young girls you've got such a pretty round wrist—"

I took it, but said, "It was for Elsie?"

"Oh, no. I told Elsie how you helped me with Leon and she said I must give it to you."

I took it, trying it on and looking at myself in the mirror. All the old passion rose between us. I flung myself into his arms and felt my legs turn to fire. My eyes were filled with tears, "Oh, Luke, how wonderful you are."

"How wonderful you are, Letty."

He edged away. When he was in the street, I opened the window and flung the bracelet at him. I didn't want him to think he had tricked me. This was a cruel night that I spent, and in it was only one consoling thought, that I had been so treated because, after all, I myself was a fraud, I had intended only to make love to Luke as an experience, to perfect my technique. And sometimes at this thought, between agonies, I would laugh slightly, "Two heels, one slightly worn."

In the morning I replied to Lucy Headlong's sticky Christmas letter with a yes. It had occurred to me that this Luke affair began after the return from Arnhem. Superstitiously I attached some spiritual power to her ancient company of ghosts, to the love potion that the air of the mysterious region was for me. I could spend three sleepless nights like the last ones there. I wondered if, on my return, another love affair as exciting would await me, for like all love-careerists I was a great believer in amulets, luck-bearers, and the evil eye. I added to my letter one lie, "Jacky cannot come."

I did not ask Jacky. I wanted all the love-luck for myself. This suited me in every way. I hoped either to forget Luke or to substitute for him upon my return from Arnhem.

I confess I was shocked at the appearance of Lucy Headlong at the station.

The snow was hard and no more fell. The square melon-lighted houses were set among leafless woods and could be seen unnaturally near, without benefit of perspective. There was this thing, the lifelessness of Arnhem's neighborhood, perhaps Death by the hand of the unwarmed North that has neither sun nor sustenance nor spring; it was the spidery weather that floated. How miserable is the northern winter where even at sunlit midday, and certainly at nightfall, a vigorous, invisible yet very sensible creature of death goes striding past over the snow, leaving faint footprints like the marks of leaves, multitudinously treading in the bare forests.

The snow spread like a dinner cloth on the shallow rim we climbed before reaching the mound of Arnhem. Slate-colored Juncos pecked in the snow beneath shriveled grapevines. There were wreaths in all the houses, from holly and seedling pines. Cherry ribbons and berries were hung up and there came the smell of baking and the sight of piled wood. By the roads, on the banks of snow, in less frequented ways, there were deer tracks; and small furred paws had pocked the snow hedges into clearings.

I spoke of the snow. From the aged woman in her yellow turban and yellow dress under the old fur coat, this other Lucy Headlong, came a bitter, crazy laugh.

"It reminds me of a Christmas when I was a child— My cousin had a little hatchet and was attacking a block of wood when he fell and cut his chin. The blood dripped from his chin and dug a hole in the snow. They all rushed out and picked him up, but I stood there laughing, and in me I felt something glorious I had never felt before. I felt no regret; and a strange wonder, a beauty in life, that this little boy that I so hated and despised—such an eanling, such a woolly lamb, such a mamma's boy—had created such a brilliant, if pathetic scene—the snow. See it, Letty, the boy's new blue coat, the scarlet blood, the sun, the bright hatchet, and my own yellow wool coat—I got my sense of color then and got it straight from Christmas Day. For the first time I felt victory and knowledge. I was superior.

"They brought me in. Father beat me with both bare hands. I bowed my head and shoulders and was secretly laughing. I was shut up in my room and thought of the wickedness of the world; but every time I calmed down I would begin to recall the scene and then a low chuckle ending in a snigger, or a loud childish laugh, would break from me. Again, suddenly, I would see his tooth showing through his lower lip, the blood-on-snow, and his silly face convulsed with howling. And I never did lose the humor of that scene! When I see snow, I still exult. Yes, how mild and stupid everyone is. He never came to any good. I knew it, I could see him as he was."

Lucy Headlong embroidered this anecdote. She exclaimed with the same note, "All the people that I'm not supposed to see, that Adrian hates, are back, of course, for Christmas. They would be calling in, but he forbids it; and I am glad to have you, at least, my lady Letty."

I looked at her through lowered lids. Her face had darkened and was clenched like a fist. She twitched and yanked at the wheel, and all the time had a desperate air. I said, "You seem tense; has something upset you?"

This time I was without fear. I had come to the country for myself and would put up with no flightiness in Mrs. Headlong. She tossed her head, "Nothing upsets me!"

I looked straight ahead. Presently I saw her biting her lips and making an effort to control herself. She spoke feverishly of the people in her class, dismissing all the male students with a tart word. "And you," she said, pouncing upon me, "you are too servile!"

I looked at her sidelong.

"Yes, the turbulency, detail, the sensitive line, all show you think with your fingers, like a typist, not with your eyes; they aren't connected! Then you're afraid to do something ugly. What has art to do with beauty, morality, its convention of idea? And you want to set down the model, that is servilely and vulgarly copy, like a cheap little middle-class advertising punk—"

"What is art if not something to do with beauty?" I was about to open the door and jump out of the car.

"What a sentimental idea for one so strong and practical as yourself!"

She began to laugh and I could feel her poise returning. I said, "In some cases in your class, there's a real soul-tussle going on! The students are trying to tear themselves away from what they have incarnated, as beauty in their own eyes. They try to please you, but honestly, not just to please; to see what you see."

And to annoy her, I said (having perceived before how much she despised the mediocre male students), "Now Parker is most conscientious, and he has vigor."

She jarred the brakes, but came to herself, and sent the car speeding along as before. It seemed a slight smile twisted her mouth. She answered me presently in a soft voice, "Letty, I have been ill for years, a nervous illness; some days, like today, I suffer. With you, the first, was I able to trust myself—the first time you came to the class. And I thought with little Jacky. You have

seen me in quite a bad moment, but you have calmed me down."
She went on hastily, "And now tell me about the flat in Jane
Street and your Susannah, and about your Robespierre and all the
Hollywood plans."

We slid easily into the narrow opening of Arnhem, past the tall
weatherboard dwelling which stood there as a decoy. The rich, always fearing local risings and those movie riots with spades and
scythes, often have these decoy houses, with tenants in them to
protect their wood-hidden mansions. Now, however, in full winter, glittering with all its panes, on the snowy slope, Arnhem could
be seen for some hundred yards along the road. It was the true
Christmas house. Its noble proportions, beauty and gaiety, promised all joy. We drew up to the small Norman door. Adrian Headlong said, "Hello, here's Baby-face again."

The guests made much of me. I almost had a love affair with a
drunken young bachelor of extreme elegance, who looked like an
old family portrait; a blond, sweet libertine, who called me *cinque-
cento* and told me the most improper jokes I ever heard.

It was the best Christmas Day of my life, and not only did Lucy
Headlong treat me as a guest of honor (which I was at a loss to explain), but Adrian appeared to take a great fancy to me. By the next
morning they had all vanished. Adrian was obliged to go to another city for a Christmas party which his wife refused to attend;
and once more we were left alone in the house. Although I no
longer felt uneasy at receiving so much loving friendship from the
eccentric woman, and, in fact, was thinking of asking her to introduce me to her friends—for the Tweed and Silk Shop—the curse of
the place got the better of me; and I was flying back to town in
Lucy Headlong's car before the third night came.

No sooner had I reached home, than as before, and almost as I
had hoped, the same cruel fever shook my body. I was alone. The
empty room, now my only true home, was bitterly cold and I asked
myself in misery if anyone in this world cared for me. Others were
loving, marrying, dancing, drinking, with hordes of friends, and if I
was in this solitude, it was because I had been hunted by a foolish
dread from a palace in the woods, lovelier than I would ever see
again. I had made up my mind not to return to it. I believed Lucy
Headlong was a mad woman, and my impression was that, in a

diseased moment, she had been going to strangle me. She had come in the night, strangely bundled, though in silk sleeping clothes, her hair in two plaits of mixed gray, and leaned over me. She would never know how ashy and cadaverous she looked in the night. When I cried out, she moved gently away, down the staircase. There I lay in a sweat until I heard her move in bed, and then had hurried through to the guest rooms empty below, where I stayed the whole night.

The winter pressed round me. I was unable to go and sit in company in merrymaking New York as I was then, so I stayed in the room without food or fire the whole night. I tore my arms and legs in the unendurable spasms of desire, and wondered, in a superstitious moment, what there was at Arnhem—it was like a sacred mount, a haunted grove. I thought of the things in legend, the shirt burning like fire, the potions, the brews, the love-draughts, and some words came into my mind rather tardily—*cantharides*, a poison. The Headlong woman thought me mediocre, vulgar, without fantasy; and had she chosen this method to show me hellfire and heaven-glint? Did she know what I was suffering at this moment; and did she too, suffer it? But why? But at this moment an unspeakable idea came to me, which helped me through the hours and days I still must suffer; for I thought, as Grandma Fox would say, "Without money there is no honey." Once more I had fancied I was admired for my wit and girlhood's pride, when it was really a lawless, unnameable, shameful possession of me she had wanted. I promised myself, at least, after this sordid episode, to look every gift horse in the mouth. But I did not. Betrayed again, but no wiser— Poor Letty-Marmalade! I hope this will be my epitaph— just a *schlemihl*, not a heel.

35

THE NEXT day I went to my mother's for something to eat, and I took along Aleck, who was disconsolate, during a reconciliation between Susannah and Brock, upstairs. Aleck made a creditable show. He was blond, naïve, and impressionable, and I wondered if he were not the man destined to me, anyhow.

At my mother's I found Jacky, Andrea, Mother, my cousin Edwige Lantar with her fiancé Ernest, anxious, and always on his toes, the born husband. Jacky had brought a very presentable man, Bill van Week, a chestnut blond, about thirty, dressed in English sporting clothes, with a British mustache; tall, with a small shapely head. We just looked at each other across the room and it was like the *Bishop of Exeter*, only that we made the sign of sex at each other; it was invisible, but sure. This instantaneous recognition of someone you've never seen before is very thrilling. There was also there Simon Gondych, a distant relative of the Foxes and the family offering to the Hall of Fame: a Nobel Prizeman. Gondych was now about fifty-nine. His thick, frizzled hair was clean, bright brown; his merry hazel eyes were clear and large. Perhaps his face was a little too red, his chin a little heavy; there he was, bright as a spark from the fire, dancing attendance on Edwige, a child not yet seventeen.

I was staring at Edwige, whose immoderate vice was apparent to every woman and scarcely to any man, except, perhaps, her poor bedeviled fiancé, Ernest, now longing after her in public, with fine, loyal eyes. When I turned my head aside to get a light, Bill van Week, petting Edwige, saw I needed a match and got me one. Smiling through the smoke, with the little usual jokes, I turned back and saw that Edwige had already captured my escort, Aleck, who looked at her with a fixed, empty smile. Meanwhile, Jacky, sitting in the corner like little Jack Horner, was looking at Edwige.

"Have you known Edwige long?" I asked Van Week.

"Did I wish you Merry Christmas, dear," said he, "it's a bit late, but since I laid eyes on you, I want to be your Christmas tree: come, hang yourself round my neck."

I did so, but pressed him, "Don't avoid the question: how did you get to know a dame like that? A man's judged by the company he keeps."

"Eddie and I go round a bit in Hollywood, dear."

"I know how to interpret that."

"Me-owch!"

"What did you do in Hollywood, honey-chile; are you a director?"

"I worked in a restaurant: also was a soda-jerker."

"Then why did Edwige waste her time on the likes of you?"

"Well, dear, a good wine needs no bush, and she has taste."

"Pooh!"

"I'm a millionaire, also, though I never mention it; it loses me friends. The fact is, dear, I went out there to start a drama school; I used up all my money, or rather my parents' money, and I wouldn't ask them for any more, also no more was forthcoming, unless I would promise to go home and attend church every Sunday. The conditions were too hard. I said, Am I a man or a deacon? Thus, like every well-found male in the U.S.A., I have ridden the rods, been a lumber-jack in Wisconsin, and sung suitable lyrics in the *House of the Rising Sun*."

"You interest me, as they say in the gangster movies."

"Eddie never mentioned her lovely cousins; kiss Cousin Bill, dear. What a woman—" he flung himself on my neck. I disengaged myself after a while (Gondych was twinkling at us too, too paternally).

"You're fun, Bill." But at this moment I turned my eyes to Edwige. Aleck wore his most foolish expression. I crossed the floor in three strides, plucked Aleck by the sleeve, "Aleck, come play with us."

Edwige smiled slyly. "He seems to like being with me, don't you, Aleck?" and she nestled up to him. With her high heels and ridiculous topknot hairdo, she barely reached to his mid-arm. I turned red and tapped my heel.

"He's mine. I brought him here. This is my beat, dearie."

"Letty—" shrieked my mother.

"Stick to the three or four dopes you've got already." Jacky turned pale. Andrea burst out laughing. The others looked vaguely about. I marched Aleck back with me, while Edwige, I am glad to say, reclaimed her fiancé. But Gondych, after staring, had an eager little smile, and Bill van Week waited for my return with a grin, "What-ho, my little tiger-cat; a woman of action, no?" I burst out laughing, "Direct action is the only way with Edwige; Eddie's a female pup, why mince words." I pounced round him angrily.

"I love you, Letty," said Bill, "the girl with the volcanic hips—how's that for a sobriquet?"

"Don't use bad words."

"You're an educated woman, dear. You know about life."

"About life? Shame! So who you are talking to, eh, *tsoo whom*?"

"I know all about complexes, but I do not know about life, wept the young New York virgin."

"It ain't what you know, it's who," said I.

During this flip interchange, Aleck had wandered back to his Edwige. Bill put his arm round me and kissed me, "Don't think about the cad, Emmy-Lou. He's too good for you. Let me try."

We had some more of Mother's modest cocktails, and went to sit in a corner where Bill, with his hand round my breast and kissing in between, told me the story of his life. It was interesting as fantasy. He said that he was the only son of multi-millionaires and he quarreled with them because they were church-goers. They wanted him to be at home on Sundays and give up the Radical Party. From time to time they gave him a hand-out (twenty or thirty thousand dollars) for his projects: plays, drama schools, ballets. He had tried to start the Van Week Ballet Company. Of course, he knew not only the top-flight society figures, the debutantes who got in the papers, and *top-name* writers, but all the *richissimi* of Hollywood and Broadway success. It was the fairy Winchell world! I listened with pleasure. Rarely do you meet a man with simple daring in his lies. It was like being a child again and hearing the boys brag.

Nothing could equal my surprise when I went over to Ernest, Edwige's fiancé, sitting quietly in his corner, to check up, and found out that every word of this story was true. Ernest even added new details, quite to the credit of Bill. I stared at Bill. He was unquestionably a good-looking man, and his strange outfit merely marked the moment of his last stormy exit from his parents' home on Fifth Avenue. He had returned from his morning ride and was still in riding breeches, when words were interchanged. The top part of his costume went with his own breeches; the pants now in presence were got from the land outfit of a friend in the Merchant Marine. Bill actually owned a theater near Third Avenue and Twenty-third Street, which he offered free to neglected talents. They had to rustle up the cast and most of the personnel. He was a big shareholder in several radical enterprises. Everything was to his credit. He had parted from two wives on the most friendly terms; they both worked for a living and so did he.

Having made up my mind about Bill van Week, who had taken a fancy to me, and observing that I had nothing to fear from Edwige, that he was through with her, I went over to talk to my sisters. Andrea wanted to show me her fan photographs. Jacky was in a melting mood. She wanted me to go into her room and listen to some poems she had written; it turned out to be nothing less than an epic. She would not bring it into the company. Standing at the door, where I could survey everything, I ran my eye down the lines. The poem was even now fifteen pages long, and all in blank verse. This is how it began:

OPUS NO. 1

Overture.

FAUST. *A high sea-crag. Faust is looking back at the distant lights of a fishing-town. His rose-colored hair flies in the gale.*

What is time? The lamps go out after midnight. Tomorrow the sun rises, a smoking, sputtering lamp, or dies—but the universe goes on creating suns, only to die, as it created me, only to die. I will speak to the sun, in a loud voice; perhaps I can stretch over the abyss to where it hurries. Daystar, plunged in night, rush forth to me, press your great lips to mine, re-create with me the spark that flashed from the skies when I stood at the gates of life. Few are brave enough to talk with the sun, but I am of a great race. The sun gave me life, poured through my cells a fluid, flashing and tumbling light, glazing and dizzying light; some men and some women know the secret of my birth, the open riddle they read on my flesh. Yes, but now—kindle, star of morning, in my heart, a deeper fire, deeper, for, O horrible, my fires smoke now; in me are ashes, the lamp is burning lower. Or spill here a rain of stars, bind me in thickets of flowers, fill my blood with new small creatures darting through the short flood of time, and make me a great vein of the earth, painlessly, without death. Turn this cup of darkness, this sea, into blue-black wine and let me drink it all at once. I am capable of that and more! Who knows what I am capable of but myself; who knows me but myself? No one can measure himself with me, but myself. I am man concentrate, all man, and on me the curse of man has come; I am old, old, old—I never thought I would get old; let others age! Old! Faust! But why did I have this irrepressible flame, if it was only to lose it, like the weak, pale man who crawls like worms? And in the very same span as other men? Why this, waste, waste, dust, misery—oh, what horror tears me—to die! And before, dances the thought, it will get worse. Love, sweet-breathing young women, in whose great eyes I see the knowledge of what I am suddenly flash, in the moment of loving me, they will not look at me after this. For I, born a king, a sun, must go in the ridiculous garments of age, with the dragging gait, the faded suit, the rags and spots of the poor scholar, ridiculous to the fat middle-aged woman flaunting the disgrace of her flesh, ridiculous to the empty-faced boy whom no passion will ever make mad, ridiculous to the monkey, the thief, the dog, the peanut vendor, the sot, the servant. I come to this? But must I die? I will not.

And the First Scene was a great room filled with moonlight. The only novelty was that Faust and Mephistopheles were one.

I said, "But you know what they say in college. It's very good, you know—but why don't you write something about your daily life? No one will ever publish this."

Jacky looked at me.

I said, "You know the old crack—only minor poets use great themes."

"As for that," said Jacky, with extraordinary boldness, "great poets also use great themes you know; and *this* is my daily life."

I laughed, "Really? Well, you'd do better with Bill van Week. Or Aleck. You're really passable, Jacky, but you don't seem to know it."

I now felt bored with the place and thought I would take a walk with Van Week. As I looked at him across the room and caught his eye, there was a flash like a short-circuit. It was the sign, the real thing. I rushed out, put my arm through Bill's, and said, "Let's go, Bill; I need a cocktail. I said a cocktail."

"I am already with you in spirit, to coin a phrase," said he; "my hat, my *New Masses*, and a low salaam to your charming mamma. I'm lucky to meet you. I'm in one of those moods. I'm sick of juggling these soap bubbles of mine. It's not good for art; it's not good for family life, and it's not good for my peace of mind. And I need plenty. My life isn't all leather medals. But I have to keep going until one of the damn bubbles breaks and some gold trickles through. Look at the bum metaphors—just like my life."

"Why don't you put up with the family portraits and family prayers?"

"Damn my family—"

"For shame—come, let's go, while the going's good."

"You're a man-stealer," he said, laughing; and went off for his trinkets.

I said good-bye to Mother, Andrea, Gondych. I said to Jacky, "I didn't know Mother was so pally with the Ancient of Days— Father Gondych."

Jacky looked pained and shot a look at Mathilde, "But Mother isn't divorced, Letty."

"Oh, when she's a couple of years older, she'll be giving us yearly beanfeasts like Grandma Morgan and asking our young advice about men. I hope so, at any rate."

Jacky was not pleased. We went out. Aleck started to come after me, but frankly, I was so angry with him that I was delighted to leave him behind. I said to Bill, "And now, tell me how you met that indescribable little witch, my cousin Edwige."

"You're an indescribable little witch yourself," he said.

I fox-trotted along the street. I was already madly in love. I could not believe my luck that I had really found the perfect man, the man, most eligible of all eligibles, and that he liked me and that we were going to spend the evening together. How would it end up? I didn't care how—I even hoped for the worst, so that he would know more about me and like me better. He hadn't a smirch on his record; his politics were like mine word for word, and I approved heartily of his manly attempt to make a name for himself apart from his family's millions. For even this was true, the existence of the millions, the marble palace on Fifth Avenue (only it was a skyscraper), and all. Moreover, as he went along, he confessed his faults and adventures to me, like an old friend, and I even told some of mine.

"I love you, Letty!"

Why shouldn't love be like this? Perhaps I had dreamed of moonlight and roses like other people, but this way is better. He said, "You're the essence of the feminine and yet you've almost no womanishness, or just enough to make a shrew, which is all right by me"; and I said, "I didn't know men could be like this, Bill, a comrade and a friend; of course, as a schoolgirl I thought of it."

It was impossible to separate. He took me to my home and for a long time we sat talking in the long room, really a salon, in which I lived. We consoled each other for the various frauds of life; and we thought much alike on this, too—the same hopes, the same disappointments, the same frankness and lack of hypocrisy.

It came to the point where I burst out crying in his plaid waist-coat, and told him almost all my story, even relating the details of these last few weeks, Luke Adams and Lucy Headlong. He made sensible remarks without taking either of these affairs as seriously as I had done. He had the kindness to stay with me until morning; and by then I knew that he, too, was in a fix. He had paid for a room in a Forty-fourth Street hotel, an old place where theatrical people often went. After a week he would be in debt and had nowhere to go. I offered him the use of my room, and at first he was tempted to take it.

"I could sweep for you, dust, cook, wash, iron, and save you the cost of a maid," he said thoughtfully, but after a while he added, "But the fact is, I have no source of income; if I could pay my way I'd gladly live with you, Letty, but I can't live on you—you're working."

I told him I was not rich, although I had a few hundred dollars I could draw upon in need, but that Susannah Ford did not need the rent badly. I was earning enough to keep both of us for a while. As to dress, I would sting my grandmother; she'd put up with it. He thanked me and seemed very touched, saying I was one of the best pals he had ever had; and indeed, I was beginning to regret very much the Christmas party at Arnhem. I could have met Bill several days before. However, Bill, after breakfast, which he cooked, told me that he had thought it over, and that if he was too proud to live on his parents, he also was too proud to live on my earnings; and that it must all wait till he got a position himself. He told me that people in the city owed him at least fifteen thousand dollars, partnerships, debts, in his various enterprises which they had not paid up; and that some of the people concerned were the best-known people in New York. He had been so hunted for debt that he had had to leave town, thus giving them a breathing space; but at present he had the matter in hand and expected, any day now, to get some of these thousands. He then told me that he was not really a beggar; he owned several properties on Fifty-seventh Street and one on Fifty-eighth Street which was a gold mine; but he had refused the rents from these places for several years, and this money was accumulating at the lawyers'. Nevertheless, out of pride, he wished to show his family that he could become a millionaire on his own hook.

I had to yield to these honest arguments, though I could just as well have dispensed with them and been glad to see Bill use my place while he was out looking for a place and trying to get the debts reimbursed. Meanwhile, I sent him to Banks, my father's old associate, the lawyer, now well-known, and promised him that Banks would get his money for him and not ask for a share; he had now become a lawyer of the highest class. He was rich and charged small fees to any friends.

"However, I don't say that a Van Week can pay it in peanuts," I said to Bill.

Bill smiled, told me we'd make the best team he'd ever heard of, and went off at once to see this lawyer. I expected him back in the evening and came home from work in a very cheerful frame of mind. I had worked at top speed that day and accomplished wonders. I was, to begin with, the shockworker of the place, and although a socialist and a believer in unions, the momentum of work and my interest in it kept me working fifteen or sixteen hours a day when in a good frame of mind. I had already caused many jealousies. The others feared I aimed at the top positions. They were right. I did. Why not? I was surely capable of them and had an overruling talent. Everything I laid my hand to, in business, was done not only well, but with that good-natured vigor which knows when and how to wink, when to lambast and when to flatter. But when I was loved and had a man in my home, I was a regular Don Quixote, conquering a flower bed.

I came home, and no Bill! Presently, he telephoned me; and we went out to eat in a steak restaurant then à la mode on Ninth Avenue. Butchers, theatrical people, brokers, and other good eaters were beginning to know it. We then went to Café Society and to a real night club and after that to a party. We rolled home at four in the morning; and I, of course, had to be at work at nine. I left Bill sleeping. Nevertheless, my satisfaction at being settled was such that I again worked all through the day and took a taxi home, preparing to go out for cocktails and dinner as usual. I had bought a dinner dress, costing $110, in Fifty-eighth Street, a rather matronly, but clearly expensive affair. I had to borrow on my salary for this; but I thought, Perhaps I will soon be a Van Week getting my stuff at a discount there, for the publicity of it.

Bill was nowhere to be seen. After I had waited an hour, he telephoned, with his *dear* and his *honey-love* to say that he had decided to become reconciled with his parents as Sunday was approaching, and he felt it a shame to deprive them of the innocent pleasure of going to church with them. He did not know how long he could last with the family butler and plate, and the alleged El

Grecos, but he had been promised some money by Banks, the lawyer, and felt justified now in facing his parents. He told me that when his parents went to the country he would take me over the mansion. This mansion in the skies was on the twentieth story, and built and furnished exclusively for them.

I sat in the dress disconsolately and wondered where to eat. I hadn't a bean. At length I wound up at my father's and borrowed some money from him. I now had to get a stand-in to go with the dress; Bobby Thompson would have to do. While at my father's, I began to discount my new hopes as fantasy; how often does one meet a millionaire radical in circulation? I was astonished that with our love and good comradeship, he could have floated away so easily, and was only partly comforted by the memory of something he had said to me, "I don't visit girls; I live with them, once I have money in my pocket. But you see, I must pay the rent."

His old-fashioned ideas had charm for me; I thought with longing of an old-fashioned life. Perhaps I was tired of struggling so hard, without knowing it? I recognized how easy it would be to slip into the old way and become a squaw with a papoose. I thought this, who all day long was writing barbed and pungent paragraphs on how to be seductive, exquisite. I thought of the witty woman with a salon who was so exhausted keeping up with Talleyrand. I might become exhausted trying to keep up with even those poor fish, Aleck, Brock, and the many others, Ken, Amos. For the woman looking for love is like a little boat meeting waterspout after waterspout. She is tired of steering, rowing, looking for land, hanging up old shirts for sails and the rest of it. But the pirates, they are not tired at all. They don't care if they don't make a landfall once in three years; they live off little craft. I went home, and felt depressed. Nevertheless, dear Bill was never able to depress me as the others had, and I wondered if this were growing up. Perhaps I would weather the troubles and begin to regard men and their passions merely as trade winds.

I won't say I was happy; in my heart I hoped always for the great love and the settled fate from which I need never look outwards. I wished never to wish for another man!

Still, Bill and I spent a lot of time together; he was a lavish man and his pockets were at present lined. He would never have anything but the best and ordered headwaiters about in an arrogant, practiced way. The only difficulty was that he often introduced into the party other women, generally of the rowdy, garish Hollywood type, the Edwige type, little high-heeled half-made-over vixens from the back of the Bronx; and when they didn't suit him, he bawled them out in public and harried them all the way home, having apparently undertaken to tame all the shrews on the east and west coasts. The best of it was that my time was filled in and I sometimes slept; for it was a time when the news and my affairs might have kept me up day and night.

36

ONE NIGHT, coming home I slipped on the ice, and after that lay in bed for nearly a week with black-outs, raging headaches, and found myself unable to take things in my celebrated style. My father and mother, sisters, friends, came to see me; in the course of the week I began to hold a levee each day, so I sent Bill van Week out to buy me a negligee, for I thought I might as well make an attempt, as the occasion was handed to me on a platter, to hold a salon. He came back with the very thing, a long, fluffy, white one, with a small train. He confessed that it had come from the wardrobe of a play that he had once put on and that flopped. The wardrobe and scenery had been impounded, but he had handed the man in the warehouse a five-dollar bill.

Bill liked women in bed and wanted to give a party. I agreed to this, but said that the party must suit my means; that is, a beer and wine party, cigarettes and homemade canapés. Bill was in his element. He was at the place in Jane Street day and night for a few days before. He washed all my dirty dishes, cleaned the paintwork, fixed the lights, bought rug-cleaner, invited everyone, bought my beer and wine, and, of course, imported drinks of his own; only, said he, because he had a certain combination in mind—the secret of gastronomic and alcoholic success was combination and quality materials. Nothing loath, I let him mix.

The day before the party, he installed me in an armchair, in the white garb, saying "Dress Rehearsal," while he fixed glasses and everything he required. He ran in and out a dozen times to get things he had forgotten. He became most irritable in the morning and would not tell me the secret of things he was mixing in the various big bowls, which he had bought or borrowed. As far as I could make out, for he never divulged his culinary secrets, one was a sort of avocado mousse, one a roquefort mousse, and one a fish-paste roll made out of thin slices of bread and butter. He carefully explained the mixing of a green salad, however. It was sharp and sour, and all his effects were male. This was for Sunday afternoon, so most of his work was done on the Saturday. He spent the Saturday night with me. He was a smooth-running lover, but this time he kept me awake half the night with his anxiety about his party.

"Oh, Jesus, I didn't get any more toothpicks," and "Green olives on one side, black on the other, and pearl onions in between, just one line, in a *coupe*."

I started by inviting ten or twelve persons (it had started out as my party), but Bill became furiously enthusiastic and insisted upon my inviting twenty others, including Luke Adams. He was almost willing to kiss the footprints of the great man. When I declared I had quarreled with him, he actually went to the man's studio to invite him himself. Luke was one of the first to arrive and came up to me, sitting down beside me with his hands on my thigh. At once the old flame started up. I took no notice of Bill nor of anyone for some time. Bill wound up with an areaway, a backyard, and an outhouse full of guests. The party went on nearly all night. Bill held court, butlered for himself, told everyone about his financial misfortunes, his flops on Broadway and in Hollywood, his divorces, his misguided parents; and presented himself, quite unconsciously, to my guests, as my possible husband. Some thought we were already a working team. My relations with him, also, were of an extraordinarily easy turn. Meanwhile, he brought me luck. I made up my quarrel with Luke. Late in the evening, while Bill was telling of his quarrel with his lovely second wife (actually she was just a high-school kid, with a fresh skin), Luke was asking me if I would make an appointment with him, "I think I can get away on Wednesday evening; will you telephone me, Letty?"

"Oh, yes, darling, yes."

"Will you, though? You have too much self-control—these last weeks—" and he looked at me darkly, without a smile.

"Oh, yes, yes, Luke."

He strained my fingers and gave me an ardent look. I thought of nothing else all night and sent Bill home, when the last guests went. At this he was surprised, for he had come to think of my flat as his tavern. I divided my night between thinking of a suggestion of Bill's, and of my decision to give up the dress publicity in the Tweed and Silk. Bill thought, with my ability, he could start to run his little free theater himself as a little theater venture. He had brought me books, plays, French's catalogue. I felt indignant with my parents, as I tossed, that I had not gone to a high-class college where I would have been able to take a drama course. I planned ways of spending what remained of my grandmother's money. Perhaps I could spend a year or two at the Yale Drama School. I was wasting time in the dress business. Likewise, I had received an offer from a man who needed a secretary with foreign languages.

In the morning my headache raged. I spent the morning playing the Razumovskys, and read Boileau's *L'Art Poétique*. But my headache increased, and I went out in the snowy air, ending up on the telephone talking to Bill; then to the Lafayette, to Charles; and elsewhere with him. When I came home, naturally, I was much worse, and went to bed with some sleeping pills which he brought me. Bill sat on the edge of my bed and we talked in French. I raved: "*Sans être prise par l'emprise de la querelle des anciens et modernes, laquelle querelle,*" I said, "*ne doit son existence qu'aux cervelles trop fertiles de quelques vieilles institutrices irréellistes, car la virginité, dit Balzac, est une monstruosité. . . .*"

All this to show my partner that I had read Proust for whom, all of a sudden, I became reimpassioned.

"Certainly one of the stylists, the most pure in the world," I said in French to Bill.

"*Quelle faconde,*" said my male nurse. "A nice little gift of the gab."

"*Pourtant, je veux dire que Boileau m'abasourdit, avec ses règles, son* rationalisme, *ses conseils.* At first, he pretends that reason should dominate; then he says things like this: *Il faut que le cœur seul parle dans l'élégie;* or, speaking of the ode, here, a fine disorder is the effect of art. On one side he destroys imagination, fantasy, declares himself an enemy of all things fantastic; on the other, he says, don't go and hitch your wagon to the moon, a thing even a child like me knows; but, bring it down to you, with the seven ways they know in Bergerac. *Enfin*—what kind of counsel is this to a struggling writer?"

"*Tu déraisonnes*," said Bill, "are you a struggling writer?"

"Yes," I said, defiantly. "Is it a closed guild? Everyone, to begin with, is a struggling writer and then, even when I played kid-games with Jacky, we were both going to write the Great American Novel."

We had an exciting heart-to-heart talk. Later on, "Well," said Bill, "we were made for each other. I think we'd make a go of it. But we ought to wait and see. We could get real bang-up fun out of running a theater, don't you think?"

I was all for giving up my job at once, but Bill advised against this. My natural excitement made me want to go and view his theater at once. He took me in a taxi, and I saw a wretched little place with brown peeling walls in Twenty-eighth Street, near Sixth Avenue.

"This will never do for us," I said; "besides, frankly, I think I ought to go to Yale."

It all ended, at that particular moment, in the air; for Bill went back to his parents in the mansion in the sky.

Now Wednesday approached when I was to telephone Luke. Probably I was calmer that week than at any other time in my life. Although at four on Wednesday I had Brock Ford with me, weeping and detailing the tricks Susannah played on him, telling me the divorce had actually been started and asking me to be his friend and confidante, I made an excuse to go out to telephone. Luke's studio secretary, some female of the watchdog kind, quite clearly fancying I was one of his *women*, told me that Mr. Adams was very ill, in hospital. He had been out at his shack in the storm of the previous night, and had been injured by a falling branch. I went to the post office to send a registered letter and came back home, in a white shock. To think that for the past day or two I had been looking at walk-ups in side streets, like Nineteenth, and thinking, "It's there we could find a place."

I had decided to move away from Jane Street. Susannah was jealous of me. The boys were dropping in on me too often, telling me their troubles with her. I thought that Luke and I could find a place to suit us, by the week, until my other affairs were settled.

The Madrid story was going down in blood and fire and I could not fix my mind on anything till I knew what was to become of Clays. For nights now, I had looked at transient hotels as I took my walks out, to cool my constant headache. Luke could hardly ever come to me. His wife kept him away. People had always gossiped about him and now they would be glad to be able to pin him down, say, to me. Now he was snatched away from me, perhaps dying, and I couldn't get to him. No one would let me know. I walked bitterly up and down the streets in the February snow, thinking:

"My God, if you exist, you punish me! Or society does. Here's a strange rule we invented. The haters, the indifferent, the cold and bitter, like Mathilde, the utterly apathetic, the crazy and drunken, the children, like Jacky, the dull and stupid and those who are willing to pass their lives parroting slogans—they can meet whenever the mood takes them. But when two people love, they cannot meet—ever, ever again. Even the unrentable street, the empty, winter night, the cast-out silence of the river banks, he can't grant me. They can't talk, nor walk, nor think together; and if they want to love—who knows if it isn't the first, the last, the true flame? —What we live for?—The secret hope in every sulking heart?— we're belittled, by the grinning, spying, loafing, straw-chewing, chain-drinking, joking, whispering, milling, chance-breeding, flea-bitten, lousy, god-damned and devil-damned bunch of baboons, who crawl into corners to butt themselves against each other and hypocritically write dirty limericks in bachelor bedrooms, but beget their children so legitimately, colder than snails, with horrible grimaces and spittling in their hands, hiccuping ear to ear, and vomiting after drunks; and talebearing so that we can't meet openly. And even fate helped them, the snow-bent branch. Is it I who am the whore? Do I destroy society? It is society, this one, which is the harlot and leaves me dissolute, desolate— It's mad that I can't meet Luke!

"But—here's the twist that makes the play! They're all mad to fall in love!"

Now I was lost in some dark street in Chelsea and walked for hours, near the Hudson, and found myself in Barrow Street and later in the coal-damp and gashouse districts near the East River. Probably I muttered to myself. Naturally, some men tried to stop me, but I shouted at them, I gave them something to chew on. I thought:

"Now there's a man in this city I love, but what is he? A pale-faced man, stooped with work and sickness; you all have seen his face, it is the face of the dear one, behind all faces that we eagerly, desperately hunt in. He's the demon-lover, himself a plain man, but his soul, a demon. When I didn't care for him I saw him often, sleeping, eating, drinking, talking, borrowing things, quite at his ease and we could have laid down on the couch, no one would have looked. But once the look is given, the first hint of the immortal embrace, the only immortality, when this took place, the jealous, flushed apes came round, getting between us—with—suitability, morality, marriage, lechery—tearing us apart, inventing, until the whole thing was a mere shallow, sordid disgrace; and, yes, my best friends, my father and mother would have rendered me this service, too. Who hasn't suffered this, that is alive today? Not one of us alive but has suffered this affront, this insult, this insult and injury—and why, because we offer life, body, heat, pleasure, all in one hour, to someone. It's not a mean act; besides death for a cause and life-giving, it's the only decent thing we ever do!"

Late, late at night, I came back to Jane Street. The house was cold; the lights were out upstairs; I suppose they were making love.

In three days I had a letter from Luke. I did not go to work, but went to the hospital. It was a long way; it took hours. He had had an operation and had just about come out of the ether. Nevertheless, he sat up, and put his foot, in its blue hospital slipper, on the side of my chair. I held it in my hand. There were six men in the same ward and I knew his wife was coming; but there are no stool pigeons among men. I thought, they'll never tell. They never did. This was how they repaid me for my outcry against everyone, of three nights before. I went back home and thought a great deal about the question of the family. Why did Adams live with his wife when he loved me? With the landless and the moneyless, I said, the family is their only possession, and it is the only property they can acquire by a mere signature. If Adams falls ill, he is sure his wife will come; it is just charity or a miracle that I come. The family is a tract of land belonging to numerous generations; a self-help mutual. All this made me very uneasy. I wanted now to become part of society myself and have a husband in the regular way. The interest of the whole world was turned on the betrayal in Madrid. I had not only their reasons, but my own. I did not imagine that Luke, who had this fatal power over me, was the right husband for me, and since Clays, I had not met anyone suitable for me but Bill van Week; but only Clays had mentioned marriage.

When I wrote to him, I tried to tell him something of all I was feeling, but naturally, I left out my adventures with men, thinking that if it proved wise, I would tell all this later; and I wrote to Clays, now escaped to London, from whom I just had a short note which said nothing.

> Dear Clays,
>   ...I thought of you today, it's a lovely evening. It's some time that I've known you, Clays. It only came to me lately that I know how to love you. The afternoon you suddenly kissed me—you remember? (Yes, I do remember, Hebe!) All week I've been thinking of you, thinking, thinking, I know the kind of man Clays is. I know he's had women. I know your history. I don't expect too much from life. But I love you. I must, because all the week I've been thinking of you, I could do nothing, I told everyone about you, read your letters over the phone; I was half-crazy, I thought I was sick, but it was just wanting you to come back. I thought I heard your voice, in the night, once sitting alone in the house, four times, more times, were you thinking of me then? Were you thinking of me all those times? I was thinking of—all love. You know...I am not selfish. I am living I really believe twenty-five hours a day. I do everything I can, except actually go to Spain and I wish I could do that. It's no life we lead, the life here. No one likes it, but we make a fantastic effort to live, just the same....
>
>   Your
>   Poor Letty.

This was the truth. I did not want to live the way I was living; and I was becoming more disillusioned about Bill van Week every day. He had too many girl friends. For a few days I thought I would never have anything to do with men till Clays came back. I had tried this before, with poor results. It is impossible to resist the pleasure of love, once tried; and I am not the kind to sit listlessly in a room. I distrust dithyrambs. I made one up about Luke and it was disproved the very next day; but *il faut que le cœur seul parle dans l'élégie.*

It was a blow over the heart to everyone radical in New York when Madrid, and with it, Spain, fell. People were blue. Also the war, with all its murderous derring-do and fire, and with the harsh, fierce flame it had lighted Europe up with, had disturbed everyone with the first truths about mortal combat in society. For most of us had not known the first European war, nor even much about the civil war between reaction and revolution in the land of the Soviets. We knew strikers were wounded and killed in our own country, and they had armored cars and regiments with steel helmets watching the streets in Paris, and hunger marchers in Britain, things like that, but international politics still seemed to us something you could tear to pieces in an evening's talk, in our strong white teeth; and we could now see it wasn't. The whole struggle in Spain had been full of diplomatic and tactical puzzles. Who was on which side of the fence and why? Who aided and didn't aid and why?

We went at the solution of the Spanish jigsaw piecemeal, but a mental fog had already begun to settle; and most people, at least in our crowd, were beginning to argue in circles. I did myself. I really didn't know anything about politics, I just had good instincts; but most people didn't even have that. If they were bright and egotistical, they drifted off into cranky Bohemia, and some, of course, joined the Government or the police; if they were good-hearted and felt a duty to society, they thought they ought to adhere unquestioningly to some party policy or another in the spirit of, "Who are we to question—here be issues greater than our small quibbles."

But I had seen at least a bit of European political life and knew you have to keep on fighting for liberty, even in a revolution when you're on the right side. This is more than most people can bear,

I suppose, especially if they belong to our soft set. New Yorkers are goodhearted, but frightfully soft, and they're afraid to come out in the open with an ideal, and they'd rather die than be Daniel in the lions' den. It doesn't show a sense of humor. Fortunately, a rough-tempered girl like I am doesn't mind looking ridiculous at times, but only when I can get away with it. That is my weakness, too. I'm well aware that after the blow, I'm only too anxious to belong, again.

Well, I knew that the triumph of reaction in Spain would encourage all the fascists in England, on the Continent, and elsewhere. Who didn't know that? The future looked sinister. And what would become of Clays and his like? As for Clays, I trusted that his Whitehall connections would pull him out of the fiery furnace. He had hinted that he might get through and back home; but I was not prepared for the letter which I received in April, from Clays. He told me that I was a wonderful girl, the best he had ever met, except for another; and he went on at this rate for a while, not too long a while. Then, with the Englishman's irresponsible love of brevity, he told me he had simply married another woman. It was not an accident, he really thought her a splendid woman who would suit him, and he hoped that I would not get too hard a blow, but would remember that in love you've got to play for high stakes and put all your eggs in one basket; but that I was too young and naïve a girl to have done this really, as he had, for a real young girl has, after all, not really invested in love. He concluded, "You may suffer, and I feel ashamed when I think of it. But what is a little suffering which may be got over, to such an experience! Would you have been without it? Love is a great experience anyhow; people are eternally grateful (you may not believe this at the moment) to those who gave them love. You and I have something in common. For the rest, my dear little Hebe, you are too beautiful to lack a man long; and it would never have done for us to marry and repent!"

I will not enlarge upon my feelings. I sent Clays a stinging reply. I thought of sending it to his wife, but I thought of the unprincipled cruelty and self-sufficiency of the British society woman and did not so expose myself. The woman was The Honourable Fyshe.

I was now in a solitude, more or less deserved, no doubt; but I suffered as much as any farm girl kissed under the blossom and deserted in the fall of the leaf. I made up my mind to marry as quickly as possible.

37

MORE BAD luck struck me. As soon as she heard my International Brigadier had wed another, Susannah piled on me and accused me of meddling with her men. Things were very cool, and then very hot, until I resolved to get out of Jane Street.

At one of Grandma's pinochle parties, I met Mrs. Betty Looper, who was still Grandma's crony. They had lived through thirty years of quarrels together. Mrs. Looper sent me to see a girl who worked in a model agency. Hundreds of girls, making their way, drifted in and out, and most were trying to pair up for a room, one of those rooms with pillows and lampshades I mentioned before. This girl was about twenty-five and lived at home, being the daughter of the owner, but she introduced me to Amy and Lorna, two girls a bit older than I was. They had a well-furnished railroad flat in Sixty-sixth Street. It had two entrances and four rooms, three of which could be used as bedrooms. The rent was high, although it was in a street of stables, because it was near the Park. The girls suited me, and as they offered to give me the front room with a separate entrance, I took it. It was properly heated and had a real kitchen.

I went at once and broke with Susannah. To my surprise, she wanted me to take Leon, Luke Adams's ward; she pretended that she had only taken the boy because I was in the house, to help me out. Of course, I was obliged to write Luke Adams about this and visited his home, where I met his wife, Elsie. Elsie had dropped the subject of Leon as soon as the unlucky boy had left her house and seemed put out to find that he was still in town. Luke, too, was put out. He had thought that Susannah had a heart as big as a whale, and now he found out that she was scatty, unreliable. For the time being, Leon would have to go back and sleep behind the watch-repairer's shop. Naturally, everyone thought that Leon was Luke's unacknowledged son, and made no move to help him; they just laughed. In the end Luke encouraged someone to start a children's colony only, I believe, for the sake of placing Leon there.

This Leon affair caused some heartburning in the Ford and Adams households. I felt obliged to tell Luke that Leon had caught some very bad habits from Blaise, Susannah's son, indolent and spoiled; and had heard corrupt conversation in Susannah's house. Easygoing Luke only smiled at me, and said the poor youngster had to knock about the world; he'd find himself in tighter places than that.

But my heart burned at all that went on in the Ford house. I don't mind a woman living with two husbands if she wants to and they want to. What angered me was the way Susannah played one against the other, pretending that she was going to take back, and reject, month after month; and, all the time, going to her psychoanalyst, to *transfer* to him. It was simple polygamy, but not the honest kind. When I left, I made some social criticism, not about her men, but about the way she tortured the children mentally and morally. She told me the pot shouldn't call the kettle black; I said, I've never done anything to children. She considered herself an admirable mother simply because she discussed Blaise's schools, *intelligence quotient*, sexual habits, and alleged neuroses in public. She was a reasonably rich woman and considered herself ideal from every point of view because she gave some of her money to radical causes, spent a lot on Blaise, and subscribed to the Book-of-the-Month Club.

The night before I left, I went up to say good-bye; and as things turned that way, I told her some of the more flagrant absurdities in her behavior. I said, "Blaise is about the worst-educated brat I've ever met; you're just a flabby bourgeois, Sue, and you're only radical because that's a kind of luxury too; everything is gilt-edged. Your brat can't hear dirty stories in the gutter; you have to pay a lot of money for him to hear dirty stories at the psychoanalyst's. You think you're a radical because you pay an awful lot of money for your radicalism. It's as plain as a pikestaff—"

"Why can't we part friends?" said Brock pathetically. "Poor Sue can't see herself the way we can see her, no one can."

"That's too bad," said Susannah, flaring up, "I know what I'm doing. I want Blaise to have a full life with no repressions."

"You don't get the point; you've got gold-leaf all over your rose-colored specs," said I. "You're just a sucker, Sue. They'll let you go along with your head in space, thinking you're a rebel and all that, till they're ready to clamp down. Radicalism is the opium of the middle class. Meanwhile, they're stealing your shirt."

She looked at me as if I were mad, "Who are stealing my shirt?"

"Why," I said, "you all kid yourselves your children are too sensitive to go to the public schools, even though every well-heeled man in this generation came from the public schools—and in those days they just had ordinary Irish and Jewish teachers who weren't respected very highly; there wasn't the to-do about education there is nowadays. But the products are all right. But your kids are too talented to go there. Private schools are just the means of encouraging the middle class to strip itself, don't you see. If you were really rich, you'd be real old-fashioned freethinkers and radicals and a danger to the State; but you are all crazy with money troubles, because Blaise and the other tots can't mix with *hoi polloi*, and so you can't think straight. You have stings of conscience, so you have, as an ointment for that, high-priced radicalism. Just the same, you can't train your kids to be radicals, not real ones, because they've got to pay you back some time and to make a living as nice bourgeois; they've got to enter the professional and government world, and for that you can't be a nay-sayer; no, ma'am. There's a very simple way of freeing little Blaise's mind and talents, and that's by saying every day, 'Be free, think free, don't kowtow to anything, Fuehrer or Dogma.' But, you know yourself freedom's just a howling wilderness to you. You don't want freedom. Heaven's Connecticut to you, and you just want a cozy little place there, in the end. You don't want freedom; it might be uncomfortable. And you don't want Blaise to be uncomfortable, or free; you want him to conform."

"You must be crazy," said Susannah, staring at me in her hard, bright way. "What is eating you? I'll bet anything you like that when you get married and get a kid you'll do just the same as me."

"Does that disprove it? I can go loony too."

I lighted a cigarette and said impatiently: "I'm sick of fake radicalism and fake education. You've got no theory at all for one or the other."

"Well, what do you know about that," she said, laughing, "so I have no theory in radicalism!"

"You know the headlines of the day," said I, smoking furiously, and through my cigarette.

Susannah said, "But all the radicals send their children to those schools; it's the best thing, they get all the newest ideas."

"It's all empiricism and parent-flattery, there's no theory," said I. "But a system can't exist without some thought behind it. The thought is just what I say, you've got to strip yourself of every cent you have, to immolate yourself before capitalism. It's a frenzy they've got you into. You're really adoring and worshiping capitalism. Because, if you were serious, wouldn't you all be starting up free progressive schools for the poor, for the slum kids? But it's only for your little doctors, artists, and teachers in embryo. So you're not serious. You're just trying to force the kids so they'll bring in big money later on."

"Let's have another drink," said Aleck, with his sweet atony. He brought one over, but did not kiss me, because the eye of his mistress was on him.

"Letty's always boiling over."

"Why not?" said I. "If I'm crazy, I like to know it, at any rate."

"Well, why don't you get out of the middle classes," said Susannah, bitterly, "if they're so bad."

"Go back to where I came from, do you mean? Listen, Sue, your Blaise when he grows up—will he be in an itsy-bitsy world with fifteen fancy bosses trying to bring out his individualism, or will he be in a world where he's got to get a job in the Metropolitan Life, or Ford's assembly-plant, or U.S. Steel, or something? The Blaise-world's a fantasy-world. And to be sure he'll go crazy, you send him to witch doctors too, who make him think there's something divine in his innermost I. There'll never be anything in his eye, but the kind of twinkle you know. And I'm damned if you're not cultivating his sex, too, so that his sex acts will be super-duper and he'll have a good time seducing all kinds of poor youngsters who work in Woolworth basements and innocents like Jacky and me who think that you ought to learn something about Aristotle and Pascal. You're just training him to be a complete rotter. And he's got there already."

We went at it hammer and tongs. Susannah would not have done defending her son's genius. Of course, he was just an ordinary pup like a million others, who would end up as a bridge-playing knight of Pythias, or something.

Well, this was my exit. I went away quite sick of them all and angry with myself. I was sick of the brainless corruption, and thought, "Business is a thousand times cleaner."

I was a ship at sea, without a port. I was no hulk nor ghost-ship, but a good freighter made to carry bread and Bibles about the world; I was a good, deep draft, built on dependable old-fashioned lines, no victory ship, no canal boat, and no ship of the line. But a freighter doesn't particularly care for the heaving billow; a freighter has a destination; and as Grandma Fox would have said, also: "A worker, I say, a worker must work, or have money." I couldn't float around for very long. I was in a bad state of mind. I could analyze anything right under my nose, and was not in want of theory—but about my personal life, I had no theory. I often wondered who and what I was. If people ran me down, I half believed it; if they praised me, I believed it, more than half. It was easy for me to come under the influence of an amoral, ignorant, but brilliant and unflinching sex-careerist like my new friend Amy Bourne.

Amy lived on a bit of income from Australia, which was her birthplace; and Lorna did odd jobs: she wrote society notes, or took photographs, or handled a gardening column, or worked in an advertising agency, or sang new songs in a record-ingle in a smart store, or took old men out dancing and necking, or sold chocolates, or designed wallpaper, or drew baby angels for stork events, or was hostess in Schraffts', or did the night clubs with a wealthy male, or mistressed it a bit, just as she could. She was a hefty, handsome brunette, who could have played lady to a nicety, but she lost her men through clumsy promiscuities; and Amy was the only natural man-hunter I've ever met. I felt like a gawking schoolchild with her. She was a short, dark chip of a girl, with almost a boy's figure; her face, the perfect, pointed oval. She was one of the few abstracted human beings alive. She regarded moralizing as a natural halting-time for some (not for her) to catch up on imperfections. She was veritably keen and penetrating, with flaw-less manners, an excellent heart; she made a good companion for women and men. While in pursuit, your game was no concern of hers: she did not man-steal until she saw something suitable, de-lectable in your grasp. At times I was less delicate. I stole out of jealousy, ambition, sulkiness.

This was the worst year of my life, perhaps, this and the one succeeding. I won't go into the numerous temporary affairs, disap-pointments, things unworthy of me, one-night stands; the disillu-sions and shames that I went through. On my twentieth birthday I would be able to say: "*En l'an vingtième de mon age quand toutes mes hontes j'ai bues,*" with an apostrophe to François Villon, "*Mon semblable, mon frère, quel escargot que tu fus!*—Brother and kin! What a slowcoach you were!"

It was the plague year for me, as if Clays had been all my luck. All the same, in the first few months when I was rooming with my pillow girls, Amy and Lorna, I had some sober entertainment. I was not free to go to the deuce, as I liked; I was obliged to take lessons from the indomitable Amy. I was thirsty for hints on the love affair and I did not despise any laboratory techniques of the Casanovas, male and female. I had suffered too much, compos-ing messages, reproaches, declarations, speeches, most of which brought simply failure and insult, not to be glad to learn the stand-bys, which save the self-respect and soul of the chain-lover who might otherwise commit suicide. All the love speeches invented by sixteen-year-olds, however banal, are an effort of the heart; and the heart is wounded when they evoke laughter. Later on, with much more experience, one suffers in the same way, and one feels less rejected if the words one proffers as the bouquet of oneself are simply a formula, part of the classic drama. They have two uses—You comfort yourself by saying, "I didn't really mean it"; and clear your conscience of crime by saying, "He must have known it was just a formula of politeness."

I listened eagerly to all the tales, trying to pick up the best-worn, most celebrated lines of whoremongers, seducers, Love-laces, Don Juans, for the words of this song are the same for both sexes, it's a sexless game, indeed. Thus, "I love you, you are won-derful to me, I was so worried because you didn't telephone me, I

sat all day waiting for your call, I couldn't sleep last night thinking of you, all last week I was dreaming of you," and the whole
juke-box story, may be blighting sentences leading to suicides
in the beginning of a career; but, after a few years, these are
slugs passed about at will, and leading only to a pleasant feeling.
Sometimes, of course, one hands these slugs to the wrong person;
likewise, when one wishes to believe, one believes, alas, these
well-worn stories, and again suffers. But this peculiar usage, common with the sex-careerist and criminal, is intended to save him
from pain, not others.

Amy had a unique idea of sex, beautiful as the finished
workmanship of any born craftsman. She admitted everything—
the troubles of youth, the difficulties of the world, the necessity of
marriage, love of children and husband, woman's traditional place
in the scheme of things, philandering, passion, love-crime and
love-sanctity. She was a kind of Prioress, and not only had her rule
and loved to guide other women, but loved to adjudicate on each
separate case. She trained us for the profession of love.

I won't discuss, at this moment, her other pupil, Lorna—a
girl able to win scholarships, but abysmally stupid; a beautiful girl,
awkward and backward; a girl with society manners who had not
the penetration of an ox. Besides Lorna, Amy had me. She said I
was just a finer Lorna, but educable. She took no notice of my foul
temper; she was sharp and cruel, pointing out all my physical de-
fects and laughing at my strategy. This baby Chesterfield tried to
make me take lessons in dramatic art and in voice, said I must
learn to ride again, play golf, and dance elegantly. I must gesture,
thus and thus; I must not tickle my nose, scratch my head, take off
my shoes; I must make the best of this line, subdue that line, and
watch out for this other line. I must smile without mincing it, and
learn all the proper tones of voice; know how to sound comradely,
languishing, angry, passionate. Nothing must be left to chance, until chance was long past and it was a settled thing. Walk properly,
relax properly, she said; and there is the whole of physical culture.
She was a thin, wiry creature. Do not jig and stretch and put your
arms akimbo, she said; this annoys a man very much, and don't
keep flirting your cigarette, spilling your ashes, jingling your ice,
pulling out strands of hair, dancing on your toes. As to what walk

to cultivate, she made us cultivate the one that suited us; Lorna was tall and hippy, I was the short, Spanish type, but without *déhanchement*. It is useless trying to cultivate the French slippy hip roll if you haven't it; much better the panther-stride or the athletic chop-chop, if it is your type. She had us walking up and down the room, lifting our feet, dragging our feet, going brittle, going languid, passing through a door looking our hostess up and down, leaving a lingering glance behind us, leaving a jolly brisk thank-you behind us; we walked in a long dress and with the brisk flirt-flirt of a tailored suit.

She had no hips, no plumpness, scarcely any breasts, and thin arms, but she was a beautiful dancer, full of muscular giving grace like an under-fed, house-blighted, but passionate Spanish girl at the onset of puberty. She studied our manners, Lorna's and mine, with the utmost particularity. She also performed for us all the usual services, such as telephoning when a beau was there, and pretending to be another beau, sending telegrams at appropriate times, telegraphing flowers (paid for by us, of course), sending orchids. Her genius stooped to anything and included anything. She actually got this heavy-limbed Lorna, a regular Flanders mare, married off, by pretending for about seven months to be an infatuated lover living in Hot Springs. She dug out a forwarding agency, which corresponded with another forwarding agency in Hot Springs, and so Lorna had a pile of love letters which greatly stirred the man she eventually married.

I did not let Amy mix in my affairs as much as this, for I never told her all my affairs. I lied about them, and I fancy Amy knew and respected this. I moved away from the girls after about three months, for, though Amy had a string of men of her own, Lorna was so stupid she lost all hers, and would cast her eyes on mine.

Meanwhile, I copy from an old notebook, in which I began to study Amy's method, some of Amy's tricks, rules, and aphorisms.

AMY'S QUESTIONS AND ANSWERS

Q. He is through with me, I think; should I make it final by asking for my love letters back?

A. Certainly, if they're good ones; you can use them again.

Q. Should I give him his letters back, instead? That would be final!

A. Heavens, no. They're exhibit A.

Q. Should I give his presents back?

A. What, he gave presents? Keep them, and he'll tag along after them.

Q. I love my fiancé, but I love another man too—what shall I do?

A. Throw up a nickel. If it comes down heads, stick to your fiancé; if it comes down tails, stick to your fiancé.

Q. What about a girl most attracts a man?

A. Other men.

Q. But how can you hold a man?

A. If there were any known way, we wouldn't have marriage laws.

Q. Still, I think a child holds a man.

A. How old a child?

Q. Mother says the only way to a man's heart is through his stomach.

A. What's her batting average?

Q. I wouldn't look at another man after I was married.

A. Well, don't let him see it in your face beforehand.

Q. I'm taller than he is; I'm embarrassed when we're walking down the street. What can I do?

A. Walk in the gutter while he walks on the curb; or let him take you about in a wheelchair.

Q. Should I have to do with him? The girls all say he's dangerous; and I feel it.

A. That's Nature's (and the girls') way of advertising their favorites.

Q. Each time he writes to me he asks for something.

A. Keep him in hopes: he'll keep writing.

Q. Can you love two men at the same time?

A. A woman is supposed to be able to love her nine children at the same time.

Q. I decided not to sleep with him before we're married; and he's too poor yet. What shall I do?

A. Conceal your decision from your girlfriends.

Q. He doesn't respect me now that we've slept together.

A. Then it's a good thing you didn't marry him.

Q. He writes me such lovely letters. Do you think he's serious?

A. More is required in a court of law.

Q. He wants me to go to Afghanistan if I marry him.

A. Is it immoral?

Q. I love him, but he doesn't make enough to live on.

A. Marry someone else.

Q. I wrote him a letter saying that I loved him, but he didn't answer; whatever shall I do?

A. Write to him saying you put a letter intended for another in his envelope.

Q. He fights with my mother.

A. Leave them to it; congratulate the winner and sympathize with the loser—separately.

Q. I'm pregnant, and the man left me.

A. Find an old man; he'll be flattered.

Q. Don't you think there is only one true love in a woman's life?

A. Said the man with the pushcart, looking up at the department store.

Q. I don't think you should flatter a man; every woman flatters them.

A. The only thing he'll ever remember about you are your flatteries.

Q. I think there should be give and take; you should point out each other's faults in a spirit of comradeship.

A. What you're describing is the spirit of barroom brawl.

Q. How can you get to know a man you like?

A. Tell some gossip, "I like X"; he'll come round out of curiosity. If it goes on long enough, he'll be fond of you.

Q. It makes me nervous when he talks about love in general and never comes to the point.

A. He's making love to you already when he talks about love in general.

Q. He must like me, because he runs down other women.

A. Never let him run down other women. He's running down you.

Q. I want to get to Act III, and he's so slow, he's still prologuing.

A. You must practice self-control, my child. Never show passion till he thinks he's stirred you to it himself.

Q. I like to have him around, and do things for him. Do you think it's wise?

A. All the fatal women in history have been sluts at home.

Q. He promised to tell me all about himself and he said I should tell him about myself.

A. Let him tell.

Q. How ought I to receive a compliment?

A. With enthusiasm!

Q. I'm very worried about the morality of all this.

A. Beauty gives an absolute power which is above all morality; so does femininity, however.

Q. But you mean I should not be honorable with men?

A. Yes, you should be frank about what you intend to do with him; and about your liking him; but keep the rest in reserve for when you will need it.

Q. What, in general, should be my attitude toward men?

A. Yield to arouse interest, resist when he expects to win; in love itself, *suaviter in modo, fortiter in re*. Further, no man can resist a long siege and even if he laughs about you to cronies, he'll yield to you in private.

Q. Should I give him a gift?

A. Generally, yes; and don't make him wait too long if you've promised it. They're impatient.

Q. But what if he thinks I am forward?

A. The rule in negotiations of this sort is, do not be easily rebuffed, and remember, he may be timid and unsure himself; but do not lay yourself open to rebuff and never let a man insult you. Be persevering, never impatient.

Q. But how, in heaven's name, am I to live through all this? I'm not a Talleyrand.

A. That I can't tell you.

Q. But do you think I'll get a man if I stick to all this?

A. You'll get one anyhow.

Q. But aren't there some general rules to adhere to?

A. Certainly! 1. *Accessibility.* 2. *Exposure*—I mean you must go out and about. 3. *Hardihood*—don't faint with shame at the first setback. 4. *Humanity*—he wants love, too. 5. *The State of Love*—it's so obvious, that while you're pursuing one, you'll probably catch another; so to be in love is a pure advantage on all counts.

Q. Isn't this mere intrigue, trickery, unsuitable for a decent girl?
A. Success is Crime.

Amy had many handsome young men and some middle-aged ones; she acquired all the vices they admired in women. She had constant escorts, fashionable men, titled men, some rich, some not yet rich and some scoundrels; all her men were good at table and at bed, yet as she had a strict code of her own (which she said was necessary for the girl who wanted to carry on this career, without going to pieces), she had a hard time of it. Her allowance was small. She was not a gold-digger and accepted only certain gifts. She let the men know this at the beginning and kept her word, thus her relations were clean, businesslike, friendly, and she had few bad moments. She hoped to do well for herself, by the use of her looks, manner, skill, and intelligence, but she lacked money; and of her eligible swains, those that were poor had to marry money and those that were rich, would not marry, but had a good time.

She was approaching twenty-four, however, and beginning to be anxious about marriage. She had her trousseau (prepared at seventeen for her marriage), and still corresponded with the man she had thrown over at seventeen for a false Rajah of Sarawak. Her intended husband, a dull, sulky, injured, blond Englishman, eventually took her back and she resigned herself to this, promising herself at least the pleasures of Anglo-Indian society. After a year of marriage, she sent me a picture of herself, the young madonna mother, with a charming child. She was at Singapore, and aped every accent, drink, and pose. A few months later and the poor woman wrote that she had met a certain British soldier of fortune, and it was "all barriers down." Yet her theory and practice was good enough. It was simply that at twenty-four one must marry, I suppose. I understand this myself.

At that time, though, what drove me out of the flat was not

doubts about Amy. I believed in her. She had a special adaptation. She was simply forced into marriage against her will, and with her philosophy, naturally accepted it in all its meanings, child, triangle, tea-meetings, and I presume, eventually, disaster. No, it was that I am not a conniving woman; I can skirmish, lay waste, and order hangings, I don't doubt; but it must be on the order of the day, it must be part of a campaign; I'm not a lone-stander, or a guerrilla fighter, or a Chapayev. I'll do anything for any social movement, even marriage, but it must be the healthy movement of others around and with me; otherwise, I am distressed, I do not know where to turn. I do not know on what they base it, those whose vision, courage, or madness leads them to stand out, seek forlorn hopes, or start movements. One is too close to lunacy. I am sure I suffer more than they do; anyone who suffers all the common fate of mankind, the way I do, must suffer more than these hop-heads and lone-rangers.

I learned very little from my Lady Chesterfield. Perhaps the thing that stuck most was the way to come in and out of doors, always, of course, an interesting moment in an evening. No, the trouble here was that we loved too much *en famille*. Sometimes we had to conceal ourselves in the kitchen, while Amy entertained an unusually eligible gentleman in the front; and at given signals we had to appear, like dashing, well-bred girls, to make a background for her; and at other times, Lorna entertained all night there, and I, if forced to stay in, felt my loneliness only too sharply. A middle-aged gentleman with a business in Bridgeport wished to marry her, but was drinking himself to a standstill, and one night about two this lover nearly died in her arms, so that I was obliged to run out in my nightdress to get a policeman; on another occasion, Bobby Thompson who was my regular escort when all else failed, and though he groused and scolded, was the kind of boy I could manage, began to admire Lorna's plump, heavy, motherly beauty. As Bobby and I for some reason were still merely friends, I realized that I was in danger. Lorna did not always take men; sometimes they oozed away toward her like something on a microscope slide: there was that about her that made her life seem purely and naïvely zoological. Men who liked the Easter Island type, wanted her at once; with this great pull, she got into nothing but scrapes, lost her admirers, and received insulting letters; she had no diplomacy, lost her temper, and when a man slighted her, in turn addressed him with the icy tones she otherwise kept only for waiters. In general, her boarding-school manners, except at the beginning of any affair, did her very poor service. Her boarding-school had been middle class and the ladies teaching in it had had nothing to teach but coldness, delicacy, ignorance, and inexperience; and all of these she had acquired. This education was the ruin of her, for she was naturally a sunny, hot-blooded, idle, pleasant simpleton. Nevertheless, without any benefit to herself, she could be a catastrophe, at least temporarily, for other girls; for she was so childishly and casually yielding to every man, that an unsatisfied lover of others often turned to her, awed at the sight of her, pleased at his ready luck. Poor creature, she was credulous and believed that every affair was a love affair, every wantoning man her fate. Seeing that she might take Bobby to herself in this way, I at once turned practical and began to take romantic walks with Bobby in the park and streets, when we talked of the misfortunes of our youth, our poverty, our problems, the mystery of our future. Bobby was of rather a melancholy turn, said that he needed help in his medical career, a long grueling one, since he was weak in the chest, had a "spot on his lung," and had to be nursed through life at least until he achieved the age of thirty, when, it seemed, most boyhood weaknesses passed. He could not marry till then, he said, and casual affairs were so unsatisfactory. With this I agreed, adding rather bitterly that for a girl the worst weakness was her bachelorhood and that this did not even pass off at thirty, unless she was lucky enough to get the right man; although the word "thirty" passed my lips with something of a smile, for I did not suppose that I would be unmarried at thirty. Bobby and I agreed with each other and comforted each other in this way, evening after evening, and I began to take a fresh interest in him. It was almost the first time I had had a serious and yet platonic friendship with an old acquaintance and I asked myself why; the thought began dimly that perhaps this was it, the real affair which would end in settling down for life. Naturally, once this thought had germinated, I looked forward to Bobby with more interest and pleasure than ever before. He made some parade of his chest-ailment, that was one of his faults perhaps, and would often get his parents to take him away for a week or two to a resort, thus interrupting his studies; they pitied him, his mother especially making him the center of her life. I had not met the parents and got the impression that they felt any girl was a danger to him, a suspicious character, in fact; this irritated me and if anything, increased my need for him. I could see that they were spoiling him and that if some girl did not take him in hand soon, his parents would soon have unfitted him for ordinary life. Of course, if they wished to have a hypochondriac, bachelor son on their hands—but perhaps they did; this is the bad side of parenthood: they go into this business blindly, invest in a commodity in which there is usually no profit, and then feel they can't give up the investment, they can't cut a loss. At any rate, with a daredevil feeling (knowing Mrs. Thompson was the kind of mother that reads her son's letters), I wrote to my friend a spirited, intelligent, comradely letter, and it must have caught him in a weak, lonely mood, for he at once wrote back to me.

Dear Letty,

I was reading the letter you wrote me today and thought you are really tops to write this way; we know each other pretty well and yet I like anyone who takes time and trouble for me and that person seems to me a particularly human person. Yes, I know all are all-too-human: all would do something for you if—but in the great quest who does things? I travel and suffer physical discomforts gladly because without food and shelter there are some people too. The benches in the parks are hard—there is independence, but such things cannot appeal to me; it is too impersonal; all things for me must have a personal quality, even the ballet, even the opera, that is why I like your letter, so truly comradely interested in me. Others pretend to admire objectively: the whistling, stamping, bravos nauseate. Because—a crowd projection of the ego? A prostitute stops and discusses her trade with a man while the pigeons wheel and the competing pavement pounder flips her hips: all for self, and least said when acknowledged; but this is triumphant independence. Lowest form of life? Or highest? The triumph of the lonely

477

key turning, the lonely floorboard creaking, the rat squeaking. So much triumph, but human. Alone in a house here; my people out. Thinking of my relations in New York and alone—independence, dependent. The opera, the theater, the movie in the greasy palm of the town. Cultureville! But in the great still empty Victorian house (unparented) is the triumph of independence—dependent. Think—an interstate license and dope in the night to keep awake as I travel across the U.S. The rain, the fog, with me, challenging our triumph. Virility, ability, sterility—all independence! The room in the Village and the bedbugs of others, the stains, the canteen of the moment, and New York and life and triumph. So much that was, until came—(what?).

The lizard on the caked earth: bordels—with other names, in the alleyways, loose-lipped, powder-caked, rouged, greasy-haired—oh, god, a million people and places and still nothing to cling to—independence still. "But how, when, where—" a girl begging, entreating—"here, now, with me—" One goes, doesn't want, yields, the mind is still that—independent. Not to be able to give up and not to want to give up. Oh, and where else—everywhere—here with parents, there with you—You see, Letty? Yes, you see. You nearly understand, as near as one can—and do not ask for love, for sadness, for understanding—there are girls like that. The magnificent modern girl. Sometimes the doubt, sometimes the doubt, sometimes the old nostalgia, and the registered faces and the unregistered real names—yes, in the night and much you would do in the night (in dreams, in alleyways) not to be independent. But it remains. Yes, I'm scared. And where is the necessity? Tell me where my love lies. Always, everywhere, here, now, when?

Why am I answering your letter like this, Letty? Am I trying to sell myself to you or another? But then, where is independence? The commodity is sold, acquired. And this is a salesman's world. Things seen, seen things done, done; all acquired; independence lost. Yes, try to hold off. Necessity to write. Life is not an independence. Try to go back, by writing. Try to triumph. That is my mood. Do you like it,

Letty? I don't care. I should be back around the end of the
month and I'll see you; telephone you, we'll go somewhere
together. Yes, I'll say, for god's sake, let us talk but not about
independence.

Bobby T.

I was thrilled by this letter which showed such tenderness, for
Bobby, and looked forward to his arrival back in town with as
much longing, love, and hope as a child. It seemed to me that this
man who was so reticent, so repressed and suffocated by his parents, and yet who could pour out his feelings to me this way, was
coming closer to me than any boy I had known till then. He arrived in town suddenly, telephoned the same evening. I made a
rendezvous at a favorite bar of ours, and met him there full of excitement. He looked well, was well dressed, and as I approached
him through the crowded alleys of the smoke-filled bar I thought
to myself that he was one of the handsomest men I had ever
seen—his only weakness was that he was too popular. We kissed
passionately, he seemed as glad to see me as I was to see him; and
in the first few words, I could see he had missed me; he did not ask
what I had been doing, which was just as well, but plunged into
an account of his life with his parents—he could not object, he
sympathized with them, he realized he was all in all to them; yet
what a bore for him: his mother did not realize that he was a man,
especially that he had any moral, mental, or sexual life. We had
several drinks and came very close to each other: we both admitted that the pretense we had made (and gallantly made) of holding
the platonic pose was *plus plat que tonique* (more flat than tonic)
and that the attempt at being disinterested friends didn't work; but
he proceeded to tell me again that the future was for him a closed
book and no attempts should be made by us to read it; we must
just read his life page by page. I accepted this, since, somehow, the
thought of not being in some way concerned with him, or hearing
from him (which was to be my punishment if I turned sibyl and
tried to look into his future), or seeing him, filled me with so
much gloom and even despair that I could not face it and I quite
honestly confessed as much to him. "Let's face the present as well
as we can," I said, then, and I refused to cringe or worry too much,

479

getting a little older perhaps. At that moment, while putting on a brave front, I felt sad that the whole episode was not transferred some four, five, or six years later, so that he felt six years older. As things stood then, he was an obsession of mine and yet, too young for me; I understood perfectly what mood of youth and even ignorance prompted that kind of letter—the one about "independence"—he shied off it and yet he needed it; he was too young to look at marriage with anything but fear: that is the trouble with these mother-jailed boys. He was subject to so many fetishisms— of family, of youthful ideals, of the idea of youth itself and as a character—I knew he was a Frédéric Moreau—and when does the *Education Sentimentale* end for a Frédéric Moreau? And yet it is a charming type of man; a dangerous one for me, for this sweet, moody self-involvement aroused that warning signal in me—the sympathetic, pitying mother feeling; I felt myself yielding and yet felt that he was sensitive and needed protection. How well I knew the signs! And with all that, this hesitating and naïve youth made me feel most alive, vibrant, anything I wanted to feel, I sparkled darkly; and I had the same effect on him. This was no silly affair, I felt, like those of the past year, and no puzzlement and flirting with a Lovelace, as the affair with Luke was; it was something decisive, which, however, masked itself (for the sake of our youth) under the figure of indecision. And, true to my pattern, I too whirled around, unable quite to make up my mind about him. But how real this was compared with the plotting and comparing of notes at Amy's. I could not bear it; I made up my mind at that moment, in that bar, to move at once. And, of course, the boy was behind it.

It was so patent to me that Bobby was in love with me—though he wouldn't admit it, and in fact went out of his way elaborately to disclaim it. But I was afraid that this refusal to admit his love might eventually lead him completely out of touch with me, and that he might thoughtlessly fall first to a Lorna and then to any number of mother-substitutes. I thought it all over as we sat face to face, laughing with each other, and I asked myself whether I was willing to wait the few years—depending on his family's decisions about him and the vacillations of his own mind, about his profession—the few years he would need to bring him to better ways of thinking. For what he now proposed to me was just what the others proposed, to live with him on a day-to-day basis; here in my bed today and gone away tomorrow with scarcely an "I'll be seeing you"; and I of course with no claim whatever upon him. We walked about a bit and I went home, the question still unanswered; but I had such a feeling of revulsion when I entered the flat where the girls were—Lorna lying back on the couch in her favorite reflective mood, her long, fine silken legs swinging, asking for the fiftieth time how the Attaché could possibly like to do what he did like to do—that was to drink one of the strangest fluids on earth—when I saw this scene, I felt so much disgust at this sexless, dull, littered world of wishing, pettifogging girls that I gave them notice at once and I put it in terms they could understand, "I am going to live with Bobby; he wants us to have a place to ourselves."

The girls made no objection, perhaps had felt the overcrowding that I felt too; they were even very pleased that I was making a settled connection, they thought it very suitable; and Lorna promised to help me look, the next day. I told Mother nothing of all this, for every new move of mine seemed to her an inexplicable wickedness, a brainless escapade.

I took a small flat up three flights of stairs in an old house in Chelsea, only on account of the cheap rent; the house was seedy and the staircarpet filthy, and the place full of rats and other vermin, the flooring half gone, and the ceiling not painted but patched. Yet it was opposite a college garden, full of sweet air in summer and not so far from the shops. Moreover, it is a home district, with children thick in the streets, a clear view toward the docks, very often sea-skies, and an unworldliness, a suburban air. I liked it very much and felt as if in a cleaner world. Lorna, who always believed in the new, made an offer to come there and stay with me, saying she would not be in the way and would absent herself whenever Bobby came. She was a good housewife, would look after the cleaning and house-keeping for me, and pay her share—but this I firmly turned down. I was glad to be alone again, and realize the strain put on my temper by the past few months of bivouacking with my own sex. I took the flat at once, making few comments about the appearance of it, made arrangements to move in what furniture I had stored, and asked for a telephone. This done, I leaned over the crumbling window sill, breathed in the dusty air, and looked friendly upon the round-limbed, dirty children in the street. I liked children and now wished to have some of my own, partly to have my own share of woman's life and partly for the parade. A young girl, newly married and expecting her baby, is simply the center of life to everyone that knows her. I was keenly jealous of the young married women in their dragging, dragged waistbands and heavy bodies. "Look, my coming child, my baby"; this is the best of possessions for a young woman.

My things came in, I worked nights, and over the weekend got the place straight, allowed Lorna to hang some curtains for me, and then put away my sackcloth and ashes, my young girl's weeds in the attic closet, and took out my Penelope's spider web, refusing to give myself the time to brood over anything or doubt. Of course, the first time he visited me, it was all over, we became lovers, officially; and (whether it was the season, the day, or the man) I realized that he was the man I really wanted. He was very constant to me for some time, which surprised me; I had not thought he had it in him; and then he left me alone for a week without even a telephone call. I was depressed, of course, but followed a new plan I had thought out, during these days—for I knew I was playing a dangerous game with this man that I wanted to marry. I telephoned Luke Adams, told him I was alone, and asked him to come to see me. I felt weary at the idea of taking up this old unhappy affair, but it was no longer dangerous; and the whole thing was an antidote to Bobby's not unnatural unkindness. I thought, this is my line, this is the only form of solace I know; I'd rather contemplate my navel than think of suicide, and I know well enough that Bobby will visit me again when it suits him. But I had to wait some evenings for Luke to visit me; I waited in the lamplight. Hardly anyone yet knew my telephone number, and I had time to think over every aspect of my present life. It was not that I felt I had gone astray; it was just that seeing married people passing below me in the street, thinking of Aunt Phyllis, Aunt Amabel, Aunt Dora, hearing the couples come home from work and light the stoves and rattle the iceboxes, I sometimes wondered at the infinite distance between the state of not being married—and what-

ever the gradation of not being married, it made no difference
—and the state of being married. How did people bridge the gap?
It seemed to happen to others—most others; never to me; and I
thought it very peculiar. I couldn't figure it out; perhaps I was
too young, anyway; but it savored to me of magic, and I felt very
miserable that in this modern world something so primary, this
first of all things to a woman, smacked so strongly of the tribal
priest, the smoky cult, the tom-tom, the blood sacrifice, the hidden mystery. It didn't seem fair. We should have abolished all that
with enlightenment.

One night, unexpectedly, as was his custom, Luke Adams came
to me. I saw him first, stooping lazily along, up the street and almost suffocated with joy, a kind of terror, and a kind of indignation; but, feeling as I did, I threw myself very hungrily into the
business of the moment, and enjoyed the pleasure with him more
than before. Perhaps it was Bobby, and I had matured a little.

It was hard for me to look back, even two hours afterwards, and
think that it had taken place, and it is hard for me now to remember it; but this victory of each over each filled us with bliss.
Leaving me, he became moral, "Now, work hard, Letty; you're all
alone, don't go to pieces; young girls—you know—all alone—Jesus
—this life—this Village life—"

And smiling in his dark, demoniac face, sweetly, mildly, he
shrugged on his clothes. I said, "Luke, I know that *omnis homo
post coitum castus est,* but why must you be such a fraud?"

He laughed and promised to come back to see me some time.
At first I did not mind, and for some days afterwards when I
walked in the streets, I floated on a cloud; I did not look at anyone
else; I almost forgot Bobby. In the office not only was I an angel of
good humor, but accomplished three times the work of anyone
else. After three or four days, however, I was surprised not to receive their telephone calls and gradually sank into depression and
became agitated.

It happened that I went out once or twice in the following week
to studio parties, and fat-chewing political groups where I exhibited a foul bad temper, and hardly recognized myself; I really
seemed to have Luke's spirit in me, I said what I thought he would
say when tired or bored. I would come out into the streets, into the

new June night, still floating with bud scales, once more bitterly unhappy, my anger raging in me like a fire. Is not his seed like a fire? All about him, his word, his smile, his hypocrisy, his darkness, was like a fire; and I burned because I could not tell people, I have Luke. I came home once in the morning and saw two street lovers getting together on the steps of a church; the little cigarette glows jigged in the dark and described, in arcs, their weavings and embraces. Another time, a man groaned in an areaway. I did not care. I could have passed murderers, not only men with the blue devils. I was possessed with this man. One night, about two, I walked over to the slum he lived in and, taking a hand mirror out of my purse, threw it into the window of their room on the second floor. The window was open; they were in bed inside; I heard it tinkle on the floor. There were voices. I looked up. He came to the window and looked down. He saw a woman. But what woman? He had so many women. He only knew it was one of his women because of the smashed mirror from a lady's handbag, and so did she, of course. I went back home and cried in fresh agony, thinking of the scene, the conjugal bed, the open window on the summer night, the jag of glass flying through the air, smashing on the floor, the delicate tinkle, and him leaping from bed. If only it could have planted itself in her eye, her cheek, her breast! But it just sang its little note like a mosquito and lay there on the floor of their room.

I recognized that Luke was poison to me, and tried to forget him by going out with other boys from college days and others met at parties. These weakling boys, looking for an easy girl, who thought they had so much of me, had nothing, and I did not see them again, very often, when I had once had them for the night. I forgot them, I forget their names. It would seem to me that I had forgotten Luke for a few days, a week, even more; and then it would all come back. I wrote to him to ask him to come to me. He would turn up, in his desultory, regretful way, with his cracker-barrel philosophy; and so it went on for nearly the whole of that year. I struggled fiercely, perhaps stupidly, to make him break with his wife whom I now hated; but he only spoke of her motherhood. This was the bitterest thing of all for me, "What about my motherhood?"

"Letty, dear, you are so young—you'll marry." He caressed me vaguely, smiled affectionately. He was not only born for love, to trap women, make them love him and make them faithful even when he betrayed them, but he had studied his art, and when making love was obedient to my whims, delicious as a boy. He was slight, formed like a Hawaiian adolescent, hairless, a bluish-bronze, smooth and muscular in all his parts and always with the feral, simple grace of a native swimmer, and a face that seemed ages old, though boyish. His straight black hair and the dark eye in yellowish eyeball seemed darker, stranger, when he was naked. He was a poor dancer, but made graceful gestures, and when he made these motions, the childish uncouthness was also charming.

I did not know what to do. He was too old for me, but I would have done anything to get him; and I had the feeling that he could have been bought, if I had had a little more money. He would have gone with me—not to marry, certainly, but perhaps for life, depending on the money, if I had money. I had not the money, and I tried to console myself with others.

I fell very low. My friends were getting married, and I could not understand why I did not, for some of them, without question, were duller and plainer than me. At this time I went out a few times with a handsome, stupid boy called Bingham. I had met him at the Tweed and Silk Shop, where he went shopping with a wealthy aunt. I had been to the opera with him a few times, standing up in the top gallery. I had had a few love passages with Bingham, who was, to look at, almost our American ideal, a blond stripling, combination of collar-ad and halfback, a little etiolated, perhaps, in the atmosphere of college and elegant aunts; I now decided to get married to him. I thought, Grandfather Morgan was no great shakes, no doubt, as a youth, but Cissie not-yet Morgan looked ahead. I have never yet had the vision to see a good husband in a college boy, or fat aunt's effete hanger-on, but I will do so this time. If he isn't good material, he's as good as another, and his relatives are rich. He seemed madly in love with me, called me every name under the sun, pretty, beautiful, charming, fit to be a princess, his ideal and the rest of it (though, no doubt, under special conditions), until I not only looked upon him as someone I could manage, but began to have the old romantic dreams about him. I truly saw once more the dancing firelight by the Christmas tree, the charming young mother in a soft dress, the charming but already grave young father, the one, or two children, beautiful, blond, photogenic. When he said, "We could live together, forever," I thought, He means it; and though he is of a weak, yielding nature, he only needs me to turn into a reasonably good businessman. I went out with him several times with the single idea of having him commit himself to this idea of marriage, a happy life together; and when it seemed to me that he could be gentled into it, and only held back because of the fear all young men have of marriage, I made an appointment with him in the Jumble Shop in the Village, and there invited my father and mother and Grandmother Morgan. They were already installed, as I had directed, before we got there, and we all sat down together, as it were, accidentally. After the first courtesies and the drinks, Solander said, "Well, young man, I hear that you want to marry my daughter." Bingham was of the nature I had supposed, for he answered, after hesitation, "We haven't put it in such concrete terms; what do you say, Letty?"

I said, "As for me, I would like to be a housewife for a year or more; or forever. I'm afraid, under my modern veneer, I'm a cave-woman."

There was a pause, and then my mother said, "Letty said something about your getting married right away; surely you are both too young to take up such responsibilities."

Bingham said, "But there's no talk of that. If we are married, I'm sure we would both work. The truth is that, at present, Letty is the only one of us that really works. Of course, she has no intentions—even if we were thinking of it—of quitting work."

Grandmother Morgan said absently, rolling her eyes round the café, "When you get married, but good and tight, legally, I'll give you a *suit* of bedroom furniture, Letty."

"Bingham can get a job at any time in such-and-such," I said, referring to a theatrical agency, "through his family. We could set up housekeeping very cheaply. And my idea isn't to work. It's to settle down and become a real wife. I haven't learned that yet, and it's something I'd like to learn."

Solander kept laughing agreeably, and as he had never been

in this situation before, he said his lines in a very crude, funny way, "So you have nothing to keep my daughter on, Bingham—Bingham what? Letty told me your name, of course, but I forget."

Bingham now became gloomy and said, "We don't have to get married; there's no rush; we just mentioned it, vaguely—but we're not in a position to."

I now lost my head, "Oh, Bingham, but I do want to get married. I'm tired of hanging around; I'm a normal woman."

He seemed puzzled, but he regarded Grandmother Morgan with speculative eyes.

My mother said heavily, "It seems a most impractical idea."

"Yes, doesn't it," said Bingham, looking at her eagerly.

My dear father at once said, and laughed, "Yes, but they're youngsters; to them it's the most practical thing going, Mattie."

Bingham looked at him, without hostility, "It isn't for me. I don't know where Letty got the idea I was so crazy about getting married. We ought to get ourselves settled, we're young yet, and I ought to get myself a job, and I think Letty ought to go back to college."

I said, "Oh, Lord! I'm sick of kid-stuff. All the rest was just playtime, experiment. I'm ready to be a woman now. No more political whirlpools, no more slogans and shibboleths. I ask them for bread and they give me a banner. I want to take in *Good Housekeeping* and wear a smock in five months."

My father ordered some more drinks, frowning a little when I chose the most expensive drink on the list (but it was a habit with me and I felt that men at least owed me this). Grandmother Morgan was studying Bingham sharply, as if to find his weakest spot. Mathilde sighed, "I don't think Bingham wants to get married; I think it's all a misunderstanding, and I don't think Letty should. She has no sense. I don't want her to make a mistake—"

My father looking across at her, Mother ceased. Bingham said, "Yes, it's a misunderstanding—of some sort—"

I said, "But I understand myself very well. Bingham and I want to settle down. All we want is a start in life."

Father said, "I don't want you to give up work, and I think you ought to learn something, Letty," but he laughed good-naturedly. "However, I know what kids are—"

Bingham had been frowning, and turned to me, saying in a different tone of voice, "Letty, did you know your folks were coming here?"

My father at once said, "Oh, no, it was just an accident. We just filed in like this, family style, the dear old Jumble, it's our hang-out in the Village, and it is yours, I suppose—who doesn't? It isn't like old Montparnasse where there are dozens of cafés and everyone has his pet; here there are practically no places to go—" and he kept on like this until the others had found their way to composure.

Shortly after, my mother, much annoyed with me, as I could see, left with her mother, and Solander, after paying for the drinks, left by himself.

Bingham said, "Well, it was a trap. Why did you do that?"

I simpered away, saying, There is such a thing as an understanding and these are modern times, aren't they; don't tell me I have to sit round making tea-cozies until you go down on bended knee.

Bingham showed some firmness, which let me see I had not been wrong about him. We had a few more drinks and then left on our separate ways. He realized at the end that it was a compliment to him, that I liked him well enough to do this for him.

But the truth is, when I got home to my lonely pillow, to what was little more than a couple of hall bedrooms thrown together, and when I thought of the humiliation and what I had thrown away, family, the easy support of Grandmother Morgan and her clan, my mother's kindness, and what I had been through with men, one and another, from Amos to Bingham, I wondered what prospects there could be for me in life. Could I live through the degradation? Wouldn't it be better to commit suicide, than to put up with this a day longer?

I went deeper. I asked myself, What is the matter with me? Am I corrupt, stupid, wanton, unlucky, somehow unattractive? Much more ordinary girls than I am are getting married, and I even know one kid who's going to have a baby next month—and here am I, Letty Fox, without luck. I'm nineteen. I no longer feel fresh. What will happen to me? There must be some way out—but is there? I can't pick up a man on the street and marry some poor workman and live all my life in Chelsea and go to the free clinic to have my babies. I'm not out of the slums, to be glad to wash floors for a wretched clerk or bartender or butcher's assistant in order to have a position in the world; I'm not déclassée; I'm not mad with ambition or talent. I'm an ordinary girl, gay, hard-working, good-natured and pleasant. Men like me. Heads turn when I go into a restaurant. Men look after me, in fact, a bit too much, as if I were a planked steak. Then, what is it—what is it—why am I just as much a failure as a Bowery bum?

This was the first night I ever thought seriously of suicide. Another thing that depressed me was the way the others went more or less smugly on their nondescript ways, my mother, Solander, Grandmother Morgan, now at her sixth or eighth beau; and what was I to them? What they to me? What a world and what a life! I had started out with the best intentions and did not wish to scheme. I wanted a clean, vigorous life. I then had the usual fantasies. I'll be a nurse, sacrifice myself, organize something or other, become known as a woman superior to human follies; but what was the use? I was born to live with all the ardor of my blood and to mate and breed, and laugh at my grandchildren. These monastic notions were not for me.

38

I WAS discouraged and had no hope. Why work? I threw up my job at the Tweed and Silk, where I had quarreled with Mrs. Patrice and where I saw too much of Bingham, spent a few weeks scraping the bottom of my pocket and getting credit at the grocer's (an easy thing for me), wearing slippers with holes and turned heels, as my habit was when I was down on my luck. Papa became anxious, fearing he would now have to set to work to support me again, so he prodded me until I got a job, this time on a journal working for racial equality. I always enjoyed a new job. It made me forget my troubles outside. There were times when I worked till two in the morning at the office, merely not to have to face my flat, where the wraiths of my follies were installed. I missed telephone calls, left letters unanswered. This was my cure.

Meanwhile, I became furiously engrossed in my new job and not only started to write a novel called *Intolerance*, which began in a little town in New Jersey, where a crazed religious printer, a nasty young boy, and an impure old maid started trouble, but took up the question of Zion and Liberia, ideas I had not come across before.

I met a young Jew named Salo, slender, slick-haired, elegant, an idealist; and a young Negro, in color like bronze, tall, smooth; and I got from them, as well as from torrents of reading, all I could about the Zionist and Liberian movements. The British supported Palestine, and Abraham Lincoln himself had thought that the Negroes should have a black state, preferably in Africa. This was what we had to go on. I was against both these ideas at the beginning, but the joy I felt in my regeneration gave me a false enthusiasm for them. I liked both these boys and created no little jealousy and race prejudice by my impartial friendship. Encouraged by Salo,

I wrote a pro-Zionist short story of quite sickly sentiment; and nearly went to the length of becoming an explorer, colonizer or the like, when it came to Liberia. I decided that I had found my walk in life. I would become an expert upon things African.

I started digging on Liberia, and unearthed tracts, broadsides, muck-raking, government puffs. I got up a theory which I wrote out and intended to print in a pamphlet. I suppose the theory was obvious as hell to most educated people. Briefly, it was this. Africa, more than any other unexplored continent or country, is in for a tremendous industrialization. The tse-tse fly will not stop capital from flowing there. Once capital discovers that not only is there immediate money to be made there, i.e., gold, which comes out of the mines daily, or palm oil which oozes out of every uncultivated bit of land, but a tremendous and constant productivity, unimaginable raw materials (contrary to the remarks of several scholarly debunkers), the largest hydro-electric potential in the world (scarcely harnessed, save in spots), and a great labor potential, which has to be concentrated to be effective, but which, divorced from its surroundings, will have only work to fall back upon, there will be a rush for investment and development. If the world picture moves faster than we think, and things start humming in Europe, given a war with a short, snappy, undemocratic end, and reinvestment after it, all over the world, Africa will soon be industrialized. Whatever the picture in Europe, they'll want colonies, dependencies, or (if socialist) friendly recipients of their goods. Then, in the latter case, it won't be for the benefit of the few, but for the African people. The Soviet Union managed to make folk cultures flourish and at the same time industry was born, and grew a thousand-fold. After all, the Sahara desert is a small part of Africa, and even that is being bridged, if the leisurely French ever get that Trans-Saharan railroad finished.

So, I was convinced that that continent would witness the next great development of imperialism (with the vague possibility that it would only be industrialization with socialism) and that a mighty struggle would result. The natural education for the people, break-up of the tribes, concentration into large settlements, etc., would follow, and more; so that there is in Africa a tribal disintegration by force, by chicane, by associations for profit or force between chieftains and so on.

Not that I was absorbed by it, but I was reborn. Everyone forgot, in a moment, my troubles, and we all began to discuss, in the family, the African problem.

I went to Harlem and to a couple of Leftist shows with this Negro boy, Jeff Mossop. It turned out that he didn't believe in Liberia at all, but was a skeptic, a radical, and a poet; but he had a fine appearance, spoke musically and with singular dignity, and was an asset to the sheet; they felt that they had to have at least one Negro as an editor. Jeff, of course, became sentimentally fond of me, even more, quite attached to me; and as he had spent some time in the West Indies (which he disliked) and had easily picked up French—for he had about the finest ear I ever came across—we spoke quite a lot in this language. He knew enough to know that the well-educated Frenchman and Englishman of color speak a fine Parisian French and was anxious to practice as much as he could with me; this was, naturally, partly an excuse. Perhaps it was partly policy, for the dark-skinned French and English feel that they have a better social position in the U.S.A. than the native Negro. Jeff was extremely handsome, tall, with an oval face and large sparkling eyes, framed in curly hair and with a small, sparse, curly beard. He was not a native New Yorker, although a Northerner. It is hard for a stranger to know where he can dine and where not, if he is a Negro, and so I piloted him round town a little. I did not think about this one way or another, as I was brought up with absolutely no race prejudice (although Mark Twain says that every one of us has one, without knowing it—but what was mine?). But Jeff Mossop liked it in me, and being a true sentimental, took an ardent interest in me; pretty soon we were thee-ing and thou-ing in French. When he left for a trip to the South, in order to get some local knowledge on racial antagonism, and when he experienced for the first time the true bitterness and shame and fright of the people of his skin, I received a number of letters from him, of such a loving and devoted nature that I made up my mind to cut off relations with him, for I saw when he returned he would propose to me. He was single, very idealistic, and a poet, and I was a beautiful young woman; this was enough. He had some wonderful vision of the future where no hate would exist, only love between peoples and races; this was fine enough, but I live too much in the here and now; this is my great weakness. It happened that I received the first of his letters in the same mail with one of Bobby Thompson's. I was longing to hear from my dear Bobby and yet the difference in tone impressed me; and for the first time, perhaps, I saw this selfish, weak, spoiled lad in his true light; and yet with insight into his nature came the desire to marry him. Of course, I opened the letter from my old sweetheart, Bobby, first, even though I knew quite well beforehand the type of disappointing, self-centered garrulity that would greet me. This is what Bobby had written the morning before, from the country house where he was summering with his adoring mamma. His tone had changed somewhat since we had gone together seriously; he now thought of me as being madly engrossed with him.

Dear Letty,

Subtlety is not one of my dominant characteristics; but nevertheless I can't get myself to call you a no-good-bitch for not writing. There are so many variables, besides your natural arbitrariness, that reservation of condemnation, castigation, and plain complaint will wait until I definitely don't hear from you for three, count them, months. Then, with the aid of a dictionary which I don't have now, your hide will burn. (It'll be Farmer and Henley's good book of bad slang.)

If you only realized how secluded we are, how vacuous our existence is, how lonely. It is away from everything, your pity alone would prompt you to at least let me know how lousy your place is, where you saw Luke Adams and your other suckers last, how the others are doing and especially, what's noo along the wires and especially "line" but not plainly, abstrusely. Haven't seen a decent newspaper, pamphlet, or spoken to a knowing soul. If you know any good people living near here, please let me live again; being confined here for the summer with a bunch of morons certainly does not result in any moral or mental stimulation. The town library is all the way over the other side of the place and almost a physical impossibility for me to get to from here. If you want to be especially kind, you could send me a couple of the latest books, doesn't your papa get them for review? Considered intellectual that is; I promise to read them. Don't know what struck me; rotten climate. In 1934 the War Dept. did away with the use of saltpeter in the food; however, maybe they use it round here, subversively, my manhood is gone, dormant, or wasting. I wake up, I am alive, but what's most interesting in me (probably) is dead: just is represented by his absence. All day lying, reading, sunning, swimming, presence of girls in sunsuits—and what then? The father of all living is dead. God have mercy on my soul if this is actually so because of my physical state. But they say the opposite; this was one thing I counted on, if I turned into a real lunger. I do not choose to live and yet be—pardon all this garbage, but am tired, have had no exercise worth a centimeter of the party Casanova you said I would turn into. Some garbage! not to say worse. What a life.

As ever, B.

P.S. I wrote another communication which I tore up and bloody nearly well tore up this one: the fact is I do nothing but crossword puzzles (hate them) or tell dirty stories (don't like them either—both too much effort) or write to you what I think of you, and tear that up. Tell me what I can do? Don't. I know it only too well.—B.

It took me a long time to really absorb this stricken note from my poor friend and it was midday before I read, without real sympathy, the sweet letter from my living bronze, Jeff Mossop.

(ABOUT TO LEAVE NEW YORK.)

Letty,

I make a gift to thee, back again, of an image of thine own; "my life is too vivid when my eyes are shut, my heart beats too much at night." Why did it have to be, Letty, that always since I can remember my life is nothing, Letty, but an immense desire stretched toward a very little thing, a very delicate, weightless thing called Happiness? All the stages of my life, Letty—since this childhood, too bled by tears, too regulated by severity, too fevered with silence, my infancy without infancy, my infancy which flowed away to the rhythm of dull days which were crushed by the inexorable severity of a man, my father, whom I cannot hate and for which I therefore hate myself: from then, up to the man I am now, nourished on repressions, this repression, Letty, that is nothing, in short, but a great ungratified desire.

But why do I hesitate to speak of myself? Perhaps the day will come—close, it may be, Letty, close, dost thou desire it as I do?—where we will make an exchange of our lives. Then wilt thou not give me, in thy voice with its tranquil inflections, this little girl again which thou wast, the girl with the long imp's curls, where floated an extravagant forbidden sequin butterfly, gift of Mme. Pauline, and who sang in the country around dear, far Paris, *Meunier, tu dors!* and *Auprès de ma blonde!* And I will give thee a boy drunk with the country air and the leaves and grasses of his birthplace, who runs after the bearded goat and the glittering insects, in the loud insobriety of a free day, a day of unchecked childhood, on my family's farms. But now that the memory of minutes too brief come down upon me from the obscured stars of Harlem, now that the night swells with all that which was "the hope of a tomorrow of dream," why must it be that there sings in my ear now the vibrant note of burning sorrows to come? From the closet of the night, orchestrates itself the symphony of beautiful dreams poignarded—it's an obscure theme, a *de profundis* of the living who sing with unrecorded voices, who are the voice of all the desires that one thought, perhaps, soon to be attained, married, possessed, and loved by the method of the heart. They drag along now in the silence and in the night, their funeral procession of mourning crape. Good night, Letty. I will tell thee what follows in my sleep, which the thought of thee will fill with a great population of fair Lettys. Good night, Letty.

Jeff.

I did not even show this letter around, for I did not know the temper of my family when it came to a man of this kind. But I felt the pleasure of being loved again and resolving to organize my life better from now on, I made up my mind to write a novel during the evenings when I was alone.

For my novel (on *Intolerance*) I had begun at the beginning, and made some notes for myself.

1. I must know different social sets. I am confined to one only, i.e., understand emotions only on faces of *my* class.
2. Must study anthropology, ethnology.
3. Anatomy, diagnosis by face, gait.
4. Current union, trade, and intellectual papers for phraseology—which avoid. Cant phrases, fads, movie wisecracks.
5. Hold forth on topic, like Liberia, in meetings, homes, to draw reactions. Slogans, headlines. Cover sleep.
6. National traditions, sexual traditions. Is there a true individual underneath? Seek.
7. Basic beliefs of all people, e.g., he is special individual, so is his wife; others are mere types.

I worked, and the events of the few preceding weeks began to lift from me like a fog-bank from a harbor. I was back in the world. I resolutely forgot the nights and days when I had sat gibbering with misery over men who were not there.

39

JACKY, now at college, and uncertain of her career, came to see me often, because I was alone at this new place. She had disliked both the Jane Street place and my friends, Amy and Lorna. She thought I was getting into trouble in Jane Street; and then she wanted to talk about herself and could not, with Amy and Lorna giving her advice about profane love. Jacky was on the classic side. She was handsome now, with dark gold hair still done in a plait crowning the oval head, hair that would become chestnut, gradually; her oval eyes fully opened, her long cheeks which in old age would droop into dewlaps, now were full, fresh, sensual. She had, above all, a remarkably beautiful skin, thick and translucent. When she was dull or dogged, her skin was dull as old paint; but at other times, she was radiant. She was well formed, more slender than myself, with an upward tug of the members which gave her an air of youthful pride. She was vain. Sometimes she would condescend to shine at a family party, but had the most curious vanity of all: she deserted the young men who clustered around her (Aunt Phyllis's days were over) for the older men; and, as there were several brilliant men in our circle, like Froggart, Gondych, Froggart's cousin, Solander, my father, and Banks, the lawyer, not to mention Joseph Montrose, all middle-aged men, she was the fancy of these men. No one else troubled about them at all. I, for one, could not bear them. But Jacky's wits led her astray. She wanted to take each clever man on, in hand-to-hand fight, and then in a general melee. She considered herself a wit. I was anxious about her future, for she had no aim. One week it was languages, the next, medicine; and the next, it was poetry that she would take up.

She came to see me one evening at the end of June as soon as college had closed. We had something to eat off the hotplate I had in my kitchenette, and sat at the window wondering what to do. I picked my words with Jacky, who, though no fool, had not had my experiences. Eventually, I got bored and would take her out to the movies. She generally paid. She was generous, even spendthrift. I had much to do with money, living alone as I did. But this evening, with her handsome, old-gold crowned face turned to the sunset across the Hudson, she was speaking so much of herself in a disordered, interesting fashion, that I thought I ought to stay there and listen to her. After all, the day must come soon when she would wake up and some man would disenchant her. Also, lately I had suffered such a revulsion from the small-minded counsels of Amy and my own horrid misadventures, that I was delighted to listen to the naïve clatter of a young girl. What a beautiful girl says can never really be stupid, whereas with a plain girl one always feels that what she is really saying is, "I am a failure."

She had been watching a man, an old carcass, who was sitting on the stoop opposite, leaning on a knotted stick and occasionally opening his mouth, like a fish. He was looking this way and that, not up into the sky, and timidly, sadly greeted anyone who would salute him.

"Oh, he's there every day, except when there's wind, or snow, or rain, or humidity, or dust or one hundred degrees in the shade."

"Yes," said Jacky, "old age is worse than death for such people; but, after all, I don't know who he is. Perhaps he is one of those for whom death is worse even than old age. Suppose you are Rembrandt van Rijn—death is then worse than old age, for it is the extinction of Rembrandt. The way they all talk—'I've only just begun, I must live; why, I've twenty years of work ahead of me— let me live another month at least, Doctor, I've got some work to finish.' To them, it's different; to the real workers. I hope I'm a real worker."

"I'd be delighted to settle down right now," I said, with feeling; "I don't want to be a real worker. Why do we have to struggle? I don't believe in the struggle of youth. Things ought to be made easy for us when we're at the height of our powers. Old people like to struggle; at least, they're used to it. Why should we get crow's-feet?"

"Tories are people who are frightened of the future," said Jacky;

"perhaps the source of life is shallow in them; anyone can see the future, it all depends on courage."

"Courage is too painful; she speaks who knows."

"The face of a really brave man—oh! how he looks at others! He never blinks," she said, smiling; "it isn't like a man turning his face to an enemy, but like someone turning his face to the sun. But, you see, even the brave get old; then they are afraid of the snow, the wind, the dust, and people who won't say hello to them. Isn't it terrible?"

"Yes. I don't know. I suppose you can keep your chin up at any age."

"No," said Jacky. "If you think about old age, you can't believe in anything but materialism. The immortal soul doesn't exist. A man like Faraday, Talleyrand, gets old; Goethe, King Lear, Faust—"

"What have they to do with each other?"

"They were all old."

Tears were standing in her eyes. I looked at her attentively and waited. She continued, "The face of Talleyrand was shrewish, with an intent glance, and a high forehead. Thought pierced through his skin; he seemed never asleep. When old, his eyes were sluggish, nothing was seen; he had spots on his skin, he limped, he was bent, and his skin was as dry as an old corpse under an autopsy, it wheezed and crackled. He was infinitely polite, he loved society. When he was old he would not let anyone in to see him. Do you think both of these were Talleyrand? Yes, they were. But there was no sole *Talleyrand*. There was Talleyrand old and Talleyrand young, the two men. Perhaps many more Talleyrands than that."

"Are you writing about Talleyrand?"

"No. He is interesting though; he was a professional cynic, so much of a crook, so to speak, a diplomatist, that his name is a byword; but as a friend he was charming, open, frank, simple. So you see there were more than even two Talleyrands. Ordinary people are just of one piece, like paper dolls."

Her skin blazed now. I saw she had something on her mind, and I waited. She led me a dance. Said Jacky:

"The sexual cells are immortal, you know. These queer beings like Talleyrand, I don't say him in particular, for I don't know about his sexual life, but such beings, hypersensitive, morbid, and what we call great, seem to understand that, for they wish to be immortal and they cling to their sexual life when it is exhausted. Now, that poor old man, well, perhaps, even now he dreams of pretty young girls who will come and hold his hand, or something else."

"Really, you ought to be a playwright. So much in that old hulk, sitting on the stoop!"

"Yes! There is no death from old age, don't you see. That is to say, no natural death, without lesion, fatal sickness, although I admit you could dispute about the fatal sickness. But there is natural death in this sense, that many generations of cells have lived in us before we die, and sooner or later they cease to regenerate themselves and so life is no longer possible. Or they begin to increase and reproduce in such a dreadful, mistaken way—but no doubt it is in us, the remnant of what once was the power to re-create unremittingly—a limb, skin, parts of the body."

"I see you've decided to go in for medicine, after all, Jacky."

"The infusoria have no corpses. The earthworm can re-create himself. Starfish put on a broken limb, lizards a new tail. We can grow new hair, and new teeth once, that's all. Our children don't have any changes, except in the womb. Once they emerge, they just grow from little to big, but no change in actual diagram. We're a fixed race."

"But those other things die," I said, thinking she was worried about death. "They die sooner than we do."

"I'm just speaking generally. Death isn't one thing, it has all kinds of factors. We ought to find a way to prolong each stage of life. They complain that the youth of the race is longer now, but also the age of the race is longer. We can lengthen it. Those people who live long have always signs of youth in them, even to the end. Men who are packed with energy contain all the men they ever were: children, youths, men in their prime, even their mothers, too. And they attach to themselves all kinds of other living things of their race, as other grand old men, which they suck up; and they consort only with the most living; and they love young beautiful girls, for example, only to drink up, unconsciously, from them the new blood, don't you see? But also they have shunned old age all their lives. So, such men are not old, but young, and you can never tell when, out of this secret drinking of new and strong blood they have always done, they will regenerate at least their energy and flash upon you, making even an ordinary young girl or man feel feeble. There are such old men and I am sure that old man there, timidly sitting there begging for glances is not one of them. I don't want to run down the poor old man, but he is not one of them."

"But King David gat no heat," said I.

She looked sad, "Yes. I am just thinking generally. Old age begins at sixty perhaps, but senility does not begin till much later, even till eighty-five if the person is energetic. Some men of genius have kept going, apparently in perfect health, till eighty-four or so. It is quite possible. In senility the intelligence dies, but until then, there is no sign of deterioration; the brains are sharper, and the judgment gentler, but—naturally, there is fatigue. Even feeling, sensitivity collapses. Especially the ability to know how others suffer. The old man wants to love, he knows he is in a situation where he might, and he cannot—then he becomes very sad. I read about one poor old man who had been a celebrity—he had to walk upstairs on his hands and knees, when no one was looking. He could not bear the weight of his body, it was too much to hold up. Other old men spend fortunes trying to get back their hair, their clear skin, their potency—it is a different life from ours. It is in another planet."

"I can't bear old men or old women. I never could."

Jacky said: "You know, poor Faust"—she laughed, as if she knew him—"he drew the sign of the macrocosm, that's the great world—"

"Look, I've been to school!"

She laughed, "He feels intense joy and cries out, 'Am I a god?' Today, he'd cry out, 'Am I a ruler, a dictator, the head of a government?' Wouldn't he? God was the highest in those days; of course, an imaginary creature. Now, we'd say, I'm fit to run the government. I suppose a very rich man, born to it, like W. R. Hearst, he naturally thinks, am I a god? Am I a king? Am I nature? He tries to do what he can to give other people his impression."

"Yes, sentimentalism leads you to defend Hearst on romantic ground."

"Not at all. I hate him. But what's the situation of a man who considers himself above the mob, for whatever reason? Take not a bad man like Hearst, but a good man like Gondych."

"Gondych who?"

"Simon Gondych; he's some vague relative of ours, or, at least, of the Foxes."

"Oh! Yes. I see. What about Gondych? What's he doing in this boat?"

"No, you don't understand!"

To my surprise, I saw that Jacky was hurt.

"Yes, yes. I understand; excuse me, Jacky, I'm so gross, really. I get used to making jokes, but I didn't see what you meant."

"You don't see now; it isn't your fault, Letty. I have to tell you, though. No one could understand. But you've been out with men; you understand."

I was silent because a premonition struck me. Jacky said, "You have no idea what he is really like.... All my life I heard things about Simon Gondych. You know last year he got the Copley Medal or something, from the Royal Society."

"Yes, Jacky."

"I went out with him several times," she said, in enraptured tones.

"Really, with Simon Gondych?"

"Oh, you have no idea what he is like."

"No."

"Oh, Letty! Such a man! I'm not afraid to rave, because it's clear he is an exceptional man—he gets medals; he got the Nobel Prize."

"Yes—evidently; of course."

"But as a man—he is charming; beyond everything; out of this world!"

I laughed.

"He'll soon be out of this world, won't he—he's a bit old for you, Jacky."

She started to cry and put her head on her two arms on the window sill.

"*Il est vieux, c'est un vieux, je sais.*"

I saw everything, but did not understand it.

"Don't let yourself go like that; explain it to me. I'm listening."

"Since Grandma's last party, about Muron, the broker, you

know—I went out with him. He's very interesting. Papa met us in a cafeteria one day and he said: 'What are you doing, Faust, with this young girl? I give you permission to seduce her, for you have not the aid of Mephistopheles.'

"Gondych said: 'Probably Mephisto wouldn't do business with me anyhow.'

"Anyhow, the next day he telephoned me. I have the impression he thought he had got the go-ahead signal from Papa."

"I know," I said. "Papa is capable of that. He sees everything, he knows everything, and he is a scandal as a papa."

"I have been out with Simon about fifteen times since then. One weekend I refused to see him because, you know, the whole week I didn't sleep, but really, not one night. It was as if I had eaten deadly nightshade, or benzedrine; whatever you eat not to sleep. I had been out three times that week—and as I thought it over in bed at night, of course, I went into simply every detail, I saw—"

"Yes?"

She said, "I saw he was trying to seduce me."

"You let him see you were crazy about him."

"I didn't mean to, but I suppose he couldn't help but see it. But I am glad that he did not know what I was thinking all that week —he would laugh at me."

"What were you thinking?"

"Why, I was adoring him, like any schoolgirl adores any professor. I was inwardly praying, 'Oh, divine intelligence, oh, god, enlighten me.' I thought he took me out to enlighten me, can you imagine? I am delighted that he can never know that about me. He would think I am a fool."

"Yes, and you still think he's a god, don't you?"

"Yes. I am still sure. But a different kind. The god of love. The true one. Supposing he is here, he has to have some human form. Why a vapid young man, with yellow curls? Why not a divine old man?"

I looked at her attentively. I knew that in a way, this way, I had never loved and did not even wish to. I preferred to have the right use of my eight senses and of my brains as well.

"At any rate, I am not mad, but everything I have ever wished for, he has given me. Absolute love."

"Well, I don't understand. Do you mean he loves you, too—?"

She was silent for a while, and I looked her over, in the dusk, now thickening. She was really beautiful. I was surprised. I could not help thinking of her powerful and white limbs and of what charms Gondych could have. He was red and yellow, bright-eyed, brisk, well-mannered.

"He loves young women, you know, because he is old," said Marguerite, my sister Jacky, "and not my sort, I know. I don't fool myself. He likes the lively sort; and I am quite a bore to him with my adoration, or I would be if I let him see it. But I don't. I go out with him—fifteen times—and I listen to the story of his adventures with other young women."

"That means he likes to confide in you."

"Why can't he tell me he loves me? Why must I hear about them?"

"Well—perhaps it's his line. '*Parler l'amour, c'est faire l'amour.*'"

"No. He doesn't love me, that's all. Imagine—I'm a little more than eighteen, not bad-looking. I love him, but so madly that I'd sacrifice my life for him if I could, and what does he tell me? 'Love is sacrifice; at one time a young woman I lived with—' and he tells me some absurd story. All the time I'm pawing the ground with impatience, and I myself would do anything just to prove to him— but meanwhile, what happens? In comes a girl of rather a gypsy type—a bit like you, in fact, Letty, and he follows her with his eyes: 'That girl certainly has gypsy blood,' he says. Of course, I have no *nous*, I admit. He places me with my back to the street, and then he tells me, 'Now I can look at you,' but it is to look at the street he wants, he is mad about company. I don't attract him. I go, look at myself in the glass, I'm beautiful! Pale-faced, disagreeable young men actually follow me, but he looks over my shoulder and says, 'There's a pretty girl with a young man, you know, my dear, an old man is fascinated, and looks to see why he has invited her out.'"

"Very ungallant! Why do you go out with him?"

"I don't know. Each time I come home very angry and swear at him. I burst into tears. As if I needed him! And I can go three or four days without thinking about him, then he calls up. I go unwillingly, and as soon as I see him, he has his claws in me—he doesn't mean to. He only sees me to tell me about the others."

"It's really extraordinary! After all, Jacky, there are lots of men. Why go out with him? Turn him down!"

"I can't."

"That's silly."

"I can't turn down Simon Gondych."

"Because he is Simon Gondych?"

"If he weren't, of course, but what is the use? I love him madly, so madly, so much with my whole soul, that if he won't have me—"

"Don't say such things," I said.

I had tears in my eyes, I didn't know why exactly. I thought her affair absurd and the result of isolation and summer. Later, she told me some of the things he had told her, old scholar's tales, fascinating researches he only had pursued and which he told her. I understood the vanity of her love. I took Jacky to the subway and took a drink at a soda fountain coming home. I was engrossed with her story. I knew she was a young college girl without knowledge of men, but the conduct of Gondych was something new to me. When I got home, I thought for a long while, and then, with a smile, I wrote Gondych a note, telling him how much I had always admired him, how I'd seen his citation in the paper, and how I had always compared him with Talleyrand, so complex and witty in company, but frank and simple, charming and human in tête-à-têtes. I asked him to come and have tea with me at my flat the next Saturday about four.

The next Saturday morning, a florist's boy brought me a bouquet from Gondych; he himself came at four sharp, appearing at the door in his usual, charming, gay way and rushing in, like a whirlwind, to give me a kiss and dispose his things, in an interesting, lively way about the place. I saw that he had a lot of charm. He made an appointment with me for later in the week. Thus, I had the chance to see whether Jacky was seriously in trouble.

I acted out of curiosity, without morality. With regard to sex, I have never been able to see where moral behavior began; it seems to me that everyone is for himself; yet, in this case, I know that I betrayed poor Jacky. I said to myself that no good could come out of her schoolgirl love for the great professor. He was happy with me, but even with me I observed his habit of looking around, in all public places, to find the most beautiful and youngest girls, and I felt rather humiliated. Of course, I was not old, but through Gondych I had first had the sensation of aging. There were others younger than me; he picked them out and showed them to me. He was fifty-nine. I wondered sometimes if he was Old Scratch. He was sharper than a needle. His anecdotes were not only the ones Jacky had repeated to me, but newer, more secret ones, that he had dug out himself, and that he brought to me, like a victor with the spoils.

When he did not telephone me, after receiving my kisses, I was disgruntled; I began to long for him myself. Yet he was a very strange person, attracting undesirable attention in public places; and he was so clearly not of my generation. People would think he was my father or uncle, even grandfather. Then he made love boldly—he was ashamed of nothing; and he would say, He was ashamed of everything, he was gentle, meek and timid. The affair was irritant, intriguing; and he was gallant and generous. He treated me always with unusual respect, and seemed, at times, somberly distracted. I was curious about what the love of a man like that could be.

One evening, after we had been to a movie together, and he was bringing me home, I began asking him in the taxi to come upstairs and have tea or a glass of beer. He said nothing to this, but held my hand and pressed close. When we turned into Twenty-first Street, it seemed to me that he hesitated. At my gate (an iron fence with gates ran before three or four houses in a row), he shook my hand and said good night, but I held him by the arm, "Come upstairs with me, Simon; I want you to stay with me a while."

"It's too late, Letty."

"I want you to—please—"

With my hand on his sleeve, I brought him through the gate. At the door, where I was obliged to insert my key, he turned back again, "No, my dear, you are very kind, but it is too late and you are a young girl; this makes it wrong—you understand—"

"Simon, I'm not a child, we're not children, I know what I'm doing."

"No, no, my dear—"

But he came into the hall and began to ascend the dark, long staircase. At the top of the first flight, he stopped again, after following me quite softly in the dark, "No, I must not."

"Simon, are you mad? What are we? What are you doing? What a noise you're making, too."

He whispered, "We shouldn't, we shouldn't—"

"We should, we will, are we children? It's the age of reason—"

He giggled softly under his breath; but on the top floor, where I lived, he made a last stand, as I fumbled for the old-fashioned iron key which would let us in.

"But, Letty, you know what it will mean—"

"Why shouldn't it mean it? Oh, gracious, what a man, what a man—"

I looked at him with rage and bit my lip as I fitted the key in the door, "The way men are—and the reputation they have—if anyone knew—"

He came in, drooping, not daring to say any more. He took off his hat and coat which he put on a chair, and sat down pretending to read a magazine till I had made him some tea, then, taking it, he said, "Letty, dear, I've got to get out of here. I'll just drink this and leave."

"Do what you like," I said amiably, handing him the cup.

His eyes were fixed on my breasts in my low-cut ruffled dress. When I had gone behind him, he said, "You tempt me, you should not."

At these charming words I came back behind him and kissed him, where I had already yearned to kiss him, on the neck, behind the ear, around the soft fringe of hair. I said in a low voice some words which I did not intend him to hear, a mere murmur, and he turned quickly, seizing my hands and kissing them. I then left him, saying, "You will sleep here with me—I've another couch."

And presently he came after me, after he had made up his mind to it; and caught me in the passageway, "Very well, get undressed, my darling; I shouldn't do this, but I will."

He pressed me to the wall and kissed me all over the neck,

arms, face, and breast. I went out tranquilly, smiling to myself. He came after me and showed himself quite simply, naked; and I saw he had not, as I had thought, any fear of me at all. I said to him all the foolish, untrue things I had said to others, and he thanked me for them all. I never had a more agreeable lover; he was grateful, obliging, and well-mannered. He wished to go home but I kept him; and in the morning, as he had a great rage for sweet things, I made him a large breakfast. Afterwards, he kissed my face and hands again, with gratitude and respect, and said to me, "I'll never come back, my dear girl, because I should not have stayed in the first place; you are a sweet young girl and I am a wicked old man; I am glad you like me though, and I shall never forget you. But because of your family I must not come back. That is all. I regret it."

With this he went, and I felt pleased at what I had done. I believed he would come back. I was wrong. I did not see him again that summer, or, in fact, till the birthday party which Grandmother Morgan, for reasons of her own, gave me in February. Meanwhile I heard both from Jacky, who was quite ignorant of my intrigue, and from Lily Spontini, who had now taken to visiting me regularly, that the mysterious Jacky-Gondych friendship had broken, but now continued. They laughed overmuch at Jacky and her professor. Indignation and jealousy kept me silent. I had also to suffer from Jacky's naïve confessions, when she came to visit me. She now thought of me as her confidante. Some might think I behaved dishonestly toward her; if so, I paid for it, hearing her ravings, that summer, about Gondych. I could say nothing but, "All this is lost; men of that age cannot even make love, you know."

She would look at me sadly, "I suffer, but I love him."

"And if it comes to nothing—?"

"All my life I only lived for one thing—a great love; and this is it. I can't be mistaken, because I've thought of nothing else. I never could tell you my ambition. That was it."

"You ought to be a bit more practical."

"Well, he is not married and what do we know about it? We are too young. We only know old wives' tales about the other generations."

"Good—but it's a risk I wouldn't take."

"No—but I would die for him, you see."

I can't say why these words cut me so deep; I wanted, for a mad moment, to give my life, too, for some man; but I knew I never would.

40

I GAVE up my job on the racial equality magazine. I had had an affair, not worth mentioning, with the young Zionist, and now that he had transferred to another girl in the office, I found everything intolerable and resolved not to stay in a place where I was daily disgraced. I therefore seized the first honorable pretext to leave my employ.

I spent several months lounging at home and wondering if I were not sinking from bad to worse; but I made an attempt to write a play, a novel, and some pieces for the *New Yorker* and the *Yale Review*, and so on. In trying to sell these, I met a number of midtown people who could help me, including one or two young men, who made good companions for a while.

The European war had opened officially with the entrance of Britain and France over the Polish question. This, of course, is still the official muddler of mid-European affairs. At that time, we were all mad for neutrality, and I even went to Washington to picket the White House and Congress and felt again for a time that my role should have been political, for it was really here that I felt at my best. Not only was I able, with a good memory, apt in quotation, sharp in repartee, unkind to enemies, but a natural strong-arm machine politician, believing in the steam roller, the goon, the lead pipe, unfair practice. Such is life! There I'm in my element and only need, in fact, a salon, which is the intellectual side of the business, to realize myself. That is what I felt. I flung myself into this political action with all my nature and neglected the small-fry, the blond wolves, and cheesecake merchants of the Forties and Fifties (I refer to streets in New York), with whom I had been passing the last few months. It was the fire in the nostrils of a fire-horse, blood in the nostrils of a charger, I suppose. Not that I cared for war and blood, what we were fighting for was peace of course. But how happy I was to abandon paper-and-ham-shifting at the call of some office boss, and the love affairs that trail around such offices, like lost paper streamers, trodden and torn, from a departing steamer. What a grand trip the passengers are taking and how bad the quays look the morning after. Yes; to me, my life was, and was intended to be, a grand tour. Meantime, as for the mad whirl, I went to several parties and enjoyed myself with two literary gents, an author, and an editor in a publishing firm, which made me think I was getting on in the literary world. I went into the office of a small publishing firm which employed non-union office labor although the manager was a radical. The fact was that he was quite poor and as a businessman had a good reputation. I had the notion that I would organize the girls and received some reproofs during the first two weeks for my rabid talk; I began to lose myself in the usual lively office scenes, quarrels over precedence, over extra work, over gossip, smut and religion, which was engaging the attention of the girls more and more, as politics went into decadence. This was during the war, when, as usual, everyone became quite distracted with conflicting loyalties; to intoxicate themselves meanwhile, every bright girl took to sexual corruption, fortune-telling, and drink, while the stupid, home-staying girls began to confuse and intoxicate themselves with religion and race-mania, which are always coupled, at least in these circles. I was accused of being an agitator, but this did not trouble me. I converted no one, but I soon became the battleground of the office. I let no one get away with an undisputed prejudice. I was no prude. On account of the sophisticated life I led outside the office, I was a perfect treasury of the stories of the town, both *obscoena* and fantasy, and the charge that I wasted many hours entertaining my colleagues was not ill-founded. However, I was popular, and this consoled me for many miseries which I had gone through before I came to the office. I was guilty of telling all the gossip I knew about the love affairs going on, not only in this office, but also all through the publishing world, the publishing world, of course, because of the material they handle, being one of the favorite secret gardens of sexual folly in the town. My informant was usually this editor, Erskine, who worked in one of the big firms and who generally invited me to meet authors and magazine editors in various showy bars uptown, on Madison and on Park avenues. Erskine and I were soon intimates and I made rather a parade of our acquaintance. I knew his reputation, but fell into one of the oldest illusions, perhaps it is the Grand Illusion in the love affair; that is, that if you have an affair with a Don Juan, it is a triumph, even though all his other women seem to you fools. Erskine's marriage was in a state of dissolution—that sounds dissolute, and that is what it meant for him; but I mean, dissolving. I didn't want to be a contributing factor in that dissolution, however, and was primmer at first than I wanted to be. I waited to hear that the angry wife had her co-respondent. I did not want to start off in life as the other woman; I still aimed at some fate flourishing and not dishonorable and thought I deserved it.

Well, there was a really complicated story that delighted me no end there, or so I pretended; and in the process of pretense, I had a lovely time with Erskine and some stray associates of his, I partied forever during this time, twelve nights in a row, was always answering the phone when in and missing calls when out, and I met dozens of nice people. That is one of the chief virtues of an eligible escort and especially of a married one. I had a lot of fun with very involved people—and they are the best. One of these days, said I to Erskine, we'll quit kidding, honey, and get down to serious talks, such as, "Where do you and I stand?" But until then, let life, wine, and *toi-et-moi* flow merrily. The trouble with a lot of men I knew at this time was that they were married, all but Bill van Week, a likely prospect, really a man made for me. He was not married, but he had already been married too often, and I didn't want to have my name on a bill of divorcement as long as the call of members at a new Congress. The fact is, with a young girl, with at least some attractions and experience, that if she meets men, they are married; and if they're prepared to do something about it, she's not such a fool but that she asks herself, "Isn't this, maybe, perhaps, a life-long policy?" I didn't want to start with a commuter, at twenty. Add to this the reappearance of a few persons I had known, such as Amos—but I stymied those attempts. I know how to cut a loss, especially when I have other investments in view; and then, I live for the day (that is, when I have a date for that day). The fact is, I'm a fool of a girl, and if I get married, as I hope, I'll have to give up all this; for I would be ashamed for my daughters to know such a fool as I have been. So I thought.

I became, for several merry weeks, almost sick of men. I had seen too many of them; and only arrived home from job hunting (for Solander kept me at this), to answer the phone and become the escort, so to speak, of some weak willy or other, who fancied I was all aglow at his call. Except for the two, the author and the married editor, I was almost sick of hearing the phone ring, for there were a great many misprints in my little red address book. How transient are women's moods! Ah, me! This was my mood at that time. Once more, I was hopping on and off a merry-go-round at their will! What a mad ex-virgin I was! Naturally, I forgot Simon Gondych (who was perhaps having moral struggles over me). But, ah, youth, if you knew your brightness—and, of course, we do and profit by it; and we expect our victims to take it into account, for we're certainly so tough with each other that we have no time for salving the feelings of the old.

I attended the family get-together at Christmas, New Year, and on my birthday in the early season; and on the last occasion, at which Jacky and Gondych were present, I was surprised to have my father and mother ask me separately what I thought of the Gondych-Jacky affair. I said, "What? It's still going on?"

My heart sank. It's true, of course, that those who love or favor me, love or favor others, but I've never been able to face it. It's the bitter, hard core of bad luck to me. I tried to argue Jacky away from it; for example, in February, I said, "But, Jacky, what can he offer you?"

"What can he offer me?"

"Good. All right. We're in the ideal plane. I see that. Jacky, do you want to live with him?"

I thought I had her there, for to me she was just a school child. But she said, "After a week, when I was out with him almost every night, I suddenly thought of physical love. I prayed, I really prayed, that I should never want him. How terrible—an old man, everything in him is repugnant. A week later, I was afraid because already the idea had come to me. For I wanted and didn't want. I know by the symptoms, it's hopeless, dangerous—"

She began to laugh, lifting her charming, radiant face out of her long hands, "To think I was born for this! It doesn't sound possible, either, does it?"

"To me it seems to be just an obsession."

"When I'm by myself, in my room, I laugh, I feel such madness, of joy; when I'm lying down on my bed I kick my legs out. I fly, I float, this is love. He's the God of Love. Naturally, he's very old, the God of Love."

I laughed, "It's not a question of getting over revulsion; love is not a dream, it's physical; even Faust had to have Mephisto to make him into a young man."

Jacky said, "I have no sympathy for the story that Marguerite fell for a young good-looking man; what's the interest of it? No, Marguerite fell in love really with a very old, wonderful man, magical, a genius, the first man in the world, and it was because of that it was a wonderful tragedy and her life was ruined; but she knew what she was doing."

"Well, how are you going to ruin your life with Gondych?" I said, laughing.

She tossed herself about in her chair, making big eyes and her skin taking on a bluish shade, "I suffer. He tells me, This one loved me, this other one sacrificed for me, this third one threw me flowers, a fourth one gave me her diamonds for safekeeping, a fifth one used her fortune to game for me, although I did not want it; and a sixth one came from the mountains to the plain, a long, long way, leaving her husband in suspense, only to shake my hand. He tells me all this, with his big eyes popping out of his head, and his hair shining, like thousands of little glassy snakes of fire, if he's sitting in the light, I mean his cheeks are red like a boy's and his mouth is smiling, and if I say anything to him, he becomes silent, and a modest expression, a flush comes into his face, for he only babbles like a boy, because in his private moments he is frank and boyish and pure in heart—"

"Like Talleyrand—"

"All the time, I listen painfully, and want to say, But I, Simon, I am like that. I am all those—I would sacrifice for you, only ask me to. And so on."

"I'd feel funny going out with him; he's quite strange-looking."

"Yes; I feel strange; he is odd-looking. He's like that old Egyptian king, the one with the stoop who was so brilliant and such a materialist—"

"Ignaton," I said, smiling wryly.

"Yes, Ikhnaton—you know everything," she flattered me.

"I don't know everything. He told me that story too. At that last party too."

"Yes, I suppose. He's a scholar; he doesn't have a regular line, so I suppose he just has stories."

"They all have their package goods."

"And did he tell you about the old troubadour songs?" she asked dolefully.

"No."

She cheered up.

"Well, I am glad he—" She laughed. "I am a fool. I'm wanting him to love me."

"Why shouldn't he?" I said coldly.

"That would be like a vision of paradise, to me."

"As far as I can tell, a good many girls have had that vision of paradise."

"I know. I've swallowed that. I say to myself, What can I expect? Do I expect a man to wait till—his age—just because I am not even born yet."

"Eh?"

"I mean—I'm getting mixed."

"In other words, you love him, you burn for him, and if only he could recognize you, if only he could reciprocate—the very situation you were in with 'Varnish,' the professor, you remember?"

She blushed and sulked.

"Naturally, this is very different. I am older."

"There's something funny about your always picking someone who can't do you any good. What do you want? The martyr's crown?"

She became silent and looked at me in doubt. For my part, I was irritated and jealous. From the above and other confidences, I realized he had confided in her a good deal. I felt disgraced that after the episode between Gondych and me he had not made me his friend. I put him down as a pure philanderer who preferred to float from butterfly to butterfly, and I accused him, in fact publicly to Jacky, of having no staying power as a lover. It made her very uncomfortable, but did not move her.

"Such things could not last under any circumstances."

"Everyone says so," she murmured, "I have asked people in a general way. They're all amazingly interested in the idea; they don't know it's about me and Gondych. They all say, it can be, but it can't last."

She took herself off, and I thought she was coming out of it, inferring this from her last words.

I confess that I had troubles of my own and forgot hers. It was almost spring, and I owed: item, one hundred dollars borrowed from Bill van Week, payment of which was promised for the previous Christmas (though he didn't dun me); item, one hundred dollars borrowed from Susannah Ford and which she now needed back as she was settling her financial and marital affairs with Brock. Although wealthy, she was making as much profit out of this, her second divorce, as she had made out of her first. She always agreed to settlements, not to alimonies, which cease upon remarriage. Brock, meanwhile, had settled out of town in a chemical factory on a site he had bought near Trenton, New Jersey, and when he came into town, came to see me. I was in danger, for Susannah had telephoned me several times, asking me if I was seeing Brock and asking what tales he had told about her. In fact, I knew that Susannah was already living with Aleck, who had now deserted me completely. I realized that I had always disliked the feeble boy. Brock, on the rebound, seemed lovesick about me, but I knew Susannah was quite a viper and would gladly put the divorce on my shoulders. As I did not care for Brock enough to marry him, I saw little of him, and did not sleep with him once.

I saw little of Bill van Week for the moment—he was engaged in some new venture for which his parents had put up a lot of money; and though I was really disgusted with him, because of his innumerable philanderings, I liked him. I thought perhaps we might make up a household between us, legal or extra-marital, at some time.

I had also really fallen in love with the man I mentioned before, Erskine, the married man; and as Erskine said he was on the point of divorcing his wife, I had some hopes of settling down at last. I had bumped into a few friends, like Gallant Stack and even Gideon Bowles, old family friends who now considered me enfranchised and did their best to make me—in fact, one of them did make me and I heard all the ins and outs of his *amourettes*. That is what gallants in New York consider an attractive line—to lie in bed and talk about other women.

Lily Spontini came to see me and, of course, I gave her dinner, which was the family system. She was a sieve of scandalous gossip with a censorship bureau, just like a Freudian mind. I heard what was juicy, but not too nasty, and what was suitable for me to hear. Lily never ran down anyone, however, whether out of a kind heart or out of provision for the future, I cannot say.

I saw my mother and sisters twice a week, but avoided Jacky, whose doting upon Gondych made me acutely jealous. Andrea was already a glamorous young miss with pictures of movie stars and singers everywhere. She was going to develop in the usual style, from the waist downwards first, but had shapely straight legs and wanted to become a model; this shocked the whole family. It was all right for Edwige—but a daughter of Solander Fox! Andrea was like Jacky at her age, with less brains—"Am I glamorous like this? Don't fan-dancers wear anything? Watch me do a strip tease! Don't you think I have come-hither legs?" and referred to herself and her friends as subdebs. She even had plans for a coming-out party. Since she had long ago found out that she had not any of Grandmother Fox's money, she made a comic stance out of it, and proclaimed herself, first, as the only proletarian in the family, and then, as the only career girl. She wanted to join up with Cousin Edwige, now a young married woman, living with her husband, Ernest, and her mother in Hollywood.

The husband was a young writer, very serious, consecrating himself to husbandhood. Edwige and her mother were carrying on a loving-mother-and-daughter pose which turned out to be nothing more than a cheat upon the husband. Edwige had a car in which she raced up and down her canyon, visited friends in Beverly Hills, and went shopping in Westwood. She was a friend and correspondent of Bill van Week, who was having a transient affair with her. She was man-mad, but she wrote to Bill quite simply that she wanted to turn her talents to use. She did not intend to turn into a raggle-taggle. She wanted to make use of some few of the hundreds and hundreds of pretty girls at a loose end in Hollywood. Most of these girls were winners of contests, or ambitious show-girls, or even home-girls, who had turned up their noses at small-town boys, broken with their families, and now had too much experience. They would do anything rather than go home. They had already, mostly, done anything: been the bait of restaurants and cheap agencies, the meat of any whorehound, the nameless party girls at the great obscene drunken feasts; and most had gone out there in the belief that they would have to sleep with everyone in the studios to make their way. Most of the girls, in spite of their concessions, had not made good and were drifting, prepared to do anything, including starve, rather than go back home with their tailfeathers missing. Those who had acted a bit in the movies were best. Edwige had written not only to Bill van Week but a few other suitable men asking them whether they could not help her set up a little entertainment house for men, in Hollywood. If it succeeded, she would come East, paying the fares of the girls back again, but in an inconspicuous way. She wished to be a *madam*. She was married; her serious husband stood in the way. She must either get rid of him, which would be a disadvantage, or contrive to carry on her business through her correspondents, Bill van Week and others.

Bill wrote to her, "Calm yourself, my beauty, can't you be content with highjacking? Have you got to go into straight business?"

He said she was probably the most corrupt girl alive, although she had many close competitors in New York and Hollywood.

One of her other friends fell in love with her and was mad enough to promise to help her. He thought it wonderfully ingenious for one so young. This was a blond curly-haired amorous man, already once married and divorced, who was completely dazzled by Edwige's wax beauty. By now everyone knew Edwige's foibles and laughed at them. The men were very weak toward her, and her mother was a mealy-mouthed church-goer, talking of her daughter and son-in-law like a character in a slick magazine, but willing to do anything for the profit-making little trull. Everyone liked Ernest, and no one had yet told him of Edwige's goings-on.

My precocious sister Andrea was childish enough to fancy that Edwige was a Hollywood star and she had to be restrained from taking the train out to join the family white-slaver. I was obliged at last to go and tell Solander the whole story. Gallant Stack was there, and before I had left, had gouged Edwige's address out of me.

The wonder was that Jacky could live in such a set as we were, Grandmother Morgan, Edwige, even myself, and could remain what she was. I had only occasional qualms about myself, for society justified me, not Jacky. Jacky no more had the line of the day than a suicide or a saint.

There were unaccountable drift-lines of gossip about Gondych at this time—that he had plans for joining the Government in Washington, that he wanted to go abroad and had an offer from London, that he felt war was coming to the U.S.A. and felt he had a duty overseas as a bio-chemist, helping civilian populations protect themselves against the yet unimagined horrors of the war; rumors, too, that he had already asked for and received his sabbatical leave, to complete some researches, in this country. Ordinarily, such straws of talk about a bio-chemist did not stick in our family's hair; there was something significant in the way they now did.

Jacky reached the end of her school year. One rose-dusted evening I was watching for her out of my window. I saw her, in a rosy dress, coming down the treeless, asphalted, brown-walled street. Coming, she seemed a stranger; when she got close I recognized her, but was surprised, still, at how far away and alien she seemed to me. It occurred to me that for years I had not been her friend, attempted to understand her. We had dinner out of some packets she had brought from the delicatessen; and then she told me that she was going away with Gondych, to Cape Cod, for the summer. He was worn out by the year in town and thought her charming; he was flattered by her love. She knew it was that.

"Perhaps he'll get to love me really; now he's just delighted that such a young girl admires him so much."

"You can go away on those terms?"

"Yes; I think over everything he has ever said to me, his laughing and smiling, his talk, and it seems to me we could become very intimate. He kisses my hand so many times, out of gratitude too, and with passion, with the passion young men haven't; and then, when we go out I look round and think, Not one boy can compare with him. I am madly in love with him."

"But you don't quite believe in it?"

"Last night I had three dreams about him. I didn't know they were about him, but each time I woke up suddenly, with my heart beating fast, and I thought, it was almost as if I had said aloud in my sleep, 'That is about Simon.' Will I tell you, I know it's boring; but they mean so much to me."

I assented, lighting a cigarette and leaning back to look across the street. There sat the daughter-in-law of the old man she had talked about before. The old man was dead. I did not mention this. Jacky said, "I dreamed I was climbing a mountain road with you; and in front of us, Mother, but she was an old woman. There were clods of earth which turned into cow-turds; and these, into patches of snow, as we came into the high regions. We were now in a plateau so high that you could see mountain tops, humps, and the tops of long sierras, covered with snow. Night came. The old woman had disappeared, you had gone; but someone I knew as well as you was there, close as my own blood. We got into a tobog-gan and now I could see the night sky thickly banded with stars and the broad Milky Way. The toboggan started off, and we flew up and down while I felt intense joy, indescribable; but we were descending as we flew. We were flying in the night sky, but I thought, Yes, but this will only end in the yellow sand of morning. Then I knew I was with Lucifer, the morning star. When I woke up I thought, That is about Simon. . . . I fell asleep and a dream flashed past. There were two or three bony fishes from the great ocean deeps, showing their ribs and with leafy decoys around their faces and mouths. One gaped and gasped till it was a skeleton; and it gaped after a bony man resembling them; it chased the man who became skinnier. They were all disgusting phantasms; but I was not afraid. The man had no chance. They fell away into an extrem-ity of extinction, there was no thought of life; they were long ago crushed, ages ago; and devouring, soul-eating creatures, one and all. I woke up and thought, That's about Gondych. The third time, the same night, I dreamed I was in an underground tomb of the Pharaohs. I was not afraid. There was a large chamber with a sealed door, leading to a small chamber, and a broad foyer leading outside. I was not afraid; and I thought, Gondych is in there, meaning the sealed chamber. Those are all dreams of death, aren't they? I am afraid he will die?" And she burst into tears.

"Is he sick?"

"No, but he is old."

"Are you really going away with him?"

"Yes, next week. I am pretending to go away to a camp at Cape Cod."

"I'll have to tell Mother, Jacky."

"No, don't do that. I'll write to them from there."

"How on earth can Simon do it? Look, I've got something to tell you—"

She said, in a deadened voice, "I know what it is. He was here. He told me. That is the kind of thing he tells me."

"Simon told you everything about that time?"

"He said that—he said, 'Naturally, I stayed there because it was so late.'"

"He was charming; he's a nice fellow; I wish some of the young men were as pleasant."

"I know you've had a few lovers, Letty."

"Yes, but Simon—"

I began to brag, flushed with my victory, my experience; I was puffed up with what seemed to me my real hold on life, and there was some goodness in me too. I wanted to let her see it wasn't as serious as she thought. Each time I said his name, I saw her resisting the pain of hearing it said by me, in this goofy, boasting, half-sneering, and half-affectionate tone. Then she said, "You see, Letty, you can't tell Mother! You're in the same boat as me. You would not dare. Why would you do that to me?"

I looked at her helplessly, and returned to my senses, "I was just boasting."

"No, he told me too. One day we quarreled and when we made it up—I ran after him; I sent him a card and offered to meet him —he was anxious and pressed me, made me hurry—when I met him I could see he had sleepless nights just like me. I said to him, 'There is something I must tell you, Simon; I can't live like this.'

He said, 'My dear, one doesn't die so easily.' But I saw how he looked. When I met him he was not waiting for me, but was cozily talking with a beautiful girl about my age. At first I wanted to go and never see him again. I couldn't do that. I saw him watching the door, waiting for me. I came up to him and he rose quickly, pleased to see me, glad I was so pretty; and when he passed the desk—it was in a bookshop—he gave a sly underhand look at the pretty woman he had been talking to, and a slight lift of the shoulders as if to say, 'You see, I must take out my young niece'—it suggested something like that. . . ."

"But if you know all that—you don't love him. Love is blind."

Jacky said, "Love sees a thousand times more than other people, and almost everything it sees proves to it it isn't wanted."

"God," I said, "I wouldn't like to be in your shoes, Jacky. You're so darned serious; where will it end? I mean, you can't take anything as a joke. This is darned serious."

"Well, we went to a teashop, where he offered me tea and cakes in his polite way, and he began to make conversation in his gay way. You know him—at first, I didn't follow the drift of his talk. I often don't. It's because he's really thinking about something else altogether. But he thinks you must chat about this and that with young girls. At last I saw that he was telling me about other women who had fallen in love with him, or at least been much struck with him at one time or another. But naturally, he wasn't bragging like a college boy. It was circumstantial, very colorful; and I gulped it down, but I was bored, bored—not a word about me. At last, I got ready to go. He put his ice-cold hand on my warm one, and I looked into his flaming face and his sleepless eyes, his face was quite sanded over with overwork and insomnia, and—it seemed to me—this was the worst thing—with unrequited love—"

"You're in a bad way—" I murmured, not liking this story, and resolved to go and tell my father as soon as Jacky had gone.

"I got ready to go, put on my hat, then he said, 'You are going to leave me so soon, I see, my dear; but what did you want to tell me?' And he looked at me with a kind of bloodthirsty hunger, and it was so clear that he expected me to make a declaration that I grew quite cool. 'Only that we must not quarrel, Simon.' Again he put his wrinkled, stone-cold hand on mine."

I said, "Jacky, it's horrible, really, if you see him like that."

She did not answer, but calmly continued, "Icy hand; it chilled me to the bone and I thought, imagine that hand reaching toward me and—here—" she touched her breast.

"Gosh," I said, distressed, "you're dramatizing it a bit."

"We got up, went outside, and he was hunched down, because he was disappointed, he wanted to have me in his power, just out of a lust of power. But when we got outside, it was a violet-blue evening, just coming down; the dusk so thick that it was like volcanic dust; and people rather idly going home, though thick as troops. He had on his squashed old hat that he must, one time, have thrown under a bus and his long-tailed coat in which he is every bit the professor; and he looked like a draggled old beetle crawling out of a pond where it has fallen. We stood side by side on the curb waiting to cross, and such peace came into us both as I never felt before; I could tell he felt it, too. It was like standing in an immense garden with no one about. We crossed and he stood hesitating at the corner, wondering if I would go further with him, for he was bitterly disappointed and hoped to get some sort of declaration of love from me. I found myself just a brisk, pert young girl. I made him bring me home. He sat in the bus beside me, patted my hand, and stole glances at his evening paper. His face was crushed, ridiculous. He held my fingers as we came down the street; and he smiled at me with his large eyes. He would not come in. I kissed him lightly on his cheek which was not well shaved, and nearly fainted from love and joy. I suppose I showed it. His face lighted up too. I walked in, quite dizzy; and was dizzy all evening until I thought I was getting something. Mother and Andrea were talking, Aunt Dora was there, and actually, at moments, there was a transformation scene. The room just reeled away, tossed itself away, and I even did not hear the voices for a moment, but saw Gondych, felt his cold hand and saw his wonderful eyes, and felt his cheek. I jerked myself back into the room, answered them. They thought I was tired. And then the smell I snuffed on Gondych's cheek—the shaving cream, the old felt of his hat, his newly starched shirt, I suppose—all poured over me at once, and I was drowned again; there was the transformation scene. At last I had to go to bed; I couldn't keep track of the conversation. Mother said, 'Jacky's overworking, the work they have to do is a shame.' Aunt Dora offered to lend us her cottage at Cape Cod; she has an old ramshackle thing there. That gave me the idea. That's where we're going to stay. It's empty this summer. I set about fixing it all up at once. I told one lie after another; but I was happy. The theory is that I'm going to paint with a famous painting class up there, which is there every summer, and by the greatest good luck, they paint just round and about Aunt Dora's little house. So I said I'd stay there with a couple of the girls, because it is hard to get rooms in the usual cottages. The class is always full to overflowing and is so this year. That's no lie."

She heaved a sigh, "Thank goodness one thing is not a lie. Simon is pleased enough, but a bit dubious about sanitary arrangements, hot water, cooking, cleanliness, and I don't know what else." She laughed nervously, but happily. "Well, it's all arranged; I can't do much, can I?"

"No. It's madly harebrained, and what can Simon be thinking of?" Jacky said solemnly, "You know what I say to myself, Letty? I'm telling you so that you won't tell on me. Don't ruin it for me! Perhaps this is my only love; you don't know. When I'm alone, I throw myself on my bed or in a chair, or wherever I am, and I feel mad with bliss, just bliss. And I say, I have been touched by the mighty wing—as it swooped nearer earth than usual—"

I said nothing, sitting there, smoking one cigarette after another, and myself almost in a trance. After a silence, Jacky said, "The wing of a great thing—death or love, or Lucifer; that is just the feeling I have. Can you imagine the wing, an immense, dark wing, as broad as the sky almost, dusk-colored, and soft but strong with a surge of power such as—" she got up—"such as you and I never felt—" she walked up and down—"such as—" she stopped in front of me with tears in her eyes and her hands wrenched together—"such as anyone, with any heart or spirit, would die just to feel? For what is the good of living otherwise? There's nothing else in our lives—this gin-milling and lechery and selling-out. We think every fraud and crime is life, reality. I don't want to sound despairing—no one could feel that—the flight of the wing and despair. You know what I say to myself when I go out at night and I wish I was with Simon, I say, 'Now I'm going out with the

Angel of Death,' and when I sit in a movie by myself, the seat next to me, which is for the Angel of Death, is always empty."

"You crazy kid," I said. "You're imagining that, at any rate."

"Oh, I assure you, it's quite true. And I feel safe; absolutely safe. And I think, if I am friends with the Angel of Death, he'll not lay hands on Simon."

"Look, Jacky," I said, spilling everything all over the floor, and looking cheerfully at the litter on my floor, "it wouldn't do you any harm to have a drink. Why don't you come out with me? I think you're alone too much. I realize Mother isn't quite the type you can rave to, and Andrea—of course—but why don't we go out and sit in a café? I don't want to corrupt youth or anything, but I think you ought to try first to get another boy friend."

Jacky burst out laughing, "Oh, that kind of advice everyone gives me. I have boy friends. One wanted to marry me. He wrote Mother a letter. He asked her in the same letter if the twenty-five hundred dollars would be paid at once and if Mother's piano would go along with me." She went on, laughing reasonably, "Simon isn't a next-best."

"You mean you really love him."

She gave a shout of laughter, "Oh, that fiery bean, that mind of flame; you do catch on quickly"; she cried out, and in the next hilarious few moments, she insulted me and I could see her flinging me off, my dull influence, paying me out for my anecdotes about Gondych, like a big terrier, throwing the pond water off his hide. We went out and I came to the conclusion, within myself, that I must tell my father the whole thing next morning. He would know what to do. He would go and see Gondych. I thought the whole thing a disgrace. Gondych was no doubt pleased to have a hideaway in a quiet place while he worked out all his plans for his sabbatical year. He was not certain of his future, whether it was to be here, or in England, or on the Continent. They were to live as friends and lovers and her youth was a guarantee to him; they would separate when the summer was over.

"But if you love him, why don't you try to marry him?"

"I will try," she said, laughing sideways at me. "Imagine how simply perfect—oh, I'd say, 'Life, you don't owe me anything.'"

I laughed, "Oh, yes, we always say that; but at the next

toothache we're not so sure; and the next man who turns us down, we're asking Life for the nipple all over again."

Jacky left me; but on the way home I met Bill van Week coming from my place, where he had been to get me. We went out, drank too much, wrangled, told each other too many home-truths; and as he was stronger and nastier than I, this went on all the way home. When I got home, I cried and then telephoned Bill to ask him to console me. He told me he meant every word. I was this, that, and the other.

The next morning I had too much to think about to even call Jacky to mind. I was then at low ebb and I was on the slide. Would I really end badly, just a slut, a rolling stone?

The unusual pair thus went off to Cape Cod without my having put in my oar; and, after all, I was not sorry. My fate is that when I interfere, all the troubles of both parties spill out over onto me. But by the next week, thinking they were well established and she ruined, so to speak, I went to my father and told him the story. By that time I felt very guilty indeed, and called myself the most selfish woman alive. Jacky wrote, telling of the northern lights, the cold water, and the eddying darkness of their dunes, and her extravagant nature seemed here to be developing out of bounds; "I wonder if I am not fated to found a love-cult or a religion; those are the ideas that now possess me; it is not only that I love such a man as this, but the climate here—"

Soon my father had set off after her, to rescue her from her infatuation under the twanging and wavering night curtains of the northern lights.

41

JACKY was indisposed for the old family life when she returned. The family was scandalized; and she, being very unhappy, had no stomach for their sermons and questions. She came to live with me. We both had to suffer reproaches for living away from our mother.

Jacky went back to college, where she slaved away to forget her disappointment over Gondych, in work. They had been very happy; so much so that Gondych had done no work, spending each fine day in her company, bathing, riding, walking, and visiting the more disreputable of the neighbors. Gondych declared that no work, especially not bio-chemistry, compared with the happiness of a summer spent with a lovely young creature; and Jacky believed in this idyll.

Solander visited them, saw nothing he could do in the strange situation, and left them on their sand dunes. At the end of the summer, however, Gondych became much irritated with the letters he was receiving, not because he felt guilty, but because he had a hot temper. He had work to do; he could not waste his hot but diminishing suns at a schoolgirl's side. She found him sitting hunched, in black moods; he talked wildly; he hurried up and down the sandy roads talking to himself; he flung his fist at the starry sky, one summer evening; he hated the worn flooring, the squeaking doors, the sand, wind, rains, birds, ticks, and gorse. He hated the place eventually, and dragged Jacky back to town. He was kind and tender, but said, "Can we live together forever, my dear? And I am an old man. I cannot be your husband; I cannot give you a child; I am more like a father. Think; it's all right now, but in a few years, five, six, how many, I will be more than old. Perhaps dead! Don't let people see you living with me. You go back to your young girl's life and we will always be friends, lovers, always love each other. Isn't that better?"

Jacky was in such dense misery that she spoke of it little, and appeared tranquil, cold. If asked about Gondych, she answered almost severely. But she began to work in this unusual way.

Conscription fell like an iron rain on our young men; they ran to cover, they hid in cellars and workshops. The hardier at once began pouring into special courses and mushroom workshops all over the greater city; the idle, squatters upon their parents' property, college boys, bore the glamour of grease and overalls. The men had something male to do and sprouted eaglets' wings; the girls at first had an inspired look—the country had something to do. But a good many, also, saw what it meant in flesh and blood. Bobby, for instance, rang me up in a frenzied way and begged me to meet him at once in a bar, to leave work in the middle of the afternoon and come to discuss his future with him. It was nearly four; I said I had a headache. I told the girls it was a man who was going to be called and an old friend. He was sitting at the bar with a Scotch-and-soda in front of him; he said irritably, "I didn't know when you'd be here; I've been waiting half an hour."

"I got away from work as soon as I could."

I had wondered, coming along, if he was going to propose marriage, for it looked like the quick way out to a lot of men I knew. He kept looking at himself in the mirror, his face dark and lengthy, and occasionally coughed hollowly.

"You have caught a cold, Bobby."

He hunched over his drink and waved to me to drink mine. After he had ordered another he said, "I want your advice; you know me pretty well. This damn war has got me worried; they'll rake me in."

Well, I thought, no choice is offered us, we're just pushed into everything and so life is all dreary aimlessness to the Bobbies. Why should they like the war? Of course, Bobby is not exactly a hero, but his parents worked hard nineteen or twenty years to make him like this. He isn't the ideal husband, but he's a nice enough boy. It's no use crying over spilt milk, I said, to myself; I'll seize the occasion by the forelock, if I can; all I need is a footing—from then on, I'll know what to do. Thus, I was very happy, comradely, gentle with Bobby and knowing him so well, I thought we would soon be man and wife. A married woman is doing her duty to the state and is happy, glad not to have to worry about the moral and financial problems of each new day. I admit it would be better if the state did it for us, but there is no state but just a man; that is our system. I thought my troubles were at an end, in short. Bobby was perspiring, sitting at the bar, tearing his hair and looking tragically into the bar mirror when I got there. He wrung my hand and pulled me onto the stool beside him.

"It's come," he said, looking at me wildly, slantwise under his low, neat, clever forehead, his eyes darting to the mirror and to me. "What'll we do now? They've got us."

"Who do you mean?"

"The tribal gods, the things of wood and stone—" he said, fiercely. "Let's get a table! I've got to talk this thing out."

"Maybe they'll reject you."

"They'll take me, I've got one year medical training; they'll take me to mop up blood and pus in their hospitals."

"You could get a worse berth than that!"

He took no notice of me, drinking his Scotch-and-soda in gulps and snapping his fingers, and sourly ordering more.

"We're in it; not you—you're a girl!—but even you girls, a whole swag of you'll live to be old maids." He stared at the floor, drenched with bile; "another lost generation! They're all lost nowadays. What do we have them for?"

"Have generations you mean?" I laughed in a sultry style for I was feeling the day rich in possibilities.

"Yes; you wouldn't have kids just to get them blown to hell; no woman would."

"The way things are, I'd say, if I can't have anything else, I'll have kids; at least that is something I got out of living."

"Yes, a woman's view," he said darkly; "the old biological urge; that's living on the instinctive level."

"If you're not instinctive why this cringing on the part of all you guys; if you all refused to march, they couldn't march you. But you're afraid of criticism."

"Afraid of dungeons dark and deep and the firing squad, you mean," he said; "you don't know what they can do to us. I've thought about war a lot. I guess it was fear of blood made me a medical student."

"Hooey!" I cried, peevishly; "you went in because your father and uncles can grease the slipways for you, when you leave dry-dock." He hunched over the table, put his hand to his chest and coughed, without answering me or raising his eyes.

"Drink went the wrong way?"

"It's my lungs," he murmured presently, "I'm afraid it's a goner."

"Which one?"

The liquor had worked in him, and now, as usual, inspiration visited him.

"A little perforation," said he, mournfully, "gives one more penetration. I would have made a good medico, but now I don't know whether I'll be able to finish the course, even if those mass-murderers don't take me. The passion of the sick, the fever of the man who's spitting up his guts. Do you know what that is? No, you're too healthy. To us, so much health seems a kind of deformity, as if you were born all in one piece."

"Is it serious, Bobby?" I asked, with a note of alarm, feeling ashamed that I had secretly thought him weak, trifling, spoiled.

"Passion sweated out into bloody handkerchiefs and sputum bottles," he said, taking fresh energy from his glass, "man spewing death, the moribund preternaturally like superman, fire in his blood and his entrails torn by his own breath knifing through —symbolizing, solemnizing our fated and ominous mission—man to make man perish from the earth. Death everywhere. They won't let me die of my sickness. No, by the awful hose spewing fire. We make a show: the vaudeville act between the risen curtains has gripped us all. War! 'Come in, you yellow dogs, and put on a uniform.' The bands play. The audience of mothers and sweethearts claps with frenzy. 'Come on, sucker, show those lousy jerks, those subhuman apes across the Rhine.' Thus, the common invectives, slinking in and out of bars, watching for the detective, 'Have you registered? Where's your selective service card? What's your name? What's your nation? What's your destination?' To the last, we'll answer, 'Hell,' no matter where they give us a boat ticket to."

"But, Bobby, maybe they won't send you across; it's just preparedness. And besides, if you've got tuberculosis, why anyone— they wouldn't even take you for hospital orderly."

He tapped his chest and said hollowly, "That's the trouble; I know what I feel, but there's just the shadow there, on the plate; it's a spot there—or two cicatrices—just a spot they would hardly call a vacuole—they're taking men who oughtn't to be in at all. Let's eat something; I may as well eat in a restaurant, while I can; I'll probably be in a sanitarium soon."

"What? You will," I cried.

"Yes," he continued, reading the menu and his mouth full of bread. "My family'll do what it can to get me into a rest home, I suppose; that ought to convince them. And if not—Ravioli, Scallopini with mushrooms and two glasses of red ink— Well, if not, I'll be in the craphouse too. The laundries of the U.S. army must be one bad smell; think of the mountains of tainted drawers when the news comes through daily; for it isn't rag-chewing any more, or the dear old rag, but another sort of rag the boys are interested in. People dead, killed in action, kids you went to class with and swapped smut and shortcuts with, men missing, what does that mean? Concentration camps, the dirthole, some chap my age and sort lying on the dirt with festering wounds and yelling for water and dying of starvation; men with skulls for heads and long useless bones that can't walk because there's nothing to hold the bones together, heaps, men with all the skin charred off them, like steaks, in oil baths—that means us, me, Letty—!" and his voice had a faint shriek—"and I must fight. God! When will the strength come to us to fight, to maim, to kill—for no reason, for no guy believes you've got to do that for your mother and sister; no, just for butchery, cruel, heartless savagery!"

"Gee, it's awful," I murmured, not knowing where to look, and feeling very miserable. "But it's awful for everyone, I mean; and they're burning up the civilian populations too now; they say this is probably the last war with armies."

"It's not fear so much," he went on, emptying his glass of water. "I'm compassionate for others because I've compassion for myself too. The spirit of the Nazi and the goon is, Be tough yourself and slug the other guy. All good doctors suffer themselves. It makes you think. Bloodshed is not moral."

"It may simply become a necessity," I murmured.

"Yes, a credo too simple. Overshadowed—impotent—when we know what we must do to ourselves and—and the threat to our homes, our lives, and I admit—our part in the straightening out of things. But who tangled them?"

"The crooks and the lethargic."

"The last generation," he said, leaning his head on his hand as he plucked up a collop with his fork; "I wish we need have nothing to do with each other: the last generation and us. We all wish that."

"Well, it's up to us; I'm taking a hand in my own life."

"You won't get anywhere unless you conform to them; where have you got? You're trying to get through the jungle alone, when there's a highroad being laid down by tractors and masses of men, right beside you—but only by men in uniforms. What's the answer? There isn't any? You see, Letty, you're a girl, you just want to get married and that settles things for you, doesn't it?"

"I guess so—more or less."

"Yes," he sighed; "and you're healthy too; it's like having only one eye, or trying to look through glass eyes. Besides, it's the fate of women to lose their identity, enter the herd as Mrs. X or Y, isn't it? Do you mind that?"

"No."

"Yes, yes; but we too! We'll be numbered, called up, registered, branded like cattle, entrained and shipped into slavery more or less long—years for some, eternity for others. Think of it! No life of our own."

"Look—but—well, isn't there such a thing as mass-feeling, Bobby? I mean, I thought men liked to be with other men; I thought that was a kind of bracing experience; and then you'll see other countries perhaps—well, other sorts of people anyway, and rub shoulders with all kinds of men; you know, I sometimes feel it's a bit mean the way we live, seeing absolutely no one but each other; we just live in a narrow lane, it's as bad as a book-worm burrowing through a library: we're men-worms, we just burrow through men, blind to all but our own set. I know I want to marry and that'll tie me up a bit tighter than I am tied now, but if they offered me a job overseas, in Buenos Aires or Kamchatka, I wouldn't mind."

He said gloomily, picking up the lumps of sugar and throwing them back into the sugar bowl, "That's what you think; that's because you expect a man to emerge from behind a rock or tree and take you out for a good time: that's a girl's view of things."

"But there are John Reeds and, well, Pancho Villas—and things—" I said lamely—"and Lenins, and practically everyone seems to have had a heroic grandpa in the Civil War; well, you see what I mean—"

He put his hand to his side, and coughed painfully, "It's this damn spot; I'm afraid I'm not of the stuff that heroes are made of; I don't believe there is anyone but an ordinary punk under anyone's skin."

"Well, don't think I'm flag-wagging," I said, "or that I'm not a realist."

He coughed desperately, drank his glass of wine to the bottom, and beckoned the waiter. He complained about the wine and ordered some more for himself. "Pasteur said wine is a disinfectant for the stomach and bowels, and I suppose if I help one part of my anatomy, I help the other parts." He was in a terrible state and filled me with pity. When we walked out, it was nearly dark, and I put my arm through his, and soothed him with friendly words; he probably wouldn't be accepted, he was studying for medicine; I'd heard that would help. But he said they were shoveling the lads in, you couldn't get exemptions like last time. His attention was only distracted from his discourse from time to time by things written on fences and walls. His eye would dart aside, and every block or two he would point out something interesting. "Say, haven't you got over toilet-literature?" I asked him. He said seriously that it was one of the oldest forms of literature in the world and you could still find personal remarks about men and women two thousand years dead in the excavations of Greece and Italy. "It makes you think," he muttered, "when you think of dying yourself; it makes you want to scribble on all the walls, Jake Jones, so that maybe something, just a wall-scrawl, will last after you. Maybe two thousand years. Who knows?"

"Not in New York," said I.

"That's what those smart guys thought in Herculaneum, too," he said; "it's just, you see, Letty, that I've joined the ages."

"Well, wait till they call you, Bobby, for God's sake."

"And naturally, a man like me has no future; I was right not to try to read it. I had a forewarning."

He coughed and put his hand to his chest, then he spat in the gutter. I could not help but feel that he was overacting it a bit, but did not dare to say anything. He pointed out an arrow, with a little design in chalk on the brick wall we were passing. Farther down he read a series of chalk-declarations, saying, "Emmeline stinks," "Izzie stinks," "Bobby stinks." "Prophetic," he said, shaking his head.

I seemed to cheer him up, though, for he called for me every night for a week or so, and even after that we went out a lot, eating, drinking, and rolling home in the early morning hours, which did not seem very good for his health, but he had turned reckless. I began to weary of his "spot" story, for instead of brushing it aside for the gruesomely unmentionable topic it was, he improved it every day and reveled in physical details and prophecies of corruption in which he outdid the joyous, black masters of groaning in English literature. For all I know, he looked them up; I never thought of that then, but became tired of a long tirade against everything which never mentioned me; I should have been glad even of a good stout denunciation; but he treated my character as negligible. I was born a woman, hence a cipher. I was convinced that he was a dependent who especially needed a woman of his own, but I could say nothing to convince him of that. I asked him why we shouldn't get married, in view of our close friendship and physical liking for each other. He would only ask hollowly if such a thing would be fair—to me, to him? He could not take on responsibilities. I said honestly, "Bobby, I admit I always meant to take up housekeeping when I married; for I am tired with knocking round the world; I've pounded the sidewalks for jobs and hurt my shins against every obstacle, and heard all the naughty words and seen the seamy side of quite a lot of men; but if it's the responsibility that's worrying you, then I'll forget it. I'll keep on working. What the hell—we're supposed to anyhow now; it's not good for the birth rate, but at least a woman has some sort of thing to live for, she's got an address she's proud of, not some hole in a wall. I like to be decent; and in the table of decency, a husband comes before anything else. So, if it's that alone that's bothering you, I'll work for you while you're making your way, going through college, or sitting in a sanitarium, or going to the wars, or whatever it is."

He groaned and said, in the state he was in, it was all out of the question. This was how it stood between us until Christmas. I was really fond of the guy, and would have done what I said, although the prospect of it made me tired; I said to myself, "I'm rather selfish and perhaps what I need is just this, a rather charming selfish grouch, who needs a nurse and mother; perhaps this will reform me; it will take my mind off myself and keep me away from other men—and that's a first-rate consideration; and perhaps I'll really be happy at last." I was very sweet to Bobby and he showed his gratitude in his peculiar way; I hoped he was transferring this inward, sick love from his mother to me. Whatever influence he had he used, and he received a deferment; and he was at last admitted for limited service. From then on my dear coward made use of every device for keeping himself not only safe from the danger he saw too clearly, but even for keeping himself near New York. Yet months passed when I did not see him and he began to go out of my mind. When he did write, he emphasized the mental old age which was coming over him. When he came to town, for a while the old flame and pleasure would be renewed. But I was also looking elsewhere.

With the passing of conscription, marriages came amongst us thick and fast; the town was gay and the girls hopeful. Sad dalliances ended happily overnight, and not only these college girls and unhappy flirts, but middle-aged women started to have babies, thick as buds in May. The men did not want to work at professions, believing they would all be in the army soon and would be getting good pay in the more romantic and professional services; and that intriguing and planning began which we are all so familiar with now: the learning of special trades, the using of influence, the taking of courses, all with a view toward avoiding the greatest danger, receiving higher pay and better grades. No woman can possibly see anything wrong in this; we do not start wars and we don't like killing. However patriotic we may be, we can't inwardly understand the madness of a nation which does its best to kill off all its healthy males.

Jacky received several proposals, but could not bring herself to cut herself off forever from Simon, who was charming to her, spoke tenderly about her, but appeared to be merely annotating it before he filed it for reference, at a yet greater age. The thought of having children tempted her; we, of course, kept urging her to marry, while she kept saying, "But he was so kind to me; no one else ever understood me; and no one understands him as I do."

She wept at all references to age; she gave money to old men in streets and stood, stony, when she had turned to look after some bent old fellow trudging through the streets between dinner and bedtime, all alone, muttering to himself. It dismayed people. They could not say what upset them so. They said, "He'll never be like that." She would not answer this.

The war came and during the first days after Pearl Harbor, people went about with a holy expression, both dumb and secretly shocked and yet radiant. Some young men were terrified; the girls began enrolling themselves for war service; the oppression of the last few months fell away. The nation was glad to be at war, and yet in a trance. Marriages fell off; when people heard that babies conceived after Pearl Harbor would not count for deferments, marriages fell off even more. As for myself, I had not been lucky enough to find the right man at the right time, in the panic, and so had to look round in the same old hit-and-miss way. The town was bright at this time, however; and the middle classes and those beginning to see money in the war were in a spendthrift, hopeful mood. A young girl like me could have a very good time, and there were still a lot of men in their twenties to take as escorts. The town was jammed with wealthy refugees from Europe, and war profiteers on the upgrade. Among the refugees we met some recent wives who had once been mistresses and café loafers in our time in Paris and London—friends of Aunt Phyllis, Mother, Pauline, and ourselves. Aunt Phyllis avoided all these, having forgotten this world and having by now deeply embedded herself in a fat, rich, middle-class, card-playing set, where nothing was spoken of but the prices of furs and apartments and the vices of servants. With some malice, though, I talked quite freely about them when I went to see Aunt Phyllis, mentioning the names she had known them under and the ones they now wore. Most of them had done so much better than she had, poor smug suburban wife. As for me, I made the rounds. Their husbands, who had been their lovers, had nearly all kept in touch with Solander, who was a merry good-natured man, with a wonderful talent for business, though not for moneymaking. The new couples, most of whom were past middle age, remembered me as a handsome, shrewd, impudent Paris child, and so enquired after me. When they saw me, they were delighted at my appearance and clever conversation; and while the husbands went about their new businesses, the wives set about inviting me out and running up lists of eligible bachelors for me; I was offered, tentatively, a colonel from North Africa, a rich young Jew from Oxford, a young psychoanalyst. I spoiled these chances, if chances they were, by my impatience and by having too many other irons in the fire. I could not play the role of interesting young girl for more than an hour or two; my hard knowledge of the business and social world, my sense of the comic, and that fierce, almost brutal energy that took hold of me when I saw a new man, and turned me into termagant and seducer, soon ripped the veil from the eyes of these women who were, after all, no such sentimental fools as they pretended to be. These women of the world made me quite sick when they played at the maternal, and toward me; "Oh, sisters, drop those masks," I wanted to say. Were they not like me, I like them? I was no more a young eligible girl than they, yet I had as much chance of success as they, if I went about, as they had, with my eyes open. I do not want to give the wrong impression about these women; some of them had paid their own expenses during their long liaisons, many were rich women; one I know for certain had bought a house, an automobile, and furniture for the wealthy man whose mistress she had been and whose wife she now was. Not only that, but she now worked day and night with him, in his business, like any proper French wife, and in all good faith did not understand libertinage or impurity in speech.

These women, who were mostly of good bourgeois families, had excellent manners and expected European manners from me. This was the turn of the screw; I had to forget them. Also, I had other fish to fry. But if I dropped them, it was not out of hypocrisy or necessity, as it was with Aunt Phyllis and Mother. Mother was ashamed before them, that was her trouble. She was a deserted wife and poor, and they were now wives moving in good café society, living in uptown hotels, wearing expensive clothes, with much forward-looking toward war speculation. All had active and quite tender husbands. Months passed for me, in this way, months of excitement and fever, alternating with dull, fretful months in which I worried about my future.

The example of Jacky, my father's good advice, and the general restlessness put me to work again. I looked at my love letters, my unfinished novels, poems, and plays, and began to think: Time's fever is all in their bloods, and I think I won't beat it by neglect. Time does not respond either to affection or neglect; and I can't close my eyes to the fact that I, Letty Fox, am now just on twenty-one years old.

In a fit of petulance, I resigned from my publishing office, but through Erskine, I got a job in the editorial office of a weekly political magazine, with smart circulation and flip vocabulary. I was forced to it, too, by my debts, which were outstanding from the previous Christmas. I learned the journalist's technique, had practice in writing, learned cable writing, read the provincial press for clippings, and wrote stories, as well, about certain things that I was supposed to know, such as modern personalities in art and music, on the radical side, economics (because I had once been such a hard-working Communist), and things of that sort, that I had honestly come by. I was on the editorial side of the fence, and was now uptown, near Rockefeller Center. As I had joined this crowd of cynical radicals—they thought of themselves as radicals, though they were completely corrupt, worked like mad for the success of the paper, and cared not a jot about the poor—I was obliged at last to give up my true political views, at least officially.

For a long time now I had been working with people with the same underlying political philosophy, the same esthetic creed, the same over-all interests in life, the same love-lives, almost; the same advanced, sophisticated views on things like psychoanalysis, divorce, writing, new trends in the movies. I had been with people who took in the same magazines, went to the same coffee shops and dances, and I had been (for all my doubts and troubles) very happy. I had felt a great compatibility with all these people, of whom some were Susannah Ford, Bill van Week, and even most of my other men; and this compatibility of views, and pure, deep-spirited New Yorkism had made me friendly even with men who had loved and left me. The sting was there, sometimes; sometimes it hurt very much; but, also, I could live with them and not feel shipwrecked, just because society or this social group had not abandoned me. I had no need of great personal passions. I had no need of being exceptional. What I had in me that gave me the most joy were two things: the capacity for an enormous output of work, and the ability to enjoy myself regardless of expense, regardless of others; a healthy trait, if a bit barbaric.

There were no *delicates* in this new job; all were New York born. I had no secrets. In my moments of suffering I told most of my troubles to everyone, men, women, and bosses. They were like me, sympathized. People are generally kind; some take advantage, but even they can be kind. The person who gives himself away as I do is more likely to receive kindness than the timid soul hiding his wounds—so said I; and it seemed to work out for me. To keep up my mental life, I began to keep a diary for myself, full of quite silly political speculation, and I found, if I didn't want to repeat editorials, that I had a few and very feeble economic concepts, nothing to enable me to solve the problems that every turn of patriotic feeling and every necessitated change of political line brought up. One of the questions was pretty common those days: "In the face of extreme restriction, what was the incentive for capital to go on capitalizing?"

That is the way I put it to myself. We mulled these things over, but I found no one knew any more than I did, for the answer wasn't, "They do it out of patriotism." It's a fairly safe estimate that no one does anything from noble motives, until you strike the exceptions like Jacky and Gondych; and Gondych, query. I am not, we are not, as they. Society itself must change; you cannot depend on individual nobility. That is what I think. We have no measures of morality and motive—someone said something like that. Alas! I copy; but the sentiment is true. And this is why, with such heartiness, I have always sunk myself in my group. There are great movements of the group to which no one can be superior. I am not wiser than my fellow; and especially, I doubt my wisdom to be smarter than the massed forward pressure of the vanguard. I would not dare to stand alone. I might be mad and not know it.

Now, inspirited by this lively work on this snappy magazine weekly, I shook myself out of a long sleep. I had been in a cocoon, it seemed to me. For instance, while loafing, I worried about my misadventures with men; but, at work, I took them in my stride. I had spent a year, no, eighteen months in a protective envelope of routine and vice and occasional moods, without producing anything. I was rewarded for this outburst of work and new adult stand by meeting, it seemed to me, the ideal man for me. One can't help these feelings of rewards and punishments.

I discussed the trivia of daily existence with the office crowd, and important theoretical questions with those that remained of the old group; with my friends too, and of course, domestic questions with Jacky. I sometimes visited my father or mother; but now I had one other to whom I could talk about more serious problems—well, slightly more serious, they seemed. I had met a *Man*. I breathed not, stir I dared not, lest something should happen: the usual misstep or mistake. As the cow in *State Fair* thought, looking at the hog hero, "She was not sure whether Blue Boy was a hog or an illusion." When you find everything you want, you hold your breath. I had created like—who was it?—created a man in my image, or the hope of one, and then, whenever I saw man or boy with the appearances of my ideal—unworthy confession, but the basis of real love I suppose—I fancied myself in love. I had never, till now, been in love. Every time, disillusioned, I said to myself, Am I never going to be in love? I don't fancy myself as a quester, but I'm a human being; I'm frail, I have to quest. And so on! But now— a man of twenty-seven, the ideal age, the perfect American, completely blond, blue-eyed, handsome, beautiful in every respect, and with an expression on his face, when he was not thinking of anything in particular (which seemed to be often), which was a mixture of natural dignity with goodness. A miracle! Well, in short, all I needed. He had been an actor, but only as a student. He had been an engineer and an economic analyst for a foreign government. Now, he was working for a big uptown firm and I met him through the newspaper. He used to cast his eye over technical articles for us. I had the job of taking the articles to him. Romantically—

pretty girl enters office and finds the man; thus, I found him. Better, he came from a very old New England family, and his general sophistication and political views were the best possible for me. All this is just a description of externals, things that can be described.

As for the rest, what you see but can't describe in round figures or on a chart—he was a man, not just half a human couple, like so many men I have met. He was a man with all the sensibilities and experiences, and even the craft of a real man; and my attitude toward him was extraordinary; that is, for me. I felt at once that I couldn't bear a cheap episode with him. I thought, if he tries to make me, it's all over, I won't see him again. But anyone could see he was not the type to go into love affairs like that; he was too serious—perhaps if not serious enough for marriage, for the great and sober emotions. When I know someone who seems fun, but doesn't really get me excited, I telephone him if I want to see him. But this time I could not. I didn't want to start things from my side; I wanted nature to take a hand. We contacted psychically, you could say, at once, at first sight; got to know each other in the first few words. It was steady, delightful, and there was the flash of lightning. We knew each other, and yet not altogether; there was an element of wildness and speed in the air, exhilaration, as if we were on the Loop-the-Loop. Then, each time I saw him, I lost my breath in this way. Curious, for me. I wasn't excessive. I couldn't be, with my new method.

I saw him once or twice a week; but, between, I didn't stay at home bad-tempered, smoking and drinking nervously as usual; I was sweetly calm. I smiled even, the whole day long, which was a mystery for my companions. The rub was—there was one naturally—that he had a mistress of years' standing, whom he could not drop in a minute. He frankly declared himself fond of this woman, although not enough to marry. Things were ambling along in this style, he told me, when he met me. At once he knew the world had turned upside-down. Now, he had something to think about.

Well, I had enough experience not to build too much upon it. Each time I saw him it was an evening like nothing I had ever passed. Each time, I was completely happy, and each time he told me more about himself. I learned to know him better and in detail; his past, character, ideas, even his affairs with women; and I plunged myself into his personality. We were suited in all respects.

I spent his birthday with him. We went home and mixed drinks for ourselves and Jacky. Then we went out together. What a delicious day! We spent the evening at a party of Bill van Week's, and then I went to his flat. Everything was so different with him, that I found myself passing the whole evening until late at night, thus, with him, in his room, without anything indelicate having been suggested. He kissed me, and then—said I must go; I gave him a feeling of real passion, and he respected me too much. Then, charmingly, he apologized for this (for both aspects of this), and we stayed still, talking, kissing, and coming to an even better understanding; and it ended without any indelicacy whatever.

I left feeling radiant. I saw that I had not sold my birthright for a mess of pottage. I could love and purely, sweetly, like any young girl. All my snifter-taking could stop short, and I could be clean and devoted. I had often seen it before. It was not that I did not love him materially—this, too; indeed, more than others. I could not sit still when he was there. It was fantastic! I was on wires; but the promise for the future, a real relation, a serious love, was so dear to me that I knew there were more important things than making sure of the night's happiness.

I naturally bored poor Jacky half the night on the subject of my new love; I told her what it was to be in love. How considerate! This time, too, I had patience and bore without a murmur the doubting smiles of all my friends. I knew I had been an idiot often enough. Even this thought kept me in hand; I waited to see what would happen. How difficult it was for me to be sensible! I loved, I, the foolish virgin, loved truly, almost greatly. I knew then that if it should happen, I'd acquire an incredible serenity; nothing would be able to touch me. I have not given the name of this love of mine, because it seemed unimportant when I recall my strong feelings; but it was Wicklow.

Once more, I was merely duped. This attractive man stayed with me for months, and we were not, unfortunately for my self-respect, always so sober; but not once did he really think of letting his mistress go. Of course, now I wonder whether he really had such a mistress at all, and whether I was not the stick-woman on which he built this touching fiction.

As I had imposed a regime on myself, however, I had more time on my hands and now went out very often with other girls. I often took Jacky, who worked too hard and was miserable about Gondych; and she told me several distressing episodes in her past which showed me she was not as childish as I had imagined. I was glad to have her to look after, and began to see that I had a good side to my nature, which I sometimes doubted.

The war came. My friends fell away, most married and soon were showing their young bodies much swollen in parks, and, later on, were sitting with their fair and dark hairs pinned up, in new cotton Mother Hubbards, playing watch-dog to baby carriages. They looked very youthful, more than I did, and very vapid, as if they had never been to school and never read a book. They looked like themselves at the age of four; and soon—after that—but I'm advancing the clock a bit—they had with them replicas of themselves at the age of four; and by that time had aged, looked careworn, a bit thinner, and were urging me to go back to Mother, get married, think of the older values. They kept asking me if I believed in those ideological salves; if ideology itself was not the soporific of the people and whether women especially ought not to go back to the old race-ways. Later on, this emptiness of head gave them heartaches. They became unhappy with their husbands. If their husbands were away at war, needing something to think about, they became the most serious possible little nuns of the progressive school movement and worried about diet, and should you spank Junior! But where were the lively, smart girls of my adolescence—where are the snows of yesterday?

Although sorry I had no husband and baby, I could no longer rub shoulders with these thwarted and miraculously stunted youngsters who had become middle-aged women, dull, smug, neurotic. One of the things I noticed about them was that they chafed themselves sore about the smallest household irritations, and the natural failings of the men they had yoked themselves to. I thought to myself, I shan't be like that; I've seen enough men to know they aren't perfect. I'll make a model wife. But my experience of men and the common-sense view I had of their lives made it difficult for me to marry those gossoons who were now marrying to escape the draft. I was sick when I looked at the beautiful babies that came out of these war marriages, and knew I should be glad to have one; but all that went along with it did not suit me.

Yet the men got better as the women got worse. Many a time I saw one of my male schoolmates married who was ten times better than before marriage, and with whom I could talk easier than his wife. His wife retained usually, some of her college habits: wise talk, solemn face, vague tags of modernism (slowly growing whiskers), an attachment to the more serious programs on the radio, at least at parties; I still clung to real life. It was to me, it seemed, the men turned. I did not trust myself enough to think, either, that if I were married, I would be different from these kids. True, I was fairly smart, but I always had that mad urge to sink myself in the heaving sweaty mass of humanity and be one of the girls (or boys). I would try to be a cave-wife, just as they did, in order to prove I was a good guy and not a prune and a prissy.

Well, apart from this, with everyone turning into a model citizen with accepted values, life on the old home front crept along, progressed sadly and sometimes gaily, when there were farewell parties to boys I knew, or weddings. The radicals I knew had fallen into line with an ungraceful bump and there was no more official iconoclasm. Some of the radicals were delighted at this, they had always felt gawky and out in the cold. Others, the hot-blooded ones, felt very mad indeed, but they could not do much. I was betwixt and between; I had enough red blood not to like a lot of things I saw passing under the name of patriotism and the war effort, but I hadn't the guts, folly, or lunacy to go out on my own hook. I had to belong to society.

New York was now the deadest place imaginable. Everyone was in the army, married, out of school, or following war courses. No one was a radical! Everyone, therefore, though they would not admit it, was slightly discouraged. Their life principle was hit. For no one, after all, can consider war, even against a hated enemy, an aim in life. No one can consider the death of your nearest and dearest as a good thing; and any woman, even unmarried, thinks, Well, do I after all bring up my boy to die like that, horribly, and unwillingly? We still have that weakness about having boys.

As to the radicals—it was finally hitting all the prize dodos (dodo, a fabulous and antediluvian bird existing in Wonderland— and that's what New York was then) that, (a) If this was a people's war, it was up to the people to make it so, and not a time for the people to retreat on all fronts; and (b) Capitalism, draped in the well-known Star and Stripes, British Union Jack, and so on, a handsome and imposing figure, supported by all that is fair, strong, young in the nation, was pulling some awfully funny stunts, for an ally of Soviet Russia; thus, refundable corporate taxes, delayed second front, mad income taxes, hitting kids like me; and other signs rem-iniscent of the detested Britisher, etc., etc., *ad imperialauseam*; and (c) That wars are pretty grim things and the people fight them, even when it's for someone else's glory and profit.

I really think the only thing that carried me through this moral bottom, which always comes in a profit-taking hour, is that I worked for the United Nations out of hours, daily talked with all and sundry about guerrilla warfare, militant action after the war, the rise of the oppressed peoples of Europe, the hope of a Republic in Britain, and the future of the world; the future in the future tense, not in the past tense.

I had, thank goodness, a very decent job with good pay; I worked mad hours for the fun of getting my back into something, all purely voluntary, without extra pay. The work came so thick and fast that it didn't get done, even with respites of gabbing and sly cokes and cocktails in between, and reduced lunch hours. I liked to see the work, so that I could sail into it, and yet I got tired, and I did not like that hurt look that bosses so easily acquire when someone (the secretary, or other inferior type of human) "lets them down." But since it was, after all, for a cause, the war—and it was wonderfully encouraging to believe in this—we did it, and liked it. It also gave me the feeling that my adventures after hours were purified by all the work. I believe they were. I had a right to them. I was beginning to feel all the oats I had eaten all my life. I wondered why we couldn't have a war-effort all the time, only without any war; a peace-effort. That's asking too much. In peace, they let you drop—with a short, sharp shock! I got into the way of nosing out journalistic scoops and wondered if I couldn't make a career in radio. I thought I saw in myself a combination of Dorothy

Thompson, Anne O'Hare McCormick, and Genevieve Tabouis rolled into one. I was young, and a voice, and a talent.

To drift out of these high altitudes and down to what was earth to me: I was still scratching round to make up the few hundred dollars I owed. My father eventually advanced me the one hundred dollars for Bill van Week, on the principle, I suppose, that millionaires should be paid first, a law of nature. I had rent coming up, thirty-five dollars in cleaner's bills, and I paid more than half in the household expenses for myself and Jacky. In short, Tillie the Toiler. My mother, as usual, had ten dollars in the bank. Grandmother Morgan, as usual, was several thousand dollars in the red. She was the one who lent me most of my needed money. She had real financial power; for this it is to be able to live entirely off debts. I have not this.

To keep up what they used to call (blissful days of Academe) "extra-curricular activities" (funny word for fun), I scrounged and sponged, worked hard and saved, labored and starved to go to concerts. I paid fortunes for my seats and usually reduced my avoirdupois by *force majeure* for two or three days before and after. With work, I returned also to the mind. The fact is, when I loaf I can do nothing, and don't even get men; and when I work, I can do everything; learn too, and get men too. But I'm such a little elephant of work that I need these periods of incubation. The worst is—if I marry will I just silt down into primeval mud like the rest of the girls? I'd hate it; but a woman as strong as I am can also be strongly, wickedly lazy, and forever; and take it out as a common scold. The weak worry about losing their souls, minds, or education. I could just be a beast, a party-beast, a kitchen-beast, a nursery-beast. I'm afraid of myself.

Well, the example of Jacky, too, helped me. I was ashamed to see her, sitting piously at the feet of Academe, goddess of dust, confinement, and bread-eating. Jacky was getting lectures with a veneer of objectivity about economic determinism, Buckle, Hegel, Marx, Mumford, food-determinists, geography-determinists, and so on (implying a restricted and rigid kind of determinism, a teacherish sort) all in one three-quarter hour. Pretty swift work even for America, where "*Alles geht auf dampf.*"

Jacky became madly enamored, even really in love with

Benedetto Croce, and was stumped, indignant, she flew into a passion, when I dared to raise the query, "What does that unsainted resident of the Naples slums think of matter?" I made her agree that there was a good deal of Platonic ideology there. Teacher told Jacky, Hegel and Marx were impossible to read. I told Jacky I could read both at the rate, say, of about six pages an hour, not guaranteeing to understand every word. I had a mission; life at home became a riot, but I was back in my stride. I thought I was doing Jacky good by coaxing her, rather forcibly, at the end of a leash, out of her Cave of Adullam. Jacky did not like Marx or Hegel because she could not fall in love with them. She was wild about Spinoza, Melanchthon, Shelley, and Bertrand Russell. Why? No need to give the answer. I never saw such a girl for marrying immortals. I don't say I understood all the rot I talked, but I had poor Jacky backed off the map every time, and only raised flushes and tears in her.

It proved one thing to myself, which was the object of the whole rousing tussle in me; that, at least, theories to me meant theories; they meant fighting and some resolution, while to the purely feminine girl they were just dreams, poems, a kind of religion.

At each new brawl with Jacky, or with others more fit for my fighting, I felt the world ought to be organized differently, so that I could keep this kind of life up forever. My marshal's baton was once more peeping up out of my knapsack and sprouting. I thought that Napoleon, too, had his lazy, worthless years, and wrote reams of vaporings. He got nowhere until he was placed somewhere by the chances of war. If only I could get in touch with a great man of action, if only I could work together with men of energy and intelligence, modern men who think the way I do. I couldn't do anything with the compatible groups in which I was happy but lazy, just chewing the rag, and I couldn't dream after stardust and live on nectar; and I couldn't do much as a stenographer, a special article-writer, or a messenger girl; and I couldn't do much, truth to tell, bringing more larval human beings into the daylight and worrying about diapers and cute little sayings and lisping geniuses for years, at least, not at my age. I felt the world was too small for me. I sprouted. Was this all due to my good plumpness, my fat, in short?

With all my other work, I found time again to begin work on a new novel, a new idea. It came about through a fluke. I was at Susannah Ford's home, where I met some refugees who were doing quite well here in the start-up of an engineering, ship-building and ship-reconditioning business. A young woman was there, very much on the outs with her young, ambitious husband. I made quite an impression on him, claiming also to be a French refugee, and out of a job. My French, which I had always kept up with Jacky, was so very good (to him, at least, a German-born Swiss) that he at last believed me and slipped ten dollars into Susannah's hand as he was leaving, for her to give to me, to secure an appointment with him, the next day. An appointment for a job, he said. But was it?

It's a kind of amusing gag starting-point for a story, a lead, but what to? That's the rub. I heard there weren't many novels around, as the boys were going into the army and were interested in flying, soldiering, techniques of one kind or another, that would improve their positions; so women novices had a better chance.

I worked on my novel for two or three days, even denying myself to my boy friends, but such a high-minded state could not last with me. Partly out of ambition, and partly out of gaiety, I had become intimate with the head of the office, a pleasant married man of thirty-six. He was supposed to be rather tired of his wife, but I was getting to be used to this and no longer built the hopes on marital fatigue that I had before. He was an ambitious man, and wanted to help me on, to see me a journalist, a radio commentator or writer. To impress him and help myself, perhaps, one lunchtime I dashed off some "Notes on Character Observation on First Sight, and Afterwards"; for I said to myself, Here I am with a huge, sprawling, mad family, hundreds of friends; I've mixed in every kind of life and know a good deal; and know men better than ten women of my age—at least the average ten women—I ought to be able to make a hit with a novel, and I admit the novel is built on character.

So this is what I wrote:

1. Esteem old wives' saws until proven false; examine commonplaces, accepted lies—often truths.
2. Remember first things, as age, sex, domestic and marital standing, finances.

3. Occupation; this gives a special viewpoint.
4. Indications are given by body-build, race, coloring, skin, gait, sitting posture, tics; etc. Examine systematically, beginning with crown of head, ending with feet, or vice versa.
5. Ask for medical standbys, e.g., heart-build is as face-build is as body-build. Peculiarities of posture indicate old or new weaknesses.
6. Indications by hands.
7. Draw easy conclusions; these are likely to be right. In analyzing motives, don't jump at once to idea of complex, egotistic, or raptorial notions. There may be temporary or permanent imitations, family, *milieu*.
8. What is the guiding motive?
9. Most things, apparent weaknesses, are really life-system of preservation. Life urge is strongest, even weaknesses utilized. Foibles are *fortes*.
10. Hackneyed situations always exist unless otherwise proven.
11. Mere observation not enough. The examiner must take part in discussion and bring out all kinds of reactions. Sympathy and antipathy are two instruments of observation for the observer.

Etc., etc.

I showed this to my new friend, as well as to the one I had fallen in love with such a short time back, Wicklow, my "American Ideal Male," and pretended that these notes were the fruit of years of contemplation; but I slandered myself! Unfortunately, in this as in other things, I was far, far too clever. I came home from the meeting with my new lover in a great flush of success and joy; but, once there, while I was congratulating myself on my ability, an unpleasant thought struck me: Why can I do so much? Why can I love so often? It would be simpler to have one clear call, like Jacky. At least, simpler; but could I stand the stupidity of such a life? I must have fire!

42

MY MEDDLING with Jacky's affairs was not successful, after all. Simon Gondych had been gone to England about a year, and was working on poison gas, gas shelters, and diet problems in a reduced economy. Jacky did not often hear from him, for he was very busy, often ill, as he tried his experiments, like all biochemists, on himself, and always in danger of some sort. Also, he made frequent trips out of town, or to the Continent, and could not reveal his address. I thought this romance was fading, and was much surprised when I found that Jacky wrote regularly to him.

I was quite satisfied with my home. It was an old flat, but looking out over a back court, quiet and private on Sundays. All around were old studios in which commercial artists, artists, and workers in the fine arts, who had done very badly before, were doing very well now, owing to war orders and the general look-up in the business world.

We were at the end of a corridor with five other doors. On the right was a young airman's wife, with a blond baby; on the left two pretty Southern girls, making hay and harlotry with the army; opposite, a couple of tired girls-about-town, who drank and brawled and pulled in their rare male visitors; then an unmarried couple who spent the week end in gin, brazenly; and next door again a hard-working bachelor girl, nearly middle-aged. Jacky knew none of them, but I could borrow chairs, ice cubes from any of them, at any time. Jacky was disliked. Nothing is easier than to be alone. She lived for, with, and by Gondych, even in absence; and so she was neglected by the rest of the human race. I often became very much annoyed with her. She did not work as much as I did either, and was becoming quite old-maidish, although as lovely as she had ever been.

My surprise was great when this child, who had shown no enterprise, came to me one day and detailed plans she had been making for getting over to Gondych. I first said, "Does he want you, Jacky?"

"What do I lose, anyhow? I'm not happy here. I don't care if I die."

"Well, little items like your family, me, your mother, your country, that is not much, of course—"

It was Greek to her. Overbalancing all that, she had a dozen or so twenty-line notes from her sage, written on small white notepaper, in extremely regular lines, in his clear, crabbed, scholar's script, and signed "Yrs" or "Your friend" or "Affectionately, Simon Gondych" or "S.G." She thought they were State documents. The pretty monogram he had invented, the precise, masculine capitals, were, for her, Simon himself. She looked at these little bits of paper with burning cheeks and glowing eyes, and something of a maternal expression. By now, his age, all that had first repelled her, attracted her. She pitied and loved him for it. In fact, it was invulnerable. She had quite made up her mind to lose her life, country, and everything for Gondych.

She had been to Joseph Montrose, with whom my father had worked half a lifetime, and had asked him to get her to Britain somehow. Montrose was very friendly with every woman in my family, and still hankered after Aunt Phyllis, even though she was twice married and twice a mother by now, rather fat, be-furred and be-ringed, interested in facials and bridge.

Jacky resembled Aunt Phyllis most remarkably, with this shadow over her, which she had always had. It made her a less blatant beauty, but to some, the older, more thoughtful men, even more enticing. Montrose behaved with great delicacy toward Jacky, and, although himself a shameless Casanova, seemed to understand and respect her *grande passion*. Like all frequent lovers, like myself, Joseph Montrose had struck once or twice in five hundred chances—to put it in round figures—the fatal woman; and he sympathized with a poor young creature who had struck the fatal man at her first going out into the world, and one, by chance, separated from her by nearly two generations!

"Such things can happen," he said, "and I am not one to laugh at love. I dare not. What would love do to me?"

He visited my mother frequently on this interesting topic, and begged her, perhaps only in obedience to habit, to arrange a meeting with Phyllis. My mother told him quite coldly that she no longer moved in Aunt Phyllis's set; she was not rich enough; an abandoned woman was a mere death's head at their feast of successful marrying and divorcing.

Joseph Montrose then betook himself to my father's. Mother was bitterly opposed to Jacky's wild plan, which was natural enough; but her poor words carried no weight, since she was opposed to any manifestation of will and considered almost every event some kind of as yet unclassified tragedy. Where did she get two or three daughters like us? She always said we were Grandmother Morgan's daughters, not hers; but she supposed she had no right to ask anything of life; she had failed, and life has no use for failures.

My father was equally opposed to the wartime (and necessarily illegal) trip to England, but Jacky managed to persuade him, with what sure signs of an invincible determination, I don't quite know. Montrose then agreed to take her over himself, by bomber, if possible; and as he had many connections in Washington, he hoped to get her a post there, preparatory to her getting over. He would finance her till she found whether it was possible for her to stay there. Jacky said my father should not be the loser, nor anyone else. Now, at length, she had found some use for Grandmother Fox's money; she wanted to use it for getting to Simon. My poor father made enormous eyes, and said, "Your little grandmother worked as a governess and housewife, and gave language lessons so that you kids could get a better education than she had; she didn't mean it to be spent on cleaner's bills, debts to Bill van Week, and trips to visit a man in England."

Jacky said, "Grandmother was a darling old lady, but one of the old school; and, by the way, didn't she tell me of a long trek she made from Wisconsin to New York, without a cent to feed herself with, all for the sake of a man?"

"Did she tell you that?"

For my part I had never heard of it; but it turned out that it had been so. Grandmother had told me stay-at-home tales, painted word-pictures of adoring humble daughters and Griseldas and Penelopes. I saw in Grandmother a gentle propagandist. Jacky she perhaps considered too mild. My mother could only think to ask Jacky, "Don't you want to get married and have children?"

"Yes, but I can't help this."

She refused to stay at home with her mother, but kept on with me, and I left her to her romance. She became tedious enough. To her mind, Gondych communicated with her, when he was in New York, by some animal means unknown to science. She knew when he was in town and when not. They could not really quarrel because, so often, their thoughts were identical. He had the simplicity and decent frankness of a young girl; she had the psychic complexity of Gondych. When she first fell in love with him, after a memorable week of outings, their meetings had been interrupted by ten days. She had daydreamed of a certain incident. He would come to Solander's place for dinner; Persia had apéritifs and wines. She would hand Gondych glass of wine; he would taste from it and hand it back to her; she would drink from it and smash it accidentally. She had thought for some hours of the smashing of the glass, how she would place it, so that none but Gondych would know it was intentional. Gondych of course would know, "because he knew everything."

The evening was actually arranged. Gondych came to the house, she opened the door, and there stood the man she loved, bowing. They looked at each other, and each thought, "Yes, it is true; it is not something I fantasied."

She thought this, in a flash, and she could see it flash through Simon. He kissed her hand, and came in. The wine scene took place almost as imagined. Persia handed them both glasses of wine —Jacky followed Gondych to the foyer; he, with a slight bow, drank, his eyes fixed on her. She was frightened at the way reality fringed her dream. She put down her glass because her hand was trembling, and saw Gondych's disappointed look. She took his and drank from it, but did not dare to smash it, although they were alone. This incident showed an "abnormal parallelism in their thoughts."

Jacky and I went for walks in the streets and usually ended up in a bar or cafeteria. She preferred to sit and walk in dark places. She did not like the way men stared at us in bars. I was pretty much on the prowl and her soul-mating made me shiver. I wanted to look about. Often, when I had dropped her at home, I'd pretend I had to get cigarettes and go back down to the Village, approaching it from the Port of Authority end of Fourteenth Street. Down that way I met few I knew, but by the time I got to Seventh Avenue, and turned down toward Sheridan Square, I was getting into my own bailiwick and was likely to run into plenty of people. I'd meet people I'd met with other men; and if I met no one, there were a few doorbells I could ring, where we could drink beer and chew the rag till I felt like sleeping. Jacky, at home, would not worry.

These empty weeks were the ones when I went most often to Mathilde's or Solander's, or called upon any relatives in town. This I only did to cut my expenses, or when I was too heartsick at my connections with crooks, self-appointed Casanovas, and the riff-raff of town.

I took to card-playing and set out to beat Grandmother Morgan. I had some talent for gin rummy, which we played mostly for a quarter of a cent a point, and sometimes going partners with her, and sometimes letting her stake me. But I lost as often as I gained. If I made two or three dollars, I'd blow it in, and if I lost, was quite sick to think of the additional hole this made in my pocket. Jacky understood none of my troubles, but she no longer reproached me. She had been blown out to sea herself; she felt she had no advice to give to the rudderless. There were moments when I didn't mind being on the town, and times when I had thoughts of suicide, for I saw a good deal of sham in my glorious life-cavalcade and I couldn't see anything much to go for.

There were one or two bad incidents. Soldiers were roaming the town, out of camp, and a few back from abroad. They were wild, and from every girl expected the works, just for the asking. I had always gone round town freely, since schooldays; but now, a lot of town became impossible. Many of the soldiers were small-town boys or country lads who thought we owed them everything because we'd been born in the sex that doesn't fight.

"Can you tie that, half the Americans there are don't ever get put in the army, what sort of goddamn luck, just because they're born with—" etc.

The others were wild guys who were pampered to death by the

Mom and *War-Loan* publicity they were putting about, and to whom most civilians in bars were afraid to say a word. The civilians hunched over the bar, drinking their drinks and not daring to put in a word to help us when we got into trouble. I daresay they had a lewd pleasure in hearing these hayseeds and regimented pool-parlor kids get after us.

We pretty soon found we were only free in the Village or thereabouts. Once I was with Isabel Cartwright, this ugly, clever girl I had been with at high school. She was a doctor of medicine now, and we had been to an old school-tie affair. Afterwards we dropped in at a place we had known for years, taking no notice of a couple of flying dinosaurs in soldier-suits drinking there, even when they came up and tried to sit in our booth. I simply said, "You're making a mistake, boys."

One of the boys, with a Texas accent, who was stinko, said, "Then what are you here for?"

"This is the result of self-appointed Southern chivalry," said I to Isabel, "or the war of the U.S.A. with Texas is still being held."

I said to the boys, "Come on, heave yourselves off that bench and leave us alone; we're not in business."

The other lad looked glum, cruel, uneasy, and got up; but the tall dinosaur harried us till we had to leave the place; and when we looked at the civilians at the bar, he started to yell, "You're so homely, no man would ever (so-and-so) and you got such a loud mouth that the feller who (so-and-so) is a (so-and-so)," and he went on to say that he had a perfectly good wife at home that he could get at when he pleased; she never said no; and she didn't sit in bars, but waited for him, and so forth.

We walked out with the dignity, I fear, of ducks taking a walk. I was pretty red, though I knew decency takes a nose-dive in wartime, with the sexes cooped up and kept from each other. Oddly enough, it's sexual freedom that makes the world decent. However, out of curiosity, for I was burning with shame and anger, I said to Isabel, "How did you feel?"

She said, "I've been an ugly girl all my life, it started with my father, brothers, and cousins, and I guess I'm used to it now. They always said to me, 'You're so goddamn plain, no man would give you a tumble.' Besides, I see more of these air-conditioned bats than you do. But I assure you, there's not much difference to me, between now and before; it's only to you, it's different."

I felt my heart sinking at these words; for somehow they revealed to me the great shame in which we all lived, and I was quite blue for about a week. However, after a few such brawls, I got my tongue ready and I also took care never to take Jacky to my old haunts, now become unsuitable for a young girl.

For my Christmas vacation I went away for a trial marriage, to a hotel, with Wicklow, the ideal "American male," since his mistress wanted to spend Christmas with her family at Seneca Falls, New York.

Ours was a lovely hotel near the Delaware, with a Coca-Cola stand across the road, an ice cream soda town at five miles, and a liquor town at eight; with this, nine holes of golf, swimming, riding, and a place full of young people. Posing as Mrs. Wicklow, the charming young bride, wore me out. There were a lot of middle-aged people beaming at us. We had to stick closer than brothers for the week of the holidays; eat, dress, sleep, walk, sit, read, and yawn together. I found it a second-rate life, and felt I was not ripe for marriage; this living inside each other's sweatshirt was not for me. I kept my eyes lovingly glued on Wicklow, while all the time I was wondering about his mistress, secretly observing the other men, and wondering if I wasn't passing up a real chance by this sham-honeymoon; for a good many men could have been better for me than Wicklow. Add to that the trifle that Wicklow was short of cash, and I had to advance the money for the holiday myself, first having squeezed it out of Papa, with promise of repayment. We did not click, and I thought with dread, "This might be a real honeymoon, and I would then be stuck for some period of months or years with this dull, vain, boorish showpiece; I'm afraid to take such a plunge."

I looked back on my life with Mother, with Jacky; I was evidently suited for life with very few people. Your life becomes channeled into theirs, you've to put up with their confidences and weaknesses, you can't let things rip, and you yourself don't dare confide your true thoughts.

To make matters worse, Grandmother Morgan, after having given Aunt Phyllis, for Christmas, a diamond ring worth three

thousand dollars, all paid for in small bills, to avoid income tax de-
tection, and bought herself diamonds and a new fur coat, had only
given Andrea, Mother, and me a couple of pairs of stockings each. I
had at once sent mine back, with an angry note, saying I knew she
gave the servants at Green Acres more, and that she was actually
paying Jape, Grandfather Morgan's crony, the old gardener, an income for life.

"Why do you do this, Grandma?" I asked her. "Is it because
Jape started to go tippling and saying you kept your husband in
the outhouse; and played around with Sid and Muron and so on?
Aunt Phyllis has just become one of your own crowd and she attracts men to the hotel, you know that. I know myself that Joseph
Montrose is making a play for her to this very day. But we don't do
this; we're your poor relatives."

I reproached her and, by proxy, Aunt Phyllis, for being war-
brides and profiteers and exhibiting their true selves in the minks,
skunks, cross-foxes, and heavy-hearted stones nothing could make
a dent in. I said, "They'll be sending *coureurs de bois* down to
Green Acres yet; aren't you crazy putting on this show and letting
everyone see your crazy war-money. I think diamonds are a disgrace." I continued, "Are we all queens in the Morgan family? It's
simply a means of shrieking to high heaven that you're not an
honest worker."

I had tried to encourage Mother and Andrea to send back their
stockings, but, with the humble life-plan which was theirs, of *a
dime here, a dime there*, they refused, although sore.

I was sweating over the injustice reigning in the family, and
the boredom of my holiday; I could hardly entertain Wicklow. I
was pining for the end of the week. I thought, Good Gosh! I might
be a real bride and having a baby with this man. What a prospect!

I wanted to quit a few days before, but he did not want to. I
sulked and found him uncivil at night, picked faults in him, invisible before; and would not say a word to him all the way back in
the train. He came to the apartment with me (Jacky was at home
for the week) and coaxed me back into a good humor. The notion
that I was free of him was enough. However, as he owed me
money, he felt free to criticize me. He told me I had no sex-appeal,
that I ought to see a psychoanalyst for it; and he recommended

one, to whom his mistress also went. This friend was a celebrated practitioner with a swank address, who had created a halo round himself because he treated poor patients free in public hospitals. Wicklow himself arranged an appointment with this man, who turned out to be one of his best friends. Wicklow was not in the army because he was doing war work in some studio of engineering design near Rockefeller Center. His medical friend was excused because he was a doctor, and doing some very valuable work in new treatments of mental disease by a combination of psychoanalysis and physical violence; this is the way I prefer to describe it. He attacked his madmen physically, either by violent drugs, or by dropping them on the floor, out of bed, or by imposing upon them slight wounds, which cured them temporarily (of course). Some of the patients screamed with fear when they saw him coming, or knew their day for treatment had arrived. He hoped to liberate some of his young male patients for the draft. This is what I heard upon inquiry from Solander, and knowing my father's style of merry hooliganism in discourse, it's possible he garbled it a bit.

This practitioner turned out to be a silky wolf who lived in a lovely house in one of the best streets in the Village, those that most resemble Mayfair. He had a white door, brass knocker, a maid, the latest furnishings, a piano painted white, silk hangings; all that, and himself, were remarkably handsome.

I was very happy to see him, because he suggested understanding and even love. He begged me to stretch myself on a padded Récamier couch, and tell him all about myself.

There were some peculiar paintings on the walls, perhaps done by some of his mad patients, all of which suggested sex in some way, although they were pictures of the sea, ships, a vineyard, and a medieval battle for a bridgehead.

The lights were low, his voice too; and after hearing the details of my life—some of them—he placed his head in his large fine hand, to think. He emerged from his trance to announce that I, unquestionably, had a father fixation, and that I must be liberated from this before I would feel free with men. This Solander-fixation was the reason I did not keep men and did not get married. I asked him if he did not think the war had anything to do with it. He said

I was resisting him, which was a good sign, because it meant I was beginning already to transfer from my father to him. He said he would treat me twice a week, for as long as necessary, at the rate of twenty dollars a visit.

My heart sank, for I believed that Wicklow had meant me to just have a little preparatory talk with the great physician of bodies and souls. I said I could not afford twenty dollars a visit, that is forty dollars a week.

He said, "Don't you want to be cured? Don't you want to marry?"

I said, "Yes, I do; but I don't want to be put in jail for debt either."

He told me, with some asperity, that the draining of my purse would be far better for me than the draining of my heart's blood, and that if I were serious, I would get some night work, or borrow from my relatives to pay him; this financial pain would cure me of my erotic preoccupations. I informed him that I did not mind my erotic preoccupations at all; I only wanted to know how to keep a man and, in fact, how to fall in love with him, and stay in love. The doctor said this was easy; I had only to be rid of my father-fixation. I told him that I had not lived with my father most of my life, and he said, "Good grounds for a fixation."

"But," said I, in great confusion, much troubled by the prospect of the forty dollars weekly, "I thought girls who lived with their fathers had father-fixations."

"They do, too," said the great doctor.

"Is there no way out?" I asked.

"Only by analysis," said the eminent prognosticator.

But before I left him, he had poured balm over my painful doubts, with his charming, loving manner, and he wrote down on his calendar the date of my next appointment.

I went out, torn between pleasure at the man's appearance and doubt about his understanding. It was an honor to be his patient and, indeed, I felt at once that I could love him; and that perhaps, up till now, I had not met the right type of man. My father had always told me I would be better off with professional men. Then there was the other thing—the money. I went to my father and told him he must give me the money for the treatments which might last a year or so, because my whole future depended on it. Didn't he want to see me married?

"What," cried my father, starting to his feet, as soon as the facts of the high-priced visits reached his ears, "are you crazy?" and I had much trouble keeping him away from the fire department, the police, the homicide squad, and other emergency outfits, for he shouted that it was blackmail and highway robbery.

"Pickpockets," he shouted, "matricides, embezzlers are nothing to this—nothing—imposing on a fool of a girl looking for a boy friend—nothing doing," and he continued to shout and stare at me with incredulity in his eyes.

Persia said, "You'd do better, Letty, to go to a fortune-teller. It's only a dollar, I think, and you can get tea-leaves read for a quarter or thirty-five cents."

I laughed, and it seemed to me that this was rather good advice, the best I'd ever heard on the subject. I myself trembled so much at the idea of the outlay that I wrote to the great doctor and also to Wicklow the very next day.

Though the doctor attempted to make me pay for the visit had, and the visit proposed, I did not, and nothing came of it. I scolded Wicklow when he came to see me. He grinned, sat down on a stool, took off his hat, and remarked, "You're more fascinating as a termagant, Letty, than as a sweet little wife."

I relented toward him for a while, and regretted it afterwards. I reproached him with the whole story of the mistress and his pretense of passion for me. He only said, "Letty, you know how to take care of yourself, don't you?"

It took him four weeks to pay me back the cost of his vacation with me at Christmas; he did eventually. The next I heard of him he was almost living at Susannah Ford's house and no one heard a word about the mistress.

The very next day, after my father's fit of temper, when I had posted the two letters, with a sigh of relief at seeing all this money saved, I went upstairs to a gypsy tea-leaf reader in Fourteenth Street and had a very amusing fortune told. The woman especially impressed me by saying that I would have some affair with a man whose initials were T. or B. The amazing thing was that I did know a man with both these—T.B., Tom Bratt.

When I went out for a walk that evening, I was in such good spirits, in spite of my misadventures, that I walked down Bank Street and rang the doorbell of the Bratts' flat. Tom Bratt had a wife called Bronte. Everyone knew Bronte for the fuss she kicked up round herself at parties. Tom was quite a rounder, and I don't suppose Bronte would have stayed with him if she could have got another man. She was a big-hipped, chesty girl, with black, bright eyes, and a white skin; she looked like a half-breed Indian, to my mind; but some people thought she was handsome.

We had a good, long chin about political affairs on which we were absolutely agreed, and Tom told me all about Hollywood, where he had been a thousand-dollar-a-week man at one time. At present he was on his uppers. They were living badly at the back of a divided railroad flat. The wife had put in a lot of Woolworth rayon goods to brighten it up a bit, as she imagined. It looked very tawdry.

Tom and I had always got on like a house on fire, and we kept chiming in with new bright ideas, while she sat there smiling like a Cheshire cat, and thinking nothing, I suppose, in the way of wives. She gave parties for Chinese relief, anything that was the fashion at the time, and the real reason was that she thought she could pass as Chinese herself. I understood why a bright little boy like Tom left her so often for transients; and everyone knew about their many and various rifts. Naturally, in front of me, she kept up the turtle-dove comedy.

Tom went out with me when I left, to get beer, rye bread and sausage for their supper, as they had had nothing to eat since lunch. Bronte did not cook very much. She stabbed at painting a bit, some of her amateur decorative efforts being exhibited on the walls and mantelpiece, like some bright progressive child's. It all made me feel quite out of sorts, and I was glad when Tom and I got into the streets. It was just as the gypsy said—everything ticked. I felt the spark when he looked at me. He held my hand at once, and as soon as we got round the corner, bent down to kiss me. "Lovely Letty," he said, "I wish we could go some place."

"I have a place; come up and see me some time."

I told him Jacky was leaving soon for England, to join her Faust, and he told me Bronte had to go to Washington for some cause or other. She dabbled quite a bit in radical politics and would go any-where where she could cut a figure. This was lucky for Tom and me. I went home, walking on air, very pleased with the gypsy and resolved to go back the next day.

I had left the publishing office some weeks back, for the usual reason. The head of the office had started fooling round with one of the other girls, and I couldn't stand this indignity. I seized the first honorable occasion, this time a question of falsifying news, to quit. Now, however, what with Tom and a general feeling I had, I got a new spurt on, and soon got a job with the United Nations in-formation offices at Rockefeller Center.

I had quarreled sharply with Bill van Week. He was playing with Edwige. I had seen them one night through the window in the café of the Lafayette, and had gone in and made quite a scene, hoping we all would be thrown out. They are far too patient at the Lafayette and too humane, like all the French, as my father, that incurable Gallophile, will persist in saying.

Since then, Bill and I had been on the outs. I heard vaguely that he was madly in love with Edwige, who was no better than a har-lot. She went in for cute little things like cocktail napkins whose motif was a coozy with skirts or drawers you could lift up, and cocktail glasses with a similar sort of design. The girl was dressed on the outside of the glass; when the drink went down, inside you saw her naked back. She had stacks of obscene books, the lowest kind, and everything the undressed girl can still wear. My wretched cousin had a crowd of young lechers in her wake, and made use of them, as she made use of her loving husband who was now in the Pacific. They were writing an indecent novel intended to be a best-seller. They intended to process it in what they considered the new scientific way. First they would make it as improper as possible, with a going-to-bed on every second page, then they would have it multigraphed and sent to as many producers, publishers, and agents as possible. At the first bite they would send out Edwige and others of her *bagnio* (she had already set up as a flesh-peddler, masquerading as a movie agency). The name of the modern (and worser) Fanny Hill was to be, "If I Had the Time and Space—"

The book was written and was now going the rounds. Bill said it was very bad but he thought it could be placed, since book publishing had entered monopoly capitalism with the movies and best-book clubs. They were crazy to get the book that would net them millions, no matter what the subject matter. The taxes—one could whistle them away, one way or other. He said Edwige and her suitors, or consorts, had a brilliant idea there; one of the best he had ever heard of. He had been all his life on the track of bright ideas, just to show his family he could make good too, and that the Van Week blood ran good and strong in him. Bill was pulling all the strings he had to put the book across.

I told Bill and Edwige a good many home-truths. It was only too easy to do this, and I felt like a fool. Furthermore, it had not the faintest effect on them. Bill said tartly, "I'm a socialist; don't you think I know the society we're living in? The common-sense thing to do is to make use of capitalists, not let them make use of you."

"Pander to the profiteers," said I. "You're a stinking social-democrat. Why don't you join the honest millionaires like your old folks? It isn't that you're too modern to go to church, it's that they wouldn't let you in even to have a look around. As for Edwige, she's just a—"

And I said everything that I could think of that she was, which was a lot and none of it complimentary. Edwige's sweet face hardened to a flint and I could see the tigress in her. She will go far, I thought.

This was a disgraceful scene and had made more than one of my days morbid. What was I coming to? First, so sentimental that every tear-jerker did business with me; and then, brawling and bawling like a fish-wife. What sort of girl am I, I asked myself madly, eating my heart out. Good Gosh, what will become of me?

It's easy to imagine that in these rages and agonies I let Jacky's departure creep up upon me, almost unnoticed, though I cried honestly enough on the last day, and told her many things, quite untrue, but which seemed honest to me at the time, as, that she was the best of us all, and I loved her more than anyone else, and never could love anyone as I did her, and so forth. In a way, too, they were true; and they did no harm, for she was quite exalted and for weeks past had been in a state where every old bent man on the street with hazel eyes had reminded her of Gondych.

43

I HAD been in this particular information office of the United Nations organizations for some weeks, and had made a lot of friends of both sexes, and become very friendly with the chiefs, mostly because of my hard work and real ability, I may say, with honest pride. I was an excellent office manager, not drawing back from show-downs and not pussy-footing when the hard and sharp word was needed; but also, in spite of my rather wild and selfish behavior, which I freely admit, I was at times a good friend of the girls and confided in them most of my troubles. This is one of the secrets of success in human relationships. He has much who can give himself away frequently and lavishly.

I worked without question, also, nights, week ends, at all times; and was no clock-watcher, overtime grouser, pennypincher. I was good at accounts, could do anything in an office, and also by this time had so much worldly experience that in a pinch or quandary I was worth ten ordinary girls. I knew where the dog lay buried; it seemed like instinct; it was just old campaigning. I got on very fast. This rapid rise which was, of course, partly due to my friendship with the chiefs in the office, and even to some night-clubbing and friendship with the wives, did not get me much in the way of salary, but I was once more in clover. I went out frequently, always had someone to pay my bills, and was able to spend most of my pay on my own marginal needs. I never lived in a small way, never could live inside my income, and indeed felt small, unhappy and mean-spirited when obliged to scrape.

I was in the midst of these hearty, improvident joys, but pretty much without a man. Tom Bratt and I had quarreled as he had turned out to be a shocking philanderer of the one-night-stand variety. I tried to shut my eyes to it, but I thought, Why should I put myself in the class of Bronte? I am not his wife.

Bill and I had not seen each other for weeks. Edwige's book, "If I Had the Time and Space—," had actually been placed and was now being combed against the indecency laws; Bill was in high feather. He had seen it, he had predicted it, and so on.

Edwige was trying to find a way of divorcing her husband, who was in the service. She could not at the moment, and hoped for the end of the war, for like many a bright lady before her, she had her eyes on the Van Week millions. Only my knowledge of Bill's history gave me courage. Bill could not stick. Bill loved all women!

Into my office came Cornelis de Groot, a tall, handsome Dutchman of good family, blue-eyed, blond, of slim elegance. Before the war he had flown his private plane to the Cape, had a factory of his own, owned race horses, and had a wife or two. He made a ripple when he entered the office the first morning on business; the men started to laugh at and after him. It turned out that his first question had been, "Where can I get me a pretty girl?"

He had been showered with replies, but my name had been mentioned. They told him I knew the way of the world, was accommodating, intelligent, pretty, witty, and knew all there was to know about night-life in New York. My best office friend, Charmian, a swarthy, tough woman, unmarried, but not an old maid, told me this in one of her good moods. With us, Charmian and me, it was off-again, on-again, most days of the week. She was a girl a bit like me, or had been, but was now coarsened, toughened, who would sleep with strangers, and was getting desperate about her chances. She was thirty-six and looked more, being one of those fleshy, hang-cheek stubs with wiry hair and a heavy bust. Charmian, however, was the one who designated me as the companion for Cornelis, for she had the sense to feel at once that he would never take her. She preferred, therefore, to have him pick her lieutenant. There were plenty of other passable girls in the office, and some, even, were well-bred enough and knew a few languages. He might have chosen one of them. I thought it a good choice. They were too babyish, or too babyishly corrupt for such a man.

We took to each other at once. We merely glanced at each other across the room and something sparked. I was delighted to have such a desirable escort, and I soon whipped him into open admiration with my sparkling wit and common sense. I had the art of being myself, or rather, of always seeming to be myself.

We had not been out more than three times before he told me quite plainly what he wanted in me, beside companionship; and I had no hesitation in granting it to him. I had known from the beginning that this was part of the unwritten bargain.

Meanwhile, he had much money to spend and he spent it all on me, with *savoir-faire*, choosing a dress or bracelet for me, which smelled of the Kalver-straat and the Rue de la Paix, and a lifetime of experience with girls. He was an excellent friend and lover.

However, in a quaint European way, before we entered upon the carnal part of our friendship, he made me a little speech to this effect: That our love relation was not to be love, but necessity, a respectable partnership without emotion, and that if we showed any signs of becoming "involved," both agreed to break it up.

I might have not liked this in another man! But in Cornelis, while it injured my pride, I thought it showed yet another of his greatly strange qualities. Cornelis was the man most suited to me that ever I met; not inscrutable, for it was always his will that was in question, and his will came first and his will was all turned to his career. He was making his way toward the Governorship of Curaçao, hence the Government of the Dutch West Indies, and though quite young, only forty-one, he was likely to get it after the war. There was the possibility of Surinam, Celebes! And later, much later, he had his eye on Java, but his head was not clouded by any dreams; he had planned each step in his intended rise in the Civil Service.

It was for this reason that he now made this unflattering proposal to me, but he carefully explained this to me, and nothing, to my mind, could have been fairer. I accepted. He explained to me that he was married, though not much to his satisfaction, and without children; but that he would not leave his wife unless a great occasion came his way. Naturally, I did not look upon myself as a great occasion, and I had good reason to fear that by that he meant title, money, a career-building woman. How bitterly now I thought of the girls I knew without ability, but with families behind them and plenty of money. When we passed one of these in the street, De Groot, while properly attentive, would observe her; it was clear enough that she was the possible great occasion, and not I.

Being hardy, enterprising, and optimistic, I yet hoped that something would happen to change his mind about me—it could not be wealth or title—it could only be love. I did not think of this all in the twinkle of the eye; but gradually, as I became accustomed to him, and to our connubial relationship, I longed to be with him in the Caribbean and saw for the first time how tired I was of my relatively successful career in the great Metropolis of Get-By. I suddenly saw the attraction of Gondych and Europe for Jacky. She had been offended by her ill success here, and probably was led by her library years to imagine that in Europe things would be different—chastity, beauty, romance, idealism, self-sacrifice, might have some spiritual value there. I doubted it, for the world is a rough and self-centered world, but in a material sense, I saw the beauties of distance; the tropic seas—Atlantic or Pacific—began to flash through my mind's eyes. Life might become a rapturous travelogue, and I knew myself well suited to entertain, to fit my place as governor's lady, to make a drawing room politically and socially brilliant.

This was the chance that I longed for and I saw it—through the looking glass. Cornelis had to go and come on various missions, and sometimes went as far away as the West Indies. He conducted himself according to his contract, with good breeding, decorum, but too much coolness. I was getting into deep water. I loved him and in a more serious way than ever before. He was too *old* for me, too clever, too cold, too ambitious. Naturally, I wanted him particularly.

The first of my troubles came on a night in spring, in 1943. Cornelis appeared truly romantic, as only Dutchmen are, *douce*, poetic, with drawn-thread silences, a languorous way of walking. How sweet he was. I would have turned to water had I dared to let myself sigh. The love affair of the past night had most to do with the good footing we were then on. Such things are rare accidents. I was serene, thinking that we were well-knit. Cornelis, at some such moment, began to tell me of his greatest love affair, a woman now in London. He had met her through a fur coat merchant. She was an ex-model who needed men and who helped the furrier to business. Cornelis had not liked her at first sight. Is this a prerequisite for the great affair of passion? He had taken her away in the taxicab from his friend's house, out of courtesy. In the cab, he noticed some of her good points, a firm, fleshy, and handsome face, a clear skin with fine, natural color. She was a blonde. She was badly dressed and her hair straggled. She was ill cared for, and seemed hungry.

Nevertheless, he became enslaved to her. Why? He told this, too—"Honey in the comb."

I suffered to hear all this. In dreamy accents he described all of his slavery. He knew her weaknesses; she was an adventuress; ugly in those subdued orchid restaurant lights, lazy, suspicious, grasping. He had come away from London, where he had been last, leaving a great deal of money, all he had to spare, in her name. She could draw it all, and undoubtedly would. My feelings were rising up and choking me, but I contained myself for a moment more.

"Are you going back to her, Cornelis?"

"Yes; and I have my wife. I've had other affairs and every time I was on the brink of love, I drew back. I already have responsibilities to too many women."

This was so typically Dutch, said I to myself, that I couldn't argue with it, but I began to flush and felt my eyes spark. I burst out, "You drive me half mad with your theosophy, psychology, mystic speculations of all sorts, the soul, the mind, the spirit, and you don't know the first thing about women, which is, that when you live with them, they begin to love you. This is because they are more earthy and also more honest than you are. When they give their body, they give their heart and soul, too. Isn't that honest? It is men who whore! What are agreements? Agreements aren't written in flesh and blood. That's the only sort that can hold. With your pen on my papyrus, you see, you wrote something, you can't wash that out; you can't reason it away with your dry, feathery, insane Dutch reason."

He stroked me down, but I could see him become wary, and he

left me for that night. I had only to go home and cry at my folly. I can never hold my tongue. But what is the use of a man if one can't be forthright with him? I would never hedge and plot with a man, thought I. It was dull living alone, but I would never live with a woman again, either.

44

It HAPPENED that he was obliged to go away just then, and our effusions of the previous nights had been a temporary farewell. I made up my mind to pick up some of my old friends while he was away; but it was rather dubiously that I spoke to Luke Adams whom I met shambling down Eighth Street one evening in June. He was in one of his Eldridge Street bargains as to suit, a snuff-colored, second-hand thing, and himself in it, older, darker, thinner, looked like a bit of ambulating pemmican, or a lost red herring.

At first I thought his charm had passed and I managed to spend the evening with him, at the back of a delicatessen, without any sentiment; but no sooner had I reached home than a black wave of hate rushed through me and I sat clenching my fists, thinking of how he had said good-bye to me in his dulcet, casual way. I did not know what to do. He ground and squeezed my heart. I knew he was miserable, poor, even hungry; he had lost his job and his wife could not forgive him; he was poor among the poor. I dreamed of him—I dreamed I was in a shack, with only rags for partitions and his wife, a blonde slut, leaning over the stove, while some thin children, like crabs, like scorpions writhed about. I went to get the dinner for them from the stove and saw only old rags and little shoes boiling there. I woke up full of remorse and crying bitterly, for his life and the life of men and women. All burned for him, with this black and sour rage. When this had gone on for a week, and I was alone one evening in my flat, sitting at my secretary, with my typewriter, wishing I could write a short story, but unable to think up a good idea, a temptation flashed across my brain. I nearly fainted with the temptation and the thought of it, but as I recoiled from it, the frightful joy of it grew keener. Instead of composing a short story, I composed a low, insulting letter, stupid, coarse, dull-witted, talking about Luke Adams and his wretchedness now, about how he was walking the streets looking for employment and could not find any, how his home was ragged, his children hungry, and how the winter was coming on, how he was faced with real starvation. I put all this into the letter and signed it at the end, "A Friend." I pretended to give him advice about what he must do—leave the woman, take to the road, bum his way. I copied this letter out again, improving it, as I felt, making it more in character, and the next day, on my way to work, horrible to relate, I posted it, in an out-of-the-way mailbox. I felt pleasure while doing it and rejoiced openly all the day, thinking of how this letter would insult her, who was his curse. Nothing came of it that I know; what could come? I did not blush, I am not sorry now. It was perhaps for Luke alone I felt the true criminal passion; but he is too old now, I no longer fear him.

In my agony I did not know what to do. All my sorrows I called down on his head. Yet he reminded me, in a way, of a younger, healthier world I had once been in, the savage joys of my youth, when everyone had believed in something in this world and not in the spiderwebs of Cornelis and the other men I was now meeting. For these men, while talking about the age of calculation and science, the men in their thirties and forties that I was now meeting, and all that I met in night clubs, were now religion-mad and I had many a boring hour arguing the soul up and down, Cornelis being one of the chief offenders.

Each of these men was in some measure a fraud—of course, practical and successful men, who had kept out of the war or got themselves ribbons or stripes without a shot for their country, and they also had now nominated themselves not only war chiefs, but shamans and soothsayers.

Luke Adams belonged to the girlish world I had now left. To tell the truth, I was feeling old. Everyone I went with was too old. There were girls ready for marriage and married younger than I; many younger than I had children. Even my smallest sister, Andrea, now thirteen, was as precocious as all the youngsters of both sexes, at this time. The boys she knew swaggered down the streets, tossing their clipped, slicked hair like dogs or cocks, and many of them at the ages of fourteen and fifteen were going about with that smooth, sly, sweet air of the successful libertine.

They all knew more than I had known at that age. I felt my infant endeavors to be corrupt, ludicrous. Besides, Andrea, a girly girl, had been boy-mad since eight; in fact, she knew the soft men, the seduceable, at four. She had quite a correspondence with her boys. She had never had anything else in her shallow, pretty head. As I heard her babble her confidences, and felt myself stiffen, my tolerant, easygoing laugh sounded positively like that of a plump maiden aunt.

My mother was now anxious about Andrea, who, during this summer, did what a lot of New York kids do, and stayed out all night, roaming the streets with boys and girls on the nights when it is too hot to sleep. Andrea and her crony Anita ("the two A's"), a girl of fifteen, were inseparables, often spending the night together at the home of one or the other. Anita's father was a war worker, gone to another city, and her elder sister, a good-looking girl and said to be a genius in precision work, was at a war plant in New Jersey; the mother meanwhile, worked in a five-and-ten. Mother did not like the Andersons, Anita's family, but could do nothing against Andrea's girlish devotion and was obliged to put up with their sleeping arrangements and with Anita herself. The plump, strong, high-colored Anita used pretty strong, cutting language and knew the seamy side of her worker's life; not only that, she insisted upon opening Andrea's eyes to the dangerous time in which she was growing up, "putting her wise," as she constantly said. She looked upon Mother and me as old women! Anita (whom I detested) was growing taller and plumper and had a magnificent skin that work and nights in the streets could not alter. She used either a thick layer of cosmetics to show that she was "in the groove," or no cosmetics at all, to triumph over the other girls with her natural looks. What she did, Andrea did. We could do nothing about this either. Naturally, the girls in the factory thought a lot about their appearance, nothing at all about the labor movement or the war; they wanted to be glamour girls, marry a rich feller; they made up, talked outright filth (that would have made even Erskine blush—or would it?), felt each other's breasts to see how far they still were from full womanhood, bragged about their good times, and exchanged addresses of transient hotels, little bars, and accommodating druggists. There was quite a lot of going together, sapphism that is, necessitated by their early awakened sex and the absence of men; but it wasn't rotten, as it had been amongst us at the aristocratic, progressive school; it was just the madness and headiness of poor youth which for a moment held the purse-strings and knew, sure enough, that this time would soon end. They were oppressed by the future, hurried forward into this riot by the worker's fear of the future and the girl's fear of men and of pregnancy. All their lives had to be pressed into this wartime, a shoddy contraption like the valises they brought for week ends, into which all kinds of shoddy finery had to be pressed.

It was a brief saturnalia and dangerous; but Andrea's was such a young spring, she had such a good home, that we never thought she would be in it at all, nor understand what Anita told her. She was with those girls when they came out of work, but she could never be one of them. Of course, Mother had her melancholy spells and blamed my father, Jacky in her absorption, and me, for leaving Andrea on her own. There were plenty of girls, twelve, thirteen, all over the country going out whoring, and plenty even younger than Andrea, who had made up their little call-houses, or went out boldly in children's socks and without girdles, with their childish obesity, to pull in young men from the services, at railroad stations, bus stations, parks and other public spots.

Mother was afraid now, on account of her dreaminess and her irregular hours, that my thirteen-year-old sister was meeting boys or men, and receiving love letters, and asked me what they should do. I said, "Have you looked in her purse?"

I looked in her purse and found some prescriptions from an out-of-town doctor.

"What are they for?"

"For headache," she said. "They're Anita's."

At the factory they used chemicals which gave the girls headaches. They had gags or respirators, but the girls still got headaches.

I took the prescriptions to David Bench, Luke Adams's buddy, and found that they were prescriptions for emmenagogues. But don't worry, said David Bench, who was the man who had helped me through my own trouble, pharmacists don't usually make them up in proper strength for young girls, who are usually scared about nothing. However, he came to visit us and see Andrea. Andrea, fraternally questioned by him and us, and bullied by Mother, and investigated by Father and Grandmother Morgan, still laughed at us and said, "Yes, it was not quite a headache powder," that she knew; but what it was, she didn't know. She thought it was some drug. The girls at work took drugs, some of them, and Anita was a bit of an addict; she didn't want her parents to see. Her mother spied on her, and so she had given it to Andrea to keep.

Mother and David Bench explained what the "headache powder" was for, to see if Andrea would change countenance, but she did not, merely laughed, and said, Perhaps the girl was frightened; she knew she had a boy friend and sometimes stayed with him overnight. In fact, said Andrea, at times this girl friend of hers was supposed to have stayed with Mother and Andrea in their Eighth Street flat.

"Oh, God," said Mother, "whatever will I say to the parents if they come? You mustn't land yourself in such lies, Andrea."

Andrea said she would not if she could help it, but all the girls helped each other, and it was the right thing to do. My mother worried endlessly about the immoral and lying life; and Papa said that Andrea must leave Anita and her crowd and Mother must keep her company at night. Thus Andrea stayed at home and scowled. She pretended to go to school, but we soon found, through inquiries from her teacher, that she had got herself a job not many streets away, where it was advertised on a loft building—

LIGHT WORK FOR WOMEN AND GIRLS, PLEASANT CONDITIONS, GOOD LIGHTING, REST ROOMS,

and so on.

As was common, the too-young applicant had forged the necessary certificates. When caught, she said, "I am used to company; I can't stay home any more, Mother." And she went off again, quite pleased to be with the girls again and have her twenty-five dollars a week. She was still such a child at this time that she had not shaken off her pubescent embonpoint; yet she was half a woman. More than that, she showed signs of being a very large woman, a

"Spanish beauty," as I said about myself, when her age. Mother wrung her hands, as mothers always appear to do, not able to resign herself to the idea of her daughter's growing up.

This went on for some time, during which I, of course, was too absorbed with Cornelis de Groot to pay any attention to anyone at home; and then Mother came to me again to say there was really something the matter with Andrea; she was again out at night, and made terrible scenes if threatened, saying she would run away and live in a flat with five or six girls she knew who had good times with men. I called for Andrea at work and saw Anita waiting there. There was something very strange about Anita, at any rate. When I brought my sister home, I observed in Mother's presence that Anita looked very peculiar for a young girl and Andrea at once said, Yes, she had had to leave work on account of a glandular disturbance. She would not see a doctor on account of the expense, but was going to get a job in the loft where Andrea worked; and when she had the money would look after her health. Anita had quarreled with her family, she said. Mother invited the girl to the house and had meanwhile arranged for a doctor to come; but it leaked out too early and not only did Anita make good her escape, but Andrea ran out and stayed away from home the entire afternoon and night, only coming home during the next afternoon. She had missed the day at work (where we had enquired) but was prepared to return, if we would stop persecuting her adored Anita. I went to see my father, who seemed to think we were a hen-coop making the feathers fly about nothing. He said, "You must not harass a child at this age; you must remember her sensitivity, and treat her with delicacy."

Cornelis de Groot was away two months during which I was able to visit my family, and it then became apparent to me, certainly, and to any woman at all, I should have thought, that our now constant visitor Anita was going to have a baby. I spoke to Andrea and told her I myself had been in a jam like that, and I told Mother the same, "You did not know, but it is true; let me handle this," and I muffled her laments so.

Andrea listened to my story with great interest and seemed to warm up to me, but she smiled at my idea and said Anita had had nothing to do with a man; she had no real boy friend. She had kissed a boy once; and could you get a baby from kissing a man? I felt I must be mistaken. However, I said, "But, Andrea, you know she does look funny, and you can't blame people for thinking such-and-such, and you ought to get her to go to a doctor just for our sake."

"She went to the doctor at work," said Andrea, "and he said it's just a combination of her age and the hard work, with some glandular disturbances like you said, but that she mustn't take anything, it wouldn't be safe."

Anita, too, when questioned, was so innocent and composed that the evidence of our senses was as nothing, and we were all defeated. She could not have a baby; her stories about her relations with men were childish. It was clear that she had not had to do with one: her corruption was only superficial.

Meanwhile, Cornelis returned, and when we met, on the first evening after my work, I, full of emotion and relief, and he, full of his trip away and the prospects for his advancement, and of kind words, though not of love (that was not his style), we went out together, as if to spend the night together, for that had been the way of it. But after dinner Cornelis refused to go to the theater, although I had bought the tickets, and said he had something to say to me, and I, although angered, because I had to pay for the tickets myself, stayed with him, in expectation. He then told me that I had broken our contract myself by becoming fond of him; as for himself, he had come to look on me as a comrade, friend, so we must never spend nights together again. He owed life and love already, he said, to the woman in London and his wife, and perhaps another woman whose affections he had engaged; he was an honorable man, and realized he was playing with fire. He would not lead me on and then let me down; better to stop now. I burst out crying. We were in a big café in the Village. There were dozens of people and I detested scenes, but I felt my heart was broken.

"Oh, how can you leave me, Cornelis? You mustn't leave me; I love you, Cornelis. It is too late for me."

"You'll get over it, dear, and you see I am justified; your attitude shows that."

This went on for about an hour, when he said abruptly, "I am going; come with me, if you like. I am very, very glad I broke tonight, before we went any farther."

As he was leaving, I got up and followed him, weeping. He went out, quite soldierly in bearing, and with a frightening composure. Even I, bowed, crying, well aware of their looks but unable to stop myself, had a flash of perception, "Is he very used to this scene? What a dangerous man! And I am in deep with him. I have nothing to live for now."

As he was getting his coat I broke out in a loud voice again, like a little girl, "Oh, Cornelis, you should have written this to me while you were away, and prepared me."

He said, "I am not so cruel. I tell my bad news in person."

I said, "Oh, Cornelis, this other woman; you met her while you were away just now. I'm not a woman. I'm only a girl; they're women, they can bear it better"; and by that I meant all of them, his wife included. His bearing was perfectly easy. He liked the attention he was attracting, and I thought, What a fool I am, putting the limelight on him, this way; this is how he gets his women; but I was too unwomaned to stop crying.

We went along the streets this way, he with his arm round my waist, wiping my tears away, but perfectly firm. He took me to my gate and there left me. I flung myself on his chest and kissed him, kissed him, and he held me, but remained chaste and cool as ever.

At the office the next day I could see they had heard part of my misfortune, and Charmian told me that that morning Cornelis had asked one of them for the address of another girl, "but, out of the office." I was grateful for this; I supposed he did it to spare me. To my surprise he waited for me after work in the evening as if nothing had happened, and when I made to pass by him, he said, "Letty, aren't we friends? It was only agreed that we should stop making love, but not that we should not be friends; why did you stick your chin out, Letty? We talked about it before; everything was fair and square. Why, I thought you were on the up and up."

"Well, so I am, Cornelis," I said, turning my face away and taking his arm; "let's go somewhere and have a drink; I'm just tired out; I'm worried about my little sister more than you."

During the next few months this strange man, this man dangerous to me, kept me company most days in the week, and was, as before, a generous friend; but his spending was a little less lavish and he told me, as man to man, about his needs for the women abroad. I could hardly swallow it, but did not want him to know that he had my number, so I grinned and bore it. Other times I roared at him like a fish-wife—I trust not so much to his advantage as the first time. He would never visit my parents' house, but he opined that Anita was going to have a baby; she was a sly one and had got Andrea to stand by her. One day when we walked by her loft, and he saw the girls by accident, he said, "Well, apparently they can argue away anything; that kid's long gone."

One summer night, after twelve o'clock, when I was not sleeping, with the heat and mosquitoes, I had a telephone call from my mother who asked me to come over and help her with Andrea and Anita, "terrible trouble," said Mother. I found a taxi and got there in about half an hour. Andrea and Anita had gone to bed in the room used by them, before my mother's arrival. Andrea was asleep when she had come in, but Anita was lying there with bright eyes and pale face, which twitched occasionally. As Mother looked at her, she groaned. I now looked in. She was very bloated, and she put a hand on her belly, twisting toward the wall. Andrea said something in her sleep. "Wake her," I said to Mother; "this'll be a terrible shock to her," I continued. "Anita! You're having a baby, aren't you?"

"No, no. I ate some lobster and it was bad for me; just get me an aspirin."

Mother looked at me. I said, "Let's get the doctor at once—it's obvious—"

Mother said, "But she said, she says—she denies absolutely—"

I rang up a doctor I knew in the Village, a good-natured middle-aged man, and told him, "There's a young friend of ours here having a baby; she's a young girl and the pains are quite close together; please come at once."

"It must be," said my mother, suddenly collecting herself. "Of course, it's a baby. How can you—?"

"Anita's mother or sister must come; I can't take the responsibility," said my mother, and went to the telephone. My sister had got up and was standing, sleepy and confused, in the middle of the floor, saying, "Is Anita sick?"

"Andrea, you're just a baby," said I. "Anita's having a baby too. We don't mind; it's wonderful—but you'll have to help, and don't be frightened."

"A baby," said my sister, looking pleased. She went to speak to Anita. She was already suffering, terribly. As soon as she could speak, however, she said, "It's not a baby; it's just something I ate."

I helped her next time she suffered, then she looked up at me with darkened eyes, and said, "I don't understand, but I'm feeling so bad, Letty."

"Every woman does—but it'll pass; it'll be bad again soon, but when you have the baby—"

"No, no; I'm not having a baby; it isn't a—"

She suffered. Andrea, in doubt, brought a chair to the bed and began to cry when next she heard the girl cry.

Fortunately for all, the labor was not long, but it was not till about four in the morning that the girl, in pain and confusion, suddenly cried out, "Mummy, Mummy! I'm frightened. I'm going to have a baby."

She was delivered about eight o'clock in the morning. I did not go to work that day, but sat with her; and all that day I did not once think of my own petty troubles, but thought of Andrea and her friend and would not let anyone bother them. As she had denied the baby to the end, I expected her to hate it; just the contrary. Anita was delighted with it, and looked at it in ecstasy. Andrea, ravished and with an expression both childish and maternal, looked beautiful, and I saw she was the handsomest of the three of us, or, perhaps, I thought with a pang, that is just innocence and love of maternity; and a hot, sad feeling went through me: I wish I were a mother too, I thought. Cornelis and all the men I had played round with seemed far away. This was the reality, and this was, truth to tell, what I, in my blind ignorant way, was fighting for, trying to make shift with one and all of them. But what chance has a smart, forward girl to be innocent or maternal? That's a dream.

Presently, I left Andrea to Mother and went back home. I felt converted, saved. It was hard to go back to the office next day. Presently, in my slipshod way, I had told them all, and was back in my old intrigues. Such is life! But what a life! I hated it.

Anita refused to tell the name of the father, though I fancy Andrea knew it by now. Andrea only admitted, after we had brought up all the science, medicine, probabilities and the like, that there had been a father. But she pretended it was no one they knew—as if she really thought that possible. She had the extraordinary naïveté to say that "sometimes in the subway men do things to you," and this little boy was the result of a pinch, or a gliding finger!

The Andersons refused to have anything to do with their daughter. They were very poor and glad enough, no doubt, to see Anita fallen into a middle-class family and one so shiftless, nonchalant as to receive her. My mother could think of nothing better than to get money from my father for the baby and mother; and complained that at her time of life she was saddled with a newborn child; but to tell the truth, she was very pleasant for once, and being essentially a vigorous woman, she seemed delighted to have someone to work for. She cleaned the apartment from top to bottom and even reproached Jacky and me for not having given her the present joy that Anita had provided. This state of things could not go on. Anita declared that she would go back to work at once.

"I was never so bored in my life as when I was lying on my back," she said; and in ten days she was up, walking about painfully, and making plans for going back to the factory. "I can't live without friends and some fun. Do you think I could live at home?"

I wondered if her boy, the father of the child, was not at work; and whether she did not miss him. No man telephoned and she would never give us any indication about him. Mother said, "But don't you want a father for your child? Don't you want to get married? Think of this beautiful baby boy without someone to look after him!"

Andrea at once said, "I'll look after him when Anita is at work."

"You mustn't count upon me," said Mother, ignoring Andrea. "The best thing is to come upon the father for support, for you can't pay for a nurse."

"No, I won't tell him about the baby."

This was actually the first time she had mentioned the father so much as to say even "him." Andrea said, "We want the baby." Anita continued firmly, standing up straight, plump, and more voluptuous than ever, "He is mine; if it hadn't been for me, he wouldn't be here. I don't want anyone to share him."

She was nursing the child as she spoke, bosom naked, her breasts full of milk, like two white gourds. Andrea stared at her with admiration, with violent desire. When the baby had finished and fallen asleep, she took the child from Anita and sat on the edge of her cot with it. We went on trying to persuade the young mother to start a suit against the father. Mother turned round, I saw her blush deeply; I turned too and saw that my little sister had unbuttoned her blouse and was pressing a small nipple between the sleeping baby's lips. The baby gave a suck or two.

"Andrea!" I thought my mother looked quite giddy. Andrea started and put the baby away from her.

"Someone's got to work for him," continued my mother mechanically.

"I'll work for him," cried Andrea, "I don't want him to go away."

She spent hours with him, crooning over his bed when he was asleep, prophesying his moods, delicate, fussy and accurate. She sang all the time she was with him, spoke to him, told him her affairs. He smiled at her first, that was a great event; she called me on the telephone at the office to tell me about it.

Meanwhile, Aunt Phyllis had heard about the whole thing and had interested a friend of hers, a lawyer, in the affair. This lawyer at once set about persuading everyone to start a paternity suit against the father and himself underwent the expense of tracking down and locating the young man. He turned out to be a very young man, handsome, disagreeable, spoiled by many affairs, but only a poor factory worker and living meanly in one room. He denied all knowledge of the affair. We had all grown sick of the idea and Anita firmly refused to prosecute. It was done for her by others at first. When she went to look for work, she found it the same day because of the war shortages. She called the baby Alex (and this was the father's name, it turned out), Alex Anderson. She could not be brought to see that this was odd.

"I'm a young girl," she said placidly; "I'll get married later on. Not now. Wait till he gets a bit bigger."

I was very curious about this independence, greater than any I had had; and I pressed her, when she was quite well and I saw how cool she was.

"Why didn't you tell us? You weren't afraid of us."

"No. But it was embarrassing; I didn't want to talk about it."

"But how could you let it go on like that? A baby is a real thing; it has to be prepared for."

"I know, I just let it go on, day after day; that was the way it happened. I didn't want to think."

"But—the father, Anita—"

"It was a love affair; I thought he meant it; and when he didn't answer my letters and told me on the phone that it must have been someone else—when there never was anyone else—I didn't have the heart. I didn't write or phone any more."

"You don't want to marry him?"

"No, not now. He didn't mean it. It was a shock to me."

Anita was now a grand, calm, splendid woman with a great rose-flush, with large, thoughtful eyes. She ate a lot, laughing and taking things easy, and when home from work loved to lounge in a wrapper and slippers. Queer it was to see her so, turned into the plump, sensual slattern. When she went out on her Friday nights (she took them off just like any other working girl, just as if she had no baby in the house), she dressed up in dazzling bad taste, in sequins and black satin, with velvet roses in her hair, and high heels; and a brilliant, sordid, shrewd flash came into her eyes, while her looks became sensual and quick, antagonistic, and almost wild. I have seen plenty of girls with that look tear a dance floor to pieces. I wilted before her myself, though keeping my looks well in hand, and felt myself weak before the woman in her. Andrea worshiped and imitated as before, but neither could now be called a bobby-soxer. They were the true sisters. They lived a secret life of their own in our midst.

The family went on in the same old way after this scandal and I began to see that was what the family and society were for—to scatter during bombshells and then calmly cultivate the back yard. Even the individual lives much on that plan. Letty next door to a

fancy-girl; Jacky gone off into the blue beyond after an old philosopher; Andrea doting on an illegitimate baby; and the Family plod-
ded along as if nothing had happened.

When next Cornelis went off, on one of his long commissions, I
was left to consider my situation; twenty-four or nearly, unmarried, no lovers to speak of, nothing but debts and no family. The
family had closed round Andrea, almost excluding Jacky and me. I
was just at this point when I thought of taking a new and better
apartment. The old place was getting on my nerves, and, finally,
was the scene of so much bad luck that I had to get out of it.

45

THIS ALL happened on the fourteenth and fifteenth of March, 1945, apparently an unlucky date, although none of the soothsayers, tea-leaf readers, followers of God and Freudians, had mentioned it to me. Probably they saw it, and found it too bad, like Max Beerbohm's palmist, or Hitler's necromancers.

On the fourteenth, in the morning, Cornelis told me that he was leaving for England soon. He had business there, and he was worried about his mistress. She had used all his money, swindled others for money, and he believed she had been absurd enough to get in touch with a spy ring; of course, "innocently," and no doubt, through the influence of some man, "for if a woman's bad, some man's behind it."

I choked with disillusion and rage, but my thoughts and the injustices I had suffered bubbled up in me during the day. I kept my eyes glued on my work and got through a mass of it, out of pure rage, but in the evening, when he met me, calm as usual, I let go.

"Damn you ambitious men and whoregoers!" I said to him, crying out in the middle of the street, "to whom one woman is a pastime and another a grand passion; is she better than I am? No. Not even you would say so, but because she's a criminal, a thief, a harlot, a spy, you're after her—that's a schoolboy's ideal. You aren't the only one I know: a sensible man, who can knock everybody else into a cocked hat, and yet who crawls on his hands and knees after the worst female in sight. If we're good, we can be beautiful; it still is no good. But if we're bad, and very, very bad, what a *hold* is there, oh, my countrymen. Sink your eyes, Cornelis," I cried out, "of all the goddamn bloody lives—I could be a hundred times worse than that blonde spy of yours, but I've got ambition and looks and I'm a good scout, and I try to get along in the world; I work my legs off for you and the likes of you, my worthy bosses, and I know as much as the likes of you; and I'm even your friend and sleep with you, and give you every goddamn thing you ask for, and you know I'm as good as you, I've proven it a hundred times, never clinging or howling, standing up to it and taking it, and what happens? You run after an embezzler and a pavement-pounder; that's all she is. And you run after a lazy, worthless, shift-less woman who's tied to you because she's got your name. You've got to work for them, but me you can't even be a friend of. Why? You might get entangled. You ducky, little tender thing. Who has to suffer? I have to suffer! I'm your pinch-hitter, a stand-in, so you don't have to suffer the twinges of insomnia, maybe, and so you can get up in the morning, fresh and bright, and carry on with your sainted, bloody, hell of an ambition. Oh, god damn you," I cried out, without letting up at all, "I'm supposed to be able to take anything, but you not. You're a man, you can wallow all over me, and I'm not even to get love out of it; not even a memory."

I burst out crying in the street, and he didn't say a word. Just walked along beside me with his head down and a twisted look on his face, partly shame, I suppose. I cried a bit, and then in a fresh gust of passion said, "Cornelis, it's you make women bad. If you didn't pay for her, she wouldn't get into debt, and if you made your wife work, she'd work, and wouldn't be shiftless; and you see, you take it out of me, a working-stiff, just because I'm not a louse and I'm not a married wife. If I were either, I'd get all kinds of consider-ation. I could stick you for blackmail on the one hand, and al-imony on the other. Oh, the world's a rotten place and a woman's a fool to stick in it. I loved you, Cornelis, I really did; I lost my head, I guess. What's the use of saying, *'We'll go to bed, but we won't love'? You know love isn't something mystic; it's a bloody real thing, there's nothing realer; and it grows out of all that madness at night, that growing together in the night, that thing without eyes, but with legs, that fit of convulsions, all that we had—you know what love is. But my love you can avoid with your mystic relations and your contracts, even though it's as real as any other; it's as real in the world as any other, I can't let you pretend it isn't. I'll admit you can wriggle out of it, just because I can't keep you, but for no other reason. You know damn well it was love," I said, turning to him, my hair loose, and my eyes streaming with tears, and I reached up and kissed him on the mouth. "My dear, darling Cornelis, you men make us bad, for we are not trying to be bad, we are trying to live, find someone to love, that's all. I always wanted to love someone. Proof is, I imagine I love each man I make love with. It's harlotry, the system invented by man alone, that makes us bad. Women couldn't invent harlotry. You are just trying to push me off with one foot, like a man followed by a dog, and I have to be, because, god damn it all, after all, I know I can get another man, and is that a reason for making a floozy out of a woman like me?"

Even when we caught up in the street with a friend of his, who turned and listened to us before he joined us, a certain Dutch friend of his, I went on, and they walked street after street with me, through all the Village, while I raved; and both went by my side, one on each side, with their heads drooping, and both looked ashamed.

In the end, we went into a café and had drinks. The other man came with us to my door. Cornelis kissed me, said, "I can't say anything, Letty; what you say is true, but I can't do anything, either; I didn't invent all that, either"; and they went away. I didn't see them say a word until they reached the corner, and then one of them just pointed the way.

Naturally, the next day, I felt very low indeed, and didn't want to go to the office, but I did, and went out to lunch with Charmian, the poor old roustabout, to whom I could at least outline this kind of tale. The others were misses and pretties and boarding-school girls who were still in the giggling and "I stayed out all night in a car with a man" stage.

Charmian soothed me, and took me to see a fortune-teller. She said I was going to tin-horn fortune-tellers; what I needed was a gold-plated fortune-teller. She met me after work and we went up to Madame Tara, uptown just off Fifth Avenue. It was a fashionable restaurant with a late-dining crowd, one to which I had been occasionally. Madame Tara was a vulture, with dyed hair, a red skin, mascara, rings, and a print dress, to look folksy perhaps. Her expression was that of an unreliable police captain who indulges in everything indulgeable.

We crossed the palm while having cocktails, and Madame Tara

predicted for me a change in the immediate future, work and a marriage in a foreign country, a sea trip, old women cackling over my fate while some one or other took a plunge, probably me, and an exit from the apparent *impasse* in which I found myself. This cheered me up. I went upstairs to make up, and found three very young tarts sitting in the powder room, dressed respectably, but with that rubbed, startled expression of the trade. They looked at me with fright and calculation.

"Madame Tara's little crew is on the top deck," I told Charmian before the ogress had sailed out of hearing. Nevertheless, I went back to her from time to time; she was a smart animal and could tell fortunes more, I suppose, from hands, dress, face and type than from any scrawlings in the hand, and, after all, I did not have to join her crew.

Later that evening I had to go to a party at Grandmother Morgan's. It was one of her big affairs to which the public was admitted—that meant, at present, Mother and me; not of course, Solander, and not, any more, little Andrea. I don't think Andrea knew Grandmother Morgan was alive.

Grandmother had been in hospital for a long time, but was up again, smartly dressed, winning big money at cards, and taking care of her health in the usual style by giving parties, staying up all night, dancing and looking for charming men. She was nearly seventy. She now felt that she had been making a mistake since Grandfather Morgan died, and what she needed was a man, like the ship-charterer, Joseph Montrose. She moaned over all the years she had let slip by since she had first met him. Without inviting my father, she therefore invited his partner Joseph Montrose, promising that lovely Aunt Phyllis would be there, and she coaxed me to come and meet a nice young man—this was to salve my father's feelings and make up for Andrea's folly.

When I got home to dress for the party, I found Lily Spontini there. It had been a year or two now since she had visited, poor woman. She was dressed in cocoa-brown, an old hat and coat like a janitress, black shoes and stockings. She was not much more than a janitress. Her kind-hearted visiting had brought her a couple of legacies from the family. Now she part-owned a couple of brown-stone houses, which she had to look after herself, in wartime. She had become the downtrodden boarding-house keeper. Her husband, who had been a hard-working man, had gone queer with fear of the draft (to which he was still liable), and with the idea of his wife's wealth had threatened the boarders and Lily.

I was in haste and frightened Lily half to death by calling up everything I could think of from the Bellevue psychiatric ward to the local fire department, and then packed off to her murderous husband my chastened and intimidated relative.

No sooner had she gone than I received a telegram from Cornelis, asking me to forgive him and wait for him, he could promise nothing, but things might right themselves eventually. On the receipt of this I shouted, "To Borneo with all philanderers, I'm through"; and tore up the telegram. I spent the next fifteen minutes putting the pieces together again. After this, before I was half-dressed, Brock Ford, Susannah's ex-husband, dropped in to see me and tell me about his disastrous love affair with a woman of Lesbian inclinations; and I had to listen to his declarations of love for another before I could at last get off.

Grandmother's party was uptown, above One Hundredth Street, in a ballroom, as usual. Uncle Philip greeted me, as soon as I came in, with unusual love, and after I had circulated a bit, came back to me, and, taking me into a corner, told me, with his great eyes wide open, that I was the only woman he always saw with pleasure. He said the tragedy of his life was that we were uncle and niece, and hence could not love each other; I was the woman built for him. He declared that he was going out of his mind with the shrewish tricks of Aunt Dora and that God had punished him for his youth; Aunt Dora was God's scourge.

Aunt Dora, who looked much older, now came up, and after a quite reasonable beginning, raved at me, saying I was trying to steal her husband, and had probably seduced him already, for nothing was impossible in this family. Grandmother came and calmed her, as she always could, by promising her things for the family; Philip and I stood there as if no hurricane had blown us apart. Philip said,

"She gave me the jaundice; it was wretchedly painful, and if this goes on, I'll put a rope around my neck."

"I can well imagine," said I, restlessly, tapping my foot and looking for a cigarette.

"Here's a light," said Philip; "you don't believe me, Letty honey, but I'm through. I haven't anything to live for. It's mad to say it, but I could love again—I haven't a chance with that witch after me. If I can't love and can't even look forward to an old age like other men, why don't I put a rope round my throat?"

"You'll find a way out," I said, "there always is. I've thought of skipping out, too, Phil, but one just can't. I don't know why; but it seems weak."

"You haven't been through what I have."

"That's true."

I wandered off. They were playing cards in part of the room, and I played for a bit. After I won two dollars at quarter-cent a point, I became restless again and walked round the room.

Templeton Hogg was there, being adored by two or three of the girls; I elbowed them away on the ground of seniority of acquaintance; but he had become foppish, shallow.

I left him, too, and walked round tapping with my heels and trying not to think about Cornelis. I had a bad headache, and its refrain was: What did he mean? "A schoolgirl complexion on my mind forever," I said to myself, bitterly.

One of my relatives, puffed up in war-profits, was wearing a diamond ring, and showing off his wife's amethysts; another was telling where he got black-market gasoline, meat and cigarettes. According to them, the land was bursting with meat, wine, butter and anything needed, but most of it was underground, going moldy in warehouses and camps, often on account of bad management and bad calculation; they all proclaimed they didn't see why they shouldn't eat when it was going to waste anyhow.

I heard amazing stories of underground ice rooms gorged with carcasses; huge sums paid in auction rooms for out-of-date old masters by war-pigs, and so on, and so on. It was their talk. They shone like satin with it, their big bodies luscious and their eyes like stars. They were in heaven. What more would anyone have to offer them?

Philip roamed the room like a hankering ghost and ran into me when he could without attracting too much attention. Aunt Dora was telling the long story of his crimes to various sympathetic old women. Men were telling sordid and obscene stories; the women were talking about their furniture and summer vacations.

"This is my life from now on, you understand," said Philip, at one of our encounters.

"Get out of it, Philip."

"How? You remember I've been in jail quite a few times and she says she'll kill me if I leave her. She would!"

"I don't doubt it."

"Then what's your answer?"

"There isn't any."

"There's one. A rope round the neck."

"Philip! You're not funny any more."

I explained to him some of my miseries, and how I had as much to bear now as he had had at his age. He could give me no advice for he had been one of the very dandies and Don Juans who were now giving me so much trouble. He could only groan and say he was being punished, which, with all my sympathy for him, sickened me somewhat. I said, "How about the girls?"

He wandered away again. This went on all the evening, and I couldn't help thinking what a weakling he was; he couldn't take his medicine, strong as it was. The one wrong woman, eh? *Il ne faut pas badiner avec l'amour*, eh?

I continued roaming; our paths crossed again.

"To think, Letty," he said quietly, one time, "that all those words, Shakespeare's sonnets, love songs, the weakest, worse lyrics in juke boxes, to die for love, star-crossed lovers, all that, mean something to me; they are enough to give me heartache. I am still looking for love, after all my bitter experience. Experience so black and cruel, it is enough to kill a man, and yet, I long to be loved. If only you and I could go away and love—I don't mean it, I mean if only—if still—at my age, with what I know; you can't kill love in a man. That, too, is driving me mad. Not that wicked, coarse old woman, Dora; but this agony and hunger for love is driving me mad. I'll never have it again. I had so much. I know what it is. I'll kill myself, Letty."

I took his hand, looking up at him, and thinking I had known him since I was a little girl. He had said then, "Then I'm afraid I'm not a good man, Letty."

Poor fellow. I talked to him for a long time, in a low voice, consoling him. He at last bent down and kissed me, "I love you, love you, Letty; we could have been happy, and see—we can't be. That's what's killing me. I see hundreds of women, and I have this one—"

I turned away,

"Oh, as to that, the ones you see, if you're going to die for that, we could all die every day, for the ones we see, we can't have."

He kept turning round me, whispering his sorrows at me, harrying me with his great lovelorn eyes on me, till Aunt Dora came at us again, giving us great blows of words in the face, racking us, tearing us apart, even though we were just uncle and niece.

"I know his pretty ways, the so-and-so—" and the women approved her. Everything the vixen did was approved of; she called on the sacred wicked names of the family gods. Presently, Uncle Philip could not stand it and left the room. I was sorry for the poor soul, but glad that he had gone, for my own troubles were nosing out, from the black lock where they had been crowded in this day of troubles, and I knew I should be with them all night. I thought I would go. There were no fish for my fry here. What a life I lead, I thought. I'm mad. I'll end up like Uncle Philip. But I hung round, talking like they were talking, telling filthy jokes, too, showing how bright I was, till a general move was made; then Aunt Dora set up a cry for Philip to bring her wraps and wake the boy, who was lying down on two chairs. Philip had locked himself in the bathroom. Aunt Dora thought he was acting up; he did that so often, at home.

Well, they called and pounded, eventually broke in, and though the window was open he was nowhere to be seen. There was a lean-to roof just underneath; not a sign of him. After a while, one of the men saw a linen towel hanging out of the window and pulled at it. It hung taut. It was at the end of a couple of linen towels that they found him. He had gone out just like that, on some sort of impulse, surrounded by that company. A fine end.

I went home to Mother's, quite unable to spend the night alone with the thought of that body dangling, without thought or feeling, outside my window. It would be outside my window, he would be dangling, trying to get me to understand some more, I felt. He died for love. But I don't want to.

46

UNABLE to bear my place after this, for I always had the sensation that Uncle Philip was outside my window, I moved to a hotel. Then, finding it too lonely and expensive, went looking for a place, until I came across the one in Eleventh Street, as I have described in the beginning.

I had been there some little time, trying to break myself of the habit of loving men, which is just a vice like taking a snifter too often, knowing well enough I could cure myself of it if I had only the grit, when Bill van Week drifted back into my life.

He had quarreled at last with Edwige, even though her book had been quite a success, and she had enough money to go into a Hollywood agency with some of the fellows back on the Coast who knew the seamy side of the game. Edwige could only stand the seamy side of things. Edwige had made the grand play for Bill and thought him hooked. She had managed to get the affection of his parents, who, for all their worldly wisdom, knew nothing about simple little crooks of her sort. Bill, whose pastime in life was splitting with his parents, could not endure the idea of a dovecote balanced up there on the twentieth story of their skyscraper, in the hanging garden they had built for themselves and him; and it was because of this alone that my Edwige, too clever by half, had lost the Van Week air castle.

Bill was like an old friend. He was a great relief. We began to go out a bit, and I was so calmed down by my misfortunes with De Groot and the Philip tragedy that I behaved better than usual.

All one summer night in 1945 we walked the streets, talking about our lives and what a mess we had made of them, and how we could do better. We didn't think of our parents. Our lives stretched behind us, for aeons, without parents or anything, just the extraordinary tangle we had invented for ourselves. It was one of those nights when everyone is out.

The brats were walking the streets on the East Side and in Chelsea till four in the morning. People were making love in corners of loft buildings, or on the steps of churches, anywhere where it was dark, and a bit cool, and I knew there would be thousands sleeping on the beaches.

It was pretty cool and we thought of going back to my place; and then Bill said, his parents were out of town and we'd go to his. I'd never been to the Van Week mansion in the skies. But just as we came to the door, I said, "Let's not go up, Bill, let's go somewhere and get a drink, or sit by the lake, and see the dawn rise, or let's go to Staten Island, or get a taxi and just rove a bit; I just don't feel like going up to any more apartments, no matter how gilt-edged, with any more men, no matter how nice; I'm tired, or something. You know me, I'm frank. I'm Letty-say-it-with-nuts. Don't tell me I'm like Cornelis de Groot. I am, like the King of Siam. I want to get married. I'm off the town."

Bill put his arm round me and said he felt pretty much like that, too. We walked about a bit more; morning came; we had breakfast and people started to go to work. I said I couldn't go. Bill said he had a job as counterman, since he quarreled with Edwige and his parents, but he'd give it up, too.

We walked for a bit, the sun got good and hot; we sat in the park, and then we went to my place to get washed up. When we had had baths, we came out again and went into Stuyvesant Park.

There were children from the East Side playing in the sand pit, and mothers with their baby carriages, children round the statue of Stuyvesant the Peg-leg, and a woman, with a big tummy, waiting for her big pains, near the hospital. There were old men and old women. Everyone seemed rested. We came back to the children.

"Why shouldn't you have one like that one of these days," said Bill, pointing out one that appealed to him.

"You can't pick 'em; it's a grab-bag," said I.

"Well, take us, for example; we're not so bad. You're good-looking and I'm a moneymaker."

"Anyhow, I'm not going to make that old crack from Bernard Shaw."

He said, "I'm serious, Letty, it's time to settle down. We've been through hell together, as they say in the Grade B war movies, even if it wasn't hell in the same spot. I'm fed up."

"Well," I said, much surprised, "if I thought for a minute that you were serious, and you meant me, I'd certainly take your name and address and let you know if anything turned up."

"Don't be so wise."

I blushed, "Well, I hate to make a fool of myself. I've been taken for a ride so often—" and I went on, blushing, thinking to myself, "I'll never meet a man who'll make me an honest proposal in plain terms."

"Sure! Let's get the damn papers, and get looked over and all that, and we'll go down to City Hall and you can have champagne cocktails at that place opposite."

"Well," I said, "excuse me taking a seat, Bill, I'm overcome. I won't fool you. This is the first honest-to-god proposal I've ever had, whatever I may say when I'm an old married woman about the youths formerly clustering round my pearly feet. Well, sure, Bill. I'm willing."

He threw his arms round me, and raised me off my feet, kissed me in his resounding way, and said to everyone near us, "We're going to get married."

"This calls for a celebration."

"We'll have a real little drink, to prove we're serious about married life."

"Good Gosh!" I kept saying, as I walked along the street. "I can't believe it. I'm going to get married. Bill, let's do it before we tell. How long does it take? I've cried Wolf so often, I mean that, literally, I'm ashamed to turn up once more before the ring is on. But who'll we get to witness us?"

I went home alone and spent the next few days in a cloud. I was obliged to go to my father and say: *This* time I had to have a reckoning, and to my sad astonishment found I had only nine hundred dollars left of all my grandmother's money.

My father couldn't get over the fact that I was actually marrying a multi-millionaire, but I had known Bill so long and was so sure there'd be a slip between the cup and the lip that I didn't dare think of that aspect of it.

My father was enthusiastically anxious to meet what he called his new "co-paternals," but gave up this idea with humorous grace when I explained that Bill was usually at loggerheads with his family, for one thing; that they still expected him to marry Edwige Lantar (now divorced), for another; and last, that he was a skeptic and they were strong for divine service; that they believed God had given them their millions because they were so devout. They were near the head of the procession on Easter Sunday in Fifth Avenue, and they sincerely thought it a religious duty to have their pictures in the paper on that occasion. "The only place you could meet them, Papa," said I, "is in the comic strip, and then—" and I could not help saying good-naturedly, "even in the comic strip they only read Mr. and Mrs., if you get what I mean."

Persia raised her eyebrows and said idly, "Well, I hope you won't cut your father and me, when you're an honest woman."

I blushed, "I admit I don't care whether I am or not; I think Bill and I will go to it anyway; but it would be better if—"

I told them Bill was even then with his papa and mamma, going into things thoroughly with them; he expected the worst. Persia said, "I knew you must have been stood up when you telephoned to say you could come."

"Shut up!"

We laughed; it was good for me to be treated so unceremoniously, and I noticed it each time as I felt the stiffening beginning to dampen; for I was obliged to have some self-respect, except at my father's, or I could not have kept going; and really, what did I do that was wrong? I lived the best way I could; I could not see how to manage any other way. Nevertheless, I thought it best to say, "You know, the reformed rake—I'm going to be a decent woman, I must tell you, so that we may avoid the grisly reference, and you ought to burn your card-catalogue on my past, I mean, in your memories which appear to be unnecessarily good; of course, Bill knows all, or about all, but sensible couples, as far as I have heard, clean up after each other's crimes; and that's what we'll do, Bill and I."

I saw my father and Persia took this very well, and Persia came and shook my hand. "I'll be a sister to you," said she, "*hypocrite, ma sœur, mon semblable*: does that satisfy you?"

"I'm a new woman! That isn't even supposed to be funny."

At that moment Bill telephoned and told me that he had blown up his family, told them exactly what he thought of them, and that they had reciprocated. His father was particularly peeved and said he would cut him off without a dollar. All the fireworks were for that little what-have-you, Edwige, whom his poor innocent parents found captivating. They had settled it between them that Edwige was to reform him, teach him how to make a profit, and that he would become a deacon and hand round the plate on Sundays to begin with. This Age of Innocence was rudely broken into by Bill, going up there fortified by several Martinis, to tell them that I was his prairie flower. I could tell by his curiously extravagant and witty style that it had been a serious blow-up and that my papa's picture of holding Mr. Van Week's hand, was a pipe dream. I rushed out of the house and met Bill in our bar at the corner of Gramercy Park, a subdued gentlemanly place with Venetian blinds, and we talked it over. He said, "The old man was not ashamed to trot out the old one about cutting me off; he might do it at that; a life in business breeds the unfortunate habit of rapid decision. They learn it in the Pelman course or perhaps just in business. I never did like business for that: human relations are not a matter of rapid decision. However, to streamline my con-versation, Toots, we are out in the cold, cold world with the wolf howling at the door."

"I've been through this before, Bill," said I; "but frankly I do want to settle down. Do you mean I must work and keep you and do my own housework? I've cleaned up so often after my casual boy friends, who believe cigarette ash is good for the rug, that I don't want to do it for you and harbor the sentiments I do harbor against them."

"I hope you have sent a circular to those boy friends, by the way," said Bill, solemnly, "for I have done the right thing by you, Letty. I went to a printer's today to get the announcements printed—I had gold print, I suppose it's bad taste, but what fun—and I will make three long-distance calls five minutes after we are married."

"Fear not," I dropped the tone of banter and kissed him. "Bill, it's all over, I didn't like it; but I had to; I told you before. I was looking for a husband; honestly I was. I was going to marry ever so many boys, just because I wanted to do the right thing. Now I've got a husband, touch wood, why should I break the Seventh Commandment? I have no leftovers from corn-syrup days; I like men but I'm done with them. It was fun while it lasted. I'm going into this in a businesslike way—oh, do I have to be so emphatic? I'm serious."

"I know; I was kidding. We're made for each other."

"I know. This is it."

"How do you like that what-is-it Edwige winding my two old-timers round her finger? You'd think they'd have had more sense," he said testily; "I'd like to skin her alive."

"You liked her once, didn't you?"

"Let us now solemnly swear, dear, that never again will either one of us refer to our pasts; let us bury them in a common grave."

"So help me God."

"So help me God.

"Well, that's that," he said; "since we're being decent, I'll take you home and later we'll look for a hotel room, for I think we'll have to pig it for a bit," and gallantly, gaily he brushed me off at my Eleventh Street flat, and went into the night. I looked after him with satisfaction and thought of all his attractions, precisely that, his gaiety, gallantry, fits of irritation when Tories blustered (and he did not pussyfoot but came out at them starkly, since he was richer than they), his ease of living and his simplicity which enabled him to live for months at a time in a slum or in a ship's galley, just in order to assert his independence. He had been bankrupt and had fled the city, had come back in state, had had mistresses and easily dropped them, he dressed well and had no hokum in his make-up; he was better than I, in this respect. He worked continually, if not always successfully, and he was a sensible fellow, when he married he expected to have a home; a decent fellow, when he married he expected to love me and to see me love him. This was the best bargain I could have got out of life, with my frowsy, lazy and yet ignorant ways. Add to this his excellent good looks, his delightful build—he had that hairless, delicate, and sinewy shield-shape from shoulder to waist which sculptors like to show, those bronze plates bearing small nipples and bronze plates at the shoulders; fine muscles in the small of the belly and the back, long, graceful muscular thighs and long arching hands and feet. If his face was a little too small and boyish for his age, he had a good short nose and pleasant blue eyes, perhaps at times a little empty. He had few faults—he could be dragged into a discussion or a drinking party; he had a hot temper. Well, still, it is by the merest, rankest luck that I, Letty Fox, could find a man like that; and I went upstairs to my lonely flat, this time with a full heart and good will toward everyone. "I will try to do something for others," I thought, "not fritter away my days," and this was Bill's feeling too. One can't make a great stir, but one can be on the side of the angels. This was the modest program we set out for ourselves.

Mr. Van Week died soon after our marriage and died unrelenting, to our great surprise. Bill saw the notice of the funeral in the papers; this was the first intimation of his father's death. The next morning a letter came from the lawyer, which said Bill was totally disinherited by his father—the money went to some institution. There was his mother left, and Bill had some faint hopes of receiving something from her relatively small personal estate; but at present his mother was bitter with sorrow and would not see her son whom she accused of hastening his father's death. People always say this, and we did not feel ourselves guilty. However, there was no help from others coming to us and we had to set to and think about getting ourselves a home. I was still at work, but was sure by this time that I was going to have a baby; and as I had been through a disappointment of this nature several times, when I was not able to support a baby, and as I was obscurely, painfully jealous of all good women who have received their inheritance from nature, I explained to Bill that, whatever our circumstances, I would not let this chance slip by. "Who knows?" Bill was a little downcast at the idea that the future was taking toll of us so soon, but fairly soon showed the usual pleasure and we made what plans we could. This still left us, however, sitting in a Twenty-eighth Street hotel. But I did not need money. I did not need society. I was never alone and never despaired. What else can one hope for?

This is exactly where this finds me now, except that I am getting a little satisfactory embonpoint in Anita's style and at last feel I have something to live for. I always did, but not in this way. I can see now why society is organized in ways that seem so strange to youngsters. It is, of course, organized to a certain extent for babies. Another thing is that all this mad and rowdy time of my misguided youth I was looking for something—union with something, an ideal, a lover; but I have a different sort of union now, and this, I believe, is it.

We had not been in our hotel more than two or three days before Mother, who now took an extraordinary pride in me, told me Grandma Morgan had nearly died of a heart attack when she heard of the suicide of her son, Philip. Dora Morgan was staying indefinitely at Green Acres. Said Grandma, "Poor woman! Why not! She is a mother; poor woman."

Grandma was now convalescing in a small suite at the Coverley.

"That's a hell of a sanitarium," said Bill; "half the theatrical profession hangs out there."

"That's why Grandma picked it," said I. It came to me suddenly that Grandmother regularly promised a *suit* of furniture to whomever got married in the family; and when I telephoned her suite, which I did at once, naturally, I told her that if she was well enough I would bring my new husband with me.

"Well enough? What are you talking about?" cried Grandma. "Come at once, my darling; don't keep me waiting; take a taxi—at my expense."

I could hear a vast murmur of gay voices as she was speaking, and I said to Bill, "This is a very bad wire, but all the wires in New York tick now."

"They're all tapped, because they trace racing bets placed in New Jersey."

"That's so."

Bill knew the ins and outs of the fascinating worldly life which never came close to our petty interests. Every day I felt more exhilarated as I learned more from my husband. We set off that same afternoon to visit Grandma, and when we tapped at the proper door were surprised to hear the same joyous buzzing behind it. Someone ran to open the door to us, with a loud squeal, but seemed surprised to see us. It was Aunt Phyllis, overdressed as usual and too fleshy. She hung herself upon my neck and kissed Bill too fondly. I became cool and went in, taking off my gloves. The suite had an entry, with kitchenette, sitting room, and bedroom. The whole apartment was jammed with women, among whom one could see one or two graying clipped cadaverous heads—their husbands, one supposed. The women had all had facials and reeked of perfume. After a moment, we battled our way through to the bedroom, which was full of doors, gadgets, and mirrors, and in the midst of which was a grand bed. There was Grandma, her thick white hair shining, newly marcelled, rings on her fingers, and a white fox fur round her shoulders. She looked radiant. I threw myself upon her bosom and knees, crying, "Grandma darling," and there was a long deep embrace full of the joy of life which bubbled in us both. Grandma then threw herself upon Bill with as much enthusiasm as upon me, and I felt rather indignant at the bright, lustful twinkle in the old lady's eye. I, however, could do nothing. I murmured, with dignity, that I hoped Grandma was not overdoing it; it did not seem to me that she was resting, and my eyes swept the room. She had been showing off some new clothes, for boxes with tissue paper were lying about, silks and rayons trailing out of them. A box of powder had been spilled on the dressing table. Seven bottles of perfume stood on the white mantelpiece. The remains of a card game were on a card table pushed into one corner. There was a tray full of bottles, and cocktail glasses were all over the room.

"My darling Letty, married at last," said Grandmother affectionately, and inviting me once more into her arms. This remark chilled me, but I felt obliged to lend myself to her rapture again. At this moment, looking over her plump shoulder, I perceived one of the grayheads approaching; it was Percival Hogg himself; he kissed me, was very pleasant indeed, and avuncular to Bill. Then Grandmother began laughing heartily and saying that Uncle Perce was off to Paraguay, because of all the women there. About this time one of the women came running with a flower in her hand, plucked from one of the hastily assembled vases in which their bouquets were choking to death, and crying, "Oh, Dr. Hogg, what is the name of this flower; we are having a little discussion—"

He said severely, "Ma'am, I'm a plant physiologist, not a seedsman's catalogue," at which the poor old thing looked quite chapfallen, or she did not understand him. She continued to look sadly at him, so that he continued, "I am P. Hogg, ma'am, I have published several monographs on plant physiology; I sell microscopes to study cell structure, I don't know their damn names: I would scorn to." He then turned his attention back to Bill and me and told us he had chartered a ship, for quickest sailing; that the ship's name was the U.S.S. *Sons of Liberty*. It was a former war freighter now idle, of about four thousand tons; he had a crew, for men in the N.M.U. were already looking for jobs, and he had a passenger list of the martyrs of alimony; he had acquired it as he chugged over the roads of the U.S.A. selling his scientific instruments. He had a captain, and he and they all would sail "without a woman aboard" to Paraguay, there to set up his colony, Parity, Paraguay.

"They have the highest ratio of women to men in the world, due to Lopez, who almost extinguished their manhood in his wars; it's impossible for women to tyrannize over men; none of the men do any work; they sit around all day long watching the women do the work. They're appreciated. I'm not going to discuss the question of equality; perhaps I will call it Imparity. I don't know."

"But, Uncle Perce," I cried, "you're a back-number; in the U.S.A., too, you're dreadfully outnumbered."

"Good God," said Bill, "look at the women in this room alone."

"I don't care," said P. Hogg obstinately, "I intend to see for myself"; and looking rather nastily at me, he stumped off, with his head in the air.

Well, this is all. The frenzied crowd of Grandmother's friends boiled and bubbled round her, and every time I brought up the subject of the *suit* of furniture, the noise was such that she could not hear a word I was saying. Still, this was not the first snag Bill and I had run into; we took it with a good grace and soon left, without even a cocktail.

We went back to the hotel and, as I said, this is exactly where this finds me now; I don't think for a moment that this is the end of everything, but I'm no tea-leaf reader. I can only tangle with situations as they come along. *On s'engage et puis on voit.* Perhaps I just love life. I certainly expose myself to it; and I'm accessible to it. I don't ask myself, Will this last? It's a question of getting through life, which is quite a siege, with some self-respect. Before I was married, I had none; now, I respect not only my present position, but also all the efforts I made, in every direction, to get here. I was not always honest, but I had grit, pretty much; what else is there to it? The principal thing is, I got a start in life; and it's from now on. I have a freight, I cast off, the journey has begun.

ABOUT THE TYPE

The text of this book has been set in Trump Mediaeval.
Designed by Georg Trump for the Weber foundry in the
late 1950s, this typeface is a modern rethinking of the
Garalde Oldstyle types (often associated with Claude
Garamond) that have long been popular with printers and
book designers.

Trump Mediaeval is a trademark of
Linotype-Hell AG and/or its subsidiaries

Printed and bound by R. R. Donnelley & Sons,
Harrisonburg, Virginia

TITLES IN SERIES